LION'S BLOOD

STEVEN BARNES

LION'S BLOOD

A Novel of Slavery and
Freedom in an Alternate America

ASPECT®

WARNER BOOKS

An AOL Time Warner Company

Copyright © 2002 by Steven Barnes
All rights reserved.

Aspect® name and logo are registered trademarks of Warner Books, Inc.

Warner Books, Inc., 1271 Avenue of the Americas, New York, NY 10020

Visit our Web site at www.twbookmark.com.

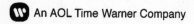 An AOL Time Warner Company

Printed in the United States of America

First Printing: February 2002

10 9 8 7 6 5 4 3 2 1

Library of Congress Cataloging-in-Publication Data

Barnes, Steven.
    Lion's blood / Steven Barnes.
        p. cm.
    ISBN 0-446-52668-1
        1. Africa—Colonies—Europe—Fiction. 2. Europeans—Africa—Fiction.
    3. Imperialism—Fiction. 4. Colonies—Fiction. 5. Slaves—Fiction.
    6. Africa—Fiction. I. Title.

PS3552.A6954 L56 2002
813'.54—dc21   2001045587

To my wife, Tananarive Due.
Truly, God answers prayers.

And my daughter, Lauren Nicole,
Whose smile is the promise of heaven.

ACKNOWLEDGMENTS

More than any other project of my career, this book could not have been written without the cooperation and input of more people than I can possibly thank.

First and foremost, I would like to thank Mushtaq Ali Shah, one of the great friends of my life. This honorable man and his Shaykh, Taner Ansari Tarsusi er Rifa'I el Qadiri, opened unto a humble traveler the heart of Islam and most especially Sufism. Any accuracies or insights in this text should be accorded to them, and any mistakes to the author.

Tananarive Due, Brenda Cooper, Todd Elner and Tiel Jackson, Judy Schultheis, Rebecca Neason, Sonia Orin Lyris, Chris Bunch, Maeve Kroll, and all the wonderful folks who attended the *Insh'Allah* brainstorming bash. To the two men who, more than any others, taught me the methods of logical extrapolation which were so vital in a work of this nature: Larry Niven and Jerry Pournelle. To Toni Young for all her input and support, her design of the Bilalistan maps, and the original drawings of the *Nasq Kabir* which grace the section breaks.

Rex Kimball, knife maker *par excellence*, with thanks for the fearsome model of Lion's Blood. Members of the Primate newsgroup for speculation upon the possible modifications of hamadryads baboons.

And a very special acknowledgment to Celtic bard Heather Alexander, her husband, Philip Obermarck, and foster daughter, Máirí. It is the beautiful and talented Heather who composed "Laddie Are Ya Workin'," "Deirdre's Funeral Song," "We Are Bound," and "The Mushroom Song," as well as other songs inspired by this project. All are the sole property of Seafire Productions, used here only by Heather's grace. As lovely as they are in print, they must be experienced in concert or recording for full effect. Ms. Alexander is an artist of the highest water, and gave herself unstintingly to the fantasy I call the *Insh'Allah* universe. Do yourself a huge favor and check out her website: www.heatherlands.com.

A very special thanks must go to my editor, Betsy Mitchell. Without her support and understanding this story might still be squatting in the back of my mind, yearning to breathe free.

Comments, constructive or otherwise, should be directed to lifewrite@aol.com.

AUTHOR'S NOTE

Bilalian weights and measures are modifications of ancient Egyptian standards. The royal cubit is here interpreted as about eighteen inches. A digit is about an inch. A kite is approximately an ounce. Ten kites equal one deben, ten debens equal one sep.

The dates given in chapter headings are rendered in both Gregorian (dating from the birth of Christ), and Hijri (dating from Muhammad's flight from Mecca). Dates within the text itself are exclusively in Hijri.

LION'S BLOOD

BLALISTAN

CHINESE
SETTLEMENTS

THE
NATIONS

VINE-
LAND

DISPUTED TERRITORIES

AZANIA

WICHITA

NEW
ALEXAN-
DRIA

NEW DJIBOUTI

AZTECA

Lake A'zam

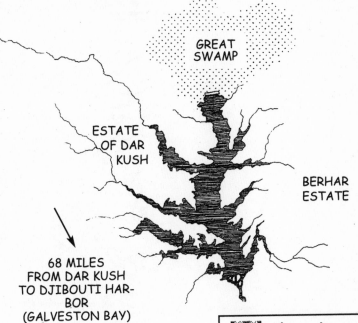

GREAT
SWAMP

ESTATE
OF DAR
KUSH

BERHAR
ESTATE

68 MILES
FROM DAR KUSH
TO DJIBOUTI HAR-
BOR
(GALVESTON BAY)

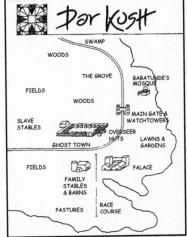

Dar Kush

SWAMP

WOODS

THE GROVE

BABATUNDE'S
MOSQUE

FIELDS

WOODS

MAIN GATE &
WATCHTOWERS

SLAVE
STABLES

OVERSEER
HUTS

LAWNS &
GARDENS

GHOST TOWN

FIELDS

PALACE

FAMILY
STABLES
& BARNS

PASTURES

RACE
COURSE

PART ONE

The Old World

"Allah hu ahad," said the Master, "God is one. Remove all that distorts or complicates."

"What remains?" asked the student.

"That which remains at the end is what there was in the beginning."

"And what is that?"

"Al haqq. Truth."

CHAPTER ONE

15 Shawwal 1279 Higira
(April 4, 1863 Anno Domini)

Therefore all things whatsoever ye would that men should do to you, do ye even so to them: for this is the law and the Prophets.
MATTHEW 7:12

Do unto all men as you would wish to have done unto you; and reject for others what you would reject for yourselves.
THE PROPHET MUHAMMAD

SPRING'S FIRST DAY WAS A WARM SWEET SONG, a time of companionable silences and comfortably shared labor in Mahon O'Dere's coracle. The boat's round woven sides bobbed gently in the Lady's arms. Aidan O'Dere, eleven years old and the crannog's best swimmer, leaned against the coracle's side, reveling in the river's timeless flow. He studied the dark darting shadows of the fish as if they held the secrets of the universe, his mind alternately racing and utterly still.

Just now, his thoughts were of his father, Mahon, a lean, strong man weathered brown by sun and wind. He pulled the nets all day without tiring, best fisherman and fighter in the village bearing Aidan's great-grandfather's name. Father and son were sculpted from the same clay: blazing golden hair, crystal blue eyes, clean angled profiles. His father stood a head and a half taller and twice as broad across the shoulders, all of it good useful muscle and well-proportioned bone.

The sun was a molten eye, gazing down from the heavens without malice or mercy, unfettered by clouds. It baked against Aidan's skin. In a few minutes he would dip beneath the Lady's waves again, seeking the shelter of her embrace.

Mahon lifted his flute to his lips and coaxed it softly, gently, as if afraid of scaring away the fish. His eyes glowed with humor.

"What have you, boyo?" his father asked, taking his pipe from his lips.

Aidan leaned farther out, pressing his thin arms against the coracle's rim. He peered more carefully now, straining to see through the chop. "Something shining in the water, Da."

The Lute River, usually referred to as the Lady, was clear as glass here. Upstream a bit, clouds of silt from an inland mudslide darkened her depths. Here, fed by a thousand eastern tributaries, the waters had healed themselves, as if loathing the idea of gifting the distant ocean with less than her best. The Lady's blue ribbon had fed and nurtured the O'Deres for three hundred years.

Mahon gazed up at the sky, shielding his eyes with one broad hand. "Well, it's a hot one. Maybe time for another dip?" Aidan needed no further encouragement. He slipped off his rough wool shirt and clambered over the side, careful not to tip the boat.

The water parted to receive him then closed over his head, sealing away the music of air and bird and flute, replacing them with the Lady's eternal rushing murmur. She was cool and bracing.

Aidan was a strong swimmer—half eel and half boy, his mother claimed—and oriented himself quickly in the water. Avoiding the nets was easy if you kept your eyes open. It would be humiliating to be caught in them; his father might be forced to draw him up and free him by knife, possibly endangering the day's catch.

This didn't happen. It was the work of moments to locate the source of the glittering he had glimpsed from above.

Aidan's heart quickened as his hands closed around his prize. For a moment he floated there, suspended like some strange river creature, the Lady's strong arms tugging at him, his bare feet clinging to a rock for ballast.

The object that had caught his attention was a knife. Not just any knife, though. Not some fisherman's blade tumbled overboard, but something wholly alien to his experience.

It was gold, wreathed with gems about its handle, its two-hand length of blade as gently curved as a shark's tooth. Young Aidan found it so beautiful that he almost forgot the need for breath.

His aching lungs would no longer be denied. Gripping his prize tightly, Aidan released the rock and kicked back toward the sun. Sound and scent and taste inundated him as he held the blade high.

His father's strong arm clasped his, lifting Aidan from the river with effortless ease. "What have you, boy?"

Aidan panted. His breathlessness owed more to excitement than lack of air. "A knife, Da." He smoothed his fingers over its surface, tracing every knob and etching. "A golden knife!"

Shadows flitted over Mahon O'Dere's face. The expression was darker than mere curiosity, but before Aidan could put a name to the shade it was gone. His father stretched out his arm. Reluctantly, Aidan placed the blade in Mahon's calloused hand.

Mahon examined it, grunting. His mouth smiled, but his eyes remained cautious. As his father wielded the blade with practiced grace, Aidan was awed by the steel's formidable size, its graceful arc. This was a knife forged for killing.

"Jewels, Da? And gold?" The dagger was a strange thing, a great thing, and if it was genuine, then it would add to his family's wealth, would increase their standing, could be traded for coin and tools and cattle.

"I know this blade," his father said. Mahon's words seemed burdened by an unusual weight and chill.

Disappointment was a sharper edge than the blade's own. "Then you know who owns it?" Never had Aidan seen such a knife, not in the crannog, nor in the villages upriver to the east. But his father had traveled far, knew many things, and certainly if any man would recognize such an oddity, it was Mahon O'Dere. But still his father did not speak.

Etched along the blade's curved edge were squiggles and curlicues, and things resembling the runes he had seen druids scratch in the dirt at Festival. "What are the markings?" Aidan said. "Can I keep it?"

Mahon thrust the knife under his leather belt and swatted playfully at his son, forcing the boy to duck. "Unhitch the nets like I told you," he said, "and we'll see."

Aidan grinned and jumped back overboard, swimming down to the bottom, finding the anchor rocks they had heaved over the side some five hours earlier. He pulled the slipknot then swam back as the net began to rise. Dozens of silvery fish were caught in its web, fish that would quiet grumbling bellies, or be traded for eggs, or straw for thatched roofs.

The Lady's currents cooled his eyes as he watched the net rise toward the light, drawn up by his father's strong arms. Aidan gazed up at the coracle, and deep within him, in a place that lived beyond ordinary thought and emotion, he had another vision of the knife.

It was held in a hand that was not his father's. It gleamed by reflected firelight. And its edge was stained with crimson.

It was early evening by the time they returned to the crannog, their island home. A stranger would find it hard to locate, hidden as it was by reeds and carefully draped moss. The O'Dere crannog was set at the edge of the lake, connected to the mainland by a gated bridge of wood and earth. There the land was cultivated in corn and carrots, with rectangular pens for cattle and sheep. The crannog itself held a dozen houses with woven wooden walls and thatched roofs. Great-grandfather Angus O'Dere and his brothers had built this hidden place. They carried rocks from the forest out to the lake, building the crannog up from the lake bed with rock and gravel and clay. Here they raised their families. Here, for generations, they had lived and loved and died.

The other boats were drifting in as well. Although the shadows were lengthening, he could see that the faces were happy: the day's fishing had been good. The sun was setting in the dense emerald forest west of the crannog, tinting the sky copper.

His father hailed the other fishermen, sharing a jest here, a barbed comment there. Most of the other boats were river craft, circular or tub-shaped. Pulled tight at the dock were also several canoe-shaped boats, oceangoing vessels, always an exciting sight. Aidan knew that the ocean lay a day's journey west. He had been enthralled by stories of it since boyhood but had never seen its endless rolling surf. Soon, his father promised, they would take a trip downriver. Aidan couldn't wait.

The fishermen were broad-chested and thick-armed, with yellow beards and faces cracked by sun and long years of grueling work. Aidan's own small face was still smooth as a girl's. He doubted he would ever grow into such splendid manhood. When he expressed those concerns to his father and mother they merely smiled and told him stories of their own distant childhoods, of streams swum with tireless strokes and green valleys run on youthful legs.

We, too, were children, they had told him in countless loving ways. *Childhood was long, and sweet. But childhood ends.*

And while a certain wistful sadness lingered in that last thought, there was joy as well. For it was only in the final days of childhood that Mahon and Deirdre first glimpsed each other at Spring Festival. Gentle Christian girl she had been, smitten by the wild river lad, heir to the Chieftain's seat at his crannog's council. Introductions had been made, families negotiating bride price and reciprocal obligations.

And when Mahon and Deirdre finished with their reminiscence, they would take hands one with the other, and share their secret smiles with their only son. "You will grow," his mother often said. "And faster than you would ever believe."

Still, watching his father work the oars, it was hard for Aidan to imagine that he would ever be so wide and tall. When would the first tiny hairs appear on his face? All that grew there was now a fine, almost invisible down, no more than might be felt on his sister's cheeks. He longed for the first sign of his awakening maturity, for the day that he might take out his own coracle, weave his own net, return triumphant with his own catch to an admiring village.

To the day, distant but quite real, that he himself might take the Chieftain's seat.

Aidan's mother, Dierdre, stood on the dock, waiting for them. She was strong herself, and beautiful—more beautiful, Aidan thought, than any other woman in the *tuath*.

"Deirdre," Mahon called up to her. "A spot of help with the line." He threw the rope up to her, and she plucked it almost casually from the air, her eyes never leaving him.

Something simmered in her gaze that made Aidan happy and a bit uneasy at the same time. He slept in the same room with his parents and had awakened more than once to hear low laughter and blankets rustling in a steady, quickening rhythm. He was almost ready to ask them just what they were doing. Almost, but not quite. He imagined it had something to do with what he had seen dogs and sheep doing, except that his parents had been face-to-face. There was something worth knowing here. Something that he knew would make an eternal difference in his life, something he sometimes suspected some of the girls in the *tuath* already understood.

Without a wasted motion, his mother tied up the line, then extended a hand to Mahon, who jumped up on the dock and gathered her in his arms for a lusty kiss. "Fire's waiting for you," she said when they came up for air.

"Good, woman," Mahon said happily. "My feet are cold."

She tilted her head sideways. "Is that all need's warming?" She said this last part with her voice dropping, huskiness flowing into it like warm honey. Aiden hopped up on the pier and tied up his own line, carefully ignoring the exchange.

Or appearing to. He peeked around under his arm as Mahon placed one fond hand on Deirdre's stomach. "Not enough to have one in the oven?" he asked.

Her voice dropped even further, but Aidan could still make it out. "Thought that you might want to poke her a bit, see if she's done."

"Did you, now?" He rubbed his nose against hers, slowly, then turned back briskly to his son. "Get the catch in, lad."

"Yes, Da," he replied. His twin sister Nessa ran up behind him, cotton smock almost impossibly clean, as if the dust and the dirt never quite managed to touch her. Once Aidan and Nessa had been exactly alike, but time and the eternal variance of male and female were beginning to mold them. Aidan was browner, muscle just beginning to tauten his arms. Nessa's hair was almost strawberry, and she stood a thumb taller, but his father told him not to worry, the coming summer would probably see an end to that.

Their spiritual upbringing had been a compromise. They had been weaned on stories of both Jesus and the forest folk, the Tuatha de Danann and the Nativity, the Gospel of Mary Magdalene and that of Ana, mother of the Irish gods. Nessa tended more toward the ways of the Druids, Aidan more toward Christianity—it made for fine, fierce family arguments.

But however much the siblings quarreled and bickered, the two shared secrets that no other living creature would ever know: Where Aidan hid the Druid stones won last Festival (since his mother wouldn't let them in the house). Who had given Nessa her first kiss (Geirig, the stonecutter's son). What bend in the Lady held the fattest frogs, the ones who fairly jumped upon the nearest spear.

Nessa helped him heave the net up onto the dock and into their wheeled cart. "Looks like a good pull," she said.

"Good weight in it," he said, strutting a bit. Together they could just manage the load their father had drawn up with seemingly little effort.

Every cook and carpenter seemed to be chattering as they pushed their way toward the squat, thatched shape of the communal smokehouse. "Thought you weren't coming back tonight," Nessa said. "You'd miss the dancing and the games." She dropped her voice a bit. "I think that Morgan would have cried."

"Go on, now." His voice mocked her, but beneath that facade lay interest. Morgan ran faster than any of the other girls in the crannog, her bare feet seeming almost to float above the ground. But she ran just a little faster whenever Aidan chased her, and many of the adults nodded and chuckled when they saw how he never caught her, which frustrated him all the more. And more than once Mahon had suggested that one day, Morgan might let him catch her after all.

He caught a glimpse of her as they trundled the net to the smoke hut. She was in the midst of some chasing game, elusive and feathery-swift as always. Heart-faced and red-haired, slender as some forest creature, she hid behind a low peat wall, but he spied her. She knew that he saw her, and raised a slender finger to her lips, begging silence. His face grew long and stern, as if considering whether or not to give her her wish. As the clutch of pursuing boys and girls ran by he said nothing to betray her position, and her thankful smile was radiant.

No words were said, but he was suddenly certain, and unexpectedly pleased at the thought, that one day soon Morgan would indeed let him catch her.

And then . . . ?

CHAPTER TWO

DEIRDRE HELD MAHON'S ARM as they walked back to the home his grandfather had built with his own hands, the single large room they had shared as husband and wife for a dozen years. She knew her man's every mood as well as she knew her own, and something about his face, his laugh, the evasive shift of his eyes, warned her that he was troubled.

"Bees buzzing between your ears?"

His eyes refocused, found her. "Pulled something out of the Lady today," Mahon said. He did a little hop-step as they walked, dodging one of the big yellow mongrel dogs that ran freely through the streets, belonging to everyone and no one.

"And what might that be?"

"What?" he asked absently. Deirdre suppressed a flash of irritation, knowing that his mind was simply wandering again, as it often did. If anything, it meant that some aspect of the recent discovery had seized his imagination so strongly that he had tumbled into the depths of some strong speculation.

"What you found, silly," she said.

"Oh, that." His face was a mask. "Maybe nothing. We'll speak of it later."

She looked up at him, curious and unconvinced, as they entered their home. Irritation would profit nothing. Patience might. In time, they would speak of it, and any other things that occupied his mind.

Any discomfort of the day had been forgotten, and town festival held sway: not so elaborate as the spring dance not two weeks ago, or the annual gathering of chieftains and kings. But on this day eighty-four winters past, the O'Dere crannog had been founded: the first child had been born. On the day of that birth, the land was officially declared alive and fertile by the forest-dwelling druids who arrived, unbidden, for the occasion.

And every year the fisher folk and herdsmen, the farmers and hunters who called the crannog their *tuath*, the core of their five generations of mothers, sons, and cousins, gathered to celebrate its birth with song and dance and merriment.

Aidan walked the periphery of the great central fire, where cook-kettles bubbled and the village shared its bounty. On a night like tonight, no one would go hungry. Tonight's celebration had brought guests from the *tuath* a day upstream, as well as families from small farms in the northern woods, and Eastern marsh folk who traded with O'Dere and came on this night to rejoice with them.

Crouching behind a barrel, Aidan caught snippets of conversation. Dearg, a black-bearded fisherman who lived next to the bridge, gestured broadly, spilling his mug of ale as he bragged. "Three days!" he said. "South along the coast, and found a shoal so rich we had only to dip the nets and they fair broke our backs."

His companion Conn, the quick-tempered graybeard who minded the smokehouse, laughed at him. "If you'd bent your back to the nets you might know that."

Conn's big-bellied younger brother Lir chortled. "Too busy giving orders to pull," he agreed sagely.

Aidan started as his father squatted next to the men. Mahon grabbed the goblet from Dearg, quaffed deeply, and slammed it back into his friend's hand. "Ah, lay off," Mahon said. "Someone has to keep you lazy-bones at work."

His voice was playful, but Aidan knew his father, and sensed that there was something serious in his mind. "Tell me, lads. While about, did you see anything of . . . unusual interest?"

They passed the flagon from hand to hand. Aidan fought his urge to lunge from the shadows and make a grab for it, knowing that if he did, the topic of conversation would instantly shift to imaginative methods of punishment.

"Of what sort?" Conn asked.

In reply, Mahon pulled the gold-hilted blade from his belt. Aidan's blood quickened. As he had suspected, there was something special and secret about the knife. And *he* had found it! Was it magic, perhaps? Surely it was the blade of a Druid king.

Lir's eyes went huge. "Where in heaven did you find *that*?"

"In the Lute," Mahon replied. He held the blade up so that it reflected the firelight. "Gold was shining in the sun, but . . . see? No tarnish on the steel?"

The men exchanged quizzical glances. Dearg held his hand out for the knife, weighed it in his palm, made a few dexterous turns and then handed it back hilt first. His sun-creased face seemed to darken. "A strange and curious thing. What do you think, Mahon?"

Mahon rested one knee upon the ground. "I don't know," he said. "I have a memory, but can't place it. Maybe on the next trading trip upriver, we could ask the *seanchai* if he's ever seen such a thing."

Aidan hoped that his father might take him along. The *seanchai* were magical folk, who held the history of the entire Lute River in their songs and stories.

The other fishermen nodded agreement as Deirdre appeared from around the fire, where she had been speaking to some of the other women. The flute music wafted across the fire, seeming to pick up heat as it passed. She balanced her fists on her hips saucily. "Will you stop talking? The boats are in, life is good, and your wife needs a dance."

She lifted one small fist and extended it to her man. The fishermen laughed and waved him away, and she pulled Mahon to his feet as if he were a great salmon reeled from the river.

A beautiful red-haired woman was playing fiddle. Aidan had heard that she lived in the forest by herself, but he did not know her name. It was whispered that she was a witch, and perhaps it was true. He did know that the spell she wove transformed the night into a living creature, alive as the forests or the river.

Two couples performed a slow, lovely jig to her music while the children clapped and the men passed a jug. Deirdre pulled Mahon out and they danced joyously, while Aidan and his sister, Nessa, watched. They laughed along to the music and the motion, and more dancers joined the celebration.

In the torchlight, their young faces shone with unfettered joy. Aidan caught a flash of bright red hair to his left and Morgan emerged from the light, all youthful promise and hope, the baby fat just beginning to melt away, leaving the mesmerizing curves of a healthy young woman. Again he felt that sense of bonding, and some part of him knew what everyone else in the *tuath* seemed to know, but the knowledge eluded his conscious mind, was present only as a mild and distant yearning.

Morgan stepped closer, her feet making little patterns on the ground. He wanted to jump up and chase her, to play the old games that they had played since before remembering. But something in her teasing smile said *New games, Aidan. New games coming.* And then the tension broke like a bubble in a brook, and he barely saw Nessa's hand as it flickered out, stinging his cheek. "Go dance with her, then!" Nessa said.

Morgan jumped back, startled a bit. Aidan and Nessa traded slaps, an old and fond game. Eyes watering, Aidan on some level realized that he welcomed the interruption, the respite from the secret in Morgan's eyes.

Morgan watched them, seemed to sigh, and slipped back into the shadows, taking one last glance at him over her shoulder. Even in the midst of the frantic action, he could appreciate the length of her lashes, enjoy the way her hair lay against her shoulder. Something about her called to something within him, and if he had yet to understand, it said to him *Don't be afraid, Aidan. I understand well enough for the both of us.*

Night fell softly in the *tuath*, the music slowly dying away, the adults wandering to their beds or back to the forest, or setting off singing in flat-bottomed boats. Fireflies rose from the edges of the lake, flitting and darting like low-slung stars.

Aidan, Nessa, Kyle Boru, and his brother, Donough, lay out on the dock, staring out at the lake and the reeds that bordered it. They spoke in slurred voices as Deirdre and Mahon ambled up to them, arms about each other.

Mahon's expression was one of sleepy satisfaction. "You children stay out of mischief," he said, and gave his wife a squeeze. "Your mother and I are yieldin' to nature."

Deirdre laid her head on her husband's shoulder, her hand caressing his side. "I saw that little Morgan chasing after you," she said to Aidan. "Red hair means trouble, boy." She gave him a lazy, knowing smile, shaking her own crimson mane.

"I can handle myself," Aidan said.

His father grinned ruefully. "I once thought as much. Look at me now."

"You're the happiest man in the *tuath*," said round-faced Kyle Boru.

Mahon snorted. "Too drunk to feel the pain, boy." He planted a smacking wet kiss on his wife's welcoming lips. "Take me to bed or lose me forever, woman!"

Arms entwined about each other's waists, they wobbled off. Behind them, the children giggled.

When the adults were safely gone, Kyle and Donough produced an ale jug. Conspiratorial whispers followed, and a soft swift gurgling liquid sound as the jug was upended into one eager young mouth after another.

Nessa protested indignantly when the boys hogged. "My turn! Don't keep it all for yourselves!"

"Mine first!" Donough said, jostling for position.

He took another swallow, then passed it to Aidan.

Nessa grabbed for it and missed. "Aidan!"

He clucked at her. "Patience . . ." Aidan drank. Liquid fire rolled down his throat. He turned as if passing it back to Donough again and was deliberately slow to avoid Nessa's lunge. She snatched it from him.

As she drank and sputtered, Aidan rolled over onto his back. The jug continued to pass from one child to another, and the alcohol took its toll in the form of bleary speech and increasingly animated expressions.

Aidan gazed up through the clouds at a luminous shoal of stars: the Great Northern Plow, the Small Plow, the Goose. He had heard a Druid claim that the stars were balls of flaming gas. But surely such fires would have burned out by now . . . ? "I heard," he said, "that there are men who sail across the ocean guided only by the stars."

Donough sighed. "I'd like to see that."

"So would I," Aidan said.

Nessa plopped down next to the others, wobbly as a wet reed. "You'll never see anything but lake and river," Aidan's twin laughed. She swept her arm out, pointing at the village and the lake. "This is all you'll ever see."

Without being able to explain how, Aidan knew that she was wrong, knew that he was meant for bigger things. The Druids said that there was a larger world out there, beyond the *tuath*, beyond even the ocean, and he was going to explore it. He thought those, and other things, but merely slurred: "I'll show ya. I'll show alla ya . . ."

CHAPTER THREE

FOUR HOURS BEFORE DAWN.

The O'Dere Crannog was utterly silent now. Even the dogs had curled up into a knot in the shadow of the central fire.

The children sprawled on the dock were still asleep. There was no one to see the arrival of the raiders. Out of an enfolding bank of mist glided twin dragons. Rearing back like sea horses, stub-winged and fanged, each dragon was perched on the prow of a ship, each ship about fifty hands in length. The ships' oars scooped water and sculled ahead silently, every motion practiced and perfect. They were flat-bottomed, designed for swift forays along smooth, shallow rivers like the Lute.

Aidan was the first to wake. He peered out across the lake, seeing the silent shapes, but certain that this was a dream following him even after he had opened his eyes. As he watched, the head of the lead ship began to glow with a strange light. Without warning, flame gushed from the dragon's mouth, directly onto the row of coracles.

Aidan's eyes widened. What a dream this was! Then he felt the rush of heat against his skin, and sat up screaming.

"Northmen!"

Nessa and the Boru boys bolted to their feet, grasping their peril in a single glance. For a moment they stood frozen, but as the ships smoldered and the flames licked at the docks, their paralysis broke and they fled back into the village.

Aidan walked backwards, watching, eyes wide. Since infancy he had heard tales of the dragons and of the village heroes who waged righteous war against them. Had been warned away from mischief with images of terrible beasts that tore and swallowed and carried away forever.

So even though he realized that these were ships, that what he watched

was the work of men, not monsters, something inside him held him transfixed by primordial, nameless dread. The dragon vomited flame again, and
another boat seethed with fire.

Now alien, vaguely human shapes stirred upon the decks. They drew
closer to the dock and a grapneled rope flew down, anchoring itself to the
weathered pier. Barely discernible in the mist, two-legged shadows
emerged from the ships.

The first thing Aidan saw was that the invaders were giants. He had always considered his father and the men of the *tuath* impossibly huge, but
these creatures were so broad and thick through chest and shoulders that
Aidan's father looked almost childlike in comparison. These were not
human beings at all. They were ogres, *sidhe* from hell, who would break
their bones and suck their marrow, down to the last screaming child.

He stumbled backwards as the first of the invaders stepped onto the
dock. Aidan was hidden behind a low wall now, but he swore that the *sidhe*
looked directly at him. The dock was aflame, and the invaders walked toward the village as if treading through deep mud, had all the time in the
world to breathe between each massive step. One raised a knife. To his
horror Aidan realized it was brother to the one he had found in the river
just that afternoon.

The fire's flare illuminated a Northman's face. It was a thing of tusks and
snout, more boar than man.

Suspended dizzyingly between dream and reality, Aidan wheeled and ran.

His feet pounded the earth. He registered distantly that the village
alarm bell was ringing. A few of the men and women tottered out into the
street shaking drink-muddled heads.

Half naked, Mahon himself had emerged, sun-burned chest broad and
bare in the dark. "Drown me! What mischief is this?" Cuaran, their left-
hand neighbor, seemed more awake: perhaps he had quaffed less deeply.

"Northmen!" screamed Cuaran. "Burning the boats!" He carried a hal-
berd, an evil mating of spear and boathook, equally suitable for splitting a
sapling or gutting an enemy. Aidan flattened against the wall as Cuaran
ran past, bellowing his challenge. Aidan had seen Cuaran hurl that
weapon half a hundred paces to behead a rabbit. Behind Cuaran was
Willig, and then Angus, the great bear. Aidan felt a swell of pride and
hope: These were the men of the *tuath*, mighty fishermen, fierce warriors.
They would send the Northmen howling back to hell!

Cuaran's arm drew back hard, and in another moment Aidan knew that
he would loose the thunderbolt—

Then Cuaran's head snapped back, and Aidan heard a sound like a whip cracking. Red splashed between the fisherman's eyes, and he flew backward to land in the dirt. The back of his head burst like rotted fruit, spattering the ground with seeds and pulp.

Aidan felt more awed confusion than fear. From his shadowed place he saw the burly, animal figures leveling long sticks, heard cracks, saw fire flash like lightning in the sky. A man behind him groaned and tumbled to the ground.

Were these gods? Or demons, emerged from the mist to hurl bolts of lightning? Hadn't the Druids made sacrifice, sung songs, danced and prayed and sown sacred seeds to the Tuatha de Dannan? Why, then, this day of destruction?

The crannog was fully awake now, and several villagers ran to those few boats still unconsumed by flames. Cennidi, the stout fisherman who tied his coracle next to Mahon's, tumbled to the ground, dead.

Cennidi's son Tirechan tried to save one of the boats, and a gout of fire erupted from the yawning mouth of a dragon ship; the youth became an instant ball of flames, screaming before he twisted jumping into the water.

Women and children scrambled from the huts now, fleeing away from the lake, toward the forest's shadowed depths.

His mother managed to make her voice heard above the frenzy. "Save the children!" she shrieked. "Quickly! Into the woods!"

Mahon had her by the shoulders, and Aidan ran to them. He grabbed Aidan's arm and pulled him close. Mahon's face was riven with strain. "Find my daughter," he said to Deirdre. "Care for our children. Pray for me." He clung to them both for a fierce, brief hug, and then was gone.

Aidan twisted and turned in his mother's grasp, trying to join his father, to fight, to die if necessary. He was old enough. He was!

But the straw roofs and wooden walls of the village were aflame, and there was another part of him that wouldn't let him tear free from his mother's side, something so completely overcome with terror that he could barely think.

Around him, men who had taught him to walk, to fish and to dance, fought and died in the dirt, their precious blood flowing in the mist-throttled moonlight.

"Nessa!" Deirdre called, voice cracking in the early-morning frost. "To me, girl!"

Deirdre called out again and again as she fled toward the rear of the village, toward the wooden bridge linking the crannog to forest and field.

With a despairing cry, Nessa crawled from beneath a hut and ran to them. As she did, another of those sharp, strange cracking sounds rang out, and Molloy the net mender fell, humping along the ground like a crushed river eel.

The night was chaos and red ruin. The men and childless women were fighting, while mothers and grandmothers attempted to flee.

"Ma!" Nessa cried.

"Come," Deirdre said, voice both soothing and firm. Framed by the wild light, her crimson hair wreathed her head in flame. "Quickly now . . ."

They were at the bridge now. On its far side lay the fields, and a hope of safety. But they were no more than halfway across when six net-wielding beast-men emerged from the shadows. Another boar, a stag, and one with an eagle's beak. Women and children were ensnared as they ran for the imagined safety of the forest.

Deirdre screamed and tried to turn back, but the masked men entangled the three of them. They fell into the dirt, the bestial eyes and mouths of their captors leering down at them. The captors' scent was a nauseating meld of rancid animal fat and caked sweat, thick enough to choke.

The net's rough strands bound Aidan's arms and legs tight enough to cut his skin. Aidan struggled until he was bested by fatigue and a gnawing, crippling fear beyond anything ever experienced in his young life.

His mother and sister strained against the tangled strands. "Mahon!" Deirdre screamed.

Nessa wormed a thin arm through the net, trying to claw her way free. "Help, Da!"

Suddenly, as if in answer to their prayer, Mahon O'Dere appeared. His shirt was red-streaked and torn, and he held a bloody axe aloft like a firebrand. His mighty arms were strained crimson, his eyes were wild. He seemed not completely the man Aidan called father; this enveloping night of horror seemed to have ripped away a facade to reveal something more primal than mere humanity. Aidan felt a strange and unaccustomed twining of fear, pride, and excitement.

One of the beast-men turned and charged just in time for Mahon's axe to cleave a diagonal chunk from his skull. A second raised his fire-stick. Mahon's arm whipped up and down. The axe flew from his hand end-over-end, blurred through the air, and struck the *sidhe*'s chest with a satisfying wet, hollow sound. Blood flowed, and the monster sank to his knees with an oddly human groan.

Then, thrillingly, Mahon pulled the golden knife from his belt, turning just in time to twist away from a descending sword, answering with a vicious upward stroke. The misery he wrought with the invaders' own weapon made Aidan's heart pound and sing in the same glorious instant.

"Yes! Father!"

Mahon's eyes met his for one golden moment. The boy was proud, hopeful. In that instant, it seemed that Aidan was on the verge of some terrific, overarching understanding of all the world's myriad things. Then another of those sharp, odd, cracking sounds rang out, and Mahon staggered. He froze in midmotion; his lips parted and crimson dribbled down over his beard. It seemed almost comical, as if he had brayed laughter with a mouthful of half-chewed berries. Then, still in that terrible slowness, he crumpled to the earth.

Aidan watched in disbelief as his father gasped like a beached fish, great hands clasping and unclasping, grabbing at the air as if he might be able to claw life from it. Their eyes met again, and this time there were no great answers there, only questions that would never be satisfied.

A giant strode into view, this one a man-bear. The beast looked down at the mortally wounded man, head tilted to one side. Thick hands rose to his own face, and peeled it away.

The face beneath was ruddy and unremarkable, windburned and bland. He had small, bright blue eyes and unruly red hair that stirred but little in the early morning breeze.

Aidan felt dizzy and sick. The bear-face was but a mask. Only a mask. The Northern demons were merely men, after all.

Almost tenderly, the invader bent down. He lifted Aidan's father's head with his left hand, and plucked the golden knife from the ground with the other.

As the Northman made the death stroke, Mahon's dazed eyes locked with his son's, blinked once, then rolled upward. And as darkness came to the father he loved, in the midst of his mother's and sister's pitiful screams, Aidan mercifully fell into a deeper, dreamless night.

And was gone.

CHAPTER FOUR

THE STENCH OF BURNT WOOD and flesh wafted with the uncaring breeze as women, children, and a few miserable, broken men were herded toward the ships, arms bound at their sides. One at a time the captives were shackled at the ankles with stout metal bands tight enough to numb limbs. Jarring hammer strokes locked them into place. Each bore a loop through which thumb-thick chain links were passed, connecting each miserable soul to another.

Aidan looked into the faces of the captive men and saw shock, disbelief, horror, and bleak resignation. Riley, the *tuath*'s massive blacksmith, was one such. Aidan understood why: the shambling, shamefaced Riley had preferred captivity to death. Aidan hated him. He should have died! Died as had Mahon O'Dere, fighting to be free, fighting for his family. Better a swift and endless sleep than this disgrace. Had not Aidan a sister and a mother to protect, he would have chosen the first good moment to jump overboard and drown himself.

He would, yes.

A brawny Northman locked the chains into place with thunderous hammer strokes. Nessa tried to kick him, and he casually backhanded her across the face so hard that at first Aidan thought her neck was snapped. She fell limply back, but the giant simply grabbed one of her ankles and dragged her forward. For Aidan, it was like watching events in a nightmare, submerging him in an ocean of rage so deep it blackened thought.

Now it was his mother's turn. Never had he seen her like this, wild-eyed, and almost like a drunkard. Her eyes were rolled up exposing the whites, and she pulled against the pig-eyed Northman's brawny arms. "Mary! Oh please, Mother of God," she screamed over and over again in a voice not entirely her own. "Do not forsake us!" Her thrashing was without aim, without real thought, almost as if she were some kind of dangle-toy twisting in the wind. After the chain was hammered on she was shoved aside and Aidan hauled into position.

He struggled without effect, and the Northman slapped him across the face. Stars exploded, the white sparks extinguished in an ocean of red, and then black. When he came to his senses, the first strokes had already fallen, linking him to the wall. His mouth felt swollen and nerveless. The boy's eyes narrowed as he ran his tongue around his mouth, tasting blood. He longed for a knife, a boat hook, a sword. Something to grasp in his hand as he leapt and died gloriously.

Like his father.

Pig-Eyes watched him, and something in the big man's face smiled, almost as if he approved of what he saw in Aidan. "Careful, boy," Pig-Eyes said, his voice guttural and unpracticed, as if he had never spoken a true language before.

Deirdre twisted about, her face pale, momentarily lifted from her own madness by the threat to her children. "Aidan!" she screamed. "Nessa! Don't fight—"

She was pushed brutally, but managed to reach back to take Aidan's hand. His sister's face, so like his own, was wide-eyed and slack. "Mother?" she asked.

His mother struggled to mask her terror with calm. "It's all right," she said. "All right. We're together."

With swift, ringing strokes the chains were hammered into place. They were walked up a plank and onto the dragon ship's deck, where they huddled on the deck in fear, guarded by armed, silent men.

Aidan put his face down. He would not let these monsters see him cry.

Like a great predator returning to its lair after a prodigious feeding, the dragon ships wallowed toward the river, swollen with their burden of living meat.

Don't cry. Don't cry. Don't—

Nessa gripped at his hand with hers, her small, sharp nails digging into his wrist. Her eyes were wide and almost unblinking, and she trembled like a trapped squirrel.

The journey from the lake to the sea was dreadfully peaceful, a silent slide between riverbanks lined with moss-hung trees and corded vines. He had fished these waters, played on those rocks, swum and run and speared frogs amid these shadowed corridors. And with every passing moment, every renewed moan from those chained beside him, the realization grew that he might never see this river again. That the village of his birth was gone. That he was in the hands of creatures whose motivations he could not begin to comprehend. That for the first time his mother and sister really needed him, and he was powerless to aid them.

The Northmen seemed to need no sleep or rest or food, remained on the alert at all times. They began to relax only after the sun began to dip toward the west and they began to smell salt in the air.

The ocean.

Its steady roar rose gradually, building to a churning rhythm. Despite his chains and sorrows Aidan's curiosity sharpened. The ocean! Ever he had hoped to see it. Never had he imagined his first sight would be in such a state.

The raid boats slid out along the river current, bucked the waves and then turned toward the south, where he finally saw their destination: another, larger version of the dragon ships. This vessel was three times the size of the river raiders. They slid past its prow, and he looked up into the dragon's mouth, seeing none of the black stains that must have marked the flow of fire. This ship was for carrying cargo, not raiding or destroying.

Under threat by axe and fire-stick their gang-chains were struck and replaced with leg irons and wrist irons. By twos, the miserable captives were dragged belowdecks into the ship's black maw. Those who resisted were clubbed and lowered into the hold. When it was Aidan's turn to descend he looked back at the coast, the white beaches he had never played upon, the dense green forest beyond. The sun was nearing the western horizon now. He wondered if he would ever see its golden rays again.

Rows of horizontal wooden shelves were mounted on each side of the hold, with a narrow aisle running between. Without another word they were shoved onto the planks. Their chains were shackled to metal claws mounted in the thick wood at their feet. Someone's feet were in Aidan's hair, and his own rested almost upon some woman's shoulders.

When the hatch banged shut the darkness was abysmal, and seemed to signal an end to all hope. A low moaning rose up from the captives, a funeral dirge for the living. A cry of lament for the dishonored, unburied dead.

There was no light, but Aidan heard the clinks as the captives struggled with futile desperation to free their leg irons from the locking mechanisms. He heard the voices of the Boru boys, heard bold little Morgan's cry, was dragged toward despair by the steady weeping of his mother and sister. The last wail he recognized was his own, torn from deep in his chest as the darkness without and within joined arms to enshroud him.

With much clanking and rumbling of the planks the great dragon ship weighed anchor. The fisherman in Aidan's bones told him that they were not headed out to deeper water but were traveling nonetheless.

It took hours for the weeping to stop and the first coherent conversation to begin. "Where are we going?" Morgan asked. Then: "Did anyone see my father? My ma?"

"Hush, child." said Deirdre. "They're gone."

Silence, and then a soft keening sound.

"They're going to eat us," said someone, the voice so thick with phlegm and misery that Aidan couldn't recognize it in the dark.

Riley the blacksmith made a heavy grunting sound. "They'll not eat us," he muttered. "They'll sell us. Sell us all for slaves."

There was murmuring, and more cries. Aidan knew of slaves, of course, although there were no bondsmen in O'Dere Crannog. Slaves were captives of war, or those with heavy debts, or farmers who could not feed themselves through the winter and so exchanged freedom for food and shelter. Without fortune or honor, they worked like beasts and were lucky if a mere ten summers passed before they could buy themselves free. Was this to be their fate?

"Slaves," someone else whispered in the darkness, and after that there was silence again.

Days passed in which misery finally gave way to numbness and boredom. Twice a day they were passed slop buckets filled with water, and each captive sipped at a ladle while Pig-Eyes watched, axe in hand. Once a day they were fed a chowder of fish guts and some kind of meal. Aidan refused it for the first two days, wanting to die. On the third he wolfed it down, and then spewed it back up again. The fourth day he managed to keep it in his belly.

They relieved themselves where they lay. Aidan managed to hold his piss for a full day, but then awoke from slumber having slimed himself. The smell of urine and feces clouded the air like a foul wet blanket, and each breath was an insult to the memory of freedom.

The chains rubbed against his ankles and wrists until they bled. Tiny insects swarmed out of the wooden floors and walls to nibble the chafed edges of his flesh. Up above, filtering down through the beams, he heard the roar of waves and wind, the harsh drumroll of rain. Despite his fear, or perhaps because of it, he felt terribly lethargic, and with the sound of raindrops pattering against the deck above, he fell asleep.

Aidan awakened as the door above them opened; the light projecting down upon them was gray and squalled.

Three armed Northmen descended, wet cloth wrapped around their faces to protect them from the stench. Despite that protection they choked and spit, glared at the captives as if the Irish had voluntarily chosen to live in such a manner. They selected several of the captives, including Aidan, Deirdre, and Nessa, and warned them with threatening gestures not to attempt escape. The metal stem was thrust into the hole beneath his leg irons as a Northman threatened Aidan's throat with a blade: there was no hope of action. Once they were freed, the Northman pulled him along and up the ladder. To his shame, Aidan hadn't the strength to resist.

Deirdre and Nessa came up on deck behind him, trembling in a thin frigid rain, looking out across a gray sea toward a distant, rocky shore. Several of their captors splashed them with buckets of salt water. Aidan winced as it seared his sores, but was grateful that the stinging waters also cleansed.

The deck lurched and swayed beneath their slippery feet, and as soon as Aidan steadied himself he began to wonder: Where were they? He could see the coastline, frighteningly distant, so far away he could barely make out individual trees. He recognized no rocks or hills. The wind didn't smell like any place he had been or known. This was beyond the edge of his world.

"Move. Quarter hour," Pig-Eyes said. "And then back down."

He understood by this that they were to move, to exercise their limbs, so that the numbness of long immobility would not cost limbs or life itself.

"Where are we going?" Nessa asked.

"South," his mother answered, her wet hair hanging to her shoulders.

Pig-Eyes was watching him with some interest. The rain plastered the man's mop of dark hair against his face. He seemed invulnerable, inured to the weather. Aidan gambled, like rolling bones in a game of chance, and approached him. "Where are you taking us?" he asked.

The man was cutting a piece of orange fruit with a knife. Aidan's belly leapt. In two days nothing had sloshed in his belly save the dreadful fish gruel. His gaze went back and forth between Pig-Eyes and the fruit. After a pause, the man cut a chunk of the fruit with his knife and threw it to Aidan. Aidan kept his eyes locked with the Northman's and handed the fruit to his sister. Nessa gnawed it to pieces in an instant.

Pig-Eyes smiled, nodded approval, and tossed Aidan the rest of the fruit. He fell upon it ravenously. The meat was as orange as the skin, sour-sweet and full of juice. Never had he tasted its like. The peel was thick and chewy, not as good as the pulpy part, but a damned sight better than the gruel. He ate half, and gave the rest to his mother.

All during this process, the Northman watched. When Aidan was finished, wiping the juice from his face, the man said: "Tarifa, Andalus."

He'd never heard the words before. Nessa turned to Deirdre. "Mother?"

Deirdre shook her head. "I don't know, Nessa. I don't know what an 'Andulus' is. But as long as we're together . . ."

"How can we be together?" Nessa said in the frailest voice he had ever heard from her. "Father is dead."

The Northman grunted and turned away, returning to his business.

Deirdre wiped the rain out of her face. "He would want us to be strong." She hugged her daughter as best the chains would allow, and for a moment the old firmness had returned. "All of us." Nessa leaned her head against her mother's breast, seeking solace. Deirdre closed her eyes tightly, then opened them and fixed Aidan with her gaze. "You're the man now."

Aidan gripped at the rail. He could vault it before anyone could stop him, knew that he could surrender to the welcoming waves, that he could be free of these monsters, free of his chains. But his mother and sister needed him, and heaven help him, he wanted to live. Even like this, he wanted to live.

Aidan marked time by the lowering of the slop buckets: two of water, one of fish gruel. The salt water that cleansed them also caked upon their skin, itching and chafing where their flesh pressed against boards or chains.

Nessa had sickened by the third day, could keep little down, and burned with fever by the fourth. He could not see her face, but her hot, wet hand clutched at him in the darkness.

"Aidan?" she whispered. "We're going to die, aren't we?"

He heard a rustling, and his mother's hand reached across to them in the darkness, joined with their own. "No," Deirdre said, managing to find sufficient vitality to lend certainty to her words. "We will survive."

Something seemed to flow out of Deirdre, and Aidan felt it, like a river of heat or light, their mother pouring desperate strength into her failing daughter. He felt her hand grow limp, and for a moment was certain she had died, then her fingers found him again, and the three of them were quiet.

Then, quietly at first, Nessa began to sing in the darkness. She sang a song loved by his father, and by the Druids, one he had heard crooned in the forest beyond the Crannog with blended voices that stirred the night sky.

"There is a distant isle.
Around which sea horses glisten
A fair course against the white-swelled surge,
Four feet uphold it . . ."

The darkness stirred around them as her wounded voice struggled against the weight of mortal fear. Another voice, this one Manannan the brewer, a thin, reedy tone heard often at drunken revels, now weaved its way through the stink and the murk like a sun-starved vine, twining with his sister's own.

"Feet of white bronze beneath it,
Glittering through beautiful ages
Lovely land throughout the world's age
On which the many blossoms fall . . ."

And one at a time the other voices joined in, beautiful in their tumbled harmony, a shared cry for a land forever lost.

"An ancient tree there is with blossoms
On which birds call to the precious hours
'Tis in harmony, it is their wont
To call together every hour.
To call together every hour . . ."

And though there were tears, Aidan was unspeakably proud of his sister, who for a few short moments had shouldered all their burdens, lifting the night so that they might glimpse, if only with their hearts, a glimmer of O'Dere crannog's gilded dawn.

CHAPTER FIVE

FOUR ENDLESS DAYS LATER, the ship made harbor. The planks echoed with clanks and groans, creaking wood, scraping iron and thumping feet, the bark of voices shouting tasks and curses in languages he did not comprehend.

Once again, the upper door opened, and three Northmen descended, two with whips, one bearing an axe. The lash fell among them, its bite etching lines of fire into their skin. Insult followed injury as buckets of brine sluiced the filth from their bodies once again. They bucked and sputtered and writhed, and begged their captors for relief, to no avail.

As they cowered, salt water streaming from their hair into their mouths and noses, the second whip man unlocked their chains. One at a time, they were herded stumbling and shaking up the ladder to the deck above. The sun blazed high and hot above them as Aidan emerged into the light. Pig-Eyes watched him as he climbed onto the deck and was herded along. Even if Pig-Eyes had thought of him as a prisoner, the Northman had responded to him with some measure of simple humanity. Aidan would have to face whatever came next bereft of even that meager protection.

Whip in hand, a burly Northman pushed and jabbed at them as they staggered along the deck, half blind and dizzy. "Come!" he growled. "Move! Move, damn you!" More seawater was sloshed over them, washing the remaining stink and caked salt onto the planks beneath their feet.

Wet and miserable, Aidan wobbled down the gangplank, supporting Nessa as he went. As his eyes adjusted to the light, he caught his first glimpse of the city. It spread behind the harbor like a crystal forest of gleaming spires and towers. His mouth fell open and he stared, certain at first that he was dead and in the heaven his mother's Christ promised him. Then he caught the smells of wood smoke and food, the ocean's clean brine scent, and knew that however impossible the vista, this was a physical place, a place in this world, not the realm of faeries or angels.

Wooden crates were piled high, the few open ones he saw filled with fish and salt. Strange animals—like horses, only with long necks and humped backs—carried loads of boxes and rolled bolts of fabric. The air was filled with smells of sweat and smoke, of blood and fresh-cut flowers.

Twice more he heard the word *Tarifa* used by Northmen, who pointed toward the towers, and he began to believe that that was the city's name, and called it so in his mind.

Colorful banners flew from glistening ivory peaks that he finally identified as some sort of dwellings, built higher than mountains, places where men ate and slept. There were cylindrical objects floating in the air, things as large as the dragon ships. At first he thought them some manner of enormous bird, then realized that they had sharp edges, like boats. Boats, floating in the air, moving as slowly as leaves drifting on the lake.

That sight drained the strength from his legs. Flying boats. Tarifa was not inhabited by men, then. Not men at all.

As he watched, one of the air-boats glided to the lip of a staggeringly tall tower. He swore he saw human shapes grabbing lines, and a gangplank of some kind fell forward. His mind reeled.

For those moments, Aidan completely forgot the bonds on his wrists, forgot everything but the impossible sights before him. The dock alone was larger than O'Dere crannog, and densely peopled. And what people! If the Northmen had seemed alien, the inhabitants of the strange, impossible town of Tarifa were stranger still.

"Is this heaven?" Nessa asked. "Are we dead?"

The weight of dread and awe in his mother's voice made it almost lifeless. "Not heaven, child. No."

No. Hell, then, and these were demons.

Tarifa's streets were filled with male and female demons that looked like human beings smeared with soot or mud. Most of their heads were wrapped in cloth, but bare heads were crowned with what looked more like black lamb's wool than real hair. They were dressed far more elaborately than either the Northmen or Aidan's own people. Their lips were thick, noses wide and blunt. They babbled in a language Aidan had never heard, more melodic than that of Pig-Eye's people. He could not understand a word.

They spoke. Did demons speak? Were they men after all? He remembered stories now, dread tales flooding into his mind, whispered around dying campfires. In a far land (so the stories went) lived a race of black warlocks. They were man-eaters and ravagers, with swords that cleft ordinary steel as an axe carves wood. The Druids spoke of their cities, irresistible armies, and vast knowledge. Traveling traders spoke in low voices of their wealth and cruelty.

Better he had died on the river, in the Lady's arms.

A hugely fat soot-man sat on a canopied chair at the dock, surrounded by alert, muscular black-skinned guards. At his feet knelt four white men, men like Aidan's father, only their eyes were cast down, as if they dared not meet their grotesque master's gaze.

Aidan stared: never had he seen so corpulent a human being. Rolls of dark meat cascaded on his face and neck. What he might look like beneath those robes Aidan could not even imagine. What kind of people had so much food they could afford to let one of their own gorge to such uselessness? Could this thing swim? Balance itself in a coracle? Hunt? Or even walk? He imagined that the guards were forced to lift this monster on their groaning backs whenever he needed to look behind him. With a dismissive flap of sausage fingers, he waved the captives into groups, while another dark man of normal human dimensions made tally marks on a slate.

The Northmen seemed proud and strong, but oddly deferential to the soot-men. As the last captive was dragged off the dragon ship, several soot-men wheeled over a box of the deadly fire-sticks. Aidan took the opportunity to glimpse one more closely: a thick metal rod joined to a carved wooden plank similar to the blade of an oar. Did these things catch lightning from the sky to spit it out again on command?

The Northmen handled the fire-sticks as if they were spun gold, and Aidan understood at once that this was their reward for the destruction of his village. The fire-sticks were fearful things, but the boy swore that one day he would learn their secrets. One day he would kill the killers.

As his fellows hauled the sticks aboard, Pig-Eye gripped Aidan's shoulder with one vast hand. In broken Gaelic he said. "Enjoy trip, little maggot." Whatever softness might once have lived in his face vanished as his northern brothers laughed.

Immediately Aidan and his family were surrounded by black-skinned men, creatures so strange they made the Northmen seem like cousins. And at this range, he could clearly see that they were men, though with dark eyes, thick lips, and blunt noses. They did not smell like men, but of flowers and fruit, as if they did not sweat, or perhaps exuded nectar. They smelled like husband-seeking girls at Festival.

Such skin! Dark as a starless, moonless night. And such clothing! So rich and variegated, robes that sparkled even in the light, as if threads of gold and silver were woven into their mesh. Never had he seen such wealth. The dark people shouted at them, poked, prodded, and forced the captives to form a line at a four-legged metal table.

One of the fat man's lackeys sat and regarded them. This man was primped and oiled, lips rouged, his black, woolly hair braided like a woman's, his lashes longer than those of Aidan's mother.

But when he spoke, his words were clearer and cleaner than any of the Northmen's had been, and Aidan didn't know whether to relax or contract with horror to hear familiar speech emerge so easily from the blunt, painted black lips.

"I am Fekesh!" he said. "Write your names!"

A guard thrust a quill pen into the blacksmith's meaty, stained hand. After shaking for a moment, he scrawled *Riley*. Fekesh glanced at it and nodded approvingly. He pushed the man toward a line of captives facing away from the docks. The soot-men supervising this line sat astride horses the likes of which Aidan had never seen. Some of the crannog's farmers had horses, of course, but they were plodding, slow-witted creatures that pulled plows or carts all day without rest. These were different: sleeker, more muscular, prouder—purer somehow.

The man who called himself Fekesh (and what kind of name was that?) turned to the next woman in line, Brigit, who made the best bread in the crannog, always somehow lighter and tastier, and it stayed warm in the belly for hours. Brigit was a thin, handsome woman who was now as dazed and haggard as the rest.

"Write! Name!"

Brigit shuddered. Her face was slack, pale, and she seemed on the very edge of collapse. "I . . . I never learned. I don't know how . . ."

Fekesh pursed his mouth and didn't even bother to meet her eyes. "*Zawariq*," he said. And two men grabbed her arms and hauled her back toward the dock. She screamed as she went. Aidan watched as if experiencing a dream, momentarily beyond emotion.

Deirdre was next. She swallowed hard, tried to stand strong. There, for a moment, was the woman Aidan knew, the ghost of her customary grace and dignity held around her like a ragged cloak. "Where are they going?" she asked.

One of the huge dark guards spoke in that garbled, choppy tongue, then took her face in one huge hand. Fekesh glared at her. "Those smart ones go to good masters," he said in their own tongue. "Alexandria. Athens. Addis Ababa. Not so good, work the fields in Bilalistan."

Deirdre's eyes narrowed in confusion. "Where?" She sounded desperate to understand what was happening.

"Across ocean. Write," Fekesh said. "Name."

With a shaking hand, Deirdre signed her name, and she was placed in the line of cleaner-looking captives. Although Aidan didn't completely understand what had happened, he had a deep sense that this was a good thing, that there was a real difference between the fates of those who could write and those who could not.

His mother turned to them. "It's all right now," she said, face glazed with a terrible, drunken smile. "You'll be with me."

Aidan started after her, but a rough hand seized his shoulders, yanked him back to the table, and thrust a pen at him. "Write," Fekesh said. "Name."

Aidan trembled now. For a moment the scene was frozen in his mind. He and his sister had always taken after their father, and Mahon was a fisherman. Aidan had loved the river more than he loved the world of books, and had brushed aside his mother's attempts to teach him the way of runes. Nessa, with her clever hands and feet, was little better. Why learn runes when there was a new stitch, a new recipe, a new dance step to learn? Why oh why had they not listened to their mother?

"No," Deirdre said, her voice a trembling singsong. She set her jaw tight, her eyes held unblinking on the man before her. "They're with *me*."

Fekesh glared at her with something so far beneath contempt that she might not have been human at all. He flicked his hand at a guard. The lash sliced her shoulders with a sound like a fire-stick calling lightning from the clouds.

Aidan's mother fell to her knees, red hair dangling limply around her face. When she looked up, the fear she had worked so hard to conceal burned in her eyes and mouth like the marks of a wasting disease.

Painfully slowly, Aidan struggled to make an X on the paper. The guard grunted impatiently and pulled him toward the other line of captives heading onto another, larger ship that looked to Aidan like the very ferry-boat to hell. All of the sailors were soot-men.

Nessa twisted piteously and helplessly, shoulders gripped by black hands as large as her head. Her frail strength had been almost extinguished by the dozen steps down the ladder. "Aidan!"

He was yanked away and dragged back toward the harbor. He stared back over his shoulder, eyes wide. "Mother . . . ?" he pled, beyond terror now. A hideous war raged behind Deirdre's beautiful eyes. Her frantic gaze lit upon the enormously large man on the canopied seat. The monstrosity was fanned by two small sunburned boys who might have been from Aidan's own village.

Deirdre broke away from the line and ran to the big man's chair, throwing herself onto her knees. The guard grabbed her feet and began to haul her away, her fingernails splintering against the dock. "Mercy!" she begged. "Please. Let me stay with my babies. I'll cook, clean, anything you want. Just don't take them away. Merciful Mary, please."

The guard tugged at her. With strength beyond reason, she clawed her way forward, and clung to the head man's swollen feet.

"Please!"

The big man gazed at her balefully, nothing but irritation in his fleshy face, then considered Aidan and Nessa. He spoke a few words to Fekesh, who walked over and presented the big man with the piece of paper on which Deirdre had scrawled. His small bright eyes glanced from the paper to her face, and back again. Then something happened that surprised Aidan. Abruptly, the hard lines around the man's mouth softened just a bit, as if he was remembering something, or thinking of something that was of pleasure to him. Incredible as it seemed, perhaps this creature had once known a mother's love.

Deirdre sobbed at his feet. The man's face gentled further, and his cheeks pouched in the barest smile. With a flourish, he ripped the paper in half, then in quarters, and scattered the pieces. "May Allah protect you," he said, and gestured sharply to the guards.

Allah? What was an "Allah"?

The enormous man spoke again in the unknown tongue. The guards replied curtly, and then Aidan, his mother, and his sister were all dragged back to the harbor. The indignity was utterly eclipsed by his overwhelming sense of relief that he would not be separated from his mother and sister.

For a brief moment Deirdre was able to embrace her children, and he squeezed tight, eyes closed, smelling her salty skin, pretending that they were home, and safe . . .

Then they were prodded up the gangplank and onto a triple-masted vessel with smoke rising from a central chimney. The back of the ship had something like a gigantic carpenter's screw trailing down into the water. It was thicker than he was tall, and turned very slowly. As it turned, water pulsed from its ridges. As Aidan's feet touched the ship's deck he felt it vibrate beneath him, chuffing in some odd way, as if within its bowels lurked one of the dragons that had exhaled fire onto their boats.

They were taken belowdecks, where the guards packed them in with the other captives. He saw the Boru boys, and Brigit the bread maker, and a half dozen completely strange faces. Hollow, frightened, resigned faces. Obviously O'Dere crannog had not been the only village raided.

Daylight receded behind them, and they seemed to enter another world. The black men hurried them along like cattle. "Move! Move!" one said, and forced them in tight, chaining them on horizontal shelves against the walls. They were crushed in like salted fish in a barrel, barely room to breathe or move, and the screams and moans were almost as bad as the lack of room.

He was startled to find himself on the shelf below Morgan. He had not seen her curled there in the dark, clothing soiled and torn. She seemed so small and frail, entirely shorn of her customary confidence. As more bodies were packed in the hold, she could restrain herself no longer. "Please!" she sobbed as the lash rained down upon her. "Have pity!" she screamed, writhing in its caress.

Finally she lay shivering, silent save for the rustle of her body convulsing on the pallet. Aidan's chain was locked into place.

"*Uskut!*" the guard commanded. "Silence!"

She flinched as he brandished the whip again. From across the aisle Kyle Boru cursed and kicked at the whip man, his leg chains somehow longer and less restraining than the others. "Bastards! You killed me Da—"

The kick thumped against the sailor's buttocks to little effect. The whip man turned, snarling, and brought the whip down again and again, cursing in that unknown language.

"No, Kyle, they'll kill ye!" his brother, Donough, screamed from somewhere down in the darkness.

"Don't watch," his mother whispered, but Aidan could not, would not take his eyes away.

Aidan *needed* to see it. See the bleeding hands as the lash ripped Kyle's fingers to the bone. See the upturned face as a lid was nearly torn away from its eye. See the nose as it broke, the shoulder as the skin peeled away. The body as it collapsed in total surrender.

"Kyle!" Donough sobbed. "Kyle . . ."

Aidan *needed* to burn this sight into his mind, into his heart. There would come a time, a way. He had to believe that. And if he could find that way, he might free his mother and sister. He would have to learn from the mistakes of others, even the poor sobbing wretch of a boy across the aisle even now pleading for mercy through a throat thickened by blood and tears.

When his time came, he would not fumble, he would not be clumsy. He would be swift, and direct, and deadly.

As his father would have been.

All that day new captives were herded into the hold, until at last Aidan lost count of them and fell into a doze. When he awakened, the light streaming through the hatch doors had narrowed and faded. Darkness deeper than night reigned absolute. Already the air grew heavy and hot, almost like breathing mud. The narrow shelves were so tightly packed that he could feel the fearful, fevered respirations of Morgan above him. There was no room to sit up. There were probably a hundred eighty captives crushed into a space that would have been grueling for sixty.

Their captors seemed to have less regard for them than Aidan had had for the village dog.

"Who here calls O'Dere home?" croaked Riley. Donough Boru, Morgan, Brigit, and Aidan's own family were the only ones to answer.

"Kyle?" Donough whispered anxiously. "Can you hear?"

"I'm sick," Kyle croaked at last. Then he added: "But O'Dere is my home." He made a sound that might have been a sob. "I want to go home."

"Who from Delbaeth?" a woman said quickly, and received five affirmatives.

"And Buanann?" said a voice younger than Aidan. "Is there no one from Buanann? Am I the only one here?"

There was no reply, and Aidan heard a soft wail.

Then the Delbaeth woman spoke. "Don't cry, little one. What is your name?"

"Cormac," the boy said. "Cormac of Buanann. Me ma and da are dead. All dead."

"Hush," said the woman. "So long as there is a woman of Eire, you have a mother."

"So long as there is a man," said a masculine voice across the aisle, "you have a father." A general murmur of agreement in the dark. "I am Niad of Cumhail, and I should be dead. I chose life over the company of my ancestors, and I must bear that burden. Coward I might be, but if you will have me, while we are together, call me father. And when we arrive in whatever hell waits for us, I will protect you as my son."

"Well spoke," Aidan murmured.

There was a pause, and then: "Niad?" said the boy.

"Yes?"

"Better a live dog than a dead lion."

And incredibly, Niad managed a grim laugh, echoed and amplified by other voices. There were no lions in that hold. Only live dogs.

But dogs, Aidan thought, could bite.

And so the dark game progressed. Villages of Cormac, of Dagda, of Cridinbhel all had lost children in that hold, and in reaching out to one another they found themselves.

For hours it seemed that there was no motion in the ship, and little sound except the distant, hollow sound of feet and muffled voices from above them and to the side. Then finally there was the gradual, soft swaying that told Aidan that they were under way, heading out to sea.

The talking had died away, leaving only an occasional sob or a whispered word of comfort in the silence.

"Aidan?" Nessa said quietly.

"Nessa?" He twisted in his chains, eyes wide, struggling to see her.

"If we die, I'm glad we're together," she said.

"We will live," he said. "And if they separate us, I will find you, I swear it."

"You swear?" Her words were soft, reedy, a child's voice, filled with a child's need to believe.

"I swear."

She sighed and rustled as he had heard a thousand times in the past. He knew that she was rolling onto her side, seeking the elusive comfort of sleep. Aidan hoped that her dreams would be sweeter than his. That is, if dreams were possible at all in such a dark and dreadful place.

CHAPTER SIX

THE SEVENTH NIGHT OUT, Aidan awakened from a nightmare to find the hold lurching and rocking like a treetop in the wind. He snapped to the end of his chains, felt them pull at his flesh and then yank him back onto his pallet.

"Christ, save us!" cried the woman below Aidan's feet.

"Goddess!" moaned the woman from Delbaeth. "I beg you, don't let me drown. Please—" Her plea was truncated by another savage lurch. Water poured down through the hatch and sloshed through the sludge of vomit and body waste slicking the center aisle.

Aidan was certain that the screw-ship would founder, bringing them a cleaner death than any other that might await. At least this way captives and captors would be delivered unto death together! And if there was a final Judgment, as Deirdre claimed, then they would see who was right, and who was damned.

The ship tilted like a dolphin dancing on its tail. Again, water gushed into the hold. Distantly, he heard screaming from the top deck and found himself hoping that some of the black bastards might have been washed overboard. A fisherman knew the peril of water: that which fed and succored could swallow as well. A fisherman made peace with the rivers and the sea, and feared it not. He hoped that every one of their captors would find death in the deep. Some prisoners wailed that they were going to die, but Aidan bit his lip and refused to scream.

Through most of their voyage, he had heard a deep thrumming in the ship's bowels, a pulse, almost as if the ship was a living thing, and sometimes he felt heat through the walls, heat that made the press of bodies even more agonizing.

But there were other times when that pulse died, and he knew in his bones, from the generations of fisher folk that had birthed him, that these were times when the ship used the power of wind to move them.

This strange ship, the flying boats, the towers that touched the clouds . . . all these things were the work of men. Black men, yes, but they were human. He had to believe that, or he was lost.

Drown us. Drown us all, now, and we die together. Not masters and slaves. Not eaters and eaten. But as folk who had wandered too far from land and paid the price fishermen have paid since God first blessed the land with life.

But they did not die. The ship did not founder. In time the waves hushed. The ship's stomach-voiding side-to-side lurch diminished, slowed, died. Stinking water drained from the hold, washing away some of the corruption with it. As the acid of mortal terror leeched from his belly, Aidan fell into an exhausted sleep.

Twice a day they were furnished with water, and once a day with food. The blacks seemed loath to venture into the dankness of the hold so great was the stench. On some days, the hold filled with tiny black flying things that swarmed over their wounds, crawled into mouth and eyes, and made sleep all but impossible. Aidan breathed the insects and the stink in and out for so long that they seemed a part of him, things he might never cleanse from nose and throat and lungs if he lived a thousand years.

He was constantly ill. Sick of his own festering wounds, which the black men daubed with a stinging, tarry slop. Sick of the sound of his own mother vomiting up her food, of the constant crying and pitiful attempts to comfort. Sick of the swarming flies, the fleas that festered, and of the rats that grew bold enough to chew the edges of suppurating wounds when a captive grew too weak or despairing to fend them off.

Sick of the dead.

Daily, now, it seemed that one or two of the captives yielded up their lives, killed by despair and unending horror. The black men searched among them every morning, and hauled the corpses up onto deck, perhaps to eat, perhaps to throw to the sharks.

It was not until they came for Kyle Boru, dragging his limp body from its pallet, that Aidan stirred from a glassy lethargy into full horror.

"No!" Donough screamed, the sound a raw-edged howl of despair. "He's not dead! He's moving! Stop!"

And Aidan watched the form of his friend, the terrible limpness as Kyle's head thumped down onto the muck-smeared center aisle. The pale palms turned upward in the thin light. The unblinking eyes, half-lidded, staring at them all without the slightest accusation. *Fear not,* he seemed to whisper. *Mourn not. I am safe, and away.*

He watched as Kyle was hauled out of the hold, trying to close his ears to the terrible, gut-wrenching howls of the surviving Boru boy. He clasped his hands over his ears, sealing them until all he could hear was his own frantic breaths echoing in his skull.

Finally, a wobble-legged Aidan was taken up along with some of the others. He feared he might be devoured or murdered. When the sunlight struck his face the agony of sudden blindness forced Aidan to forget his fears. He threw his hands in front of his eyes and shrieked, and the others joined their voices in choral protest.

When Aidan finally adapted to the light, he recoiled in horror: in every direction, as far as he could see, there was nothing but water. Endless rolling waves, no sight of land, nothing but sea in all directions. He was stunned out of his pain, transfixed by the sight. Who would have thought there was so much water in all the world? To hear tales of something called an "ocean" was one thing. To be adrift in such an impossibly liquid world was something else altogether.

"Where is the land?" murmured Niad of Cumhail, close behind him.

"Don't know," said a man in front. His wild pale beard was matted with black and yellow specks. "Water has swallowed the world."

The air was so still that the smoke from the ship's chimney rose almost straight up. From where he stood Aidan could not see the screw turning at the back of the ship, but felt the vibration beneath his feet.

He heard a splash to his left, and turned in time to see a woman's body rolled over the side into the ocean. Had one of her hands struggled, feebly, to cling to the rail? No, he couldn't believe that, couldn't allow that image to remain in his mind.

The black sailors bent down and hefted up a smaller, male form. Aidan watched, numb, as it cleft the water.

Even when the whips cracked and their captors forced their unsteady legs to walk around the deck, Aidan could but stare out over the rail. Water, only water. An endless blue hell, restless and avid.

Every few days a clutch of the captives were brought up on the deck, lashed until they shambled about the boat, told to _banjala-t! Dance!_ as whips fell about their shoulders. They lurched and ran and hopped as the blacks threw buckets of brine on them, noses wrapped in wet rags to ward off the stench.

But their sores, from shackles and fleas and rats and near starvation, never healed. The brine could not rinse away the blood and pus, and the fish slop ran in the mouth and out between the legs without pausing to offer nourishment.

The black men examined their miserable cargo, and seemed to feel that too many of them were sick, too many dying. As a result, the quality of food increased, they received more time out of the hold and on the deck, and the abysmal depths of the ship were sluiced out daily with brine mixed with some kind of sour-smelling potion.

Sometimes Aidan was allowed to lie on the deck for an hour at a time. He gazed up at the sails, or the smoking chimney, or watched the eternally rotating screw as it chewed its way through the water. Half sick and half asleep, half alive and half dead, he wondered at such times if there had ever been an existence before this one.

Then Nessa might find his hand with hers, and he would see in her haggard face the shadow of her old smile, and he knew that there had been a past for them. And if a past, then perhaps too a future.

He had life. And therefore, hope. Given that much, he would create the rest.

When the sea water slopped down into the hold, Aidan prayed for death. At other times, he prayed for life to a God who had apparently forgotten he was ever born, or worse: was angry with him. Nessa seemed to collapse into herself, lost the ability to speak although their mother sang to them in a weak voice, seeking to comfort with song what her arms could no longer reach or hold.

What strength she offered was given at great price to her own mind and body. She could barely move, herself. When the hatch lifted he could see her, just across the aisle, lying on her side, chained to the wall, coated in her own filth. Deirdre was mortified by her sickness and helplessness, and one night, thrashing and screaming at phantoms, she awakened with a wail of despair.

"Ma," Aidan whispered. "What's wrong?"

For a time she didn't answer, and at first he thought that perhaps she wouldn't. "I've lost my baby." Her voice was bereft of hope. "I've lost Mahon's child."

He was dumbstruck, amazed that he had forgotten that she carried his father's seed. And realized that she hadn't mentioned it, had carried that burden on her shoulders, alone, hoping against hope that the rigors of the voyage would not tear his unborn brother or sister from her womb.

"Forgive me, Mahon," she sobbed. "Forgive me . . ."

And there was nothing that Aidan could think to say in comfort.

          *   *   *

She had muttered "Forgive me . . ." for seemingly endless hours when the hatch opened and the food bucket was lowered once again. Three of the black men, cloths tied across their faces, followed it and were moving along offering ladles of slop to the captives.

He could see his mother's face, now all hollow eyes and slack mouth.

"I'm not eating today," she said.

"Ma," Nessa whispered. Aidan prayed that she might say more, but his sister fell silent.

"You've got to eat, Ma," Aidan said. "If you don't eat, you'll die."

She gazed at him. "We're already dead," she whispered. "I remember stories about hell, and a river the dead cross to reach it. This is that river, Aidan. My people were wrong. There is no Christ. There is no heaven. There's only hell." She began to weep.

"Ma," he whispered as the bucket grew closer. "If you don't eat, they'll just pour it down your throat. Please. For Nessa."

Deirdre stared at him, and he saw the tip of her tongue extend to wet her cracked and bleeding lips. Then she nodded, just a tiny one, and when the bucket came to her, she ate.

At night, often one of the black men descended into the hold, carrying a lantern. He would study them, and select one of the women, and unlock her chain, forcing her to climb the ladder to the deck. They protested and some-times struggled, but ultimately always went. When the woman returned Aidan noted she had been washed clean, but walked as though she had waded through a river of filth, and sobbed until dawn brought restless sleep.

Once one of the women was simply too sick and weak to move, even when struck. The black man called up to the deck, and two of his com-panions came down. The sight of the new men seemed to galvanize her. She struggled to rise, but her weakness was not feigned, and she collapsed back onto her pallet. They unlocked her and hauled her away.

"Why?" she begged. "I'm sick. I'm sick. Please don't—"

Only minutes later, Aidan and his family were brought up onto the deck, blinking and struggling to shade their eyes against the light. Each step felt as if his legs had turned into dead eels.

Nessa, still almost completely silent, was actually a bit stronger than his mother now, perhaps physically stronger than Aidan. Their tattered, stinking clothing flapped in the breeze

Then he saw the sick woman. She was broad-hipped and bony, pocked with wet-lipped sores, her hair a deeper red than Deirdre's. He didn't know her, but thought that perhaps she was one of the three women from Cumhail, east and upriver of O'Dere. A burly black man struck off her chains. Two others hauled her to her feet, and to the edge of the ship. Then they simply threw her overboard.

The woman who had been chained next to her howled "Goddess! Why do you forsake us! Let us die, let me die—" Despite her travails, she had fewer sores than most of the others, and her flesh seemed more firm. The black men poked at her, lifting her tattered dress, squeezing her leg and thigh as she shrieked. Her cries seemed only to excite them, and laughing, they unlocked her chain. She scraped at the deck, pulling at the muck with her fingernails as the men grabbed her legs and dragged her away. Her prayers became unintelligible howls as they shoved her behind one of the smokestacks.

Her howls grew ever more anguished, then, as Aidan listened, assumed a deeper, more wrenching quality.

Deirdre pulled her children close. Together, they shivered in the ocean spray. Her cries became prayers again, mixed with deep male laughter. After a few minutes the prayers became numb, brute sounds, and even those sounds, in time, surrendered to the eternal, merciless roar of the waves.

CHAPTER SEVEN

29 Safar 1280 A.H.
(A.D. August 14, 1863)

AIDAN DREAMED OF SWIMMING IN CLEAR, cold water, surrounded by salmon and trout, ever flashing just beyond his reach. He was wrenched from that dream by a sudden, violent sound and a flood of light, and emerged along a tunnel of pain and fear back into the world of captivity.

The ship lay at rest, and the upper hatch had opened. Through it, a stream of dust-speckled light assaulted their eyes. The black men swarmed down into the hold, unlocked the chains from the restraining hooks, and herded all the captives up onto the top deck.

Aidan clung to Deirdre, all of his pretense to manhood vanished. Oddly, his fear and weakness seemed to give her strength. She lurched upright, eyes ringed darkly, cheeks gaunt, but standing straight. Her body radiated heat, as if the fever within her were banked, but might never be extinguished.

Finally, Nessa found her voice. "Ma," she asked. "What now?"

"We don't know," Deirdre said. "We'll find out soon. God won't ask more from us than we can give." Aidan was both shocked and humbled. How could she, again and again, put faith in her Christ? Even in such a state, his mother had infinitely more strength than Aidan had ever imagined. He tried to believe. Needed desperately to believe.

Aidan shaded his eyes from the light and waited for normal vision to return. His first glimpse of the world above made him fear the strain of captivity had broken his mind at last.

Standing astride a stone island, its titanic back turned to them, stood a colossus. Taller than thirty men, the great columns of its legs were like the spurs of a mountainside, its shoulders as wide as the horizon.

Aidan gawked, his mind refusing to connect what he was seeing to the world of flesh and blood.

The captives, bound as they were, were silent as their ship glided past the titan. Runes of some kind were carved at the base. Nessa turned to Deirdre. "Can you read it, Mama?"

Deirdre merely shook her head. "No. And I don't think I'd want to know."

As they glided into harbor Aidan was finally able to see the man's face, towering above them. It was strong, but not cruel. After a moment of superstitious awe, Aidan realized that this immense statue was the work of men, not some living being frozen by ice or magic. The unknown artisans had given the face a sublime nobility. The features were clearly those of a black man: thick lips, blunt nose, and hair like wool. However mortal, this was also a man of great spirit, suffused in full waking with the kind of vision that most mortal men could barely hold in their dreams.

The screwship slid past a dozen resting steamscrews and sail ships, then nestled into a dock fronting a half-mile of wooden buildings. After the lines were tied on, the captives were herded down, still blinking against the sunlight and fighting for balance.

When his feet touched solid ground he almost fell to his knees in thanks. He had lost track of the time that he had been at sea. Had a moon passed? Two? Perhaps. Too many days had been spent in a kind of stuporous haze.

They were immediately surrounded by black people wearing costumes as strange as those in the last port, without quite so much gold and jewelry. They wore brightly colored robes and hats of wound cloth, and save for the color of their skin and blunt features, reminded him of his own *tuath*: these were strong, hardy folk, filled with physical energy and vigor. They stood and walked erect, and their words, though beyond his comprehension, were bright and loud. Nowhere did he see the likes of the fat monster who had sent them on the ship, or his effeminate lackey.

There were no buildings here even half so tall as those in "Tarifa," and Aidan saw none of those strange flying boats. He sensed that this was a newer world, one still being built, as his great-grandfather had once constructed O'Dere crannog. Some buildings were mere skeletons, still gathering flesh. Most of the walls seemed constructed of stone or some kind of hard, grainy mud: there wasn't much wood in use. In addition, this city contained far more open, cleared spaces, where in Tarifa he had seen only a tight-packed confusion. There were still trees and grass and bare ground in sight. It would take endless labor to transform this world into the one he had seen a few weeks before.

Was this their fate? Lives of endless labor, constructing a kingdom for these dark demigods?

Many of these blacks wore leather aprons, gloves, heavy boots, and he guessed them to be laborers and workers. *Not gods, humans.* They stared at him with open contempt, speaking in voices that seemed guttural and unrefined. Some of them carried fishing hooks and some variety of fancy netting. Fishermen, then.

Some say they are going to sell us, he thought. *Perhaps they will sell me to a fisherman.*

A very few members of the crowd wore more gold and jewelry. One woman had something that looked halfway between a tiny man and a hairy squirrel perched on her shoulder. It had a gold ring about its neck. One of the Little People?

Her mate was half a head taller, wore a crimson robe trimmed in silver and jeweled rings upon his black fingers. They looked soft-bodied, their wealth obviously produced by the labor of others. The couple was unmistakably high-caste, perhaps even king and queen of this place. Wealthy, at any rate, and Aidan revised his hopes. *This* was the preferable fate. Sell his family to one of these soft ones. He would kill them, escape, steal a boat, and find a way back to their homeland. Somehow.

The black men evaluated them with hungry eyes, ravenous eyes, caressing every curve of the women who had survived the journey. They yammered amongst themselves, obviously speculating about the slaves. Despite her haggard state one bone-thin man leered at Aidan's mother. Through huge fleshy lips he laughed something to a shorter companion. Deirdre pulled her tattered dress around her, covering a length of exposed thigh, and turned her face away. Aidan wanted to leap and savage the dark throat with his teeth.

But as they were marched onward, one man grabbed Deirdre's arm, gobbled something in that alien tongue, and pulled at her soiled dress. Aidan snarled, but before he could move the whip came down on his head. Stars exploded behind his eyes and Aidan sank to his knees, could only lie there dazedly as his mother's breasts were exposed, as dark fingers poked at her belly. She kept her face tilted up at the sky, as if there were answers hidden in the clouds. When the men were finished, Aidan was hauled to his feet and marched onward.

Behind him Nessa seemed to shrink within herself, perhaps trying to make herself appear as young as possible. Where before she had been proud of her budding breasts, now as the soot-men stared at her they seemed a source of terror.

The men clearly bid the captors expose the girls to view, and Brigit was halted right then and there, roughly turned around, her remaining tatters torn from her so that she stood naked and trembling before the crowd. They cheered and laughed, appeared to be making bets with each other about something.

Aidan was numb by now, felt little or nothing. The blow to his head seemed to have broken some crucial connection between heart and mind. This was a dream. *A dream.* This was a dream, and he would awaken. He *had* to awaken.

A black man in fine purple robes stepped forward and examined Brigit more carefully. She slapped at him and he snapped his head back, braying laughter, and spoke to their captors, holding up three fingers. In reply, the guard held up seven. The man laughed and stepped back into the crowd. The procession continued.

They walked between rows of shops and market stalls for a half hour, pelted, laughed at, and spit on as they did. At last they reached a long, low building that smelled as if it had been used for animal storage. The floor was strewn with straw and the walls set with rows of the loathsome iron restraining rings. The gang-chain was unfastened and they were herded in lots of ten into small rooms walled with metal bars. The door clanged shut on them; Aidan stared out.

What was this world? What possible horror would tomorrow bring? Nessa trembled against him, and their mother wrapped her arms around them both. In this cruel place such a gesture seemed more symbol than substance.

Suddenly Aidan could no longer restrain his emotions. Fresh tears streamed down his face. He felt as if someone were standing on his chest. He pushed his way through the crowd of captives until he reached the barred doors. "Let me out!" The scream was like some clawed bird that had nested in his throat.

His scream was taken up by the others, and soon more than a hundred of them wrung the bars and stomped the floor in a shouting, screaming cacophony.

A gigantic brown-skinned guard approached the bars and peered at him. For just a moment, Aidan thought that the man might have understood. Certainly the blacks didn't know that Aidan possessed land, and cattle, and skills. That in time he might have been leader of his *tuath*, and that his great-grandfather had founded O'Dere crannog. Certainly, if they knew those things, they would free him and his family.

With casual brutality, the guard slammed a leather truncheon against Aidan's fingers. Then with a roar he slammed the club against anyone in reach, sending them reeling back with bloodied hands and gashed scalps.

Aidan gasped and reeled back, sucking at his wounded hand, trying to dampen the bright flare of pain. The holding pen was filled with screams and sobs. Aidan wanted to curl up and seal himself off from the world, shut himself away from everything but his own pain and misery.

Deirdre drew Aidan close, trying to comfort him. "It's all right, Aidan," she crooned, as she had a thousand times before. "We're together."

But as she spoke a growling sound just outside the bars caught her attention. The sun had passed the line of the horizon behind the giant's statue. His shadow swelled to fall across them, dimming the streets. The alleyway between their prison and the next building was now dark, growing darker by the moment.

Something lived and moved in that darkness. Aidan clambered back to the window, peered out. A strange, quasi-human shape lurked just outside the bars. He couldn't see what it was, but it seemed to be something misshapen and hideous, perhaps as tall as he. It shambled by in the darkness, and Aidan pulled back before it passed, not wanting to attract its attention. What in heaven's name?

The holding area was closing up now, and their captors laughed, one of them making some kind of mocking, bestial face as he left. He heard the single word *"Thoth-maimûn,"* then the door clanged and there was silence, and deeper darkness.

They heard the animal sounds again, growling sounds. Distant and bestial. Close, and then distant. Aidan's nose wrinkled: this was an animal stink, something unfamiliar, something that made the hair on the back of his neck twitch and creep. *Danger. Danger here . . .*

Nessa's eyes narrowed. She smelled it too. "There's something out there, Aidan. It's not a man."

"What, then?"

She shook her head. "I don't know." She sounded less afraid than he felt. Once again, the strength seemed to be flowing between them, among them, fluid as the tide of the lost Lady.

A water bucket sat just beyond the bars. As the night grew deeper and day's heat abated, their thirst grew more intense. One of the men gazed at the water bucket, and finally, unable to repress his thirst any longer, he reached out through the bars, his fingers almost brushing the bucket. Just a little further, just a little more . . .

With blinding speed, something that looked like a thin, hairy human arm lashed out of the shadows. Aidan heard a sharp doglike bark as a furred, taloned claw raked skin from the thirsty man's outstretched hand. The captive reeled back, holding his bloodied fingers. Animal snarls mingled with brays of human laughter from beyond. Beast? Demon? Aidan didn't know, couldn't be sure, but their human captors were grotesquely amused.

Hatred raged within him. To kill or capture men and women might be considered the fortunes of war. His people had many stories of heroes and bloody battles, villages burned and pillaged, captives taken.

But to rejoice in their pain was something else, an evil for which he had no name. What he could not define made him uneasy, and he would rather feel hatred than the weakness of fear.

Beside him Deirdre held his sister with desperate strength. Nessa's hands no longer clenched in return. They hung limply. By the poor light remaining to them, it seemed to Aidan that Nessa's life was simply draining away from her. Her skin seemed almost translucent, the cheekbones protruding, eye sockets clearly visible, and he felt he could see her skull despite the layer of flesh.

*   *   *

Morning came at last. The door swung open in the corridor, and brown guards bearing whips entered the cell area. The slaves huddled back as their door was opened.

One of the guards had white skin. Aidan's heart leapt as he realized that this man might be an ally, might have been of Eire or even one of the neighboring villages . . .

But a steel collar clasped the white neck, and there was no kindness in his eyes or manner. When Brigit stumbled, his whip strokes fell just as readily as those of any black man.

A chain was threaded from Aidan's neck collar to Nessa's, and then to their mother's.

When they passed out of the holding cell they stumbled down a narrow alley and into a wider courtyard packed with soot-people. Here there were buildings with six or seven horizontal rows of windows, fewer than those in Andulus, but still dwarfing anything in the land of his birth. Rectangles of crimson cloth emblazoned with a crescent moon and the face of some great catlike beast flew at their corners and upon poles. Some buildings were flat-roofed, and seemed constructed of white stone or precisely hewn wood, of a workmanship such as he had never seen.

The ground beneath his feet was plated with carefully joined stone, or hard-packed gravel set in a binding of dried mud.

As they were herded into a corner of the courtyard, hundreds upon hundreds of the strange dark people jabbered at them. Blue-black and brown-skinned, gaping and gawking and chattering in the strange language as the captives were poked and prodded, forced to display hands and breasts and genitals. Those who resisted were beaten to their knees, then pulled erect and forced to submit.

The black men wore billowing, colorful shirts, their women generally less colorful dress, and often a rectangle of thin cloth across their faces. Sometimes the facial cloths completely obscured their features, but in other cases he could clearly see dark cheeks, full lips, white teeth.

The captives were filed past a table where their wrists were stamped with black paint in the shape of a crescent moon. Then they were ushered through another double row of gawkers who chattered to each other and pointed and laughed.

Some waved a fistful of paper. Others displayed gold coins. *They're bidding against each other,* Aidan realized. He had seen fish and grain sold in such a fashion. These people were . . .

Buyers. He had to let that word into his mind, that realization into his consciousness. Buyers. They were being bought and sold.

* * *

Sick and weak at the knees, Deirdre watched the entire process of wrist stamping. A wooden dowel as thick as the circle of her thumb and forefinger was pressed into dark paint, and then rolled against the outstretched arm.

The stamper then took a thinner stick, dipped it in ink and made marks upon a sheet of paper. This man was branding and counting, as she had seen merchants and traders do since girlhood. It was then that she fully understood what this was all about, what she and her children faced. Late at night, when the children were asleep and the adults of the crannog gathered around the fire, some of the Druids and the older folk told stories of the Northmen and how they raided villages, stealing women and children to sell to dark people they called "Moors." A very few of those had escaped and found their way home, with tales of a fabulous land of unbelievable wealth and power. But they also whispered that many were sent across the sea to another world, from which no one had ever returned at all.

This was, she knew in her numbed and aching heart, that very land. She felt a shell of herself. The weeks of breathing foul air, eating foul food, and drinking water not fit to slop hogs had broken her. But with the power found only in the depths of a mother's loving heart, Deirdre summoned up what strength remained to her and hardened her spirit. If there was no hope of ever finding a way home, then she must resolve to find the best life she could for her children here in this new and alien world. But how?

Blurred by fever but sharpened by fear, her mind raced. She had all but given up hope when her time came for the wrist-stamp. Then, inspiration struck. She lunged forward, snatching the ink-stick from the trader's hand. The guards leaped to restrain her, but before they could she had scrawled the letters DEIR on a piece of paper.

The guard ripped the stylus from her hand, but the trader stopped him before he could strike her. The interest and intelligence in the trader's dark, slightly slanted eyes was evident. Her heart almost stopped. *This* was what she had prayed for. In the previous land, the place they called "Tarifia" or perhaps "Andalus," it seemed that those who could write were destined for a better quality of life. Perhaps the same applied here. She could only hope that among these people, reading and writing might be skills of sufficient value to give her the slightest bit of leverage.

The trader studied her with open curiosity. Then to her astonishment and vast relief, began to speak to her in her own tongue.

"You can write?" he asked.

Her answer tumbled out with desperate speed. "Yes," she said. "And read."

"Ah . . ." His eyes did not see a human being standing before him. His eyes counted gold.

"Keep my family together, please." She reached back, grasped Aidan and Nessa by the arms, and pulled them close. "My son and daughter. Please. I'll work myself to death for you."

He examined her collar and noted the number thereon. A smile curved his lips, then was gone. He waved her on, glanced at Aidan and Nessa's collars, then returned to his papers, first scrawling something illegible by their numbers.

She and the other captives were taken to the block, paraded back and forth. Deirdre shuddered at every bid, every jeer and catcall. A brown-skinned man was bidding fiercely. Some around him laughed and repeatedly said *Ob-Kob*, as if it were his name.

The auctioneer slammed his palm on the podium. A guard tugged at her chain, and she turned to Aidan and Nessa, who had watched her machinations with wonder and hope.

"Come, now . . ." she began, but as they stepped forward a guard stepped brusquely between them, pushing Aidan toward his mother and pulling Nessa away.

Shock followed shock as another guard grabbed the chain between Nessa's wrists and pulled her toward a tall, imperious black woman in butter-colored robes. Three white girls Nessa's age or younger already cowered in the dust at her sandaled feet.

Nessa's eyes rolled white, flashing from the tall woman back to her mother.

"Ma?" she whispered, the single syllable repeated again, growing from a disbelieving whisper to a banshee's wail. "Ma!"

Aidan surged toward her, and was whipped across the face. Deirdre felt that blow as if it were her own flesh that had been torn. Aidan stumbled bleeding to the ground. Deirdre was able to take only a single step before a tug at her collar chain nearly ripped her feet from under her. She turned to meet the pitiless face of a burly white guard, his own throat collared. He held her chain in a hand broader than her head. "Please. She's supposed to come with me!" she begged. He could not, or would not, understand.

Nessa dug her feet into the ground, but to no avail. She was simply dragged toward the tall woman. She fought and bit and clawed and then was cuffed on the side of the head. She slumped, and they dragged her the rest of the way, then chained her to the other girls.

Deirdre's heart raced, breaking. Despite her prayers, her fears of death on the ocean, she had always known that this moment might come, that Aidan or her precious girl-child might be torn away, sent down hell's own road to an unknown fate. Eyes wide with terror, somehow Deirdre managed to raise her voice. "Nessa! Nessa! Be strong, darling." Then grief seemed to close her throat, and she could only cry, her hands reaching out, clawing for her daughter, body pulling against the chain until her neck shackle cut off her air and she sagged sobbing to her knees.

The hands were closing in on them, separating them. Forever. Aidan had risen to all fours, trembling. "Nessa!" he called. "Remember what I promised you."

"What?" Nessa's single word could barely force its way through a throat filled with tears.

"That I'll find you. I swear it."

Her eyes were locked on his. To Deirdre, drinking in the sight of her children's yellow hair, their round pale faces and bright blue eyes, they seemed more alike than on the day of their birth. A single bright soul trapped in two captured bodies. "You swear?"

Somehow, Aidan managed to sound certain. "I swear on our father's life."

She nodded, tried to smile, her golden hair ragged and dirty around her shoulders. "I believe you, Aidan. I'll wait for you. I'll—"

Deirdre would never forget her last view of her daughter, Nessa's arms extended, face distorted, stretched taut like a skin across a coracle frame. "Ma! Aidan!" she cried. "Oh, God! I love—"

She was shoved away, and Deirdre lost sight of her. Deirdre and her son were stunned into silence, and before they could gather their senses were herded along a narrow row between stacks of wooden crates to a wider spot far from the market. There Oko met them and passed money to their guard.

Deirdre babbled out words. "My family was supposed to stay together," she wept. "Please. There's been a mistake—"

Without a word in answer, they were prodded and shoved through a bustling black mob into a waiting cart crowded with several other slaves. Although in her heart Deirdre knew her efforts would mean nothing, still she had to try. "It's a mistake!" she called. "Oh God, oh Mother Mary, won't someone help us? Please, please, it's a . . . mistake . . ."

But no answer emerged from the sea of alien black faces. Deirdre sank weeping to her knees, could not be made to stand. All of her strength was gone, and sobs wracked her with such violence that she could barely breathe, and had to be lifted up just so her chains could be fastened to the inside of the cart.

Aidan stood over his mother, teeth bared and eyes wide, struggling not to remember his last view of Nessa, dragged off to heaven knew what fate. Slavery? Rape?

Worse?

He squeezed his lids so tightly shut that lines of light and color erupted through the darkness. He bit his lip to drive the images from his mind. That way lay madness, and it was not a distant journey.

Nessa would live. He would live. And somehow, he would keep his promise.

The cart began to roll away. He watched the slave block and market square recede, then vanish in a maze of stalls and shops and clay-roofed buildings tall enough to blot out the sun.

CHAPTER EIGHT

THE CART ROLLED OUT OF THE MARKET onto a hard-packed clay road and began a slow and steady journey to the northeast. The intervening territory was mostly sandy soil and scrub brush. From time to time they passed rows of white slaves laboring in the sun, under the watchful eye of white and black overseers. Aidan did not recognize the crops being worked: strange plants in neat rows that extended almost to the horizon. Little dusky woolen-haired children ran alongside the cart, yelling and jeering at them. Aidan longed to jump down from the cart and beat the little boys into the ground. He was as good as them. Better! He would show them!

By the time the sun was a hand's-breadth above the western horizon, they reached a river. There they were unloaded onto a boat similar to the one that had taken them across the ocean, only smaller. A single chimney belched clouds of white smoke. The rear of it was another mighty screw-shaped device. Even now it turned lazily, shucking waves of water into the river.

They were marched aboard and anchored to bolts set in the inside walls. Aidan watched everything, missed nothing, and saw that despite the apparent casualness with which they were treated, there was no moment at which escape was possible. They were chained, or escorted in small groups, under the threat of whips and fire-sticks at every moment. This thing that had happened to his family had been going on for a very long time, and their captors knew far more about it than he could possibly imagine. Captivity was their very trade, and they knew it as Mahon had known fishing. A time would come—Aidan had to believe it. But that time was not now.

Before the sun had vanished completely, the boat finally pulled away from the dock and began its journey north.

Besides the captives, there was only one other white face on the ship: an elderly man, all bone and gristle, tufts of gray hair sprouting from his ears. He mopped the deck with slow, measured strokes, as if he had all night to complete his task.

Deirdre watched him for some minutes before venturing an attempt at conversation. "Do you know where they're taking us?"

He never looked at them, and spoke without moving his lips. "It's inland you're going," he whispered. "Dar Kush. Now let me work."

He turned away from them. Aidan tested his chains. He could not budge them, and knew there was no chance of breaking them. He watched the water flow.

The river was wider, flatter than the Lady. Unknowable. Somehow, watching it, the sheer irreversibility of his situation seemed to settle about him. *Even the waters here are alien,* he thought. He had half a mind to free himself, leap overboard and drown. But it would not be the Lady's waters that filled his lungs, not her cool and crystalline arms that welcomed him, and without them, he could not find his way home.

PART TWO

The New World

"In the universe," said the Master, "there are three forces: affirming, denying, and reconciling."

"How does this manifest in the world?" asked the student.

"In many ways. For instance: there is Life, there is Death, and there is the Transcendent."

"I do not understand. Can you tell me how these forces manifest in the affairs of men?"

"Yes, and from your own experience. There is Master."

"Yes."

"There is Slave."

"Yes."

"And there is Friend."

The student paused, then said, "Yes. I see."

CHAPTER NINE

22 Shawwal 1280
(March 31, 1864)

You cannot escape God. You will meet Him in foreign lands.

NAMIBIAN PROVERB

IN THE SPRAWLING TORCHLIT FIELDS adjacent to the Wakil's castle, six horses thundered toward a red flag posted at a mile-distant stand of juniper. Their hooves tore clods of grass and dirt from the pasture as with crop and heel their riders urged them to ultimate effort.

On the sidelines laughing, bearded nobles and highborn in brilliant raiment raised their fists to the night sky, waving clutches of tan banknotes and rectangular gold coins. They hailed from Abyssinia, from Zululand and Moorish Almagrib. There were even a few aquiline visitors from great Alexandria herself. Their skin shaded from blackest black to a creamy coffee, but they were one people in their appreciation of the evening's sport.

The Wakil himself, Abu Ali Jallaleddin ibn Rashid al Kushi, pushed his way to the fence as the lead horses rounded the trees and flag torch and headed back toward the main house. He was the tallest in the crowd, and wide to proportion. His nose was broad and regal, the whites of his eyes so clear they seemed to sparkle. The Wakil's skin was so dark and shining it was almost bluish. Although his waist was thicker than it had been in youth, he moved with the authority and dignity of a born warrior and leader. He was in his vigorous fifties, his chest still as massive and imposing as that of the champion wrestler he had been in his youth.

Now bound to his desk by duty and scholarship, the Wakil was perhaps the second most powerful man in all New Djibouti, responsible only to the governor, who in turn answered only to the Caliph himself in New

Alexandria. The Wakil's name literally sang the song of three generations: "Jalal father of Ali, son of Rashid the Kushite."

Although his people were of the Aderi tribe, originally from Harar in the province of Hararghe, it pleased Abu Ali to wear a Magribi *djebba*, a simple dark robe of Egyptian cotton, decorated with vertical stripes. The *djebba* was suited equally to hot, dry days and cool nights.

His keen eyes measured the action as the two lead horses, a gray Zulu stallion and a white Egyptian mare, raced neck and neck, so evenly matched they might have been yoked. The Egyptian was on the far side, and Abu Ali had to watch carefully to spy his elder son, bent low and forward, Iraqi-style flowing pants clamped around the flanks of his mount, jacket fluttering in the wind, his flowered shirt stained with sweat. Ali's handsome face corded with the strain of his effort.

The Wakil raised his fist and called "Ali! Hai!" across the field sharply, fully aware how unlikely it was that his principal heir would hear his voice above the din of hooves.

Ali ibn Jallaleddin ibn Rashid was a striking, athletic lad of sixteen, all wiry muscle and fine bone, high Abyssinian cheeks and eyes like black diamonds. At times still quite playful, at others he radiated sufficient intensity to frighten boys his own age. Girls tended to react to him with cautious curiosity, and giggled behind their veils. Ali spurred his mighty white mare Qäldänna to greater effort, and the pureblood obeyed as if they were of a single mind.

Abu Ali's attention wavered for a moment as he heard a voice that he recognized. He searched the crowd of laughing faces to his right and spied his younger son: Kai ibn Jallaleddin ibn Rashid. Twelve years old, thinner and less confident by far than whipcord Ali, Kai was almost too beautiful to be a boy. His eyes were soft brown and long-lashed, his cheeks round, neck long and gracefully poised. Kai's muscles were stringy, and the boy spent too much time in the book stacks, entirely too little practicing sword strokes.

Beside him, Kai's sister, Elenya bint Jallaleddin ibn Rashid, was but ten. Her hair was braided in tight, precise oiled rows, her skin so shining and flawless that he often called her his *teqit tequr lul*, his little black pearl. Elenya was the flower of Abu Ali's existence. Her mother Kessie (Allah protect her name!) had been sorely wounded in her birthing and died three years later, yet Ar-Rahman, the Most Merciful, had given her beauty back to the world in Elenya, like a flowered spring following a killing frost. Life, the Wakil knew, turned in cycles. Thus had it ever been, and would ever be.

When all was measured in the scales of Paradise, despite the long and lonely years, Allah had been good to Abu Ali. "All praises unto His name," he whispered.

"Ali! Ali!" young Kai shrieked. His eyes were so bright, his lips red, his thin body animated beneath princely robes. He was a mischief maker, his hair worn in the plaited rows of a young scholar, not close-cropped as was his brother's.

Abu Ali sighed. Praise Al-Hakim the Wise that this boy was born second, spared the pressures and obligations accorded the first. Ali would inherit most of the estate and the Senate seat; Kai would study law and business and help his brother administrate. At times Abu Ali felt he had married plump little Kessie too late in life, that he had not enough years left to guide his family. Times when he felt the snows of the coming winter already settling upon his broad shoulders. But he had confidence that these lands his father and grandfather had earned, that he and his brother, Malik, had fought for, would ultimately rest in safe and capable hands.

The rider on the Zulu mare challenged Ali all the way but the Wakil's son snatched the final flag from the pole with an arm's length to spare.

He wheeled his mount about, letting her slow to a trot as he raised his fisted arms to the cheering crowd and crowed an exultant "Yes!"

As the other contestants sulked, Ali walked his horse over to his father's station. The mare knelt, and Ali slipped off. He lowered his head.

"Father," he said.

Abu Ali smiled. "Well done." He reached into his robe and extracted a gilt-edged scroll. "You make me proud." He handed his son the parchment.

Makur, heavy with muscle, his face showing the flat, strong lines of his Dahomy ancestors, jumped off his horse with surprising lightness for his size. He pretended to glower. "Next year, Ali."

"Only if you learn to ride." The boys grabbed each other behind the neck, banged foreheads hard enough to make their eyes water, and then laughed.

As onlookers spanked their palms together in appreciation, Ali opened the scroll. In a cursive Arabic script it read: THE BEARER IS PROCLAIMED THE WINNER OF THE IDD-EL-FITR FEAST DAY CELEBRATION.

Kai and Elenya had pushed their way up behind their older, taller brother, trying to read the scroll. Ali teased them, holding it out of their range, making them jump about like fleas just to catch a glimpse. It was an old, fond game, one Abu Ali watched tolerantly. At last, deciding that there had been enough of such mischief, Abu Ali took his son aside. Then he pulled his sacred knife, his jambaya, Nasab Asad—Lion's Blood—from its scabbard.

Nasab Asad's three debens of weight and fourteen digits of sleek, curving, razor-sharp steel and bone was his most precious personal possession. Its hilt was crafted of black rhino horn, bolted to the tang with six heavy steel rivets. Legend held that the steel blade was smelted from a fallen meteorite by Benin smiths, its white-hot length quenched in the living blood of a lion.

Men of the Wakil's line had carried Nasab Asad into battle for ten generations. It had seen more war and death than any dozen men, and it was said that its wisdom and strength flowed into he who held it. Nasab Asad had protected life, and taken life, until the blade had come to symbolize the power of the family it protected, and the fury of its warriors.

"It will be yours one day," said Abu Ali. "Feel it now."

"The Lion, Father?" He barely seemed willing to touch it, as if it might awaken and claw him.

"Why not? Of all my possessions, my children are most precious. The Lion," he said, twisting it so that the polished blade caught the firelight, "is merely steel."

"Merely . . . ?" Ali's eyes sparkled. The blade was beyond magnificent, bordered on divine, almost as fabled as Zul al Fikr, Lord of Cleaving, the sword of the Prophet's son-in-law and faithful follower, he for whom Ali had been named.

Ali's fingers dug into the black bone handle. This was a deadly scepter. Whoever held such a blade need fear no man. He made a few dexterous cuts in the air, then respectfully handed it back to his father.

Ali made a shallow bow. "I pray I will one day prove worthy of the Lion." He grinned. "One very *distant* day."

Abu Ali smiled proudly. *"Insh'Allah,"* he said. "If it is the will of God."

Oko Istihqar, the plantation's head overseer, approached with his customary gliding strut. "Sir," he said, "we need your attention at the main gate. Shaka and his men have been sighted."

Abu Ali sighed. "Well," he said. "The great man himself. Honor indeed. At once. Again, well done, Ali."

As their father left, Kai dashed to his brother, pretending to cut and thrust at him with a slender branch.

"Great warrior!" he cried. "I'll show you!"

Ali defended effortlessly, then deliberately left a gap in his defenses. Kai "stabbed" him in the side, and Ali reeled against a tree, holding the imaginary wound.

"Ah," he moaned. "You have slain me! Ahh . . ."

Elenya shook her finger in Kai's face. "You *qattâl!* Father will skin you—"

"—and roll me in salt," Kai finished for her. "A threat like that, and it might make sense for me to finish what I started!"

Kai stalked toward her. Shrieking, Elenya hid behind her eldest brother, seeking safety.

Ali grabbed both scamps and spun them like little tops, then hugged them hard enough to creak ribs. Then they returned to the festivities.

Their father's estate was the grandest of all in New Djibouti, the southernmost of Bilalistan's four provinces. Today, its rolling hills, forests, and fields were crowded with guests celebrating Idd-el-Fitr, the most important Muslim festival of the year.

Idd-el-Fitr celebrated the end of Ramadan, the month of fasting. For a month, the Muslim faithful had gone from dawn to dusk without food or water passing their lips, and all eyes had watched the horizon for sight of a new moon.

Now, a thousand happy celebrants filled the grounds.

As the three siblings crossed the lawn the crowd parted respectfully and they were feted by musicians, tumblers, and magicians. The performers displayed skills of voice and agility and sleight of hand sufficient to resurrect memories of the old sultans, of djinn and flying carpets, of Persian wedding celebrations or Alexandrian holidays.

The estate was one of two sharing the waters of Lake A'zam, famous for boating and fishing, with tributary streams running all the way south to the Azteca gulf. Some said the Wakil's manor was the wealthiest in all New Djibouti.

Banners fluttered from the turrets of Dar Kush, the main house, which had been disassembled and shipped stone by stone from Andulus fifty years before. Its hundred rooms, Moorish vaulted ceilings, six fountained gardens lined with roses, miniature date palms and thousand-pillared hallways were the envy of Djiboutis New and Old. It was rumored that the Ayatollah himself had demanded his carpenters and architects specifically trump Dar Kush's gilded inlay in his own *masta*, his winter home.

But it mattered not how the head of the Ulema, Bilalistan's spiritual government, might imitate their home. There was only one Lake A'zam, only one Abu Ali, to whom thousands owed fealty, and for whom three children lived and breathed.

Only one Dar Kush.

CHAPTER TEN

WITH A BRASSY, BLASTING TRUMPET FARE, a detachment of ten mounted soldiers arrived at the front gate, led by the imperial figure of Colonel Shaka kaSenzangakhona, usually referred to as Shaka Zulu. *Inkosi*, or hereditary chief, among the Zulu, Shaka was the most powerful non-Muslim in all New Djibouti, perhaps in all Bilalistan. Thousands of Zulu fighting men owed allegiance to the giant, and those *impi* battalions had proven themselves against the Apache, the Northmen, and in skirmishes with the west coast Chinese settlements.

Shaka's deadly tactics and absolute battlefield discipline had earned his family impressive land grants in northern New Djibouti and Azania. There, with his younger brother Cetshwayo, Shaka ruled like a king. Mounted on a night-black Zulu stallion, the colonel was a sight to inspire awe: lean and muscular as a desert lion, cheeks prominent as an Abyssinian's but grooved with the vertical marks of his traditional Zulu scars. The arrival caused a ripple among the guests, especially the women, who whispered that Colonel Shaka actively sought a *thanthu*, a third wife to manage household affairs.

Abu Ali strode to him, smile wide. "Colonel! Please, welcome to my humble abode. The blessings of Allah upon you."

Shaka reined his horse and declined his head slightly. *Regally*, Abu Ali thought. *This one has ambitions.*

"*Sawubona*," Shaka said in Zulu. "Have I leave to enter?"

"With my whole heart," said Abu Ali. "Come. Refresh yourself."

Shaka dismounted in full formal military coat and cloak. An ostrich feather angled from his triangular red cap, and a necklace of leopard teeth graced his neck. Not strictly military, of course, but who would challenge him? The man was an animal, and Abu Ali always felt just a breath of alarm on the back of his neck when the Zulu visited. A servant took the stallion. Shaka barely noticed the man, who bowed low, common sense or some primitive survival instinct preventing him from meeting the great man's eye. Shaka had slain more than one clumsy servant, flipping the *riwâl* blood tax disdainfully over his shoulder to fall beside the hapless and writhing transgressor.

"I feared you would miss the festivities," said the Wakil.

Another man approached from the direction of the castle. An unwary observer would have thought magic was at play, for in face and form he was nearly Abu Ali's image. But instead of the Wakil's *djebba*, this man wore the same military garb favored by Shaka, and had even more medals arrayed on his chest, including the coveted gold-and-purple Pharaoh's Crest, the highest honor a living officer could receive.

This was Malik ibn Rashid al Kushi, the Wakil's brother, younger than he by only ten months. Malik, often called Al Nasab in honor of his battlefield prowess, was more warrior than statesman, and when he clenched his jaw or chewed, the pale angry line of an old dueling scar appeared just above the left jawbone.

But for the absolute leanness of his waist and thickness of his forearms, he was Abu Ali's double. They had even married sisters, Kessie and Fatima, although the marriages had come years apart. When the Wakil looked at Malik, he felt himself gazing into a mirror reflecting another, simpler, perhaps better life. A warrior's life was better than a statesman's: steel might slay and scar, but it never lied.

Malik held out his arm in sincere greeting. Volatile the Zulu certainly was, and Abu Ali did not entirely trust him, but any man who had witnessed him in battle knew Shaka to be a fierce and valuable ally. For the sake of the nation, Abu Ali kept his private feelings to himself.

"Shaka," said Malik. "How goes the frontier?"

Shaka gripped his old comrade's arm. "The Aztecs nip, we bite back."

Malik's eyes narrowed, merry hell burning within. "They will learn."

"Not too soon, I hope." Shaka grinned. "The game is good."

Abu Ali called to his eldest son, who had maintained a respectful distance. "Ali!" he cried. "Come! Join us in the study."

"Yes, Father," Ali answered, both grateful and obedient.

A hawkish smile split Shaka's scarred and coal-dark face. "Ah. Young Ali!" He clasped hands with the boy, and the boy's fingers were swallowed in the gnarled fists. "Is the Empress's niece still in your household?"

Ali coughed. "Yes, sir."

Malik nudged him insinuatingly. "And it seems likely she shall remain, hey?"

Even Abu Ali laughed at that, despite his son's evident embarrassment.

"To unite Rashid al Kush with the royal house of Abyssinia is quite an accomplishment," Shaka said. "If certain matters ever come to a head . . ."

"Certain matters which I fear are inevitable," Abu Ali said soberly.

"Perhaps. If they do, such alliance will prove invaluable."

"Allah be charitable," Malik said. "But never was an alliance forged more pleasurably, eh, boy? The Empress finds soul mates for her nieces and nephews, and we callused veterans speak of politics."

Ali couldn't meet the older men's eyes, and they roared merrily at his discomfort.

Abu Ali noted Kai and Elenya mousing around the discussion's edge. "Can we come?" Kai asked eagerly.

Uncle Malik's fingers dug into Kai's tightly braided hair. "Your friends would miss you, young ones. Represent us at the party. " And the men began to walk back to the house.

Kai watched them leave. He just knew that they were going to have serious man talk, the kind his father rarely indulged in around him, and more than anything in the world he wanted to know what they were going to say. *"Hail kilal,"* Kai muttered. "Horse balls."

Elenya balanced her little fists on her waist. "Ooh, Kai. I'm gonna tell . . ."

"You do, and I'll tell him who stole the *berbere*," he said, referring to a pot of Kushi pepper gone mysteriously missing from the kitchen.

"But I stole it for *you*," she sputtered.

Kai's mind was already haring off in another direction. What might he do? Almost immediately, a plan came to mind. "Come on," he said. The two of them raced after the grown-ups.

At the home of the Wakil, it was vital that three-storied Dar Kush be even more impressive inside than out. From the exterior, the countless hand-formed roof tiles, the intricately detailed stucco relief, the white dome of its Mosque, and the peaked height of its bell tower radiated wealth and power. But through the massive double wooden doors lay another world, one which eclipsed even the grandeur of the external edifice.

There were times when even Abu Ali considered his home ostentatious, but if luxury was a burden of power, it was one onus Allah would hear no prayers to relieve.

The surface of the central pool was like a rippling mirror: the Wakil could easily shave himself in its reflection. The walls, ceilings, and columns gracing the eight thousand square cubits of the ground level were worked in low-relief planes of finely molded, colored and textured plaster which caught the light and drew the eye ceaselessly from one wonder to another.

The central atrium caught the sunlight so perfectly that even at dusk he sometimes paused to read the thousands of verses of Qur'anic poetry inscribed on the walls or contemplate the murals depicting the wonders of Paradise. The interior walls were also covered in paintings, sculptures, captured armaments, and maps. Shaka nodded in admiration as he passed this or that treasure, although his only comment was to wonder whether "polishing all these fine things mightn't tax even the fabled sword arm of Abu Ali."

The Wakil chuckled politely, but mused that there had been a time, not so long before, that Shaka would not have made even so carefully veiled an insult. Although his brother Malik was the duelist, in matters of honor any free citizen had recourse to trial by sword or knife.

Ali was oblivious to his father's discomfort, strutting the halls as if he personally had led the charges and sacked the cities, delighted to be in such august company. Malik was quick to notice his nephew's affectation, and his lips curled up in amusement.

"So tell me," he said to Shaka. "Do you believe the Aztecs actually eat human flesh?"

Ali flinched, but Shaka nodded gravely. "In ceremony, yes. The heart of an enemy for courage, or to give praise to their god."

"Quetzalcoatl?" Ali inquired. "Is that the name of their demon god?"

"The feathered serpent," said Abu Ali. "Yes."

Shaka grunted. "These Aztecs fight like demons, and die like men."

Malik let out a deep sigh of regret. "I envy you. One more campaign . . ."

Shaka barked laughter and slapped his old friend on the back. "And another after that, and another after that, hey? Such games are the only fit practice for men like us, Malik. If there were no Aztecs, we'd have to fight each other, hey?" They laughed roundly, the kind of dark, guarded laughter that said: *How right you are.*

The four warriors turned the corner and disappeared. For a moment the hall was clear, and then Kai and Elenya appeared, creeping down the corridor after them. They were the very soul of stealth. Outside the Wakil's study, Kai slid a rectangular metal insulation plate away from the wall, revealing a grille. These grilles were part of Dar Kush's central heating system, and the plate on the other side was usually open. Elenya nudged to get up next to him. They jostled each other, contending for position. Elenya put her lips next to his ear. "What are you doing? What are they going to say?"

"They'll talk about the Aztecs," Kai whispered in return. "Quiet, or they'll hear."

They peered into Abu Ali's study as their elders settled around a central table. The athenaeum was part trophy room and part library, crammed with scrolls, armor, and maps of past and present military campaigns. On the floor lay a lion skin, trophy of Abu Ali's first spear hunt with the Masai. Weapons from around the world were arrayed on the walls and above the double-wide fireplace: muskets, javelins, krisses, daggers, triple irons and bola knives. Schematics for armored boats and steam catapults decorated the walls, alongside captured flags from Vineland and Azteca.

Although Kai knew his father considered him too bookish, Abu Ali's own study held thousands of volumes, including histories, tomes on strategy from China and India, and of course the fabled *On Warfare* by the Pharaoh himself. Kai had read it and been terribly surprised that instead of bloodthirsty exploits, Alexander had expounded at length on the value of administration and supply lines. Fascinating. Kai loved his father's study and treasured every minute he spent in it, wrapping himself in the memorabilia of the man he loved and admired most in all the world.

When big brother Ali entered the room, one of the first things he did was glance over at the grate, and Kai knew they had been spotted. Ali said nothing to their father, but did seem to position himself in front of the grille each time bodies shifted in the room.

At one point Ali moved away, and Kai got a clear view of the great map on the western wall. It delineated the territory of New Djibouti, which stretched from the Bay of Azteca all the way north to Wichita, so recently purchased from the eponymous tribe. North of Wichita was Azania and a no-man's-land of disputed territories, and further still was the Viking settlement of Vineland. A disputed strip ran north-south between New Djibouti and the aboriginal Nations. The western Nations were often at war with Azteca, but sometimes traded with them.

To the east was New Alexandria, which held the capital of Bilalistan as well as being its major economic and manufacturing nerve center. Those four major provinces—New Djibouti, Wichita, Azania, and New Alexandria—were detailed closely: major settlements and towns were marked, as well as some of the larger personal holdings.

Perched on the Wakil's main table was an intricately crafted three-dimensional map of all New Djibouti. Kai's angle from the grate was irritatingly obscure. He climbed a trophy case to a louvered shutter at the top of the wall, where he could look down on the display.

There had been changes since last Kai examined the table model. Little red flags marked out vital points, or perhaps battle sites. Miniature Aztec horsemen were poised on the west side of the Chinaka River, Muslim and Zulu horsemen on the east.

"—you may well get your chance, Malik," Shaka was saying. "The Infidels have rattled their spears at the Shrine of the Fathers."

Ali looked shaken. "They wouldn't dare!" The Shrine of the Fathers was one of the most sacred sites in all Bilalistan. There lay the bodies of the holy men who had first blessed this region over two hundred years ago. Pilgrims they were, seeking only to fulfill the dream of honored Bilal (Allah protect his name). *"The sun will rise in the west,"* the great Abyssinian had declared upon his deathbed. *"Seek to the west."* The "sun" he spoke of was thought to be Islam itself, its new dawning symbolic of a chance to begin anew, without the divisive power struggles that had tainted the Prophet's teachings in his own land.

The bravest, strongest, and luckiest of those who followed Bilal's instructions now held a land of unparalleled wealth and opportunity.

Ali's disbelief still echoed in the room. Abu Ali rested his fists on the table map, glared down at it. "They *would* dare," he said. "The *kufurin* fear nothing but their Feathered Demon."

Ali's face was tight with rage. "Allah grant me the honor to strike blows in His service."

The model of the shrine was fist-size, out of proportion to the other map details. It was a two-storied mosque with a golden dome in the very center of its flat roof. The shrine was rather curiously set away from most of the other, marked-out settlements. Ali traced his finger around its periphery reverently.

Malik watched his nephew with interest. "Tell me, Ali."

"Yes, Uncle?"

Kai could not see his uncle's face, but guessed that it was composed in the same kind of relaxed intensity that he wore when administering a lesson. Kai cringed at that thought. He both loved and feared his uncle, and in some ways was closer to him than to his own father, the august Abu Ali. Fathers, especially men of the Wakil's stature, sometimes had little attention for their younger sons, but Malik's weekly combat lessons were both intimate and awe-inspiring. It was Malik, not the Wakil, who had taught Kai to walk and ride. Malik ibn Rashid Al Kushi was New Djibouti's greatest sword master, a blooded warrior and accomplished duelist whose mere presence in a room sufficed to hush the voices of hard, dangerous men.

"What actions," Malik asked in measured tone, "would *you* take in defense of the shrine?"

Ali hesitated for a moment, perhaps knowing that the adults were watching and judging him. Kai glimpsed Shaka Zulu, and the challenging expression on his lean scarred face.

For a long moment Ali seemed frozen. "Well . . . I, uh—"

Then the cloud passed from him as inspiration struck. Ali began swapping bronze horse and cannon figurines about. "The Al'Amu is in a very defensible—"

Kai's father snuffled. "'Mosque Al'Amu' is an offensive term, Ali." Kai had to stifle a laugh. That was a slip on Ali's part. *Al'Amu* meant "a crazy place," and the mosque was certainly located in the middle of nowhere. Pilgrims traveled a thousand miles afoot to visit it. The pious called it the Shrine of the Fathers, but the labels "Crazy Mosque" or "Mosque Al'Amu" were probably in equal currency.

"Sorry, Father," Ali said. "The *shrine* abuts a gully, and the front gates are thick. The plain before it is very vulnerable to rifle fire from the roof."

Shaka nodded approval. "Good," he said. Shaka was not Muslim, did not believe in Allah, so his interest in the shrine was purely political. Whatever beliefs he did have he kept to himself. The Zulus were their own people and a force apart. They lived by themselves in their *kraals*, generally in northern New Djibouti or in Azania, where they had been granted large tracts of land, and served as a buffer between Bilalistan and the Northmen. Zulus tended to marry other Zulus, and voted in the Senate as a bloc. When it came to fighting, however, there were none better, and it was their lethal and indomitable skill in this arena that had secured them special privilege in both the old world and the new.

Ali was warming to his task. Although he had never been to war, he had studied his military texts faithfully. "A defending force in the mosque could hold off an army. I would order my men to create an outer perimeter, and bolster them with riflemen."

Malik grunted approval, but Shaka was not satisfied. "Good, but passive."

"Passive?" Abu Ali said, curious.

"Weak," Shaka said more bluntly. "My men are the hammer. The mosque is the anvil." He indicated the positions of each with chopping, stabbing motions of his hands. "I divide my forces, create a diversion, appear to send half my men away. When the enemy falls upon the walls of the mosque, we strike from the forest, trapping them, crushing them." He snatched up one of the Aztec horse models, his thick fingers squeezing. "We take no prisoners," he said. "We make them eat their own hearts."

Shaka was shaking, something rhythmic and hungry working its way through his body. He danced up and down where he stood, and in a near frenzy swept his broad, thick hand down like a crashing wave, smashing the little Aztec soldiers from the board.

The room was utterly silent. Kai held his breath. There was an intoxicating intensity to the man. For a moment Kai tried to imagine someone like Shaka bearing down on him, bloody spear raised on high . . . and felt a wave of nauseated horror sweep over him. Could anything or anyone stand before such a creature? Al-Muhaymin preserve him!

Abu Ali, ever the statesman, made a placating gesture, turning his palms up to the ceiling. "Yes, well . . . let us hope it won't come to that, shall we?"

Malik and Shaka exchanged glances. These men could hope no such thing. His uncle and the awful Shaka lived for war.

Abu Ali rubbed his hands together smartly. "Well," he said. "We will have more time to speak of war, but later. Today is a day of celebration!"

Shaka stared at Abu Ali as if he were a stranger, perhaps an enemy. Or was that just an illusion, just Kai's overactive imagination? Because in the next moment Shaka's energy had transformed, and he was expansive and friendly, a jolly bear, just another party guest. "Yes," he said. "Of course. I thirst! Lead me to food and drink. I carry half the road in my throat."

Laughing and talking, they left the room. Kai scrambled down from his perch and grabbed Elenya by the shoulder, pulling her into a cubbyhole behind a display case for armor. The men passed without seeing them—

Except for Ali, who cast them a single backwards glance, wagging his forefinger mockingly.

Kai stuck out his tongue in reply, and as soon as they were around the corner, took Elenya's hand and headed into the recently vacated room.

Elenya couldn't bring herself to cross the threshold. "Kai . . ." she said nervously. "We shouldn't be here."

But Kai wasn't listening to her. He was staring at the board, studying it. So intense was his concentration that he barely noticed when she tiptoed up behind him.

"Kai . . ." she finally said, fascinated. "What would you do?"

He spoke dreamily. "Call up a thousand balloons, and drop fire on them from the sky!" His voice arced up, in his mind the sky filled with flying carpets, far beyond the reach of Aztec spears and arrows. Infidels milled in confusion as death rained from above. Elenya clapped her hands delightedly.

"Whoosh!" he cried, and imagined a fireball splashing atop a hapless Aztec soldier. "Whoosh! Whoosh!"

CHAPTER ELEVEN

WHITE CLOUDS SHROUDED THE FULL MOON, casting a diffused light upon the celebration. The merriment had died down a bit, and most of the three hundred dignitaries had seated themselves at the long, low banquet tables erected in preparation for the evening meal. Eight hundred commoners sat on linen squares, each large enough to accommodate an entire family. Servants in gloves and aprons as pale as their skin attended to all needs and wants, serving steaming portions of chicken *wot* and Kenyan *samosas*, Moroccan lamb *tandine* with pears and spiced vegetables simmered in ghee.

Kai always loved these fancy dinners, the servants buzzing around them like smiling bees. At times like this, everything seemed right to him, all in the world in its place, by Allah's design. There were unfamiliar servants at this party: a new clutch had arrived only three months ago and were only now integrated into the household staff. He spied a new woman and boy who looked to be mother and son, the woman red-haired, the boy's yellow as the sun. The woman's smile was shy if tired, but the boy seemed less happy.

Why? Kai wondered. It *had* to be fun to work in the kitchen. Kai wished he could spend time there, stealing *fufu* grits and slices of *bobotie* meat loaf, sharing song with the others. A servant's life was good, an easier, simpler one than that demanded of the noble class, full of obligations and choices. Many times Kai wished that he had nothing to concern him but following simple instructions and honorable labor. The servants were lucky.

The red-hair served him a beautifully rendered chicken *doro alicha*, a dish said to be a favorite of the Empress herself. Presented on an edible plate of *injera* teff bread, *doro alicha* was an utterly succulent collation of *berbere* spice, clarified butter, eggs, lime, and onions. "Yes, fine," he mur-

mured, and bowed shallowly in dismissal. The red-hair backed hurriedly
away.

He ran his hands over the tableware, the plates, the napkins. Everything was in its place. Still, he had little appetite and a pale mood, and
knew precisely why:

Next to Kai sat his brother, Ali, and across from Ali was Ali's betrothed,
Lamiya Mesgana.

The Empress herself had declared Lamiya his brother's soul mate, his
feqer näfs. On a day prophesized by the Empress, when both had achieved
their majority and the stars were properly aligned, the two would wed.

Of fifteen summers, Lamiya was small compared to most noblewomen,
but sweetly proportioned as women of the Afar tended to be. Her folk
hailed from the shores of Lake Abbé on the edge of the Abyssinian
province of Djibouti. Her grandfather, now wealthy in land and shipping,
had once been a herdsman, and that good sturdy bone and blood helped
make her what she was.

Her dark eyes were luminous, her hair dressed in the Afar fashion that
turned a coiffure into living artwork. For this celebration her maids had
braided and beaded her hair into a complexity that would have baffled a
mathematician.

Her nose was slightly pointed, her ears small and perfect. Beneath her
partial veil she seemed always on the verge of a smile. She had the Afar
habit of leaning her head forward slightly, in shyness perhaps, but perhaps
also because it allowed her to present her very best profile to the world.

No, that was wrong. Lamiya *had* no lesser angle, no perspective from
which she was less than a jewel. It was all Kai could do to find appetite to
eat in her presence, to remember how to bite meat from bone, or loosen
his throat sufficiently to swallow.

Lamiya. *Light of the World*, indeed.

A servant whose colorless hair was bound back from her face ladled rice
onto his plate. Kai accumulated a respectable mound before raising a hand
in acknowledgment. She continued on another half-motion, then seemed
flustered and tried to scoop some back up.

"*Gafar*," she said in a thick and clumsy accent. "Pardon."

Kai could only shake his head, trying not to become irritated. The stupidity of new servants never ceased to amaze him. He was surprised they
had ever been able to survive on their own.

The Wakil stood and raised his cup. "To my children. And to Lamiya
Mesgana, of Abyssinia's Sultânî-y Dar, the Royal House. In the two years

you have lived among us you have become like a daughter to me . . . and it will be a proud day when you are closer still."

She glanced at Ali, then lowered her eyes to the table, the slightest of mysterious smiles curling her lips. "Thank you, Wakil," she said modestly.

Kai felt his own face heat. Oh, to win but one such glance!

The men at table pounded fists and knives, cheering the couple.

The Empress had dreamed a dream of love, a vision of Lamiya and Ali as soul mates, joined before birth and for all eternity. So it was proclaimed, and so it would be.

But for all the talk of *feqer näfs* the Wakil had implied to Kai that it was curious that the Empress's more than thirty nieces and nephews had all obeyed her dreams, and that all had married into wealth and power. It would be crass to suggest that political necessity wore the mask of true love, but Abu Ali had winked and suggested that Kai would profit by a careful study of history in the matter of royal weddings.

A political union it might be, but that hardly detracted from its obvious joys. Kai raised his glass of nectar high and managed a smile, but it was impossible for him not to think, *She reminds me of Mother. Why is Ali always the lucky one?*

Pony snorting, the knight swept down from his corner, bringing swift and certain death to the hapless Mamluk. Blood spattered the Mamluk's face and he dropped to his knees, fluid dripping from his scalp.

Then he dipped his fingers in it, licked them, and loped grinning off the *satranj* board, escorted by the referees.

The onlookers cheered.

Here on the manicured lawn fronting the main house, a great canvas *satranj* board, thirty-two cubits to the side, had been rolled down, that the house of the Wakil and that of his honorable neighbor Djidade Berhar might once again contest for highest prize. Pieces were played by young servants and children of the guests, each wearing a badge to proclaim his role: Sultan, Sultana, Vizier, Mamluk, and Castle. All were afoot except the Knights, who rode ponies specially bred for live-action *satranj*.

Djidade Berhar's estate shared Lake A'zam with Dar Kush, and although larger in land area was not so wealthy in minerals or plowable acreage. And Djidade Berhar, of course, had not nearly so much influence with the Senate as the Wakil, who had been appointed by the Caliph himself. But the corpulent Djidade was perhaps the second wealthiest man in New Djibouti. He also fancied himself a *satranj* wizard, and had once traveled to Alexandria to challenge the Pharaoh's champion.

More fascinating to the observers was the fact that representing Dar Kush was none other than Kai's sister, Elenya. She was a recognized prodigy in the game, the third-ranked junior player in all Bilalistan. Elenya had first beaten her own father at the age of six, and tutors from India's Mogul Court had declared her a future world contender. Still, she was young enough to wipe greasy fingers on the loose sleeves of her Moroccan caftan and lick her mint *ablûj* stick while Djidade Berhar fretted and fumed over his next move.

Kai wore a red hemp robe, as befitted his position as a Mamluk, a slave-soldier of the lowest rank. Mamluks could move only a single square at a time, and only straight forward unless capturing. Kai felt absurdly vulnerable, certain to be wantonly slain. And it was *disgusting* to be controlled by a little sister, be she genius or dolt.

Lose a Mamluk to gain a Sultan was ancient and irritating wisdom. It made his death as certain as the next sunrise. But if by some miracle he did survive, if Elenya, in her infinite mercy, would move him safely down his file to the last row, he could be promoted to the level of any piece on the board except Sultan. Usually a player who successfully advanced her Mamluk chose promotion to Sultana or Knight, the Sultana being the most deadly, the Knight capable of unpredictable movement.

If that happened he could swoop down the board, swinging the cow bladders filled with cherry syrup that ended an enemy piece's "life." That fate had befallen Kai last year, and he purely loathed it. With a dab of luck, vengeance might be his.

"Ah!" Ali was saying from the sidelines. "The Knight! Beware!"

The Knight was portrayed, with gusto, by Djidade Berhar's son, Fodjour. Fodjour was as plump as his father, an earnest but not brilliant student, an exceptional bowman but only mediocre on horseback. He and Kai had been rivals since they had learned to walk.

Fodjour's father leaned back in his enormous rattan armchair. Despite the cooling night breezes, droplets of sweat collected in the dark folds of his neck. Two slave girls fanned him with silken paddles.

"What say you now, Elenya? Your move." Berhar's gaze went to the dual-faced, freestanding *satranj* clock imported all the way from Benin. Taller than Elenya, it was all flesh-toned ebony, glass, brass, and spring steel, handcrafted by the greatest clock makers in the world. It cost more than some sharelanders earned in a year.

Every eye shifted to the little girl, all but swallowed by her chair's plush cushions. She examined the board, tongue flicking at her candy, and narrowed her eyes and mouth. "These things take time, sir," she said in a mock adult voice. "*I have the clock.*"

Kai watched Elenya's eyes. He knew that contemplative expression well. She was taking in the entire board, thinking moves ahead in a way he had never been able to manage. Kai felt a single drop of nervous perspiration roll down his neck and wend its way under his robes.

From the corner of his eye he watched Fodjour and his pony. The Knight was just one jump away. If Elenya didn't move Kai, Fodjour's father might well choose to pick him off. It would give Berhar a very slight advantage in manpower, without compromising his position. Elenya, on the other hand, could choose to further develop her own attack, at the slight expense of one humiliated older brother.

Fodjour leaned forward and whispered: "I'm gonna *killlll* you." He hefted his hand, in which rested a heavy bag of cherry syrup. Kai sighed. It was going to be a long game.

Or worse yet, a short one.

He had all but resigned himself to his fate when, scanning the crowd, Kai realized Lamiya was watching him.

She smiled, which only made everything worse. This would be the third time she had seen him played, and every time he had died like a pigbelly. He smiled tentatively at her. Lamiya wiggled her fingers in greeting, made a sad face beneath her veil, and then turned and giggled to her maids.

Kai's ears burned. This was simply too much. It was more than any boy could take. Even if he caught a whipping, something had to be done, and quickly. He had planned for this eventuality but come to doubt his own resolve. No more.

Another red-garbed pawn stood beside Fodjour. This boy was a skinny thing, golden-haired and freckled, pale as a ghost and a little sunburned. One of the new ones. Kai thought that he had seen him once or twice over the last month. He was standing stock-still, playing his Mamluk role with desperate stolidity. Kai calculated distances and probabilities, thinking hard.

Elenya finally made her decision. "Sultan's Vizier takes Mamluk," she said.

The Vizier was personified by one of Abu Ali's younger guards. Experienced warriors almost never participated in such games, but the unblooded ones found the simulated combat amusing. The Vizier slid down the file in his lethal diagonal, thumping a white pawn with a pouch of cherry syrup. "Blood" flew in all directions, and the servant boy fell to the ground, thrashing and bucking piteously before being led away.

The "dead" Mamluks, all Kai's age or younger, were being fed hot punch and cake over to the side, stuffing their pale faces. The new "corpse" was cheered by his fellows as he joined them.

Kai's sense of humiliation increased. Why was he only a Mamluk? Why couldn't he have been at least a Knight? True, some of the other landowners had children on the board, but he was the oldest of the black Mamluks, and in his own mind, old enough for higher rank. This was terrible.

His remaining reticence dissolved. It was unfair. *Never bow your head to injustice, boy,* his father had often said. While he doubted Abu Ali intended for that philosophy to be applied to a game of *satranj,* Kai was determined to be guided by paternal wisdom.

"Pssst!" he hissed to the yellow-hair in the square adjacent to Fodjour. When there was no response, he tried again. "Psst!" The lad was staring straight forward. Perhaps he did not hear. Poor hearing as well as slow of wit? Why oh why had Allah made such creatures? To be servants, he supposed.

"Psst!" At last the boy glanced at Kai from the corner of his eye. "Boy! I want you to do something!"

The boy didn't respond. Kai was about to give up in exasperation, when it occurred to him that perhaps the lad wasn't entirely dim. Perhaps he didn't speak the language. *"B'tekbe Araby shway?* Do you speak even a little Arabic?" he asked.

Again, no answer. Kai gestured to his lips. *Do you speak Arabic?* he mimed, to no effect. He glanced up at Fodjour. Luckily, the boy wasn't paying any attention. Nor, so far, were any of the spectators.

This time, the slave boy shook his head a negative. He didn't understand. Well, maybe he would understand *this.* Kai reached into his robes and extracted a piece of candy. It was hard rock candy, a big crystal of sugar, hard and sweet enough to last half the day.

The boy's eyes fairly bugged out when he saw it, and he licked his lips. "Candy," Kai whispered seductively. "Sweet. You help me?"

He mimed sucking on the chunk of candy. The servant boy's eyes gleamed. He nodded eagerly, as if he hadn't had such a treat in all his life. Kai wanted to turn somersaults with pleasure. Revenge! He reached his left hand into his pocket and extracted the square of folded paper containing that which Elenya had stolen for him earlier.

Kai gave a quick glance at his sister and Djidade Berhar. Berhar's clock was running down. He had a habit of waiting until the very last moment to make his own moves, in an attempt to rattle his opponent. A worthless stratagem against someone like his sister, who existed in a separate world while playing. Nonetheless, it aided Kai's cause.

Pointing subtly toward the pony's nose, he twice mimed a throwing gesture. "Understand?" he whispered.

Again, the servant boy bobbed his head up and down. Kai passed him the *berbere* pepper, and made the connection just in time to yank his hand back before the grinning Fodjour turned back to him, drawing his finger across his own throat like a knife.

Not this time, Fodjour . . .

But Kai kept his thoughts to himself and lowered his head as if abjectly depressed.

Finally, Djidade Berhar spoke. "Knight takes Mamluk!" he announced grandly, as if no one could have anticipated *that*. Fodjour eagerly touched up his pony, but had to pass the blond boy to reach Kai. In the moment the pony's muzzle approached the boy most closely, the servant's hand made a swift jerking movement.

Kai held his breath, eager to see the results of his little experiment. It was even more spectacular than he could have hoped. Fodjour's pony snorted irritably and made a great, blubbery sneeze, blowing mucus and slobber everywhere. It reared up as if trying to throw its suddenly terrified rider, then bolted.

Chaos erupted across the game board. Adults watching the game laughed uproariously as the children scrambled in all directions, diving out of the way of the panicked pony.

Fodjour's eyes were huge. "Whoa! Whoa!"

Spectators might have considered it low comedy, but Kai was running for his life, the servant boy scrambling just behind him. Heart pounding, he glanced back over his shoulder and saw that the pony was almost upon them. Kai threw his arm around the servant's shoulders, hurling them both to the ground.

As it had been trained, the pony jumped the boys, but landed sharp and clumsily, just in front of a hedge marking the game board's western edge. Fodjour went rump-over-shoulders over the bushes, landing with a *thump* on the far side.

Kai rose to hands and knees, dizzied but also exhilarated by the sheer energy and turmoil he had unleashed. Next to him, the servant boy was watching the action as well, wearing a grin of wonderment that Kai knew had to mirror his own.

Djidade Berhar lumbered to the rescue. "Fodjour!" he called to his son. "Are you killed?"

That was the question on every tongue as they converged on the far side of the hedge. Fodjour sat up dazedly from a pile of leaves and small branches one of the gardeners had swept together in a pile. "I don't think so . . ."

Kai sidled up to the scene and was standing just behind Shaka Zulu as the colonel arrived with Uncle Malik. Shaka leaned over to his old compatriot and whispered: "No fall kills a boy with such a backside. My troops could eat a month on such a rump."

Malik's scarred face creased with silent mirth, but he said nothing.

Djidade Berhar stormed. "This is outrageous!" he screamed. "I demand a forfeit."

The Wakil held up his hands in a conciliatory gesture. "Agreed, my friend."

"Father!" Elenya pouted, and shot a glare of pure hate at Kai. *I am going to torture you for this. Slowly.*

I know, I know, Kai shrugged. *Skin me and . . .*

Malik leaned toward Shaka. "A stroke of luck for Djidade Berhar," he said. "It was mate in seven."

Shaka closed his eyes for a moment, his fierce lean face becoming surprisingly mild as he calculated. He shook his head. "Six, my friend."

Djidade Berhar appeared somewhat mollified, but wasn't finished yet. "And the boy must be punished," he said.

"Which boy?" Kai's father asked innocently.

Berhar was so angry that Kai would not have been surprised to see small lightning bolts dancing above his head. Kai choked on his laughter. This time, he might be in real trouble.

"We know who was responsible," Fodjour raged. "Who is *always* responsible?"

Kai glanced at his father, whose moods he knew intimately. Abu Ali was clearly secretly amused, but protocol demanded that the miscreant be punished. He turned, seeking out Kai, who tried to duck behind the hedge, but to no avail. Spotted.

Abu Ali strode toward him purposefully, stopping with big fists balled and set on his waist. He looked down at Kai, his face angry, but enough twinkle left in his eyes to tell Kai that neither death nor dismemberment was imminent. "Kai," he said sternly. "Did you do this thing?" A lie now would be a thousand times worse than the act itself, unforgivable.

"Father," Kai began, "I—"

And then suddenly, and utterly to Kai's surprise, the pale-haired servant boy stepped forward. Kai realized the boy had been watching everything, and there had been a certain animal shrewdness about his face.

In a thick and clumsy accent, the boy said: *"Nî."* Me.

So shocked was Kai that he temporarily lost the power of speech. Abu Ali, Djidade Berhar, Shaka, and the entire group of witnesses turned to look at the boy, whose pale face was flushed and trembling. He could not meet their eyes, and dropped his own to the ground.

Malik was the first to speak. "No one spoke to you, *walad.*"

The boy managed to tilt his face up a bit. Just a fraction. "*Ni . . . ya 'mal.*" *I do it.*

Shaka shrugged, grim laughter dancing in the dark eyes. "The little pig-belly says he did it."

Djidade Berhar fumed. "He lies. I know it was . . ."

Abu Ali turned back to his son. "Kai, did you do this?"

"I was not near the horse when it bolted, Father."

The Wakil's eyes narrowed as his father judged the comment, decided not to challenge it—praise Ar-Rahman the Merciful!—and turned to examine the young servant. The boy was barefoot and dressed in scruffy but well-mended pantaloons. He looked painfully thin. A half-healed bruise darkened his left cheek, and his hair had been chopped short, as if someone had simply hacked away at it with a saw. His eyes were very blue, and there was something about the bones in his cheeks, the long thinness of his arms, that said that he might grow tall.

"I don't know this one," mused the Wakil.

By now, the reliable Oko had arrived, dressed in a sparkling aqua *djebba* and leather sandals with silver buckles. Festival or not, the Ibo chief overseer always seemed to be overdressed. "One of the new batch, sir. Barely speaks the language."

Abu Ali considered. "Harder to lie, then."

Berhar strode forward and his arm blurred, the flat of his hand striking the boy's face hard enough to snap his head around and stagger him backwards. He strode forward for another blow, but the Wakil slipped between them. "I can punish my own servants, Djidade." The words were spoken in a host's conciliatory tones, but there was no mistaking the steel within. "Oko," he said. "See to it."

Oko grabbed the boy and pulled him away toward the barn. There was a little general chatter and the adults began to drift away, the excitement concluded.

Kai watched Oko dragging the scapegoat to justice, a tremor of guilt tickling at his stomach. It was only a servant, he told himself. Only a *hinzîr-batn,* a pigbelly. And yet . . .

"Kai?" his father said.

Kai's head snapped around. "Yes, sir?"

The Wakil's eyes were narrow and unamused. "There will be more about this, later."

Kai dropped his eyes to the ground. "Yes, Father." he said, and did not dare look up until he heard his father stride away.

When he looked up, Uncle Malik and Ali were both following his father off toward the house. Ali winked at Kai as they passed.

Feeling both shame and relief, Kai wandered, feigning aimlessness, in the general direction of the barn. When he was certain that no one was watching, he began to sprint.

CHAPTER TWELVE

THREE MINUTES' WALK WEST OF THE CASTLE, adjacent to the great field, stood a large building serving as barn and stable. Similar structures were scattered around Abu Ali's vast holdings, but this one housed the personal mounts of residents and guests.

Peering around its corner, Kai watched as Oko took the boy to a short whipping post and in quick guttural phrases ordered him to grip the handholds. The boy seemed a bit dazed, confused, eyes searching out any potential means of escape. He took the position as ordered.

The post was erected behind the barn, out of sight of either the main house or the guests. In one way it was a mercy, in another it seemed to increase the sense of isolation. In such a setting, anything might happen.

Oko ripped the boy's shirt away with one ring-bedecked hand. Even from Kai's hiding space he could see that the servant's pale body was bony, and crossed with three or four partially healed whip scars.

Next to the post were a choice of a leather bullwhip or a slender switch. Oko examined them, and then looked at the boy. "I know the young master, and the *satranj* business seemed his work." He wagged his head in sympathy. "How you got mixed up in it, I don't know, but we all follow orders here." The boy's eyes met his angrily, and Oko nodded with satisfaction. "You aren't afraid. Good."

Oko took hold of the switch. "You've been a good boy, so I don't want to hurt you, but you have to learn your lesson."

The stroke descended. The boy winced. Another stroke. The boy shuddered now: it had to hurt! Kai's own skin quivered in empathy.

Another stroke. Oko's gemmed fingers glittered as he raised the switch again. Kai winced. This was enough: honor demanded that he take action. He strode forward from his hiding space. "Oko!"

The overseer turned, and Kai noticed that he wasn't totally startled. It was quite possible the Ibo had expected an intercession of some kind. *So be it.*

"Young sir?" A short bow.

Kai drew himself up imperiously. "It was *my* game this scoundrel disrupted. I claim the honor of punishment."

Oko's eyes narrowed a bit. "Sir?"

Kai waved a hand in dismissal. "Go, now. I would do this alone."

Oko examined them both. The man was a peacock, but no fool: he saw what was happening, and he managed the impressive feat of simultaneously frowning and smiling.

"As you wish, sir," he said, and handed the switch to Kai, retiring from the scene.

For a moment Kai brandished the switch threateningly. The slave boy still gripped the post, but he looked back over his shoulder at Kai, blue eyes meeting Kai's brown without a flinch.

The contact lasted for a long moment, and then Kai smiled and lowered the switch. "All right." Kai sighed. "Come over here." At first the boy didn't move, and Kai was forced to pantomime his request. "Let go of the post," he urged. "I'm not going to hurt you."

Slowly, the servant boy released his hold. Keeping his eyes on Kai as much as possible, he slipped his shirt back on. His hands trembled, and he thrust them beneath his armpits as if to steady them. He stared at Kai's hands, an unspoken question on his face.

For a moment Kai didn't grasp the significance, and then he groaned as memory flooded back. "Oh, yes," he said. "Here." He handed the boy the promised candy. The servant snatched it greedily from his hands, gnawing at the hard crystal surface. Kai wrinkled his nose at the boy's smell: a sour sweat stench that suggested he understood little of proper bathing. Why didn't they use oils, or even good honest soap?

The yellow-hair watched Kai as he chewed, almost like an animal cornered in its lair. Almost. There was something else there, too, and Kai had a hard time putting a name to it. Some shrewdness, perhaps. It was just possible that this one had a brain.

"You look awfully skinny," Kai said finally. "Why don't you come with me to the house?" He mimed taking a step toward the mansion, then turned back. The servant regarded him doubtfully. "Come on," Kai insisted. "Don't be scared."

He gestured again, and finally the boy followed.

In a servant's nook off the main kitchen, a banquet was spread out before the boys in a fan shape: cookies, sandwiches, sweet cakes, rolled pastries in the style of a dozen lands. Fruit salad laced with papayas, mangoes, pineapples, and bananas, iced with cellar-fresh packed snow and diced and served in a scooped-out melon rind.

There was also leftover food from the main course, including a cane rat *saté* so tempting that the servant boy wolfed down four skewers in a row, barely stopping for breath.

He crowded his mouth greedily and seemed to have completely forgotten the whipping, although he did cast a suspicious eye at Kai from time to time.

The young master was enjoying himself too, but watched the servant lad as carefully as the boy watched him. They were about the same age, the same size. Watching the expressions of delight on the servant's face, Kai found himself smiling, shoveling handfuls himself, reveling in the boy's simple pleasure. Through some strange alchemy, the servant's enjoyment had become his own.

"What's your name?" he asked. The boy just looked at him blankly. "Name?" he said again, and pointed to his own chest. "Kai," he said.

The servant boy laughed, a few crumbs falling out of his mouth. "Aidan," he said.

Aengus, the kitchen master, approached them carrying two enormous lamb-filled pastries. Aengus was as wide as he was tall, face as pale as the bleached flour he magically fashioned into the world's tastiest confections. He was both fat and muscular, with a huge flat face and bright, watchful eyes. He studied Aidan with disapproval as he rested the platters on the table. "Master Kai," he said deferentially. "*Qalîl tawwâf*, little ghosts like this should eat in the barn."

Kai swallowed his mouth clear. "Are you questioning me, Aengus?"

Aengus's answering smile was as mild as cream. "No, young sir. Of course not." And he carried away his pastries, grinning to himself.

* * *

Aengus had enjoyed that exchange. The blacks could be terribly easy to manipulate. Just push them in one direction, and they would push back just where you wanted them, if you were careful.

And Aengus *was* careful. The kitchen was his domain, and he was allowed to run it almost as he pleased. It was enormous, with three ovens and an ice cellar, but still barely enough to keep up with Dar Kush's household demands. At the moment it was crowded with servants who chattered and laughed as they ground and folded and cooked and served.

Only one black face besides young Kai's was in the kitchen: Lamiya's formidable head woman, Bitta. A mute, Bitta had traveled from Abyssinia with the Empress's niece, taking over half the household management before anyone could blink. When Bitta appeared in the doorway she filled it, all broad hips and shaven, gray-stubbled pate, her Kushi-style shawl flowing across her strong shoulders and cinched at her thick, powerful waist. In her early fifties, she carried herself with that special gravity exclusive to women beyond childbearing years. The room fell silent whenever she appeared, and the servants tiptoed about like mice.

She gestured rapidly. All within the circle of her influence were obliged to learn her hand signals. *Is the punch ready yet?*

Aengus managed to bow without lowering his head. "Not quite, missy."

She tossed her head. *Put a fire under your ass, or I will.*

Aengus broke eye contact. "Yes, missy."

Somewhat mollified, she left. One of the other servants—in fact, the boy Aidan's mother (what was her name? *Deirdre.* An attractive woman if she could ever learn to smile again)—brought him the punch bowl. Bawling orders to the others, Aengus filled the bowl from the steaming container on the sink and announced: "I trust none of you to carry this safely. Some things, a man must do himself." He set his hands on either side of the bowl and carried it through the door out toward the celebration.

Just beyond the door was a small alcove, where Aengus could not be seen either from the kitchen or from the yard. There he set down the bowl. He glanced left and right, his expression first furtive, then excited. Aengus unbuttoned his pants-flap. Then, extracting his ample *zakr*, he gave a great sigh of relief, and began to urinate. With only the softest of gurgles, the golden stream flowed into the punch bowl.

A satisfied smile creasing his face, Aengus fastened his pants, laced them up, and grunted. "Now," he said, "it is ready."

As the evening wore on the last of the day's heat dissipated into darkness, but by torchlight and bonfire the celebration continued in full sway.

A troop of acrobatic jugglers amused the children at the eastern edge of the house; to the west, in the fenced field, Malik, Shaka, and Abu Ali laughed mightily as several of the local townsfolk jousted on horseback, displaying more enthusiasm than skill. One after another the commoners spilled to the ground, staggering up or rolling quickly from the threat of horse's hooves.

"Hah-hah!" Malik roared at one moderately impressive effort. "Well done."

Aengus set up the punch bowl carefully on a small table, draping a cheese-cloth over it to protect it from flies, making certain that the punch glasses were arranged in perfect order. For a time he stayed to watch the jousting.

Finally, laughing and settling bets, Malik, Shaka, and the Wakil headed back to the refreshment table. Aengus stood by, beaming, as Malik and Shaka served themselves fragrant cups of hot punch. Shielding his eyes, Shaka sipped, his thick lips curling with satisfaction.

"Ahh . . ."

Malik slapped Aengus's shoulder. "Aengus!" he said jovially. "You must tell my cook how you do it. He tries to follow your recipe, but it . . . just never has that . . . that . . ." Malik floundered for words.

"*Mahsus jauhar?* Special essence?"

"Precisely!" said Shaka Zulu, and drained his cup.

Aengus chuckled. "I will try to describe it more precisely next time. Wakil?" he called. "Have a drink, warm your bones!"

Abu Ali turned back from the competition, beaming. "Thank you," he said, accepting the cup. "What a night, what a night."

The three warriors enjoyed the gaming, as well as refreshing and pungent cups of Aengus's *very* special concoction, as the celebration wound on into the evening.

CHAPTER THIRTEEN

ON A WINDING DIRT ROAD CONNECTING the estate of Wakil Abu Ali with that of his brother Malik, a single horse-drawn cart trundled north in the late-morning sun.

Kai and his footboy Aidan dangled their legs off the rear of the cart, enjoying the day as the horseman drove them on. Kai pointed to a gnarled and spreading oak. *"Sajar,"* he said. "Tree."

Aidan's eyes followed Kai's finger. "Tree," he repeated.

Kai nodded approval. He pointed down at the tufts of green sprouting along the edges of the rutted road. *"Hasis,"* he said.

"Grass."

It was good. Kai was satisfied with the boy's intelligence. He had been right to befriend Aidan. A good footboy was a valuable thing, and Kai thought it possible that he might keep this one for years, perhaps eventually promoting him to head servant of his household. *"Zarrab,"* he said, pointing to the twisting wooden rails stretching along the sides of the road.

"Fence," Aidan said, and immediately looked at Kai for approval.

"You're pretty smart," Kai said. "You'll get it."

"Get it," Aidan repeated, and Kai spanked his palms together, delighted.

Another half an hour brought them around a sweeping gentle curve to the castle of his uncle Malik. Of Moorish design, it wasn't as large as his father's, but it didn't need to be. Malik was wealthy, of course, but his wealth had also been granted from the government as a result of long and intense service. While there were dozens of servants to provide his every need, Malik and his wife, Fatima, had not yet been blessed with children.

The cart crossed the castle's moat and pulled up in the circular courtyard, and Kai hopped down. The horseman said, "You have a good lesson, sir, I'll be here when you need me."

"Thank you, Festus," he replied, and then indicated the gear in the back of the cart. "Bring those," he told Aidan.

Aidan hesitated for only a moment, and then began to pull down the weapons and light armor piled in the back of the cart. It was quite an armful, and the boy bent and stumbled under the load. Kai almost pitied him, but stopped himself. If Aidan wanted the privilege of being a footboy, he would have to learn to handle the responsibilities as well.

The castle door opened at their approach, Aidan balancing the gear in both arms.

Fatima greeted them. She was a tiny thing, barely three cubits tall, the youngest sister of Kai's deceased mother, Kessie. Fatima was so perfectly proportioned that she might have been one of Elenya's porcelain dolls. Her skin was the color of burnished copper, and betrayed the slightest touch of the Egyptian stock that had long ago twined with her Hausa blood to create an exotic, irresistible beauty. She was quite young, barely eighteen, but Malik's first wife had died childless, and his adoration and indulgence of Fatima was legendary.

Her smile was dazzling. "Young Kai," she said. "Here for your lesson?"

"Yes, Fatima," he said. She bent and kissed his cheek. She smelled of flowers and honey and fresh baked bread, and he thought that, truly, Al-Musawwir, the Fashioner, had fashioned his beloved uncle a jewel in human form.

"Well," she said, "he's just finishing up another. Your timing is excellent."

She led them through the hallway, and Kai chuckled as Aidan's eyes seemed to swell from his head. The entire house was filled with the memoirs of a life spent in warfare. It seemed that every digit was filled with armor and weapons, maps and paintings of their warrior ancestors astride muscular, dark steeds.

Kai's pulse quickened whenever he strode these halls. These were his people. These were the men of Dar Kush. He felt a terror deep within him, knowing in his bones that he would never measure up to them, and in those moments glad that he was the younger son. Ali was the diplomat and legislator, the leader with an inherited military ranking. He would win glory, and inherit his father's castle. Kai's destiny was a different one, a quieter one that lay in Ali's shadow. As Malik would have remained in Abu Ali's shadow, had he not transformed himself into the greatest warrior in New Djibouti.

But certainly Kai could not do such a thing . . .

Could he?

Malik's main training hall was in the very center of the house, a wide courtyard with a glass ceiling imported all the way from Alexandria, both natural and artificial light illuminating the place where young men learned to survive on the field of honor. The sounds of combat rang loudly: clangs and thuds, scuffles and shouts.

Kai entered to find his uncle conducting a practice dual with one of Ali's friends, a round, rubbery boy named Kebwe. Kebwe looked as though he should have been clumsy but moved with the explosiveness of a leaping frog, with deceptive balance and a tigerlike aggression.

Kebwe wore leather armor, Malik none at all. Every muscle on Malik's body was etched like a surgeon's chart, his every motion spontaneous, reflexive and yet calculated for maximum effect. No slightest breath was wasted.

His sword was a miracle of fluidity: here, there, to the side, a flickering fire in the waxing light. Kebwe was intuitive, precise, strong, fast . . . and a straw in the wind compared to his teacher.

A second student sat on a bench, heaving for breath and perspiring profusely. Obviously, he had just finished a round with the master. His dour expression suggested that he wasn't eager to begin the next.

Malik and Kebwe stood on a silver floor painting of a triangle within a circle, about four cubits in diameter. Even from where he stood, his eyes wide and heart tripping to the lightning pace of the engagement, Kai could tell that Uncle Malik's footwork moved precisely along the corners of the triangle. His thrusts and parries were, more often than not, in parallel to its lines.

Kai glanced at his footboy, curious as to the effect of this display. Wide-eyed Aidan seemed utterly entranced. Kai deliberately and elaborately slouched into a bored posture.

Malik's arm corkscrewed, and Kebwe's sword clattered to the ground.

"Pitiful," Malik snapped. Kebwe could not meet his teacher's blazing eyes. "Sit. N'Challa!" Malik called out to the second student. "Once more!"

N'Challa rose heavily to his feet. He tried to elevate his spirit to the challenge, but it was clear that this round-robin had been going on for some time, and both younger men were near exhaustion. Malik was still uncannily fresh, as if his exertions had consisted of little more than a brisk walk.

N'Challa was clumsier than Kebwe, but quicker, lurching into position with unexpected speed. Time and again, Malik countered him with casual and unnerving ease.

After a quarter hour of thrust and parry, in which Malik touched the armor over N'Challa's heart a dozen times, the master called a halt.

"Enough!" he roared. "If you are going to waste my time, restrict yourself to kitchen cutlery. Bah!"

Without a word, the boys slunk out of the training hall, heads down.

Malik stood in the middle of the silver triangle within the circle, his point pressed against the ground.

"They were good, I thought," Kai ventured.

The very thinnest of smiles shaded the warrior's face. "Improving," he granted grudgingly. "Most men respond better to blisters than to praise." Then almost as if a spell had been broken, the darkness slid from him and he embraced his nephew warmly. "You, on the other hand, are another matter entirely. " Malik finally seemed to see Aidan, who stood huddled in the corner, his shoulders tight. "Outside, boy."

Aidan nodded humbly and scurried out. The door boomed shut behind him.

Malik turned back to his nephew. "Now, Kai. Let's see what you retain from last week's torture, eh?"

Kai drew his sword and took his place on the triangle. As Malik spoke, Kai automatically executed one short, choppy series of set patterns after another.

"One!" Malik called, triggering a set of six motions: high circle, low circle, riposte, attack at a left oblique, straight right, straight left. Very formalized, keeping his balance well forward on a deeply bent knee, concentration focused to a tunnel. Malik nodded approval.

"Two!"

Kai shifted to the left, passed the sword from his right to his left hand, and lunged. Then low parry, high parry, a thrust to the outside, beginning to enjoy himself—

"No!" Malik called. "You were sacrificing clarity for speed." There was irritation in his voice, but Kai didn't flinch: Malik's occasional irritation masked a deep well of affection.

"Now," he said, as he had a thousand times before. "Count with me." He stood at Kai's side, right hand forward. "One." Kai swooped his sword up, then down toward the center starting from the top right corner of an imaginary box. "Two." The sword glided up to the top left corner of the imaginary box, and slashed to the center. "Three." With a flick of his wrist, the sword went down to the bottom right corner and slashed up to center. "Four" took it down to the bottom left corner, slashing up to center in a kind of backhand, and "Five" took him in a lunge directly down the center.

"Now you," Malik said. And slowly, Kai repeated the motions. In his mind was the square, divided by lines, each of Malik's Five Strikes taking a different line. According to Malik, all of physical motion could be subsumed under those five angles of attack. All other motions were merely variations or combinations. Kai bent himself to the purpose as Malik called them out.

A One was a One regardless of the hand holding the sword. It merely became a backhand motion if in the left hand. And a Two was a Two, and so on. It made a pattern reminiscent of a starburst, and it was dynamic, and could rotate a bit so that the lines of entry were parallel to the ground.

Some systems of combat have seven angles, or twelve, Uncle Malik had said time and again. *They are organized despair. The fewer choices you have to make, the faster you can respond. Think five angles. They are the only directions from which an opponent can attack. And if he hops or twirls or leaps or spits, still your defense against the line remains the same. Think simply. In combat there is no room for the complicated, only the complex.*

"Halt!" Malik called, and the boy froze in position, a human statue.

Malik circled Kai, checking legs and shoulders, adjusting here and there, prodding and probing. Finally, at the point when Kai's thighs began to burn, Malik deigned to nod approval. Then he faced his nephew and took up position with his own blade. "Begin."

Now Malik made the classic strokes to provoke Kai's defense. Thrust, block, parry, a series of motions practiced countless times, engraved upon Kai's mind by the chisel of a master sculptor.

But despite frequent encouragements and proclamations of excellence, his father was right: his heart was more in scrolls than swords. He would sweat his way through his exercises because he loved his uncle, who had taught him to walk. More importantly, he loved and obeyed his father. But the concept of actually facing a sword-wielding Aztec, a barbarian who intended to drive that unyielding sharpness into his guts, made him wilt internally.

For just an instant he allowed himself to fantasize that Malik was actually attempting to kill him. Kai's concentration faltered, and sweat beaded beneath his arms. Panic crawled in the pit of his stomach, but despite the wandering of his mind, his reflexes had served him well: the rhythm remained unbroken.

"Good," Malik nodded. "Better than last week. Let us begin again, and freeze on my command. One—"

Kai began the motion, and Malik cried, "Stop!"

Kai froze, sword extended toward his uncle. Malik tapped his blade against Kai's.

"Look," Malik said. "Granted that you are fast, but you opened the line here. Do you see that man?" Malik pointed toward a full-size model of a scowling Aztec warrior in leather armor and feathered mantle. Next to it was an equally menacing image of a fur-coated Viking carrying a double-bladed axe.

"Yes, sir?" Kai said, trying to keep the quaver out of his voice. Allah preserve him if Malik grew angry!

Malik leaned forward. "He would be eating your liver. Or the Viking? Cleft you in two." He swept his sword down, the tip coming within a digit of Kai's nose. Kai fought not to tremble. Malik sighed. "Boy, you have lived your life in comfort and luxury because your father, and *our* father, took their lessons very seriously. I expect you to do the same, so that your sons may enjoy the same pleasures, hey?"

Kai nodded his head vigorously. Malik squared Kai's shoulders and set him to practicing his lunges against the Aztec dummy.

"Now!" he said. "Lunge!" And Kai lunged. "Recover. Roof block! Recover. Stroke number two! Recover—"

Kai performed each technique with full energy and commitment. If not all of his most secret heart was in it, his uncle either didn't sense it or pretended not to notice.

Every stroke touched a vital spot. Every lunge was accompanied by a sharp exhalation that precisely matched the duration of the strike. Kai's eyes narrowed, mind simultaneously on the target and roaming though his body striving to keep the arm aligned, the hip properly positioned, the rear heel flat on the ground to transfer the shock. If fate was with him, if his technique lanced his blade into the dummy, then that additional leverage would insure that steel would drive deep, not be deflected by armor or bone.

Again and again and again, until the circle of his concentration had contracted to exclude fear, and all awareness of self was consumed in the flame of focus.

And as he entered that strange and special place, his uncle smiled.

Night had fallen. The cart was trundling along the road slowly, as if Kai had all the time in the world. The moon hung swollen on the eastern horizon, its lower edge kissing the Tägaday Plain, named for an Abyssinian wrestler fabled to have won land concessions from the Tonkawa native tribe by besting their champion.

Kai had been quiet for the last half hour, reveling masochistically in the ache in his legs and arms and back. It would fade into stiffness in the morning, leaving behind a sense of greater connectedness. And in a few years, he knew, the same lessons would shape his body into manly perfection. Not the awesome machine that was his uncle, or his father as he had appeared in old portraits, but manly nonetheless.

Finally, he turned to the boy next to him. They had shared a basket of warm pastries sent by Fatima; after all, the footboy had carried some quite sweaty clothing and light armor. *Ai-Den* would clean them, too, in the morning. It was only fair for him to share in some of the good things. And he was, Kai suspected, sharing more than the food. He chuckled to himself when the servant made subtle thrusting and blocking motions in the air.

"You were watching, weren't you?" he said. Aidan looked at him curiously, but without recognition. Kai gestured with his sword, and said it again, raising his voice and pronouncing the words more carefully. "You . . . were . . . watching?"

Aidan's eyes sparkled. He picked up a stick and pantomimed his response. *"Wahid, atnen, yudafi!* One! Two! Block!" he said, moving clumsily through the paces.

But Kai rather liked what he saw. Aidan had learned more by just watching (through a grille? through a crack in the door?) than did some of his uncle's students in the actual presence of the Master. "Not bad," he allowed.

Aidan mimed a salute, his hand to his heart. "Yes, sir!" he said.

Kai grinned. Just like a little monkey, Aidan was. Kai lay back against the grain bags, resting his sore muscles. Indeed, he had made a good choice of footboys. This was going to be fun.

CHAPTER FOURTEEN

FESTUS STOPPED THE CART before the gate to Ghost Town, the blacks' derogatory name for the slaves' compound. The wire fence around the entire settlement was shoulder-high, but not barbed. Try as he might, Aidan was unable to avoid comparisons with O'Dere crannog, the home that he had been torn from barely a year before.

"Here y'go, boyo." Festus grinned. Festus would take master Kai up to the big house, drive back to the barn, rub down and feed the horses, and then, finally, return to the compound for his own meal and a night's sleep.

Kai waved his hand and said something in Arabic. Aidan was learning as fast as he could, but there was so much to learn, so many things that he sometimes despaired. There were only two words he recognized: *"Gadan."* Tomorrow. And *"Ma'ab Salame Aidan."* Good-bye, Aidan.

He waved his hand back. *"Gadan,"* he said in return. The alien word felt odd in his mouth, and he felt a little chill, knowing that in time those sounds would be natural to him. If he did not find a way out of this trap, a way to return to the land of his birth, he was afraid he might become as some of the other slaves, speaking Arabic more readily than Gaelic.

Luckily, most slaves in the village were from Eire, and spoke the same tongue. He had heard that this was unusual, that on most farms and land holdings they were mixed from over the Isle and the Far Lands as well, forced out of their languages and customs and made to accept those of their new masters.

He would not. He would learn this terrible, ugly speech, but never forget who he was. And one day, he would find a way to take his mother away from this place, and they would find Nessa . . .

The utter helplessness of his situation suddenly threatened to overwhelm him. Since arriving in the harbor he had seen so much, done so much, and so much had been done to him. Weeks of the meanest, most mindless labor as he learned enough basic Arabic to respond to commands. Then rotations in the fields, weeding and hoeing. More weeks in the barns shoveling shit, and heaven help him if he touched one of their precious horses! Then weeks of kitchen duties: scrubbing floors, carrying wood, shoveling ice in the ice cellar. If he hadn't found a way to catch Kai's eye, he feared he might have been unhinged by the mind-numbing combination of boredom and fatigue.

Topper, a strapping black-hair who was one of the village's two blacksmiths, saluted him. Topper was a kind man, with a round face and a back like a boulder. Knowing that Aidan had yet to learn their master's language, Topper addressed him in their own tongue. "Had a good day with the young master?"

"It was all right," he said, grateful to feel, for a moment, sane and free. "He's not all bad, I guess."

Topper's wrinkled face creased in a smile. He laid his slab of a hand on the boy's shoulder. "They're all bastards, boy," he said. "It'll be easier on you if you learn their speech and their ways. There is no way home."

Yes, there is, Aidan said to himself, but his mouth replied, "Of course not."

Topper slapped his shoulder and swung his way past, whistling. There was something haunted in the man's eyes, and Aidan knew that he was not as cavalier as his words implied. Not at all.

A pretty, freckled, red-haired girl walked past, carrying two buckets of water in a yoke across her shoulders. "Hello, Aidan," she greeted him. She was only a year older than he, but there was a wealth of sad knowledge in her eyes, concealed behind the joviality. Her hair and smile reminded him of Nessa.

He greeted her in return. "Molly," he said, and she seemed to glow at him, which made him feel uncomfortable. He wanted to avoid her. He had enjoyed poor Morgan's flirtations, yes, but now any fascination with girls had been lost to his overriding preoccupations: Survival. Freedom. Nessa. Home.

He had been here for ten months. In some ways the village was reminiscent of O'Dere crannog. But there were new elements added by their masters, strange mud that dried like stone and cloths from someplace called Kush and *Ee-Gyp*, which he now understood to be worlds away but somehow still influenced *this* world. So many things, so many dizzying sights and sounds. He wore the blacks' cast-off clothes, he would learn their language. He gawked at their houses, so much larger and more luxuriant than anything he had ever known. He had to understand. He had to know this world, and was afraid that he wouldn't ever be able to truly grasp it.

What kind of strange beings were these black men, who built such terrible and wonderful things? Were they really human, or something else?

Could they possibly be gods? He didn't think so. Kai, whose favor he had carefully cultivated, certainly seemed to be much like an ordinary boy, except for his power and knowledge. He had watched Kai piss against a tree, and what he pulled out of his pants certainly *looked* human, but with demons and fairies you couldn't be sure.

Aidan had to be very careful indeed.

He strode the narrow streets of Ghost Town, long since memorized. About two hundred slaves lived within its walls. There were a few more on the grounds, living in the main house or in shacks next to the quarries. Aidan struggled not to become overawed by the wealth. Slaves he had known in Eire, but he had never known anyone who owned more than two. Over two *hundred?* The "Wah-kill" was unimaginably powerful, and if his son seemed nothing but a normal human, mightn't the "Wah-kill" be more?

These and other riddles plagued him as he returned home. It was a mean shack by O'Dere standards. The wooden walls were flimsy, the roof thinly thatched. It was hot in the day and cold at night. The floor was earthen, but not the good dark clay he had known only months ago. He could smell the difference, *feel* the difference when he ground his bare feet against the reddish dust. This was alien, all alien, and the pleasant, sympathetic faces of the other slaves were no more than a further snare to entrap him.

When he walked through the door, the first and most wondrous sight was his mother, Deirdre. Without being able to halt himself, he burst out in his "Mama!" and ran to her, grasping her around the waist. *"An airíonn tú ceart go leor?"* Are you feeling better?

"Tá mé go maith," she replied in Gaelic. Hardship had stripped flesh from her body. She was gaunt now, and her hipbones dug into his arms when he hugged her. There was plenty of food, but Deirdre had not eaten or slept well in the months since their arrival.

There were stories that slaves on other farms were treated far worse. The overseers would sometimes imply that they were lucky to be here—thereby subtly threatening them with removal to one of these fabled terrible places.

But that was little relief, little comfort. His sister, Nessa, was out there . . . somewhere. Aidan knew his mother's prayer was to ingratiate herself to her new masters, and plead with them to find her child and buy her. That would take time, and God only knew what might happen to Nessa in the meantime.

Aidan began to babble, barely in control of the words as he complained of his hardship in learning the new tongue. *"Tá beagán cúthaileachta orm fós faoi bheith á labhairt—"*

Deirdre interrupted. Her face was drawn, once-flawless skin blemished and pulled tightly across her cheeks. She was still beautiful to him, but he could see clearly the old woman she would be, and knew that that age would crumble her before her time if he did not find a way to get them out of here. Their home betrayed the pitiful efforts she had made to create beauty and maintain dignity in their new surroundings. Candles, flowers, small shining rocks—anything that might create a pattern of their own in this place, something to remind them of the rhythms and spaces of their own world.

"We are here in this land now," she said, then lapsing into Irish continued: *"Tá sé tábhachtach nósanna na tíre a choinneáil i gcuimhne agus aird a thabhairt orthu."* It is vital to learn and practice these new customs.

"The words don't fit in my mouth," he protested.

"De réir mar a dhéanann tú botúin foghlaimeoidh tú." As you make mistakes, you will learn.

Then, as though angry with herself for lapsing into her native tongue, she stumbled through her Arabic sentences. *"Aidan, la tayyib.* Not good. Learn to speak. Practice speak." She fought over the words, but he was suddenly ashamed that she had done so much better than he. He was the man of the house now! "This our home," she concluded, and there was a touch of exhaustion about her, as if the alien words were chunks of iron in her head.

Aidan thought, searching his meager store of Arabic words and phrases. *"Níl agam ach beagáinín Araby."* I speak only a little Arabic, he said, lapsing into Gaelic again.

"Isti'mal. Practice," she said. "Get good. Here. *Akal.* Eat."

He sat. *Speaking* that damned devil tongue made his head spin, as if he had to learn to think like the black monsters in order to just speak their chittering, awful speech. Deirdre placed a bowl of stew on the table before him, and he sniffed deeply. Mutton, thickened with vegetables and teff flour. He wanted to turn his nose up at it, but his stomach rumbled. Aidan dipped his wooden spoon and lifted it to his lips.

"Miswab. Spoon," he said, pulling the word out of his mind. *"Batiya-t.* Bowl."

He took a bite of stew, and his face relaxed into pleasure at his first taste of the savory collation. At least they were not starved. That was a good thing. A warrior had to remain strong. To remain strong, he would have to eat. Eat and *isti'mal*. Practice.

Deirdre watched him for a few moments. He met her eyes, saw the tiny trace of a smile that curved her lips, wished that he could offer more to her. She tried to be strong for him, but he heard her crying at night, every night. Knew that she was not whole without his father, who had died trying to save them. Knew that she felt she had failed his sister. He had to be strong, for her, for both of them.

He finished another mouthful and sat, studying the spoon thoughtfully. He made a slashing gesture. At *Mah-lick's* castle he had found a ventilation grate close to the ground. There he had squatted, watching the lesson as Kai and his terrifying teacher swirled through their paces. He was sure that Kai and the big man were related. Perhaps Mah-lick was an uncle: Aidan hadn't picked up enough of the language to ask that question yet, but there was a family resemblance. The teacher looked like the Wah-kill would look if he lost some belly. Not that the Wah-kill looked fat, or slow. Just that the teacher was as lean as a wolf, and moved faster than any human being he had ever seen. If only O'Dere's warriors had possessed such skill! Certainly, these blacks were more powerful than the Northmen. They probably had greater weapons as well.

If Aidan could be a friend to Kai, he would have the chance to learn things, things that he might use one day to kill many of the black men, and perhaps the Northmen who had destroyed his village. Yes, that would be good.

Hatred, raw and corrosive, welled within him, gnawing at the emotional mask that he wore in the presence of the black men. That much he had learned. *Never let an enemy know how you feel.* The whip scars on his back had taught him as much. Smile and nod, do your work, find ways to make yourself useful when they are watching, and creep off when the work is done. Yes. These things and more he had learned.

He swept the spoon up and down in the air, making sword strokes.

He looked at the spoon. *"Battar.* Sword," he said in perfect Arabic.

Yaqtul.

Kill.

CHAPTER FIFTEEN

BELLY FULL AND WARM, KAI WAS CLIMBING to his bedroom on aching legs when he heard a faint voice originating from one of the far rooms on the second floor. His pulse quickened and he immediately abandoned his notions of heading to bed, where nothing more riveting than a book of local history awaited him. Who cared how much net profit his grandfather Rashid had accrued when the first boatload of wretched whites arrived in New Djibouti? The Wakil wanted Kai to memorize vast columns of financial data, but the idea of more study tonight made his head hurt.

This wing and floor had been consigned to the royal Lamiya and her entourage, and the voices could only mean that a late-night lesson was under way. Kai tiptoed along the hallway and then paused outside the broad double doors of the library that had been converted for the use of Lamiya's brilliant tutor, Babatunde.

Now in his fifties, Babatunde was the son of a Yoruba prince and a shepherd girl of Yoruba and Turkish extraction. Denied palace comforts and tutors by reason of his tainted blood, he was a true genius, renowned for his poetry and scholarship by the age of twenty, holder of a spiritual lineage at least forty generations old, extending back through Nur Addin Qwami and Jafar Al Siddik to Bilal, and ultimately to the Prophet himself.

By twenty-five he had come to the attention of the Pharaoh, winning a royal appointment to serve the imperial house. During a cultural exchange between Alexandria and Addis Ababa, Babatunde had been hired by the Empress to educate her own family. It was her throne Babatunde had served for the last twenty years. Babatunde accompanied Lamiya as friend and tutor, and while in Dar Kush, the household's children had access to his wisdom. Education was a combination of lecture, guided self-study, and spontaneous discourse. Math, history, philosophy, science, theology, and warrior craft were Kai's disciplines. Elenya and Lamiya's educations were similar, save for the combatives. In early adulthood, varying, but usually between the ages of seventeen and twenty, children of the wealthy traveled to New Alexandria or even Addis Ababa for college. This would be Elenya's eventual journey, and perhaps Kai's. Ali was receiving a far more practical education at his father's side.

Kai came close enough to the door to hear clearly. The air was a bit warm, and the door had been left ajar to enhance circulation. Babatunde's voice was melodic and distinct, well articulated in any of the six languages he spoke fluently. "And by what is the Royal House of Kush bound to the throne of India?" he asked.

Lamiya answered so precisely she might have been reading from a book. "The Alexandrian Concords of 770 established trade and were the first of many mutual defense and assistance treaties for the Pan-Indian trade sphere."

Kai felt his knees wobble a little. Her voice was the very epitome of feminine perfection. He thought that it reminded him of his sainted mother's, although he had not heard that voice in many years. It had the same calming effect on his heart.

"Very good," Babatunde said patiently. "And the only interruption to that pact?"

Lamiya answered without the slightest hesitation. "In 1008, during the Persian Insurgence, when India refused to impose trade restrictions."

Kai heard a book slapping shut. "Very good," Babatunde said. "Let's call that all for the day, shall we?"

Lamiya sighed. "My head is very full," she said, and Kai could easily imagine her holding it between her hands. "I would be grateful."

There was a general rustling sound, as books and papers were ordered and arranged, then Lamiya and her maids filed out of the room. Kai had already hidden himself behind a bookcase, a position from which he could watch unseen. They were all lovely, but beside Lamiya the most striking was Bitta, Lamiya's chaperone and companion, a tall, broad, shaven-headed woman of mixed Zulu-Ibo extraction. Her scarred cheeks and exceptionally alert eyes seemed more appropriate to a blooded warrior than any woman. Oddly, her hands and feet were delicate. He had glimpsed the black handle of the knife hidden beneath her shawl, and guessed that she wielded it with skill sufficient to shame most men.

The women chatted among themselves as they headed for their rooms. When the hall was empty, Kai crept back to the door.

Babatunde's back was to him. The great teacher seemed always in motion, engaged in this or that project, lecture, or experiment. Kai crept toward him. Babatunde seemed completely absorbed by shelves of beakers and bubbling vials containing whatever arcane project currently occupied his vast mind. Transmutation of gold? Kai had heard rumors that the Yoruba knew that secret. True? False?

Babatunde gave no external sign that anything had impinged upon his consciousness. He picked up a hard rubber ball that sat on the table next to him and weighed it in his hand. What was Babatunde up to? Was this part of a precious secret? Kai felt almost ashamed to be spying on the great man. So a ball of India rubber, immersed in one of the bubbling vats, yes . . .

Babatunde tossed the ball over his shoulder, bouncing it off the ceiling. Kai's eyes followed it, confusion momentarily clouding his reflexes. The rubber sphere descended at a steep angle, and bopped him squarely on the nose.

"Ow!"

He stumbled back, rubbing the offended body part, eyes smarting.

When he had recovered, Babatunde regarded him mildly, muscular arms crossed. Babatunde's face was kindly and sharp, with no more than a touch of chalk about his cheeks and brown skin. His black eyes twinkled with mischief above a strong, prominent nose. "Shouldn't you be studying, young sir?"

"Your lessons are more interesting."

"Did you learn much, crouching in the shadows?"

Kai blinked the water from his eyes. "Lamiya was wrong," he said.

Babatunde's expression was mild. "Really?"

Kai nodded. "India didn't refuse to impose restrictions on Persia."

"Hmmm," Babatunde said, as if his mind had already moved on to something else. He picked up a piece of red cloth from the back of a chair and tied it around Kai's face, effectively blindfolding him. He smelled of cinnamon. "Tell me why you think so." Babatunde picked up a stick and drew its tip carefully and lightly across the wall. Kai pivoted, pointing with his finger, following the sound. "Tell me what you think happened."

In darkness, Kai used his ears. As he spoke, Babatunde changed the direction of scraping stick, using the sound of speech to mask his action. Tricky. But not tricky enough. "According to Al'hadif, who chronicled the event for the Empress . . ." up, and then in a circle, Babatunde moved the stick. *Listen carefully, carefully.* Kai fought to create a still, silent space within himself. He became very quiet, which is difficult when simultaneously attempting to answer questions. "The Abyssinian Pan-Indian trade sphere was the Empress's attempt to balance Egypt's military power. The throne of Egypt disapproved and wanted to punish the Empress, but only unofficially."

Babatunde had changed the game. Now he was pushing the little red ball with the tip of his stick. The ball made almost no sound at all, and Kai had to pause and concentrate in order to hear it. Wait . . . *there* it was. Kai began tracking again, following a whisper-thin thread of sound. Then the sound ended. Pause. A moment later, a thump on the floor.

Babatunde had pushed the ball off the edge of the table.

"So that . . . ?" Babatunde asked, as Kai fought to keep track of the bumps and thumps as the ball bounced across the floor.

"The whole trade thing was just . . . a convenient . . . excuse for the Pharaoh's punishment."

Kai snatched at the ball, and caught it on the third bounce. He took off the blindfold, and Babatunde applauded delightedly. "Excellent," he beamed.

Kai smiled with pride. It had taken months to learn how to track the ball. Babatunde was always coming up with new tricks and tests. It sometimes seemed that El Sursur, the Cricket, lived for nothing other than teaching.

A few of the beakers in the racks were smoking, heated from beneath by chemical flames.

"What are you doing this time? Making gold from lead?"

"Another convenient fiction, I'm afraid," Babatunde said, though Kai still suspected that El Sursur might be keeping secrets from him. Crickets were wily insects. "The world is not its symbols, Kai. The form is not the essence. When wise men speak of creating gold from lead, they speak of any transformation of lesser to higher form. Usually it is a reference to the growth of the human spirit itself. My intent here is nothing so lofty. I am precipitating solids from a solution. Do you remember what I taught you about that?"

Kai searched his memory. "Super—super . . . saturate the solution, and it forms precipitates."

Babatunde clapped approval. "Very good. Hand me that, would you?" He indicated a leather pouch next to Kai's elbow. Kai hefted it. It weighed a kite or so, and contained some kind of powder.

"Why are you so interested in these things?" the boy asked.

Babatunde opened the pouch, then began examining a rack of little scoops and spoons of various size, finally choosing one with a bowl the size of Kai's thumb, measuring a cubic digit. "Al-Mubdi, the Originator, created a miraculous universe, and expects us to learn its marvels." He took two heaping scoops and placed the contents into a metal pan. Then he chose a second container, which was filled with a thick clear liquid. With a second, clean spoon, he scooped out a glob of the stuff, and seemed to be measuring it with his eyes. "You're actually quite good at this, you know." Kai glowed. The occasions on which Babatunde allowed him to play in the lab were some of the very best times in his life.

Babatunde mixed the gel with the powder, took a step back and produced a timepiece from the folds of his robe. He counted to himself. In fifteen seconds, just as Kai was becoming a bit impatient, fire flashed with a sharp *crack!* followed by a tiny puff of black smoke.

Kai jumped back a step. "My soul!"

Babatunde nodded to himself. He may have been pretending to conduct some sort of experiment, but Kai knew that that particular demonstration had been just for him. "Yes. Useful." He became more animated as he turned to face Kai. Now he looked to be at least twenty years younger than his half-century. "I would like to speak with your father again. I think sending you to school in Addis Ababa would refine certain qualities of mind . . ."

Kai frowned. As the flames died down he found a little flat wooden stick and stirred the mess. It hissed at him. "Father will never agree. He doesn't like me to spend so much time with you."

Babatunde shrugged. "Well, there are sometimes ways to make even the strongest change his mind. Turn up the burner, would you?" Babatunde turned his attention to a bubbling beaker on the other side, and found the dial controlling the fire vent. While Babatunde wasn't looking, Kai managed to secure a bag of each of the volatile ingredients beneath his shirt.

"Very interesting," Babatunde said behind him, and Kai gave a guilty start. "Did you know it is possible to predict the color of a solution by its components?"

Kai breathed a sigh of relief. "Really?"

Before another word was said the great door opened. Faster than conscious thought, the boy dropped down behind the nearest counter as his father swept imperiously into the room. Kai crouched and hid, barely able to breathe.

He crept around to a corner until he was slightly behind the Wakil, staying low. Kai watched Babatunde bow, nothing in his face or manner betraying either amusement or nervousness. "Wakil. Can I be of service?"

Abu Ali shook the tutor's hand, wrist to wrist in the manner of equals. A high complement to El Sursur indeed. "Babatunde, my friend. We are entering negotiations with the northern Gupta settlement, and I wished to make a present to the lady of the greatest house."

Babatunde's fingers combed his beard. "Ah. That would be the Benares. And this concerns . . . ?"

"Quarry sales. Several thousand cubic cubits of granite."

Babatunde stroked his beard. "Excellent," he said after a few moments. His gaze was distant. "They will probably be building, expanding the settlement. Let me see—"

Kai knew that his father would be completely involved in Babatunde's comments, and that this was his best chance. He began to sidle his way out of the room, holding the bag of stolen treasures.

"Some in their settlement worship Shiva," Babatunde mused, "but Allah has touched the hearts of the Benares." He snapped his fingers. "I would suggest a gift of silk, something that might decorate the new home."

"A curtain." Abu Ali sounded excited. "Or wall hanging . . . ?"

As the conversation continued, Kai scampered out of the room with his prizes. At the door he glanced back. Babatunde held his father's attention, but simultaneously managed to make eye contact with Kai. He winked.

That night, Djidade Berhar visited Abu Ali, and the two friends smoked, drank nectar, and spoke of business and the eternal political wrangles between the Senate and the Ulema. Meanwhile, their children played. When they weren't feuding like natives, Kai often hosted Fodjour for the night, and many were the times they were up until all hours, talking of the mighty deeds they would accomplish once they had reached their majority, and which of them would make the greatest mark.

Such conversations had been suspended this evening, in favor of outdoor adventure. Kai, Fodjour, and Elenya crept through the shadows, across the access road toward the servant quarters, Kai carrying a little pouch of the mixture purloined from Babatunde.

Ghost Town's privies were just outside the gate, generally downwind from both servant and master. They were of simple design: holes dug in the ground with chemicals sprinkled in to hasten the breakdown of waste and mute the odor. The privies were covered up or pumped out every few months, with an eye to limiting disease and making the settlement as pleasant as possible.

Fodjour crept close to Kai as the three came within sight of one of the privy hutches. They hid behind bushes. "Are you sure this will work?"

Elenya's round little face glowed with worshipful confidence. "If Kai says it will work, it will work," she said.

Kai shushed them as he scrambled up to the back of the hutch. He took a few minutes to attach his innocuous little bundle, and then amidst giggles and shushing sounds they scampered off again.

*   *   *

Kitchen Master Aengus had enjoyed a wonderful meal. Not the garbage he fixed for the blacks in the big house, concoctions of ground beef and lamb that they would probably prefer spiced with beetles and grubs. They thought themselves so civilized, but didn't appreciate the value of a side of roast pig, of good honest simple raised bread. He could work all day in their kitchens to produce a banquet to their taste, but what Aengus really wanted was to get home and savor the chicken and potatoes he had simmered in the pot all day, his good wife, Ana, having added whatever garlic, bay leaf, and shallots she could obtain. Ana would have stirred slowly and carefully for hours, blending in sufficient native herbs and mushrooms to produce a truly wondrous meal.

Aengus was filled almost to bursting with her current efforts. Another spoonful and they would have to roll him to bed. That and the beer that he was allowed to brew. Another alien and disgusting thing about these damned blacks was their aversion to alcohol—the followers of Muhammad, at least. The Zulus and Ibos were rarely Muslims, and those he sometimes provided with beer or imported Roman Provincial wine or fermented milk.

Tonight it served him well. He was so drunk he could barely walk, which was not an uncommon occurrence. Beer helped him forget, helped keep him from wringing a neck or slitting a throat, or more pointedly from putting ground glass or poison into the food and killing every black man and woman in Dar Kush, an act that would be suicide for the entire settlement.

So he smiled, and dreamed, and practiced his culinary arts, learned as a boy on far Eire. Aengus barely remembered those days anymore, and often managed to forget them until the next batch of slaves came in, emerald memories still alight in their eyes. He envied them the sunsets they had seen on the shores of his youth, and pitied the awful freshness of their loss.

Then he could remember, *then* their pain was his, and he attempted to make their lot a little easier, to warn them against rebellion, or attempted escape. Damnably clever, Abu Ali favored the purchase of intact family pairs whenever they could be found: daughters with fathers, mothers with sons. Always hostages. Always another to share the cost of punishment if one struck out against the masters.

And one of the most effective punishments was the simple threat to sell one from the relative comfort of the Wakil's settlement to another, less pleasing place. Oh, yes, there were worse by far, and Aengus knew it. There were mines where healthy boys became toothless, broken old men in a single year; swamps filled with fever, pit-fighting circuses where men fought to the death for a crust of bread or a single night with a diseased whore.

Yes, there were worse.

Aengus waddled into the nearest hutch and dropped his pants, settling his ample buttocks onto the round wooden seat. The seats were low, so that his knees were a bit higher than his hips: not his favorite squatting position, but truth to tell it did seem to facilitate evacuation. He could already feel gravity doing its work. Aengus hummed a song to himself as he alternately grunted and relaxed.

The smell was awful, of course, but not as bad as some privies he'd known in his youth. These black bastards *did* have their uses.

Suddenly, he realized that there was another smell mixed in with that of urine, feces, and stale old farts. Something that was like fire, a faint burning smell—

He had a single instant to feel alarm, and then the back of the privy simply vanished with a flash and a roar. The floor beneath him groaned, and he fell into a ghastly sour soft wetness.

Fear warred with anger as he thrashed in the awful muck, slimy fingers finally finding purchase and hauling his bulk up (and for once he was glad of that mass! If he had been a lad or a lass, he might have sunk right into the midst of the filth, never to be seen again!). With deceptive strength he pulled himself out, covered toe to chin in stinking slime.

He heard their laughter without being able to see them, and wrath's red tide boiled behind his eyes. He took a step, slipped, and almost slid back into the pit, finally lying there and sputtering at them. "You . . . your father will 'ave your 'ide for this!" he shrieked at them. "I . . . I'll 'ave you!"

Three of the little bastards were running away, doubled over with hilarity.

Behind him, the other slaves were pouring out of their houses, through the gate. They had heard the muffled explosion, of course. Perhaps at first they had been afraid, but when they saw its target, recognized an irresistibly perverse sort of justice. As a result, they began laughing too, pent-up emotion and fear breaking free to a torrent of cleansing mirth.

"Aengus," one woman called out, hands cupped to her mouth. "Are all yer dangles in order?"

Aidan joined the edge of the crowd, his young eyes narrowed. Everyone was laughing at the sight of Aengus lying in a pool of shit, greased from head to toe in foulness. Smoke and stinking steam wafted from the pit. Why were they laughing?

He felt something brush his elbow and looked up to see Brian Mac-Cloud, a tall, golden, charismatic rogue, neighbor and crony of Topper the blacksmith. The Wakil could vest power where he would: old Auntie Moira was designated the official village leader. Aidan and most others chose Brian. He was a spellbinder and a schemer, fast with his fists and his wit.

"Well," Brian said. "Serves him for pissin' in the punch."

"What?"

Brian grinned his wide, white grin and lit his pipe. Aidan loved the way it smelled and hoped that the wind would hold steady. "Ye never heard it from me, boyo, but come party time, I'd suggest ye stick to water."

"Aidan?" a familiar voice called. "What happened here?" It was Deirdre, dressed in the thin blanket wrap that substituted for a shawl. Thank heaven that most nights were warm, because with the loss of body fat, his mother would have suffered terribly. There were never enough blankets. The food, while sufficient to ward off hunger, never seemed to be enough to make them truly full, unless one was lucky enough to sit at Aengus's hearth.

"Evenin', ma'am," Brian said politely. "Just one of the good Lord's thunderbolts, I reckon. All sins accounted for, eh?"

Aengus struggled up, then slipped again, and for a moment seemed destined to slide back down into the pit.

Aidan turned in time to see a goddess saunter out of the shantytown. Her hair was yellow, her face an oval vision. Aidan felt his breath quicken and then freeze whenever he watched her approach. Her name was Máirí. She was Brian's frequent companion, and probably the most beautiful woman in the village.

He felt a moment's shame and disloyalty that he would think that about someone other than his mother, and snuck another glance at Deirdre. His heart sank. Her eyes were dark-rimmed and her posture was slumped, as if she were still chained in the terrible narrow spaces in the slave ships.

Aidan swallowed hard.

Máirí's clothing was disarrayed, and a shimmering aura of heat seemed to envelop her and her man as she linked arms with him. Brian looked at her with lazy-lidded eyes, his long strong jaw working around the pipe. "Now, girl. Where were we . . . ?"

Murmuring to each other, they returned to the village. Aidan knew that they were bound for Brian's bed. Since arrival in this land, he had seen and heard things that shocked him. Men and women seemed to pair off and couple with no concern for possible pregnancy. There seemed no shame, no guilt, little morality.

He let Deirdre shepherd him back, but her attention was split. Her eyes focused beyond him and across the road to the distant big house.

Guards roamed on horseback, just visible in the distance. The village gates were open, but not for a moment was Aidan gulled into believing he could just walk out and away.

He had seen the scars of those who had been ridden down, seen the missing eyes and fingers, and heard whispers of night riders and death in the swamp. No. When he made his move, he would be certain. He would be sure.

And right now, his mother needed him.

Her eyes were far away, further even than the great house or the imagined limits of the estate. He knew that she was seeing, lost in the verdant mists of time and distance, the O'Dere crannog. She imagined she was seeing her husband, Mahon, his da, wishing she could join him in whatever heaven or hell he reposed. She was remembering Nessa.

What else did she see? Lir, the fisherman? Kyle and Donough, his old friends? And little red-haired Morgan? The thought of her crimson tresses saddened Aidan, a sweet-sour ache in his chest. Her smile, so warm and challenging. She had known something, held within her some secret about life. Perhaps about their life together, and if he had not awakened to that reality in the crannog, it gnawed at him now. Where was she? He had not seen her since the slave market, and there he had been too panicked and frightened even to say good-bye.

"Come," Deirdre said, as if she could read his downward-spiraling thoughts. "Morning comes too soon. You need your sleep." He found her hand, a dear, thin hand, and held it tightly as they returned to their simple shelter.

CHAPTER SIXTEEN

SO THE DAYS TURNED. The servants worked in the laundry or the kitchen or dusted and cleaned; they hoed and irrigated and planted in the hemp and bean and teff fields; they mucked the stables and groomed the horses; they bent their backs with hammer and pick and shovel in the northern quarries.

Dar Kush had found a home for Deirdre's skills: she was the only slave capable of reading and deciphering complex sewing patterns imported from Alexandria or Djibouti. She labored by candlelight fashioning or mending clothes, embroidering sheets and stitching pillowcases. When she had a spare moment she stitched rags into clothes for the villagers, trading for extra food or labor. Despite the indignity of patching their owners' clothes, his mother was at least spared the hardship of the fields, and Aidan was grateful for that.

Aidan rubbed his hands raw scrubbing pots in the kitchen. He spent so much time raking straw in the barn that he could recognize individual horses by their droppings, and began learning the theory of crop rotation and the value of the fallow field where Kikuyu herdsmen ran their hardy cattle.

Above all, he was on call to take care of Kai's needs: polishing, cleaning, sometimes just simple companionship. Kai was a mysterious creature: elegant and effeminate yet well versed in fighting. A lover of scrolls yet quick to mischief, lonely and yet surrounded by slaves, family, and would-be friends.

He was the favorite of his father's seraglio, the six women, black and white, who slept in a second-floor wing of Dar Kush and seemed to have no function save slaking the lust of Wakil Abu Ali. Plump and giggly, they plied Kai with sweets and pinched his cheeks, but the smiles never remained on his dark face for long.

Abu Ali's business and political contacts—men from New Alexandria, Wichita, and as far as some place called India—often brought their children with them, as if hoping that Kai might bond with them. The boy was rarely more than polite, as if wary that they wanted something from him or afraid that someone would use him to influence his mighty father.

And so, curiously, Kai sought Aidan's company frequently, as if comforted by the constraints upon such a formalized and limited pairing.

The artificial camaraderie might have seemed demeaning if Kai had been a less agreeable sort, but in truth Aidan rather enjoyed his company: he felt a soothing quiet emanating from Kai that he had previously experienced only in his mother's presence, and from the teacher Babatunde. It was strange, and deep, and he had to caution himself not to relax in the other boy's presence, to constantly remind himself: *This is not your friend.*

In fact, Aidan's connection to Kai served him quite well. He was able to learn, to gain privilege, to become an invisible set of eyes and ears around the grounds.

He learned that servants often moved with great freedom in the household, if they were plausibly going about their duties. Aidan spent the days practicing his Arabic until he could stumble his way through a conversation without making a complete fool of himself.

Most important, he learned to mask his true emotions. For days after the incident in the privy, Aengus had glared at Kai, but his genuinely murderous anger seemed reserved for Abu Ali, who declined to punish either his children or their guest, Fodjour. Twice Aidan had seen Aengus spit in the master's food, then stand beaming with pleasure as the Wakil cleaned every morsel from his plate.

Once a week Aidan traveled with his young master to Malik's castle, which lay three hours north by horse-drawn cart. Malik's home was squarish, perhaps two-thirds the size of Dar Kush, a sandstone-walled, moated, turreted fortress enclosing a central atrium crowded with strange, fleshy-leaved, spiny-flowered plants. Twice Aidan had been allowed to spend his waiting time in a kind of glass-walled house of flowers, where he reveled in blossoms of phenomenal delicacy, perfumed beyond anything he had ever imagined, a place which bore no slightest imprint of the mighty Malik. This was his wife, Fatima's, sanctum, and Aidan had only invaded it on those occasions when she desired his clever hands to work the pruning sheers.

All of this land belonged to the brothers, and Aidan was drop-jawed with amazement at its wealth and extent.

At Malik's mansion, Kai tested the limits of heart, mind, and body. Usually Aidan stayed outside the room, but on a few occasions—for instance when Malik wished Kai to practice a new throw or hold—Aidan was invited in. These sessions, when Aidan left skin and sweat on the floor, were the most painful and rewarding of all.

Of all the things that confused Aidan, none puzzled him more than the old man, Babatunde. He was tiny, hardly one of the massive warriors who seemed to hold all the power in this bizarre land, yet the black men treated him with the utmost respect, as if he were a kind of *seanchai*. Babatunde treated all the slaves with a certain degree of consideration: the very first time Aidan met the little man, Babatunde held a door open for him as he struggled under a load of firewood. But whatever concern for slave humanity Babatunde might possess, it didn't translate into the kind of help that might mean freedom or even ease, and expecting favors from Babatunde was like watching a campfire through a wall of ice, hoping for warmth.

But he did enjoy the fact that Kai, who grew weekly more proficient with sword and empty hand, was never able to sneak up on Babatunde. The little man had the same phenomenal level of awareness displayed by some of the crannog's best hunters, a kind of animal awareness that was never completely set aside, even in sleep.

Then why were they slain by the Northmen? he asked himself at night.

And would these black warriors have been taken so easily? It had been a matter of surprise, he told himself. Surprise, and sleep, and ships that spit fire. The black men would die just as easily.

And one day, Aidan promised himself, he would prove it.

Sometimes Kai treated his footboy like a pet, a mere plaything. Aidan never had the sense that his young master was being deliberately cruel— just treating him with the casual dismissal that Aidan might have felt toward a nameless village mongrel.

About once a month, especially after a particularly brutal lesson with Malik, Kai dressed Aidan in ludicrously oversize leather armor and lunged at him as his footboy sought to scramble in evasion. No matter what he did, Kai would inevitably thump him about the head and shoulders with his light wooden sword. Other times, Kai practiced the throws and holds he had learned from his uncle, inviting Aidan to attack him (often while Ali or Abu Ali watched approvingly) and then pounding Aidan into the dust while his family applauded.

Following such sessions, Aidan limped back to his bed, enduring the laughter and catcalls of the village men. One particularly ache-filled night Brian MacCloud took pity on him. "Are ye not weary of having the tar whaled out ye, boy?"

"There's nothing I can do," Aidan said, begging his eyes to cease their shameful watering.

"Not true, boyo. Not true. In fact, you're about the only one of us who could thump these black bastards and not take a hidin' for it."

Aidan was shocked by Brian's words, but intrigued as well. "But how? He's so good."

"Bosh. I seen that fancy nonsense they call fightin'. If they were really any good, they wouldn't need their damned guns. They're not even strong enough to do their own work." Brian knelt down and looked him squarely in the eye. "Don't be so focking impressed." He hunkered closer. "I kin teach ye to knock the shite outa that boy, and make him like it. You game?"

Aidan nodded eagerly. Brian walked him to the rows of vegetable gardens at the back of the village. There, on furrowed but unplanted earth, in relative privacy, he began to teach Aidan the holds and locks, the throws and sweeps of wrestling. Aidan had seen such skill in the crannog, of course, and there were times when boys and men from his village would match with those of other villages, either traveling troupes who competed for food and a place to rest (and the favor of the village's unmarried girls), or at spring festival, when the prizes were even greater: pigs or goats or sheep or even lumps of gold.

He reckoned that Brian would have risen high in such competition. He was strong, and fast, and knew a thousand different painful ways to tie a man up.

Aidan demonstrated Kai's holds as best he could, and Brian worked with him to find ways to counter, or slip out of them before they were tightly set. "Fancy crap," Brian said. "Trust in your courage and strength, not a bunch of dancing fit for girls."

So he said, and more than once. But Aidan knew that part of that was just Brian keeping his courage up against the forces arrayed against him, a most difficult thing given their current circumstances.

Aidan was afraid he was demonstrating Kai's holds incorrectly, that as a consequence he would never learn anything useful. On one glorious day, however, he learned differently. Kai had been tossing him about on the tall grass behind the barn. For the twentieth time Aidan thumped ignominiously to the ground, the victim of some kind of twisting hip throw. For a moment Aidan's vision clouded, and he rose to hands and knees, feeling some of his carefully suppressed rage boiling to the surface. The next time Kai pulled him close and shifted his hip in for a throw, Aidan crouched, grabbed Kai around the waist, hoisted him into the air, and threw himself backwards so suddenly that Kai wasn't able to counter or adjust.

Kai landed heavily on his shoulders, spreading his arms to absorb the shock of the fall, eyes wide and mouth pursed in an "o" of surprise.

For a moment the young noble just lay there, blinking. Aidan held his breath, cursing at his temper. Why had he done such a thing? The young master had the power to have him beaten, to have his mother cast into the fields—or worse. *Oh God, Mother Mary, what have I done . . .*

Then Kai looked up at Aidan with genuine curiosity and pleasure and said: "That was good."

"Yes," Aidan grinned, relieved beyond words. *It was, wasn't it.*

The two boys laughed, and began again.

Kai was greatly amused by Aidan's lucky throw, and it tickled him to keep the boy by his side more often, even allowing him to sit quietly in the corner and listen to his lessons with the all-knowing Babatunde. Delightfully, as Aidan's Arabic continued to improve, he even seemed to understand a bit of the little man's history lessons.

One stormy spring day, the windows of Babatunde's chamber misted and streaked with rain. El Sursur lectured Kai on the man usually referred to simply as the Pharaoh, with the kind of emphasis that implied an almost mythical status.

"And what was the Greek name for Pharaoh Haaibre Setepenamen?" Babatunde asked. The rain had stopped and started all day long. Just an hour ago the sun had shone brilliantly through the east window, and Kai found himself hoping that it might again. If the lesson ended soon, he and Aidan might enjoy a game of kites or even a bout of grappling.

Kai was seated on a tall stool next to a wall map of the world. At first Aidan had seemed astounded to see just how much world existed. When he asked Kai to show him the location of Eire, his face fell to see just how insignificant his homeland was in comparison to the rest of the map. Too bad, Kai thought, but such realities were the way of the world.

"Alexander," Kai answered.

Babatunde nodded and opened a book to a page framing a picture of an impossibly noble-looking black man with hawklike eyes and a strong chin. "Is this a picture of Alexander?" he said.

Kai nodded. Then, detecting an odd inflection in Babatunde's voice, asked: "Isn't it?"

Babatunde shrugged. "So some say. But his father was the king of Macedonia, and at the time, Macedonians were more similar to the light-skinned peoples of the Mediterranean."

With a conspiratorial air, Babatunde withdrew a scroll from a drawer in his desk. It looked cracked and stained—older than the others, and as he unspooled it, the lettering looked like little pictures. Etched on the scroll was the picture of . . . a *white* man. He had curly hair, an aquiline nose, and a strong, uplifted chin. Kai's interest was pricked, but Aidan seemed riveted. Could this be true? Could the Great Pharaoh actually be closer in blood to Aidan than Kai? Absurd.

"Why," said Kai, "would you think this could be Haaibre Setepenamen? All of his descendants are of Kushi blood." He said this challengingly, but already there was doubt in his eyes.

"The Pharaoh conquered half the world during his roaming days, when he was known as Alexander. When he returned to Egypt and took the throne, it was years after his first wife died that he took a second, a Kushi princess named Mesgana, and she gave him twin sons. He sat one on the throne at Alexandria, and the other in Abyssinia, also known as Kush, Sheba, or Ethiop." Babatunde liked to walk when he talked, and the spectacle of the little man pacing back and forth through the endless stacks of books was always amusing.

"Men create history to suit themselves, Kai. Most scrolls bearing this image were destroyed."

"Where did you get it?"

Babatunde merely smiled. "As your people marched out of Africa to conquer the world, they burned old images and created new ones, as men have always done, and the Great Pharaoh became a black man. The evidence is there if you choose to look for it, if you are unafraid to question the common wisdom."

Kai went quiet and thoughtful for the rest of the lesson. Much of it was review of material he had heard before. But the speculation about the Pharaoh was fascinating.

He knew the history of Egypt's relationship with Abyssinia, of course: every schoolboy did. Generations after the death of the Pharaoh the thrones of Egypt and Kush, allied with a man called Hannibal, ground Rome, the only power to challenge Africa, into the dust. Egypt then controlled southern Europe as well as eastern empires as far as India.

Alexander's empire lasted for almost a thousand years, but the Egyptians, wealthy beyond reason, felt less and less need to send their own sons to patrol their borders, to fight and die in wars with the northern barbarians.

To spare their own blood, they looked again to the kingdoms south of the great desert. For centuries Egypt and Kush had worked together, creating a great trade route along a river called the Nile. Over hundreds of years the Nile and its tributaries had been tamed, and vast networks of canals constructed. By two hundred years prior to the birth of the Prophet boats powered by water and fire routinely plied their currents. These steamscrews traded with kingdoms deep in the central continent, dominating culturally, economically, and militarily.

Gold and ivory, precious metals and skilled labor were also traded. Schools disseminating the knowledge collected in Alexandria followed the Kushi armies and traders, as most of sub-Saharan Africa fell to the combined empires of Egypt and Abyssinia. Arabic became the great trading tongue, uniting a thousand tribes, a hundred nations.

When Alexandria's decadent citizenry called for warriors, central Africa's dusky children answered, and throughout southern and eastern Europe there was no sight more common than the legions of blacks who patrolled the empire. Known as fearless, peerless warriors and administrators, they channeled a river of wealth back to the royal houses. For hundreds of years, all seemed peaceful.

And might have remained so if not for the Prophet. There were no drawings or paintings of this giant, but again, Babatunde seemed to imply that Muhammad looked more like a Turk than a black man. Muhammad's vision and his recitation of the Qur'an changed the face of the world. Ultimately, his teachings challenged the throne at Alexandria. Holy man, charismatic leader, and brilliant warrior, Muhammad was a thorn in the side of the royal house until his death of natural causes in the month of Safar in the eleventh year after his flight from Mecca, the Hegira. Following his death, his followers fought over Muhammad's legacy, his teachings, and his empire. As jealous and petty men too often do, they tore the Prophet's carefully wrought alliances to pieces, and very nearly slew his holy daughter, Fatima, whom they perceived as an obstacle to their power.

But a fabled warrior and staunch follower of the Prophet, named Bilal, would come to her rescue.

Bilal ibn Rajah was a former Abyssinian slave, tortured by his owner, Umayyah ibn Khallaf, due to his acceptance of Muhammad as the true Prophet. In fact, Bilal was only the seventh man to embrace Islam, and as such would be celebrated even had his life not been such an exemplary one. Due to his extraordinary voice, Bilal was chosen by Muhammad to be the first Muslim *muezzin*, the first to utter the *adhan*, calling the faithful to prayer.

Bilal prayed and fought with the Prophet, distinguishing himself in both battle and piety. After the Prophet's death, Bilal returned to his homeland. He was stirred back to action only by reports of growing instability in the Prophet's empire, and a possible risk to Fatima.

Rousing his followers, Bilal lead a daring mission of rescue, defying the throne of Alexandria and carrying Fatima south to Abyssinia, where she was sheltered and protected by the Immortal Empress, Mesgana. Mesgana's refusal to bow to the Egyptian throne's demands for Fatima's return and probable execution began the ancient, bitter rift between the thrones.

Fatima continued her father's teachings, with Bilal as her loyal guardian. She was an impassioned leader, considered by some of secondary importance only to Muhammad himself. Fatimite Islam, a doctrine of complete surrender to the will of the one true God swept through Africa like a desert wind, consuming totemism and polytheisms like a divine wind. It was this unified force that spelled the doom of Egypt's royal house.

How exactly the fall of Alexandria was engineered was debated to this day. But it *was* agreed that a legend, told by a dozen river tribes, of black barges cruising north on the Nile, seemed to have some substance to it. It spoke of a killing spirit brought from the depths of central Africa.

Somehow this spirit death entered the palace at Alexandria. Some said it was a judgment by Allah for the thousand years of rule the Egyptians had enforced upon the righteous.

"Was it magic?" Kai asked Babatunde.

The teacher paused before he answered. "No one knows for sure," he said, "but I think that it was a disease. The royal houses died first, but that year a plague swept the city, and then passed around the lesser sea to Jordan, to Greece, to Rome. Whites died more readily than blacks—said to be a sign of divine grace, but it may have been something else. Do you remember your biology? The djinn theory of disease?"

"Tiny spirits which drain the life from the unfortunate?"

Babatunde nodded. "The truth is that there are insects too small for our eyes to see, which are to ants as ants are to elephants. It is these insects that we once thought were djinn. I believe that the 'black barges' brought exotic animals infected with these tiny insects. The royal houses thought them fashionably attractive, and adopted them as royal pets. And somehow became infected, perhaps by contact, perhaps when royal servants smeared animal blood or feces in the food. And the disease spread."

Kai looked over at Aidan, his pink mouth open in wonderment. He looked like Kai felt: overwhelmed by these fearsome stories of an older, more savage time.

"They say this thing, be it djinn or disease, swept Europe in waves that left corpses piled so high that there weren't enough of the living to bury the dead. Survivors were driven into the country, and the entire economy collapsed . . ."

The tale went on, growing more horrific with every new revelation. In combination with raiders from the east, Europe was a ruined land, torn by conquerors, wars, and disease for hundreds of years.

Abyssinia took the throne of Egypt, splitting control between the children of Kush's royal family. Alexandria, with access to greater trade routes, once again became the dominant power. The only difference: this time full-blooded black Africans sat upon both thrones. The bloodlines of Greece and Egypt only gradually reinsinuated themselves over the passing centuries.

Bilal lived an extraordinarily long life, long enough to see (and perhaps engineer) the fall of Alexander's bloodline. It was said that he was the last of the Prophet's companions left alive, and therefore much revered. He saw the way politics and religion had intertwined, and the chaos that unholy union engendered. He feared that Africa and Egypt were tainted already, and with a heavy heart realized that he had not the power or strength to halt the deterioration.

On his deathbed he had a dream, in which the angel Gabriel came to him and told him that there was another land, a land to begin anew, where the sins of the old world would not follow. And with his last breaths he told those with ears to hear that a continent beyond the ocean would be the promised land, and that the faithful should find it, and populate it, and claim it in the name of Allah.

It was African Muslim explorers plying the oceans in their great steam vessels who first landed in the New World, trading with the natives for gold and strange fruits. It was Muslim pilgrims who founded the first cities on the new continent, New Djibouti and New Alexandria. They pushed further and further into the wasteland, leading group after group of the faithful. And when the last of those original pilgrims died, their burial site became the foundation of the Shrine of the Fathers, far to the west at the very edge of the empire men called Bilalistan.

Bilalistan had existed formally for just over a hundred years. By treaty, the entire New World was under the rule of Egypt, but its population tended to come from southern rather than northern Africa, and even from the very beginning, the New World sought greater independence.

Kai's father had said that Bilalistan would be free one day, free to chart its own destiny. *"You and your brother will be a part of it,"* he had said. *"There will be blood and fire, and at the end, you will stand free."*

Blood and fire. He felt a little sick, a bit alarmed . . . and on some even deeper level, excited. His father and grandfather had made history. And mightn't the day come when a boy like him would sit before a teacher like Babatunde, hearing of a hero named Kai? Someone whose strong arm wreaked havoc among the unbelievers, whose keen mind wrote impassioned legal documents to be argued before the Senate by the Wakil of lower New Djibouti, his elder brother?

Eyes wide, heart racing in his chest, Kai hung on every word his teacher spoke, as Babatunde made dead days live again, so that even a boy eager for sunshine might, for a time, forget the rain.

CHAPTER SEVENTEEN

5 *Dhu'l-Hijjah* 1280
(May 11, 1864)

There is not friendship either, since there is not justice; e.g. between crafts-
man and tool, soul and body, master and slave; the latter in each case is
benefited by that which uses it, but there is no friendship nor justice towards
lifeless things. But neither is there friendship towards a horse or an ox, nor
to a slave qua *slave. For there is nothing common to the two parties; the*
slave is a living tool, and the tool a lifeless slave.

ARISTOTLE, *NICOMACHEAN ETHICS*

AIDAN'S LONG DAY HAD BEGUN AT DAWN, scrubbing the kitchen floors and
walls. He never prepared food: those who worked in the stables never did,
even after multiple bathings. These blacks were insane about their clean-
liness! After long hours with scrub brush and soap pot, he was sent to the
stables for shit-shoveling and grooming, smelly work that lasted until
midafternoon. Sometimes he assisted Topper with shoeing.

A caftaned Kai wandered in and found him at work but said nothing.

Aidan smiled to himself: he knew Kai by now. In all probability he had
sought audience with his father and been rebuffed, tried to engage brother
Ali in a game and been sent away. *Quiet. Quiet. He will come to you.*

Aidan and Kai were almost the same height, but frequently Kai seemed
smaller, even less mature. Aidan couldn't completely explain it. Certainly,
Kai had suffered far less in his life. Aidan wondered how Kai would have
coped with the horrors he himself had endured, and allowed himself a

cold smile at the thought of the bookish Kai chained in a screwship's dark hold, squirming in his own shit.

Sure enough, in about a quarter hour Kai returned.

"Aidan," he said, "come with me for practice."

"Three more horses to groom, sir," Aidan said automatically, but knew what Kai's answer would be.

"I've already cleared it. Come, now."

Aidan "reluctantly" agreed, dropped his brush, and followed Kai out to the matted area in the courtyard behind the great house, between the canopied back porch and the lake. Aidan knew that Kai's father could observe them from his study, and supposed that that was a major motivation for the exercise.

For the next two hours Kai practiced throws, using Aidan as a dummy. When Aidan grew tired of it, he tried one of the throws that Brian had taught him. This time it didn't work. Kai countered his counter, and Aidan thudded to the ground. Even before the breath whistled out of him, Aidan eeled around, his feet whipping Kai's legs from beneath him, and the two boys ended up tussling about on the ground.

Out of the corner of his eye Aidan saw a dark shape at the Wakil's study window. Abu Ali himself had seen that last exchange. They were too far from the house to see the Wakil's expression, but Aidan bet that he had been smiling.

At any rate, he certainly *hoped* so.

Smiling or not, Wakil Abu Ali drew his curtains closed as Kai and Aidan wrestled and laughed. And whatever Aidan's secret thoughts might have been, for those moments his smiles and joy were genuine. His sweat and bruises were his own. Sometimes he won, usually he lost. But here, in these moments with Kai, they were just two boys, and Aidan managed almost to forget that Kai could have him killed and suffer no punishment at all.

Night fell before Kai and Aidan were exhausted, and Kai tottered off to wash and dress for his dinner. They had taken one break, while Kai said his fourth set of prayers for the day. These Muslims seemed to do nothing but pray. Five times a day, by Aidan's count. He could only figure that their Allah was deaf to need so many prayers.

Aidan returned to the village, thinking of hot stew and a soft bed. He was whistling to himself, making up a tune joining two of his favorite songs into a single unified whole. He seemed to have a talent for it and thought that he might ask Brian to make him an instrument of some kind, a flute perhaps. Brian was a master whittler and seemed expert at making anything out of nothing.

But he was just thinking of this, and other things, when strong arms gripped him from behind, binding arms and legs. Before he could scream a rough sack was yanked over his head, blinding him. Pure panic surged through him, grotesque and mind-crippling memories of his capture in the crannog, echoes of his old helplessness as light and breath were constricted. "Wait!" he cried, voice muffled even to himself. "What do you want . . . ?"

No answer was forthcoming. He was hoisted off his feet, rough, strong arms lifting him around the legs and bustling him away. He could see nothing, but after perhaps a hundred steps his abductors placed his feet back on the ground. His hands were lashed behind him, and when he tried to shout a belt or strap was wound around the bag, muffling his sound. He felt something sharp poke into his back, and at once he understood the meaning: *walk, don't talk.*

He stumbled on, frightened now as he had not been since the terrible night almost two years past. The soil beneath his feet was hard at first, then turned grassy, and then moist. He knew that they had entered the outskirts of the marsh that ran into the lake up north of the village. The acid in his stomach boiled hotter, stealing strength from his legs, making him feel hollow and sick.

He had been told in no uncertain terms never to enter this densely wooded area. There were stories of swamp *sidhe* and lost lives, of runaway slaves whose bodies had never been found. And he knew by the smell, a kind of warm heavy green miasma, that they were entering this forbidden zone.

He tried to turn and run, but the binding hands clamped more tightly, rendering all efforts fruitless.

At last he stood, and the arms left him. He could sense that he was not alone, that in fact there were eyes watching. For a time, no one spoke. Then with a whispering sound the ropes were cut from his wrists.

He stood, unable to move, uncertain of what was expected. The terror grew within him like a worm that consumed thought and courage to increase its own substance.

Dimly through the mask he saw torchlights in the darkness, then he heard a muffled cry next to him, and recognized his mother's pleading voice. What *was* this?

"Take the mask from your eyes, boy," said Auntie Moira in good Gaelic. "And forget that A-rab double-tongue in this sacred place." Hands shaking, Aidan removed the bag.

They stood in a vast arching canopy of ancient trees. Hundreds of them: oaks, date palms, gnarled mossy giants he didn't recognize, crowded closely enough to blot out the sky. Two other recent acquisitions, male field hands named Cormac and Olaf, had likewise been bound and brought here, and were also freeing themselves.

With hands as unsteady as his own, Deirdre stripped the bag from her head. "What is this about?" she asked when she had regained sight.

The entire village seemed to be here, every adult and young adult, and they were humming some song that Aidan did not recognize. Despite himself, he found the tune oddly soothing.

"What is this?" she demanded again.

"Our past, lassie," said Moira. "Your future."

Aidan's eyes, blinded by the bag, had adjusted quickly. From the village, the grove had simply seemed a stand of trees bordering a deeper darkness. Many of the trees, he knew, bore fruit. From time to time the dates and oranges and mangoes were harvested and the women of the village made sweets and pastries, which were distributed in ceremonies. Although the desserts were delicious, none of the adults smiled when consuming them, and he never understood why.

Now that he was within the trees their mossy trunks and branches encircled him, hundreds of thick-bodied ancients and thinner youngsters that now felt more protecting than foreboding. The villagers stood in a clearing, and the more he examined the ground beneath his feet the more convinced he became that it was good growing soil. There was no natural reason why trees would not grow there. Nor were there stumps suggesting that it had been cleared by axe or saw. No, this special place had been created by planting a ring of trees around the edge. Now that he looked more closely still, the largest trees stood at four corners, and a line of smaller trees stretched out behind them. So men had planted a square, and then filled in the spaces, but continued to pluck away the saplings that tried to grow in the middle clearing.

That much he could guess, but the *why* of it continued to elude him. "Where are we?" he asked in the strongest voice he could muster.

"You built this," Moira said, arms indicating the vast arching emerald canopy. "Not in this body, or this life, but the hands and hearts are yours. Like you."

"Like me?"

"And your mother, boy. Slaves, stolen from their land. Taken across the sea." A sober smile split that withered face. "We're the lucky ones. Abu Ali doesn't take our names, or try to take our gods. He's a good man, compared to most."

There was a rustling, and then a line of children approached. Each carried a tiny sapling. One at a time, they offered the trees to the new slaves.

Deirdre took hers in trembling hands. "What do I do with this?" she asked.

"Plant it. Love it," she said. "It's your seed. Pray over it. Here, we worship the Cross, the Lady, the ground and stars . . . anything but Allah." She hawked and spit on the ground. "That's not our way. Here, we're all one. Druid or Christian . . . pray as ye will—God hears, and one day, He will answer."

Much to Aidan's surprise, Brian led him to the tree line, then knelt and scooped a hole in the earth.

"You plant this now," he said. "And pray that your own son will eat its fruit as a free man." Aidan heard the words and realized what they represented. A life in exile here, in a hostile land. His knees sagged, and in the wake of that sudden wave of dizziness he saw things more clearly, and deeply regretted that clarity.

He knew what they were telling him. *Give up your dreams, and make your peace,* they were saying. *This is now your world.*

Vision blurred, and his eyes stung. "Maybe you'll be the one to pluck the fruit as a free man, boy," Moira whispered, as if she could read Aidan's mind. "Free."

Aidan looked into Brian's eyes, and then back at Deirdre, who stood with her hands clasped together, tears sparkling in her eyes. She gave an almost imperceptible nod. Aidan took the rough shovel in hand and completed the digging. One at a time, each of the newcomers came to the tree line, dropped to their knees, and dug with hands, knives, or shovels. And when they had holes of sufficient depth, they planted their trees. The onlookers began to sing.

The song swelled in an odd way: the adult males began first, standing in their outer ring. Then in an inner ring the young working-class adolescents, male and female, began to sing. Then finally, in the inmost ring, protected by the men and the youngsters, the women, children, and elderly raised their voices as well.

"Eastern sun, southern sky
Western rain, northern star
Circled within, kith unto kin
We are bound . . ."

The women joined in next.

"Walk we now through this glade,
As our ancestors made.
Here lies revealed, our truths concealed
We are bound . . ."

And now the men of the village joined in as well, and the refrain swelled in the torchlit darkness.

"Sea and Stone
Salt and Loam
Hearth and Home,
In us resounding—"

Aidan didn't want to feel pulled along, but he was, felt something swelling inside him, a pressure in his eyes. They were tears, the tears he had sworn not to cry since first setting foot in this terrible land. His eyes stung and watered, but he was not ashamed.

"Pressed are we to be slaves unto men
Yet we be blessed beyond mortal ken
To be freed and reborn once again
We are bound—
To your tasks, lay your hands
Though we tread foreign lands
Still we may part, heart unto heart, we are bound—"

Haltingly, he took up the refrain, stumbling his way through it but somehow needing to mouth the words, painful though they were.

"Sea and Stone
Salt and Loam
Hearth and Home,
In us resounding—"

He was weeping now, and could barely hear the words that followed.

"Severed still from the land we adored
Of one will, of one law, of the Lord

By the Cup, by the Cross, by the Sword
We are bound—"

Managing just barely to control himself, to find the strength to join in as the song ended, hearing the words and more than the words, the strength, the plea that he join with them in the only weapon they had to stand against their omnipotent foe.

Faith. In the future, in their gods, in each other.

Faith.

On the balcony of his mansion, Wakil Abu Ali stood sipping coffee, gazing to the north toward the densely wooded patch of land bordering the swamps. From time to time he detected the barest flicker of light. When the air was still, and the wind blew just right, he could hear a whisper of song. In the night, distant torches burned like a dim nebula.

Djidade Berhar and the other nobles criticized him for allowing his servants to keep their names, their faiths, as much of their culture as he did. It had even been commented upon on the floor of the Senate, that the second highest official in the largest province of Bilalistan favored such indulgent treatment of a conquered people.

On most holdings, these men and women stolen from their homelands were mixed into bastard villages with a dozen languages and cultures, and given Arabic or African names. Those who worshipped trees or sky or the spirits of their ancestors were forced to renounce their pagan beliefs at the edge of a sword.

This was wrong, he felt in his heart. Slaves deluded enough to believe in an undead Jew were usually left alone. Isu ibn Maryam, the *real* name of their supposed Messiah, was indeed a great prophet, even if he had never actually died upon that Egyptian cross. Allah Al-Mujib (preserve His holy name) had saved Isu personally, a blessing that should have satisfied any craving for miracles. But no, they had to say the Jew was a god of some kind, venturing further into blasphemy as they insisted upon his multiple aspects. Father, Son, and Holy Ghost indeed!

However disturbing such nonsense might be to one of the true faith, Abu Ali knew that Christians, like Jews, were children of the Kitab, the Great Book. And being so, one day might well find true salvation. He saw no sense in forcing a change upon their bodies that their hearts were not prepared to embrace. To the Wakil, no conversion motivated by anything but purest faith had meaning. False conversion was, in fact, an abomination, a pretense more vile than the worship of a thousand-headed god could ever be.

He would leave them their beliefs, for these and other, more personal reasons. A bit of guilt, perhaps—after all, his father, Rashid, had built Dar Kush on the importation of slaves.

But that was a long time ago, and even if built on the backs of wretched Irish and Germans this was *his* land, deeded to him by his father and held against all odds for three generations. *His* land, and he would manage it in his own way.

Abu Ali managed a smile, one that warred with a certain sadness in his heart, and returned to his bedroom, refreshed.

CHAPTER EIGHTEEN

IN THE DAZZLING AFTERNOON SUN, imperial niece Lamiya Mesgana and her fiancé, Ali ibn Jallaleddin ibn Rashid, raced across the field southwest of the great house, their white thoroughbred Arabians laboring for victory.

As the women of her house had been for centuries, Lamiya was a master horsewoman, strong and sinewy beneath her royal robes, the strength disguised by her grace and beauty until she gripped the reins. Then the muscles in her shapely forearms leapt into relief, and her jawline jutted sharply.

She was strong, fit, and as she raced felt nothing but the sheer excitement of the moment, the thrill of competition coursing through her veins. Her glances at Ali pleased her: judging by the fierce line of his young mouth, it required every speck of his concentration just to stay even with her.

Curiosity overwhelmed her competitive streak. *What if I let him win?* She reined her horse back just enough for Ali to draw ahead.

Sensing victory, Ali spurred his mount to an all-out sprint and drew ahead just as they reached the agreed-upon terminus of their race, a stake driven into the ground with a kerchief dangling from its tip.

Ali panted but still crowed, arms held to the sky. "Victory is mine!"

"This time," Lamiya said, noting that Ali and his mount were more fatigued than she.

He wiped his glistening brow and grinned at her. "I claim my prize," he leaned toward her, seeking to steal a kiss. Lamiya smiled sweetly at him and then lashed her whip at his horse's flank, yelling, "Hai!" It nearly jerked the reins from his hands and pulled away, as Lamiya spurred her own mare into flight. Riding with him without a chaperone was bad enough. Kisses were out of the question!

Blood up, cursing under his breath but eyes riveted to the intoxicating form of his intended, Ali wheeled his reluctant mount Qäldänna in a circle and began pursuit. Qäldänna meant "joker" in Abyssinian, and at times like this, the name was especially fitting.

Lamiya maintained her lead all the way into a sheltering thicket. There, lengths ahead of Ali, she managed to lose him in a cocoon of branches and leaves that offered deeper shadow.

Ali entered, but turned the wrong direction. She knew that the subterfuge would not work for long, but meantime, the game was good. She liked Ali: he was strong, and smart, and a true nobleman, with the courage befitting a young warrior. And, of course, according to her royal aunt they were soul mates. When the stars were right they would be wed, and the union would bond her house with the boundless resources of the New World. Since childhood she had known this would be her fate, and if her heart remained sometimes unconvinced of their divine predestination, she was still satisfied that her life partner would be a man as handsome and good as Ali. Perhaps she would even learn to love him. Things could be far, far worse: letters from home said that a cousin had been forced to marry the old, fat sultan of some desert tribe. Soul mates indeed! Still, no one questioned the Empress's word or wish without the direst of consequences.

In fact, for a thousand years, once a *feqer näfs* marriage had been arranged, it could not be undone. From time to time a potential mate died between engagement and wedding. In such a case the *feqer näfs* was expected to return to Abyssinia and a cloistered, spiritual life. A hundred fifty years ago one niece, promised to a Gupta prince who died on a battlefield, had actually immolated herself on his pyre, gaining great honor in the process. It was this loyalty and bond that made the Empress's *feqer näfs* the most prized mates in the civilized world.

Lamiya sometimes felt like a piece on a *satranj* board, to be moved and placed where the Empress thought best. If this was the price of privilege, mightn't it be better to be born a commoner, or even a slave? At least they married whom they chose.

Lamiya was suddenly startled by a sound beside her, and turned to see Kai mounted on his black mare, Isis. He watched, lips curled in amusement. "Excuse me," he said.

She glared at him. "Don't sneak up on me like that!"

Kai managed to bow in his saddle. In spite of herself, Lamiya felt a giggle working its way through her system. "I'm sorry," he said, with a tone that said he was anything but.

There was nothing she could do save plead for quiet. "Shhh . . ." she said, a slender brown finger pressed to her lips.

Ali was circling around, not two dozen cubits distant, although he had yet to pick up her trail. "Lamiiiiiya," he called. "I'm going to fiiiind you."

Her heart raced, although she couldn't have said why. "Please don't make a sound," she whispered.

Kai cocked his head. "What is it worth?"

She sighed in exasperation. These Bilalians! "Does *everything* have a price?"

The boy studied her, and for a moment she wondered if he was going to request the same price his brother had. That would be odd, for Kai was like a younger brother to her, with all of the mischief and fondness that relationship implied. Still, there were times when he confused her a bit, and this was one of those times.

"What if I said . . . your smile?"

She felt her lips pull up, felt a warmth within as he surprised her once again. Their eyes met. His eyes were so *direct* for just a twelve-year-old. He was more than merely a gifted scholar, a lover of poetry and sculpture. For the first time, she realized that Kai's feelings for her were not entirely fraternal, and it flustered her.

On the far side of the thicket, Ali remained aprowl. "Lamiya . . ." His call was like a soothing hand, warm and seductive.

Kai pulled his horse up next to hers, ostensibly to decrease the likelihood that either of them would be seen. In her heart she knew that he also wanted to be close to her. In her stillness, Lamiya heard him sniff her hair.

She knew what he was doing, and her reaction, comprehensible to her at last, was some blend of flattery, indignation, amusement . . . and curiosity.

Her thoughts were catapulted out of that odd and shadowy space as Ali turned and peered through the leaves directly at them. "Hai! I see you!"

He galloped toward them. Without a backward glance to Kai, she wheeled and ran, and once again the chase.

Kai's heart raced as Lamiya's horse pulled her away at reckless speed. He was uncertain how to react to Lamiya's behavior: she hadn't simply swatted him away! Did she like him? Maybe *really* like him? That possibility made his head swim.

He started after Ali, watching the chase as it neared the barn. He understood the implicit rules: if she made it to the barn, she would jump off the horse and the race would be over, and she would have won. If Ali caught up with her before she could do that, however . . .

Considering that his workday was only half completed, Brian Mac-Cloud was in a fine mood.

The black masters of Dar Kush controlled his time from dawn till dusk, but after that the nights were his. Brian owned his own cottage, and his own vegetable patch to grow the herbs that most pleased his taste. During the days he put his considerable carpentry skills to use around the big house, and on Sundays, the day the blacks called *al-ahad,* he patched and fixed things around the *tuath.* Sometimes, the masters gave him leave to spend time fixing things in Ghost Town during workdays, almost as if they really gave a piss. There was no more caring in them than men might have for beasts of burden, or perhaps horses—except that the blacks weren't afraid of their horses. Horses rarely rose up and massacred their masters, and Brian knew that save for the awful cost of a failed uprising, there would be more such events.

But the day was warm and comforting, and at times like this he could pretend that he was hired labor, that at night he returned home to his own roof and four walls, where he was the master.

His powerful arms carried a load of bamboo poles that would have tested the strength of two men. Brian balanced them comfortably as he headed toward the barn, enjoying the slow and steady play of sinew and muscle. It helped that Máirí was watching.

Máirí had been acquired only last summer from one of the Hindus to the north, and she was one black-haired, wide-hipped, healthy, lusty lass. Few women could keep up with Brian in bedroom matters, and he had experimented widely. Máirí was different. Everything about her appealed to him, and Brian had a sense that maybe, just *maybe,* he might want to tie up with the wench. He laughed at that: there was no such thing as a *real* marriage for Bilalian slaves, no sacraments that a black man was bound to respect. But the masters were happy to give their blessing to what passed for a wedding: marriages meant children, and children meant more property. It was obscene, but unavoidable.

His fury at the thought that his children might belong to another man was balanced by the urge to procreate, to see his own eyes in the face of a newborn child, to pray that his own progeny would have a better life than his own. And he swore that would be the case.

Máirí was returning from the fields. She wore a raw hemp tunic cut in the Egyptian fashion, corded at the waist and flowing at the ankles. Although a castoff from the seraglio, hemp lasted forever, and damned if Máirí didn't look better in it than the Wakil's fat sluts ever could. Her freckled cheeks shone with life and energy. Brian felt a drumroll of anticipation. He knew what that smile meant, and he could hardly wait for nightfall.

Máirí eyed him speculatively. "Looks a little heavy for you," she said.

"Worried I'll hurt my back?"

She came closer, peering toward the house to make certain they were unobserved, then cupped his groin with her left hand. "You'd be useless to me then."

He laughed and blushed. "All my parts are in proper order," he said, although the evidence was already well in hand. "I'll drop by tonight and show ye—"

Máirí laughed, and stole a kiss. "Till tonight, then."

For a moment, it seemed that there was nothing in the world save the two of them, nothing in all the world save her eyes and lips and the promise of fire to come, a moment so intense that neither of them heard or saw anything but each other. So it was as much Brian's fault as Máirí's when she backed directly into the path of Lamiya's oncoming horse.

Lamiya's mount threw her, and she tumbled from her saddle, landing with a resounding thud and a great exhalation. Her face was slack with surprise, and Brian's first thought was how funny she looked. His second, traveling instantly behind it, was a prayer that she wasn't injured. The girl wasn't a bad one, less imperious than most highborn blacks. In fact, it seemed to him that the worst bastards were the lower-class blacks who had nothing to offer the world except the shade of their skin. What shites *they* could be!

But Lamiya was also the intended of Abu Ali's heir, and therefore this was very bad indeed. Alarm squeezed the air from his chest, moistened his palms.

Máirí's thoughts seemed close to his own. She ran forward instantly, although nothing seemed really injured except Lamiya's pride. "Oh, miss!" she called.

Her call was all but drowned out by Ali, who galloped up and jumped off the horse with a single, effortlessly fluid motion. "Lamiya!" he called.

As if the accident had been viewed by the entire house, the manor seemed in an uproar. It seemed that all the servants, free and slave, white and black, were running to see what had happened. "It's the miss!" they cried. "She's been hurt!"

"Here, miss," Brian said, dropping the poles. "Let me help you." She extended her hand, and he clasped it firmly, set his balance, and drew her up. At the first moment of contact he noted how incredibly smooth and cool her skin was. Brian found himself thinking *how can that be? The day is so warm . . .* then forced himself back to reality.

She was unsteady, unfocused, and any smallest trace of haughtiness that Lamiya might have ordinarily communicated had completely vanished. What remained was a woman. For a long moment Brian was simply awed by her beauty.

Suddenly a hand was on his shoulder heavily, pulling and then pushing him away. "Do not *touch* her!" Ali snapped, and helped Lamiya the rest of her way to her feet.

Máirí hovered. "Are you all right, miss?" she asked.

Lamiya seemed to have caught her breath. "Yes," she began. "I think—"

Enraged, Ali turned and lashed Máirí's face with his open hand. She reeled back, gasping.

Ali's face was twisted with rage. "You clumsy *hinzîr-batn* idiot! You could have killed her! I'll flay the pale hide from your—"

He raised his hand again, and Máirí flinched away, eyes wide with fright. Before he could strike, Brian interposed himself. He held a three-cubit bamboo stick in both hands, and knew in his heart that he had almost made a potentially fatal mistake. *Never, ever show the blacks what you really feel.*

Never.

He calmed himself, softening his grip on the bamboo. "No, sir," he said. "It wasn't her fault. It was mine. If someone must be punished—punish me."

Challenge and danger crackled in the air. Ali recognized it, that much was certain. He also, just possibly, had felt the moment of contact between Brian and Lamiya, the challenge in the way that Brian had interposed himself. He was the young lord of the manor, and the way he handled this would be a signature of things to come.

Ali relaxed his shoulders. "As you wish," he said. Oko Istihqar had arrived, cloaked in a caftan inlaid with tiny silver threads, his long sour face creased with concern. "Oko," Ali said. "Take Brian to the stocks. Twenty."

Oko nodded and took hold of Brian's wrist. The carpenter wanted to jerk his arm out of Oko's grasp, longed to simply grab the smaller man and break his back, but this was not the time or the place to resist.

As he was led away, the look Máirí gave him was one of naked thanks and affection. Brian felt in his heart that those twenty strokes, as painful as they would be, were less than the stature he had gained in her eyes. He could sustain himself through anything to see a look like that. And without a spoken word, the relationship between Brian and Máirí shifted in that moment. It was no longer a thing of passion and convenience. It became, quite simply, a joining.

Kai had watched the drama from horseback, the higher perspective serving him well, allowing the youngster to avoid enmeshing himself in the events or difficult decisions. As the big carpenter Brian was led away for whipping, Kai jumped down from his horse and helped Ali support Lamiya, who was wobbly but recovering swiftly.

Babatunde rushed out from the house to meet them, somehow moving at a jogging pace while maintaining a walking gait. He must have seen the collision from a side window, and his lips were pursed with concern.

"I've told you," he chided Lamiya. "They are terrible animals. They should all be driven over a cliff."

"The Irish?" Kai asked.

Babatunde glared at him. "*Horses,*" he said. "Allah's greatest joke."

Lamiya's mouth twitched, and she stifled a burst of laughter. "Ha! Ow! Don't make me laugh. I think I bruised a rib . . ."

Babatunde prodded her side a bit, watching her wince. "We'll have that taken care of," he said. "How exactly did this happen?"

"Never fear," Ali said grimly, with a glance back over his shoulder. "I'm having that taken care of as well."

Without offering resistance, Brian was fastened into the stocks behind the barn, wrists securely fastened. His shirt was stripped away, exposing tanned skin. Old whip scars, now healed, ridged his back.

"As master Ali prescribed," Oko intoned. "Twenty lashes." He dug a hard rubber bit out of his pocket, and silently offered it to Brian, but the slave refused. He gazed straight ahead, eyes hard as flint. Oko nodded approval. "Proceed."

Bari was one of the white overseers who lived in the overseer's hut outside Ghost Town, separate from the other slaves. A giant with stunted legs and a colossal torso, Bari had accepted Islam as a youth, gaining favor thereby. He was a flat-faced man with a tight, wet mouth and ears too small for his head. Bari uncurled his whip and leaned forward. "Do not fear," he whispered. "You are safe in the hands of Bari the Mighty."

He grinned, exposing a row of yellowish teeth. He drew his arm back, and began the stroke.

"One," Oko called soberly. "Two . . ." and with each counting, the lash cut Brian's flesh. He shuddered, but did not speak. He turned his head slightly, enough to see Máirí radiating love through tear-filmed eyes.

Amid the parlor's silk curtains, Bitta and Babatunde applied cold compresses through Lamiya's dress to the small of the royal niece's back. Stomach-down on the couch, she flinched at the touch, her muscles spasming. Distantly, she heard the cry of the lash. With each stroke, she trembled.

Stricken, she turned to Ali, who watched with his arms folded, face emotionless. He might have been a stone statue. She set her small teeth into her lip to steady herself. "It's not so bad, Ali," she said. "Perhaps not . . . twenty."

He folded his arms and seemed to consider her words. "You think not?" The corners of his mouth turned up. "Perhaps you are right. But the barn is too far away. The punishment would be over before I could reach Oko."

Before she could answer, Bitta stood. *All men leave*, she signed, and then turned to Kai's sister, Elenya. *You may stay*.

Her posture left little room for question, but Ali posed one regardless. "Should I leave?" he asked. "She and I will be married soon."

She glowered at him, unimpressed. *Go. Go.* And shunted Ali, Babatunde, and Kai out of the room.

After they were gone, Bitta's demeanor relaxed a bit. Elenya's eyes were wide and frightened, and Bitta guided her as they pulled apart the layers of silk and woven hemp.

"It's not so bad," Lamiya protested, then yelped as Bitta probed a bruised rib.

Silence, Bitta commanded.

Lamiya was quiet for a few seconds, and then managed to twist around to face Elenya, who dampened cloths in a pan of hot water. "Little one? Is your brother always so angry?"

"Not always," she said, wringing dry a small towel. "Just usually."

Hold still, Bitta signed sternly. Lamiya yelped again, and Bitta daubed without mercy.

Behind the barn, Bari administered the last of the twenty lashes as Kai and Ali arrived. Brian hung in the stocks, exhausted, sobbing for breath, blood oozing from his lacerated back. His legs sagged, all endurance fled, unconsciousness near. If not for the manacles and Máirí's adoring, tear-streaked face, he would have collapsed. By some miracle she had transmitted strength from her heart to his.

Ali looked at Brian as if inspecting a slaughtered goat. "Is it concluded?" he asked mildly.

Oko bowed. "It is done."

"Good." He stepped closer. His breath smelled of bitter spice. "Brian? Are you awake?"

Brian struggled, puffed air, and managed to pull himself erect in the stocks. "Yes," Brian said, teeth gritted. Then he forced himself to add: "Sir."

"Good," Ali said. He walked around the stocks, his hands joined behind his back. "You know," he said calmly. "I know you. I know your type. You smile in our faces, and behind our backs, think yourself of some strange, high station. You put on airs." He leaned closer. "Don't you, *binzîr-batn?*"

Brian met his eye, and fought the almost overwhelming urge to tell the truth. Instead, he said, "No, sir."

Ali clucked at him. "I think you dissemble. When men do these things, it is generally to impress women. Are you the kind of pigbelly who likes to impress women?"

Brian watched him warily, but remained silent. Bastard. Fucking black bastard. Humiliating him and beating him weren't enough. What now?

Ali seemed almost merry. "I think you are. But we have years of good service left in you. I would hate to see any of them spoiled. So we will remove the motivation." He pivoted, heel-toe. "Oko?"

Oko snapped to alertness. "Yes sir?"

Ali smiled at Brian again, and suddenly every nerve in the slave's body, even those deadened by pain, flared to alarm. He stood upright, pulling against his wrist cuffs, eyes wide and comprehending.

"Sell the woman," Ali said. "Immediately."

"No!" Brian heard himself croak.

At first Máirí barely comprehended, and then as Bari laid his pale meaty hands upon her the full impact of the words seemed to wash over her in a flood. "Brian!" she called, struggling, reaching her arms out for him. Brian twisted helplessly in the stocks, grunting like a whipped camel.

"Please," Brian pled, all haughtiness stripped from his voice. "Please. Don't do this."

"I'm sorry," Ali said. "It is already done."

Brian sagged, and then struggled back to his feet as Ali turned away. Brian screamed his woman's name over and over again, and she craned her head trying to see him as the giant Bari dragged her toward the house. Brian pulled at his wrist manacles until his wrists bled, to no avail.

Ali placed his hand on Oko's shoulder. "Leave him there for another hour," he said. "Until she is gone. Then turn him loose."

Now, Máirí gone, hope gone, Brian sagged. Blood ran down his arms and puddled in the dust, dead as his dreams of love.

CHAPTER NINETEEN

NIGHT HAD FALLEN HOURS BEFORE. Máirí had vanished, borne by wagon to Djibouti harbor's slave market, where she would be auctioned to the highest bidder. The story of her clumsiness, of injury to the Empress's niece, might lower her price, and this was a genuine hazard. Each diminution in value brought the very real possibility of a crueler master, a poorer station.

Máirí had not even been allowed to pack her few meager belongings, or say good-bye to her friends. She had simply been dragged to a wagon and trundled out the gate.

Brian was shoving food and tools into a woven hemp ruck sack when Aidan entered his room. The shack was no larger than Aidan's own, but its door was stouter, its tables sturdier, its roof more finely patched. In these and a hundred other small ways Brian had improved his living conditions as only an accomplished handyman could.

Brian did not seem to notice him. The big man moved stiffly as he threw a few vital items into the tan sack. His handsome face was a mask of rage. "I know what you're planning," Aidan said.

"Really? And what might that be?"

Aidan's heart raced. "Brian, please. You'll never make it."

"I have to try," he said grimly. "I will escape, I will find my woman."

"And then what? North is Vineland. South are the cannibals. You're dead both ways, aren't you?"

"The Northmen need good workers." Brian never paused, digging through his clothes to find the few items he deemed vital to his flight. "If not, to hell with them. We'll find our way to the Nations in the west."

The Nations? Aidan had heard of the red men the blacks had pushed west, and it was rumored that they sometimes gave shelter to runaways. But how could a lone white man possibly hope to cover the hundreds of miles to safety?

Suddenly, and with an intensity that shocked Aidan, Brian wheeled. "Listen, boy," he said, his breath sharp and acid. "Come with me. You still have fire. Leave, before it's beaten out of you."

Aidan was locked into Brian's eyes, fixed by his passion, and something inside him answered: *yes.*

Deirdre was cleaning house, one careful motion at a time, as if afraid that a quick or poorly judged movement might shatter something within her. The coldness that had seeped into her lungs on the Great Crossing had never entirely left her, and in the last months she seemed unable to warm herself, or to throw off a cough that now brought blood up onto her handkerchief.

She lived her days terrified she would die and leave Aidan alone in this horrible place. Countless times she had prayed that God might tell her what sins she had committed to be condemned to such an awful existence. So she made her daily ablutions, cleaned, sewed, did what she was told, and worked until she could collapse at night into dreamless sleep. But now with Brian's flogging and Máiri's sale a new possibility had emerged. She had to be stronger than she had ever been in her life.

"Ma . . ." Aidan said, his voice faint behind her as he entered their home.

In her own world, Deirdre barely noticed. "Supper will be ready soon, boy."

"Ma," he repeated. "I need to talk to you."

"No talk needed," she said in a small, measured voice. "You eat, then rest. It's a long journey you face."

Aidan stood frozen. "What are you saying?"

She turned to him, face filled with all of the lost hope and pain in her heart. Now the emotions locked within her heart boiled to the surface. "Don't you ask stupid questions," she said. "Your Da taught you better than that. Are you the stupid fish that won't swim away when the trap is opened?"

"Ma, please," he said, trembling in place. "I . . ." he seemed stumped. Then he blurted out: "You need me."

Deirdre was racked with coughs but managed to squeeze her throat shut on the last one and quiet herself. Her fingers dug into his shoulders. "Aidan," she said. *"I'm going to die in this place.* I can feel it, have since we landed here. Get gone, boy. Brian can get you out of this hell. You've got to try, for all of us."

"I can't do that . . ."

The flat of her palm cracked across his cheek. Then she grabbed her own hand, as if afraid it might betray her. "Then you're no son of mine," she whispered. "Perhaps you're a daughter. Is that you, Nessa, come home to Mother?" She turned her back on him. Tears burned her eyes, streaked her face. She knew her boy, knew that he was wavering, weighing the risks, knowing that she had opened the door and all but booted him out. She tried to hold her breath, but her body, weakened and frail, betrayed her, and she vented a wet, weak cough.

Aidan tugged at her arm, and she pulled away. "No!"

"Let me help you," he said, and she could not shake him off. Then, very quietly, he added, "So long as you live, I will not go."

Crying, softly cursing the God she had worshiped her entire life for failing her in her moment of greatest need, she sat heavily on the edge of her bed, her face in her hands, as Aidan began to sweep the floor.

CHAPTER TWENTY

Ghost Town was wreathed in shadow as Brian slipped out into the night, rucksack on his back. He looked carefully in all directions, waited until the mounted patrols had passed, and then headed north, staying to the shadows.

Ten minutes later, he was in the grove.

The trees welcomed him, and Brian searched by starlight and moonlight until he found a date palm with his name carved into the trunk. He had planted that tree at the age of fourteen, and carved his name three years later. Brian bowed his head and prayed.

"Mother Mary, as a boy I prayed that I might be free before this tree grew tall. I failed. But no son of mine will rot here. If I stay, I'll wring every black throat these hands can reach, and my people will suffer for it. Give me strength tonight." He crossed himself and stood, breathing deeply. No turning back now. He shouldered his rucksack and trotted through the grove, heading toward the swamp. A bloody moon overhead provided just enough light for Brian to enfold himself in its embrace.

A solitary figure roamed Ghost Town's streets while the rest of the village slept.

He slipped into Brian's empty shack, probing and checking to be certain that crucial items were missing. Now certain that Brian had indeed left, and was not merely spending the night in another shack, the man slipped back out. Keeping to the shadows, he exited through the gate, and made his way stealthily toward the overseers' huts.

Before he reached his destination, he was stopped by Bari, on routine horseback patrol. Whispered conversation followed, and if anyone had been watching, they would have seen little save two dark twists of shadow joined in conspiracy. Then the shades separated.

Bari met quietly with the overseers. No immediate alarm was raised: the great house remained in slumber. One group of men mounted and doubled their patrols. A second group headed west of the house, out beyond the barn.

South of the barn on the edge of the lake stood a cluster of fences, and beyond the fences a small group of huts. The men who lived there rarely mixed with the other overseers; they worked with the animals, and if truth be told, they enjoyed the company of beasts more than that of human beings.

They were low-born Danakil, men who had performed these functions for over a thousand years at the behest of the Egyptian Royal family. They were still awake: legend said that they never slept, but trained and worked with the horses and camels by day, and with their other, grimmer charges by night. In the darkness they sat circled around their cook fires, smoking, and hoping.

And waiting.

The wait was over.

Kai lay sprawled on his bed on Dar Kush's second story, asleep but not at rest. Some deep instinct worried at him even before his conscious mind registered a sound.

He tossed restlessly, the sticky web of dream ensnaring him so that his last shudder before awakening was a convulsive lunge that threw him into wakefulness, the way a fall from a boat tumbles one into the sea.

For a few moments he lay there in bed, unable to move, unable to think, knowing that something was out of place but not knowing what or why. Then, faintly, he heard a hideous gobbling sound, punctuated with sharp, vicious barks, and his skin felt clammy.

Wondering if he had merely traded one nightmare for another, Kai levered himself out of bed and walked to the window. The moon was wreathed in clouds and the stars seemed even more distant than usual.

The clouds slid by, revealing a swollen, bloody moon. The entire estate seemed heavy with mist. The sound rose once, like something not quite human speaking in the night. He knew what that was, knew what it meant, and he shivered, returning to his bed, searching for sleep that did not come for the rest of the night.

Aidan awoke on his thin straw mattress, shivering despite the fact that he was not actually cold. Across the room, Deirdre snored lightly. He thanked God that she wasn't making the faint sobbing sound that had stolen her sleep during the first months of their captivity.

What had awakened him? Curious, he rolled out of bed. He wiped his forehead, looking at the sheen of thick cold salt water on his hand. Nightmares again. He cleaned it on his naked leg. Aidan tiptoed to the door and looked out. From the doorway, he could see between the rows of houses onto the grounds, which now were heavy with fog.

For an instant he thought that he saw something moving in the fog and backed up a step, primal horror chilling his blood. *What in the world . . . ?*

A sharp chorus of barks rang through the mist, and his breath caught in his throat. He remembered that sound from his days in the pen, when an unseen force had raked a captive's arm. And had heard them also from the direction of the lake, out south of the pasture, where no slave was allowed to trespass. Whispers passed among the slaves, the words *"Danakil,"* and *"Gruagach."* Mothers told tales of demons to keep recalcitrant children in their beds.

As a new shudder coursed through him, a gibbering howl wound up out of the gloom, and Aidan closed the door, knowing that death, and things worse than death, were in the night.

CHAPTER TWENTY-ONE

MIST HUGGED THE VILLAGE STREETS as the first breath of morning began to dry the dew. A single aged woman walked the narrow rows.

Moira was Ghost Town's oldest inhabitant. She remembered eighty summers, which meant that she was perhaps eighty-two or -three. She had come to this new and awful land as a grown woman, sold to Abu Ali's father Abu Wakim after a raid by one village upon another. She had thought it her fate to be some Northman's wife, perhaps, or a slave to a Scot clan, but never had she dreamed she would endure the horror of the Big Water, or that the lush beauty she had once thought might bring her a highborn husband would be ravaged by black overseers, her dusky issue born into a lifetime of service and shame, and often sold away.

When Moira reached sixty or so Abu Ali's father died, and the Wakil declined to grind more work from her brittle bones. She was given a monthly stipend of meat and grain which she supplemented with home-grown vegetables. Additional creature comforts were gained in her capacity as priestess and midwife. She was mother to all, knew every leaf and mushroom, knew the songs and stories of a dozen Celtic peoples, and was the leader of the informal Elders Council that delegated work, resolved conflicts, and decided which slave complaints would be brought before the master. It kept her days as busy as she cared to have them, but still, in quiet moments, she wondered what had become of her children. Were they slave? Free? Alive? Dead? She had never been able to find out. Once, five years ago, a coach had drawn up to Abu Ali's estate. The reins were in the hands of a brown-skinned man with curly hair, and she thought she saw in his profile something of her own father. She could not go to him, could not ask him the question she longed to ask, and had never seen him again.

But she wondered.

She didn't sleep much anymore, and on this morning she was the first to awaken, carrying her slop pot out of her cabin toward the gate. The privies were kept far enough away that the smell wasn't offensive, and the truth was that they were better cared for than they had been in her own village in Eire.

She yawned and stretched, trying to straighten her back, but it was too tight, felt as if it had been fused into an unyielding column. She was looking down, not really paying attention to her path until she reached the gate. There she fumbled with the latch. As it opened she looked up, seeing quite clearly what lay beyond the gate.

The slop pot dropped from her hands, spilling its vile contents onto the ground in stinking rivulets. She was too busy screaming to notice as the filth flowed over the toes of her sandals.

The village was waking now. The slaves poured into the streets, limping, yawning, but responding to Moira's cries. It took them mere moments to grasp what had happened, and their shocked, blanched faces revealed the depths of their distress.

Moira waited until there were four or five good strong men gazing up at the terrible sight before she unlatched the gate. "Come with me," she said, her voice very deliberately held as low and strong as possible.

The men followed her out of the village.

At some point in the night, the masters had quietly erected a stocks four cubits in height. Roped into the middle of it, sagging and unconscious, hung Brian MacCloud.

Brian was no longer pretty. Half of his face was crusted with blood, and one of his eyes was torn from its socket. Cuts and scratches scored his naked body. One of the men turned away and vomited. Moira saw a few of the children gawking up at the sight, and snapped at their parents: "Damn ye! This is no sight for such as them. Get those children indoors, fools!" And the parents obeyed, probably glad to close their own eyes to the sight.

"Is he dead?" one of the men asked, trembling.

As if in answer to his question, Brian moaned. A bubble of blood slid from his mangled lips. His remaining eye opened. He looked out at them without recognition or focus.

"Sweet Mary . . ." one of them cried.

Again, almost in answer, a single gobbling bark rose up in the morning air, something from far out behind the barn, and the villagers trembled.

"*Sidhe,*" Moira said heavily. "The ghoulies were out last night. And they've taken one of our best. By the Lady, take him down."

Brian was swiftly unfettered, and the wounded man collapsed into their arms, too weak to move. But he did manage to gasp a single word: "*Thoths,*" he said. Then: "*Gruagach.*" *Hairy goblins.* Then his one good eye rolled up, and closed.

"Take him to my hut," Moira said. "His wounds need cleaning." She peered out in the direction of that last, terrible cry. The sun was brighter now, higher. The mist was burning away, leaving the sweet green grass. But by the faces of the villagers, it might as well have fallen for all time.

Despite the shock and horror of the morning's discovery, and the low cries of pain from Moira's shack, the routine of Dar Kush continued. The servants went about their tasks, displaying even less emotion than usual to the masters, as if life had been squeezed from their marrow.

In the fields, the barn, the kitchens, there was no laughter, little camaraderie or joy, but there was work in plenty. Oko, the overseers, and the masters of the house watched, each immersed in his own thoughts.

By afternoon Brian's screams had quieted, the pain eased away with the application and ingestion of herbs and plants picked carefully under Moira's supervision. He lay abed now, face swaddled in bandages. His left eye, the one remaining, peered out at the room, bloodshot and murderous. Crimson seeped through the bandages. The herbs coaxed him toward dreaming, but judging by his restless slumber, dreams were even more hellish than waking reality.

That night Topper and some of the other slaves grumbled of revolt and murder, of the terror that might descend upon them when the Wakil passed the torch to his son Ali. But no hand was lifted, and no murderous deeds were done: none would lead, and without leaders, there was no hope. And ultimately, the long day's fatigue beckoned their heavy limbs to bed, where a few troubled hours' sleep might prepare them for the rise of a new dawn.

In the barn, Aidan brushed down Kai's horse with one smooth, controlled stroke after another. The motions were peaceful, and he found in them a kind of soothing rhythm, a way to keep his emotions tightly leashed.

Kai appeared at the door, dressed in flowing Maghribi-style riding pants and a woven hemp tunic. Ready for the day's ride. He nodded approvingly at his horse's sheen. "Very nice," he said with little emotion. "Thank you. That will be all."

Aidan noted that Kai's voice was more formal than it had been just yesterday. Over a year of daily practice had given him a basic facility with Arabic, to the point where he was able to detect nuance. Kai was barely paying attention to him today, all focus directed at the great mare.

"Kai?" he asked.

Kai turned to him, a little warily. "Yes?"

"What happen to Brian?"

Kai's answer was as stiff as his spine. "He tried to run away."

Aidan bit back his anger and searched his mind for the right words. "But what was it? What tore him? *Gruagach?* Demon?"

Kai's face was like stone. "That is none of your concern, so long as you remember your station."

Frustration bubbled inside Aidan like acid. "He just want to be free."

Kai turned to Aidan, his bearing imperious. "Just as we have the obligation to take care of you—feed you, clothe you, house you—you have the obligation of obedience."

There was dismissal in his tone, but Aidan bore in. "He just want to be free."

Now there was something cruel and distant in Kai's face, and for a moment Aidan felt he was dealing with a stranger. Or perhaps, more realistically, this was Kai's true face. "Learn from his lesson, Aidan. Life can be good for you, if you just accept your place."

Be silent! His common sense, his mother's pleas rang in his ears, but Aidan couldn't leave Kai's statement unchallenged, even if it cost him a beating. "And who decide where my place?"

Kai paused and then replied, his voice as flat as a sword. "I'd say Allah has already decided."

"I was free!" the words burst from Aidan's lips, unbidden. "I had father, and sister, and a mother who sing and danced . . ." Words failed him, and he was left empty-throated, hands trembling.

"And now," Kai replied, "you have a barn to clean. I suggest you get to it."

Without a backward glance, Kai mounted and rode out. Aidan watched him ride away, hand gripping a straw rake as if it were a weapon.

As he watched Kai ride, Aidan saw Babatunde's ghostly figure, almost ethereal in the morning light, standing near the barn door. No word passed between master and student, but Babatunde's face was set in disapproving lines. Had he heard? What was in his mind? Babatunde mouthed so many pious words, words of love and wisdom. It was even rumored that he had a pale grandmother, or a "pigbelly shadow" as some of the foremen whispered. Could it be true? And if so, could he have exchanged both his precious spirituality and his blood for a little privilege? Aidan longed to grab the little man, to shake answers from him, but finally, inevitably, merely returned to his grooming.

After a few days, emotions in Ghost Town were less raw, less volatile, and the Irish could perform their duties without constant remembrance of Brian's suffering. The routine of days stretched into weeks, and at last most things on the estate seemed to return to normal. Aidan generally accompanied Kai during his lessons with Malik and Babatunde. When he was not in his young master's company, Aidan worked around his shack, caring for Deirdre, who seemed to grow weaker and somehow more ethereal daily.

Aidan kept himself busy, striving to stave off the lethal depression that hovered over him, a grim sense of hopelessness that might prove crippling. As time went on, he saw the many ways the other slaves fought off despair. There was much coupling on the weekends and in the depths of night. The slaves were allowed to brew their own beer, and some smoked the rolled leaves of the hemp plants. Hemp seemed to make them quiet and jokey, while beer rendered them boisterous and quarrelsome.

And in one way or another, almost everyone in the village worshipped. Whether the scrolled teachings of Christ or Mary or the oral traditions of the forest Druids, prayer seemed to offer some kind of inner fortress.

Nearly a fifth of the slaves, or about forty, had embraced Islam. Five times a day, morning to night, slave Muslims would cease their labor, unfold their rude blankets, and bow toward the east. Aidan suspected that they might have done it just to gain precious minutes of rest denied the Christians and pagans, who glared at them as they chopped and hoed in the hemp or bean fields. The white Muslims ignored the glares as best they could, performed their prayers, and then returned to work.

Aidan had to admit that the Muslims seemed fresher at the end of the day: they carried their loads more readily, suffered fewer apparent bouts with despair. And although the Wakil had instructed the guards to treat Christian and Muslim identically, clearly overseers leaned more lightly on the lash with fellow travelers on the Prophet's well-worn road.

And Aidan watched. Somewhere in all of this, in all of the comings and goings, the alliances, there was a way out for him, for his mother. They would find lost Nessa, they would find freedom. This was *his* worship, his preoccupation, marking his time each day.

The blacks were not demons, although demons danced at their command. There was the reminder of Brian's face. Brian would not speak of what had happened to him in the swamps, but dear God, his *face*. It was said that other slaves had attempted to "follow the Plough" and escape to the north. Some had been brought back dead. Others had been recaptured and then sold north to mining concerns on the disputed edge of Vineland. A few had ghosted about the village for a few months, bearing terrible wounds, their will and pride and spirit utterly broken.

Six weeks after his return from the swamp, Brian removed the last of his bandages. His beautiful face was gone, but Aidan knew that deep within, Brian was still Brian. He bowed low when a master walked past, but his remaining eye flashed fire.

At night, Brian helped Moira with prayer services in the glen, but there was something so intense and incendiary in his teachings that it was actually unnerving. His torn face and eye patch seemed to add an eerie weight to his words, almost as if his dead eye saw nothing of this world, but everything of the next.

Blended together with a kind of spicy *imbuzi* goat salad, the scent of steamed cabbage and carrots together with a side of *izidumba* yams created an explosion of color and fragrance. Aengus had exceeded himself, adding a master's flourish to the traditional Zulu fare.

The meal was held in the Family Hall, one third the size of the Great Hall on the eastern side of the ground floor. The Wakil's full household was present, with Malik and Fatima in attendance as well. The candled chandeliers glowed orange, casting a warm, earthy light across their faces and over the woolen wall hangings, which depicted the Mosque of the Fathers. No silk tonight: Shaka was the guest of honor, and any fabric so effeminate would have been tantamount to an insult.

Tonight, the Family Hall seemed a celebration of war. Four empty sets of leather Aztec armor stood at the corners of the room. Newly acquired, their feathers were fresh with blood.

"That one!" Shaka roared, quaffing his beer with relish and pointing at Kai. The boy started, then realized Shaka was pointing beyond him, and turned toward a set of deeply scored armor in the corner.

"That one was a madman!" Shaka said. His three officers, battle-scarred Zulus like their chief, pounded the table. "He came at me as if he had already thrown his life away. As if he longed for the tip of my spear, and wished only to cleave my own head in the process. Hah Hah! I *liked* him!"

The Wakil grinned and shook his head. "You mean you liked killing him."

"Well, that too. But I wished he was one of ours. What I could have done with such a man. See?" Shaka leaned his head to the right, exposing a fresh scar on his neck. "A little more luck, and we would have met our ancestors together."

Abu Ali snapped his fingers and Brian stepped forward from the shadows and filled the Wakil's water glass. His single glaring eye was carefully lowered. Kai felt queasy about the presence of the eye-patched, scarred servant. This was some kind of adult game, one-upmanship. Perhaps Kai's father wanted Brian as a kind of trophy. Perhaps he was their way of saying, *See? See, Shaka? You are not the only one who can inflict damage on your enemy.*

Shaka took a great forkful of the steaming goat and closed his eyes with pleasure. Zokufa, Shaka's first cousin and chief lieutenant, spanked his palms together, grinning. Half the teeth on his upper right side were broken, and that section of lip was missing. The right ear was but a scarred nub. "Shaka! Tell the story again."

Shaka didn't need to be reminded which story. The Zulus leaned forward in pleasurable anticipation.

"Zokufa and I were cornered, cut off from the rest of the men and surrounded by five of the devils, swinging and cutting at us with those razored clubs."

"I thought we were dead!" Zokufa laughed. "I could smell my intestines already!"

"Please, Zokufa," Fatima protested. "Some of us still have ears to offend."

Zokufa's eyes widened and he roared with laughter, and the other Zulus pounded the table until the cutlery danced.

"We fought like men!" Shaka said. "And they fell before us. *Ssshut! Ssshut!*" He made cutting motions in the air, and Kai could almost see the blood spray. Appetite was a distant memory. "One, two, three, they die. The fourth ran. *Ssshut!* I throw my spear, and he falls like rotten fruit."

"The fifth," Zokufa said slyly, "we . . . detained for conversation."

The six Zulus suddenly became very quiet and polite, glancing at each other with barely concealed mirth. Shaka made a slight bowing gesture, as if withholding details in deference to the ladies. In actuality, of course, the lack of details merely made the implications more obscene.

Apparently energized by the vile memories, Shaka plucked up a knife and flipped it in the air, caught it by the blade and hurled it point-first into the leather throat-guard of the Aztec armor.

"Excellent!" Malik laughed and followed suit, his own blade landing within a digit of the first.

And then it was a game. Ali and then Abu Ali snatching up their knives, spinning and hurling them into the armor, demonstrating their skill. The air buzzed with cutlery.

Even Kai joined in. He hadn't practiced knife-throwing for a month, and his first effort hit handle-first and clattered to the ground.

Malik chuckled. "Wrist straight, boy," he said, meaning *Don't embarrass me, boy,* and tossed Kai another blade. The entire table was quiet as Kai aimed, murmured a little prayer to himself, and let fly. This time his wrist was straight; the blade revolved exactly five times and sank a half-digit into the leather.

Kai sighed relief, the men roared approval, and even Elenya and Lamiya clapped their hands.

"More knives!" the Wakil called. "The game is just begun!"

Servants bustled in and out of the room, ducking and dodging the flying kitchenware. When Brian resupplied Shaka, Malik's throat was momentarily within reach. Kai imagined Brian thrusting in a knife with all of the desperate speed he could muster. Imagined the screams and consternation, the pulse of blood from the awful wounds, and a beatific smile on Brian's face as he died knowing he had dealt death to his enemies.

But even as Kai thought those thoughts, he glimpsed Malik's eyes. They were peaceful, watchful, almost playful. Daring Brian to try it. *Please,* they said. *Give me an opportunity to display my prowess.*

Brian laid the knife on the table. Malik smiled as he would to a child, and deliberately turned his back on him. "Fatima, if I can pierce the armor's eye hole, can I win a kiss?"

She blushed and whispered something to Malik that Kai could not hear. His uncle's eyes widened. Malik stood and hurled his knife. It pierced the eye hole in the leather war mask. Malik beamed down at his bride. "Tonight," he said. Then he turned and gave Brian a particularly warm and friendly smile.

CHAPTER TWENTY-TWO

I<small>T WAS</small>, K<small>AI</small> <small>DECIDED</small>, a fine day to fly a kite. The winds gusted from the east, pushing clouds before them, a strong steady pulse that caught the tissue of his lacquered red box and lifted it to the sky, a dancing red dragon.

He felt a little bit wistful, remembering the days when his father had first taught him to fly kites, gifting him with dancing boxes of light wood and gilded tissue shipped all the way from China. It seemed his father had more time for him in those days. Now Abu Ali would listen to his younger son recite poetry, or the Qur'an, or sometimes watch him practice his swordplay against his more accomplished older brother. At such times Abu Ali's darkly bearded face warmed with pride. But he just didn't seem to have as much time for Kai as he had just a few years previous.

Nor did Ali. Even little Elenya seemed busier, more involved in her lessons and in her relationship with Lamiya, which grew more important to her with every passing day.

So the plunging and capering of the kite, with its delicate control strings, sometimes seemed a salve to Kai, a way to concentrate his attention on something other than the turmoil and isolation roiling within him.

The kite, Kai thought in a poetic fancy, *is my own heart.*

Its tissue and balsa frame began to rise as he spied Aidan's figure approaching, pushing a cart filled with firewood toward the house.

When Aidan drew closer, Kai called: "Aidan! Come play!"

Aidan regarded him deferentially, emotionlessly. "I'm sorry. Bitta told me to bring wood."

Kai smiled. "I could write you a pass?" There was a question in that, almost a request. Of course, he could *demand* that Aidan stay with him and play, but he could not bring himself so low.

Aidan replied in flat, lifeless tones. "No, sir," he said. "That won't be necessary. Excuse me, sir, I have work to do." He bowed politely, but coolly, and went about his business.

Kai looked after him, saddened. Why couldn't Aidan understand? Brian had virtually begged for his punishment. The maintenance of a household demanded order—his father had said so a thousand times. Such a savage thing would never happen to Aidan, who was obedient and polite. Never.

Why couldn't he see that? Why wouldn't he play?

It was disturbing, and confusing, and just a bit irritating to be so dependent upon the availability of a slave.

All afternoon Kai played with his kite, while the business of Dar Kush went on about him. The Great Wakil was expecting ambassadors from the Ayatollah, head of the Ulema, the sacred branch of Bilalistan's aristocratic theocracy. They would probably ask him for intercession in some deadlocked matter with the Senate, or perhaps even a personal letter to the Caliph. It was said that the Ulema favored declaring *jihad* against the Aztecs, but the Senate opposed such total war, and without the Senate, there could be no Federal troops to back up the wild-eyed radicals eager to march to the frontier, waving swords they had never learned to wield.

Below him to the south, the Danakil were breaking a trio of new horses in the pasture. He did not like the wiry, braid-haired Danakil, despite—or perhaps because of—their great skill with animals. Part of the Danakil's charge was to handle the man-hunting thoths. Kai rarely looked out toward the lake, and the thoth pens, without grimacing.

He reeled in the string, walked up to the slight hill rising above the manor and let it out again. From his new perch he could see everything: the servants in the fields, the house itself, the distant sparkling blue of the lake. The wind shifted and he turned with it. Now he was looking out to the west, toward the end of the fields and the vast undeveloped land owned by his father.

"Kai," Lamiya said behind him, and he turned with a start. She wore peasant sandals and a print dress strewn with purples and ocher moons. Behind her the silent Bitta was swathed in a spotless white smock.

"Lamiya." His heart brushed the clouds. "Will you try my kite?"

She smiled, and in answer took the thread from him, playing the line expertly. A great sense of peace descended upon him. "You're really the best at this," he said, and was rewarded with a smile.

Kai watched Lamiya out of the corner of his eye. At fifteen she was three years older and two digits taller than he, so beautiful and utterly unreachable that his heart ached until he was certain that her slightest glance would reveal every secret in his heart. He rushed to find words to fill the deadly silence. "This summer, we are taking a trip north. There will be hunting and fishing. I hope you're coming. And Bitta, of course." He nodded toward the stern, gray Bitta, who seemed oblivious, her eyes calm as still water.

Lamiya shook her head. "I can't do that, Kai. I wanted to talk to you. It's been decided: the Empress has requested my return to Addis Ababa. I must complete my education."

Kai felt as if someone had torn a hole in his chest. Always had he known this might happen. Never had he allowed himself to contemplate how it would feel. "Leaving? When will you return?"

"It will not seem so long, little one," she said. "You will have so many things to fill your time."

"Nothing . . . no one like you."

She played the line of his kite, made it swoop, performing its lonely dragon dance in the sun. "I will miss you too, Kai."

His eyes felt heavy, and he couldn't raise them to hers. What did he want her to say? More than she had. More than she could.

When he finally looked up, she was gazing at him fondly. She seemed to be struggling with herself, coming to some kind of small but important decision. With a single glance at a disapproving Bitta, she pulled a little pearl-handled knife from her waist sash and pricked her finger. A single scarlet drop of blood welled up.

She stood, holding her bleeding finger up for him to see. For a moment he didn't respond, then reached out and took the knife from her hand.

"In my homeland," she said, "it is a way of joining."

Hand shaking, Kai cut his finger, and Lamiya pressed it against her own. She stood so close to him that he could smell the scent upon her breath, something of roses and mint.

"You are now my little brother," she said.

Kai felt a deep stab of disappointment and realized that, impossibly, he had hoped for something more. Lamiya took his head in her hands, leaned close, and pressed her lips against his forehead.

Then she smiled again, a bit sadly this time, and turned to Bitta. "Come," she said. She handed the kite string back to Kai, and they left him there on the hill, the kite pulling helplessly, seeking freedom, leaping in the wind.

Kai sleepwalked through the rest of the day, barely said a word at dinner. He excused himself as quickly as possible and returned to his room. There he sat gazing at the wall and its hangings of kites and lions and flags of a dozen nations. None of these bright and gaudy things appealed to him at all today.

He gazed into his room's raised fireplace, idly studied the flames for a few moments, and then reached under his bed, pulling out a notebook bound in wood. Within were a set of drawings, the products of his eye and heart. Sketched in a young but talented hand were images of sky and tree and lake—and Lamiya.

Lamiya, drawn from memory. Against a sunset, laughing at table, riding on the ridge and in the forest. One at a time he pulled the drawings out, and one at a time fed them to the fire, watching them smoke and curl and blacken as they were consumed.

Then he drew a basin of water, washing his face and hands. He stood, hypnotized, as a thread of blood drifted out of his finger into the water. Numbly, Kai wrapped a piece of cloth around his cut finger, then gazed at himself in the gold-veined mirror above the basin. What did he see? The face in the mirror seemed very, very young, but also lined and heavy with sadness. Kai squared his shoulders. It was time to be a man.

Miserable but struggling to mask his misery, Kai helped Babatunde pack. As he did, he realized that he would miss the little Yoruban almost as much as Lamiya. For all Babatunde's eccentricities, the scholar seemed the one who best understood Kai. Who could ever replace him?

Babatunde hemmed and hawed to himself. "Now . . ." he said. "Where is that Aztec scroll?"

"This one?" Kai was digging through a table piled so high with books that a lion might have hidden there successfully.

Babatunde smacked his palms together. "Thank you," he said. "Rush rush. So much to do." A thought seemed to occur to him. "Pity the airships are so primitive. One day, they will make an ocean crossing almost tolerable."

Kai felt a panic hammering at him, crumbling his enforced calm. "Babatunde," he said. "Why do you have to leave?" He couldn't meet his mentor's eyes, because he already knew the answer.

"The Empress commands." He said it with finality, and it should have been answer enough, but something in Babatunde's face said that he knew that such an answer would never soothe a young heart. He laid a gentle hand on Kai's shoulder. "Young Kai—we don't want to leave," he said, "but none of us are our own masters. As you said to Aidan in the barn, not so long ago: each of us has our obligations. The whole is more important than any of the parts."

Kai recognized, and was stung by, his own words. "You were spying on me."

Babatunde answered fondly. "Not spying. Just . . . listening." He scrubbed Kai's head with his knuckles. Chuckling, he turned away. "Here, Kai. I have something for you."

Kai's mood brightened. "You do?"

Babatunde didn't answer, just continued rummaging about until he found two books, then handed both to Kai.

"What are these?" Kai asked.

"Poetry of Yunus Ernre, and more important, *Sirral Asrar.*"

"What is that?"

"'The Secret of Secrets.' These are the lessons you are to memorize by the time I return. They will speak to you of your future, young Kai."

Kai's brows drew together in puzzlement. He thumbed through the books. "My future?"

Babatunde's expression was studiedly neutral, but there was something in his eyes that was as deep as the night sky. "You are no small part of the overall plan, Kai. You must study. Must prepare."

"What are you talking about?"

"Your future," Babatunde said. "You pray five times a day, as the Prophet proclaimed?"

"Of course."

"There are those who say that it is the Ayatollah who opens the road to Allah. This is not true for the Sufi. We open our own road, are responsible for our own salvation. We stand directly before Allah. We are responsible for our actions, and punished or rewarded for our intentions. No human laws can save us. There is no court of appeal."

"Sufi?" Kai asked. He had never heard that word before.

"I have no greater gifts to offer you than this," Babatunde said. He took a crescent moon medallion from his neck and held it for Kai to see.

"My grandfather gave it to me when I achieved my manhood."

Kai could not take his eyes from the medallion. It was a simple thing, but he intuited that he was being given much. "Babatunde," he protested. "I can't . . ."

"I have no son, Kai," El Sursur said simply. "I would ask you to take it, and give it one day to your boy."

Against the simple affection in Babatunde's eyes, there was no defense. "I will," Kai said.

"And this also," Babatunde added. He reached into his bag and extracted a second piece of jewelry. On the end of a chain swung a triangle and a many-pointed symbol embedded within a circle.

"What is this?" Kai asked. The way Babatunde extended it to him, one would have thought it held the Sufi's heart.

"The Naqsh Kabir," he said, almost whispering. *"Al Naqsh Al wajid Allah."* *The sign of the presence of God.* "It is a secret, Kai. The books will speak of it, but you will not understand. Think on it before you go to bed, and your dreams will tell you what you need to know."

Kai's head spun. "I don't understand."

"Understanding is not necessary," he said, and hung it around his pupil's neck.

CHAPTER TWENTY-THREE

Death is the poor man's best physician.

IRISH SAYING

THE ROYAL STEAMSCREW WAS TO LEAVE on first tide, so Lamiya and her co-terie began their journey to Alexandria Bay at night by the Wakil's coach, a luxuriant black-tasseled ceremonial conveyance drawn by four white Arabians.

Abu Ali and his family were at the main gates, all resplendent in black-and-red-striped robes, ceremonial swords at their belts. Elenya wiped away tears, knowing it would be years before she again saw her adopted sister.

At the Wakil's order, the servants had gathered to sing good-byes to the beloved Lamiya. Their songs proclaimed her graciousness, beauty, and kindness above all mortal women, and though a reasonable man might have doubted their sincerity, their volume and sweet harmonies were above reproach.

Abu Ali was the first to speak and give blessing. "Lamiya," he said from horseback, "the daughter of my heart. May your passage be swift and joyous, and your return like the wind."

Ali joined in. "I will sing a prayer for your safe return every night, and every morning, until we are wed."

Sitting by the coach's red-rimmed window, Lamiya turned her gaze shyly away, as befitted a maiden of her standing.

Elenya edged her mount forward. "I made this for you," she said, handing Lamiya a garland woven of twigs. It was a simple, beautiful thing, and the Imperial niece mounted it on her head with pride.

"I will treasure it always," she said, and gave Elenya a kiss.

"Your ship awaits," Abu Ali said. "Travel well!"

As the Arabians began to trot forward, Lamiya's eyes meet Kai's. He had said nothing. He didn't wave as the slaves sang a song for safe passage.

Instead, in a reaction that confused him, he searched the crowd, hoping to see a certain pale face.

When he could not, he bent and asked old Festus, "Have you seen Aidan?"

The gray-hair nodded sadly. "His mother is very sick, sir."

In the darkness of her hovel, quietly and without any fuss, Deirdre lay dying. Aidan, hands shaking as he moistened a small towel and applied it to her forehead, knew this to be true. As did Deirdre. Auntie Moira provided food and herbs and poultices, and more important, whispered the words of the *treoraich anama* soul-leading ceremony that would guide her soul to the gates of heaven.

> *"Now is the wistful soul set free*
> *Outside the coich anama*
> *Christ all-knowing, all-seeing, thy blessing*
> *Surrounds with love in your good time . . ."*

Moira sang this and other songs, and soothed Deirdre's brow, and when there was nothing left to do, at last left to claim a few precious hours of sleep before returning to begin once again.

Now it was just Aidan and his mother, and the last painful hours of her life. Deirdre was hot-eyed and haggard. "Aidan?" Fever had run her voice ragged.

"Here, Mother," he said.

Distantly, through the open window, he could hear the sound of the slaves singing. He knew that that meant Lamiya and her party were leaving. Good. He wished to God that they would all leave. Or curl up and die.

Or allow him to board that ship with his mother and go home.

"Aidan . . . ?" she called, more distantly this time.

"I'm here. Right here."

"I'm so sorry." She tried to sit up but had no strength. All strength had been exhausted in the effort to stay alive another night. Her eyes were rimmed with dark wet crescents and she struggled with every breath, as if her lungs were filling with a viscous fluid.

He eased her back down. "You have nothing to apologize for. Rest."

"I'm leaving you here," she said in a thickened voice. "In this terrible place. This awful . . ."

She cried out in a garble of languages. "Oh, God, *An labhraíonn éinne anseo Gaeilge?* Who will take care of my boy! My boy!"

Aidan felt panic hammering at the doors of his control, splintering them. "Mother. I'll be all right. You'll be all right."

"No, I won't," she said, rejecting his desperate lie. "No, I won't. I pray . . ." But her strength had failed, and she could speak no longer. The sounds issuing from her mouth were no longer words. Aidan leaned his head against her chest, and she placed one frail hand on his shoulder, even now, at the last, offering what comfort she could.

Aidan held her. "I'll be all right, Mother," he wept. "I swear. I'll find a way to live. I'll be free. We'll be free, I swear, Mother, I'll be free for both of us. I'll find Nessa. We'll be a family again . . ."

Her hand seemed to squeeze his briefly, and then it drifted down, as gently as a leaf.

"Mother?" There was no answer. The next sound torn from Aidan's throat was a raw, hopeless sound, brutal in its intensity. *"Mother!"*

The room seemed emptier, darker now. Aidan O'Dere, boy lost in a monstrous land, held his mother's cooling body, and shrieked his pain into the night.

CHAPTER TWENTY-FOUR

"Short is the span of the mortal heart
Long is the length of grieving,
Deep is the wound only time can heal,
Shallow the words of comforting—"

Bearing torches, ringing the tree line in their hundreds, the inhabitants of Ghost Town had gathered in the grove in Deirdre's honor, offering their hearts and voices to her spirit.

Tears glistened on Aidan's cheeks, but his mouth did not tremble as the songs wove through the trees.

"Dark is the day when the news is first heard
Bright is the sun with its passing.
Brief is the crossing from life into death,
Endless, the soul everlasting.

Great is the loss of those left now behind
Small are the troubles of ord'nary day
Tightly we hold to thy memory,
Freely we wish thee upon thy way . . .
Freely we wish thee upon thy way . . ."

As they concluded, the slaves filed out, one at a time offering condolence. Brian clasped Aidan's shoulder. "Be strong, boy. You'll never need for meat, or shelter. I swear it." His voice was husky, but in it Aidan could have sworn he could detect an echo of his father's own strength. "She'll sleep well here, among her people. God gave her life. Our masters gave her death." An edge as hard as steel lurked in those words, and Aidan gazed up at Brian, who was looking mildly upon the earthen mound. "Be strong," he said. "A time will come, I promise."

"When?"

"When you're man enough to strike blows in Deirdre's memory. Would you like that, boy?"

Little muscles twitched at the corner of Aidan's jaw. His blue eyes, though filmed with tears, were like fire.

Brian squeezed Aidan's shoulder, then left the boy alone with his agony. When the last of the villagers left the grove, Aidan's legs turned to wet straw. He collapsed, clinging to the rude cross above his mother's grave, struggling not to revile the God who had brought them to this accursed land. He struck his forehead against the wood over and over again, lost in pain and fear and grief.

Late the next day Kai walked beside one of the western streams that fed into Lake A'zam, mired in his own thoughts. His father's lands extended for miles in all directions save east, but much of it remained undeveloped. More cultivated was the northern land, where grew endless fields of hemp and teff. Further still lay ground scarred with quarries, where hard, dangerous work produced more stone than any mines in the province.

The wealth was divided between Abu Ali and his brother, Malik, as it would one day be divided between Ali and Kai.

No thoughts of future wealth or power brought Kai the slightest bit of pleasure. He felt disconnected from himself, his life, his station—even his family. Kai just walked, thinking, trying to find a way to hold his feelings that made sense. Why was the world as it was? Why did we care about people only to lose them? Why were feelings not entered into whatever calculations adults made when they designed their days?

And in Allah's name, what exactly was it that he felt for Lamiya, and was he sinful to feel it?

Until he found an answer to those questions, he would be baffled and bothered and heartbroken.

He was turning the pieces around and around in his mind when he saw Aidan sitting on the edge of the stream running through the woods west of the pasture. The slave boy sat alone. Kai knew of Aidan's loss and felt momentarily guilty that he had not sought him out before now. He had seen but six summers when his own mother died and remembered little of her but her ethereal beauty, the warmth of her breast, the sound of her voice whispering his name, and the liquid-rose scent of her hair oil. He remembered kneeling at her bed during her final fever, praying that Allah might allow her to utter one last word of love, afford him a last precious smile.

Allah answers all prayers, but sometimes the answer is no.

Kai approached carefully and sat at Aidan's side in the grass on the stream bank.

For a long time neither spoke, and then Kai said: "I'm sorry about your mother."

Aidan said nothing, but he dug into the dirt at his side, palmed a small rock, and tossed it out.

"My mother died when I was six," Kai said.

Aidan didn't look at him. "You have a father," he said. "A brother, a sister. An uncle."

Kai felt the truth in those simple words. For a terrible moment he saw himself as this boy, lost and alone. No mother, no father . . . it was fortunate that Kai's father provided all needs to the servants, or Aidan's suffering might have been unendurable indeed.

Aidan tossed another stone out into the stream. "I have a sister. Somewhere." Aidan leaned forward and sank his face into his hands.

Kai picked up a stone and skipped it out across the water. "I hate this place," he said, shocking himself with the admission.

Aidan stared at him in utter disbelief, and opened his mouth as if about to say something poisonous. Then he seemed to realize that his young master was being utterly sincere. The absurdity of it struck him, twisted his mouth from an expression of grief to one of shock.

"Hate it," Kai repeated.

"That's really strange," Aidan replied, with blackest irony. "Because I *love* it."

Kai stared at him, and Aidan turned away, and was suddenly laughing and crying at the same time, and Kai laughed too, utterly hysterical laughter, laughter on the hot edge of tears that rang through the woods and swelled to drown even their pain. But it lasted just a moment, and then the moment was gone.

Kai watched the water flowing south, to the lake and then to the ocean beyond. And reached a decision.

"Come on," he said, and stood, tugging at Aidan's hand.

"Where?" Aidan looked up at him in irritation.

"Just come," Kai said, and then added: "Please."

The storeroom was dim, and a bit dank. The boys had snuck through the kitchen, pretending to be on their way to Kai's room, then ducked through the pantry into the dark of the stairs.

Kai tested the door, turned the knob and opened it stealthily, trying to prevent it from creaking. He poked his head it. "Shhh," he said.

"What is this?" Aidan said.

Kai silenced him until the door was closed, then found the firegun and used it to light the wall lamp. "We keep the *qinnab bûza* here. It's for the workers, for harvest celebration."

"Hemp beer?"

The room was filled with boxes and kegs large and small. Kai rummaged, and finally picked out a keg the size of his head. "Come on," he whispered, and Aidan helped him with their illicit load. The Prophet, peace be upon him, forbade the drinking of spirits, but surely, Allah Ar-Rahman, the Most Merciful, would pardon a small transgression on a night such as this.

Together they spirited it up the stairs. Kai scouted ahead, checked to see that no one in the kitchen was watching, and then motioned Aidan onward. Together they escaped into the yard.

No one spied them as they climbed through the pasture fence and headed out to the woods, finally reaching the clearing where a few months earlier Kai and Lamiya had met by chance.

When they had settled themselves safely behind a bush, Kai scraped the layer of wax off the cork, knocked it out of the bunghole, and took a mouthful, spraying half of it back out before managing to swallow some. It was sour and vile, but remembering Ali's oath that it cured all pains of the heart, he managed to gag it down.

"Here, I'll show you," Aidan said, and got Kai to hold the keg steady for him as he poured a golden stream into his mouth. His eyes went wide.

"You've done this before?" Kai asked.

Aidan nodded enthusiastically. He swallowed, took another mouthful, and swallowed again. "Good!"

A half hour later the two boys were roaring with sick, helpless gales of mirth.

Kai upended the keg, gulping another mouthful and choking it down. He didn't quite manage to swallow it all before the residue exploded from his mouth in another hysterical spray.

"Oh, no," he gasped. The world wheeled like a kite with a broken string, and he fought to find the thread of conversation they had begun just before the last round of drinks. *"You're* the one who has it easy. You work a'day—" He paused, fighting to keep his speech coherent. *"All* day, but then you go back, and you can do wha'ever you want, with whoever you want, whenever you want." Kai wiped the back of his hand against his lips. "Me? It's study study study, responsible for the whole place one day, marry who they tell me."

Aidan glared at him and snatched the keg away. "You are so full of *zibl.*" Aidan took a long pull and bolted down an entire mouthful of the powerful stuff.

Kai knew he should have taken offense at that last comment, but somehow the *qinnab bûza* just made everything seem sort of warm and mushy. He was having trouble putting his sentences together. The hemp beer seemed to have a double effect. One wave of intoxication hit suddenly, and then a second seemed to come on more slowly, pulling his feet from under him like a patient opponent waiting for him to drop his guard. "Ahh," he said as Aidan choked it down. "If you really knew, you'd be happy to be white. An' a slave. When the Aztecs come, *you* don't have to go off and fight an' die. Oh, no—you have strong black arms to protec' you."

"Not all that strong," Aidan sneered.

"Oh yeah?"

"All that fancy fightin'? I'd kick your arse."

"Well," Kai said belligerently, slapping his chest. "I'm right here."

"I'm here," Aidan replied. "Stand up."

Kai tried to stand, but wobbled, and Aidan had to catch him. "Whoops!" They were both giggling now.

Another couple of attempts and they were finally standing fairly straight. "Ready?"

"Ready to send you to Allah," Kai said. "Should have been praying."

"Praying?" Aidan said. "Praying that I don't kill you." He paused, considering. "Too much."

Kai threw a punch. It hit Aidan's shoulder and he spun, but grabbed Kai and wrestled him to the ground. Kai scrambled up and looped another punch. Aidan dodged, and Kai nailed him in the mouth with the left hand, and then another right. Shock ran up his wrist, but the second punch made a perfectly satisfying *splat* as it split Aidan's lip.

Aidan collapsed to one knee, and levered himself up unsteadily.

"See there?" Kai said, fists balled. "Infidel slave-dog, the righteous shall—"

Aidan rapped him squarely in the mouth. Kai blinked, more startled than hurt. Aidan hurled another punch but Kai slipped it, grabbed him and they both fell down. They tangled in the grass, flailing about and laughing like a pair of loons. Then finally collapsed.

"I win," Kai managed to pant.

"Crap," Aidan said. "Let's start again."

"I can't stand up," Kai complained. Then tried, and failed.

"I win," Aidan said, and collapsed on the ground next to him.

Kai looked at Aidan for a long moment, and then pulled his knife. Aidan watched, more puzzled than fearful as Kai pressed the blade against his own left thumb. Kai flinched, and then a red drop of blood welled up. Kai stared at it, fascinated, then remembered his purpose and passed the knife to Aidan.

Aidan looked at the blade suspiciously. "What's this?"

"It's a knife."

Aidan snorted. "I know that. What do you want me to do with it?"

"You don't have any family," Kai said matter-of-factly. "And I don't have any friends. Blood to blood."

Aidan looked at Kai's bandaged right thumb. "Like that?"

"Uh-huh."

"You're running out of thumbs," Aidan said. He paused, then nodded and pricked his finger. He leaned over and pressed his thumb against Kai's.

Perhaps due to the effects of the *qinnab bûza*, Kai felt something. A warmth, perhaps. A tingle, spreading up his arm and into his chest, and he was startled by the impact as their eyes met.

Then the intensity of the moment was broken by laughter and they tumbled back down to the grass, head to head under the swirling sky.

Aidan blinked hard. "It's like the sky in Eire," he said.

Kai stared up, the stars doubling in his wavering gaze. "What's it like there?"

"Beautiful," Aidan said. "Another world." He pressed his palms against his temples. "Ohh, my head is spinning. Another, other world. So close to here." He turned to Kai, grinning. "And in that world, *I* live in the palace, and *you* work in the fields."

Kai started to bark laughter, and instead, somewhat to his surprise, it died on his lips. Instead, he asked quietly, "Do you think we'd still be friends?"

Aidan smiled. *"Insh'Allah,"* he said.

"Insh'Allah," Kai replied, and for a long time they watched the sky, and listened to the night wind moving through the grass, saying nothing at all.

PART THREE

Sophia

"The unifying and transcendant aspects of the Creator impinge themselves upon the universe," said the Master. "What we cannot understand of His process we sometimes consider miraculous."

"What is this called?" asked the student.

"The Divine Theophony."

"And what is an instance of this miracle?"

"The Prophet once said that there were three things that gave him peace: prayer, perfume, and women."

"And the miracle?"

"Prayer joins us to the divine. Perfume to the world of the senses."

"And women?"

The Master laughed. "I am an old man," he said. "You, my student, have a lifetime before you to answer that question. That, young sir, is a miracle."

CHAPTER TWENTY-FIVE

21 Muharram 1288
(April 12, 1871)

Those who hate you are more numerous than those who love you.

HOUSA SAYING

It is sad to have no friends; sad to have unfortunate children; sad to have only a poor hut; but sadder still to have nothing good or bad.

IRISH SAYING

KAI BIINKED HIS EYES OPEN, for a time just watching the billowing clouds sliding through the sky above him. He felt a fine emptiness below his belly, one just now beginning to fill again. The glen was quiet except for the soft nickering as a fine pair of mares nibbled at the grass.

Then came a welcome sound, the lilt of a young, feminine voice calling: "Here we come!"

Aidan sat up from the grass beside him, chest and flat stomach still slicked with perspiration from the afternoon's sport.

At nineteen, Aidan was just a hair taller than Kai and a deben or two heavier, with a quarryman's tight, dense muscles. Save for Kai's greater flexibility and grace in motion—and for the color of their skins—they might have been mirror images.

Aidan turned to Kai and raised his right eyebrow. "Here they come. Ready, boy?"

"On your life!" Kai replied. The heaviness low in his gut increased. Juices were flowing now, and he felt the familiar tingle of anticipation.

A pair of slave girls greeted them; returning from the river, wrapped in sheets that clung wetly to their ripe bodies. These were Bahati and Mumbi, a pair of plump blond vixens bound to Djidade Berhar's estate across Lake A'zam. Known to be of high spirit and negotiable morals, both girls were willingly available to the province's highborn in exchange for gifts and trinkets. Truth be told, Kai suspected the freckled, short-haired Mumbi actually desired a brown baby. Berhar enjoyed the increase in his servant stock, and rewarded fertile women with extra food and privilege. The other serving women might scorn them, and their own men revile them as sluts, but Mumbi and Bahati were well on their way to being the wealthiest white women in the district.

Bahati, a giggling pug-nose and at sixteen summers the younger of the two, flashed the edge of her sheet open. "Catch us if you can," she said.

Kai and Aidan glanced at each other, two minds sharing a single thought. They leapt up as if spring-driven and were off on the chase. The brush scratched and flapped at them without diminishing their enthusiasm. Sheets were soon lost, all four of the youngsters as naked and wanton as any forest creatures.

"Victory!" Kai called, gazing down on Bahati, whom he had tackled softly to the ground. She lay panting, breasts high and nipples erect, firm broad thighs parted, her green eyes huge.

"And to the victor . . ." Aidan said beside him, already squeezing himself between Mumbi's legs.

"Go the spoils," Kai said, and sank down into softness, and a pair of very willing arms.

The day had grown cooler, and then faded into early evening. Passion had been slaked, grown sharp, and slaked again, and had finally devolved to conversation and affectionate murmurs.

The girls were buttoning their clothes, casting back over their shoulders glances that were part coquette and part slattern. Kai opened his purse and extracted a few small coins, dropping them into Mumbi's open palm. "Playtime's over girls. Get off with you."

"Will we see you next week?" she pouted.

"Now, lass," Aidan said. "How could we stay away?" He followed his words with a swift flurry of gropes and kisses.

Aidan sighed and collapsed onto his back, his shirt unlaced to the waist. "Now *that* was a pleasant evening."

"I think I'm in love."

"Not very likely," Aidan snorted. "You'll fall in love with some ugly Wakil's daughter with ten thousand head of fat cattle in her dowry and live happily ever after."

"Not the way it works," Kai said. "Among civilized people, the man pays the dowry."

"Ye been robbed."

Kai regarded Aidan sourly. "Flogging," he said, "is not out of the question."

Aidan levered himself up and mounted his speckled brown mare, digging his heels into her sides. "Have to catch me first!"

Kai rose as swiftly as fatigue and inebriation allowed. He buckled on his sword and took a running jump, vaulting onto his own mare, heading down the darkened road after Aidan.

By boat or horse, home lay an hour's ride from the Berhar estate. As they rode along, Kai sang songs and exchanged bawdy jokes with his companion, enjoying the deepening night and the perfection of the moment.

Suddenly, dirt flew into the air, spraying them both. Twanging like a harp string, a rope sprang up and across in front of them, rising as high as his mare's neck, barricading the road.

Before shock could sweep away the effects of the beer and hemp, three hooded men had stepped out on the road in front of them. Kai glanced back over his shoulder swiftly. Two more men behind them. All were armed with sticks and knives. Their hands were white.

Runaways!

"What the hell is this?" he said indignantly. Any idiot could guess what this was, but the more oblivious they thought him, the more likely they were to make a mistake. From the corner of his eye, he noted with satisfaction that Aidan's hand had drifted to the short cudgel strapped beside his own saddle.

The largest of the hooded men ignored Kai's question and turned to Aidan. "Stay oot a' this," he warned, then whipped his cudgel at Kai's shoulder.

The exchange was brisk and violent, a flurry of clubs and knives. Kai moved before he could think, countering and slashing from horseback. One of the attackers fell to his knees in the dirt, screaming as he struggled to staunch the flow from his severed fingers.

As the highwaymen crowded beneath him Kai wheeled and spun, keeping his mount moving constantly, forced to be more defensive than aggressive, blocking and warding off.

He caught a glimpse of Aidan, who had backed Kai's actions with gratifying speed. Although clumsier on horseback, the Irishman wielded his cudgel with strength and vicious accuracy. In the brief view he was afforded before wheeling his horse about again he saw Aidan block a knife with one end of his two-cubit stick and pound the face of an attacker with the other, splitting his nose and making him spit teeth. Blood gushed.

Three men came at Kai at once, and he knew he could deal with only two before the third wounded him. He steeled himself for the pain and deflected a cudgel stroke that would have spilled his brains. A knife nicked his left shoulder, then the knifeman ducked aside to avoid decapitation. From the corner of his eye he saw the knife coming for his side, then Aidan's club smashed down on the extended arm. Bone cracked.

Then one of the attackers yelled: "Enough, boys! Take off!" and they began to run.

One of the others yelled back over his shoulder, "White bastard! Traitor! We'll 'ave ye, coal-licker!"

Aidan ignored him and drew his horse closer to Kai. "Are you all right?"

Kai examined his right arm. His shirt was rent a few digits above the elbow. "Just a little nick," he said.

"Who the hell were they?"

"Slaves, probably runaways seeking gold or blood." He grinned. "Good work with the stick. I saw a bit of Malik's style there."

"You've been beating me for years. You think I've learned nothing?"

Kai clasped Aidan's arm. "Thank you," he said. "You saved my life."

Aidan nodded but didn't reply. They continued on down the road, quieter now.

They were ghosts, Kai thought. *Aidan is white. For even a moment, did he consider joining them . . . ?*

They parted ways as they passed through the front gates of Dar Kush. While Kai headed toward the mansion, Aidan reined his horse toward the shantytown. In the intervening years a small barn had been built for the slaves who owned or used horses in their work, and Aidan sheltered Imi, his own mount, there. Imi was on permanent loan from Kai: Aidan could not sell or lend her, but she was his to use so long as he was the young master's companion.

The village, their *tuath,* had swelled to almost three hundred souls now, the passing years filled with acquisitions and births.

He was most often greeted with a polite wariness: as the chosen companion of Abu Ali's youngest son, Aidan was a man to be reckoned with, even if one ignored his breadth of shoulder and strength of arm. Some of the men seemed a bit cautious of him, resentful of his status as a favored pet. He knew that they sometimes whispered "coal-licker" or "shadow-boy" behind his back.

On the other hand, young women often greeted him more warmly, perhaps believing that he could provide them with greater status and comfort.

Molly, once a playmate but now grown into a flame-haired, wide-hipped vixen, greeted him saucily. "Aidan!" she said, noting his disheveled condition. "You needn't travel so far for company. My hearth is warm."

Aidan pulled her close and whispered: "Why not build a fire for me to-morrow night?"

He smacked her lips and she yielded for a moment, then twisted away with a wink and a satisfied smile, swinging her ample hips about her business.

Aidan stepped around the corner, coming face-to-face with—

Brian. Two digits taller than Aidan, but no longer the village's angelic protector. His face was a mass of old scar tissue and his hair had gone coarse and gray. He seemed ten years older than his age, but still as dangerous as a timber wolf. Thinly veiled murder danced in his eyes. "So, Aidan. Been oot a' night with the young master, have ye?" He blocked Aidan's path.

Aidan locked eyes with him, a challenge. "And if I have?"

Brian sneered at him. Putting a straw to one of the lamps lighting the village's center path, he lit his pipe. Aidan smelled a mixture of tobacco and hemp. "Nothing. Nothing. Except despoilin' our womenfolk. Do ye sleep easy, Aidan?"

"They're eager for it," he said, a touch defensively. "No one forces them."

Brian exhaled a slender plume of sweet smoke. "No. I suppose not. They're free to make their choices, free to feel what they feel. As are we all. I'm sure that when they were wee girls they played with their cornhusk dolls and thought, 'When I grow up, I want to be used and thrown away, to bear the wee bairn of the men who own and sell us.'"

A flash of shame warred with anger and lost. "Get out of my way," he said, and pushed past his former friend.

"I'm sure you're doing the right thing, Aidan. I'm sure yer Ma would approve."

Aidan's muscles still burned with the fire of recent combat but he quelled his urge to smash Brian's face and brushed past him, stalking off.

"Did you never wonder if one of those girls is your sister?" Brian called after him. "Or who's dipping his black wick in *her* hot wax?" A thousand vile visions, suffered through every night's dark dreams exploded to mind. He couldn't breathe, couldn't think. His fists were balled painfully tight. If murdering Brian could have given Aidan the slightest hint of his sister's whereabouts, the slightest chance of rescuing her, Aidan would have torn the other man's throat out with his teeth.

Instead he merely squeezed his eyes so tightly that darkness exploded into light, then breathed deep, forced himself to relax, and continued on.

Aidan slammed the door of his house behind him. The room hadn't changed much in the years since Deirdre's death, and her presence was still sorely felt. Her sewing kit still sat on the table, her favorite chair still pulled to its edge. He never allowed another to sit in it.

His flippant smile, worn bravely passing Brian, had faded like the table-cloth, as had his anger, leaving an empty pit of shame and self-loathing. He tore off his jacket and opened the cupboard, taking down a piece of dried meat and a hunk of bread. He stuffed a pipeful of hemp, lit it from the lamp beside the door, and drew deeply, almost savagely, as if trying to punish his lungs.

He ate and drank slowly, hunched over his solitary table, loins empty, mind filled with odd thoughts that flew like moths in a whirlwind.

I'm still here, Ma. I have more freedom than most. I'm alive. I eat more meat, get my pick of the work details, and wear better clothes than most of the others. I can read and write their language, and their youngest son thinks I'm his friend. Hell, maybe I am. He's not bad. He's all I have.

Today, I might have had a chance for freedom. Instead, I fought men who might have been of my own tuath, and saved my master's life.

Perhaps I am no longer fit to be free.

What promises had Aidan made over the years and not kept? Despite a steady stream of inquiries to every visitor to Dar Kush, he had not heard a word of Nessa's whereabouts. He had not avenged his father's death. All of his dreams were fading. He was more comfortable than most—even most free blacks. Ate in the kitchen when it pleased him, had few tasks besides being Kai's companion and almost the run of the place. When Abu Ali died and Kai inherited, Aidan would probably be his overseer.

Kai certainly trusted him: on occasion they had even gone shooting to-gether, and the Wakil's son had taught Aidan how to load and aim the fire-sticks that had killed his father. Little did Kai know that when Aidan fired at a target, he was seeing a Northman, or a black, wooly head.

In time, he might earn his freedom. Mnyamana, a slave on Djidade Berhar's plantation, had done it just last year! And if he earned that precious gift and decided to stay on in Kai's employ, Aidan might eventually be quite well off. It was not unknown for former slaves to become wealthy merchants, if they conducted their trading under the protection of their former masters.

Legality and *custom* were two very different things. And he didn't think he was selling too much of himself in order to find a measure of comfort and security . . .

He took another bite, chewing carefully. Thinking and evaluating. No. He was doing all that he could to stay alive, and sane. Brian should talk. Look where his big attitude had gotten him! The man was half mad. Children ran when he approached.

Who fills your bed now, Brian?

Aidan finished his meal. There was more. All year long, there was food. There were no lean times here on Dar Kush, and that was just fine. He remembered lean times in the O'Dere crannog, when the fish were not running, when the salted pork was gone and winter hunger had been a live rat in his young belly.

Never here. He was fine. He ate again and stared at his home.

Four walls. A floor. A straw ceiling.

Home.

CHAPTER TWENTY-SIX

KAI GRITTED HIS TEETH against the leather bit as Jimuyu, the Wakil's short round Kikuyu doctor, put needle and thread to his wound. "Damn!" The chunk of leather fell from his mouth. "Ow! I need a surgeon, not a boot maker—"

Jimuyu merely smiled, his receding hairline and slow manner concealing a knowledge of health and sickness both intuitive and scholarly. His people's herbalism was famed as far as the Ayurvedic schools of India, their knowledge of energy healing comparable to anything

China's *chi gung* healers could muster. But he had also mastered the Greek and Egyptian methods, and because of that complete knowledge was perhaps the finest doctor in all New Djibouti.

Wakil Abu Ali and Ali entered Kai's room.

The air around his father seemed to crackle. "Kai!" he raged. "I wish they'd hacked that arm off! *Then* you might learn your lesson."

"Father . . ." Kai began. The Wakil waved a hand curtly.

"Is that what I am? How could I be when my son won't listen to me?"

"Father," Kai protested. "I listen . . ."

His brother Ali leaned closer, sniffing, his neatly trimmed black beard twitching as he did. He wrinkled his nose. "Beer."

Abu Ali's face creased in disapproval. "My son," he declared, "is a drunkard. You are the disgrace of the district, boy."

Kai dropped his head. "Father . . ."

Abu Ali paced back and forth and back again, his hands linked behind his back. "No more of this. You are a man soon, with responsibilities. I have been willing to turn a blind eye to your childish antics—but . . . finish them now!" He turned and glared, and again Kai was unable to meet his father's eye. "When you are a man, it changes. No man of my household will carry himself thus. Do you understand my meaning?"

"Yes, Father," Kai said meekly.

More quietly this time, Abu Ali asked, "Were they white?"

"Yes, Father."

"Runaways," Jimuyu said placidly. "There have been reports of runaway brigands waylaying travelers. Now stay still—"

"Ow!"

Abu Ali turned to his eldest. "Have the constabulary double their sweeps. I want their livers on a pike by sunset tomorrow." He turned to leave the room, then paused and asked: "How many attackers were there?"

"Five, Father."

Kai wasn't certain, but he could have sworn that he saw a slight, prideful lift to his father's shoulders. He might have even been smiling, but *that* he would never show his son. "Next time, I wish them better hunting."

Ali lingered behind a moment, grinning openly, and slapped Kai's sore shoulder. "Well done," he whispered.

Kai groaned. He floundered around for the leather bit and set it between his teeth again as Jimuyu put down his needles and began the application of salves that first stung, and then soothed like ice.

*   *   *

Kai was alone in his room, the ache in his left shoulder reduced to a dull throb. He remembered the moment when he had left his right upper quadrant vulnerable and cursed himself. *Now* he understood some of the concepts Malik tried to teach him. The need to maintain soft eyes and wide focus, to put the conscious mind into a kind of servant position, merely maintaining awareness while the deeper mind was allowed to spontaneously express its learnings. What had been repeated to him in a thousand lectures was made clear in a single crystalline instant of actual combat. Strange, how that happened.

And if Aidan hadn't been there, Kai might never have lived to learn it.

He stood on the balcony, looking out across the yard and the road to the village, where lantern lights still burned bright. Aidan was a good sort. If not for an accident of birth he might have made a decent laborer or horse trainer, might have eventually owned his own land, or business. It would have been hard, but he would have managed: Aidan was no ordinary ghost. Still, Aidan was fortunate to have the Wakil to protect and feed him. The whites were often hardworking and loyal, but not capable of much above that. Oh, once the Romans had had some sort of primitive empire, but books said most of their architecture and philosophy had been stolen from Greece. And most Greek philosophers had fled to Egypt along with Socrates, a clear testament to the superiority of African culture.

In the house were hundreds of books and scrolls that touched on doomed Rome and its defeat at the hands of Egypt and Carthage. Kai had read a dozen of them. They all agreed on the fact that the poverty, disease, and war that ravaged Europe had been ended only by the rise of Abyssinia and the subsequent capture of the Egyptian throne. Black soldiers patrolling Egypt's European kingdoms a thousand years ago had filed reports filled with tales of horror and unbelievable poverty. Much of this misery existed in the very shadow of mystifying ancient ruins. While such relics suggested a forgotten culture, the buildings and statues were doubtless the remnants of ancient Egyptian conquests.

If Aidan was a good fellow, he was doubtless the very best of his breed, and they were lucky to have found each other. When Kai had his own estate, he would need a trustworthy aide, as the Wakil had Oko and some of the others. Perhaps he would begin to speak to Aidan about converting to the true path.

Kai had to laugh at that: as if the Prophet would be happy with Kai as a messenger! But the world of responsibility was so infinitely wide, and

Kai had so little time to enjoy the youth remaining to him. He would enjoy it all.

And then he would settle down.

One day. Not today.

CHAPTER TWENTY-SEVEN

DAR KUSH'S ROLLING LAWNS WERE CROWDED with highborn and share-landers from the surrounding district. Sharelanders, blacks who contracted to work the Wakil's vast holdings in exchange for a share of the crops—usually worked hours comparable to that of the servants. On holidays, however, they were invited to lay down their farming tools and join in the festivities.

It was Kai's nineteenth birthday, and although dignitaries above the local level had merely sent gifts and notes of congratulation (unlike Ali's birthday, or the Wakil's, which drew visitors from as far as New Alexandria), it was still a joyous, festive time.

The weather was mild and sunny and the tables filled with friends and good cheer. Kai's uncle Malik observed the proceedings with an unusually broad smile softening his bearded face. Perhaps his mood had something to do with the presence of his wife. Still childless, Fatima remained as slender as a girl, and Malik doted on her famously. At the moment, however, his gaze was locked on his nephew. There were more threads of gray amid the black of his beard, but the fire in his eyes was undimmed, and the passing years had only lent strength and agility to his sword arm. "And in honor of his majority," Malik said, "I offer Kai the finest mare in my stable, that his enemies may always be a length behind. I present . . . Djinna!"

To much applause, a magnificent black Arabian mare trotted out of the barn.

"Uncle!" Kai was wide-eyed. He had not seen such a mount since his father had chosen Isis eight years before. "I have no words!"

Malik's hand fell heavily on Kai's shoulder. "You are a man now. We want deeds, not words."

Kai's teeth flashed. "Deeds it is. Here, girl . . ."

Kai set his cup down and walked toward the horse, first with nervousness, then growing confidence. Her eyes were very calm and startlingly direct, and he could sense the intelligence behind them. Kai ran his hand along her neck, marveling at the strength and grace of that ebon column. Djinna turned her head to watch him as he examined her flanks, and the firm muscles of her legs. Magnificent! Kai could have sworn that she nodded her head yes, as if offering him permission to mount. Grinning, he set his hands on the saddle and pulled himself up. He dug his heels in and triggered Djinna into motion.

Kai had ridden almost before he could walk and was a superb horseman. To the delight and applause of all, he weaved through the crowd and jumped the pasture fence. He put the magnificent creature through its paces, jumping fences and bushes, racing as if pursued by a band of Aztecs.

He couldn't believe how responsive she was, how powerful. The whistle of wind past his ears was intoxicating. Monthly drill with Amin's regiment would be a joy with such a glorious beast at his command!

He trotted the horse back in a great circle and stopped before the guests, who applauded loudly. Malik and Abu Ali stood shoulder to shoulder and applauded loudest of all.

"Well done!" Malik said.

Kai was breathless and bright-eyed. "Uncle," he said. "Djinna is indeed her name. I will strive to be worthy of such magic."

"You have my blood," Malik said as Kai dismounted. "I expect no less." The two men embraced warmly.

Kai's head swam. "I have been blessedly gifted today. It is hard to imagine any greater good."

His father smiled. "It is my turn, Kai. A father's honor to present the final gift. As you all know, my son is famed not only for his riding and scholarship, but for his . . . nocturnal adventures." Kai's ears burned at the ripple of good-natured laughter.

Abu Ali continued. "It is time childish things were put aside. I believe in enjoying the fruits of labor and courage, but the responsibilities of manhood cannot be ignored. There are many delicious temptations in this world." The men at the table pounded their fists on the table while Elenya averted her eyes. Fatima gave her husband a polite but disapproving frown. Malik hugged her around the shoulder and merely laughed.

Kai didn't like the sound of this. Abu Ali continued expansively. "But my son is also a man, and I thought it best if he distracted himself from such temptations with a tutor."

Kai groaned.

"—and since Babatunde will not return for months, I imported the very finest tutor available for my son, that his studies might last far into the night." The Wakil removed a red scarf from his pocket and waved it broadly. A pair of servants scrambled from beside the table and jogged toward the front gate, a quarter mile distant.

Just as Kai wondered if a protest would serve any purpose, he heard a distant creaking of wheels and hinges, and the estate gates opened. The Wakil's new personal coach approached, even grander than the one that had borne Lamiya to the harbor. Of lacquered ebony with veins of gold, it was certainly too ornate for use by any Muslim warrior, perhaps reserved for guests from India's royal house. Drawn by four brown Spanish stallions, the tasseled window curtains bounced as it rolled forth, concealing whoever—or whatever—awaited within.

The prancing horses pulled to a stop. For a long moment nothing happened, and the tension made Kai's neck itch. Then the door opened, apparently by itself. Kai realized that he was holding his breath, although as yet there was nothing to be seen.

Then a hand appeared around the frame of the door, tapered brown fingers tipped in lacquer just a little darker than her own skin. A face appeared next, and Kai's heart leapt.

He had seen such women before, knew that they were children of Andulus, the product of the Moorish empire's influence on the bloodlines of southern Europe. They were beings of grace and fire, prized as dancers and courtesans.

Her eyes were slanted, half-lidded. When they opened a trace more and fastened on him, he thought his heart would stop.

Her smile was the promise of a perfect sunrise following an exquisite night. Her every motion glided like honey-water down a parched throat, but restrained in a manner that promised the absolute limit of what mortal flesh could bear. Although her skin was pale her lips were full and African, her hair and eyes dark, her nose more broad and sensuous than any of the poor thin-blooded Irish girls.

Had a lion licked the back of his neck, Kai could not have taken his eyes from the girl as she approached and knelt before him. Her hand made a single rolling magician's flourish, and a long-stemmed rose appeared. When he accepted it, he was embarrassed to note that it was his hand, not hers, that trembled.

Her eyes met his for just a moment. They were deeper and darker than the night. Kai felt as though he were balancing on the edge of some massive revelation.

"Her name is Sophia," his father said.

In what was clearly a very choreographed motion, several of the female servants appeared, and swept Kai away from the table.

Sophia floated behind, barely seeming to bend the grass beneath her feet.

With agonizing slowness, the servants removed Kai's clothes one piece at a time. Then they led him to his bathing tub, which had already been filled with steaming water, where they cleaned and anointed him in precious oils. Not since childhood had Kai been so pampered, and the entire ritual seemed dreamlike.

Then Kai slipped into a plush saffron robe, and was led to his bedchamber. The door was closed behind him. The bed was deeply canopied, its shadows inviting and somehow mysterious. He had not been a virgin since an occasion in the barn soon after his fifteenth birthday, but he had never brought a woman into his own bed, or into his father's house.

The curtains around the bed obscured Sophia's form. Only a single hint of a shadowed breast pulled him forward.

He drew the curtains aside, and stared. The sheets were covered with rose petals, and Sophia watched him with an expression he could not read. Expectation, perhaps. Judgment, perhaps.

She was a sight to steal a man's breath. He slipped into bed beside her, his hands seeking eagerly.

She set her palms flat against his chest, and said in perfect Arabic, "Not like that." Her voice was heavily accented, as sweet as syrup.

He pulled back, mystified but not angered. "Then, what?"

She took both of his hands in hers, and kissed the fingertips. Every touch sent tremors up his spine. "Slow," she said. "Touch. I am not a horse, to be driven to speed. In exchange for each day's labor, Allah gives us one glorious night. Let us take them a moment at a time."

He was dizzied. Her scent was unlike that of any woman he had ever known, heavy with a hint of her own musk, and some essential oils that he could not name. He sensed that she was the door to mysteries undreamed of. Kai had believed himself to be a master of these, but the loss of illusion was the beginning of wisdom. This woman would teach him the secrets that his father and uncle and brother knew, secrets that had only been hinted of in the frantic tumbles with servant girls in glens and barns and hovels. Sophia was the doorway to lovemaking as an art.

"Teach me," he said, and she drew him close.

As the night thickened, Abu Ali, Ali, and Malik reclined on the lawn, enjoying a bit of Turkish tobacco in the hookah and Kenyan tea in their cups. When the wind blew just right, they could hear sounds from Kai's window: creaks, and groans, and the mingling of male and female voices raised in pleasure.

One groan was more exquisitely prolonged than the others, and Abu Ali raised one bushy eyebrow. "Such sounds! The torture must be exquisite."

"I think the prisoner will soon succumb," Ali chuckled, and raised his cup in salute.

The night rolled on. The grounds were deserted save for the pacing overseers and guards.

Kai rose naked from his bed and walked to the balcony. He felt that he could sense every blood vessel in his body, that his sensitivity to every muscle and motion was enhanced, that his very nerves carried their messages more quickly.

He felt . . . older. Changed. He looked out across his father's estate with a man's eyes. He would own a healthy part of this, and his brother would control the rest. And he would be ready, when the time came.

Slender arms twined around his neck. Sophia leaned in, her perfect breasts pressing against him from behind. Her lips nibbled at his earlobes. "The lesson is just begun," she whispered with honeyed breath.

He turned into her kiss, drunken with the music of lips and tongue, lost in the depths of her hips and breasts, so recently explored. Burning as she molded herself against him.

Already she had drained and rebuilt him three times. He should have been exhausted, but miraculously felt himself responding to her yet again. "Are you a witch?"

"I am whatever you desire," she said.

He scooped her up in his arms, and carried her back to the bed. And there, on a mattress of rose petals, they rejoiced until the dawn.

CHAPTER TWENTY-EIGHT

KAI HIT THE MAT HARD, then rolled onto hands and knees and mule-kicked into Malik's rock-ribbed gut. His uncle slid to the side and swept Kai's supporting foot, miming a crippling stomp to the knee.

Sophia sat at the side of the room, wide-eyed with amazement as the two warriors practiced, astounded that neither had accidentally crippled or castrated the other.

Groaning at his gaffe, Kai stood, wiped the sweat from his brow, and began again.

The two warriors had been practicing for over an hour, and even the indefatigable Malik now moved with a certain heaviness. His burly bare chest glowed with perspiration. This was an empty-handed session ("*Occasionally one loses the sword, or is attacked before one comes to hand. A warrior must be prepared for all things*"), and Kai seemed to be actually enjoying this kind of play more than the sword skills she had also watched him perfect.

Although he left sweat and sometimes blood on the mats, Kai's rigors were ennobling, quite different from the severe training to which Sophia herself had been subjected.

Sold into slavery at thirteen to pay her father's debts, Sophia De Moroc had understood her eventual fate even before leaving Andulus. At Dar Hudu, Alexandria's House of Submission, she had not only been deflowered, but indoctrinated in the thousand arts of love, taught to pamper her body with dance and lotion, and how to prevent conception with an herb-soaked sponge.

Then, fully trained, the girls had been told that a few, just a few of the very best of them, might charm their eventual masters into privilege and possibly even freedom.

The night of her rape she had been fourteen. God! The pain and humiliation! If not for the hashish ball they had forced her to swallow, she swore she would have killed herself. Four years had passed since then, and every day of those years she reminded herself that she would be free, no matter what it cost her. Her body was just her body, and might be used against her will. But her mind and heart would be hers alone. The other girls might weep and wail at night, calling for parents who would never come for them. In Dar Hudu, Sophia learned to bury her heart and forget childish dreams, and spent her nights reading scrolls from Persia, or translations of erotic texts from India and China.

She swore that she would master any man who purchased her, using the only tools in her possession: her mind, heart, and body.

She might have no say in where she lived, in whose bed she slept. She would trust in her beauty and high price to bring her to a man of wealth. When she learned that she would be the manhood gift to a boy of Kai's breeding, she had sighed with relief, knowing that, however small, *here* was a chance to make her mark, to possibly earn more than mere freedom. The other girls at Dar Hudu spoke in hushed tones of one "graduate," almost legendary, who had convinced her fat and wealthy master to marry her. She not only made him an excellent wife, but lived to inherit his estate!

Lies? Reality? It mattered little. If there was a spark of hope at all, Sophia would fan that spark to flame, and become that myth other girls whispered to bind the demons in their dreams. And Kai, unformed, earnest, beautiful Kai, might well be the key to her prison.

She wrested her mind away from the past and to the present. If there was an answer for her, a way out, it lay in mastering this boy's heart. So far, praise Allah, that heart had proven to be kind.

To her dancer's eyes, Malik's combat technique was like wrestling, with the addition of short, fast blows. The practice was brisk and often painful, but knees, elbows, and head-butts were usually pulled before contact, to avoid crippling injury.

Three Benin drummers provided the rhythm. Kai danced to their improvisational beat, arcing and inclining his body in a hundred different ways to avoid, change distance, feint, shift angle or position, alter footwork, counter, or manipulate the pace.

Neither man spoke, but occasional sharp cries or exhalations accompanied a forceful strike. Malik grinned as his nephew landed a solid elbow to his gut, a blow he had taught Kai only a week before. *"Paralyzes the diaphragm,"* he had said. *"Not a killing blow, but one guaranteed to cause disruption in the opponent's breathing. A gift from heaven—a golden second, perhaps two, in which to find a sword."*

He spun away, depriving Kai of the opportunity to follow with a finishing technique. "Ahh! Good, boy. But not good enough . . ."

Malik hip-faked to the left. When Kai turned that way to block, Malik twisted to the right and spun like a darvish. He swept Kai's legs from beneath him so that the young warrior corkscrewed in the air, landing in a jarring breakfall.

A few cubits away from her, Fatima applauded lightly. Malik's wife more or less ignored Sophia. She leaned toward Mani, a young Dahomy girl engaged to one of the drummers. "See how well young Kai moves," she said, as Kai sprang back up lithely. "He might almost be an acrobat." Mani nodded agreement.

Sophia sidled closer to them. "He learns new movements very well," she said.

Fatima's answering gaze was utterly frigid. "Speak when spoken to, girl."

Stung, Sophia immediately lowered her gaze, biting her lip hard. Malik's wife saw her as little more than a whore. She was not! She was *yaqid imrat*, a fire woman, a teacher of erotic arts. Given time she could win a place in this world, she knew it. But first, she must learn to hold her tongue.

Kai attempted a fancy kicking maneuver, beautiful and sweeping. Malik simply leaned out of the way, then stepped in and slapped his face hard, smacking Kai unceremoniously to the ground.

"Enough!" Malik called. Kai seemed immensely relieved. He rolled over onto his back, panting with open mouth. Malik knelt close to him. "Boy, such leaps are pretty things to display for women. Try them on the battlefield, and you'll leave your head on a pole."

"Yes, Uncle," Kai said humbly, struggling for the breath to speak.

Malik's fierce expression softened. "Aside from that effeminate insanity, you are doing well." He smacked Kai's left thigh hard enough to make Sophia wince. "That concludes our lesson for today."

Kai rolled up to sitting. "I fear I will never learn."

"Hah! So speaks the prodigy." Malik extended his hand and hauled Kai to his feet. "Keep a secret." He put his arm around Kai's shoulder, pulling him close. "You began this path with only half a heart, but always had the seed of genius. Your brother gives me his heart and mind and body, without reservation. He will never be more than excellent."

Kai's eyes went wide. "Truly? But I am no match for Ali."

"So you think. And so long as you think that, it will be true. Also, so long as you waste your practice time pirouetting for pretty slaves."

Kai cast a glance at Sophia. She took the cue, produced her prettiest blush, and turned away.

"And she *is* a pretty thing," she heard Malik continue. "Tell me . . . is she for sale?"

Fatima's heart-shaped face grew taut. Brows furrowed, eyes spitting daggers but mouth drawn into a thin, genteel line, she rose and left the room, slamming the door behind her. *Good,* Sophia thought. *His wife doesn't like me, and wouldn't want me in the household. A young man like Kai will be easier to bend than an experienced warrior.*

Malik laughed.

Kai was confused. "I don't think—" he began.

Malik slapped Kai's shoulders again. "Oh, I was merely teasing Fatima." Sophia wasn't certain whether Kai's uncle was serious or not, but Malik's voice dropped a bit, became slightly conspiratorial. "But . . . would she be? A man might be tempted to make an excellent offer."

"No, Uncle."

Thank heaven.

Malik shrugged. "Very well, young Kai. *Hai!*"

Without further warning, Malik snatched a spear from the wall and hurled it at his nephew. *God!* she thought, shocked. *Kai is dead!*

Kai twisted to the side, and the lethal dart missed him by a digit, burying itself in the wall behind him.

Kai blinked, then grinned, stunned by the excellence of his own reactions. Confusion and pride warred in his face. At last he bowed to his uncle and mentor, right hand over his heart.

The sun was waning but still strong as Kai and Sophia crossed Malik's moat and headed south toward home. Distant eastern mountains caught the last of the light, sparkling with quartz and mica.

Kai guided Djinna without thought, his mind far away, nerves still tingling with the last three hours' lessons. True, his uncle had been operating at mere practice intensity, but still Kai had managed to touch him three times. Unheard of!

Virtually mirroring his thoughts, Sophia said, "You were very good."

Kai was still dazed. "Uncle says I may be his best student. Ever."

"I'm sure it's true."

Kai yawned and stretched, feeling the weight of fatigue in his arms and legs. Once he had hated that sensation. Now he welcomed it as a herald of greater strength and skill. "Once, on this very road," he said, yawning again, "I fought off five bandits!" Well, it wasn't actually *this* road, but country roads looked much alike.

Sophia made an appropriately impressed sound, and Kai began to elaborate. "Left and right! They cut and thrust, but I was too quick . . . they wounded me, here." He pointed to his left shoulder.

Sophia brushed his shoulder with her hand. "I remember," she said, and lowered her eyes as they rode on. Indeed she did. She had brushed that scar with lips and tongue a hundred times, and the very thought of it made his blood race. She was not black, though far darker and more beautiful than the fishbelly-pale slave women. And yet . . . she was still *other*, exotic, in a magical, tantalizing manner. Never had he suspected the existence of a woman like this! Truly, she had mastered the arts of love as had Malik the arts of war.

"Five men, all by yourself," she purred. Even her accent was exotic. He had learned that her father was from Andulus, her mother from Greece, and the blood mingled in her veins to produce an extraordinary creature. "You must be *very* brave."

Kai's chest swelled. He knew that tone of her voice, and could hardly wait to get her alone in his room. First she would bathe him, and then . . .

He leaned back in the saddle, humming, thinking back on that glorious and pivotal night. Then he remembered Aidan. He frowned a bit, and decided to be fair. "Yes, well . . . I did have a *little* help."

"Whose?"

"My friend Aidan."

Sophia laughed derisively. "I have seen him. I am sure it is *you* who saved *him*."

Kai laughed and squared his shoulders.

Within another hour, Sophia sighted Dar Kush's front gates. Kai had been digging, hurrying Djinna along the last quarter hour, and she was not at all surprised when he said: "I'm afraid I drank too much juice before I left Malik's."

"Shall I see that the horses are fed and watered?"

"You've saved my life." He jumped down, trotting toward the house, and relief.

"It is my pleasure." She laughed. Again, her offering kept him from ordering. He *wanted* to forget that she was a slave and bound to obey his wishes. Deep in his heart he wanted to believe she was enamored of him, and a slave only to his *zakr*. Malik would never make that mistake, and the mere thought of his calloused hands sobered her.

Sophia walked the mounts to the barn, humming to herself and swaying her hips to the music. She liked the barn, its dark shadows and deep, rich aromas. There had been horses in Andulus, and when she allowed herself to stray back to those memories, thoughts of riding with her father and mother were some of the best—

" 'It is my pleasure,' " Aidan said mockingly.

Sophia hadn't seen him there in the shadows, and her hand flew to her bosom. "Oh! You surprised me."

Aidan was combing the horses, cleaning their coats to a high sheen. He had doffed his shirt. She noted that his body was as muscular as Kai's. Perhaps a bit thicker through the torso. Kai was as lean as a whip. Aidan, well . . . Aidan resembled one of the animals he groomed.

"Did you and Kai have a good ride?"

The double entendre lingered in the air between them. Sophia half-lidded her eyes, but pretended not to notice. Animal, Aidan might resemble, but a splendid animal, whose eyes held hers in a most disconcerting fashion. His face was both sad and mocking, his smile lines deeply grooved. "Very pleasant," she said. "He is an excellent horseman."

"Ah-hah. And you?"

"I enjoy the sport," she said, and handed him the reins.

"I'm sure," Aidan said, and led Djinna to her stall. His pants rode low about his hips, and the muscles in his lower back bunched and flexed with every step. "I am allowed to exercise the mounts. Perhaps we can ride together one day."

Such impertinence! Sophia balled her fists and set them on her generous hips. "I think not," she said. "If you have such an urge, I suggest you ride by yourself."

And with that, she turned and strode away. The nerve! But despite, or because of, the fact that she was certain the upstart was watching, she put a little extra swing into her walk. Just so that he would know what he was missing.

CHAPTER TWENTY-NINE

28 Jumaada thaany 1288
(September 14, 1871)

A DAY CAME WHEN WAKIL ABU ALI decided it was time to orchestrate yet another change in the life of his younger son. So, gathering his household together, he told them to make preparations for a trip of several days to the *kraal* of Cetshwayo, elder half brother of Shaka Zulu.

A caravan was mounted: horses, wagons and carts, and an unadorned carriage for Abu Ali and his family, accompanied by six servants, attendants, cooks, and two beautiful mares just entering season.

The Wakil and his children rode on horseback or in the carriage, depending on their energy and inclination. Elenya, now sixteen, wore her hair in tight, thin braids, with bangled golden earrings cascading to her shoulders, golden links across her scalp-line, gold nose ring linked to a mesh cap of wrought gold and silver that dangled over her cheeks and eyes in the Afar fashion, forming a veil that provided modesty and proclaimed her station at a single glance. She rode her jet-black mount like a princess. Soon it would be time for her to travel to Alexandria, perhaps attend the university at Al-Ahzar and be presented at court for marriage.

"Mating season is a wonderful time, Kai," said Abu Ali to his son, who rode beside him.

Kai started, almost as if the Wakil was reading his mind. "Yes, Father," he said.

Abu Ali seemed in a whimsical mood. "One must make certain that the stock is properly combined. Such arrangements are often made years in advance, and are for the mutual benefit of both lines."

Kai raised an eyebrow. "We *are* speaking of horses, are we not?"

His father and brother laughed. Kai tried to take his mind off the obvious truth: that at long last, "arrangements" for his future were being made.

Kai trusted his father without reservation, but the fact that someone other than himself was choosing his life partner was absolutely unnerving. He tried to concentrate on the countryside, a mix of low trees and scrub brush, irrigated farmland, and cactus patches. This was exciting: He had been to Djibouti harbor, of course, had ridden across every cubit of his father's holdings, and traveled to several neighboring estates. But unlike Ali, Kai had not been to New Alexandria or Azania. In all his nineteen years, Kai had never been more than a hundred miles or so from home, and the taste of adventure was sweet indeed.

Abu Ali's family was in the lead, supply wagons and livestock rolling the road behind them. Aidan drove the main wagon, his hands sure on the reins. He was quiet and watchful, and just a little cautious.

Sophia sat on the seat beside him, keeping a careful distance, although he knew she was *aware* of him. She was a spoiled, pampered thing who thought she had Kai on a string. And since she arrived his relationship with the Wakil's son had diminished from its former nightly ramble to occasional hunting and gaming trips. That was fine: in time all fleshly fires died. Things would return to normal. Meanwhile he, Aidan, had lost no privilege at all.

According to Kai, Abu Ali had tried to discourage Sophia's presence on the trip, but had at last relented. Aidan guessed that the coming marriage would thin Sophia's influence, and so was inclined to temporarily indulge his younger boy's carnal appetites.

"*And when you marry, boy?*" Aidan had once heard the Wakil ask.

"*It depends on the contract,*" Kai had insisted. "*Perhaps I won't need to send her away at all.*"

Probably true. The Wakil had had but a single wife, but many of these blacks had three or more, if they could afford them—and if the first wife permitted the expansion.

Abu Ali had laughed knowingly. "*You sound like I did, boy,*" he said. "*Many a man has dreamed of multiple beds, only to be stripped of his illusions at the marriage table.*"

They were rolling along through a bountiful golden teff field. Slaves were raking and hoeing between the sun-baked rows, singing a song that drifted up to the road:

"*Darkness hangin' in the sky in the morn,*
Moonlight dyin' as the sun is reborn—
Crops are swayin' in an island of green
Hemp and teff and corn in between—"

And then a familiar refrain:

"Cut her low, swing her 'round
Iron wire, tightly bound
Thresh the teff by the morning lark,
Lie in her arms in the still of dark,
Laddie are ya workin'?"

Aidan watched bleakly as Abu Ali and his sons took up the refrain, enjoying the muscular rhythm and drive of the song, nodding in approval as the field workers timed their motions to the refrain.

"A very musical people," Ali said.

"In all truth, yes," his father said. "Our composer Al-Hadiz wrote a recent piece building upon a white composer named . . ." Abu Ali squinted. "Amadeus. Mozart, I think. Wrote some perfectly respectable songs eighty years ago or so. Found patronage in Alexandria, I believe."

"Even monkeys can do tricks," Ali said dismissively.

"Al-Hadiz said that it was more than a trick, that Mozart's work was equal to that of Jeffari—"

"Impossible!"

"Or even Mubutu himself. His early work, at least."

Ali shook his head. "Listen to them," he said, and another chorus drifted up from the field. To Aidan's ear it was a mournful song, a song of loss and pain, and it was hard to believe that his proud, educated masters could not hear the fury behind the sweetly twining melody.

"Storm clouds gather as the hands to the field
Raindrops scatter as the land's made to yield.
Body separate from its fine golden head
Stalk and sheaf and chaff for a bed—

Cut her low, swing her 'round
Iron wire, tightly bound
Thresh the teff by the morning lark,
Lie in her arms in the still of dark,
Laddie are ya workin'?"

"Listen to that," Ali said. "Their rhyme is crude, and the rhythm is barely fit for scythe swinging."

"It's a work song," the Wakil said patiently. "We may find, in time, that these people are capable of much more."

"Father," Ali said. "Sometimes you astound me."

"A wise man," said Abu Ali, "strives to be both astounding and astounded at least once a day." And they laughed and rode up toward the head of the column.

Aidan merely watched. Some of the field workers were close enough to the road to meet his eye, and there were tiny, subtle nods passed between them, greetings. Questions: *Who are these black folks? And who are you and where do you go?*

He would have loved to stop and speak with them, trade stories: *How did you come here? Where are you from?*

And more importantly: *Have you ever met a woman named Nessa . . . ?*

"They work hard," Sophia said, jarring him from his thoughts.

Aidan felt an almost unreasonable irritation. This woman nettled him. Perhaps it was the fact that they were too damned similar. She was a whore, certainly, but then, so was he. Each of them sold an illusion to the blacks in exchange for favors. Her illusion was passion, his was friendship. Hell, perhaps Sophia was better than he: in some ways her status might have saved some Irish girl from a similar fate. No matter which way he thought of her, she unsettled him mightily. "Certainly less agreeable work than yours," he replied, instantly regretting the comment.

Sophia stiffened, then smiled sweetly. "I see few calluses on your hands." Then her eyes widened. "Oh! My error—your right is quite calloused. And I see more added in your future." Then she settled a small, satisfied smile on her face and watched the road.

In spite of himself, Aidan had to laugh.

A day later, still half a day from the Zulu holdings, the party of nine reached a sign reading WELCOME TO ABABA, POP. 730. Ababa's architecture was a mixture of Egyptian and Abyssinian styles, turreted castles and adobe domes. The most common building materials were brick, rock, and molded clay. Half the buildings stood two stories or higher.

Sophia hadn't seen a town in months, and was eager to be in even so mean a place as this. Her trip across the Atlantic had been alternately terrifying and exhilarating, the landing in the harbor a bit of a disappointment after the wonders of Alexandria. Abu Ali's estate was incredible, but she had been there for three months now, and her curiosity reached beyond its fences.

She had to learn this world, and her visit to the miserable town of Ababa was a beginning.

The streets were hoof-packed dirt, crowded with horses and camels. Pedestrians strode clay sidewalks rising a few digits from the ground. Slaves, masters of noble birth, and many black commoners mixed on the streets. The thing that she noted most quickly was that the slaves were shabbily clothed, filthy, often pock-marked, thin, and gap-toothed, as if waging a constant battle with starvation. They also kept their eyes down, rarely smiled except nervously, and seemed more . . . *servile* than Dar Kush's servants. They moved as if lost in dream, shuffling at a sluggish pace. They seemed to have had the life and light flogged out of them.

These openmouthed knuckle draggers were beyond pathetic. They were barely human, and the thought that she could end up as one of them made her dizzy and nauseated.

Skin tones were not limited merely to black and white. Natives of dark, ruddy skin and proud bearing walked the streets and seemed to be trading freely. Sophia had seen Turks and Hindus in Alexandria and recognized them. Hindus were almost as dark as the Africans, but with limp hair and more Frankish features. Still, when a dark-skinned, turbaned Hindu walked the clay, white slaves stepped off into the dirt to allow him passage.

A merchant leading a pair of camels blocked their way for a moment, and as the ungainly creatures moped past Sophia saw a sidewalk drama commence. A tall, thin, arrogant black man brushed haughtily against a pitiful young slave boy arranging fruit in the front of a produce stand. The black man lost balance and was forced off the clay into the gutter. "Pig-belly bastard!" he screamed, and grabbed the boy by the arm, yanking him down into the dirt. He jerked a small whip from his belt and began to lash the cowering boy. The sudden explosion of violence ripped Sophia from her reverie. She had seen whippings before—had even suffered them herself. But the randomness as well as the focused, mindless rage vented on the lad made her shrivel.

"No, please—! I sorry. Din't mean no harm—"

Again and again the riding crop lashed down. Sophia watched as if it were all a dream, the whip rising and falling, rising and falling, the red beginning to creep through the frayed and tattered remnants of the boy's white shirt. People on the street stopped and stared, and even the wizened store owner was cowering. Clearly the whip wielder was a local power of some importance, someone used to having things his own way, and no one wanted to interfere with his pleasures.

Please, she pled silently. *Someone stop it.*

No one answered, no one moved—

Except the Wakil. Abu Ali swung down from his mount, and as the townsman began his next downstroke onto a bleeding face, Abu Ali grabbed his whip hand.

"Hold!" he cried. "Is this your man?"

The townsman was as tall as the Wakil, but thinner. In any other context he might have seemed fierce and frightening, but face-to-face with Abu Ali, he seemed frail. "What business is it of yours?"

Abu Ali lowered his voice, so that Sophia could barely hear it. "I have had a long ride. My temper is short, shorter perhaps than yours. If he is not your man, you have no right to damage another's property. And if this is a town where one may strike others at will, perhaps I will try my own hand."

The townsman glared at Abu Ali, but the Wakil's gaze was strong. After a long hesitation, the townsman backed down. His voice turned plaintive. "But this blue-eyed baboon ruined my pants—"

Without breaking eye contact with him for an instant, Abu Ali opened his purse, extracted a gold coin, and tossed it to him. The townsman snatched it from the air.

"Here," he said. "Have them cleaned."

The townsman glared, but bit the coin. Sophia watched his eyes widen a bit at the denomination: it was gold enough to buy three such pairs of pants. Without another word, he scurried along as if afraid the Wakil might change his mind. Abu Ali helped the cringing slave to his feet.

The slave bent deeply, tried to press his lips against the Wakil's feet. "Thank you. Allah bless you, sir."

Abu Ali helped him up. "Be more mindful about your tasks," he said.

"Yes, sir."

Abu Ali returned to his mount. "Well done, Father," Kai said.

"I don't expect my horse to sing or my slaves to think. Allah has granted each a stout back, and I am content with that." Abu Ali rubbed his ample belly. "Coping with fools gives me an appetite. Come, let's eat. I have heard good things about the Empress restaurant." He called to his black attendants. "Majir, Kabwe," he said to two black retainers, "tie up the horses and find us rooms for the night, then join us inside. Aidan—you and Sophia will be cared for in the back."

Watching the entire encounter had been frightening, and more than a little exciting. Had the Wakil interceded to save a boy's hide, or only another man's property? Perhaps a bit of both?

Kai leaned over to Sophia and patted her arm. "You'll be fine," he said.

"What?" she asked, pulled out of her reverie.

"In the restaurant kitchen. They will care for you there."

Sophia smiled broadly and nodded, as if Kai had read her mind.

Kai guessed that the Empress was Ababa's finest and most luxuriant eatery. His father ordered an acceptable combination of shrimp-based *yeassa-wote*, rich with pepper, cinnamon, and cloves, and heaps of *yedinich-selata* salad, tart with onion and lemons. His children and their four freeborn retainers ate while continuing the friendly debate that had begun in the street.

"The question is not whether it is right to own slaves," Abu Ali said. "There have always been slaves. The question is: how does one witness to Allah at all times? *La Ilaha ill Allah.*"

Ali seemed doubtful. "But you allow our slaves to be beaten," he said.

"Only to correct them, that they might serve us better, and in serving us, serve Allah as well." He turned to Elenya. "Pass me the figs, please?"

She did so, and as she did glanced at the wall. Upon it was a picture of the Empress of Abyssinia and her royal family. Lamiya was one of the images, and Elenya spanked her hands together smartly. "Kai, Ali, look! It's Lamiya!" The painting must have been made when Lamiya was only eight or nine: a pointy-nosed, wide-eyed urchin with a perpetually mischievous smile, adorned in silver robes.

When Kai saw it, he winced a bit. Worse, Ali noticed him.

"A poor likeness," Ali said. "Lamiya is far more beautiful."

Abu Ali nibbled at a date. "When she returns, she will be ready to wife. I hope you are ready for the duties of husbanding."

Ali gave a slightly shy smile, an expression that Kai rarely saw on his brother's face. For a moment, he looked more boy than man. "What was your wedding day like, Father?"

Abu Ali leaned back into the deep cushions of the booth and sighed with deep satisfaction. "Your mother was so beautiful a hundred veils could not conceal it. Too beautiful for Allah to allow in this world. She made the sun and the moon jealous." He closed his eyes, slipping into the memory easily. "There is no man who has ever loved his love more than I did that day. Allah grant my work in this world swiftly done, that we might be together again soon."

Aidan sat on the porch at the Empress's back door, savoring the aromas drifting from the kitchen. Within, meals were being prepared with infinite care and great skill by immigrant chefs from Ghana and Cameroon, aided by the usual flotilla of servants.

As Aidan's stomach rumbled, a busboy carried a food platter back through the hanging curtain to the spot where the slaves would take their meals.

Four local slaves clustered about, breaking bread with them. Aidan had immediately noted that they seemed poorly clothed, shod, and fed in comparison to the Wakil's servants. Their accents were so thick that he had difficulty understanding them.

A blond, red-faced streetsweep who introduced himself as Mwaka prodded and pulled at Aidan's simple *djebba* cloak. "'Ooo. Ye dress so swell."

Aidan shrugged, discomfited by the attention. "These are just the clothes we've been given."

Zaso, a chubby woman with nervous eyes and an insincere laugh, examined Sophia's dress covetously. "And ye talk so pretty." She sidled closer. "So, girl. Ye bundle with the mister? That how ye arned the pretties?"

Sophia flinched a bit, apparently just a little frightened by the attention. For once, Aidan noted with satisfaction, she couldn't think of anything to say.

Zaso continued. "I ha' three bairn by old mister, an he never ga'me aught but another fling on me backside."

Mwaka hooted. "Fat as ye are, Zaso, yer lucky ya got that."

She cut him a dark glance. "Ye watch yerself, boyo—next time ye'come aroond, ah'll turn ye right oot."

Aidan tried to catch his balance. "Zaso. That's an African name, isn't it? But you're . . . Irish? Don't you have a Irish name? A Christian name?"

The big woman's bray of laughter triggered another from the men. "Born here, bred here. Don't want no animal Irish pigbelly name. Don't bend knee to some Jew the Egyptians nailed to a cross. Allah, he save me. Bilal, he show me the way."

The other ragged slaves began to murmur "Allah! Allah!"

Mwaka put it more bluntly. "There ain't no God but Allah, an' Muhammad was His man. I put me trust in Bilal, an' if either you say different, we can jus' start up right now, you think yer so swell." He spat on the ground.

Aidan raised his hands, the peacemaker at work. "*La Ilaha ill Allah*, my friend. Share some of our food?"

Mwaka's fierce glare softened. "Yeah, well—why the hell not?"

The plate was heaped with salad and fried shrimp, and the slaves dug their grubby hands in, stuffing their mouths and laughing as they choked it down.

Aidan managed to keep his smile plastered in place, but Sophia seemed to have lost her appetite.

The main meal had already been savored, and the conversation had turned to *satranj*. Kai, his father and brother were enjoying small cups of thick sweet Kenyan coffee. On his father's recommendation Elenya drank hers thinned with milk, but the others' were completely black. Even with her coffee thinned, Elenya's speech had accelerated, and she rattled her small feet against the ground like a Benin drummer. "I favor the Gupta defense, Father. When the Empress's vizier leaves the protection of second Mamluk—"

Kai sighed. *Satranj* again. The girl was obsessed!

Abu Ali held up his hand. Prodigy his sister might be, but his father still had greater understanding of the game's technical aspects. "No, no," he said emphatically. "The Vizier is most useful at the *end* of the game, when minor pieces have been eliminated. That was the mistake that Djidade Berhar made, some years ago . . ."

Kai noticed his father's attention seemed to be wandering, and his dark eyes were focused out through the front window. Kai followed his gaze to see a crowd gathered across the street, in front of the redbrick building housing the Ababa land office, responsible for the dispensation of over a million square miles of real estate. The crowd had been forming for the entire half hour his family had been in the Empress. Kai wasn't certain what was happening, but his father's eyes had narrowed, and that was always a sign to take care.

"—but, Father," Elenya protested. "You yourself used the Gupta when you took regional champion in '68."

The Wakil pulled his attention away from the action across the street to answer his daughter. "Ahh," he said. "My opponent expected a more traditional opening. I deliberately threw him off by mismatching attack and defense, leaving an unfamiliar middle game. By the book, he would win. Our family thrives on improvi—"

He broke off, studying the crowd across the street again, where some of the spectators were waving fists in the air. "There seems to be a problem," he said calmly.

Kai mopped his mouth with a napkin. "Here we go."

"Hush," Ali said.

As they watched, four Aztecs arrived at the land office on horseback. Three men and one woman, all were regal in dress and bearing, wearing feather-crested red and gold robes. The men's robes split to bare their light bronze chests. All four carried steel swords and ceremonial obsidian knives.

Townsfolk at a nearby table bristled.

"Aztec infidels," one whispered.

A townsman next to him made a spitting sound. "I remember Khartum. What nerve to come here!"

Ali's hand strayed to his knife, but the Wakil's hand clamped his wrist, to stay him.

"They must be leasing land," Ali said. "This crowd could start another war."

The tallest of the Aztecs looked at Kai through the window, and they locked gazes. The Aztec's eyes were like coals. Kai could not match his gaze and looked away. The Aztec warrior gave a dismissive shrug and dismounted.

"I spit on them!" a diner at the next table muttered. He wore a bright green robe and had a single scarred eye, won perhaps in some long-forgotten skirmish with the Aztecs. "They steal our land, and then sell it back?"

The second townsman groped for the blade at his waist. "The Ulema has the right of it. We should pay their price—in blood."

Abu Ali raised his hands high. "Men," he said. "Listen to me. We paid a sore price for the peace. If we have war again, let it be for higher reason than this!"

"You took the side of a slave against Fazul," the second townsman said. "Who the devil are you?"

Abu Ali seemed to swell, but when he spoke his voice was deadly calm, almost a whisper. "Wakil Abu Ali Jallaleddin ibn Rashid al Kushi. Watch your tongue, dog."

Their shocked expressions told Kai they recognized the name. "We meant no disrespect, sir. But this is our district, and not a year ago, those murdering pigs burned a farm in Kwami province. We can't just let them dance into town!"

One-Eye leaned over to his companions. "Perhaps," he said to them more quietly, "this is best discussed amongst ourselves . . . outside." Without another word, the three men left their table. One-Eye slapped a few coins down to settle their bill, and they exited through the front door.

For a few seconds, no one spoke. Then Kai leaned over and said quietly, "Father, what do we do?"

Abu Ali settled back down. "Finish our coffee," he said.

Reluctantly, Ali and Kai settled back to their Kenyan. Abu Ali sipped, but his slitted eyes continued to watch the front window, and the street beyond. Ali had to crane his head around to see. His father rapped Ali's knuckles. "I have eyes for both of us. Drink."

Ali and Kai drank, but Elenya was only pretending to sip now, her eyes saucer-wide. Kai's blood boiled with tension. Would this situation explode? Would he finally see his father in combat? Of course, he had seen the Wakil in practice, with both Ali and Malik. Despite his greater girth, the Wakil and his brother were closely matched, and Malik had to exert himself fully to gain any advantage, a wondrous and terrifying sight. But despite those exhilarating memories, Kai had never seen his father's legendary skills in mortal application.

When they completed their meal, the restaurant's owner, a bushman of fine proportions who stood no taller than their waist, presented them with the bill.

"I wanted to thank you for the fine repast," the Wakil said.

"You are most welcome," replied the little man. "It is an honor to serve the illustrious Abu Ali."

The Wakil inclined his head magnanimously and began to speak, but suddenly there was a roar from the street. Abu Ali's head whipped around. "I believe it is time for us to go," he said. "Kai—stay and pay the owner. Elenya, remain with your brother."

"Oh, Father . . ."

He held up his hand, shushing her. "Ali," he said almost formally. "Would you accompany me?"

Ali wiped his mouth and stood. Kai's heart trip-hammered. Fear for his family, disappointment that he was not to prove his own manhood, relief that the burden was on stronger shoulders than his own. "Gladly, Father."

Kai put a wad of bills on the table, waited until his father and brother had left the restaurant, and then went immediately to the window. This, he had no intention of missing.

Elenya pressed her face to the window beside him, her eyes wide, her palms pressed flat against the glass. Kai looked down at her, wondering if he should warn her away—what followed might well be unpleasant. Then he realized that he would have to rope her to the table to prevent her from watching. Even then, she might chew through the ropes.

From his vantage point within the Empress, Kai watched the four Aztecs as they walked through the land office's front curtain. They scanned the crowd with no apparent sign of emotion, despite its obvious hostility. The plumed warriors seemed utterly disdainful.

"Kill the cannibal *kufiran!*" one of the crowd yelled, and hurled a brick at the Aztec with the most impressive plumage. The Aztec slid his head a digit or two to the side and the brick hurtled past and shattered the land office's front window.

The crowd roared its disappointment. "Kill them all!"

Before a full-scale riot could erupt, the Wakil and his son interposed themselves between the mob and its intended victims.

Abu Ali raised his hands. "No!" he yelled. Again Kai had the strange sense that his father was actually swollen, had somehow increased his size. "The Treaty of Kwami clearly states that the Aztecs may lease their land at fair price with safe conduct."

"*We* didn't sign that damned paper!" someone in the crowd shouted.

The Wakil fixed his gaze on the shouter scornfully. "I *did*. I, and my brother, and a dozen other landowners and men you are sworn to obey. Attack these men, and you are dishonoring my house, and that I will not allow."

Suddenly, from the corner of his eye, Kai caught a flash of bright green, and he shifted his gaze to an alley next to the land office. Green robes. It was the three restaurant patrons, who had exited earlier to play an assassin's game. Slowly and steadily, they were working their way into sword range.

When he had worked a bit closer, the scarred man screamed "Hai!" and lunged at the tallest Aztec's back.

For all his years of training, Kai could barely decipher the blur of motion that followed. One, two, three whirlwind strokes. Abu Ali half severed the head of one man, sent a second's arm flopping into the dust, and whirled to meet One-Eye only to find that Ali had already pierced his heart with a cubit of good Benin steel.

Ali withdrew his blade and One-Eye sagged to his knees, mouth drooling a crimson stream into the dust. One-Eye collapsed onto his side and was still.

Kai found himself halfway out the door before stopping again, his urge to aid his family balanced with the need to obey his father.

Ali was staring fixedly at the blood on the blade. "Ali!" Abu Ali said sharply, jarring his eldest son from his reverie. The Wakil pulled his pistol from his waist and cocked it.

Kai watched, goggle-eyed.

Abu Ali's blade had tasted blood, and he held it on high, fully aware of the spectacle he made. The crowd was thunderstruck, fear and awe mingling to paralyze. Good. Ungoverned fear turns men into sheep, and sheep responded swiftly to a strong shepherd. "Whoever moves next against this family, when he stands before Allah will be judged a suicide. Do not test me."

The crowd grumbled, but the evidence of his intent was plain before them. If heaven was kind, there would be no more death this day. There was a disturbance at the back of the crowd, signaling the arrival of the local constabulary.

The man was all feathers and attitude. Constable indeed! Abu Ali wouldn't have such a peacock guard his henhouse. "What is this?" he said. "Disperse!" The captain was a tall man, of brown complexion. The Wakil detected a touch of chalk in his limp hair and sharp nose, and the pomposity of his quasi-military bearing suggested a festering insecurity. He examined the corpses, and then stood imperiously. "Who killed these men?"

The Wakil made the slightest bow that courtesy demanded. "I, Wakil Abu Ali," he said. "And you are?"

The captain clicked his heels. "Captain Banjul, at your service." The name suddenly seemed to register with him. "Wakil," he said. "Your fame precedes you. An honor to have you in our humble town."

Abu Ali was less than impressed. Ababa was a small town, but important: the land office coordinated leases for thousands of farmers and quarrymen. He expected better than this mixed-breed fop. "An honor sullied by blood. Where were you when this family needed protection?"

Banjul took the Wakil aside. Ali peered after them, as if trying to overhear. The Aztecs stood impassively, as if there had never been a threat. "Sir—feelings run a bit hot around here. Certainly you can understand—"

Abu Ali snapped his fingers in a dismissive gesture. "I understand that you were appointed to keep the peace. These men entered your town on legal business, and deserved the protection of the law."

Banjul sputtered, obviously outraged at the reprimand, but managed to restrain his anger. "Yes . . . *sir*," he said. He turned his back, collecting himself, and then swirled to face the crowd again. "All right!" he yelled. "Return to your homes and businesses. Disperse immediately!"

Satisfied, the Wakil returned to the land office. Elenya ran through the crowd to meet him. "Father! Are you all right?"

Abu Ali felt a thrill of alarm at the sight of his only daughter exposing herself to harm. He swiftly clamped a protecting arm around her shoulders. "Quite well."

The Wakil turned to the Aztec warrior. Judging by the wrinkles around his almond eyes he was in his forties, his woman the same age. Her hair was straight and black as coal, her eyes like flakes of gold dancing in a green pool. The skin on her throat was weathered and sun-beaten, but her mouth was the sort of proud, haughty line that never faltered, even in the face of danger.

Magnificent, he thought.

His eyes locked with the tallest of them. "Your way is clear," he said.

The Aztec inclined his regal head. Abu Ali noted that, although none of the four had drawn swords, their palms rested lightly near the hilts in relaxed readiness. He could almost believe that they had never been in real danger at all. They returned to their horses, mounted, and trotted out of town with their retinue.

Ali produced a folded leather square, and with it cleansed the blood from his sword. "What do you think, Father?" The Wakil noted that his eldest son's hands trembled. That was understandable: this was the first time Ali had taken a human life, and no good man could do that without glimpsing the eye of Allah. In time, every true warrior made peace with his own mortality. Taking a life with righteous cause is no sin: both slayer and slain would stand for judgment on that last great day, and all truths would be known.

When Ali had finished, Abu Ali held out his hand, and his son gave him the cloth. "I think I do not like this town."

"You did well, my son."

Ali's mouth twitched upward in the slightest of smiles, and they clasped hands wrist to wrist.

Aidan and Sophia had emerged from behind the restaurant, the more servile slaves with them, gawking.

"Come!" Ali called to them. "We go."

Mwaka whispered to Aidan. "That yer mister?" Aidan nodded. The slave seemed to be awestruck. "Well . . . ye git, then."

Aidan helped Sophia onto the wagon as Kai and his family mounted their mares. With a final look at the town of Ababa, they were off.

CHAPTER THIRTY

SOPHIA SAID LITTLE FOR THE FIRST HOUR after they left the town. "Poor pitiful bastards," Aidan said, echoing her own private thoughts. "Their only language was Arabic. They'd forgotten their God. Malik and Berhar don't take as much away from their slaves."

Malik and Berhar are influenced by the Wakil, she wanted to say. *If you had traveled, you would know.*

She could not take her mind from the pitiful wrecks she had seen in the town, human in form only. They had forgotten everything about themselves. For all the misery of her own existence, she knew who and what she was, knew that this was not her natural station, knew that her aspirations were hers, and not merely thoughts and dreams imprinted in her mind through pain and discipline. "Why does the Wakil allow his people to keep so much of themselves? It is not common."

Abu Ali was on horseback again, and riding marginally closer to the wagon. Still, she doubted if he could hear. Aidan seemed to ponder her words. "Kai told me once that his father believes that men may serve men, but that our souls belong to God. Abu Ali commands our labor, but not our souls. Or so he said."

She thought for a while before speaking again. There had been three official dinners since her arrival at Dar Kush, and Sophia had lurked close enough to hear the guests' whispers. They thought the Wakil "coddled" his servants. They especially seemed offended that the Wakil allowed Ghost Town its grove and worship services. A strange man. "It is . . . harder for him, isn't it?"

Aidan nodded. "There are many who oppose his ways." Then he grinned. "I'm not complaining, though. Are you?"

"No," Sophia said sincerely. "I think he is a great man."

For half the next day, they were traveling through the *kraal*, the personal holdings of Cetshwayo, brother of famed colonel Shaka Zulu. They suffered a brief burst of rain, which served to both muddy the roads and settle the dust. They passed vast green and yellow fields of teff and corn, and logging roads stretching up to the low, jagged iron gray western hills. Here and there, groups of slaves were monitored by overseers. There seemed to be little central organization to Cetshwayo's holdings, more like a series of smaller villages branching from the central homestead like rings of mushrooms sprouting from a central stalk.

The slaves looked ragged in comparison to the Wakil's, even more hollow-eyed and desperate than those in Ababa. Sophia felt herself wilt as she met their eyes, realizing how easy it would have been for her to fall into the hands of men who would make her present owners seem saintly.

The slaves eyed the Wakil's party as it rambled past the endless rows of a marshy bamboo field. A leather-skinned woman in her fifties studied Aidan's jacket, and Sophia's dress, compared them to her own crudely stitched rags, and spat into the dust.

Sophia couldn't find it in her heart to be angered. She watched an overseer pawing at a chubby, yellow-haired slave girl who couldn't have been older than fourteen. He touched the girl's breasts, probed her backside. The man made a coarse jest, and she reddened and fled as the men laughed. Sophia knew that sunset would bring an unwelcome visitor to the girl's door.

Sophia's heart ached. Whatever her personal miseries, what this girl, and women outside the Wakil's protection, suffered was certainly hell itself.

The girl didn't understand how to play the men off against each other, or to turn his sexual excitation into laughter, to trick him into remembering his own mother and sisters, or any of the thousand other maneuvers she had learned in preparation for her role. Painfully and shamefully at first, Sophia had been brought to understand her sensuality and its power, to understand it better than any man she was ever likely to meet. That simple understanding gave her leverage, even when logic and reason said she should be powerless.

But these girls . . . she knew, could *feel* that they were the lowest kind of sexual chattel, and for just a moment allowed their terror to touch her heart. It coursed through her dizzyingly, and she wanted reassurance, wanted Kai to hold her, tell her that she was more than that. Always more than that.

She looked over at him, enjoying the ride and the day, tall in the saddle, handsome in his white *djebba* and leather pants. He was not the elder son, the one who would bear primary responsibility for continuing the lineage. But . . . if she could only maintain control, his heart would remain in her hands, and she might well earn freedom, or even more . . .

She needed more allies. Would Aidan prove one? She had hoped that she would find others, but she was viewed with suspicion and resentment by the women at the Wakil's residence. There would be even fewer allies outside that immediate environment, both because they were too distant to help and because, it was increasingly obvious, the gap between her station and theirs triggered nothing but resentment.

So she was neither fish nor fowl, neither free nor slave. And was therefore more alone than any of them.

The Wakil led them through a wooden gate constructed of weathered logs. The cross-beam above their heads sported six skulls that Kai could not recognize, some kind of horned animal. As they passed beneath the sun-bleached skulls, he turned to his brother and said, "Brother—what manner of beasts are those?"

"Savannah buffalo." Ali's voice filled with pure excitement. "Prepare yourself, little brother. We shall return home with tales to tell!"

Runners preceded them, carrying messages back to the distant ranch, and before they had traveled down the dirt road another hour they crested a hill. On its far side stood a hundred warriors. Their muscular chests were bare save for necklaces of beads or cow tails. Zebra and antelope skins had been fashioned into loincloths or kilts. Their feet were bare, or sandaled. Some wore broad *isicoco* rings bound into their hair, denoting marriage. All carried *umkhonto* spears, not swords or muskets, and Kai knew that this was a purely ceremonial greeting, that here within the *kraal* they occasionally entertained themselves or guests by dressing as their ancestors had.

They pounded the butts of their spears rhythmically against the ground, chanting and stamping their feet. Kai was awed. Certainly he had known Zulus, and had heard of their prowess. But never had he encountered them on their own ground. There was something about them that was actually frightening, and he gripped his reins tightly, straightened his spine, composed his face, and showed as little emotion as possible.

As the procession passed, the warriors trotted into line behind them.

Alarm warred with wonder in Kai's heart, but wonder triumphed. The chanting, running, and stomping was fascinating. These Zulu carried no modern weapons, no rifles or tempered steel swords. With their headdresses and painted faces, keloid scars and tattoos, absolute physical and psychological readiness, they were as their ancestors had been for hundreds of years—the finest fighting men on the planet.

By Kai's estimate the procession went on for four miles before they reached the outlying barns, where they were met by the grooms. "Please," a thin, white-haired attendant said. "Rest here, and the master will join you shortly."

Kai dismounted, and was happy to do it: he loved riding, but they had been on the road for three and a half days. Frankly, his rump was sore.

They led the mares into the barn. As he was settling Djinna into a comfortable stall, Kai heard a snorting sound behind him. He turned to see a magnificent black Zulu stallion. From fetlock to mane the Zulu seemed more an elemental force than a mere beast. It tossed its head angrily, challengingly, as if aware of its impact on humans. "Father," Kai murmured. "If Djinna is a spirit, this one is a demon!"

From behind him came a voice as strong as his own, but edged with honey. "His name is Mnyama, Black One. He is the finest stallion for a thousand miles."

He turned, and despite himself, his heartbeat increased in speed. A girl, almost as tall as he, emerged from the shadows. She wore no makeup or facial paint, and needed none. Her eyes were wide and deep and filled with laughter, her nose generous, her lips full and curled in a half smile. Her cheekbones were high, her ears small and delicately shaped. A single golden braid surrounded her neck: no multiple strands, no gems or strands of other precious metals, just that single braid, as if any further ornamentation would draw the eye away from the perfection of her face and form. She wore a golden flower-print dress that seemed a winding of fabric from her knees to her shoulders, modest and yet at the same time deeply sensual.

"Nandi?" he asked, pulling her name from the depths of memory. How she had grown! He had only met her twice, the first time on his father's birthday ten years before. Cetshwayo's daughter had been a shy, awkward thing then. There was nothing awkward about her now!

Nor was she shy. Unlike any Muslim maiden he could imagine, Nandi was unhesitatingly evaluating him in return: no fawnlike eyelash fluttering or bashful head turning here. If he knew his father, a bit of matchmaking was in the works. Was this the Wakil's idea of a *feqer näfs*, a soul mate? If so, Allah give him strength!

Abu Ali flung his arms wide. "Nandi!" he called.

"Uncle!" she responded with unfeigned warmth, and embraced him. Behind them, chuckling fondly, came Cetshwayo. He had once been as lean as Shaka, but was now heavier, and limped to favor his left leg. His moon face bore three horizontal scars on each cheek, and his shaven scalp betrayed a few gray bristles. "Abu Ali!" he cried, throwing his arms wide. "Welcome to my home."

"Ngiyabonga." Thank you.

"Wamukelekile." It is my pleasure.

"It has been far too long," Abu Ali said, and the two friends clasped arms. "Little Nandi has become a rare flower. Has she not, Kai?"

Abu Ali raised an eyebrow at Kai, encouraging him to join in the pleasurable speculation. Somewhat to his surprise, he felt a stirring in his loins that was almost embarrassing. He couldn't take his eyes from her mouth. What would it feel like, taste like, to kiss those lips, to feel them part and welcome him? And merciful Allah, what of her other lips? What peerless embrace might they offer as well?

Senses swimming, Kai managed a polite nod of agreement. Ali had moved around behind Nandi, managing to examine her flank without betraying his intention to her father. He gave Kai a secretive, approving grin.

Nandi strode boldly to Kai, standing closely enough for him to smell her perfume. Her scent was like cocoa and honey, with a touch of wild, sweet grass. "How long has it been, Kai?"

He had to be careful not to stutter. "Since . . . Idd-el-Fitr, four years ago . . ."

"Yes," she said. "Too long." Then, as if timing their interaction to the second, she turned and left the barn. Abu Ali coughed politely as his younger son gawked. Elenya and Ali spanked the backs of their right hands against their left palms in appreciation.

The five of them left the barn, talking amongst themselves, leaving Aidan and Sophia behind them. Aidan was nominally inspecting the younger of the Wakil's mares, but managed to eye the retreating Nandi as he did. And as he did, was amused at the way Sophia seethed at Kai's reactions to the Shaka's exquisite niece.

"Beautiful creature," he said, examining the mare.

Sophia pretended to give the horse her full attention. "Her rump is immense," she said.

"Some might say that makes for a smoother ride."

Sophia growled at him and stalked away, fists clinched, her tight little backside switching angrily.

There was something about Sophia that intrigued Aidan, some combination of sensuality and reserve that he had never encountered before. Something that reminded him of . . . who?

An image came to mind, fleeting. The image of Mahon and Deirdre holding each other. Kissing. So natural, so right, bodies molding like two halves of a melon fitting together . . .

Strange, that. Never had he had such a sense with any other woman, and he had known many. And now that the image was in mind, it seemed that he couldn't banish it.

Somehow, being here, many miles from the pitiful little home he had created for himself, the tiny oasis of sanity in an insane world, surrounded by the wealth of Zulus who would consider him less than a goat or horse, his isolation and loneliness struck him like an avalanche, so suddenly that his knees sagged.

He had *nothing*. Kai had everything, and didn't appreciate what he had . . .

But that didn't justify what Aidan was thinking now, didn't make rational the emotions surging in his wounded heart.

Nothing did.

But it didn't matter at all.

CHAPTER THIRTY-ONE

CETSHWAYO'S OLD HUNTING INJURY prevented him from riding, but his twin sons Keefah and Darbul wouldn't have missed a hunt for a fistful of Alexanders. So as the sun dipped low above the *kraal*, Kai and seven highborn men, Zulus and Abyssinian alike, gathered their restless mounts in a mesquite flat abutting a conifer woodland. A dozen lean, alert Zulus accompanied them afoot.

The lead hunter was Shaka Zulu himself, a giant of a man who rode like a centaur. He raised his brawny arms—an ornate spear in one hand, a hunting bow in the other, with a quiver on his back—and screamed to the moonless sky. "Let the hunt begin!"

Like Darbul and Keefah, the unmounted warriors were lean, muscular, agile men, trained from infancy to be athletes on a par with any in the world. They gripped short stabbing *umkhonto* with elongated steel blades. Kai recalled Malik's sober evaluation of Zulu skill: *"Avoid close-quarter combat if there is any chance at all."*

"And if I cannot?"

"Then consign your soul to Allah and prepare to enter Paradise. Just do your best to ensure you reach those gates together."

Abu Ali, Ali, and Kai carried rifles as well as spears. Despite her pleas, Elenya remained behind at Cetshwayo's mansion. On a normal hunt the Wakil might have considered allowing her to accompany them. "Why can Nandi go?" Elenya had pouted.

Cetshwayo himself had overheard that last and had laughed heartily after Elenya stalked out of the room. "In the old country, Nandi would not ride to the hunt." He sighed. "But this New World gives girls airs. What can I say? I can't control her any longer." He dug his elbow into Kai's ribs hard enough to make the boy chuff air. "I wish you better luck!"

Shaka's white teeth shone in the torchlight. "Only here and on the battlefield do I feel so alive."

Abu Ali pulled up next to him. Kai's family rode Cetshwayo's mounts, specially bred hunting stallions of imposing strength and size. Kai's seemed responsive to a feather touch of his knees, and Abu Ali already rode his as if he had raised the monster from a colt.

Abu Ali glanced doubtfully at Shaka's spear. "Can you really make the kill with such a weapon?"

Shaka's broad, scarred face glowed with amusement. "You had best hope so, my friend."

Distantly, there came the mournful wail of the hunting horn.

Shaka grew ruminative. "We bring the calves five thousand miles and raise them here, that we might honor the ways of our ancestors. He dies today. Perhaps he will claim one of us as well. Haiii!"

With the suddenness of a lightning stroke he wheeled his horse about, as if sensing something that the others had missed completely. Abruptly, out of the brush not three dozen cubits away charged two hundred *sep* of the most fearsome creature Kai had ever seen in his life. Its black horns looked as if they could punch holes in steel, its breath snorted from its broad wet nostrils in clouds of condensation, its hooves furrowed the earth.

Savannah buffalo. Magnificent, and the most dangerous game animal on the African continent. Crafty, powerful, and fast, the buffalo had killed more hunters than lions and leopards combined, and had no natural predators—save men like Shaka Zulu.

Abu Ali's face went grim and he reined his horse closer to Ali. "They are insane," he whispered. "Hold back a bit. Give Shaka and his men the honor of first contact."

"Gladly." Even gallant Ali looked unnerved.

Kai was still formulating his answer when Nandi rode past them. Her tan riding pants were unadorned, as simply functional as any of the men's. Somehow, the garb merely enhanced her sensuality.

As she passed Kai she spurred her steed and grinned back at him.

As the very wind of her passage ruffled his face, Kai felt her call: primal and wild and stronger than he had anticipated. He felt dizzied. "You would have me marry into this family, Father?" Kai called to Abu Ali. "They are all mad." *And perhaps I am as well*, he thought. "Hai!"

Kai spurred his own horse forward into the fray.

Ali laughed. "Allah, preserve us! I think the boy is in love." And raced after his younger brother.

The footmen's shielded, gas-burning lanterns probed the darkness, but deep patches of shadow remained in the forest. Death lurked within them.

Shaka, his nephews and footmen worked forward in a practiced arc, clearing one segment of grass after another. The buffalo seemed to have disappeared.

Kai's heart was in his throat. How could so large a beast vanish so completely? Twice he had seen the buffalo erupt out of shadows, and the mounted Zulus had scattered, hooting, as its horns came within digits of their horses. Insanity! Worse yet, they treated it almost like a game. Almost. These men were in the finest, highest physical condition he had ever witnessed. Clearly, they were competing with each other not only physically, but in display of courage. And Nandi was right in the thick of it. What manner of man could ever control such a woman?

There! Their prey had raised up again, and snorted as it charged. One of Shaka's footmen thrust at the beast with a spear, and it wheeled, hitting the man from the side. This time, the hunter was unable to spin out of the way, and the horn pierced his ribs. With a despairing wail, the footman collapsed bleeding into the tall grass.

Two more men veered in, jabbing, and the buffalo turned. Shaka galloped back in. "Hold!" he cried. "He is mine!"

Deferentially, the footmen backed away. Almost as if it understood that some ultimate moment had arrived, the beast pawed the earth and faced Shaka. Had the Zulus trained it for such an encounter? Did they somehow prepare the calves to provide such moments of drama? Certainly no wild beast would behave in such a manner. Kai glimpsed, and in a shadowy manner understood, something new about the culture whose daughter he was to marry.

Kai and Nandi were eighty cubits to the side, and Kai was ready to wheel and run for it if the monster broke in his direction. But he was also transfixed by its power, by its lethal sweep of horns and breadth of shoulder. In the darkness, partially lit by torches, it seemed more a creature of myth than reality, and Shaka some conquering hero of legend, not a man of flesh and bone.

Shaka and Keefah drew their bows, pulling steadily . . .

Suddenly, as if finally comprehending its danger, the animal flickered its tail and turned, vanishing into the high grass. As it turned, Shaka loosed his first arrow and it struck behind the buffalo's shoulder. Keefah's shaft, only a moment later, missed the flank and drove into the ground. Roaring with pain and anger, the buffalo made a *chuffing* sound as it disappeared.

Bearing lanterns and spears, the footmen beat the long grass, pushing ahead in a horseshoe configuration. They were supported by horsemen, all holding to the rigid pattern.

Shaka rode along the outside, striving for position. When their prey tried to break away, it was herded back with shouts and spears. The buffalo seemed confused, but far from fatigued.

Shaka raced for a shooting position ahead of his prey, but without warning the animal changed course, racing back straight for the footmen. With insane courage they thrust their spears, shone their lights in its eyes and shouted. Again it wheeled, running for the open, where Shaka waited, bow drawn.

Then the beast doubled back again, suddenly ignoring the shouts and spear thrusts. Several of the men cast their *umkhontos*. Two struck the beast, the hafts flagging out from its back and side like dreadful bamboo stalks, blood running black in the darkness.

The center man was little more than a boy, perhaps seventeen summers. He lost his nerve, cast poorly as the buffalo came straight at him, and missed his mark completely. The men scattered as it charged their line. The beast caught the boy who had missed his cast, gouging his back and sending him flying.

The boy landed hard in the grass, screaming and thrashing, reaching back spastically for the bleeding wound.

"Fool!" Shaka yelled as he rode by. There was a sheen of madness on his face now. His eyes were too wide, lips pulled tight against his white teeth. The footmen had been left behind now—it was up to the horsemen.

Shaka was racing beside the wounded prey now. He gripped his bow and aimed, horse and buffalo seeming to match each other stride for stride.

He released his bolt, and it entered just behind the left shoulder. The buffalo stumbled, rose again, and thundered on. Shaka released a second arrow. As it struck, the buffalo's knees crumpled, and it dove nose-first into the ground with an earth-shaking impact that would have shattered a lesser creature's spine.

Kai held his breath, unable to fully grasp what he had just witnessed, beyond any doubt the most intense experience of his young life. Allah preserve him! He did not even know that men such as these existed!

Shaka raised his hands to the stars. "Haii!"

"Who is the greatest hunter in all creation?" Darbul roared.

And his footmen, gasping now as they caught up with him, cheered in expected response. Shaka trotted his horse over to his trophy—

And it lurched up, catching Shaka's horse in the belly with its left horn. Mortally wounded and neighing in agony, his mount tumbled over backward, and Shaka spilled. Despite his awesome athleticism he crashed awkwardly to earth.

Shaka seemed momentarily dazed, disoriented, and for a moment the entire party was frozen, as if they shared his confusion. As Shaka's mount whined pitiably, the buffalo lurched to its feet. In that instant it could have slain Shaka, but instead it seemed to stare at him, blood drooling from its nose.

The Zulu's face was gaunt and strained. Kai knew that in that moment Shaka Zulu, great hunter, great warrior, was gazing into the face of his own death, and that his soul had recoiled from the awful sight.

Then, twin shots rang out. The buffalo staggered to its knees, then collapsed onto its side.

Kai turned, startled. His father and brother both had their rifles to their shoulders. Smoke drifted from both barrels.

Composing himself as best he could, Shaka rose. His limbs trembled a bit. Perhaps it was the chill of night, but Kai thought otherwise. Shaka gave a perfunctory nod of thanks to Abu Ali and his son, and walked on unsteady legs to the buffalo.

Kai found himself looking deep into the beast's eyes. The mighty buffalo's breath huffed in painful bursts. Its black eyes were filmed with dust. Kai's next reaction startled him. This poor thing had been stolen in childhood from its native land, raised only to die for the entertainment of its captors. It had struggled for freedom and life, that Kai could understand. Pointless and absurd as it seemed, he wanted to tell the felled creature *well done*.

Shaka snatched a spear from one of his men and drove it into the wounded beast's side. It heaved in pain. Shaka bore down with all his weight, working the spear back and forth until the heart was pierced and the buffalo lay still.

Shaka raised his arms in victory, yelling in musical, staccato Zulu. The men replied in kind.

"Ngikhuluma isiZulu kancane," Kai said haltingly to Nandi. *I speak only a bit of Zulu.* "What did he say?"

"He said that this was no ordinary creature, it was a demon, and in slaying it he has become more than a man." Her eyes shone with admiration. She had apparently seen nothing that was not glorious, nothing in the least disturbing in her uncle's behavior. Was that pragmatism? An understanding that even the bravest men know fear? Or delusion, an inability to acknowledge what she had seen? He wasn't sure which, and that uncertainty troubled him.

To Kai's gaze, Shaka had not yet fully recovered, and his trembling was not from the cold. His men apparently noticed nothing of their leader's momentary weakness. They cheered, beating their spears against the ground. Kai and his family smiled politely, but shared searing sidelong glances.

Shaka wrenched his spear from the dead animal's side. Its tip glistened black with blood. He rubbed his finger slowly along the edge. Ignoring his dying horse, Shaka then ran to the spot where his second man had been injured. Kai broke his mount into a trot to keep up.

The wounded youth was curled onto his side like an injured lizard, his right arm still groping back for the bleeding wound.

"You are hurt," Shaka said coldly.

The wounded man looked up at Shaka, his teeth chattering.

"Your stupidity could have killed me," Shaka continued, in a conversational tone.

The wounded man said something in Zulu. Kai had the very clear impression that he was begging for his life.

Shaka spoke to him in the same language, his face calm and comforting. Then with shocking suddenness he raised the spear and thrust it deeply into the hunter's stomach. Kai's stomach fisted as the boy's body arched, as if trying to take the spear more deeply into his belly. Then with dreadful finality, he went limp.

Kai felt dizzy and sick with rage.

"Allah preserve us!" Abu Ali said in disbelief. "What have you done?"

Shaka withdrew the spear and wiped it on the dead boy's chest. "What is my right." He shrugged as if it was of little consequence. "He would have died in some days. To die on your king's spear is an honor."

The Wakil's face was as stone. "There are no kings in Bilalistan."

Shaka grinned and pointed to his men, who had moved to encircle the party. "Tell *them*," he said.

Kai scanned them. Fourteen now, standing proud and silent, chests high, gripping their spears, ready to kill or die for the man they followed. Kai felt a deep and pervasive cold seeping into his bones.

"There were kings in the days of my fathers," Shaka said. "Mark well—there may be again."

His mood had shifted completely, as if killing the hunter had purged him of all stress. He turned to his men. "Bring me the head! Put my steed from its misery. Bear your brother on a stretcher, he burns tomorrow."

Shaka ordered one of his men off his horse and mounted without a trace of hesitation. If he had been injured in the fall, the injury was already forgotten. His men scrambled to fulfill his orders.

Abu Ali and his sons rode together quietly, watching. Nandi pulled her horse up next to Shaka, clearly worshipful. "Uncle," she said. "You were wonderful. But weren't you afraid?"

Shaka Zulu rode proudly. "Nandi, fear is neither ally nor enemy. I never see fear, my child."

Ali whispered in Kai's ear: "You cannot see what lives behind your own eyes."

"Father," Kai said. "What do we do?"

Abu Ali shook his head. "The Zulus are allies of the Empress—and Shaka is as much royalty as Lamiya. On their land, it is their world. We can do nothing."

They watched the dead man rolled onto a stretcher. His eyes were open and turned up. Blood leaked from his side.

"It is not right," Kai said quietly.

"No, it is not," agreed Abu Ali. "But it is done."

CHAPTER THIRTY-TWO

DINNER THAT NIGHT WAS A FINE ZULU FEAST: mountains of *inkukhu-bhakiwe* baked chicken, *inyama yezinyane lemvu-yosiwe* roast lamb, and *amazambane* potatoes and *imbuba* beans with corn meal, served by an army of slaves. Nandi was seated next to Kai, wearing a modest white-print wraparound emblazoned with crimson buffalo horns. In this setting she was far more restrained, deferring to her father, uncle, and brothers in a fashion that was disorientingly demure. Her every gesture was calculated and fluid, and Kai found himself nearly wondering if he had actually seen this delicate creature indulging in the bloody pleasures of the hunt.

She intrigued him. She was every bit as cultured as Lamiya, but it was impossible to forget what she had been in the previous hours. The exquisite darkness of her face seemed to dissolve her into the night, so that all he could see was her energy, her almost overwhelming *aliveness*. She was unlike any other woman he had ever known . . . or even known *about*.

And that reaction in his heart both confused and gladdened him, because any fool could see what was in the air. Cetshwayo and his brother Shaka were the most powerful men in northern New Djibouti, and Abu Ali wished to join Dar Kush to Cetshwayo's *kraal*. If Kai wished to remain in his father's graces, he would agree to the plan.

Cetshwayo and Abu Ali ate heartily of *imbuzi* goat ragout, talking business and laughing. Keefa and Darbul sat on either side of their father.

"The hunt sounds glorious," Cetshwayo said. "Damn this leg!"

"Oh, Father," Nandi purred. "You would have loved it."

Shaka hoisted a glass of fermented cow's milk. Kai was glad that, as a Muslim, he could beg off the imbibing of spiritous drinks and settle for springwater. "He was a great one," Shaka said. "Perhaps the equal of he who took your leg. I give you his head."

Cetshwayo hoisted his glass in salute. "To the *kraal!*" he said.

"The *kraal!*" Shaka repeated. And they drank. The Wakil and his sons had been relatively quiet during the dinner, and perhaps Shaka sensed that. "Wakil! I hear you had adventure yesterday, in Ababa."

"The Aztecs," Abu Ali said modestly. "Yes."

Although Kai's father was reticent, Ali seemed eager to talk about it. "I tell you, he was five cubits tall. I do believe Father struck to save the crowd from *him!*"

Cetshwayo's largest son Keefah snorted. "They die like any other men."

Darbul, the shorter and squatter of the two, laughed in agreement. "Uncle Shaka says the time will come when we will push them back across the Swazi and give their feathered God all the hearts it can eat."

"I hope it won't come to that," Kai said sincerely, then paused, cursing his callowness. This was one of the first occasions in which he was being treated like a man, able to hunt and speak with the other men, not re-stricted to near silence like his sister. And his first comment had flirted with cowardice.

Nandi looked at him curiously. "Aren't you eager to fight?"

"I know this one," Cetshwayo said, reaching along the table to grab Kai's arm. Despite his infirmity, his grip was like the jaws of a crocodile. "He has the hell in him. He has the Blood, like his father and his uncle."

The Wakil seemed uncomfortable. "Cetshwayo, I—"

Shaka cut him off. "Modest, the whole family! Or scared of the fire in their veins. Has your father never told you the story of Khartum?"

"Of course," Kai and Ali said together, and then laughed. Their father was looking at the table.

Shaka leaned forward. "Something tells me that you don't know the whole story. Your father. Your uncle. And me. Haii! What a day that was, a day when the Aztecs poured over the walls, looking to feed our hearts to their god. Corpses to the hip, boy! We were men no longer, we were lions, mad with blood, hungry for more, in that red place all men should experience once in their lives."

"Please," Abu Ali said. "Al-Wadud, the Loving One, has taken that beast from my heart."

"You deny your nature," Shaka said. Kai had the distinct sense that he was enjoying the Wakil's discomfort. "The beast *is* your heart. Wait until the horn sounds—Kai will be first into the fray." He raised his cup, look-ing from Kai to Nandi, laughing again.

Nandi looked away shyly, and Kai's heart pounded. Was that beast within him? Could Nandi see something within him that he himself did not see, and was she responding to it? If that was what she needed in a man, he hoped that the blood of lions ran in his veins, for he was certain that the marriage deal had been struck.

Oh, well . . . he had to admit that if Nandi was the burden he was bound to bear, it might have been far heavier. He hoped he would be able to keep Sophia. Traditional Zulu men often practiced polygamy, but as their women became more educated, that custom had become less common.

That thought had just barely formed in his mind when he felt something soft and warm sliding up his leg. A bare foot . . . ? It was all he could do to keep himself from starting. He looked across the table. Nandi was looking at her father, but when Kai faced her she shot him a quick, hot glance that all but set his shirt afire.

Suddenly, Kai realized that he had pushed his chair back and was standing erect, in every sense of the word. Every eye was upon him. Embarrassed and seeking to avoid humiliation, he hoisted his cup. "To peace." he said. "Or a swift and devastating victory. *Insh'Allah.*"

The others nodded approval and stood, glasses raised in accord.

"*Insh'Allah,*" Abu Ali and his eldest son repeated.

"If it is the will of God," the Zulus intoned.

Elenya was watching Kai, and she glanced from Nandi to her brother and back again, a gleeful and infuriatingly knowledgeable smile on her face. He realized she had been watching him the entire time, and unlike her elders, hadn't been fooled at all.

CHAPTER THIRTY-THREE

FROM THE KITCHEN, SOPHIA COULD GLIMPSE THE TABLE. Nandi and Kai were obviously flirting outrageously. She burned with anger, and something quieter and stronger than anger. But what could she do?

A curvy little Frankish serving girl passed, carrying a plate of fried plantains. Sophia stopped her.

"May I take that out?" she asked. "Please?"

The girl was confused, but agreed. Sophia balanced the plate, and then walked out into the living room with a studied sensuality in every step.

* * *

Sophia served the men, presenting the platter as if making an offering of herself. The Zulus laughed and responded by reaching for her. With a dancer's grace, she fleetly eluded their grasp.

Nandi watched through slitted eyes, her mouth pursed with disapproval.

At last Sophia knelt before Kai, her body carefully arranged for display, tray out, face down, a light dew of perspiration on her cheeks. "May I serve you, sir?"

Before he could respond, Nandi plucked a piece of spiced flattened meat from her own plate, rolled it, and popped it into her mouth. Then, in a conversational tone, she began an odd line of discourse. "There is a Zulu story, Kai, of two rivals," she said. "It may be of interest to you. Zwide of the Ndwandwe gained spirit control over Dingiswayo of the Mthethwa by sending his own sister to steal Dingiswayo's sperm."

Elenya's eyes widened and she glanced swiftly from father to brothers, as if seeking advice on how to react to these intimate details. Kai was too surprised to offer any help. However embarrassed he and his family might have been, the other Zulus felt nothing of the kind, and were already leaning forward in anticipation of a favorite tale.

Abu Ali tried to take control. "I am not certain that the dinner table is the place—"

Very smoothly, Nandi cut him off, somehow managing not to seem rude in the process. "But it is interesting how many cultures have their version of this story, how a woman can weaken a warrior in bed. Even the Jews have the story of Samson, and how Delilah 'Cut his hair.' Hah! We all know what they *really* meant."

Nandi was looking steadily at Sophia as she spoke. Her voice was warm, her eyes cold.

Kai was genuinely confused. Sophia stood very still, as if belatedly aware that she had strayed into dangerous waters.

"I'm not sure I understand," Kai said.

"I only say that a man must be careful where he seeks relief," Nandi purred. "A lover must not only be of a man's own social station, but of goodwill as well. Otherwise she will bring him low."

She popped another morsel into her mouth and chewed carefully. The table was deadly quiet.

Sophia rose and backed out of the room, face down. Her shoulders trembled, though whether with fear, humiliation, or rage Kai could not say. As the door closed behind her Kai shifted in his place, determined to follow her.

Before he could disgrace himself, Ali clamped a hand on his arm. "No," his brother said with quiet force, barely moving his lips.

Kai sat back down. Nandi smiled sweetly at him and cut a small slice of fried banana, offering it to Kai on a skewer. "This is really quite excellent, Kai," she said. The entire table was watching him. Time slowed to a crawl. Finally, he leaned forward and took the morsel with his teeth.

Nandi glowed.

CHAPTER THIRTY-FOUR

FOR TWO MORE DAYS THE WAKIL'S FAMILY enjoyed Cetshwayo's hospitality, although there were no more outings quite so exciting as that first hunt.

Chaperones ever present, Kai and Nandi spent hours walking, talking, and riding, allowing whatever natural sparks that existed between them to fan into flame.

To this end, it would have been counterproductive for Sophia to share Kai's bed, and at Cetshwayo's urging she spent her nights in the servant quarters. During the days she was free to entertain herself, but that very freedom grew chafing. She had no part in the picnics and dinners and dancing. There was no way for her to insinuate herself into the conversations and games, and most frustratingly, she watched as Kai began to share with Nandi the secretive, boyish laughter she had once thought reserved for her alone.

Through great exertions she managed to catch Kai alone near the breeding pen where the mares and stallions were quartered.

"Sophia!" he said in pleasant surprise. "I had not expected to find you here."

"I hoped to witness," she said, "what I have missed these last nights."

Kai grinned and combed her hair with his fingers. "You have been lonely?"

"Terribly." She sniffed.

"I have hurt you?"

"More than I can say. I fear you no longer care."

Kai drew her closer. "This is all politics," he said. "Fear not. Whatever plans my father and Cetshwayo have for me, they will include you. How could I put you aside?"

"Talk," she said. "Words are ever less costly than actions."

"If it is actions you wish," said Kai, "it is action you shall have." He brushed her lips with his.

"When?"

"Tonight. Find your way to my room."

Her smile was radiant. "If you are not ready for me, I may never recover."

"Readiness is never the issue," he said. "All we require is opportunity." Kai kissed her again and began to walk back to the house.

Sophia sighed in relief. This was good. If Kai was willing to break Cetshwayo's house rules to sleep with her, then she still had a chance.

All the rest of that day Sophia's heart was lightened, and she seemed to dance through the few chores given her by Cetshwayo's wives. She even had a few flirtatious words for Aidan, who was spending his days in similar idleness.

In fact, something seemed to be eating at the Irishman, disturbing him. From time to time she caught him staring at her, and realized that when their gazes met both held the contact a moment too long and too warmly. *Ah*, she thought. *He is smitten.*

It was no fault of hers if Aidan was taken with her. She had certainly done nothing to encourage it.

That night, she waited until the house was quiet, then rolled out of her cot and rouged her mouth in the darkness of the servants' quarters. So long had she practiced perfecting her face paints that she knew she could make herself delectable without mirror or light, and she had been careful to bathe before bedtime. Tonight, she would give Kai something special, a touch of magic that that virginal bitch Nandi couldn't imagine.

Timing her motions to the snores of the women around her, Sophia crept out of the room.

Cetshwayo's mansion was built in the round, with an open central courtyard serving all the rooms on the main floor like the hub of a great wheel. She would cut across the courtyard and slip into the kitchen, take the back stairs up to the guest quarters, and then—

She had only passed halfway through a deserted stand of lilies and roses when she heard a familiar voice and froze.

"—thought that you might like a walk," Nandi said. Something else was said, followed by quiet, throaty laughter.

"—for sleep." Kai's voice.

"—else to do? No assignation?" Teasing. "Your little slave girl is pretty, after all."

Despite her disappointment at finding Kai and Nandi together, Sophia had to smile. So, even Nandi had to admit of her charms.

"—means nothing to me," Kai said. "Truly, I received two mounts that day, and Djinna is the better ride."

Sophia froze in disbelief as Nandi and Kai, arms linked, passed within a few cubits of her and headed toward Cetshwayo's study.

She trembled in the grass for almost two minutes before she forced herself to follow them. Why, she did not know. There was nothing in their plans that included her. Nothing in this night that she needed or wanted to see. But still, Sophia had to follow.

"Truly, this is magnificent," Kai said, and he meant it.

Nandi had come unchaperoned to his room only a half hour before, startling him. He had expected Sophia, and the timing of Nandi's arrival made him wonder if Zulu women had the *asmat*, the magic. Perhaps all women did.

Certainly she considered Sophia an irritant, if a minor one. Through rough words he had attempted to downplay his "plaything's" importance, although he doubted Nandi had been deceived.

But if she had ruined his assignation, saying, "I wish to show you a treasure," he had to admit that she had delivered on her promise.

Her father's office was on the east side of his circular house, on the ground floor, with a fireplace the size of the Wakil's. Its coals still glowed, whereas the Wakil was careful to extinguish his at night. "It is a custom among my people," Nandi told him, "never to let the fire die completely, to begin each day's cooking with the fire from the previous day. It is a continuance of life." She placed a log on the embers. Almost at once, it began to smoke.

Nandi took a tube of fire paste from her father's desk and put a daub from each end on the thick lamp wick. In a few seconds the mixture began to smoke, and then puffed into flame. She slipped the cover on the lamp and turned the wick up.

Placing a finger against his lips to warn Kai to silence, Nandi searched in her father's desk until she found a key, then tiptoed to the wall next to the fireplace. She placed the key into the wall, turned it, and a cunningly concealed door popped open.

A number of scrolls and parchments were stacked inside, nestled into a metal box lined with heat-resistant ceramic. She extracted a velvet bag, untied it, and extracted a scroll. "Here," she said, and spread it on her father's desk.

"What is it?" he asked, absorbed despite himself.

"You tell me," she said.

As it unrolled, Kai caught his breath. "The Pillars of the Nile." He instantly recognized the design. The Nile had long ceased to be merely a natural waterway. The major artery of travel through Egypt's empire, it had been dredged and deepened and dammed, made more navigable with a series of locks and artificial channels. But if the Nile had, over the centuries, become one of the Wonders of the World, no part of it was more fabled than the Pillars supporting the Empresses's private bridge, the royal span twenty years in the building, a marvel equal to the pyramids themselves.

And this diagram was, unquestionably, a painstaking copy of the original, designed by a mad Frank named Da Vinci in about 700. Da Vinci had possessed genius unknown to others of his kind and found patronage with the royal house of Abyssinia. Even in the darkness of Europe, Allah had birthed a spark of light. Although genius or no, the idiot had killed himself testing some manner of flying machine off the top of Khufu's pyramid. Pigbellies.

A copy, yes . . . his fingers traced the almost absurdly delicate and precise lines, the mathematically perfect arches and spires. Babatunde was right. He should have gone to school in the East, where wonders like this . .

"No copy, Kai," she whispered, her mouth very close to his ear. He had been so absorbed in this drawing that he had heard rustling sounds behind him, and now her nearness reminded him of what he had heard and not registered. His throat felt thick.

"Not a copy?"

"No. The royal architect was also something of an artist . . . this was authenticated because of a preliminary sketch on the reverse side."

Swallowing hard, feeling her fingers moving in light circles on his shoulder, Kai slowly looked at the other side. A sketch, certainly. Several men seated at table, each of them turned reverently and expressively toward a bearded man in the middle.

"Original?" An original blueprint for the Pillars? It was priceless. He should not even handle it. "This is treasure indeed."

"It is not the treasure I spoke of, Kai," she said, and turned him.

In the glow from the fireplace, the Zulu princess was an onyx statue, flawless, almost mythical, her clothing about her feet. Kai's mouth dried. Her breasts were heavy and dark as ripe plums, the aureoles darker circles at their tips.

Incredibly, Kai had never seen a naked black woman before. He felt as if standing on the threshold of some mighty shrine, each curve and fire-light shadow an awesome revelation. Never in his life had he beheld such beauty, and the sheer power of the experience rendered him speechless.

"You can frolic with all the whores in New Alexandria," she said, her voice soft and commanding. "But none of them can open the door to who you really are, Kai. What we could share is something different. With me, you enter the hall of your ancestors. With me, you open the door to your future, and your children's future. Together, we will have sport that would make Allah wish himself a mortal man."

The sheer staggering blasphemy of her words inflamed him. He could not take his eyes away and reached for her. She pressed her palms against his chest, keeping him at a slight distance.

"No," she said. "I must be a virgin on my wedding night."

"What, then . . . ?"

"There are other ways," she said. "Zulu ways. But you must let me lead if you would embrace *ukuHlobonga*."

Powerless to resist, Kai let her unbuckle him. When his pantaloons settled about his ankles, her calm, warm hands fondled him, as if affirming his readiness. He pulsed against her fingers. Her eyes locked with his as she moved forward, her hand still gripping his manhood as Nandi kissed him for the first time. Her lips were impossibly lush, the offering of her wetness and warmth enough to threaten explosion.

She never closed her eyes, never pulled away, but increased her hand's pressure, her fingers and thumb finding secret places at the base of his scrotum so that the impending release was forestalled.

She drew him down to the zebra skin rug arrayed before the fire. She lay beside him like a reclining lioness, turned her back and then nestled herself against him. Her body was taut and muscular as a boy's but fashioned as lushly as a woman's could possibly be.

Just when he thought she was offering him her back door, she reached back, found his hardened *zakr* and glided it between her thighs. She had lubricated the skin of her legs with something that smelled faintly of butter, and when he glided between them she arched like a cat and gripped him deliciously, every muscle flexing and then releasing, holding him with such control that he might have been milked by hand.

As she ground herself back and onto him the sensation was astonishing. Kai wrapped his arms around her waist, right thumb and forefinger finding the rough flesh of her left nipple and rolling it tenderly. Slowly, she accelerated the rhythm, the slick skin between her legs gripping and pulling at him, the friction and wetness creating waves of heat that rolled up his spine until he feared the top of his head might fly off.

The room seemed to disappear, and it was just the two of them, before the fire. They might have been in a mansion, or on the veldt, two human animals with nothing in the world to cling to save each other.

Kai groaned as she quickened, her thigh muscles fluttering against him, the pressure building until he lost control, stabbed forward. Uttering a low cry he voided, lost in a world of liquid fire, pulled into a whirlwind created by a woman beyond his experience or imagination.

For a time he lay there, spooned to her. Nandi cooed to him as if she was speaking to a child. *"That* is who I am, Kai. Who *we* are. In all the world, there is only knowledge, and pleasure, and power. I offer all three."

Kai cupped her breasts and held himself tightly against her, unable to think or speak. Faintly, he had a sense that a breath of cool air was blowing against him, almost as if a door had been quietly opened and closed. Very distantly, his warrior's mind heard the fall of small footsteps retreating with an animal's stealth. The sound was swiftly gone, and forgotten almost as quickly as Kai buried himself against the nape of Nandi's neck, luxuriating in the scent of musk and butter, and the heat of the woman with whom he might—just might—spend the rest of his life.

CHAPTER THIRTY-FIVE

THE NIGHT STARS WERE BRIGHT AND PITILESS as Sophia fled from the house out to the horse barn. Tears flooded her cheeks. She felt confused, embarrassed, humiliated, as if all of her dreams and plans were tumbled about her like shards of broken glass. Why had she deceived herself? Why?

And she knew the answer: her dreams were the only things that had helped her keep her sanity. The myth of what might be between slave and master was fed to the girls to keep them in line. It was the ancient game of carrot and stick, and the slave-sluts of Dar Hudu were the donkeys. There was pain and disfigurement for the wenches who disobeyed, but there were also elusive and fabled rewards for those who discovered or pretended pleasure in their hideous station.

Her pretensions and illusions crashed around her. She was a fool! A fool! Because Kai had treated her with kindness, because he was handsome and good, she had allowed her desperate dreams to blind her to reality. She was a slave, no better than any of those in Ababa or those working in the fields along the road. Worse, because those slaves had no illusions.

The death of dreams was killing her, ripping out the lining of her heart, and she couldn't stop the tears.

"Sophia?" Aidan said.

She whipped her head around, realizing that he had followed her from the house. What had he seen? What did he know? Her entire world was crumbling about her, and she simply could not deal with him now.

"Leave me alone," she said.

Instead of leaving, he came closer. "Sophia," he said. "I'm sorry for your pain. I tried to warn you: you are not his woman. You are his plaything."

She turned on him fiercely. "I could be more!" she said. "If only . . ."

"If only what?" In the moonlight, his face seemed to have been leached of color. He was silver now, not quite flesh. More than flesh . . . and his words rang out remorselessly. "Don't you understand? There is nothing there for you, Sophia. He could not marry you. He won't even free you. You are nothing—"

She didn't let him finish. Her hand lashed out, cracking him across the cheek.

Aidan's head rocked but he didn't even blink in response. He merely watched her steadily. "You are nothing to *him*."

The implication in his words electrified her. Frightened her. He had voiced what had shimmered in the air between them since their first meeting.

"To *him*, Sophia." What was it in Aidan's voice? There was a pleading there, a vulnerability she hadn't seen. He wasn't laughing at her, wasn't mocking her. *See me*, he seemed to be saying. *Open your eyes*. "He could never build a life with you. Could never really love you."

"How dare you," she said, and realized that he had taken two more steps forward, that she was very nearly trapped against a stall. She slapped him again. This time he grabbed her arms and pulled her close. Aidan was actually stronger than Kai, his body that of a worker, while Kai's was more that of a muscular dancer, the result of endless hours of swordplay. Since her arrival and partial supplanting of Aidan's relationship with his young master, Aidan had thrown himself into physical labor, punishing himself.

Now, with his hands on her, she could smell his scent, knew his power. She felt her body responding to him, and was terrified of that reaction.

"Do you think this is a game?" Aidan said. "That the exotic slave girl will win the master's heart and live happily ever after? You are a toy to him. A slutty. Little. Toy."

Their lips were almost touching. His eyes were like those of a bird of prey. "If I were Kai, I'd never let you go. Who owns you, owns magic."

She struggled in his arms as Aidan kissed her savagely. She pulled her head away. Their eyes sparked fire, and he kissed her again and drew her down to the straw.

She gasped at his strength, but knew that her protests were a lie, knew that she was not resisting with her whole being. This was not love. Was not really even lust. It was revenge: she wanted to punish Kai, needed something to wash away and replace the pain she felt. Wanted to feel alive and desired. "You will die for this," she said.

To her surprise, his eyes had softened. They were filled with hunger, a hunger to hold and be held, to understand, to open his heart to another human being. She felt the depths of his loneliness, and it startled her how deeply they echoed her own. "Die?" he said. "It would be cheap at the price."

This time, her lips found his. She fumbled with his shirt, drawing it off. For a long and aching moment her fingers traced his body's rugged contours tentatively, with gentle wonder.

Her breath came faster, and she shucked herself out of her dress. Sophia twined herself around him, snaked his pants down with her locked legs. As he pushed himself up over her, the muscles in the backs of his arms leapt out, and her nails clawed at them. One of her hands slipped down to his groin, positioning him. A moment later, he thrust forward.

Sophia arched with pleasure, crying out as he entered her. Their lovemaking was intense, beyond mere passion, two desperate slaves who had found, for however brief a moment, freedom in each other's arms.

CHAPTER THIRTY-SIX

THEIR THREE ELDERLY FEMALE CHAPERONES monitoring at a discreet distance, Kai and Nandi stood together atop a dusty low hill overlooking Cetshwayo's *kraal*.

Using skills developed by their ancestors over a thousand years, Zulu herdsmen worked the vast herds of cattle stretched off across the unfenced lands, ranging all the way to the horizon. Orange dust of earth and pungent powdered droppings rouged the horizon. The Zulu raised *umkhonto* spears to their chieftain's daughter. That was what Kai now understood Cetshwayo to be. Not just a landholder, or an employer: a chieftain. And possibly, Shaka was their king. The Zulu were citizens of Bilalistan, but they had brought their culture with them.

"Mine," Nandi said. "This is what I would bring to our union, Kai, but none of it has any meaning. I could have nothing but the clothes upon my back, and you would be a fool to turn me away."

She said that without a trace of irony. It was simple knowledge, an understanding of her worth that went deeper than mere self-respect or ego.

"That is truth," Kai said, and found her hand with his. If this was his fate, he could face it well. He could find a way to embrace it. Nandi was beautiful, brilliant, passionate . . . and if he could believe her, had loved him since childhood. Why could his heart not simply surrender?

Perhaps it was best that parents take these choices from the hands of their children. *After all, your father chose Lamiya for Ali, and see how well . . .*

He turned his thoughts away from that direction and managed to smile at Nandi. Her braided, beaded hair was held in a silver scarf. Her face was a queen's, black as the night in which she had offered herself to him. *Join me,* she seemed to be saying. *Together, we could rule.*

He leaned over and kissed her, felt the warmth and wetness of her lush mouth against his, hungry and searching. This was not mere political posturing. This woman wanted a mate who could match her own strength, her own hunger for life. She had placed herself before him as vulnerably as she could. When she pulled back, her fire was unabated, and if it had not completely burned away his reservations, he would be lying to say his blood had not quickened.

Together they rode back down the hill. When they reached the house an hour later, the slaves were packing his family's luggage onto the wagon. The mares, well serviced, were tied up behind the coach.

Nandi's father noted their approach, and his left eye raised in question. Nandi's spine was absolutely straight, her face without shame. These Zulus!

"*Ngiyabonga*. Thank you for your hospitality, Cetshwayo," Abu Ali said.

Shaka seemed to have completely recovered from his brush with death, and his smile was radiant. "I think your mares are heavier than when they arrived, eh?"

The laughter was general, and appreciative, but Kai noted that Abu Ali was watching Shaka carefully. There would be conversation later, he was certain.

Aidan and Sophia were seated on the wagon, but neither reacted at all. Good. He certainly didn't need any comments from those two.

Abu Ali clasped hands with Shaka, locking eyes. "And such hunting! It is a fine thing to finally take the measure of the famed Shaka Zulu."

To either side of the wagon, the Zulus pounded their *umkhonto* against the ground. Kai felt certain that Abu Ali's double meaning had utterly escaped them.

Cetshwayo drew Kai aside. "So, young Kai," he said. "I think my daughter favors you."

Kai squared his shoulders, determined to take every step in this process with full intention. "I would be honored to see her again," he said.

"Make it so." Cetshwayo's face crinkled happily. "*Uhambe kahle*. Travel well!"

The wagon rolled out, and the procession began its trip home. Nandi trotted her horse by Kai for a moment, waiting for him to turn to see her. When he did, she wheeled sprightly away, laughing.

Ali shook his head. "These Zulu women are bold!" he said.

Kai remained silent, but both his face and his loins burned with her memory.

"But about Shaka . . ." Ali paused, and then continued more heavily. "I am not happy with what we saw, Father. Is this the best match we can arrange for my brother?"

Abu Ali considered carefully. "Her father is saner than his brother. Nandi would make a good wife, Kai."

Elenya's smile was mischievous. "If you can handle her."

Ali and Abu Ali laughed. Kai's cheeks flamed, but he noticed that Aidan and Sophia showed nothing at all in their faces. He thought on that a bit, but decided that they were being discreet, for which he was grateful.

The Wakil's party took a different route south than the one they had followed on their way to the *kraal,* circling east before angling home. Midway through the second day out they passed a river dock, where a screwship was unloading a shipment of terrified, confused slaves.

"Gauls, by the look of them," Abu Ali said. "They are good in the house. Franks are better in the fields."

Aidan merely held the wagon's reins, watching without comment. Most of these miserable wretches were adults. Was that worse than what he himself had experienced? His memories of home were growing more and more distant, like a dream that would dim but not quite die.

"There are bills before the Senate prohibiting the importation of more slaves," Abu Ali mused. Instantly Aidan felt his attention focus. What was this?

"Why, sir?" Ali asked.

"They are stolen from their homes," the Wakil said. "Although care is taken not to harm them—"

Ali laughed. "Who would harm a valuable cargo?"

Aidan bit his tongue. At that instant his hatred and resentment boiled so high that it was all he could do to keep from throttling one of them. How dare they!

"Indeed," the Wakil mused. "Still, many feel that it is . . . better to breed them here."

"Hah! Well, breeding is easier than catching, I'm sure."

"And more pleasurable."

Kai had been quiet. Now, he pointed out another steamscrew passing the slave ship. "Where is *that* ship going, Father?"

Abu Ali shaded his eyes. "That is . . . a trading vessel. I am not certain. Perhaps to the bay, transfer their cargo to a larger ship, and off to Andulus . . ." He extracted a spyglass from his pocket and peered out.

"Six-pointed star," he said. "The flag of Judea. Jews. Merchants, most likely. They ply every river in New Djibouti, and by the Treaty of Khibar pay less taxes than Persians, or even most Egyptians." He took the spyglass down. "They trade with us and the Northmen and show no favoritism, but they don't mix with us any more than do the Masai."

Jews were white men who sailed the rivers? Aidan was boggled. Free white men who had favorable treaties with the government of Bilalistan?

Or perhaps even fabled Alexandria herself? Unbelievable. Could they be a help to him . . . ?

His hands had tightened on the reins until his knuckles were white. Beside him, Sophia was staring off at the screwship with, he thought, the same questions in her heart.

Could we ever escape? Leave this place? Find a life somewhere, where we could forget all of this . . . ?

Very tentatively and secretively, Sophia reached over and brushed her fingers against his right hand. He dropped that hand between them, and their fingers intertwined. And just that simply, without any words spoken, their pact was sealed.

CHAPTER THIRTY-SEVEN

IT WAS THE MONTH OF SHA'BAN, harvest time. Dar Kush's fields teemed with stalks of golden teff. The slaves worked the fields from dawn till dusk, singing and sweating in the sun that marked the passing of their days.

In the northern quarries the mining operation ran at minimum, every available worker recruited to the fields. It was a good time: no hand was idle, every man and woman knew his place. At the end of the season would be the month of Ramadan, a time of fasting and reflection. At its end would come Idd-el-Fitr once again, and celebration.

Kai's life had settled back into a routine. He studied, he managed the estate, and once a week he and Sophia or Aidan traveled to Malik's estate for practice. Once a month he and Ali drilled with Malik's regiment: musketry, cavalry formations, the psychology of command, tactics and strategy.

On the surface, not much had changed. Sophia still warmed his bed, he and Aidan still rode and hunted. But Kai had a sense that his true destiny was now beginning to unfold. Although he felt more distant from Sophia, she was still the only one to whom he spoke of his emotions. When he considered their future, he vaguely supposed that marriage to Nandi would necessitate a brisk negotiation to keep his favorite servant available.

He was certain Nandi would never allow Sophia as a second wife, but there were other ways to protect their relationship.

Aidan remained Aidan. The young Irishman was still the person who knew Kai best, still his closest friend and confidant, although he found the servant quieter than usual, less likely to share his own feelings. Kai supposed it was just a natural part of maturation, that each man must keep his own council and to his own station. That was a saddening thing, but he knew that as the years rolled past, Aidan would come with him to his new home, and eventually manage the estate. Perhaps one day Kai might even free him, and wouldn't that be something? He would have the Irishman's lifelong gratitude for such a magnanimous act, and the blessings of Allah Al-Karim, the Generous, besides.

Beneath Malik's watchful eye, Kai practiced sword. He could best most of his uncle's senior students now, although Ali still excelled him by a narrow margin. It was absolutely depressing to see how easily Malik thrashed his brother.

Countless thousands of hours of practice, and still Malik was the master! But there was pride and camaraderie between the three men now, and every day Kai felt himself drawn more tightly into the arms of an elite brotherhood.

At night he studied Babatunde's Sufi scrolls. Beloved Babatunde. His name meant "A father returns" in Yoruba, but Kai's mentor had been gone for so long that Kai sometimes wondered if he had ever actually existed. Returning seemed an even more distant improbability. He studied the diagrams of the Naqsh Kabir in the book, the odd geometrical design within the circle. Kai had covered a dozen notebooks with speculations and designs, seeking to find the secret in the patterns. They were intoxicating, and Babatunde, who was the wisest man Kai had ever known, had told him that there was something there within that pattern, something alive and mysterious that would help him grasp the meaning of his life.

So he studied, and sought to understand how the different points on the diagram related to varying processes. How *well* he understood it he could not say, and if the mail brought him a letter a year from his erstwhile teacher, he counted himself fortunate. The answers to his questions were almost always obsolete, the ensuing months having been filled with study and pondering.

And sometimes more.

After a day of endless study he pulled the draw cord, summoning Sophia to his room. Swiftly she arrived, wafting perfume, all soft smiles and hard kisses, ever ready with some new and alluring approach to love-making that would make him forget his studies and fall into a physical reverie that lasted until well after midnight.

In sleep, his mind, saturated with his studies to the bursting point, fell into dream.

In his dream, Kai sometimes found himself in a world in which every pattern and object seemed related to the elusive symbol.

Surrounded by them, he found himself shrinking, until he was minuscule, tiny, running along the titanic symbol, his feet tracing its inner lines. Behind him, nipping at his heels, raced a line of fire. As it caught up with him—

He awakened, huffing air, instantly humiliated, and hoping that the sounds of his distress had not penetrated beyond his bedchamber. At least no one but Sophia would know of his affliction.

Then he saw that he was alone in his bed. The place where Sophia had lain was empty, still depressed, the sheets still warm and scented of her. The curtains blew gently in the night wind. He wondered where she was: perhaps gone for a moonlit walk, perhaps in her own sleeping chamber. It was not unusual for her to leave his side, and he was glad that she felt free to do so. After a night such as she had given him, he would deny her nothing.

Calling her name once, softly, he surrendered to the arms of night and sank back down into sleep.

If Kai had risen, and walked to the window looking out across the estate, he would just have been able to make out Aidan's house behind Ghost Town's fence, one of dozens clustered together there on the edge of the woods. No light glowed in its windows, but if he had had the eyes of an owl, he might have pierced that darkness. And there in the depths of Aidan's bed he might have seen the woman he owned and the friend he loved embracing, each kiss a betrayal, each murmured endearment an invitation to the sword suspended above their heads.

Each tear that coursed down Sophia's cheek was testimony to the cost of her nights with Kai, her screams, muffled against Aidan's chest, her only impotent protest.

CHAPTER THIRTY-EIGHT

TWO LITTLE WHITE BOYS RAN FROM THE GATES to the great cast-iron alarm bell at the eastern edge of Ghost Town, jumping onto it so that their weight forced it to ring back and forth, rocking as the clapper tolled joyously across the estate.

The servants emerged from the village, wondering what the disturbance might be, alarmed at first. Was it the Aztecs? Could a band of savages have struck so far east . . . ?

But as the servants gathered they saw only a fabulous golden coach drawn by a white horseman in pantaloons and turban.

The excitement seemed infectious, and the servants were running now. "They're here!" old Festus cried, so excited he was virtually dancing a jig. "Young missus has come home!"

Lamiya allowed a deep sense of satisfaction to wash over her. Dar Kush did indeed feel like home, and she was almost as glad to see it as she had been to place her feet on dry land again after weeks at sea.

Beside her, Babatunde wore his customary inscrutable smile, the one he had worn since first landing, the expression that had wavered only when he saw the horse-drawn conveyance that came to carry them.

"Infernal beasts," he whispered as one of the horses relieved itself in a steaming golden stream.

Six years had passed since Lamiya last touched the earth of Dar Kush, and many faces were utterly strange to her now. Children had grown, new ones had been born. But the adults were not so unfamiliar as she might have thought. She had first arrived in New Djibouti when she was twelve, already betrothed, knowing that she would have to learn to love this rough, wild country. Bilalistan was so young, and so potentially strong. Treated like a child by the throne of Alexandria, this land was a sleeping giant. Hers were among the hands that might shake it awake.

In the last six years she had matured into womanhood; at twenty-one her training was now complete. In that time she had traded many letters with Ali. Those letters were affectionate if not passionate, respectful if not adulatory. He was a good man, and their union would be a strong one.

She was tall, slender, with perfectly formed features and skin the color of unadulterated coffee. Her hair descended onto her forehead in a slight widow's peak and was kept short, tightly curled and oiled. Lamiya fairly glowed with health and energy.

Babatunde still grumbled. "I want to be on my own feet. I don't trust boats, and I don't trust these animals."

"Perhaps we'll be better off when the airships can cross the ocean."

"So we can crash, and then drown?"

"I thought you liked airships."

"That was before I rode in one." The carriage bounced. *"Arrgh!"*

The conveyance rolled up to the main house and came to a smooth stop. Lamiya and Babatunde emerged, the Yoruba muttering and exaggerating his aches and pains with every step.

Lamiya's pulse raced as the house grew nearer. She had spent so many happy days here, and knew that this was her destiny: to stand by the side of a warrior and statesman as he carved out an empire and freed a nation.

Fawning and bowing, the house servants graciously helped them with their mountain of luggage and goods, carrying them up to the rooms prepared in anticipation of their return.

Kai and Aidan had spent most of the day in relaxed companionship, mending fences in the western pasture, where the foals were exercised in the spring.

It was not hard work, but it needed consistency. The hundreds of miles of wire winding around Dar Kush were subject to rust, wear, and breakage both natural and human. Every cubit of the fence was inspected yearly, the more critical sections monthly.

Aidan was pulling two broken strands together for Kai to twist and fuse when Kai heard the distant tolling of the gate bells. He glanced at his friend. "What day is it?" he asked.

"Yarum al-arbâ?" Aidan replied.

Kai grinned. "Lamiya!" He sprinted for Djinna, leaping onto her back, Aidan only half a beat behind. They spurred their horses toward the house, two superb horsemen at rough play.

An informal reunion was already under way by the time they reached the house. Kai stripped off his gloves as he strode through the door. He was just in time to see Lamiya present her hand for Ali to kiss. She turned, a smile of greeting blossoming on her face like the rising of the sun.

"Kai!" Lamiya said warmly, and enfolded him in a sisterly embrace.

Kai reveled in that embrace, his emotions a confusing meld of excitement and guilty pleasure. Fearing an embarrassing physical reaction, he pushed her away to arm's length.

"You have grown!" Kai said fervently. "By the Prophet, you have grown."

"And you are a sapling no longer." Lamiya gazed at him with eyes so guileless and filled with pleasure that Kai felt almost shy, at the same time that he was proud of himself. By seeing himself through her eyes, for the first time he truly realized how much he had changed in the last years. Since Lamiya left he had grown five digits and gained five sep or more. He was a young warrior now, a guardian of his tribe, and her frank appreciation of him made all of the work and sweat and labor worthwhile. "So tall and handsome." She chucked him under the chin. "Why aren't you married yet?"

He leaned close. "Father arranges that even now. You should see Nandi! I think she may eat me alive!"

"Relax and enjoy it," she whispered, and they laughed together. His heart was happy, and he found himself thinking, *She is my sister, and that is enough. That is right, and appropriate.*

Abu Ali interrupted them. "Lamiya, let me show you to your rooms. You must rest. We have a great feast planned for you! It will be the event of the season."

She held Kai's hand lingeringly. "We have much to speak of, Kai," she said, and left with her retinue of retainers.

Kai stared after her, temporarily speechless. He had so much to say, so much had happened! And he realized how much he had missed her. Lamiya was more than just an impossible fantasy figure. She had been, before Aidan, his closest friend. And now that Kai was taking on more and more duties as a man of the household, perhaps it was unseemly that a mere servant be his closest confidant. His heart swelled. Lamiya was home!

"I see you have no greeting for your old teacher." Kai had been so preoccupied that he hadn't really noticed Babatunde's approach.

El Sursur seemed not to have changed at all. His hair was still grayish brown and short, but full. His vast nose still perched in the middle of his face like a boulder, and his eyes were still piercing. If there was a difference, it was that once upon a lifetime ago Babatunde had been taller than Kai. When Lamiya left the country, he and Kai had been almost the same size. Now, Kai towered over him. "Babatunde. Forgive me. How was your trip?"

"Ghastly," the teacher grunted. "Please, help me to my room."

* * *

Kai carried three of Babatunde's bags. El Sursur walked with his hands knotted behind his back, studying the walls as if checking for new furnishings. "So . . . have your studies progressed?"

"Yes, sir."

One of Babatunde's bushy eyebrows raised. "So? We will see. Who formulated the Djinn theory of disease, and when?"

Kai did not hesitate. "Al Khartoum, four hundred thirty six years before the birth of the Prophet."

"Its direct application?"

"The extinction of the sleeping sickness along the Nile."

"Good. And its negative consequence?"

That took Kai aback. "Sir, how could there be? Lives were saved!"

Babatunde looked at Kai severely. "There are always consequences, young Kai. Lower mortality meant greater soil depletion due to the increased need for protein. It also meant a need for greater irrigation works, which placed Abyssinia in greater debt to the throne of Egypt." He grunted in disgust. "Did you read those books, or merely use them to swat flies?"

Babatunde's library hadn't been disturbed in years, and a squadron of servants buzzed about the room dusting and straightening while El Sursur sat, immobile, seeming to revel in the return to familiar surroundings after long weeks of travel.

When they had departed, Babatunde opened a flat black leather case and spread several odd, hand-sized pictures on the table. They were like no drawings Kai had seen before. Paintings? He wasn't certain. They had no color, only shades of gray and black, but there was a quality to them that was shockingly lifelike. Kai studied them. "What manner of drawings are these?" he asked.

"They are light paintings," Babatunde replied. "Chemicals spread on paper react to the light, which is focused on them with a mirror or lens. It is the new thing on the Continent."

Kai grew excited. He had seen paintings of some of these images before, and engravings in his textbooks. "This is the Great Pyramid. And the Sphinx! And the Pillars of the Nile!" Kai felt heat flash through his loins as that image reminded him of another, far more intimate association.

Babatunde smiled approval, unaware of his pupil's carnal musings. "You will see them all one day."

"When I make pilgrimage."

"That will be a day," Babatunde said.

Kai reached into his teacher's bag and spread out an additional collection of maps and charts. His eyes glowed. He studied a multicolor map of the heartland: Africa, lower Europe, and the near eastern states. "The borders of Persia have changed," he noted. "By war or treaty?"

"The threat of one, the promise of the other." El Sursur rummaged in another bag. "I have something for you, Kai."

Babatunde opened a little silver box, extracting a crescent moon medallion. "Before I left, we spoke of another, harder spiritual path. One day, you may decide to accept its responsibilities."

Kai stared at the medallion with wonder. "It's beautiful," he whispered.

"And you are strong," Babatunde said. "You are the image of your father as a young man."

"No?" His mouth denied the truth, but his chest lifted in pride.

"But are you prepared?"

"For what, precisely?"

Babatunde's smile was a sphinx's. "The Ulema passes religious teachings to the citizens of Bilalistan. The public thinks they fight with the Senate, but they are but two hands serving a single mind, a mind that thinks only of commerce. The number of those who merely swallow their pronouncements is great indeed."

Kai had a brief image of a vast throng waiting to gain admittance to Paradise, and was amused.

"There is a smaller group," Babatunde said, his smile disappearing. "They strive to understand Allah more directly. They care not for expediency or propriety. They care only for what is *right*, young Kai. The ways of Allah and the ways of the Ayatollah may not always be the same. Would you place your salvation in a politician's hands, or indeed any hands but your own?"

Kai looked at the amulet in the mirror and experimented with hanging it around his neck. Then he looked at Babatunde suspiciously. "Now comes the moment when you tell me I must change my sinful ways."

"Oh?" the teacher said cannily. "Have you sinful ways?"

Kai stared at him, and then burst into laughter. "Oh, Babatunde," he said. "For a moment you deceived me. I know my father has written to you in despair."

"What has he to despair of?"

"Oh, no you don't. I'm not ready to settle down yet." A series of images: of Nandi, of Sophia, and then of Lamiya, flashed through his mind, warming him. Then there was another, darker thought. He had assumed that

Babatunde was acting as moral watchdog, concerned that Kai's fleshly pleasures might interfere with his coming marriage. But could the Yoruban mean something else entirely? He felt a tingle of alarm. There was something here that he did not understand. Something that he was not prepared to deal with.

Kai handed the medallion back. "Why don't you just hold this for me?"

"As you wish."

One of the charts was the fabled Naqsh Kabir, the circle with a triangle embedded in the center and six mirror-imaged lines arrayed to either side. Kai studied it, as if hoping that there was something hidden in Babatunde's copy that had not been present in his own. Finally he threw up his hands, despairing and then disparaging.

"Now *this* is what I speak of. You told me to study this symbol. More important than sleeping, you said. But I can't make heads or tails of it. As esoterica, yes—but of what practical value . . . ?"

Babatunde smiled, noting the sword at Kai's side. "Have you learned to use that?"

"Uncle thinks so," Kai said.

"Show me."

Kai drew his sword and began a lightning series of airthrusts, mentally slaying an entire army of wild-eyed Northmen. Babatunde watched for a minute, a faintly amused expression on his face, then plucked up a wooden wand and disarmed him with a single swipe.

Slowly and disbelievingly, Kai picked his sword back up. "Let's try that again."

Babatunde nodded agreement, spreading his arms in clear invitation.

Aiming to slit the edge of Babatunde's robe, Kai advanced. The little man sidestepped—not with Malik's blinding speed, but with an economy that was baffling nonetheless, so deft it seemed almost as if he had simply disappeared and reappeared. Kai felt a pressure at his ankle, and suddenly he was on his backside.

Kai got partway to his feet, and then thumped back down, staring up at Babatunde with brows furrowed. "What . . . what are you doing to me?"

In answer, Babatunde slapped his hands on a table and said: "Help me move this."

He and Kai pushed the table aside, removing it from the rug that covered the floor. When it was removed, he saw the bare floor for the first time in memory. Beneath it was a Naqsh Kabir large enough to stand upon, fully five cubits in diameter.

"Stand here," Babatunde said, positioning Kai on the lines within the circle. "Thrust . . . *so*." Babatunde made a lunging motion. He was not lunging as deeply as Malik might have, and the motion was quite relaxed and fluid, almost casual, not at all martial.

Kai sighed and extended his arm as requested.

"Hold!"

Kai froze in place. He felt himself to be in a very strong stance. Hawk's eyes, a leopard's grip on the ground. Babatunde chose his angle with precision, pushed along the line of Kai's shoulder, and toppled him to the ground with a single finger. Kai glared up at Babatunde as if he wanted to kill him. "What was *that?*"

"That," his teacher replied, "was the fact that every position has both stability and instability. Viewed as a physical pattern, the Naqsh Kabir teaches both. When you are stable along *this* line," he said, indicating one of the inside lines of the symbol, "you are instable *here.*"

Kai took in the symbol as if he had never really seen it before, his eyes slowly widening. Then he sprang to his feet. "Teach me more."

"Oh, no. It's too impractical for a sober young man like yourself."

"Please . . ."

"I am old," Babatunde said, stretching. "And have traveled far. Perhaps after rest . . ."

"Babatunde!"

Babatunde allowed a grin to soften his face. "Very well," he said. "Traverse the lines of the Naqsh Kabir, feet *so*, body *so*—"

Excitedly, Kai began to practice.

CHAPTER THIRTY-NINE

ENGRAVED INVITATIONS HAD SPREAD ACROSS the country by steamscrew and horseback for a month. Dar Kush was filled with music and guests, the scents of *doro-wote* chicken and *kitfo* chopped seasoned beef, and food from a dozen exotic lands. The music of lute and drum and human laughter pulsed steadily in the background. The betrothal party drew dignitaries from as far as the Northeast coast: New Alexandria, Iroquoi, Delaware, and the Yoruba settlement of Lafia.

As the hired band performed, men and women separated into groups by gender, and began the age-old rituals.

Kai's clan: Malik, Ali, Abu Ali; the Zulus Cetshwayo and brother Shaka, Cetshwayo's sons Keefah and Darbul; their neighbors Djidade Berhar, his son Fodjour and as many of the others as could manage the moves performed a traditional stick-dance, testing each other's endurance and coordination in a blinding display of warrior gamesmanship.

Then the mood and the tempo changed and the women—Malik's wife, Fatima, Nandi, Elenya and Lamiya, and Berhar's wife, Uchenna—danced together, for their own pleasure and the gratification of the men.

Then the men and women formed into lines facing each other. They danced close, and then separated, and then close again: teasing, taunting and celebrating each other.

Later in the evening came a performance by belly dancers drawn from professional troupes and Abu Ali's seraglio. They were quite skilled, and pretended to offer themselves to the noblemen, who responded with enthusiastic trills and whoops while their wives politely restrained them.

Afterward, the servants performed. They played crude handmade instruments, their music a blend of Gaelic, African, and Egyptian, their dance also an energetic hybrid, with high-kicking steps that set the guests roaring in approval. When they were done, they were rewarded with applause and taken away to their own banquet of sweet cakes and roast lamb.

The guests were seated at a low table, cross-legged with backs straight. When the main entertainment concluded, Kai watched as Shaka Zulu dipped his finger in fermented milk, and drew a line on the table. Then he pulled a basket of sesame rolls from the center setting. "Now," he said, aware that every eye was upon him. "Let this bread basket represent the Mosque of the Fathers."

Malik nodded reverently. "Allah preserve its sacred name."

"Pilgrims are imperiled as we speak," Shaka said, "if we allow the filthy Aztecs to violate our sacred ground."

"*Our* sacred ground," Abu Ali said. "More *amahewu*, my friend?"

"Yes," Shaka said with relish. Kai held his smile as a servant poured a pinkish stream of fermented sorghum into Shaka's glass: the Zulu was completely blind to Abu Ali's irony. Not a member of the Wakil's family was unaware that Shaka was eager for war, and that the shrine meant nothing to him. He was not Muslim, but would mouth such phrases as served his political purposes.

Shaka drank deeply. "Excellent," he proclaimed, then warmed again to his previous subject. "Whether a sacred place or political symbol, we cannot have the cannibals so close to us. If we do nothing, we deserve the loss of respect. We deserve whatever the gods rain down upon us."

Kai felt uncomfortable. Here he was entertaining the niece of the Emperor, a pious woman if ever one existed, and this creature of war ranted of "gods" as if he had never heard of the Qur'an. Blasphemy!

Even the Wakil himself dared not chastise Shaka publicly. He did, however, seize the opportunity to change the subject.

"Indeed, my friend, thoughts to ponder. But we have something more joyous to occupy us tonight." Abu Ali stood. "Ali. Lamiya. Please stand!"

Lamiya looked away a bit shyly, but stood. At her side, Ali seemed proud to take her hand.

"Today," said Abu Ali, "I have the very great honor of announcing the betrothal of my son Ali and my beloved Lamiya, Imperial Niece. May their union bring our two great houses into deeper accord. Hai!"

The assemblage cheered, including Kai, who applauded, smiling stiffly. Nandi looked shyly at him, and then away. She had been entirely circumspect since her arrival, as if the interlude in her father's office had never happened at all.

Kai boiled inside. For all of her aggressiveness, and despite their intimacy, there was no mistaking the fact that Nandi's own shyness was as genuine as Lamiya's. What a paradox she was! Would he ever understand women at all?

After the toasts were complete, the adult men retired to the garden. Smoke curled and dissipated from several hookahs. Their multiple mouthpieces branched like friendly snakes as a servant fed tobacco into the holder.

One of the guests puffed deeply. "So, Abu Ali," he said, letting the mouthful out slowly. "Do you see a new line of trade opening with the Continent's east coast?"

Another interjected, "More important, would a tie of blood prove problematic if Egypt and Abyssinia war?"

The questions were greeted by nods and murmurs of interest.

In his divan chair, Abu Ali took a small sip of smoke, and let it trickle from his nose. "In such an instance, I would hope that I might serve as a peacemaker."

"As you did in the Senate on the Manumission Act," said Cetshwayo. The Wakil had spoken in favor of a national policy allowing slaves to purchase their freedom, and been defeated. It was said that the Ulema had used its influence to secure a negative vote.

"Not a shining moment," Abu Ali conceded.

Cetshwayo laughed derisively. "If they were capable of enjoying freedom, Allah would not have made them slaves."

"A bit simplistic, but I hazard that the Ayatollah agrees."

"They have no honor," Shaka sneered. "Nor did their ancestors. If they did, they would never have been taken alive. It is simple. Such 'men'—if men they are—could never bear the weight of citizenship."

"I think you might be surprised. What think you, Babatunde?"

Babatunde thought briefly before speaking. "Slavery is the process of turning wolves into dogs. You kill the ones that bite, and feed their pups until they forget how to hunt for themselves. Allah placed courage and intellect in many packages, with widely varied shading."

Shaka's teeth gleamed. "I can understand why you would think so, philosopher."

Babatunde remained silent, his expression studiedly neutral.

Shaka turned to Kai. "And young Kai. What think you? Could ghosts ever make citizens?"

Kai shrugged. "Probably not. Their children, if raised carefully, might make good free workers, but give them the vote? I think not."

"Free workers, to compete with our own people?" Cetshwayo sneered, disbelieving. "Babatunde, with what are you filling his head?"

Babatunde seemed to have had enough. "An excellent question," he allowed, and rose. "A good evening to you, gentlemen."

Babatunde stood, and retired.

Cetshwayo watched him go, and then leaned forward. "I heard rumors that Babatunde is actually a Sufi. What do you say, Wakil?"

Abu Ali smiled. "There is no traitor or heretic in my house. Rumors are easy to start, harder to prove."

Kai caught up with Babatunde before his teacher could reach the hallway leading to his room. "Babatunde!" he called. "Wait!" Had the talk of slaves had anything to do with Babatunde's talk of medallions?

"No, Kai," the little man said fondly. The sounds of music and merriment drifted up from the floor below. "Your father would want you at the party, not puttering around with an unfashionable old fool like me. Go." There was force in that final word that stole the words from Kai's lips. Babatunde turned and left.

Kai sighed, then walked back the way he had come. Halfway back he looked down from a stairway and saw Ali and Lamiya. They were together in the moonlight, alone. At that moment, Ali seemed very much the man, the inheritor of the estate; Lamiya's expression was affectionate and as calm as an oiled sea. Ali leaned forward and kissed her.

It was the first time that Kai had ever seen them kiss, and it caused a twist of pain that he would not have credited.

Stricken, he turned and fled.

Kai managed to reach the horse barn without encountering any other party guests, for which he was profoundly grateful. He needed to think through this sudden, unexpected misery. He hammered his fists against the horse stall, distantly aware that the animals were skittering away in fear.

All but Djinna, who attempted to nuzzle against him, seeking to comfort. "No, girl," he said. "Easy, girl—I'm sorry." Sudden inspiration occurred to him. "Hey, how would you like a nice ride? Maybe that's what we both need."

Stroking Djinna's head, Kai smiled, struck by a new thought. He would ask Aidan along. It had been too long since the two of them had taken a night ride. This might be a night for breaking the rules. Too long had he been confined by what others thought were appropriate actions. Tonight, they would play!

Kai chose Aidan's customary horse, Majii, and took both fine animals out into the night.

He led them over to the village, where the slaves greeted him. In the distance, he could still hear the sounds of the party.

He tied Djinna and Majii in front of the gates.

"Evenin' sir," said a straw-haired servant boy of perhaps fifteen summers. Kai searched his memory, and finally produced the name. "Evening, Dingane."

On the way into the village, he passed two men passing a pipe of hemp. One was Topper, the burly blacksmith, now gone largely white-haired. The other was a big, eyepatched man sucking at his pipe. Brian. The fragrance of hemp drifted from the pipe, awakening another hunger.

Brian bent low. "Evening, sir," he said. "What brings ye from the party?"

Kai didn't like to think what the thoths had done to Brian; he reminded himself that, sometimes, a few had to suffer for the enlightenment of the many. "I thought it a good night for a ride. Felt like some company."

Topper chuckled and Brian smiled, an affectation that if anything made his scars all the more terrible. "A good night indeed," he averred. "Peace with ye, sir."

"Thank you, Brian." The man had done nothing at all to suggest disrespect, but Kai was still a bit off-put by Brian's very obsequiousness. He didn't like turning his back to the man.

But perhaps he was putting too much there, starting at shadows as might a child. He walked on through Ghost Town's narrow, muddy streets.

The servants scattered out of Kai's way as he passed. He had been this way many times before, and could have found the way to Aidan's blindfolded.

He reached his friend's door but held his knock when he heard a laugh from within. A woman's laugh. Kai smiled, arching an eyebrow. He sneaked around to a side window and managed to find a slit in the cloth through which he could watch. Now *here* was the cure for a sagging spirit!

Aidan and a woman were making passionate love on his rude bed. Kai's eyes widened in delight. This was a capital idea—it had been too long since he and Aidan sported. Perhaps he could even join in the current entertainment. He doubted the wench would object—

Then the two lovers rolled over, and Kai saw her face.

Djinna might as well have kicked him in the chest. He staggered back, a sulfurous anger seething through his veins.

Barely thinking, only feeling, Kai burst through the front door into Aidan's single room. For a fraction of a second the tableau was frozen, the two lovers entwined, kissing, but in the next instant Sophia screamed and threw the covers over herself. Aidan scrambled up, and Kai slid in a long step, clinched his fist, and crashed it against Aidan's cheek.

Kai grabbed Sophia, murderously furious, and slapped her. "Whore!"

Aidan scrambled up, pulling Kai away from her. For another long moment the three of them stood frozen in some kind of static opposition. "No, Kai, it's not her fault—" Aidan began.

Sophia was babbling too, the sheet only partially covering her nakedness. The sight of her, and the sweat glistening upon her, Aidan's juices upon her thighs, drove all thought from Kai's mind, brought him close to madness.

"Kai," she begged. "Don't punish Aidan. We love each other."

Aidan managed to wind his arms around her, as they attempted to present a united front. For a moment, Kai just looked at them; then, with an inarticulate cry, he launched himself at Sophia.

A moment before he would have struck her to the floor, Aidan interposed himself.

Kai drew his sword. It gleamed in the dull light. "Get out of my way."

Aidan's eyes were wide and desperate. "You need a sword for this? To fight for a woman?"

"You are both my slaves. I can do with either of you as I wish."

Aidan caught Kai's sword arm. Kai struggled to pull it back. If he had succeeded, he might well have impaled his friend.

"Do you wish to *command* her love," Aidan said, "or to earn it?"

Kai was able to hear the sound of his own breathing, but little else. Then, as if stepping away from the edge of a pit, he sheathed his sword.

"Dress," Kai said. "And then, outside."

Kai took several deep breaths. Pure slaughter seethed through his veins. He needed this, somehow. This would be a purging of the poison in his heart, the pain that had controlled him for the last sour days. It would end. Now.

Ghost Town's entire population seemed to have gathered outside Aidan's house. Kai removed his sword belt and laid it against the side of the house. He rolled his shoulders, then turned to address the crowd. "I swear upon my honor that the bondsman Aidan has the right to defend himself freely, without fear of consequence. Do you witness?"

There was a general murmur from the assembled, but the only one who responded openly was Topper. "Aye, sir," he said. "I witness." Kai paused, and looked into the blacksmith's eyes, seeing something there that he had never seen before. Suddenly, the entire village of slaves was foreign to him. He had spent countless hours here since his youth, and thought them simple folk, largely content with their lot. Now he could feel that they were rooting *against* him. How dare they! He fed and cared for them! Didn't they understand that?

Well, they would learn a lesson today on the difference between black and white.

The tension built for a few seconds, and then Sophia, clutching a blanket around her body, ran between them. "No," Sophia said. "Please. Both of you."

Kai shoved her aside. When he was finished with Aidan, he would deal with her. First he would use her sexually, drown Aidan's seed with his own. And then he would cast her down into Ghost Town, down among the wretched until she begged, *begged* to return to his bed. "Quiet, woman," he said. "Watch and learn."

He and Aidan squared off.

For years Kai had practiced punching and kicking tactics to complement the swordwork. He was absolutely confident in his ability to take Aidan apart, make him beg for mercy. He watched Aidan, who crouched almost as if he were some kind of ape, his thin lips and pale eyes narrowed. He stank of fear, of the primitive, of an unevolved people still trapped in a stone age of ignorance and superstition.

The two men circled each other, and Kai lunged in, nailing Aidan with a jabbing right. Aidan reeled back, and Kai shuffled forward. As Aidan ducked under Kai's next short and scientific swing, Kai brought his knee up, nailing Aidan on the side of the jaw, spinning him back with blood smearing his mouth. As he did, Kai punched again, a trip-hammer left-right left-right, in his enthusiasm forgetting Malik's clever combat moves. Who needed them against such an untutored opponent!

Then Aidan charged in again, as if the knee and the pounding hadn't deterred him at all. He seized Kai around the waist. With unexpected and disorienting strength, the Irishman heaved Kai into the air and hurled him to the ground.

Kai's breath *whoofed* out of him, and stars danced. It had not been a pretty throw, but it had certainly done the job. Aidan, to his credit, did not step in and kick, which was more restraint than Kai would have expected. All right, then, this was a fair fight, not mortal combat. He would teach the pigbelly a lesson, but perhaps it wouldn't be necessary to cripple him.

Aidan charged in again. Kai stepped to the side and targeted Aidan's temple, hammering him two, three times, then uppercutting. Aidan went down, blood gushing from a broken nose.

There. Perhaps this time Aidan would stay down.

But the Irishman sprang up with an agility that suggested that he wasn't tired at all, whereas Kai was disconcerted to realize that while they had been fighting for only a few minutes, he was already feeling winded. Why couldn't he breathe properly? It seemed that he was fighting while holding his breath! Battered but unbowed, Aidan charged back in, and Kai realized something: he, Kai, had had his weekly lessons, but Aidan had been a servant competing among the others for status and women since childhood. And that experience, that confidence in his own ability not merely to hit but to *absorb* punishment, was serving him quite well just now.

Aidan dove under Kai's arm and got hold of him. His shoulder smashed into Kai's ribs, driving the breath from him again. Kai hammered at Aidan's back, alarmed to realize that he was swinging wildly, that too much of his carefully cultivated technique was vanishing under the emotional and physical pressure, the sheer adrenal exhaustion.

Aidan picked Kai up, heaving and grunting as he pitched his master over his shoulder, backwards to the ground. If Kai hadn't twisted like a cat, he might have broken his neck. He landed hard on his shoulder, and was glad not to have fractured anything as he struck the packed earth.

"Kai!" Sophia called. He stood again, dazed, blood starting from his mouth. Triple Aidans danced in his vision.

Hit the one in the middle.

The two men commenced pounding on each other. Kai got in one, two, three good shots to body and face. He had good leverage, fought to get torque and remember the other things that he had been taught. Aidan snuck in a blow to Kai's abdomen. It was like being jabbed with a hot poker. Aidan's body was so *hard!* How could it be so hard? He, Kai, did his exercises daily, as prescribed, and a reasonable man might expect him to be the better conditioned. But Aidan had labored dawn till dusk for years. His barrel of a midsection, while not pretty, was simply a wall of iron around his internal organs, against which Kai battered with little apparent effect.

Losing the fight against panic, Kai charged Aidan. Together, the two of them crashed through the door of Aidan's house, across the room, and almost onto the bed itself. Before Kai could right himself, Aidan was up, face bloody and grim, and hammered a right fist into Kai's jaw, knocking him sprawling. Kai managed to stand, all of the strength drained out of him, and Aidan knocked him down again.

He tried to rise to his hands and knees, vision blurred. Aidan stood over him, gazing down, his fists clenched, the muscles in his pale forearms swollen, and Kai looked up at him, thinking, *I don't know this man at all.*

"Stay down, Kai," Aidan said quietly, his voice deadly quiet. "I don't want to hurt you."

Kai stared at him in amazement, and then slowly rose to his feet. He didn't look at Aidan, filled with shame and confusion so deep and pervasive it was physically debilitating.

He didn't speak to Sophia, but he did look at her. She was as pale as the ghost she was, all blood drained from her face. She couldn't meet his eyes for long, and turned away.

Kai buckled on his sword, and for a moment the crowd of witnesses at the doorway held its collective breath, perhaps wondering if he would slay Aidan now. And *estafghuar Allah*—Allah forgive him—he wanted to, so badly, so fiercely, that it was shocking. He wanted to drive his sword into

Aidan's guts, watch the smug bastard's eyes roll up, listen to him scream, smell his blood in the night.

You gave your word, on your honor, that he had the right to defend himself. Even though he wronged you. Even though you have the right. You gave your word.

Kai had to leave, and right now, or it wouldn't matter what he had promised. The urge to avenge his honor, to reassert himself in the eyes of these miserable creatures, was almost more than he could bear.

Instead, he staggered away, away from the house, and then out of the village.

Aidan watched Kai leave, Sophia clutching him so tightly he could barely breathe. All of the emotion he had repressed during their fight boiled out of him now: regret, pain—and most of all, fear. What had he done? Only now, watching Kai's battered face attempting to compose itself into dignity, did he realize that it was not merely Sophia's betrayal that had wounded the Wakil's son. It was not just his loss of status in the eyes of his human possessions. Kai had thought Aidan his friend, and betrayal was betrayal, a knife that cut deeply regardless of station.

Worse, Aidan realized that that bond's rupture had gutted him as well.

And after the flash of grief and regret another layer opened up: despite Kai's promise, both Aidan's life and Sophia's could be forfeit at a single word. And the only thing that kept his fear at bay was his belief, his trust, that Kai was still his friend, and would respect his promise.

And if he was, if Kai *was* his friend, and a man of honor, then what had Aidan done?

He ground his fist against his temples as his heartbeat slowed, the adrenaline fading. No! He had done nothing wrong! This was madness! He was a man who had been torn from his home, his father killed, sister sold away and mother destroyed, that Kai's family might profit by his misery. And after long years he had found love. If Kai was worthy of friendship, then on some level he had to understand that.

But if he was . . .

If he wasn't . . .

Aidan felt as if the top of his head was about to fly off. Sophia clung to him desperately, and at last he gave in to his own fatigue and fear, and held her, trembling in her arms.

"Come, please," Sophia said. "You're hurt." Unprotesting, Aidan let her lead him back into his ruin of a house.

As they went, Aidan saw Brian, who leaned back into the shadows and lit his pipe with a flaming straw. The mixed aroma of tobacco and hemp wafted through the darkness. His smile was like the night stars, conferring light, but no warmth at all.

Not speaking, Aidan sat staring at his cottage's shattered door as Sophia mixed soap and water, dampened a cloth.

She swabbed and daubed his wounds, her own hands trembling now as the enormity of the events crashed down upon her as well. For a time she was able to maintain focus, but as soon as Aidan's wounds had been cleansed, the gaping hole at the center of her heart drew her back down. This was beyond disaster: it was death and destruction. There were some mistakes that you cannot undo. You cannot uncook a fish, then set it free to swim. Cannot unscramble an egg and set it beneath a hen to hatch.

Their fate was utterly in the hands of the man who owned them both, who had every reason to consider himself betrayed, and the privilege to enforce his will. "What will become of us?" she asked.

"I don't know," Aidan said, and meant it.

Kai staggered away from the shantytown toward the lights of Dar Kush, leading Djinna and Majii by their reins. He made it about halfway, and then sank to his knees. He sobbed for breath, disoriented, unsure where he was or what he needed to do. He rose again, staggered halfway to the barn, then collapsed again. He had made a wide circle around the house, where the party was beginning to wind down. Many of the guests had already left, some had turned in for the night in one of the many guest rooms.

How would he explain his injuries? What if a slave's whisper found his father's ear? Or Nandi's, or, Allah save him, Malik's? The shame was almost unendurable. He held his arms up in supplication to the moon.

"There are no answers there, young Kai," said Babatunde, appearing suddenly and quietly behind him.

Kai was too exhausted and wracked with pain to be surprised. Instead, he felt an almost pitiful gratitude. "Babatunde," he croaked. "Help me. Please."

Babatunde studied Kai carefully, coming close without actually touching him. "What has happened?"

Kai considered. Did he dare tell the truth? And then realized that if there was anyone in the world who might help him through the labyrinth he had constructed for himself, it was the little Yoruba scholar.

So there, in the moonlight, Kai spoke his heart, and when he had concluded, Babatunde breathed deeply, and stood, staring up at the moon and the stars for almost two minutes before speaking. "I have no power to help or heal," he said. "But Allah does."

"I hurt," Kai said, his voice a child's.

"The body follows the mind." Babatunde's voice was kind. "The mind follows the heart. Open your heart."

Kai had no strength to resist, and something deep within him craved the peace that Babatunde seemed to promise.

Together, they knelt in the damp grass. "My prayers have not been heard," Kai said. "Help me, please."

Babatunde clasped Kai's arm. "Men have divided Fatimite Islam into two paths," he said. "One of the spirit, and one of the flesh. The Ulema has taken what once was a hard but true path to Allah and bent it to the petty needs of men."

"What other way is there?" Kai asked, confused.

"When you are truly ready for the answer to that question," Babatunde replied, "you will know what to do."

CHAPTER FORTY

THERE WERE FEW COMMENTS upon Kai's bruises when he bid Nandi and her party farewell the following afternoon. He mumbled a response about a "midnight ride" that had ended in a tumble. No one challenged him directly, although Shaka shook his leonine head with ill-concealed derision.

There was only one surprise among his interactions with the guests. Before mounting her horse, Nandi touched his face, a softness in her expression he had never seen before.

"If you were mine," she said, "I would heal those wounds. All your wounds."

He held her hand, unable to answer her unspoken questions. "Travel well," he said. "And write to me."

She smiled, and kissed his cheek, pausing only to whisper in his ear: "Remember our night, Kai." And grazed her cheek along his as she pulled back. He winced at the contact, but managed to maintain his smile.

Then the Zulus departed in coaches and on horseback, beginning their three-day journey home.

His sense of relief was enormous: one hurdle passed. His body was stiff and sore, and his face felt lumpy.

Kai's father did not ask him what had transpired, although his keen gaze clearly saw the damage. Instead, he put his arm around his younger son and asked him to supervise the construction of a new corral in the northern pasture.

Kai changed clothes, dreading the moment he would face the slaves again. If he saw one slack-jawed grin he might well skewer the offender . . .

Fortunately, the crew assigned him displayed no slightest sign that they knew anything about the fight with Aidan. They shouldered their tools and accompanied him quietly out to the work site.

By late afternoon Kai was immersed in the minutia of corral construction. If anything, the men on the work crew were a bit more deferential and nervous around him. *They're waiting for the explosion,* he thought. The knowledge that they respected his authority if not his fighting ability gave him scant comfort.

He was still directing the crew when Aidan rode up on Majii. Kai tensed. He noted that the rest of the work crew ceased their casual conversation as well.

Aidan seemed uncertain of himself, and even more so when Kai glanced at him once and then turned away. "Kai," he said. "I wanted to speak to you."

Kai did not turn around, focusing all of his attention on the crew of whites digging holes for the fence posts. "We have nothing to speak of."

An edge of desperation crept into Aidan's voice. "That's not true, Kai. Please—"

Now Kai turned. There were still bruises on his face, but the wounds in his spirit cut more deeply still. Finally Kai nodded, and the two of them took a few steps away from the others. Once they had a bit of privacy, Kai said, "What you did can't be undone."

"I love her, Kai. Can *you* say that?"

"I don't need to say that," Kai said coolly. "Do you realize that you could simply disappear?"

They gazed at each other, the overt charge between them surprisingly mild. On the surface, they might have been two old friends discussing the market price of beef, rather than master and slave speaking obliquely of torture and death. Aidan didn't blink. "Yes. I love her. I would marry her. Answer my question."

Kai searched his old friend's face, looking for fear, uncertainty. Lies. Fear he saw, but no uncertainty, and no lying. Kai remembered Sophia's touch, her lips, her whispers in the dark, thought of the peace he had experienced in her arms and knew that in another world, a different world, he could have found contentment there. He would have been tempted to ask her to be his. Knew in fact that he would have already, for better or for worse.

Such a union could not be, not even as second or third wife—it would be ruinous to his family name. Were he of lower birth, even a merchant, then perhaps. But the son of the Wakil? Impossible. He might have kept her for the seraglio. Perhaps even had some sort of private ceremony, bonded to her while presenting a different face to the rest of the world.

But he could never treat her as an equal, never really join with her in the eyes of men, let alone the sight of Allah. And if not, what was he thinking? Just how selfish was he?

Aidan had him trapped, twisted around his own ethics and obligations. But did that explain why his anger was fading, replaced by a deep and numbing sadness?

For the first time in years, he appreciated anew the trap he was in. Sophia had touched his heart. Perhaps he loved her, perhaps it was just the inevitable masculine need to possess and control. He was honest enough to admit that he could not be certain which. He tested his emotions by asking himself a question: Did he want Sophia to know the joy of growing old with someone who cared for her?

A thin wind blew from the east, and its chill cooled his anger even more, left him feeling distant from his own heart. In Aidan's face he saw all of the things that he could not give Sophia. Sadness swelled within him, became almost unendurable.

So be it.

"Then be with her," Kai said, offering the only gift he had to give in reward for all of Aidan's years of friendship. No, not friendship. Brotherhood. And he had just told himself another lie. He gave no gift. Aidan had earned her. "I give her back to my father. She is now merely another household servant, and may choose whom she will. You have your world. I have mine. *Asslaamu alaykum.*"

"*Waalaykum salaam.*" Aidan paused, perhaps hoping that Kai would bend, would throw his arms wide in embrace, that the barriers between them might fall. Kai's face was impassive, but from long years' experience

Aidan knew that he had given all he was capable of. There was no more. "Thank you. I think . . . that I have work to do."

Kai nodded, not looking at Aidan as his former friend donned work gloves and began the labor of wrapping and repairing the wire, tightening, inspecting and nailing firm to the posts the endless strands of fence.

Soon Aidan was indistinguishable from the others, just another servant in service to Dar Kush, and the family of the honorable Wakil Abu Ali.

The day's work was done at last. The Wakil noted that Aidan, from long habit, had slowly taken over the supervision of the fence project, leaving Kai with less and less to do, so that ultimately the Wakil's son had mounted and returned to the house, his room, and his study.

Abu Ali found Kai immersed in his books when the bell rang across the estate grounds, and he heard the cry of "Quittin' time!" passed from throat to throat with joyful anticipation.

When the Wakil entered the room, Kai rose at once, smiling, and a brief paleness flitting across his face told Abu Ali that his son had hoped for rather a different visitor.

"Father. I didn't know you were there."

Abu Ali noted the bare walls in the small room branching from Kai's. Sophia's room. All of the furniture had already been removed. A pair of empty bookshelves sat in the middle of the floor, not yet nestled against the wall. This was to be Kai's study, and one day soon it would be a fine one. "I see you are remodeling."

Kai nodded. "Yes. I needed more room for my books."

"Study is good," he said. He had sensed his son's pain, regretting the never-ending stream of day-to-day concerns that drained his own time and energy. "I have been busy of late. Is my son well?" He came closer, studying the bruises on Kai's face. The swelling had gone down, his young warrior's resilience asserting itself, but traces yet remained. Of course, the Wakil knew what had happened in Ghost Town. In fact, he was glad it had; the slaves had seen that Kai was a man of honor, a good thing once Ali assumed control of Dar Kush. They would fear Ali, and trust Kai, and in such a manner would his household endure.

Kai tried to smile, but failed. He turned away from his father, balling his fists and planting them on his desk. "How can one know what is right, and what is wrong, Father?"

Abu Ali could clearly hear the anguish in those words, and had no easy answer for his son. He went to the window, looking out on the estate that he had inherited from his own father, that he had expanded with his own hands. The lands that would one day go to his sons as their legacy.

From the window he watched a familiar figure, his son's servant and friend Aidan, returning from the northern pasture with a line of other slaves. He looked dusty and sweaty, but happy. They were all returning to the shantytown that was their world. Their camaraderie protected them from the grief and pain that he sometimes suspected was the lot of bondsmen. Was the lot of all men, Abu Ali thought sadly.

A slip of a girl ran out from the direction of the village, along with other women. From the quarry, from the fields and the village, the men and women of Dar Kush greeted each other with hugs and kisses and laughter. Their world. He recognized the woman Sophia, who should have been with his son, running to Aidan. They embraced, kissing lustily, then twined arms around each other and returned to the village. It seemed as natural and right as the sunset.

Abu Ali sighed, and without turning around, began to speak. "When we stand before Allah," he said, "we will have nothing but our hearts and actions to present to Him. That is the moment we prepare for. It is only in that light that we know what is right and what is wrong."

Kai's face was tortured. Abu Ali gathered his son in his arms. Kai gripped at him desperately, as might a child. "You are on the cusp," said Abu Ali. "And crossing it is always difficult, and often feels like death itself. This is the moment, this is your time. It is not sex that makes a boy a man, not feats of arms, nor wealth, nor worldly responsibility."

"What, then?" Kai's voice was muffled by his father's chest.

"The understanding that other human beings have a spirit, an essence equal in the eyes of Allah, whatever their station in life. That we must measure our actions and reactions in this world lest we pay dearly in the next. It is this measured consideration of every word and action, and their consequences, that makes a man a man. Nothing less."

His son clung to him like a child years younger, and the Wakil stroked his neck as though Kai were a panicked foal. With his whores and his studies, his casual brilliance, Kai had never had to make a truly adult decision in his entire life.

The first was always the hardest. The first left blood on the sheets.

CHAPTER FORTY-ONE

6 *Dhu'-Hijja* 1289
(March 16, 1872)

LAKE A'ZAM WAS FED BY STREAMS from the northern mountains, waters filtered through the swamp and diverted through irrigation ditches into the fields. A'zam itself birthed a waterway, dredged more deeply by human hands, leading all the way to Djibouti harbor. At the northwestern edge were the marshes, partially natural, partially created by dams further north that had reshaped the waterways a hundred years before.

And at a northeastern corner of Abu Ali's land, on the edge of the marsh, sat a small square adobe mosque, given to Babatunde by the Wakil in perpetuity in gratitude for his service. Willow trees sheltered it from curious eyes.

If one drew close to its clay walls on a night such as this, the sounds of worship would have been heard, and voices chanting: *"La! Illaha! Ill Allah!"*

It was a beautiful, melodic chant. Come closer, and the sound became more intense, as if the words are merely the carriers of some higher energetic. Lights flickered within the building.

This was zikr, the Sufi ceremony where prayer and motion blended together in a dancelike confluence. The tiny room was crowded with fifteen men and women who sat in a great circle, facing each other but separated into groups by gender. Most of their faces were black, with a few paler faces of Arab descent mixed in. This small, secretive group represented every Sufi for two hundred miles. While not illegal, Sufism was persecuted and suspect. Sufis had been driven off their land, jailed on trumped-up charges, murdered in midnight raids. All of that was forgotten during zikr. For these precious hours, they basked in the light of Allah.

A drum beat rhythmically, and their shoulders twisted in time to its beat. Babatunde's eyes were half-closed, his face suffused with ecstasy, as if the hands of Allah Himself were lifting him up.

"*La!*" he chanted, "*Illaha! Ill Allah! La! Illaha! Ill Allah.*"

There is no God but the One God, he chanted over and over again, burning the holy phrase into the minds of each and every one of his followers.

As he sang, hymns called *ilahes* were chanted in counterpoint by the others, creating a consistent and hypnotic rise and fall of melodies.

Then, suddenly, the music stopped.

Babatunde looked up, his eyes still fixed on a distant horizon. "All praise Allah and His most holy messenger Muhammad, peace and blessings be upon him. One comes before us today who pledges himself to the deeper mysteries, to place his heart in the hands of He who made the universe. Come forward, Kai."

There was a swift and brief disturbance in the back of the room, and the rows of worshippers parted. An elder darvish approached, Kai walking behind him with his head down, hands on the elder's shoulders. Around Kai's neck he wore the crescent medallion that Babatunde had once offered him, a symbol whose responsibilities he had merely postponed.

Babatunde noted his posture with approval. "We who love only Allah must beware of those who twist His holy word for power in this world. Who vouches for this man?"

There was a pause, in which no one spoke. Babatunde himself was forced to pierce the silence. "I myself will speak for him. He is my student, and my friend. As it has given me pleasure to see him grow from child to man, so it now is greater still to see him pass into the brotherhood of those who seek to unite man to the creator of the universe."

Kai still stood behind the elder. Now, finally, he spoke the words he had been taught. "Peace be unto you, and the mercy of Allah and His blessings, O man of the path."

"O man of the law and seeker of the law," Babatunde replied. "The *Shariya* are the words of Muhammad."

"Blessed be his name."

"Do you accept Allah as your God?"

"I do accept," said Kai.

"Do you accept Muhammad as His prophet?"

"I do accept."

"Do you accept all of the other prophets: Jesus, Abraham, and the others?"

"I do accept."

"Do you accept my *pirs*, my great teachers, as your *pirs*?"

"I do accept."

"Do you accept my sheiks as your sheiks?"

"I do accept."

"Do you accept me as your teacher?"

"I do accept."

Babatunde joined his hands together and began to pray over Kai, evoking his lineage back to Bilal and the Prophet himself. When concluded, the Sufi raised his head. "When the Prophet's son-in-law Ali asked, 'What is the best way to reach Allah?' the Prophet answered, 'Through zikr.'"

He reached out and traced the word "Allah" over Kai's heart with his finger. Then Babatunde took Kai's hand, right to right.

"Repeat each of these back to me three times," he said softly, and Kia nodded assent.

"La illaba ill Allah," he said, and Kai repeated that precious phrase three times.

"Ya Allah." Ob God.

"Ya hiyy." Ob Alive.

"Ya haqq." The Truly Real.

"Ya Qahar." The Compeller and Dominate.

"Ya Latif." The Subtle.

Now Kai's breath stopped as Babatunde asked Kai the question that would separate him forever from other men. "The Prophet Muhammad says: 'Die before you die.' In *Hadith Qutsi* it is written, 'My servant hates to die, and I hate to disappoint him.' Reconcile these two."

Kai paused but for a moment before repeating what had been patiently learned, and what he still only fleetingly understood. "What dies," he said, "is what that person is other than Allah. What Allah preserves is the divine essence that came with the first breath."

Babatunde's eyes shone, and he bade Kai stand.

Then the *rabar,* the darvish who originally led Kai into the mosque, took Kai around the circle. He shook hands with each of the men reverently, and bowed to each of the women with his hands over his heart.

When he had navigated the circle, his teacher addressed him again. "Kai," Babatunde said. "Do you witness that God is the only God, swear to profess your faith, to act in charity and piety, to keep holy the sacraments, and to protect, at cost of your own life, the inner chamber?"

"I do," Kai said.

There was a collective sigh from the assembled. Babatunde nodded in satisfaction. "Kai, greet your brothers and sisters."

CHAPTER FORTY-TWO

THE WORKWEEK HAD ENDED. There was music and dancing, and slave men and women from Djidade Berhar's estate had arrived to add their wishes to the festivities.

"Good day for a wedding!" a slave girl called, and received a chorus of greetings in return.

In Aidan's house, Sophia was nervous as a cat. She was surrounded by the women of the village, who were busy preparing her, sewing her into her wedding gown. Now that she had given up the comforts of the big house, and they had embraced her as one of them, it was strange to remember that there had ever been a time she had not known their companionship.

She looked down at the frilly thing as they busied themselves happily. The dress had been cobbled together from scraps donated by the Wakil, but so cleverly constructed that it might have cost fifty Alexanders.

Around her neck was a tiny silver cross, one of the very few possessions she had brought with her from her former life. She had never worn it for Kai, and never thought about the fact that she hadn't. Not until she had thought of the day of her wedding had she been consumed by the urge to wear the thumb-sized crucifix, a present from her long-dead father.

"Now you hold still, girl," said Auntie Moira, who had been ancient in Aidan's youth and now seemed more spirit than flesh. Most slaves just called her Crone or Rune Woman. Her fingers were twisted with arthritis, but still nimble enough with a needle and thread.

"What if it won't fit?"

"Bah. Every woman in the *tuath*'s been married in this gown. Every one of them looked beautiful." She completed her stitch. "And none more than you. There!"

Moira produced a bit of mirror, held it so that Sophia could see herself clearly. The dress made her ravishing, and the breath caught in her throat at the sight. Still, she couldn't quiet her butterflies. "I'm so nervous."

The crone cackled. "Don't be, girl. Just say yer vows, and do yer wifely duty tonight. Ye'll be fine."

Sophia squinted. "Wifely . . . duty?"

The old woman gave her a gap-toothed, bawdy grin. "Bumpty-bump, girl. Nothing strange to ye. Now get on!"

One of the other girls handed her a bouquet of posies, and Sophia stepped out of the door.

The celebration outside quieted as she went to meet Aidan. Rows of slaves stood watching expectantly and eagerly. She walked between the rows like an empress. At the village square waited Aidan, dressed in tattered but freshly mended and washed work clothes.

Sophia smiled shyly at Aidan, and stepped forward.

Moira stood between the two of them, holding their hands in hers. "Do you, Sophia De Moroc, and you, Aidan O'Dere, vow to hold and help one another, and leave off all bundling about with others?" There was a general chuckling at the words. "If so, by the Good Lady we love, by the powers of earth and sky, and the heart of the mighty Christ, I say you are married."

They turned. Two of the male villagers stretched out a strand of fence wire at knee level. Aidan and Sophia stepped backwards and then jumped the wire, landing with a laugh. "Green pastures!" the Rune Woman cackled, and the new couple kissed greedily.

With a cheer, the gathering broke into song and dancing. Sophia and Aidan stepped together to the clapping and shouting of the village. The song ended. Aidan gathered Sophia into his arms for another kiss, to which she responded with relish.

Auntie Moira clapped in approval. "Bumpty-bump!"

Aidan broke off the kiss and laughed. Both of them were handed flagons of beer, which they quaffed heartily. As Aidan drank, he searched the crowd, warmed by the warm and joyous faces. Still, something was missing . . .

Sophia slipped her hand to his cheek, turned his face back to hers. "My love?"

He slipped his arm around her shoulder. "Nothing," he said. "Nothing at all."

And he smiled at her, and they entwined arms and drank from each other's cup.

Night had fallen and the party was torchlit but still going strong. Brian performed an energetic version of "Laddie" for the dancers, adding a verse that was never, ever sung when the masters were listening. It was a variation that inevitably raised eyebrows and nods of grim approval from the assembled:

Cut us low, swing us 'round
Iron shackles tightly bound
Thresh your soul by the mornin' lark
Lie in your dreams in the dead of dark—
Laddie are ya workin'?

Suddenly the music died. Aidan and Sophia paused in the middle of their dance, and the crowd parted.

They turned, and there stood Kai. He was dressed in black robes and a turban, and black slippers. His face was carefully composed, placid, adorned with a small, polite smile. When he moved, it was with a slightly stiff, puppetlike quality, as if he were watching himself rather than living fully in his body and the moment.

For a long, nervous moment he stood before Aidan and Sophia, then extended a small cask, one similar to one that had begun a friendship, long years before.

Kai inclined his head in the merest suggestion of a bow. When he spoke, his voice was soft and precisely measured. "Once, long ago," he said, "we plundered my father's cellar for hemp beer, spirits intended for the servants. Occasionally, my father entertains guests who are not Muslim, but possess a more rarefied taste. I thought, on this special night, you might want to consider yourselves guests of my house." He extended the cask. "Our best," he said.

Sophia and Aidan were unable to speak. Then Aidan stepped forward and took the cask from Kai. "Thank you."

Kai nodded in acknowledgment. Sophia darted uncertainly forward, planting a kiss on his cheek. Kai gave no visible reaction.

Then he turned and walked away, almost floating with each step.

The village gates closed behind him. When he was gone, the slaves gathered in tightly.

"Well, Aidan," Brian said. "We're dyin' to know."

Aidan raised an eyebrow. "Why the hell not?" He poured some of the cask's contents into a goblet. At the first sip his senses glowed. The golden brew slid down his throat, intoxicating even before it reached his belly.

The crowd waited in an expectant hush. Aidan nodded enthusiastically, and they began to cheer as he passed the keg around. Sophia drank from the goblet, and her eyes widened with delight. Then she was spirited away by giggling friends. Aidan handed the goblet to Brian. Brian drank deeply. The men watched the dour, scarred face, waiting for him to pass judgment.

"If they can afford *this*," Brian said, "I can understand why the blacks won't let themselves drink."

"And why is that?"

Brian took another swallow. "For the same reason a man can't lick his own balls. If he could, he'd never give two shites for aught else." An absolutely evil grin split his face, and the *tuath* cheered and gathered around, eager to sample.

Spring swelled sweetly, and with it came word that Allah had blessed Ghost Town with fertility: among the children due come winter would be the fruit of Aidan and Sophia's marriage.

Soon after came even greater news: Malik and Fatima had, at last, conceived a child. Malik seemed to swell with pride and expectation, bending every ear that would listen with tales of how his son would outride and outfight the proudest sons of New Alexandria. Fatima herself seemed to accept the news with as much relief as joy, spending her days in her hothouse, her nights in Malik's arms as they watched the sky and spoke quietly of the future.

Harvest time came, and with it the mellowing of leaves from green to brown and a growing edge of chill in the air. Bondsmen labored in the fields, harvesting beans and teff. They cut wood, and began the laying of a foundation for a new barn. Aidan worked out in the fields or quarries at Brian's side, the two of them in a harmony that was more like family than anything Aidan had known since the early days with Kai.

Sophia worked with the women: cooking, cleaning, mending, carrying food to the men out in the fields, sometimes working at their sides.

Aidan grew accustomed to the rougher food eaten by the other slaves, often corncakes and a little beef. Sometimes he would look enviously at the overseers, white and black, who feasted on roast beef or turkey or lamb. But his envy lasted only a moment, and then he would stuff his mouth greedily. He would not have changed his current state for theirs. Despite the limitations of his life, he was a happy man.

On *al-ahad*, the first day of the week, Aidan sang and worshipped with Sophia beneath the grove's shadowed canopy. His own voice was rough but strong, hers tutored and sweet, focused now on worship rather than seduction.

Their small community, made up of workers, had no trained priests or druids. They did the best they could, however. Several translations of sacred Christian scrolls sat on the Wakil's shelves, and Abu Ali had made a compilation available to Tom Leary, who served as the community's lay priest. Moira spoke to those who chose the druidic path, as she had longer than anyone could remember. Tall, sour, and dark of hair, lantern-jawed Leary shared her stump. Their words were crafted to blend the village, not divide it, so the services were often a meld of Celtic Catholic, Gnostic Christian, Druidic, and the Gospel of Mary Magdalene.

When Aidan sang, he forgot his troubles. When he cast a glance at Sophia's swelling stomach his heart soared far above Dar Kush, into another landscape entirely. Since the night of their marriage, when she had cast aside the herb-soaked sponge that had prevented Kai from impregnating her, the potential for creating new life had warmed their bed, sweetened the already aching tenderness of their lovemaking. Now that his seed had caught . . .

Sophia noted his glance, caught his hand and placed it over her navel, as if by so doing he might sense the warmth and life of their unborn child.

He closed his eyes, praying as he sang, as the voices of his *tuath* rose to enfold him, and for that blessed moment, neither he, nor his wife or child, belonged to anyone but their God.

CHAPTER FORTY-THREE

As Lamiya completed her morning ride, a gentle mist rolled across the lawn from the east, as if driven by the dawning sun. She enjoyed the infrequent gift of time alone and unfettered by obligation. Always, it seemed, it was state dinners, excursions to the homes of the wealthy and powerful, who longed to hear of affairs at court. Or time with Ali, more important as the day of their marriage approached.

Would that she could have followed her heart! Simply married whom she loved, like any slave girl could do. And who might that have been? A dreamy smile warmed her face as she contemplated. If she had been a simple peasant girl, mightn't she have found love with a shepherd, or a cobbler? And mightn't a simple home and hearth, warmed with love, have been equal to a palace . . . ?

Her eye was pulled to a solitary figure standing on the crest of the northern hill overlooking the estate. It was Kai. As had been his preference for some months now, he was dressed in black robes, and stood with his hands behind his back, looking out toward the eastern horizon.

She pulled her horse up and dismounted. He didn't seem to notice her. "Kai . . . ?" she asked.

He held up a hand, shushing her. She suppressed her flash of irritation and followed his gaze, and watched as a single, solitary eagle flew in front of the sun's blinding golden disk.

"Beautiful," she said, and again noted his lack of reaction. He seemed to be walled away from her, his family . . . from everything. Ali had the same ability, to simply disappear inside himself, and at such times she wondered if he had feelings at all. She thought it was probably just his way of preparing to assume power.

But Kai was different. Even when he retreated, as he recently had, she knew that he was still present. Hiding. Frightened of his own feelings. "Kai," she said as gently as she could, almost as if afraid to startle him. "You've been so alone the last few weeks. You barely talk to me anymore."

He clasped his hands behind his back. "I've had much to think of. But you've been busy. Plans for the wedding, certainly."

"But not too busy to see that my little brother is troubled."

Kai's hand gripped the medallion around his neck, a meld of the Islamic mooncrest and the enigmatic symbol Babatunde called the Naqsh Kabir, doubtless one of the mystic mysteries locked in the scholar's esoteric little heart.

Kai held it almost as if he believed it would ward off evil, or unwanted emotion. "For now," he said, "I have Allah to hear my prayers. I need no more."

He seemed completely sealed off. She leaned forward, and kissed his cheek. He turned and looked at her, and there was such love and hunger in his eyes that she was taken aback. "I must go," she said.

He nodded, and watched as she mounted her horse.

"I miss you," she said.

She turned her horse, her heart sad and confused, and rode away.

Kai said nothing more, lost in the mist and the light.

* * *

Standing in his study, Wakil Abu Ali made a few elegant cuts in the air with Nasab Asad as Kai entered. His younger son's eyes lighted on the sacred blade, then ranged back to his father.

"You called me, Father?"

"Yes, Kai. These are perilous times. You have seen the new map?"

Kai nodded. "The Aztecs are on the move again." The Wakil waved his hand at the relief map sprawled across the wall above his fireplace. Across the hills and ridges, valleys and rivers, lines were drawn, fiery symbols representing aggressive actions on the part of the Aztecs. The lines had come close, too close, to the Shrine of the Fathers, which was marked with a silver model. Kai knew that several frontier homesteads had been burned by the Aztec prince, said to be the tenth Montezuma, a mighty horseman and warrior. The wealth of the New World had induced the first Muslim traders to part with horses and steel as early as the year 300. The trading had been good, but now the wisdom of their choice seemed questionable.

Behind their strange, feathered armor, the Aztecs were said to be as rapacious and innumerable as the sands of the desert. And the frontier was but a week's ride from Dar Kush.

"Just a few days' ride from here, Montezuma has burned estates." The Wakil dropped his head. "My dear friend Akbar Muhammad is dead."

"I am sorry," Kai said. He was shocked as well. Akbar Muhammad had accompanied Abu Ali and Malik on one of their most notorious campaigns, pushing back the Tawakoni and the Comanche, defining the current western boundaries. He remembered Akbar as a rotund, jovial man who enjoyed Abu Ali's hemp crop for other than purely constructional purposes.

Abu Ali tapped Cetshwayo's estate, where months before their mares had been impregnated. "I wish you to court Nandi. In times like these, our families must stand together, bound by blood."

There it was. No more dancing about, and Kai supposed that he should have felt relieved. Instead, he felt irritation. "They are not true Muslims."

"Nandi is a Zulu woman. She will be obedient to her husband."

Oh, yes, I just bet, Kai thought. He remembered their night in her father's study. *Who was providing stud service for whom?*

"She will convert," his father continued. "This is important, Kai. You will respect my wishes."

"Regardless of my heart?" Strange. He felt Nandi's pull powerfully, and perhaps left to himself might have taken her to wife. But his contrary heart betrayed him: his father's insistence seemed offensive.

The Wakil's face went cool. "It should be your heart's wish to respect my command."

Kai's irritation increased to anger. *This is why you were born. This is the obligation of privilege.* Kai bowed. "Very well, Father," he said.

Stud service indeed.

12 *Shawwal* 1289

(December 10, 1872)

Although Aidan's cottage was still humble, it had been more thoroughly decorated by a woman's hand and eye, and was now more a home than a mere house. Lace hangings softened the room's corners, and embroidered tablecloths and chair cushions reminded him of lost boyhood in Eire.

Aidan slept, comfortable in dreams of his lost homeland. At his side, Sophia was swollen with child, and lost in an even deeper slumber.

Distantly, he began to register the tolling of a bell. He rose groggily and dressed, kissing Sophia before he went.

"Whazzit?" she said, not even a quarter awake.

"Sleep, little one," he said. Certainly, whatever this latest problem was, there was no need for the love of his life to wake herself.

By the time Aidan reached the swinging wood-and-wire frame of the main gate, he understood the nature of the alarm.

The Wakil's private road, which stretched north to Malik's estate and then continued for ten miles beyond, linked to other trade and travel routes and was the broadest, best-paved road for a hundred miles. Refugees streaming from the west crossed that road north of Malik's holdings, intending to travel to the more civilized territories bordering New Alexandria. In the past few days dozens of them had come south to the Wakil, where they knew charity could be found. Some were afoot, others mounted on horse or camel, and driving wagons packed to creaking with their furniture, tools, and children.

The caravan at the gate now was the most pitiful Aidan had yet seen: black dirt farmers scratching out a living raising hemp and beans on land leased from the Aztecs fifty years ago and recently claimed as part of Bilalistan's western territory. They looked hungry and frightened, and were dressed more poorly than most of Abu Ali's servants. Five small black children stared out from the mountain of lashed-down shovels and seed sacks.

Aidan felt sorry for them until one of the children looked at him, his thick lips curling into a sneer. *We may be poor,* that expression said, *but at least we're black.*

The Wakil and his sons were already parlaying with the family. Elenya and Lamiya were heading out from the mansion leading a pair of servants carrying plates of food, an oft-repeated ritual in the last few days.

"No, sir," one of them was saying to the Wakil as Elenya handed fresh bread to his daughter. "I have no urge to return at all. The Aztecs are demons."

Ali bristled. "But you can't just leave your land to the infidels!"

"If I don't," he said, "they'll water it with our blood. My son must grow to be a man."

Ali was unconvinced. "But—"

"Be silent, Ali," the Wakil said. "Sir, if my humble house may be of comfort to you, consider it yours. Provisions, a place to rest—whatever I can provide."

"If we can camp by your lake. Water for our horses—perhaps fresh food for the children?"

Lamiya smiled graciously. "You shall have a banquet."

"Help them," Abu Ali said to his servants. "Show them to the camp." No surprise there: from three to five families were camped out by Lake A'zam constantly now, eating the Wakil's bread, drinking his water.

Alongside the other servants, Aidan helped to unload necessities from the wagons. He turned to address Kai, who was helping an exhausted and disheartened woman down from the buckboard.

"What happened here?" Aidan asked.

"Refugees heading east from the frontier," Kai said, his manner still formal, as it had been since their skirmish. "Their encampment was wiped out."

A sad-eyed boy of about thirteen spoke. "We nailed one of them to a cross for stealing horses, and the next thing, our town was burning."

Now Kai's eyes widened. "Crucified? But the Kwami treaty specifically—"

Abu Ali shushed him. "They made a mistake, and paid for it," he said softly. "I hope the blood already spilled is sufficient price."

"*Insh'Allah,*" Kai said, as his father walked on.

Chewing at his mustache and brooding, Ali approached his brother. "Father hopes for peace," he muttered. "Meanwhile, the Aztecs feed our hearts to the fire, and refugees clog the roads. Keep your sword sharp, little brother."

Chester, Aidan's short, husky next-door neighbor, came running from the direction of Ghost Town. "Aidan!" he called.

Aidan turned, face tense and a bit fearful. "What?"

Led by the ancient Rune Woman, four of the village women had gathered in Aidan's cottage, preparing with herbs and boiled water and candles to help Sophia give birth. When Aidan arrived his wife was red-faced and panting. "Aidan, my love," she groaned. "The baby is coming."

His heart pounded at him. "What can I do?"

"I'd say ye already done it," Moira cackled at him. "This is women's work. Just leave us to it." She turned, speaking sharply to one of the other women. "I'll need more rags," she said, and then glared pointedly at Aidan. "And someone to get this *man* out of here."

Aidan bent to Sophia's side. "What do you want me to do?"

She gripped at his hand, in pain. "Have the baby for me?" she suggested, then arched her back. "*Oh!*"

She cried out as another contraction hit her, and one of the old women bustled Aidan out of the room. "Come along now. We can handle this."

"Breathe, now," Moira said. "Low in your belly. Pant, push . . ."

Aidan paced outside the house, cringing every time he heard Sophia scream. Brian handed him a pipe. "Here, boy—calm your nerves."

Aidan took a rough inhalation, held it and then expelled slowly. Almost immediately, his load felt a bit lighter. "How many times have you been through this?" he asked.

"How high can you count?" Brian laughed, smoke puffing from his lips. "I've made more money for the masters than all the teff and hemp in the fields."

"What do you mean?"

"You know what I mean," Brian said evenly. "You just don't want to think about it. Smoke up, boy—you're about to be a father."

Two hours passed, and still they stood outside the house. The world felt a good deal brighter and blurrier to Aidan by this point, and he handed the pipe back to Brian with somewhat bleary eyes. "And Abu Ali, and Ali and that damned Malik never take a puff?" he asked, and laughed.

"They ain't human," Brian speculated.

"They think they're more than human, and that we're less. The bastards sell our families off because they think marriages don't mean anything to us. That our children don't."

"That what master Kai told you?"

Aidan nodded sourly. "Implied as much. All just a lot of animal humping."

"If yer lucky," Brian said. They laughed for a few seconds, but the brief spate of humor quickly died. Brian puffed at the pipe again.

"Once upon a time," Aidan said, "I heard Oko say that if the Wakil could be white for just one night, he'd never want to be black again."

Brian stared at him, and then laughed uproariously, snatching the pipe from Aidan's hands to puff again.

Aidan suddenly shook himself out of his growing intoxication. There had been low cries in the background, but now there was silence. "What's that?"

"What?"

"That."

"Nothing."

"That's what I mean."

Suddenly, a baby's screams filled the air. The front door opened, and the Rune Woman emerged. Her brittle, wrinkled face had softened. For a moment Aidan could see what she must have looked like in her youth. "Stop laying about," she said. "It's time you saw your child."

Time seemed to stop, sound to cease. He swallowed thickly. "My child?"

"Your child. Go on, boy."

In the bedroom, Sophia's face was still flushed and damp, her hair tied back from her forehead with a string. She held their child close to her breast. She looked like she wanted nothing in the entire world so much as a week's sleep, but still had a smile for him. "There's someone I want you to meet," she said.

She tried to hold the swaddled infant out, but her strength failed. One of the women helped her, and Aidan took the child. So small, so impossibly frail, red-faced and damp. Aidan searched the infant's blue eyes, and for the first time realized that on some level he had wondered if this child would have dark skin, dark eyes. If his woman had miscalculated, if her herbs and sponges had failed her . . .

No. No chance of that at all. From the first glimpse, the first whiff of that unique and priceless baby scent, he knew that this was his flesh, his blood.

"Kiss your son."

"My . . . son?"

Aidan held his boy, and kissed his wife, tears streaming freely down his face. One of the old women cut a lock of the boy's thin hair and gave it to Aidan. He kissed Sophia again, and left.

Brian watched as Aidan left, smoking his pipe, keeping his thoughts to himself. "You know what to do, boyo?"

Aidan nodded.

Night was quiet in the grove. He carried the lock of his son's hair the mile to the swamp's edge, accompanied by four of the old women. They entered, making as little sound as possible. The night stars and crescent moon cast dim shadows into its depths. He found his way by memory and instinct.

Then, finding the right place, he knelt and dug a tiny hole with his hands. When it was as deep as his forearm, his fingernails clotted with earth, he put the lock of hair down in the hole, and nestled a sprouted date palm stone atop it. Then he filled in the hole.

His hands trembled as he wiped them against his face, and he realized that he was leaking from nose and eyes, that he had been making inarticulate mewling sounds. He looked up, and his eyes had adjusted to the light sufficient that he could see everything clearly.

Until this moment, he had kept a wisp of his dream of escape, of making his way back to that verdant land whose memory faded even now. But the birth of a child . . . that changed things. *This* was his world, and he would find a way to make a good life here.

"I, Aidan O'Dere, son of Mahon, give this bit of my own child to the earth. May the tree I plant here grow strong, and my son grow stronger still. May my son eat of the fruit of this tree as a free man."

The old women chanted alongside him, and he stood, allowing himself to take in the thousands of trees in the grove. Realized far more fully than ever he had that each and every tree in this grove represented a man or woman who had come to this land, or been born here. Each of them thought they were unique, and doubtless had their own special dreams. And so far as he knew, every single soul had been forced to abandon those dreams, and find what peace they could in the lot of a slave.

Then, with soft hands beneath his arms, the old women guided him gently from the grove, and back to his home.

CHAPTER FORTY-FOUR

THREE DAYS AFTER HER BABY'S BIRTH, Sophia returned to Dar Kush's kitchen to work, carrying her new son in a stomach sling. Mahon reacted to the bustle of cooks and serving girls by burrowing deeper against his mother.

One of the kitchen women abandoned a bubbling stew kettle to chuck the newborn under the chin. He drooled, his head flopping to the side, stubby arms moving blindly. "Oh! Isn't he just precious? And his name?"

"We named him for Aidan's father, Mahon." Sophia felt a bit flustered as the staff gathered around.

Round gray kitchen master Aengus looked at the baby almost as if he were examining a turkey roast. Then he smiled broadly, and Sophia's unease vanished. "Don't you need another day off?"

"It's time I'm back to work," she said.

A door opened and closed behind them, and a hush came over the kitchen staff as Lamiya and Babatunde entered, Lamiya in a simple saffron dress and the Yoruba wearing a tan robe. Instantly, Aengus deferred to them. "Miss," he said.

"Please," Lamiya said, holding her hands up. "Proceed. I just heard that there was a new member of the family."

She smiled at Sophia. Sophia had had a hard time relating to the masters since the dissolution of her relationship with Kai, and this unexpected kindness made her feel shy.

"May I?" Lamiya said.

"Certainly." She appreciated the courtesy, but knew that under it was the fact that any member of Abu Ali's household could sell her, or her baby. The realization caused a brief, hot flash of panic. She handed Mahon to Lamiya. Lamiya traced the child's face with one gentle finger.

"Beautiful," she said. "Motherhood is a precious thing."

Babatunde poked at one of the child's cheeks, and Mahon gurgled in delight. "Blessings upon you both."

"Do you have needs?" Lamiya asked, and seemed genuinely concerned.

"We are fine, mistress."

Lamiya nodded. "If you need anything, please let me know. Kitchen Master—what is that glorious aroma?"

"Roast bison, mistress."

"May I?" Babatunde asked. He dipped a spoon into a pot, and sipped the contents. Every slave in the kitchen waited anxiously for the response.

Babatunde seemed to roll the fluid around in his mouth. "You are . . . an artist."

"Thank you, sir," said Aengus proudly.

"Remember," Lamiya said. "If there is anything . . ."

Sophia managed to curtsy. "Yes, ma'am."

Lamiya and Babatunde left the kitchen. The slaves were silent for a moment, and then began talking again.

"You know," said one of the kitchen girls. "She meant that. When I had my third, the mistress was just a lass, but she talked the Wakil into extra meat rations for a month."

"Really? I—"

The women in the kitchen suddenly froze. Sophia turned anxiously.

Kai stood in the doorway, dressed in his rather severe black robes. He nodded to the kitchen staff, and they bowed in return. Kai walked slowly forward to where Sophia held her baby. Kai leaned close without speaking.

His face softened, and for a moment Sophia saw a glimpse of the old Kai, and it was such a happy sight that she wanted to reach out and touch him. Then he straightened without saying a word, and left the room. The slaves looked after him, and Sophia held her baby as tightly as she could without cutting off his breathing.

CHAPTER FORTY-FIVE

On a tile square beside the atrium's reflecting pool, Uncle Malik conducted a lesson for Kai and Ali, providing both instruction and amusement to the household. Malik was in fine fashion, more jovial than Kai had seen

him in months. Understandable, of course: just last week, Jimuyu had pro-
nounced Fatima well and fully pregnant!

Moving as lightly as a man in his twenties, Malik exhausted the brothers one after another, in rotation. Lamiya, Babatunde, the Wakil, and
Elenya watched. From time to time, in response to a particularly well executed thrust or parry, they cried "Hai!" or "Ho!", or appreciative catcalls
upon an error.

Through great exertions Kai managed to get a touch in, and grinned in
satisfaction. An instant later, Malik's spiraling disarm wrenched his blade
from his fist and made his fingers sting. Kai watched in dismay as his
sword clattered to the ground.

"Well done!" his uncle cried. Then, chidingly, "Next time, don't stop to
admire your thrust, eh?"

A white servant in robe and turban approached Malik, offering a tray of
refreshments. "Coffee, sir?"

Malik took a cup of coffee as Elenya bounced up to Kai enthusiastically.
"You're getting better." A recent growth spurt had raised Elenya to three
and a half cubits in height, with a round face that had yet to shed the last
of her baby fat. Recently, she had taken to dressing in the fashionable Afar
style: simple peasant blouse, dress, and sandals, her hair worn short with
tight, well-oiled braids in precise rows, studded with glazed beads.

"I'm still dead." Kai shrugged.

"And a fine-looking corpse you make." Malik slapped Kai on the shoulder. "Tell me, Kai, how goes the courting?"

Kai's cheeks burned. "Nandi? Well, we write letters."

"I'm sure they singe the paper, eh? She is a worthy prize, yes?"

Kai grinned and, rather uncomfortably, extracted himself from the conversation. He accepted a cup of coffee from the servant, and sipped, waiting for his heartbeat to slow back down. Despite his ignominious
disarming, and subsequent chiding, he had done almost as well as Ali.
High marks indeed. His work with Babatunde, while a mere supplement
to Malik's teaching, was helping him to visualize the line of engagement,
the angles of attack and defense, and was beginning to make a difference.

In watching his uncle spar against Ali now, he was able to determine
how Malik chose his attacks, watch *how* he separated a single second into
fractions, and managed to conserve emotion and energy so that he had all
the time in the world. Truly masterful, but no longer an absolute mystery.

The sparring ended. He watched Malik's head turn in distraction as a
pair of servants walked the edge of the atrium toward the front of the
house. Ah, it was Aidan and Sophia. Aidan often came to the house after

the day's work, walking Sophia back to Ghost Town with their little Mahon. And if Kai felt a wrench at the double loss, he was also relieved to find that part of himself could rejoice in Aidan's happiness.

Then, almost as if sensing Malik's eyes on her back, Sophia turned to face him.

Their eyes locked across the distance. Malik's gaze bored into her with a boldness and directness no Muslim ever displayed toward a woman of his own station, or indeed any black woman. Sophia seemed taken aback by his intensity. Aidan, slower on the uptake, turned to regard Malik.

The sword master smiled and hoisted his cup of coffee in a silent tribute to the new mother. Sophia found the strength to place her right hand over her heart, and bow courteously. Then, turning, she gripped Aidan's waist with her arm and hurried away, somehow managing to maintain her dignity with every step.

Later, after a fine dinner, Malik and Abu Ali led a stroll out to the barn, to examine the most recently foaled horses. "Our youngest," said Abu Ali enthusiastically. "Fine, strong creatures, with great spirit."

"It seems the season for them. Tell me, Kai," he said, turning to his younger nephew. "How is your riding?"

"Djinna is magnificent," Kai hedged. He sensed a contest in the wind. He hated competition, always had. Probably because he almost always lost, but that was besides the point.

"Excellent! Ali?"

Ali bowed, his ego having recovered completely from Malik's most recent humbling. "At your service." Kai groaned to himself. Ali would take out his frustration on his younger brother, and it would not be a pretty sight.

Abu Ali was interested. "What do you propose?"

Malik grinned. "A race, of course. Your sons, these fine steeds, a peerless day. Say, ten Alexanders?" Ten Alexanders was more than most sharelanders earned in a year.

"Twenty?"

"Done!" Malik smacked his palms together with relish. "Sport!"

"Kai?" Abu Ali asked.

Kai was hesitant. "I don't know, Father. Who would wager against Ali? I've never beaten him!"

Malik put his arm around his nephew's shoulder. "Today may be your day. Come!"

*　　*　　*

Outside, on the vast pasture grounds, the two brothers trotted their horses back and forth, preparing. Malik examined Djinna with satisfaction. "A fine animal," he said. "I think today is a day for risks. I'll bet on you, Kai."

Kai nodded glumly. Now he would not only be embarrassed, but cost his uncle gold. Allah help him come his next lesson!

He noted that a pair of servants had wandered over to the fence. They were a pair of shaggy scoundrels named Olaf and Cormac, the sort of men who disappeared the instant a job was done and were rarely found again before suppertime.

"I like the young master," Olaf said, perhaps not realizing he was in earshot.

"Tell you," Cormac replied. "Ali can't be beat, not on that monster of an animal."

He's smarter than he looks, Kai thought.

Olaf grinned. "You draw my water all next week, I'll cut your wood."

Cormac spit in his hand, offered it in a firm clasp. "Done."

Grumbling to himself, Kai mounted and pulled his horse up to the starting line. Ali wheeled his own steed into position. Malik motioned to Kai. "Kai! A moment?"

Kai walked his horse over to Malik. "Uncle?"

Malik's voice became conspiratorial. "Remember how I told you to hold the sword last week?"

"You said that I should relax more, let it be softer—"

"More alive in your hand. Yes. But I can only say that to a student who has already learned to grip. You grip the saddle with your thighs. Think of your best lover. Come now. Who was she?"

Kai felt a flush of heat. "Uncle!"

"Come on," Malik crooned.

"Well," he stammered, and then dropped his voice. "The slave girl, Sophia."

Malik wet his lips with the tip of his tongue. "As I thought. And how did she grip you with her thighs?"

"There are no words."

Malik laughed softly. "Grip your saddle in such a fashion. *Feel* what the horse is thinking. One body. One mind. I have wagered on you. Have I ever before?"

"No . . ."

"Because never before did I feel you could win. I am right about this. Do not argue. Do not doubt. Trust your teacher—go and win."

A thunderclap roared in Kai's chest. His uncle believed he could win? *Would* win? Impossible. Yet . . .

He studied the scarred face of the man who had taught him to hold a sword, and saw no doubt there. "Yes, Uncle," he murmured, then with greater feeling, shouted, "Yes!"

Shivering with excitement, Kai returned to the line. More servants were arriving, choosing sides, cheering them on.

Abu Ali took his pistol from his belt. "Ready—luck to both of you, my sons. Ride proudly."

Kai stroked Djinna's neck and then turned to Ali. "Good luck," he said.

Ali grinned, hunching over his saddle. "Keep it for yourself. You'll need it!"

Abu Ali fired, and they were off.

It was a glorious race, the two brothers pushing each other well. True to form, Ali took the early lead for the first quarter mile or so, but Kai kept his focus, and finally Ali had to stop laughing and bear down.

They leapt fences and dashed through puddles, speeding their way to the agreed-upon halfway mark, where they made the turn neck and neck.

The crowd roared its approval, and Abu Ali's gambling blood was aboil. This was a race the Prophet himself might have enjoyed! Even little Babatunde, for all his hatred of horses, applauded as the two brothers gouged grassy clods from the pasture in their efforts.

Malik stood close by Ali. At such moments, moments of intensity, the darkness within his younger brother seemed to retreat, and Abu Ali was happy to share this time and place. "Kai has never ridden so well," said the Wakil, "but I think Ali will carry the day."

"I disagree," Malik said. "And would be willing to increase the stakes."

"Indeed? How high?"

Malik seemed to consider. "You know that stallion, Nightwing, that you tried to buy from me last year?"

Abu Ali grinned, delighted. Nightwing was Malik's most prized stud animal, worth a small fortune. "And against what?"

Malik shrugged. "Against, let us say, any two slaves."

A fine wager! And one that displayed confidence on Malik's part. Then again, his younger brother had never lacked for nerve.

"Done," he said, and as the crowd roared, they shook hands. For just an instant then Abu Ali saw something glitter in Malik's eyes, felt a bit of unaccustomed moistness in the contact of one hard, flat palm against another, and wondered if he had made a mistake.

* * *

Kai bent to his task, concentrating until his body seemed to disappear, and there was only Djinna. The two of them, master and magnificent black beast, labored as one. He allowed himself to think of the way Sophia had held him. For the first time the memory caused no pain, but rather seemed to flow into pure energy. He felt as if he were sprinting, running at top speed, as if he and Djinna were a single creature with four legs and two heads.

Glancing to his side, Kai saw that he was slowly, steadily pulling ahead of Ali. Saw the strain on his brother's face, the muscles in cheeks and jaw straining as he realized that his younger brother was, for the first time, gaining ground.

Kai's heart soared, and he pierced the fiery veil of exhaustion, bore down fiercely, Djinna thundering against the reins—

And *won*.

The crowd erupted into cheers. Kai himself was absolutely ecstatic. "Huzzah!" he cried, and raised his fists to the sky.

The servants hoisted him on their shoulders, especially Olaf. "Thank you, master—ye just earned me a week of water!"

Kai laughed until he reeled, giddy with victory.

"Well done, young Kai," Malik said.

"Uncle!" Kai crowed. "It worked!"

"What worked?" Ali said suspiciously.

Malik put his finger to his lips. *Our secret.*

Ali was insistent. *"What* worked?"

Kai just grinned at his brother mysteriously.

"Well, Kai," Abu Ali said. "You cost me a beautiful horse, but I'm proud. *You*, though, boy—"

He glared at his eldest son, and Ali squinted back, and then they both laughed.

"You bet him a horse?" Ali asked.

"No, he bet me."

"And your end?" Kai asked.

Abu Ali shrugged. "His pick of the slaves. A fair trade, I thought."

Kai was thoughtful. Slaves were traded all the time, especially between neighboring estates, where an hour or two of travel might reunite families. Why, then, did he feel a touch of alarm?

"Cormac!" Abu Ali said to the bondsman. "Fetch Oko."

"At once, sir," Cormac replied, and dashed off. Within three minutes he had fetched the overseer. Abu Ali explained his purpose, Oko bowed, and five minutes later the denizens of Ghost Town were lining up by the fence.

At his command, the nearby bondsmen fell into line. Broad-backed men, women hardened by scrubbing and lifting. Dressed in rags and tags, if cleaned up some of them might have been quite handsome in their sunburnt, pointy-nosed, limp-haired fashion. Malik scanned them, seeming to inspect each carefully. Kai grew more quiet and still, and thoughtful.

Malik had scanned twenty, and seemed unsatisfied. Abu Ali was sympathetic. "Nothing that you like? We could ride out to the quarry."

"No," Malik said. "I see what I want."

His gaze went out beyond the servants to the great house. Two white women were carrying water out of the house, pouring it on the ground. The more graceful of them was Sophia.

Malik's eyes widened with pleasure.

Abu Ali shook his head. "Oh, Malik—she has just borne child. Certainly one of the other girls . . ."

"That one." His voice was dead certain. There was no room for discussion.

The tingle of alarm at the back of Kai's neck grew more urgent. He fought to keep his voice neutral. "She is a good worker. So you will take her and her husband?"

"No, I don't think I will. I take the infant as my second choice."

Abu Ali straightened. "The baby? But I would think the child automatically accompanies its mother. I would not consider the infant a separate person."

Malik combed his beard with his fingers. "I could not cheat my own brother in such a way. The babe will give many more years of service than the buck."

"Father," Kai said. "Couldn't we give Aidan to Malik as a gift?"

Abu Ali stroked his beard. "I suppose . . ."

"There is no need," Malik said. "I don't require him."

At last, Abu Ali's voice softened. "Just the girl?"

Malik regarded his brother blandly. "Fatima will soon need a wet nurse."

Abu Ali sighed. "Of course. Well"—he smacked his palms together—"a wager is a wager."

"Excellent!" Malik replied. "My wagon will fetch her in the morning."

The blood rushed in Kai's head as he understood the implications. "Uncle," he said. "Wait. Isn't there another selection . . . ?"

Malik's eyes were flat and cold. "You waste your breath, nephew. I know my mind."

As Malik's hand squeezed his shoulder, Kai realized for the first time that he did, indeed, know what his uncle wanted. And that he had allowed himself to be used.

Kai stalked up and down across the rug in Wakil Abu Ali's study, as he had been for the past ten minutes, his arguments passionate but unsuccessful. "Father—we can't do this. Aidan is not a mere slave, and neither is Sophia."

His father was seated behind his desk. He had given up the hope of completing his paperwork, and was trying to come to some kind of understanding with his younger son. "I know how you feel, Kai, but a wager is a wager. Perhaps if she were still in your bed I might make a case. But you gave her up, and she is now merely another household asset. I cannot break my word, Kai, and Malik will not change his mind. I know him."

"But it's wrong!"

The Wakil pinched the bridge of his nose. "Yes, perhaps it is wrong," he said quietly. "I have tried to change many things I think are wrong. There is only so much a man can do."

"But you are the Wakil!"

"Yes," said Abu Ali. "I am the Wakil. And because of that, I have great power in the Senate. But if I were to speak out against the institution that supports our entire way of life, that provides the comforts you have enjoyed all your life, I would lose that power. Already, men whisper that I am too lenient with my servants. And more: some suggest that I lack respect for the Ulema, which has formally sanctioned slavery."

Kai bristled. "How dare they criticize you! On what grounds?"

A trace of a smile softened the Wakil's mouth. "Oh, don't look so outraged. Do you think I don't know what Babatunde does in his mosque? That my own son has chosen the Way of Sufism?"

Kai was dumbstruck. "Father, I . . ."

The Wakil waved his hand dismissively. "Some say Sufis are traitors. That is a political judgment, motivated by men who seek worldly power, or those who distrust the wisdom of their own hearts."

"I don't understand, Father."

"Traditional Islam is a religion of rules. If you perform them perfectly, you will join Allah in Paradise. Sufism is esoteric Islam, a path to direct knowledge. A path of heart, of freedom."

Kai caught his breath. "Are you . . . a Sufi?"

His father smiled. "No. The Ulema is as much political as spiritual, and if it were ever suspected that I was a Sufi, they would do all in their power to destroy me. Traditional, hierarchical religions have little tolerance for those who seek direct union with the divine."

Kai stood very still, striving to digest this new information. If he interpreted his father's words correctly, he disapproved of some aspects of slavery, but could not speak out or act against them. Approved of his son's spiritual choice, but could not join him on his path. This was the world of politics? A plague upon it!

"So there you have it, Kai. I understand your disapproval. I am proud that my son has such a heart. But legally she is now Malik's property. I regret the wager, Kai, but there is nothing to be done now."

His last court of appeal exhausted, Kai bowed with his hand over his heart and left his father's study.

Sophia and Aidan met Kai in the hall outside the Wakil's room. Their faces were heartbreakingly hopeful, expectant.

Kai could barely meet their eyes. "There is nothing I can do," he said. "I am sorry."

Sophia's hands gripped his arm, her cheeks flushed. By some miracle she had so far restrained tears, and that very strength shamed him. "Kai, please. There must be *something*."

Kai tried to put the best possible face on it, loathing the lie in his voice. "Malik is only two hours away. You will be able to visit once a week on *al-ahad*, certainly."

It was all Aidan could do not to explode. "This is my wife!" he said. "I have seen the way he looks at her!"

Warring emotions flooded through Kai: haunted anticipation, then regret. Powerless to stop the inevitable, he straightened his shoulders and took refuge in indignation. "Aidan. You forget your place. There is nothing I can do. I suggest you resign yourself to that truth, however harsh it may seem."

Kai and Aidan stared at each other. Aidan's gaze was absolutely corrosive, chewing away at something that, even now, had remained between them. A ghost of past friendship, perhaps. The bonds of a childish blood ritual performed on a moonless night, long ago. Something frail and precious. Gone.

Kai tried to be comforting. "Besides, there is nothing to fear. Malik is very happily married, and his contract with Fatima has never included a seraglio. He would not take advantage. Excuse me."

And fearing that he had just told a terrible lie, Kai left them to their preparations, and their despair.

CHAPTER FORTY-SIX

THE FLICKERING CANDLES CAST FRANTIC SHADOWS across the wall of their single room. Fighting to avoid sheer paralytic fear, Aidan and Sophia threw food and clothes into a canvas bag. At first Sophia seemed determined to cram in everything they owned. Then Aidan caught her trembling wrists and forced her to gaze into his eyes.

"Lightly, Sophia," he said. "Take only what we must. We must move quickly."

She froze, looking at him with haunted eyes. "Are you sure?" she asked. "Has anyone ever made it away?"

"A few, I think. At least—their bodies were never brought back. I think they made it."

"Brian didn't."

He paused for a moment, looking deep into his woman's eyes. She was afraid, but she would take her chances with him, this he knew. "We will," he said. "You, and I, and Mahon will make it."

Instead of calming her, as he had hoped, her shaking grew more pitiful. "We have to," she said, her speech breathy and panicked. "I can't go there. I see how Malik looks at me. I was . . . trained to lock my feelings away, Aidan. Trained to use my body to get what I wanted, and never let anything touch me." She tore her hands out of his grip, and sank her fingers into his wrists. "I can't do that again. Not after you. After us, and Mahon. I *can't.*"

"You won't," he promised.

Three other slaves appeared in the doorway. Topper, a short, stocky quarryman thirty years Aidan's senior, and the newly married Molly and her husband, Ches. Aidan sometimes suspected that the ever-agreeable Molly had remained unmarried hoping to lure him into a promise. But after he wed Sophia she had yielded to the entreaties of Ches, a square-faced, stolid field hand.

Topper was white-haired, with few teeth left in his mouth. His body was as hard as the rocks he had spent his life smashing. "Are you for it, Aidan?"

"On my life."

"Then I'm with you," Topper said, and held out his flat, hard hand.

"Us too," Molly said. Her eyes sparkled with fear and excitement. "Always trusted ye, Aidan. Knew ye'd make a move one day."

"I don't want to encourage you," Aidan said. "I don't know what's out there. I have a decent map from Brian, but even he tried to talk me out of it."

"If there is any chance at all," Molly said, "we're taking it. What's the plan?"

"Cut through the marsh north, and then travel by night. Follow the waterways to the mountains. I've heard tell there are folks in the Gupta settlement who might give us shelter, help us get to Vineland."

Molly started. "But the Northmen stole ye from yer home!"

He nodded. "True. But they need workers and fighters like everyone else. A man might make a new life up there."

The five slaves were silent, each lost in his own thoughts. Finally, Sophia stepped into the gap. "All right, then. If any of us make it, all of us make it."

"I reckon," Ches said. And the five of them clasped hands, hard.

Hidden in Ghost Town's deepest shadows, Aidan watched the mansion. He was flattened against the wall of one of the outlying houses, near the fence. The front gate was unlocked, but more likely to be watched. He would slip out through the north side fence, away from the manse.

From his position, he could see the balcony, even glimpsed Kai as he gazed out across his father's estate. He would have recognized Kai's slender outline at twice the distance. Could Kai see him? He wasn't certain. And if he did, and he realized what his former friend was about to do, how would he react? It would be suicide to think him sympathetic.

And what would he do if Kai stood between Aidan and his family's chance for freedom?

Aidan couldn't allow his mind to travel in that direction. There was no life, no love there, and no hope.

He waited until Kai turned away, then motioned for the others to follow him. Sophia carried the baby in her stomach sling. If Mahon became too heavy, they could swiftly shift the burden to Aidan, but there was a very real chance that the sleeping child would awaken and cry. In that terrible instance, only a mother's breast might purchase silence.

They fled across the shadows into the dark of the forest beyond.

There was only a minute when someone watching from the house might have sighted them, and then they were in the grove. It was wreathed with fog that made it seem mythic, eternal, almost like a mosque.

They stopped and briefly knelt in prayer. Topper was the only one to find words. "Goddess," he said, "protect us this night. Lead us to open country."

Nervously, Aidan watched the forest behind them. "The Goddess helps those who help themselves. Come."

Kai lay half-asleep in his bed, plagued with wet, ugly dreams. Repeatedly, he bobbed up close to the edge of waking, only to submerge again into the arms of nightmare.

Aidan. Sophia. Mahon. Uncle Malik. The terrible wager.

A crazy quilt of fear and guilt and half-formed suspicion warred in his mind, clawed at his rest. He sat up abruptly, awakened by a distant barking sound, and he stared out through his open window into the night beyond.

Would they run? And if so, would they succeed? He knew Aidan might well risk the danger of the swamps. Did that barking mean that the thoths were out in the fog?

If they were, Allah preserve Aidan and Sophia. If they weren't . . . did he have an obligation to look, to see, to share his suspicions about Aidan's decision? His mind buzzed, plagued him, gave no answers.

And finally, he rolled back over and gave himself up to the demons waiting in his dreams.

The marshes of southeast New Djibouti were crowded with twisted black trees, dank with hanging moss, alive with snakes and owls. Half of the marsh was natural, half expanded a hundred years before by the damming of natural and artificial waterways. The marsh stretched for hundreds of square miles, and it was said that no man knew their depths.

"This is an evil place," Sophia said.

Aidan shook his head, holding his shielded lantern high enough to push the fog back a bit. "There were marshes in my homeland. Dangerous, yes. Evil, no." He paused, and looked up to find the moon. "This way."

"We've been walking for three hours," Molly said. "Can't we rest?"

"All right," Aidan said. There was no use in pushing too hard. Exhaustion would cloud their judgment. "Ten minutes, then we go on."

They sat heavily on damp stumps and rocks. Sophia began to nurse her child.

Aidan watched. Pride and fear warred within him. "Mahon hasn't made a sound."

"He's strong," she said, "like his father."

"Sophia . . ." Aidan said. "You didn't have to come. Kai is right: Malik is a righteous man. Life might have been good."

She looked at him with quiet dignity. "You are my heart and my home." Her upturned face shone in the moonlight. Very gently, he bent to her, and they kissed.

Ches was still jumpy. "I think I heard something."

"What?" Sophia asked.

"I'm not sure. Just a sound."

Aidan narrowed his eyes, trying to see something, anything, through the trees and the mist and the night. *Anything could be hiding out there*, he thought. He could see nothing, but the hair on the back of his neck was raising up. He gripped his staff hard enough to hurt his own fingers.

"Move. Hurry."

No one argued. All were suddenly aware of the need to move more quickly. They picked their way through the forest, trying to set their feet carefully on solid ground. The fear they felt was swelling up from deeper and deeper wells within them, diluting their resolve.

They were running now, and the ground turned their efforts into a nightmare. Within another mile, Molly was gasping for breath. Sophia stumbled.

Gritting his teeth, Topper turned and drew a wicked-looking knife. "This is as far as I'm running," he said through clenched teeth. "Aidan! Ches! Get Sophia and Molly the hell out of here, boys."

"Topper, no. Come with us." He looked up at the trees. They bent in an invisible wind, black against the stars.

"This is as good a place as any," Topper gasped. His white-tinged sideburns glistened in the night. "I just wanted to die free, boyo. Now, *git*."

Finally, Aidan nodded and pulled the others on. They were frantic now. Within a few minutes, Topper was lost in the mist behind them.

Aidan battled the agonizing sense that he was fleeing in a dream, that his legs were not his own, the feet pounding against the marshy soil those of a stranger.

Rising like a flock of ravens, a shriek of mortal agony shivered the woods behind them.

"Gawd!" Molly said, face gone the color of whey.

"Move!" Aidan screamed. They were stampeding now, running in blind panic through a maze of branches and mushy earth.

His arms and legs were burning. Once he almost fell, and Sophia helped him to his feet. Twice he helped her. With a cry of despair, Molly plunged into a muck-hole disguised by standing water. For a moment Aidan was torn. Wanting nothing but to continue his blind, seemingly hopeless quest for freedom.

Ches pulled at her arms, but the mud seemed to suck at her lower body. "Help us!" Ches said harshly, and Aidan came to him, gripped one of Molly's plump arms and set his heels, pulling with the power of his legs.

Molly came free, but there was no time to celebrate. No time for anything.

Aidan turned to face a forest filled with eyes.

Emerging from the shadows were eight creatures half the size of men, shagged with coarse black hair. Their faces were long and humanoid, shiny skin beneath tufts of beard.

Gruagach. Hairy demons.

Aidan had never seen them before. He doubted that any slave had, save Brian, who must have glimpsed them in the dark before his eye had been torn from his head.

Thoths. Now he knew what had lurked in the darkness of the slave pens of his youth, what monsters had captured Brian, what secret lurked in the huts by Lake A'zam.

Babatunde had once spoken, obliquely, of apes specially bred at the command of the Pharaohs, selected for intelligence, ferocity, and hunting ability. *Baboons* he had called them. Hamadryad baboons, used as pets and palace guards.

Thoths.

"Mere" animals they might be, but Aidan felt the supernatural terror of his fathers, knew that these creatures were as deadly and unknowable as any swamp sprite.

Aidan felt his stomach crimp, squirting bile into his throat, but he swallowed and pushed Sophia behind him.

The escapees were encircled. The thoths watched them, still as statues now that their prey was trapped. One of them raised thin, fleshy lips back from its yellowed teeth and barked sharply. Suddenly all of them were barking and howling, although they still had not moved. Signaling?

Of course. The slave catchers would come now, and the thoths would not move to injure their prey, unless . . .

Ches drew his knife and screamed, slashing at the thoths. "Well, come on, then!"

"No!" Molly screamed.

Three of the lethal animals leaped. Ches impaled one before the others struck him and bore him to the ground, his screams lost in the snarls.

Molly started toward them, and Aidan grabbed her, threw her to her knees. "Help him!" she sobbed.

"They'll kill us all," he said coldly.

Molly writhed in his grip, cursing. "Ye cowardly bastard. Ye . . . Ches!" She said more, but it was unintelligible, and by the time she found words again, Ches was long past hearing.

Muzzles and claws stained red, the thoths scampered back away from Ches's corpse, and once again ringed the captives.

Mahon was crying now. One of the thoths looked at the child curiously, its tapered muzzle seeming almost to smile. It was perhaps the most horrible thing Aidan had ever seen.

While Molly sobbed on her knees and Sophia tried desperately to quiet her son, the Danakil arrived. There were four of the slave catchers: low-class black men in heavily patched work clothes, men with wiry sparse beards and cruel eyes, men barely more cultured than the baboons they trained.

"Hope ye enjoyed yer little stroll." Their leader grinned.

Then, leveling their breech-loaders, they motioned the survivors onto dry land, and back into the arms of captivity.

CHAPTER FORTY-SEVEN

IN ALL THE WORLD, NOTHING EXISTED but pain and grief. The Danakil had dragged him the last half mile back to Ghost Town, and if the road had not been slick with mist and dew, the skin would have been flayed from his body. As it was, his shoulders felt dislocated, his wrists raw. At last Aidan was lost in a world of bruised flesh, unable even to scream Sophia's name.

He must have blacked out at one point. When consciousness returned, he was lying facedown in the dirt before Ghost Town's gates, and most of the villagers had gathered to witness his punishment.

Slowly, as if fearing that it might come off if he moved, Aidan craned his head to see Sophia. She and Molly sat in a buckboard wagon under Danakil guard, feet tightly roped. Molly looked almost drunken, her plump pretty face doughy with shock. Sophia clutched Mahon to her bosom fiercely. Her face was red and strained. "Stop it!" she screamed. "You're killing him!"

The slave catcher spit, grinning through a mouthful of broken yellow teeth. "He's strong. He'll cope."

Breathing dirt muddied by his own blood, Aidan watched as Malik rode up, took Sophia from the slave catcher's wagon, and threw her onto his own so roughly that he feared for Mahon's safety. Aidan struggled, to no effect. He managed to get out one protracted, tortured word. "No!"

Malik's smile was deadly. "Then stop me," he said. The sword master drew a knife from his belt. With a contemptuous gesture he threw it to the ground beside the bruised and exhausted Irishman.

Aidan's eyes burned in the silence. Watching to make certain that this wasn't a trick, with shaking hands Aidan found the blade, and sawed through the cords binding his wrists. All fear, even fatigue and pain, were burned away by the intensity of his hatred. He was an animal now, as much of a beast as the thoths that had destroyed their dreams of freedom.

Malik smiled at him coldly. Aidan seemed to quail before that gaze, losing his nerve and turning away—then leaped at Malik, slashing. Malik barely seemed to move, barely even flinched, but in one instant Aidan was armed and lethal, and in the next he was disarmed, hurtling though the air, somersaulting and smashing into the ground as if he were a thing without bones.

Malik looked down at his robe, and seemed mildly surprised to find it nicked. "He is fast."

He flicked his hand at the slave catchers, who responded by shackling Aidan to the shantytown's whipping post. Malik grabbed Sophia's face. "Watch," he said.

The first stroke split Aidan's shirt and striped his skin. The second spilled blood, and forced a grunt from between his clinched teeth. The third made him scream. A fourth. A fifth. He sagged, unconscious again.

And still the whipping continued.

"Stop it!" Sophia sobbed. "Please stop it! I'll do anything."

Malik seemed interested. "What do you offer me that I do not already own?" he asked.

She trembled, fighting to think of an answer that he might accept. "My word," she said. "I swear not to run away."

Malik's heavy lips curled in a dark smile, unimpressed. "Oh?" he asked. "As long as you are alive."

There was a clear and murderous threat in her words, but for some reason, that intent seemed to please him more than her promised subservience. "Good," he said to her, nodding. "Good. Enough!" he called, and the overseer ceased the rain of blows.

As Aidan hung limply in the stocks, the wagon bearing Sophia and his only child rolled toward the gate. Aidan's world dwindled and swelled with his heartbeats, thoughts flashing like fish in a stream. He managed to clear his head long enough to see the wagon disappear through the gate with Malik. Her face was a tiny, pale oval staring back at him. He could not see her eyes, but knew they wept, as did his own.

That night, long after the crowd dispersed, Kai's father came to him in his room, where he had taken refuge in books and scrolls. Kai had read a hundred pages that evening, and barely remembered a single fact. If ever he had felt ashamed to be a Bilalian, this was the moment.

"Come," Abu Ali said. "It is time."

Aidan still hung in the stocks. He watched their approach balefully. His face was battered and scraped, but thankfully not deformed.

Oko Iskahan had set up a little fire near the stocks, over which he heated coffee in a little ceramic pot.

Abu Ali glanced at Aidan, who lowered his eyes. "Release him," Abu Ali said. "He has had enough."

Oko nodded agreement, and cut Aidan down. The tortured man sagged to the ground in physical surrender. Blood was caked beneath his nose and along a gashed cheek. His right eye was swollen shut, his shirt hung in bloody rags, his back was sliced in a dozen places. He managed to push himself up onto hands and knees. He looked at Kai, and their eyes locked for a long moment.

Kai looked away, ashamed. Oko called out to Ghost Town, and as if they had waited the call eagerly, three servants emerged and helped Aidan back into the compound.

This man was my friend, Kai thought. *And now it has come to this. But I did not* make this world. Al-Alim, the All-Knowing, did that. He cast Aidan's people in such a station.

He did it.

Not I.

Aidan lay in his cold bed in his emptied house, screaming and cursing as the Rune Woman salved his wounds. He writhed every time Moira touched the mass of shredded flesh that was his back. Pain exploded behind his eyes like logs bursting on a campfire.

"Ye scream," the old woman told him. "Let it out. T'will quicken the healing."

She busied herself about him for another hour, salving and powdering. Her hands were sure—this was work she had done many, many times before.

At last the pain began to recede, some mixture of exhaustion and poultice drawing Aidan toward sleep. Just before he reached its shore, Moira's hands withdrew. Groggily, Aidan turned to see a man standing in the doorway. It took him a moment to put a name to the shape: Brian.

Brian nodded to Moira, and she left the house. When the door closed behind her, Brian knelt beside the bed. "I'm sorry, Aidan," he said. "Sorry it took this to teach ye that ye have no friends in the big house. That the blacks have no more soul than the rocks in the field. Sorry that it took this to make ye ready . . ."

He leaned closer and began to whisper. Aidan's left eye blinked once, shedding blood onto his pillow, and his hand reached out and gripped Brian's as they continued to talk into the night . . .

CHAPTER FORTY-EIGHT

THE SUN WAS HIGH OVERHEAD by the time Malik's horses and wagons reached his castle. On the wagon's front seat, Sophia clutched her child, watching each mile pass with increasing dread. Once, she had watched the fields and forested regions between Abu Ali and Malik's estate pass with joy, at Kai's side, knowing that she would spend a few pleasant hours watching her young master practice, and that if he had done well there would be good love that night. If he had done poorly, it would be up to her to ease his mind, soothe him, take him out of himself. She had imagined herself a vital part of his life . . . then.

But in allowing herself to fall in love with Aidan, she had left whatever small shadow of protection Kai had afforded her. Her illusions of freedom, of importance, were crashing down around her. Her legs felt weaker than they had since landing in Djibouti harbor.

She looked about herself wildly, trying to take in as much of the surroundings as possible. Somewhere, there was something that she would be able to use to her advantage. There had to be hope. There had to be. Otherwise, there would be nothing for her but death.

Malik, riding ahead of the wagon, dismounted a bit stiffly. Old wounds had leached away some of his almost miraculous fluidity, until he seemed no more than an ordinary, superbly fit man in his fifties. Ordinary, that is, until he picked up his sword. In combat he seemed to transcend the flesh, becoming in those moments something both greater and more primal than a common man.

Fatima waited beneath the castle's arched main doorway, her belly distended with child, her dark face outwardly impassive. Even at this distance, Sophia could tell that Fatima's emotions were boiling.

"So," Fatima said. "These are your winnings?"

Malik kissed her. "Fatima, my heart. You shouldn't be out of bed." His hand crept down to her belly, rested there. "It is nearly time. I merely bring you a wet nurse, and twenty gold Alexanders with which you may do as you wish." He extracted his purse and emptied it in her hand. Fatima tried to maintain an angry visage, then laughed and slipped her arm around his waist.

Malik gestured to his overseer, a big half-caste with sullen eyes and heavy, furred arms. "See this slave to her quarters."

Malik and Fatima returned to the house together, Malik's arm around her shoulder. As the overseer supervised the unloading of a few meager possessions, a straw-haired servant girl helped Sophia down. Sophia trembled, moved like an old woman, her dark hair falling across her face.

"My named is Tuti," said the girl with a nod. "You can come with me."

Always before, Sophia had entered through the front door, even if only as Kai's . . . slave. *Slave.* There, she had said it. She was a *slave.* This was her *prison.* She had been the worst kind of fool.

She saw everything through new eyes now, every digit. In comparison to Abu Ali's mansion, Malik's castle was spare indeed, inelegant and utilitarian if still fabulously rich. The wall hangings and tapestries spoke of war and conquest, with only infrequent hints of Fatima's personality.

Tuti led Sophia to a tiny room in the back of the house, on the west wing. A bed, a wardrobe, a window onto a green field. "This will be your room. We'll have a crib built, if you like."

"Yes, please," Sophia said. "Tuti?"

The smaller woman turned. "Yes?"

"Why does Malik want me here?"

Behind the veil, Tuti's eyes roamed over Sophia's lush body, and her lips twisted in a cold smile. Then she left.

Sophia hugged her baby and sobbed.

A minor sheik's gift of camels having finally overcrowded the animal quarters, Abu Ali declared the need for a new barn.

Kai and Ali supervised in its construction, and the work helped to distract Kai's mind from the feelings of guilt he experienced whenever he remembered that Sophia no longer lived with her husband.

As he had for the last week, Aidan worked far longer than anyone else on the crew. He carried more board, climbed the ladders to the most dangerous beams, hammered until his hands were covered with blisters, and then continued until they broke and were slicked with blood.

Kai's gaze met his for a moment. There was barely a flicker of recognition. His old friend turned away.

Kai's father rode up with Lamiya. "Come," said the Empress's niece. "Ride with us."

Ali slapped his brother on his back, and both brothers mounted up and followed. From the corner of his eye, Kai saw Aidan turn and glare.

The four of them rode up to the top of a rise, from which they could see the entire estate. Fields, rolling hills, Moorish house, slave quarters. Slaves working hard at their measured labors, timing their efforts to their work songs.

Distantly, he could see a steamboat chugging along Lake A'zam. Abu Ali seemed deeply satisfied. "This is my land," he said. "Mine, and my father's before me. When I die, it will be yours, Ali, yours and your brother's." He drew Lion's Blood and slashed the air with it. Then he passed it to Ali.

Kai's brother weighed it reverently.

"Does it fit your hand? Does it sing to you?"

"It sings, Father." Ali held it aloft, balancing it in his hand as if trying it on for size. And then handed it back to his father.

"This," said his father, "this is the world we have made. There is luxury and comfort, but it can only be maintained by strength and wisdom. We have dangerous days ahead, and both will be called for. Can the two of you work together, now and always, for the continuance of what your grandfather and I built?"

"Of course, Father."

"Yes, Father," Kai said.

"Good. Good." Abu Ali let a touch of weariness seep into his voice, and for a moment they saw the weight of his years. Kai wondered if he himself would carry them as well, when such a burden became his own. "It is hard for a warrior to reach that point where his body grows a bit heavier every day, when he knows he is closer to the end than the beginning. But I am prepared to stand before Allah and give account of my life, and that is all a man might do."

"You have many more years before that day, Father," Kai said.

"*Insh'Allah*. But no man knows the day of his own reckoning. I wish to avoid the taxes, to divide my lands and give one part to you and Lamiya, Ali, as your wedding present."

Lamiya lay one slender hand on Abu Ali's arm. "Father—that is too kind."

"No, it is only right. Your aunt needs Bilalistan's resources, and Ali will have my seat in the Senate only if he also holds my land. He must speak for me in the conflict to come."

Her face grew concerned. "And it *will* come, won't it, Father?"

Abu Ali seemed heavy and tired, older than Kai had ever seen him. "As the night follows the day. Bilalistan cannot forever remain an Egyptian colony. We must be free. Too many of us have blood ties to Abyssinia. If there is war between those two great powers, we will be torn."

"Egypt will not free us without blood and fire," said Ali.

Their father nodded. "All the crows in the sky could not pick the bones of the men who will fight that war. It comes," he said. "It comes."

A cloud seemed to have slid across the sun. Kai felt a chill that no cloak could relieve.

The Wakil seemed lost in himself for a time, and then roused himself to continue. "But I digress. Kai, on your marriage to Nandi, one-third of the estate will be yours. I will keep only a small piece of land sufficient for my house and servants."

"Are you sure, Father?" asked Ali.

"As sure as I am that I love my sons, and know that all Malik and I have built is in safe hands. It is your turn now."

Kai nodded, but watching the workers tilling the fields, felt an unaccustomed anxiety stealing over him.

CHAPTER FORTY-NINE

THE CANDLES GUTTERED LOW, flickering as to an unfelt wind, as Fatima writhed in childbirth, her brow wet and tight. Her fingers furrowed the crimson sheets. "Oh!" she cried. "Allah, deliver me!"

The doctor Jimuyu was grave. "Boil the instruments," he said to the nurse. "It is begun."

He had delivered hundreds of children, and knew every moment of the process well. But there was something about the position of the child in this woman's belly that disturbed him. When he probed with his hands he could feel that the infant was twisted wrong, and in his heart he knew what that meant. The midwives had massaged in Kikuyu fashion, trying to turn the baby around, but they had run out of time.

He tried to keep the fear from his eyes and voice, but Fatima, abnormally aware in her pain and fear, had already caught a glimpse of his true mood, and it had very nearly undone her.

Just outside the door, Malik paced restlessly, hand on his sword. His servants were terrified to approach him: never had they seen him in such a mood. Terrible screams echoed from inside the room, and he slammed his fist into the wall, cracking wood and plaster.

The servants scattered.

On and on he paced, until the first light of dawn rose in the east, visible through one of the castle windows as a rose blush seeping along the horizon. Finally, the door to his wife's bedroom opened. Jimuyu and the nurses filed from the chamber, their faces sad, eyes downcast. "You should enter now. Swiftly."

Malik felt his heart freeze. He entered the shadowed confines of his wife's bedroom, eyes swiftly acclimating to the absence of light.

Fatima looked drained of blood, and life. Emptied, barely conscious, fighting for each and every breath.

"Malik," she whispered. "I held on long enough."

He smoothed his fingertips along her cheek. "Shhh. Shhh."

She tried to gather strength, to rise to a sitting position, but could not. "Malik . . . hold your daughter. Please."

"Rest. Keep your strength for healing."

"It is too late to speak . . . to speak of healing." Her voice and spirit found the strength her body lacked. "Hold your daughter."

Only then did he notice the nurse standing to the side of the bed, or hear the wails from the blanketed bundle in her arms. Nervously, she stepped forward and handed Malik his girl child. He stared at the child, its tiny wrinkled face, stubby arms, hairless head. It felt as frail as a bird in his arms. So tiny. So helpless. What did one *do* with such a thing?

Fatima's wavering eyes found enough focus to fix upon him. "Is she beautiful?"

"She is your child."

"Malik. I'm sorry I was not stronger." She shuddered as if she was cold, or perhaps in the grip of a fever. "Malik," she begged. "Hold my hand." She groped her hand up toward him.

He clutched it. It seemed as small and frail as his newborn daughter. "Fatima . . ."

"Malik . . . please don't leave. Stay. Stay until . . ." She didn't need to finish, and he couldn't have borne it if she had. Fatima relaxed as he held his daughter, sitting on the edge of the bed, counting each and every breath. Finally there were greater and greater gaps between breaths, and finally, two hours after dawn, there was no breath at all.

The door of Sophia's small room burst open. Malik filled the doorway, vast and seething with a kind of cold power that, for a moment, convinced her that he meant her harm. The nurse stood beside him, carrying a bundle, and it took only an instant to realize what it contained. Why his mood? Surely this was a joyous . . .

The nurse thrust the bundle of blankets at Sophia, and she saw, within, a newborn black child. It seemed so impossibly small and tender, even as it cried and thrashed, that she lost her capacity for breath as compassion swept her.

She raised her face to Malik, meaning to reassure him in any way she could, but he was glacial. *"Yuraddi,"* he said. "Suckle her."

Hesitating, and with trembling hands, Sophia unbuttoned her blouse and allowed the baby to nurse. It did, greedily, its tiny black lips settling over her brown nipple as if they had been made for each other. Instead of joy, she felt shame as Malik stared at her. His eyes glittered, and then he turned and left.

Fatima's body was washed seven times and anointed with camphor, then wound in a burial shroud and, in the morning, taken south to the family graveyard. Kai thought the sky was almost damnably beautiful, too bright and cheery for such a somber occasion. There should have been rain clouds and a cold, sterile wind blowing from the east.

Only family attended the service, in which Babatunde spoke of hope and service, of the martyrdom of death in motherhood, and the love she had had for Malik. Afterward, he led the brief prayers that consigned her soul to Ar-Rahman, the Merciful.

When the formal words were complete, Abu Ali stood beside his younger brother. "I am sorry," he said.

Malik spoke slowly. "We married sisters. They are together again. We will all be together again."

Kai gripped Malik's shoulder. "Uncle."

Malik turned and looked at him with vast, dark eyes, almost as if he did not recognize the boy he had taught to walk. Then he seemed to pull out of it, and gave a shallow nod of acknowledgment.

They accompanied Malik back north to his estate, not a word exchanged during the entire ride. When they arrived, Malik nodded to his brother and nephews, dismounted, and handed his reins to a guard. Without a backward glance, he entered his home and closed the door.

As Kai rode away with his father and brother, they passed a fenced-off square of grass next to the greenhouse. Sophia stood beside the fence. Both babies, white and black, lay in a wood and ivory carriage beside her. She watched Kai as he passed, her face like a window onto a desert. He could feel the bond between them, stressed but in some way still unbroken, and felt a jolt of pain that went beyond that which he already felt for the death of his aunt.

Although the sun had set, Aidan was working still, as if the burning in his arms and legs would drive from his heart the images of love lost. Nothing he could do in the fields was enough. Although he fell into his bed exhausted, still his dreams would not come, dreams in which Sophia might have joined him.

He spent the days in a state halfway between sleep and waking, his body working and his mind wandering, remembering what his life had been only weeks before. He remembered feeling joy when Sophia would bring his lunch to him—her stride saucy, the full sensuous lips pouting as if chiding him for not *feeling* her approach, and he raised his hand to wave to her . . .

It was not Sophia, it was Molly. She still limped from the whipping she had suffered, and her eyes often seemed glassy, as if seared almost to blindness by what she had seen in the swamp.

The sight of her took him out of himself a bit. He was not the only one who had suffered. If anything, his relationship with Kai had protected him from the realities of slave life.

He took the water cup from her hands and drank, his eyes never leaving hers, as if her inner ice were a protection from the fire that threatened to consume him.

When he was done, she went to offer water to another man, and then another. Aidan had a fleeting thought—of childhood, of games of running and seeking. Molly had been his first, his very first, and she had given herself to him in the shadow of the grove, laughing and guiding him.

That special girl was gone, killed beyond that very grove. In truth, he wondered if he had not died there as well.

With the sun's approach to the horizon, the bell began to ring. The servants created an informal line, walking the two miles back to the village, and many of them laughed and joked and sang, slapping each other on the back.

"Saw ya whack yer thumb on the post. Swelled up like a melon, did it?" said Cormac.

"Still throbbin'," Olaf replied. "Figgered I'd get yer wife to help me with it. Wouldn't be the first time Jenny's helped me swellin' go down . . ."

Aidan walked alone.

He returned to find a communal cookout in progress. Cormac offered him a jug. He pushed the man away and started to wander back to his solitary room, where he could lie on his back and stare at the walls, his habit for weeks now.

Then Brian clapped a hand on Aidan's shoulder and forced him to take the jug. Aidan looked at Brian as if he wanted to hit him, but then, almost desperately, upended the brown bottle and began to drink.

The other members of the *tuath* cheered their approval. Now, more than ever, Aidan was one of them.

In the corridor just outside Malik's training hall, the servants were terrified by the grunting and clanging emanating from behind the locked oaken door.

Within, stripped to the waist, Malik slashed and thrust with his sword. His attacks were eye-baffling in speed, heart-stopping in both implicit and explicit violence. Gathering intensity, Malik worked himself into a deeper lather, screaming with each new stroke. His chest was gilded with sweat. Spittle flew from his lips with the effort, as if he were trying to push himself hard enough to kill his body.

Suddenly he froze and turned. His eyes were tight, bloodshot, frenzied. He screamed and lunged again. Stopped.

Distantly, a baby's scream echoed through the halls.

Sword in hand, he stalked from the room.

In the isolation of her room, Sophia struggled to quiet the infants. Side by side, one white, one black, they wailed as if glimpsing the end of the world. "Hush, Mahon," she said to her own. "Azinza, please. Shhh."

She heard the footsteps before her door flew open. There stood Malik, sword in hand, glaring at Mahon. "I hear my daughter cry," he said. "Perhaps you have not milk enough for two children."

The thinly veiled threat staggered her. Would Malik do such a thing? Or order it done? "No. I do," she stammered. "She just knows I am not her mother. It is natural."

"Is it?"

Sophia stood, putting herself between Malik and Mahon.

Malik took another step forward, closing the distance between them. "Then perhaps it is your heart," he said. "Perhaps your heart is not large enough for two."

Malik brushed the tip of his sword along the underside of her jawline. Sophia closed her eyes, expecting death at any moment.

"How large is your heart?"

She shuddered. Malik grabbed her, pulled her close, threw her to the bed, and descended upon her. In their twin cribs, the babies screamed.

"No . . ." she said, a single pitiful, inadequate syllable.

And then there was only pain, and humiliation. She could not even remember the craft taught to her in Alexandria's house of submission, the methods of walling her heart away. Malik was too demanding, his assault too overwhelming, giving her no time to find her balance.

She could not think of Aidan, lost Aidan, or the home that she had struggled to build in Ghost Town. Or of her brief and intense happiness there.

As Mahon and Azinza yowled their hearts out, Malik thrust his irresistible weight onto her, pinning her to the sheets with a driving, merciless rhythm.

Please, she could only think. *Not in front of my child . . .*

As usual, even before the sun crept across Aidan's window, he was up and awake, washing his face in his basin with water drawn the night before. He scrambled eggs over the coals of the previous night's fire and ate them, staring into the ashes. A week's growth of beard darkened his face. His eyes were flat and lifeless.

He had heard of Fatima's death, and knew that Sophia now cared for both infants. *You have nothing to fear,* Kai had said. But Malik was no longer married. Malik was a thing of war and blood, and that frightened Aidan all the more. He knew that a man such as Malik pushed all of his strength to the surface, to deal with the worst the world could offer. But that could leave a fragile core, an emptiness that could only be filled by the love of a woman. He had seen the toughest fishermen in his *tuath* break down sobbing when their wives died, never whole again. He knew that slaves on Berhar's estate had torn out their hair and eaten broken glass when their wives and children were sold away.

Strong men. Brave men. Aidan knew himself no coward, but the images of Sophia, alone in Malik's castle, were enough to make him want to cut his throat. Malik was the strongest man he had ever seen in his life. What aching void might he even now be seeking to fill . . . ?

After eating he dressed, joining the stream of workers heading to their daily labor.

Barely paying attention, he noted a wagon heading in from the north, and for a moment hoped that Sophia was on it. He had not seen her since her departure four weeks ago, punishment for his attempted escape.

But that faint hope of reunion died. She was not on board, although he recognized a few faces, including a house girl named Tuti, who hopped down and approached him.

She stood before him, and his heart trip-hammered even before she began to speak. "Malik has taken your woman," she said, the words unadorned and scathing. "We thought it best that you knew."

Tuti hurried away, leaving Aidan standing alone. He felt nothing, the words he had dreaded hearing seemed to have consumed his heart, leaving only ashes.

The fields to either side were filled with workers who sang, their efforts in rhythm with their words as they began a new day.

Cut us low, swing us 'round
Iron shackles tightly bound
Thresh your soul by the mornin' lark
Lie in your dreams in the dead of dark—
Laddie are ya workin'?

Brian shielded his eyes against the glare of the morning sun. There was no shade to be found up here, atop the half-fleshed skeleton of the new barn west of the main stables. For the last week he had directed the gang applying shingles to its roof. It was hard, dangerous work. Due to his careful management, they were on time and without a single accident, and that was something to take pride in.

He looked down to see Aidan standing in the barn's shadow, staring up. There was something in Aidan's eyes that he hadn't seen before, something cold and merciless. Brian sensed that the moment which he had awaited so patiently had arrived at last.

Without a word, Brian climbed down. As he came closer he could see that the young man's face was as pale as milk, his eyes wild and unfocused, his hands clenched into fists.

Brian touched down, and looked at his friend carefully. "What is it, boyo?"

Aidan's mouth moved without words, and Brian saw the tracks of dried tears in the dust on his cheeks. Aidan swallowed hard, and Brian had a sudden, terrible feeling that he knew what the boy had to say. The wagon had just come from Malik's castle. Yes. Malik's wife was dead now. Yes. Beautiful Sophia was there with no one to protect her.

Yes.

Brian rested a strong hand on Aidan's shoulder as the younger man dropped his eyes to the ground.

"Well?" Brian said, as gently as he could.

"I'm ready," Aidan said, his voice swollen with misery. "For whatever you want."

CHAPTER FIFTY

DRESSED IN A ROBE OF UNBLEACHED Egyptian cotton, Kai crouched over his desk, sipping lemonade and studying maps, the most important of which displayed the current position of the Aztec battle lines. The closest were less than fifty miles outside the incorporated territory of New Djibouti. So close—but not close enough to draw the aid of federal troops. If the Djiboutans wished to repel the threat, they would have to muster troops loyal to the Wakil and the other nobles . . . and seek aid from the Zulus.

His heavy thoughts were disturbed by a knock at his chamber door. Kai called for the supplicant to enter.

To his surprise, it was Aidan who answered his call. Aidan, with eyes cast down and his hand over his heart in a bow. "May I?"

The familiar face warmed him. It was uncommon for servants to come to the third floor of Dar Kush without a pass, but long custom allowed Aidan that privilege, although he had not used it since their altercation. "Please. It has been too long. Refreshment?"

"Please."

Kai poured him a glass of lemonade. Aidan sipped, and made grateful sounds.

"It is hot today," Kai said.

Aidan sat his glass down. "I want to ask your advice, Kai."

Kai stiffened, expecting the inevitable. "You know that there are matters in which I am helpless."

"I understand. Not . . . that."

"What, then?"

Aidan touched a black leather-bound copy of the Qur'an sitting on Kai's desk. "I need answers, Kai. I don't know why the world is as it is, and I need to be able to live in it. I can't do it with just my own strength."

"There are men and women of spirit among the servants. Perhaps you should speak to them."

"I have. I can't believe in Jesus. God smiles on those who walk His path. He isn't smiling on my people."

Aidan's words pained Kai, but he felt a trill of hope. Perhaps it was not too late for their friendship after all. "Aidan . . ."

"Kai—I'm not looking for special privileges. For my wife to be returned. Or to be free. Just help me find peace with my lot in life. Help me to Allah."

Kai sighed. "Allah speaks to each of us in His way. In His time. If you have heard the call, I must help you to answer."

He took Aidan's hand. "Repeat after me the *Shihadah. A'Shadu an la ilaha illallah wa ashadu anna Muhammadan rasul lilah.*"

"There is no God but Allah," Aidan repeated. "And Muhammad is His prophet."

In the courtyard, Babatunde watched as Aidan and two other slaves re- cited their prayers, and knelt in obeisance to Allah. Babatunde watched, his face studiedly neutral. The scholar had no words for his student, but he did have thoughts.

A righteous man did not kneel before Allah for alms, or worldly bene- fits. And the status of slaves made it inevitable that they would struggle for any small advantages. There was no way that a true Muslim would not grant greater privilege and leeway to another Believer than to a Christian, Jew, or infidel. These facts made any slave conversion . . . problematic. Yes. Yet he chose not to voice his doubts. For now, he would watch.

Was that watchfulness, that reticence to speak purely his desire to see a soul find its way to Allah untrammeled by suspicion? Or did the eighth of Turkish blood in his veins give him empathy inappropriate to one sworn to protect the house and honor of his host? These were questions that he would have to resolve.

Eventually. For today, he remained silent, and watched. And prayed.

According to little Tuti, who had quickly become Sophia's guide and companion, of all the rooms and features of Malik's castle, the spot Fatima had most loved was the greenhouse east of the main residence. There, flowers from around the world grew all year round, their gardeners main- taining perfect temperature and humidity through a series of steam-vents and baffles. Green glass walls filtered the sunlight.

Sophia sat with the babies, taking the sun, breathing the warm, moist air. She was gazing south toward the distant, invisible plantation of Wakil Abu Ali.

Tuti appeared in the doorway.

Sophia tensed inwardly, but did not let it show on the outside. "It is so calm here," she said. "I remember the sun, shining on the Mediterranean. My father built houses, there by the side of the sea."

"Sophia . . ."

"I don't clearly remember. Something about building materials. Wood. Plaster. A floor collapsed, and a magistrate's wife died. My family was ruined. I was sold."

"I've come for the children," Tuti said.

"I don't remember. But I remember the sun."

Tuti took the children, and left.

For a minute or two Sophia was alone in the hothouse. Then Malik appeared, dressed in dazzling, sterile white, the contrast with his skin almost startling. His fingers gripped at her like claws as he bore her to the ground. With his left hand, he pinioned both her wrists while he pushed her dress up, then pressed himself into her. She was dry; the violation hurt abominably.

Refusing to flinch or make any display of pain or shame, face a mask of unnatural calm, she turned away.

She did not hear him as he grunted atop her. She did not see his straining face. She saw only the warm waters of the Mediterranean, shimmering blue. Her own reflection in the water. Had she ever been so young? She turned, and looked at the beautiful house, built by the gifted hands of her father. He stood on a scaffold, and waved to her, and she waved in return.

Life was good.

A quarter hour later Malik exited the greenhouse, adjusting his clothing as he did, walking away without a backward glance.

Sophia followed him out, still rumpled, breathing rapid, tears streaking her cheeks. As soon as he was gone she snatched a glass flowerpot from its rack and smashed it against a support beam. Trembling, she picked up a single jagged shard and pressed it against her flesh. A thin rivulet of blood welled up. Then she threw the glass to the side, collapsed against the wall of the sun house, and sobbed.

Between the golden rows of teff, half a dozen servants, Aidan included, knelt in prayer. The rugs beneath their knees were poor in comparison to those owned by the heads of the household, but were presents from the Wakil on occasion of their conversion.

Astride Djinna, on the dirt road separating the teff from the hemp field, Kai watched the ritual with mixed emotions. As some of the other slaves headed to their beloved prayer grove, Aidan was not among them.

"Allah rejoices when a new lamb enters the fold," Kai said.

"Yes," Babatunde agreed. "He does." His eyes were sharp. He seemed not so certain as Kai. Not at all.

Other eyes judged Aidan as well, eyes from the shadows. They were cold and blue, cynically interested, and utterly unconvinced.

CHAPTER FIFTY-ONE

FROM THE LONELY SHADOWS OF HER ROOM, Sophia listened as the *muezzin* called the faithful to prayer for the third time that day. She knew that the five daily prayers were one of the five pillars of Islam, the most important remembrances of the sovereignty of God, and the core of Muslim life. The prescribed prayers were performed at the same time of the day throughout most of Bilalistan by all who could manage it without disrupting vital work or commerce. At those times masters and slaves knelt together, and in theory nothing separated them, not race, not station. In theory, in the eyes of God, no man stood above another.

From Wakil Abu Ali and his sons to the lovely Lamiya and young Elenya, at those hours when the call was given, all else came to a halt.

But once here on Malik's estate she had discovered the sword master prayed only in the morning, that from noon until night his mind burned with a restless fever even as his servants and slaves knelt in obeisance. That his mind danced from death's abyss to his ownership of her body, and back again.

From her window she watched, her face a mask, her heart lost in some deep place inside her where Malik's hands and manhood could not reach. She could only pray that she could find a place deep enough to keep her soul safe. It felt to her as if Malik would not be long satisfied with just her flesh. The unquenchable flame in his eyes said that he wanted her spirit as well. He wanted her response, her passion.

She was no longer that girl, that egotistical child who had been so proud of her erotic talents. All of that seemed so terribly far away, those memories a stranger's.

For now, for this time, there was only one way she knew to keep her essence safe. Sophia closed her window and removed her most precious possession from her chest of drawers.

Her silver cross, the one worn during her wedding to Aidan. A small thing, one of the last reminders of the life she once had known, the girl she once had been. She attached the cross to the wall, and knelt in prayer.

I feel you, Sophia, Aidan whispered to himself.

He knelt beside his old friend Kai. The two performed their ablutions together, but as he bowed, Aidan secretly fingered the crucifix hidden beneath his shirt, and thought of the woman he loved, and prayed that she was well.

We've both lost so much, he thought. *Please, God, don't let us lose each other. Just a little longer now.*

Lord, help us both endure.

Mounted on Djinna and Qäldänna, Kai and Ali watched as the slaves returned singing to their shantytown. Some of their songs were from the old country, others composed since landing in Djibouti harbor. Some crooned Muslim prayers.

Several were accompanied by their children, who seemed to have journeyed with them to the day's labors. Their father did not generally force servant children to work before the age of eight, but they often accompanied their parents into the fields, helping with the gathering or weeding. Judging by the smiling faces, this was what had happened. Five or six of the youngsters toddled along at their parents' sides, holding wicker baskets filled with wildflowers. Such flowers would probably decorate their homes, bringing a little cheer into their drab lives.

The children waved at Kai, and he waved back.

When they rode on their way, Kai thought no more of it. And when they passed a meadow and saw four children picking mushrooms under the supervision of a young red-haired woman, he thought less still.

Until Kai and Ali rode out of sight, the children plucked rather aimlessly, playing at their appointed tasks. But as soon as the brothers vanished, they returned to serious work. Crooning a bit of doggerel taught them by Moira, they picked mushrooms under the direction of the Rune Woman's apprentice, Kelly.

Quite innocently, one of the youngest started to put a blue-tipped mushroom in her mouth, and Kelly slapped it out, shook him until he cried, and forced him to spit several times. Only after he had drunk from her water skin, washed his mouth and spit again, did she relax, or did any of them continue with their task.

Most of the *tuath* was asleep when Brian entered Moira's hut. She and two other women were rolling mushrooms and dried herbs into powder, and Moira chanted softly as she worked:

> *Sleep of the Earth from the land of Faerie*
> *Deep is the lore of C'noc na Sidhe*
> *Hail be to they of the Forest Gentry*
> *Pale dark spirits, help us free.*

> *White is the dust of the state of dreaming*
> *Light is the mixture to make one still*
> *Dark is the powder of death's redeeming*
> *Mark but that one pinch can kill—"*

She stopped her singing and cast a look at the two women helping her in her efforts. "Careful, careful. Grey with white. White with black. Roll, roll, yes."

"When will they be ready?" Brian asked. He had known Moira his entire life, and she had always looked old to him. Now he both loved and feared her. Being in her presence while she worked her weirdling ways made his skin creep.

"Want them all dead?" she cackled. "It is ready tonight. Wish for some to sleep, some to wake? Ye must wait. Wait."

He peered into her bowl, which contained pellets, some dark-colored, some light. He shuddered. Everything was in its place. For years, since his own dread night in the swamps, he had planned his revenge.

With Dar Kush in his hands, Ghost Town would join him. The neighboring slaves would rise up as well, he was certain.

He would have freedom at any cost, even death. But Brian wanted to live. The Danakil and their thoth hunters had to die. And the overseers and guards. But the Wakil and his children should live, both as hostages and because if he murdered *them* there would be no place on earth his people would ever be able to hide from Bilalian vengeance.

There was just one exception to that. Malik. Malik had to die. He was simply too dangerous to live. Brian had not been able to recruit any of Malik's kitchen staff, which ruled out poison for the sword master and his men. But other arrangements could and had been made. With Malik dead, the rest of the plan just might work.

Molly was third in a line of four slaves charged with carrying firewood and baskets of clean clothes to Dar Kush's occupied bedrooms. As they passed a hall off the kitchen she split off from the others and sneaked down a corridor to a heavy iron-bound door. Since the nightmare in the swamps Molly had feigned acceptance of Muhammad as her Prophet, praying faithfully five times a day. Despite the Wakil's orders, it was inevitable that Muslims were given freer reign, observed less closely, enjoyed more privilege.

She had several keys upon a brass ring and tried one after the other, but none opened the door. Molly stamped her foot in frustration, spitting a string of expletives most unbecoming a Muslim lady.

She left the corridor and searched the fields until she found Aidan, then whispered to him urgently.

Sophia sat in Fatima's hothouse, caring for Mahon and Azinza as the third call to prayer sounded through Malik's estate. The scent of Abyssinian orchids transported her back to her father's house. Its memory seemed her only refuge.

Her solitude was interrupted as Tuti entered the hothouse. She came to stand beside Sophia, whispering in her ear. "We need the key," Tuti said. "And only you can get it."

Sophia knotted her hands into fists, eyes widening in fright. Then she forced herself to relax, and nodded. "Yes," she said. "I understand."

After Tuti left, Sophia stood, looking down at the children in their baskets. Carefully, almost as if sleepwalking, she picked them up and carried them back into the house, eyes open but her mind a thousand miles away.

She passed several of the other slaves, but said nothing to any of them, said nothing until she had sealed herself in her room and placed Mahon and Azinza in their cribs.

Then she put the flat of her palms against her eyes. "Aidan," she whispered.

Malik had provided her with a mirror, that she might properly adorn herself for his use. If he had thought that she would be for him what she had been for Kai, he had been disappointed. Her body he owned. Her artistry was her own, and the girl who had learned all of the ways of paint and carriage, of muscle tension and musical phrasing, had gone forever.

Or was she? Sophia studied her reflection. She saw a pale woman with dark hair and a sad, care-lined face. She smiled, lifted her posture, threw her hair back over her shoulder.

Yes. *There* was the little slut. Pretty little thing, who had been used by men on three continents. On one of them she had nurtured a dream of romance, that she might win a boy's heart and thereby her freedom. Pretty, silly little whore.

But there was something about that girl that Sophia admired. That girl had not broken. That girl had found a way to protect her heart, even when there had been no hope at all. That girl, not the woman Aidan had married, could do what was now required.

Malik must think he had won completely, that his little slave's heart had been won by the power and majesty that was New Djibouti's greatest warrior. He was invulnerable to men, but she had seen something in him since his wife's death. A crack in his emotional armor, perhaps. To her woman's instinct, his air of strength and assurance seemed slightly labored, not entirely convincing to her.

What was it her teachers in Alexandria had said? *You will belong to a strong man, but do not fear. The stronger the man, the more he has pushed away all that is soft within him. Men are not all muscle and bone. They are heart as well. And men who cannot touch their own hearts are vulnerable to women who can.*

Once, she had been afraid of Malik, had thought Kai would be the easier conquest. That was almost certainly true, but there was one other factor in play: Kai was young. Youth had flexibility. Kai's heart could be broken a hundred times, and he would heal. But what of Malik, who was stronger . . . but *older*, more brittle? Whose first wife had died young, and whose second had died in childbirth.

Beneath his armor, his lethal skills and muscle, he would have to be terrified of ever caring again. He had wanted her, desired her enough to wager his most valuable horse to gain her. She saw how he looked at her, felt how he touched her. She might not be able to make Malik love her, but she could make him *feel*, and once he did that, his guard would drop.

Sophia had hardly realized it, but her hands had begun to move, to organize Malik's paints and ointments into a palette. *The face is a canvas, the body, clay.* She had been trained to be a master artisan, fit for a Wakil's son. She looked at herself in the mirror. Already, the married woman Sophia had disappeared behind rouge and lip-paint. What remained was the girl from Alexandria, a woman now, all her illusions behind her.

Hello again, for the last time.

Sophia smiled, and was chilled by the sight of it.

*   *   *

Dar Kush's slaves had their own mosque, a converted shed that they had been allowed to clean and decorate as a place of spirit. A statue of Bilal himself graced the exterior, smiling down on his children who passed beneath him, his dark hands outstretched.

Within, they prostrated themselves in prayer. Devotions concluded, Brian shook hands with Molly, who opened her hands afterward to find four pellets wrapped in paper.

CHAPTER FIFTY-TWO

NIGHT'S STARLIT MANTLE HAD ENGULFED Malik's estate. Tonight, things had been different. Tonight, there had been no rape.

Tonight, Sophia had come to the master of the house with a rose between her teeth, every hair in perfect place, clothed in a cascade of veils. Tonight, she had begged him to forgive her former coldness, and to believe that she had been taught to be a companion worthy of a Caliph. That if he gave her a chance, she would show him a different woman.

Tonight, the other servants had been dismissed, although they had heard music and laughter from the dining room, and later from the master bedroom itself.

Tonight, Sophia had shone brighter than the stars, had deliberately nurtured the suspicion that she was plying Malik for favors: for perfumes, for silks, perhaps for her child's future freedom. He was the master, she the slave, and she strove with every word, motion, and touch to convince him that she was, indeed, the treasure he had sought.

And now, long sweet hours later, the swordsman lay asleep, stretched on his stomach beneath damp linen sheets.

Sophia opened her eyes, slowed her breathing, sucked it down into her belly to loosen the hard, sour ball of fear that pressed against her heart. Cautious as a cat in a roomful of sleeping wolves, she listened to Malik's breathing, struggling to be certain that he was deeply asleep.

His soft snores finally reassured her, and she rolled out of bed, wrapping herself in a robe. Searching silently, she found a key in his bed stand,

and slipped out of the room with it. She handed it to Tuti, outside the door, then turned and watched Malik, who still snored heavily.

He stirred groggily, pulling himself out of dream, and opened sleep-gummed eyes to see her standing there. With a lazy smile he beckoned to her.

"Come here, girl," he said. "I had a dream. I expect you to exceed it." Watching his shoulders to time his breathing and then swaying to the rhythms of inhalations and exhalations, Sophia returned to the bed and slipped between the covers.

"Whatever you command," she said. "Tell me what you wish."

Malik rolled atop her.

Her chin rested on his shoulder, and he could not see her face. If he had, he would have seen that it was dead, save for the fires smoldering deep within her eyes.

Tuti carried the key swiftly to the servants' quarters, where an ancient Frank named Musawwir awaited her. Every step now was a betrayal. If she was caught by Malik's guards, and they grasped her intentions, crucifixion was almost inevitable.

Musawwir was a tall, thin man. Despite his evident strength and health he was balding, with thatches of white hair framing his pink brow. He had long, agile fingers and a slightly hunched back. He was also Malik's armorer, and the estate's general fix-it man. He opened the door for Tuti at her first tentative knock, and took the key. He held it up to the light, and turned it in his hand.

"This is the key to the Wakil's armory," he said. "Each brother has keys to both weapon rooms, but I don't know where the Wakil keeps his, or where Malik keeps the key to his own armory. If I hadn't been a coward, I would have made a copy years ago."

"You ain't no coward," Tuti said. "You're our only hope."

Musawwir grunted. "Then I'd better get to it. I will need five minutes to make an impression, and then, I think, two hours to make a key. Yes?"

"Yes," she said.

"I do this, you take me with you, yes?"

"We'll need you, Musawwir."

"My name," he said, "is Hans."

Hours passed, hours in which Sophia did not sleep, even when Malik rolled over and began to snore once again. Only when the first light of dawn began to paint the horizon did she allow slumber to take her, and a restless, fearful sleep it was.

When she awoke, Malik was on the balcony performing his morning prayer, his back to his bedroom and the door. What had awakened her . . . ?

Tuti was at the door, silently carrying a breakfast tray. Sophia wrapped herself in a silk robe and rose from Malik's bed. She took the tray and the master key Tuti passed from palm to palm. As Tuti left Sophia slipped it back into the drawer. She composed herself as Malik rose from his prayer.

"I go to serve your child," she said. Malik nodded as she bowed and backed out of the room, as if her presence or absence were of no consequence at all.

It was commonplace for slaves to travel the dirt access roads in wagons, carrying straw and other goods between the estates. They sometimes used the Wakil's main road as well, but then had the obligation of carrying a pass at all times. Slaves caught by patrols without a pass, or with a stolen or forged pass, were severely punished.

As the cart rolled into Dar Kush estate, the house servants directed the unloading, and Tuti passed a copied key to Aidan.

Aidan walked and then ran to the shelter of a tree, holding the precious object tightly. He, more than anyone, could guess the price Sophia had paid to obtain it. He brought the key to his lips, giving thanks for her strength.

He spent the day laboring in the teff fields, the key burning a hole in his pocket. He could have sworn that every guard who glanced at him knew his secret guilt, could read the fear in his face.

But dinnertime finally came. Servant women emerged from Ghost Town and the main house, pushing food carts out to the fields. Molly, wearing the same drab gray dress she wore every day now, broke away from the others and offered him a mutton sandwich on coarse dark bread. As she passed it, she very cautiously took the key.

With a barely discernable nod, she turned and circulated among the other men, passing out food.

Chewing his sandwich without tasting it, Aidan watched Molly finish her job and then push her cart back to the main house.

Luck to you, Molly, he thought. But even as he thought it, Kai rode past. Kai glanced briefly at Molly, the beginning of a question on his lips.

"Kai!" Aidan called, and waved his arm, smiling with his face. "Half a mutton sandwich?"

Kai's curious expression vanished, replaced by one of amusement. "Dinner's waiting," he said. "But why not come by tonight? We might take a ride together."

Aidan clasped his hand over his heart in salute and Kai wheeled, heading home. When Kai turned, Aidan's smile remained in place, but any warmth that might have lived within it was gone entirely.

Molly ran to the house, and quietly reported back on duty, donning her apron. After a few minutes stirring a spicy, simmering pot of *yebeg-alecha merek* lamb curry, she made an excuse and left the kitchen.

Down through darkened corridors she passed, her nervousness shrouding her like the stench of something rancid and toxic.

The cellar was hung with dried fish, red and black peppers, beef, and garlic, and filled to the ceiling with kegs of flour. She approached the armored door, and with trembling hand, inserted the key.

The door opened.

The room was filled with rifles and barrels of gunpowder. Molly was breathing hard and fast now. Her hands stroked one of the gleaming barrels slowly, gingerly, as it were something other than steel. As if it were, perhaps, the body of the man who had died protecting her in the swamps.

The next morning, Kai joined his family in the dining room for a breakfast of *genfo* porridge and savory *gengelfel*, a peppery meat dish served on *engera* flat bread. Its smell alone usually set Kai's mouth to watering, whether served for breakfast, brunch, or snack. This morning, however, his appetite seemed to be drowsing.

"Kai!" his father beckoned. "The mutton is especially fine this morning."

"Coffee and rolls for me," Kai said. "My appetite is thin."

"Come," Lamiya said. "A forkful and you'll change your mind."

"We'll see."

"Kai," Abu Ali said, "I would like you to ride to the quarry. Our tonnage has fallen in the last two weeks. See if you can determine the cause."

Ali leaned forward. "Would you like me to go along?"

"No," his father said. "I'd like you to examine the fences by the lake."

"Is anything the matter, my friend?" Babatunde asked.

"No." The Wakil sipped at his coffee, his brow creased with worry. "Well, perhaps, but I can't quite grasp it. For now, let's just say I have a feeling."

Like fish in a reef, servants glided in and out of the room. Silent. Almost unnoticed.

* * *

The largest of Dar Kush's three quarries was just under an hour's ride north, a great unhealed gash in the gray earth. In its depths, workers pounded rock with long-handled hammers or worked with pick and shovel to move earth.

As Kai approached, he watched Bari, their white overseer, signal with a white flag then hunch his head down as an explosion pummeled his ears and filled the air with smoke and powder.

As the cloud drifted to earth, Kai could finally make out a few human figures, Aidan standing closest, hammer in hand. His face was grayed with powdered rock, and he wiped his face with the back of a dirty hand. "Kai," he said. "*Asslaamu alaykum.*"

"*Waalaykum salaam.*"

"What brings you here?"

"Just making a routine check. Tonnage has dropped twenty percent over the last weeks." He strove to make his words as neutral as possible. "Are the men content?"

"I'd say so." Aidan's voice was as flat as the blade of a shovel. "We just got the new shipment of blasting gel yesterday. I think that will make a difference."

"If there was . . . anything wrong, you'd tell me?"

Aidan's eyes were expressionless. "It is my duty."

Those answers were precise, and simultaneously evasive. The other slaves watched and listened to the exchange, their callused hands gripping hammers and pickaxes. Something had shifted, changed, some strangely hostile energy in the air even though no one approached him, no overtly threatening move had been made. His skin crawled.

"Well," Kai said, hand creeping closer to his sword, "I suppose my father may be worrying at nothing."

"The Wakil has many things on his mind. He needn't concern himself with this."

"Very well." Kai swung up on his horse. He looked down, troubled without being certain exactly why. "God be with you."

"And Allah save you, my friend."

Aidan's smile was warm, perfectly friendly . . . and chilling. Kai rode off.

The giant Bari gestured threateningly with his rifle. "The master may give a shit about your soul—but your asses belong to me. Get to sweatin'."

This is how it began . . .

That night, at the final call to prayer, the slaves bent in worship, but several of them glanced at each other as they bowed, exchanging fierce grins.

As they sat down to dinner that night the mood was almost celebratory. All laughter seemed a bit brighter, the voices a bit louder if not quite shrill. Sequestered in their special corner of the village, the overseers were pleasantly surprised when laughing Irish girls presented them with bowls of stew, rich with mutton and potatoes, and special spices that brought a certain something special to the dish.

In one of the last cogent comments of his life, Oko Iskahar would remark to his comrades that he had especially enjoyed the mushrooms.

CHAPTER FIFTY-THREE

13 *Muharram* 1290
(March 13, 1873)

AIDAN O'DERE CREPT TOWARD Dar Kush's unnatural stillness, dreading what the night would hold.

He knew that Abu Ali, Ali, and Lamiya all lay quiet in their opulent rooms. Kai, Elenya, and Babatunde as well. Quiet, but not asleep. More than asleep.

Mere sleep might have been disturbed by the sounds of doors opening in the night. And if they had been awake and alert enough to glance out of their windows, they might have seen the shapes creeping across the lawn, admitting themselves into the house one at a time.

They were led by the scarred Brian. Bari, sleeping in a cot in the kitchen, rose groggily, blinking as if trying to brush away cobwebs.

Aidan clubbed him, cracking his skull against the wall with an axe handle. The sound was ghastly, as was the almost childlike confusion in the giant's face. Brutal wielder of the Wakil's whip he might be, but no man was a stranger to fear.

"What—?" Bari's voice was thickened with pain and confusion.

"*This*, ye bleeder," Brian replied, and set the edge of his knife against

Bari's throat. "Safe in your arms, was I?" The big man opened his mouth to scream, and Brian sliced the skin above his artery. "A sound," Brian said. "Any sound but one and you are dead."

Bari's eyes were frantic.

"I want a name," Brian said. "Who betrayed me? Who betrayed Aidan? Who is your spy in Ghost Town? I want the name, or you're dead."

Bari paused, and Brian nicked the giant's throat again. Gurgling, Bari spoke a single word.

Brian nodded. "That was the right name," he said, then stabbed Bari a dozen times in the chest and belly.

When the big man's body spasmed into death, Brian turned, panting, to Aidan. Bari was a human sieve. Blood was everywhere: the wall, the floor, the knife. It soaked Bari's clothes. His strangely soft eyes stared out at them, uncomprehending. Nausea at the sudden violence leached strength from Aidan's limbs.

Brian grabbed his shoulders, shook him alert and pushed him toward the stairs. "No turnin' back, boyo."

Brian descended to the basement and used the stolen key to open the armory. He opened the door, and the expression on his face was exultant. "All right, boys," he said. "Have at it."

The instant Aidan's fingers closed around the cold barrel of a rifle, he felt almost faint. Then that sensation passed and raw, almost irresistible confidence surged through him. He had fired rifles at Kai's side, bringing down rabbits and pigeons and once even a cougar. But he had hardly dared dream that this great day might actually dawn.

After the others armed themselves Aidan headed back upstairs, slowly, a step at a time, until he and his men were in the bedroom wing. They began to open the doors.

Abu Ali sprawled sleeping on his bed. His eyelids fluttered and then opened suddenly, although for another few seconds his mind was still groggy and sleeping. As night's strong arms released their grip he gained enough wit to realize he felt heavy-headed, furry-tongued. A foul gut told him that he had been drugged.

The Wakil's every sense burned with alarm. Every instinct told him something was amiss. He felt like a man balanced on a floating cork as he climbed out of bed, and reached out for his sword . . .

Barely able to walk, he made his way to the door, and opened it to see—

Brian. Standing in the hall just outside the door, holding a bloody knife to Lamiya's throat. His future daughter-in-law was in her frilled nightshirt, with full undergarments, but still . . . ! Fear for her life and honor burned away the poisoned fog. Swiftly, he noted that the girl's throat was, as yet, unmarked.

Another man's blood, then. Whose?

Lamiya was barely conscious. "Shhh," Brian said. "It's a lovely throat. Let's keep it that way."

Ali's bedroom was at the far end of the hall, and as Abu Ali watched in shock, his elder son was pulled out, helpless under the threat of three rifles. Thank Allah that Ali had not attempted some idiot heroics! Nothing to do now but wait . . . their time would come. "By the Prophet," he said, voice cold as the grave. "Harm any member of my family, and I will harry you beyond the gates of hell itself."

He watched Ali's face, realized that the boy was readying himself for some kind of suicidal action, and barked: "No!" Then amended in Abyssinian: *"Gäna näw."* Not yet.

"Bastards," Ali fumed.

Brian nodded and smiled unpleasant agreement. "Yes, most of us. And whose fault might that be?"

The night wind plucked at Kai as he gingerly edged around his balcony's ledge, dressed only in his white cotton nightshirt. Although his poor appetite had saved him from all but a spoonful of the narcotic mushrooms, he was still fog-headed, frantic and afraid, but determined. He climbed down to the second floor along a trellis. As he did, through the first-floor window he saw his family herded together, the damned camel-fucking servants were using Lamiya to secure cooperation from the men: Wakil Abu Ali, Ali, and Babatunde. Rage and terror warred like fire and ice in his veins.

Where was . . . ? For a moment he dared to hope that Lamiya's bodyguard Bitta had escaped immediate capture, then saw her gray-stubbled head atop what seemed to be a bundle of clothes. For a moment he thought she was dead, then managed to discern the ropes binding her arms, saw the line of blood on her scalp where she had been clubbed. One of the slaves nursed a gashed arm. He kicked Bitta's ribs as he passed her, and Kai smiled with grim satisfaction. So, Lamiya's bodyguard had managed to fight back, even under such constraints. In fact, it seemed Bitta had been the only one who had.

There were cries above him, and Kai strove to conceal himself in the shadows.

Voices: "Do you see him?"

"No. Try the kitchen . . ."

Kai climbed to within eight cubits of the ground, then jumped down, landing in a crouch. He steadied his breathing, listened until all footsteps seemed to be heading away from him. What to do? Which way? The lake? The barn?

The overseer's hut lay between the main house and Ghost Town. He crept through shadows masking the front of Dar Kush until he could see the hut's outlines. Darkness. Perhaps, just perhaps, they were still asleep. A cloud masked the moon, and he used the darkness to dash across the road. Kai pushed the door open as quietly as he could, and peered within.

Oko Iskahar was sprawled on his side, twisted in an obvious posture of death. Agonized death: his face was distorted, eyes open, pink froth dried at the corners of his mouths.

Kai was horrified. Horror turned to shock and dismay as a hurtling body caught him from behind, apelike arms gripping him about the shoulders. Kai's trained reflexes were faster than his mind: he dropped to one knee, gripped the grasping arm and twisted. With a howl, his attacker flew through the air, smashing back-first into a table, reducing it to splinters.

The rebel slave was just a field hand, but tenacious. He tried to scramble up, but Kai was faster, meeting him with a kick under the jaw that relieved him of teeth and consciousness in a single instant.

Fighting to control panic, Kai went back the way he had come, crouching and crawling across the road, then creeping along the bushes in the front flower bed, skin itching as he heard guttural voices as slaves ransacked Dar Kush in search of hostages. When he reached the west side, he was dismayed to see a pair of whites with covered lanterns striding out toward the barn.

His heart pounded as he watched them, and was unable to determine their identities in the dark. He *had* to get to the barn. If he could reach Djinna, he could get to Uncle Malik's. And once there . . .

Kai was about to turn back when the two men emerged from the barn, heading back toward the house. A swift search had doubtless convinced them that no blacks quavered in the straw. When they came closer, he recognized them as Olaf and Cormac. Kai cursed under his breath that, once upon a time, he had been foolish enough to think them harmless. As soon as they were safely back in the house, he sprinted toward the barn.

Cries from the house betrayed him long before he reached the door. As he flung it open the servants came shouting and running, their lanterns casting ghostly glowing fingers. Without saddling Djinna he leapt astride her, wheeling as the slaves came on.

"Go, Djinna—" he yelled. No need to whisper now! The servants attempted to drag him off the horse. He slashed left and right with sword and boot. Olaf flew back howling, clapping his hand against the stump of a severed ear. With a jolt that nearly unseated Kai, his boot struck squarely into Cormac's cursing mouth, cracking teeth. His way momentarily clear, Kai galloped out of the barn, directly into a volley of rifle fire. The shots were ill aimed, but one plucked at his nightshirt, drawing a line of fire along his ribs.

He pulled Djinna's mane and sped toward the pasture.

He charged toward the fences, servants struggling to strike and bring him down. Djinna jumped the first fence, almost jolting him from her back, but as she landed he caught sight of a slave, face masked in shadow, running at him swinging a shovel.

The blade caught Kai flat on the chest, driving air from his lungs, and himself from Djinna's back. He tumbled to earth and struck the back of his head hard against the ground. Arms and legs gone soft and rubbery, Kai tried to rise, then all strength failed and he collapsed into darkness.

CHAPTER FIFTY-FOUR

IT TOOK AN HOUR FOR AIDAN to row across Lake A'zam to the Berhar property. As yet, all of Berhar's windows were still dark, and his entire grounds quiet. So far, then, no hint of alarm. He tied up his boat on the dock and stealthily made his way to the slave quarters. Berhar's estate, while smaller than the Wakil's, was laid out in a similar fashion, with a separate slave village within a walled stockade.

The gates were locked. "Open!" he called.

Only an old woman answered him, her face barely visible behind the slats. Her pale red hair was streaked with gray. "Away! Ye bring death."

"I bring freedom."

"Freedom of the grave." She spit on the ground at his feet. "Ye'll fail. And die. They'll peel the skin from *our* shoulders for yer sins."

There was a jostling behind her, and three strong young men came to the gate. Their hair was as red as hers once had been. Her sons.

"Aidan? We got your message—we're with you."

"No!" the old woman groaned, clawing at them. "Don't go. It's hopeless." Aidan stood his ground. "Where there is life," he said, "there is hope." The gate opened, but only a few slaves slipped out.

"Come!" Aidan called. "Hurry!"

After they were gone, the old woman gave him a withering glance. "God help ye," she said, and shut the gate.

Malik slept alone, one arm still splayed out as if embracing Sophia. An hour had passed since their lovemaking, and the sheets had cooled and dried. Contentment calmed his angry face, as if he dreamed of her surprisingly receptive body, her singularly passionate response to his caresses.

He awakened suddenly, responding to subtle cues that would have escaped the attention of an ordinary man. Soundlessly, he rolled out of bed. His naked skin glistening in the moonlight.

What had awakened him . . . ? His eyes narrowed. His chamber door was three digits open, increasing to four as he watched.

"Who goes there?" he cried.

With no further warning the door flew wide, hard enough to crash against the wall. Three slaves burst in, bearing swords. He recognized them, of course. Musawwir, his handyman and armorer; Quami and N'Bonga, brothers who were Scot-Viking half-breeds. There was no need for words: upraised swords spoke eloquently.

Naked and unarmed, Malik snarled, a wolf at bay.

He charged and hurled a chair at Musawwir, the man in front. The chair smashed the armorer's legs and tumbled him to the floor, and as he went, Malik plucked the sword from his hand. He pivoted so that the staggering Musawwir fell between him and the others. A precisely judged knee to the jaw collapsed Musawwir into a boneless heap. Malik pivoted just in time to parry N'Bonga's clumsy thrust.

Malik snarled, possessed by a kind of wild and crazy rapture. He struck N'Bonga in the face with the hilt of his sword and rolled down, pivoting and pulling the half-breed with him, thrusting his heel into the servant's stomach, heaving upward to catapult the man across the room. Quami was forced to dodge his hurtling body. Before Malik could rise, though, Quami was on him.

On all fours, Malik scuttled like a crab, fighting from the floor, parrying, blocking, and finally pivoting to slash strongly, cutting halfway through Quami's left calf. Blood spurted from the severed artery and the slave toppled, screaming and writhing to the floor.

Malik stood as N'Bonga rose unsteadily to his feet. Almost casually, Malik thrust his sword into N'Bonga's stomach. The man made a high-pitched keening sound, mouth open as if someone had cut the wires controlling his face.

"Look at me," Malik whispered. Slowly, N'Bonga raised his eyes. They were wide and red-rimmed, devoid of all hope.

"Farewell," Malik said, then twisted and withdrew his blade.

Musawwir had recovered from the knee to the face and returned to consciousness with Malik's sword at his throat.

Malik smiled and turned his head, intending to gloat to Sophia that her friends' little plot had failed miserably. For the first time, he noticed that the bed was empty. Unreasoning rage exploded behind his eyes, and he screamed her name until his throat went raw, but there was no answer at all.

Sophia and her baby were already miles down the road, hunched down in a horse-drawn wagon crowded with eight other slaves. She held Mahon desperately tight, praying that Malik was dead, and that despite all odds Aidan and Brian had succeeded in their part of the plot.

And hoping that someone would find Malik's daughter Azinza soon, bundled safe in her crib in Sophia's room. Safe but alone, and if awake, then probably frightened.

So are we all, she thought.

I am afraid, Aidan thought. *And this is a time for boldness, not fear.*

After another hour's rowing, Aidan was exhausted, but still managed to run from the dock to Ghost Town in time to watch the members of his *tuath* rouse themselves from slumber, emerging from their huts into Ghost Town's square to face Brian, who stood before them wearing his facial scars like a badge of honor. Aidan felt as if his insides had turned to ice water, but Brian seemed as solid as rock.

"My people!" Brian called to the slaves, who no longer yawned and stretched, but stood wrapped in thin coats or blankets, shivering in shock. "Tonight is the night we have dreamed of, prayed for in the groves, since many of us were children. It is a time for action. A time for freedom."

"What have you done?" old Festus asked, wringing his hands nervously.

"Freed you!" he cried. "To die, or live, as free people, as some of you were born. If not you, your parents, or grandparents. There's not a one of you who doesn't remember, deep inside, that your labor, the sweat of your brow, used to be yours . . . that your children were yours, not things that could be sold away. Your women were yours. Your bodies and hearts yours. We worship our good Lord Jesus Christ, or the very earth and sky and trees—not some filthy black Muhammad and his Allah. Rise up!" he screamed. "This night is the night. Take sword and rifle in hand, and we will have our lives again—or bathe this land in blood!"

Judging by their faces, they had been roused from slumber to be thrust into nightmare. Some of them began to display a bit of excitement, but most looked like they wanted to find a hole and crawl in.

"We're with you, Brian," Molly said. "What do we do now?"

"First," Brian said, "we finish old business."

A general commotion among the assembled was accompanied by kicking, thrashing, and screaming as Aengus, the kitchen master, was dragged out. He was no longer laughing and confident. In fact, he was a bloody mess of rags and torn, bruised flesh, his corpulent face swollen and pocked. His arms were bound behind him.

Brian held his hands up, and the crowd quieted. "Here's part of the reason none of us have ever escaped. We fought more than the bloody blacks. We were betrayed by one of our own!"

Aengus managed to rise to his knees. "Please—you can't do this."

Brian came close. "We can't? How could you? We *trusted* you, and you sold us. Was it good, licking up after the masters? Was it worth it?"

Aengus's neck was noosed, and the rope pulled tight. Hands tied behind him, he could not loosen the knot. Slowly, his face darkened as he struggled for breath.

Brian lowered his voice to an intimate whisper in Aengus's ear. "You just lie there and strangle awhile. Think on your sins. Decide which God will judge you. And hope you picked right."

The traitor sputtered, a thin string of spit depending from the corner of his mouth, his eyes red and staring.

As if that had dismissed the matter, Brian addressed the crowd again. Most of them stared at Aengus, who twitched, purpling, in the dust.

"Now—who's with me?"

"They'll hunt us down!" old Festus quavered.

"We've speared the thoths in their pen," Brian said. "They were just animals, not demons at all. Their handlers are with them in hell. Who's with me?"

Muttering, only half of the servants stepped forward. The others looked aghast at the dying Aengus, muttering and turning away in fear, perhaps wondering if that would soon be their fate as well.

Brian was disgusted. "The rest of you—stay the hell out of our way." He turned without another word and returned to the house.

* * *

As Aidan watched and paced, Sophia's wagon drew abreast of the estate gates. Several of the villagers drew the latch and swung the door wide; she stepped down, her eyes fixed on Aidan so intently she seemed entranced.

His feet seemed to move of their own accord. His eyes took in all of her at once, including the blessed sight of Mahon bundled in her arms.

Aidan crushed her to him, their mouths fusing as if it were the first and last kiss of their lives. He brushed his lips against Mahon's smooth warm brow, drinking in his scent. Their three hearts beating in harmony, any doubts he might have harbored, any fears that their love couldn't survive its terrible trial, dissolved in that moment.

"God," he murmured. "Sophia. Mahon. My family."

"Don't say it," she murmured. "Not any of it. It's all past now. All past." She soothed his hair as if he were a child.

It's not past, he thought. *It's just beginning.* But if there existed any hope for freedom at all, he would take the chance.

Then Aidan held Mahon on high, tears standing in his eyes. His small, precious, fragile family was together again. Aidan, Sophia, Mahon. Together.

I'm keeping my word, Mother, he said in silence. *I'm keeping my word.*

CHAPTER FIFTY-FIVE

FIRST CAME SOUND: LOW, HARSH LAUGHTER, the kind used by desperate men to mask their anxiety. In gradual degrees, Kai returned to consciousness. His mind awoke before his body began to move, and he kept his eyes closed. From the mutters and grim chuckles, he believed that no one noticed his return to awareness. Vertiginous waves of nausea hammered at him, but he forced himself to remain still until his wits had further returned. He wiggled his arms experimentally, and discovered that they were bound.

He fluttered his eyes open a fraction, saw endless shelves of books and scrolls, and realized that he was lying on his side in his father's downstairs study.

When he opened his eyes more widely he saw brother Ali's face, purpled with rage. Ali was seated on the floor, only a few cubits away, arms apparently fastened behind his back. His legs stretched out straight on the floor, bound by leather thongs. The next thing Kai saw was Olaf, the right side of his face tied with a bloody bandage. He was armed with a muzzle loader, a wicked-looking kitchen knife thrust into his belt. He heard Brian's voice behind him, and struggled to turn over to see him.

Brian was darkly exultant. "Well, masters, a new day is dawning, one I'm sure you never thought you'd see."

"Burn in hell," Ali said.

"After you, *sir*," Brian said, and lashed Ali's mouth with the back of his hand. Ali spit red onto the Persian carpet, but his disdainful expression never changed.

There seemed no purpose in continuing to pretend unconsciousness. With a loud groan he sat up and opened his eyes. The guards glanced at him, one of them checked his bonds, and then they ignored him.

Kai searched the room, recognizing the five servants who had gone rogue: rough, hard men, good workers all. He shuddered to think how that muscle and animal endurance might now be turned against them.

Why hadn't he seen this coming? Damn! In retrospect, it all made sense. But then, almost everything does. In retrospect.

He still had courage. These scum temporarily had the upper hand, but he was a black man, blessed with the intelligence and clarity Allah had denied these savages. That was all the edge he needed. They had but to make a single mistake, and their pitiful rebellion was done.

And they would. No matter how well planned this part of their plan appeared to have been, they would make a mistake . . .

Kai's head throbbed abominably, and he could taste a thread of blood leaking from a bruised cheek. Still, he was relatively fortunate: Abu Ali's scalp was clotted, Ali's eye was swollen and he bled from nose and mouth. Babatunde, Lamiya, and Elenya lay bound in their nightgowns, apparently untouched. Bitta was just now stirring to groaning, bleary consciousness.

Brian squatted next to Ali, balanced easily on the balls of his feet. "I promised Aidan not to kill ye or yer brother, you know? But I would take great pleasure in peeling off yer pretty face, leave it hangin' on the wall."

Ali glared at him.

"Ye like that?" Brian grinned. "Would Allah still know ye? What do ye say, Babatunde?"

"Al-Wasi," the Sufi said, "the All-Comprehending, knows His own."

Brian pressed the point of a knife into the flesh beneath Babatunde's jaw. "Yer a good man. Are ye ready to stand before Allah?"

Babatunde met his eyes unblinkingly. Despite his flowing, flowered blue nightshirt, he maintained his dignity. "Today I stand. Tomorrow, so stand we all. We will meet again, hands untied, no sword between us."

Brian's voice was as soft as snakeskin. "And what *will* be between us, pray tell?"

"Truth."

Brian's grin widened, as if he appreciated that answer. Before he could reply Sophia and Aidan entered the room. Aidan refused to meet Kai's gaze, but Sophia glared at him defiantly, clutching Mahon as if his mere existence justified any action.

Brian nodded. "Good boy, Aidan," he said. "She'll be safe with the other women." He waved to Cormac, and the slave took Sophia's arm, leading her away.

Kai and his family were all bound in one corner of the room, under guard. Brian and a few of the others were gathered around the Wakil's desk, talking so softly that Aidan had to join the circle to hear their words.

A map was spread out on the great table, and they were whispering plans.

"We have choices," Brian said, "a thing that they never wanted us to know. It's been damned near impossible just to look at a good map."

The new freemen looked at their leader with hopeful, frightened eyes. "What are they, Brian?"

"Choose your direction," he said.

"North."

"North," said Brian, "is Vineland."

His followers grumbled.

"True!" Brian whispered. "They're the ones sold us, or our grandparents, to begin with. But I hear gold can buy safety, and there's gold in this house. Gold earned by *our* sweat and sacrifice."

"South?" Molly asked. "What about south?"

"The Aztecs."

"They'll eat us!"

"Not so loud," he cautioned, glancing over at the Wakil and his clan. "If they hear us, we have to kill them. They'll chase runaway slaves to the edge of the province. Kill the Wakil, and you'll never stop running."

Molly nodded ruefully.

"So," Brian said. "So we've been told the Aztecs eat human flesh. Could be truth . . . could be lies. West are the Apache. They've been pushed off their land, and have little love for Bilalistan."

He turned to Aidan. "How did it go at Berhar's?"

"Poorly," he replied. "Only a dozen joined us."

"This is bad," said Olaf. He scratched at the crimsoned bandage lumped over his earhole. "This isn't what you promised!"

"Shut up!" Aidan said. "No one believes we can make a go of it. Let us take a few homesteads, raze a few farms, and they'll come flocking."

"Or maybe we'll get the skin ripped off our faces—"

"Then go back! We don't need you—"

Their argument was interrupted by the sound of shots. Aidan's head whipped around. "What the hell . . . ?" One of the field workers rushed into the room, his chest bloodied. He collapsed in Brian's arms. "Malik!" he groaned. "Malik has come."

Sophia looked stricken. "God! I thought he was dead!"

Raw panic clawed at Aidan. "Brian!" he said. "What now?"

"This house is a fortress," their leader snapped. "Gunter! Troy! Spread the word. Draw those damned curtains! Guard the hostages and take your stations. This thing is only beginning."

Swiftly, the rebels assumed their positions. Brian sent runners to the slaves downstairs, and Aidan heard hollow thumps as furniture was dragged or tumbled against doors and windows.

The minutes dragged on, and Aidan grew even more alarmed at the nervousness displayed by the other men in the room. It would only take one foolish action to bathe the entire affair in blood. It was a clutch of very frightened slaves who held the Wakil, his family, and a few loyal servants under rifle point. From time to time he could hear shots and screams from outside. Unable to repress curiosity, Aidan peeked out through the curtained window.

Just beyond rifle range, Malik reined his horse back, a demonic black mare snorting gusts of steam from her nostrils. Chaos and death were abroad in that night. As rebel slaves struggled to pull him from his mount, Malik slashed and hacked with his sword, and with every swift, brutal motion a man reeled back damaged or dying.

The night filled with wails and carnage. Malik seemed to look directly at Aidan's window, shaking his sword, before confronting two more slaves who rushed in wielding flaming torches. Sparks and sword-strokes flew. A scream. Two screams: one of rage, one of anguish. One man stumbled to the ground, right hand gripping the stump of a left wrist. The other tried to flee. Malik drew his jambaya and threw. The fleeing man went down like a felled tree, a strange new stalk growing at the base of his skull.

"Bastard!" Brian said behind him.

Abu Ali shook the blood from his face. "Brian. Listen to me. There doesn't have to be any more bloodshed."

"Oh," Brian replied quietly. "I'm afraid there does."

A voice cut through the chaos, freezing them all. *"Brian!"*

Aidan and Brian peered back out. Astride his steed, Malik held his bloody sword out like a firebrand in his right hand. In his left, he held a severed head by a rope of limp blond hair.

"Brian!" Malik screamed. "I know you're behind this, you son of an Irish whore. Come out! Let's settle this, the two of us!"

The slaves looked to Brian, wondering if he would take the challenge. Brian's answering laugh was bitter. "Champions? I know enough about these bastards to know that they'd never offer single combat if the odds were even. We have what he wants."

He cracked the window. "Malik! I have your brother and his precious whelps. I want safe passage to the west, and you can have them. My word for yours!"

"You'll never get there, Brian!"

A half-dozen of Malik's guards had joined him by now, breathing hard from their frantic night ride. So: these were all who had avoided the evening's mushroom-laden stew. Aidan recognized Quami, Malik's stout Afari lieutenant, a veteran with the scarred face of a war eagle. He conferred with his master, and then headed off to the flank.

Grave danger.

Malik raised his voice. "One for one, Brian? One of yours for every one of mine?"

Brian spit on the carpet. "That's no deal at all. Malik! It's all of us, or nothing."

"You drive a hard bargain—" Malik called. Then his sword hand swept down.

Aidan heard the sound of broken glass, and screams, and a howl of warning.

"Stand fast!" Brian yelled, but his eyes shifted side to side and he cocked his head, listening. Gunshots echoed from the direction of the kitchen. More screams, and a crash. Every man in the room strained to hear. It was almost impossible to resist the urge to run to reinforce the guards.

"Let 'em do their job," Brian said. "We have more men than Malik. The advantage is ours."

For three more minutes Aidan gripped his rifle, watching the imprisoned Wakil and his family, wondering what would happen next. Would

Brian actually kill Abu Ali to gain freedom? What of Kai? And if his heart was cold enough for that, what of the women?

Suddenly there was cheering from the kitchen. A distant voice followed: "Got 'em! We whipped 'em! Look at 'em run!"

Peeking sideways through the window, Aidan watched several of Malik's men running from the kitchen, sprinting back across the lawn to safety. Several shots were fired at them, to little effect.

But Aidan's spirits soared.

"How do you like *that*, great Malik!" Brian screamed as Malik's men scrambled away. To Kai's eye he seemed to be trembling, his excitement raised to absolute fever pitch.

Kai took sober stock of his family's chances. It was possible, perhaps even likely, that they would all die in this conflict. There would be no easy answers. Having gone this far, Brian could not allow himself to be taken alive.

They had whispered around the map, hoping to conceal their intentions. Useless, of course. There would be no coordinated flight. Slave rebellions always fractured in the end. Some would flee to the swamps, some try west. They would be tracked and retrieved, or slain.

These slaves thought they had some measure of control, when the truth was, they had none at all. They would never be allowed to escape, unless recapture was certain. If they had killed in their flight, there would be payment in blood levied against them or those left behind. In a world dependant upon the labor of men, there was no level of force or terror too great to insure Brian's efforts would end a miserable, lethal failure.

Kai could just see his father's back, and realized that, slowly and steadily, the Wakil had been twisting and testing the leather strap binding his wrists. By dint of strenuous effort he had worked himself halfway free.

No, by Al-Aziz, the Victorious, Abu Ali had one arm completely free! Ali was still worrying at his own bonds as his father leapt up.

"Shite! Look out!" cried Olaf as Abu Ali sprang at him.

Abu Ali twisted the sword from Olaf's hands, and the Wakil's massive shoulder smashed the slave into the wall. One of Berhar's redheaded slaves raced in with upraised club. Abu Ali impaled him, then wheeled to face his next opponent.

Cormac leveled his rifle at the Wakil's back. Cormac's rifle discharged deafeningly, and a black scorch mark with a ragged center opened low on Abu Ali's back. "Father!" Kai screamed in horror.

His voice was lost in a concatenation of grief and rage. Only Elenya's venomous "Bastard!" registered above the general outcry.

"Shut up! All of you!" Brian said, and tore cloth away from the smoking wound.

Kai watched the entire thing as if through soot-stained glass, unable to credit the scene with reality. Even from where he lay, he could see that crimson pulsed from his father's mouth with every breath.

"Fool!" Brian snarled. He smashed Cormac across the face with his fist, then crouched back at the Wakil's side. "Damn!" His head shook slowly, with genuine regret. "I said there would be more blood, Wakil. I'd hoped it wouldn't be yours."

Abu Ali gasped for breath. "These things . . . are easier . . . to start than to stop. End it now."

Father. Kai longed to crawl across the rug, to hold his father, touch him, comfort him. His inability to move made him burn with shame.

Malik's voice sounded distantly from the outside grounds. "What was that shot? Is my family wounded? I swear by Bilal . . ."

Brian went to the window. "Your brother was accidentally shot," he called. "*Accidentally.* He needs a doctor. Time is running out, Malik."

"For both of us," cried the Wakil's brother, voice trembling with rage. "By dawn I'll have enough men here to take the house, and crucify every one of you. Any slave who leaves the house now, with the sole exception of the dog who pulled the trigger, will receive no more than a whipping— I swear."

Kai watched the servants exchange nervous glances. Was this truth? Would it prove to be their only chance for life? For his father's survival? Any personal fear had vanished. *Help my father,* he prayed. *Please.*

Malik clarified his position. "Every slave who defies me, I swear by almighty Allah I will impale him alive—he will be insane days before he dies. You have half an hour to decide."

Kai knew this was no idle threat. Malik was perfectly capable of such a thing. And at this moment, Kai was capable of assisting him.

Brian turned to his allies. "Any of ye who want to go—go."

The servants muttered among themselves, but held firm. "We wait. He'll break."

"No, Brian," Elenya said. Her young voice was strong. "He won't."

"Ye don't think he loves his brother?"

"Of course he does." Seated against the wall, hands bound in her lap, Elenya straightened with pride. "But he loves honor more. If my father dies, nothing will stop him."

Kai saw Elenya square her shoulders, her face fierce as any wild thing, and for the very first time knew that his little sister had become a woman. Pride warmed his blood. *Well said.*

Brian considered the girl's words. Kai could see that he was taking them seriously. More seriously, perhaps, than if the words had come from any of the men. "Have ye a suggestion, girl?"

Elenya was quiet. Bitta had regained her senses, her eyes sharp despite her scalp's ragged wound. Lamiya whispered to her, and Bitta nodded, her eyes never leaving Brian.

"May I speak?" Lamiya said. Despite the fact that her hands were tied behind her back, she had managed to regain a bit of her imperial bearing.

Ali's voice rose in alarm. "Lamiya. No! Stay out of this."

"I am already *in* this," she said. "The *men* seem to have made a mess of this entire business. Perhaps it is time that the women try."

Brian nodded. "What 'ave ye?"

"Ali is right," Abu Ali said, struggling for breath. His face had grown ashy and sunken. "I am an old man. Don't place yourself at greater risk."

Lamiya's face was filled with love and concern. "You have many more hunts to ride. And I make up my own mind."

Lamiya's hands were untied, and she stood. Her legs were numb from lack of circulation, and she would have wobbled, had not her will been like iron.

"My maid," she said, pointing to Bitta. No man here had ever seen Bitta's lethal skills. It was quite possible the slaves would underestimate her, give her temporary freedom.

To her delight, Olaf cut Bitta free. Her bodyguard's fingers danced subtly, making silent signals. *Shall I kill him?*

Lamiya pulled at her right ear. *No.* A swift hand sign. *Wait.*

They were escorted out of the room and down the hallway to the stairs. With every step, Lamiya strove to compose herself. This situation was extraordinarily dangerous. Too many lines had been crossed. Men had already died, and the Wakil himself was gravely wounded.

This was, possibly, the most important action she had taken in her young life. Her aunt made decisions more important every day. Lamiya had never held men's lives in her hands before, and she found it both terrifying and exhilarating.

Were they watching her? She raised her chest, walked as she had been taught, that practiced stride that gave the illusion of floating along the ground. Even in her nightgown, she was royalty, and it was vital that they not forget.

She might have been wearing a jeweled gown as she descended the stairs, Brian and three of his men just behind her. The slaves at the bottom, rifles in hand, watched her, slack-jawed.

"Open the door," she said. A short stout quarryman started to do it, and then shook his head and glanced at Brian.

"What do you want me to do?" asked the quarryman, dazed.

"As she said," Brian snarled.

Lamiya refused even to acknowledge the quarryman's presence as she strode out into the night, Bitta at her side.

Malik and his men met them a hundred cubits from the house. His fierce eyes softened a bit as he greeted her. "Lamiya," he said. "Have any of these misbegotten ghosts—"

"I am untouched."

Malik gave a grim nod, and then let his eyes focus on Brian again.

Lamiya had the strangest sense at that moment. It was as if she did not exist. As if Dar Kush itself did not exist. In all the world, there might have been only Malik and Brian. Malik was still. Utterly still, until his calm seemed like the eye of a hurricane, only inverted: this inactivity contained a force of monstrous violence, held back only by an iron discipline.

She found herself momentarily unable to speak, then almost blurted out her words, as if fearing what terrible action might erupt in that silent void. "By authority of the Empress," she said, "I request that you make truce with this man, that Wakil Abu Ali may receive medical treatment, and the lives of the hostages be spared."

"What manner of truce?" Malik asked, a malevolent rage concealed behind the formal reply.

"The two of you talk."

Malik and Brian faced each other, hate shimmering the air between them like a mirage.

"I will give you your brother," Brian said, "to whom no harm was intended."

"What manner of truce?" repeated Malik.

"My people need time," Brian said. "We flee to the west, with our hostages, but will release them at dawn—if we see no sign of pursuit."

Malik paused, thinking. *Please*, Lamiya pled in silence. *Do this, Uncle. It is the only way.*

Finally, he spoke. "I give you until Asr, the day's first prayer."

"And for what, I wonder, will you pray tomorrow?" Brian asked.

"That my sword finds your liver."

Lamiya held her breath.

The corners of Brian's mouth lifted. *"Insh'Allah."*

Malik's grim smile might have been a mirror image of Brian's.

"A slow death if any member of my family is hurt," Malik said.

"And a quick death to them if you follow before dawn. Agreed?"

Brian spit on his palm and extended his hand. The two warriors clasped, and Lamiya exhaled.

It was done.

Kai could do nothing but watch as his father was bound to a stretcher constructed from two bamboo spears and the spun-hemp wall painting of the Shrine of the Fathers. Then three slaves moved the Wakil from his patch of bloodied carpet onto the makeshift sling. Although it was clear that every movement pained the Wakil, still he attempted to command and advise. "You should not do this thing," he said to Lamiya.

"Forgive me, Father," she said. "I cannot obey you."

"Wakil," Aidan said. "For what it is worth, I swear that no harm will come to the miss."

Abu Ali's eyes bored into him. "Swear to my son, who was your friend."

Aidan turned to Kai. "I swear, Kai, my life for her honor."

He had known Aidan O'Dere for half his life, and knew his mannerisms well enough to win at lying games. This game was being played for far higher stakes than a slave girl's favors, or a joint of beef. Emotions knotted, Kai managed to nod. "I believe him, Father."

Step by laborious step, the Wakil was carried from the house to the front yard. Armed men faced each other across an invisible line, with rifles held at the ready. One step at a time, the hostages approached the exchange point under rifle coverage. Kai's mind raced, trying to anticipate what his uncle was thinking. What Brian might be planning . . .

And then he caught a glimpse of his brother's face. Ali's cheeks and lips were taut with strain, his eyes wild and fixed on his wounded father.

Kai could actually see Ali's temples quivering, the cords standing out in his neck, and knew that it was requiring every bit of strength in his brother's soul, and more, to restrain himself from suicidal action. Kai knew he was measuring distances, calculating movements.

The Wakil moaned in pain as one of his bearers stumbled. Ali's lips drew back from his teeth.

Cormac was very close at hand.

Allah preserve us all.

Malik stood with a pair of wide-wheeled wagons and several sets of horses. As the Wakil was exchanged for transportation, Brian continued to hold a pistol to the patriarch's head.

"You are a man of honor," Brian said to Malik.

"When my word is given to another *man*."

"Malik!" Lamiya said sharply. "Your word is given to *me*."

Malik bowed slightly, without taking his eyes from Brian for an instant. "Of course."

Brian whistled, and slaves began running from the house, crowding into the wagons. Horses were fleeing from the stable, almost as if they were being driven. What . . . ?

Kai had no time to ponder that as he and Lamiya were moved toward the wagons as well. Ali twisted furiously at his bound hands, keeping his eyes all the time on Cormac and his rifle.

Kai had barely begun to formulate his own plan when Ali's hands slipped free of their bonds. He ripped a sword out of a slave's hands and crashed it down on Cormac's collarbone, nearly cutting him in half.

"Ali!" his father cried hoarsely.

"Die!" said Ali as he raised the sword again. Shots were fired on both sides, and one of Malik's men dropped from a shattered leg.

A thunderous explosion shook the earth, and Kai turned in time to see the roof fly off the stable on a column of gray and white smoke. So, the quarrymen had indeed utilized that new shipment of blasting gel. Damn them.

Burning bits of wood rained from the sky, panicked horses galloped through the rolling smoke, and bullets sent men diving for cover. Kai felt hands fall roughly upon him, felt the breath *whuff* from his lungs as he was dragged to the ground. Dizzy, unable to think, he was dragged by three slaves as chaos exploded in a melee of swords and rifles, screams and flame and frenzied shouts. He heard Lamiya shout: *"Bitta! Protect Elenya!"*

He tried to shout for help, but a canvas bag was pushed over his head and he couldn't breathe.

Now his only concern was a breath of air. He felt himself carried on shoulders, heard whispers and cries and distant explosions of gunfire. None of them meant anything. He couldn't breathe, couldn't draw a breath into his lungs, and he sucked against the bag and drew nothing and then again, and nothing, and a red-black cloud boiled at the edge of his perception, pain and panic bursting behind his eyes and—

Darkness.

*   *   *

Malik had secured his wounded brother, his niece, Babatunde, and Bitta. It took two men to restrain the Ibo bodyguard when her sharp eyes spotted a horse-drawn wagon racing to the west.

Qwami followed her pointing finger, and understood at once.

"Let us give chase," he said. "The woman is right!"

"No!" Malik thundered. The chains that bound his own actions now ensnared those in his service. This matter would be played out as Allah had written it. In the end, all those responsible would be carrion. "To my side! The house and barn are burning." This was truth: black smoke boiled from the kitchen wing, and the stench of burning hay curled from the horse barn.

"But the slaves are escaping!" Qwami protested. Bitta's eyes were wild as she strained against Malik's men.

"Tend to the house and stable." Malik's teeth were pressed tightly together. "I gave my word."

"Malik!" Ali cried. "They have Lamiya! They have Kai!"

Malik grabbed Ali by the vest. "I gave my *word*."

"I didn't give mine."

A flash of lightning crackled behind Malik's eyes, and a single whisper of rage slipped between the links of his control. Before he could stop himself his fist had flashed out, striking Ali to the ground. The younger man lay stunned.

"There will be time for steel later," Malik said between clenched teeth. "I know where they go. Not north: that is toward my own castle, and my men would intercept them. Not east, toward Berhar's estate. Too many guards. The ocean lies south—they would be trapped. No, they will head west. Quench the house fires first, those of vengeance later."

He bent to Abu Ali, manner gentled by his concern. "Brother. Let me see." Malik peeled back the cloth.

The Wakil's wounds bubbled crimson. Abu Ali struggled for breath, each inhalation a heroic effort. "I fear you got the worst of your deal. One old dog isn't worth fifty slaves."

"Rest, Brother. Life's road has not yet ended."

Ali crouched at his father's side. "Father, we will make pilgrimage together."

Abu Ali shook his head, his crimsoned mouth curling in a sad smile. "I fear not, my son. Your father is closer to Paradise than Mecca."

CHAPTER FIFTY-SIX

ALTHOUGH THE KITCHEN FIRES had been extinguished, Ali still tasted smoke from Dar Kush's blackened west end. His father lay with his back resting against a tree. With each breath a bit more life seemed to seep away. Bitta, Babatunde, and Elenya ministered to him as best they could. At last, as the sun began to rise, he bade them perform their morning prayers. Nasab Asad, unsheathed, gleamed beside him.

Ali did as he was commanded, then rose and went to Abu Ali, whose lips still moved in prayer. Ali waited for him to finish, forcing himself not to think of Lamiya, his future wife, gone and in the hands of the pigbellies. He could not think of her, or he would go mad.

At last the Wakil opened his eyes. It took him a moment to focus on his elder son. "Here, Ali," he said, voice a raspy blur. "This is yours now." He handed Ali the precious jambaya.

Ali's hand shook as he accepted it. "Father . . ."

"No time for pleasant lies," said Abu Ali. "You have completed Asr, and Malik's word has been kept. Bring back your brother, and your wife." Elenya, weeping, washed his brow with a moistened towel.

"I swear." Ali kissed Nasab Asad's blade, and then slid it under his belt. "On your soul, I swear it."

Malik and nine warriors approached them on horseback. There were two empty saddles, and Ali swung up on one of them. Malik looked down on Bitta.

"You may accompany us," he said.

She said nothing, for she had no tongue to speak, but her dark eyes gleamed and she climbed up on the second horse, seated so firmly that she might have been born there. Malik laughed without humor and threw her a sword. She caught it by the guard, examined its edge, lashed it through the air twice, then caught a belt and scabbard tossed by another of Malik's men.

Her teeth gleamed.

Elenya, still kneeling by her father's side, stared worshipfully up at her brother. "Ali. Bring them back."

He reared his horse up. "I swear!" he cried. *"Hai!!"*

And the twelve of them rode like demons. Ali spared one brief glance back at his father's shrunken form, wondering if that would be his last sight of the living man who had sired him, vowing to complete this, his first quest, with honor.

Driving his horse without mercy, Ali and the rescue party pursued the wagons. The tracks had traveled north and then west along the teff field's access road, transferring to a narrow path beside one of the canals, and then finally to a trade road heading toward the frontier.

Malik lead the pack, Ali immediately behind him, but Bitta was third, ahead of all nine of Malik's seasoned warriors, her black robes fluttering around her as though she were some kind of avenging spirit.

Ali did not want or need the rest, but twice Malik forced them to pause, giving their horses a chance to drink, the men a chance to stretch their aching legs and backs. The rebels were getting away! Still, he was heartened by the confidence that men on horses could outpace wagons.

By dusk, sharp-eyed Bitta had spotted the wagon on the horizon ahead of them.

Distant explosions proved that the escaping slaves had spotted them, and were wasting their ammunition at impossible range.

Ali's horse foamed at the mouth as he drove his heels into her side. The mare seemed to have been caught up in the race, seemed to understand what was needed of her. As she, too, spied the wagons ahead of them, he needed no crop or spur to push her to extreme effort.

Bitta drew even with Ali, and her face bore nothing gentle or feminine: it was pure hellish will, and for an instant Ali was taken aback by the intensity. Never had he seen rage or purpose or any other emotion so distort the woman's visage.

They halved the distance between them, then halved it again. The escapees ventured another rifle salvo, and one of Malik's men screamed. Ali turned and glimpsed him fall, a hand clapped to his throat.

The rear wagon hit a rut and jounced into the air. A slave flew through the air, landing headfirst against the packed earth.

Panicking now, the fugitives fired another volley of shots. Ali heard a bullet buzz past him like some impossibly accelerated bee.

Then Malik was among the escapees, slashing left and right. One of the white horsemen wheeled and came at Bitta, swinging his rifle like a club.

Ali had an instant to watch her lean out of the way and answer with a hacking stroke that sent his arm flopping into the dust.

Then Ali had engaged his own enemy, and there was no more time for thought. Blood seemed to run into his eyes. His mind seemed to go blank, was like a blanket stretched for shadow-play, momentary flashes of an arm . . . a leg . . . a sword . . . a screaming face . . .

And his sword behaving as if it were a living thing, a creature that sought vengeance, that craved flesh for sustenance. As if it were the master, and he the obedient servant.

The lead wagon was trundling completely out of control, a dozen servants packed into it screaming in horror as the reins flopped beyond their reach. One servant tried to jump out on the horses to take command, only to fall beneath the hooves and wheels, howling as his ribs and spine were crushed.

The wagon hit a rut, a wheel buckled, and it leapt into the air, spun ninety degrees, and arced down and plowed thunderously back down into the earth.

The wounded and the dead sprawled, crawling blindly, sobbing and crying out, struggling to stand and hobble away toward the imagined safety of the west.

The single intact wagon wheel rotated slowly, and then stopped.

"Surrender!" Malik called. "On your knees, hands behind your heads, damn you!"

As the survivors struggled to obey, Malik and Ali drew abreast. The road behind them was littered with dead. Wounded servants were sprawled like crushed insects, mothers protecting their children, men trying to protect their women.

"Do you see them?" Ali called, anxiously searching among the littered bodies. No sign. *Oh please, Allah, please, let her be well.* He did not always know what he felt for Lamiya: she was beautiful and proud, too willful perhaps, but she was family. She was *his.* And if the slaves had hurt her, if their actions had caused her any harm . . .

Bitta jumped off her steed. She gasped for breath, face slicked with sweat. Her anxious gaze went immediately to the overturned wagon, and she set her back against it.

"Help her!" Malik called, and Ali leapt down and pushed with her, heaved it up and onto its side to reveal the crushed and bloody figures of—

Two more servants.

With shocking suddenness, Ali realized that they had been tricked into believing the slaves would go west, and while they had pursued the wagon, Brian had spirited away his fiancée, and his brother.

"Lamiya!" he screamed. The scream reverberated through the trees, across the sky, and down the empty road . . .

Far away, in one of Lake A'zam's tributary streams, floated a flat-bottomed boat barely large enough for its passengers. Brian, Aidan, Sophia and her baby, Olaf, and Tom Leary crowded together in the skiff. Kai and Lamiya lay bound and gagged at their feet.

From where they lay, Kai could see smoke rising from the direction of Dar Kush. He heard the distant shouts and gunshots as slaves were rounded up. All day he and Lamiya had lain camouflaged in the brush, silently suffering the biting of insects and the chafing of their bonds. Rags binding their mouths prevented cries for help, and although twice searching parties had come within a stone's throw, they had gone undiscovered.

When night fell again, Brian used an oar to push them out into the stream, heading south toward Djibouti harbor.

"It's been hot," Olaf said to the gagged Lamiya. "If I untie your gag to give you water, do you promise not to scream?"

Lamiya glared at him, but at last nodded agreement. Aidan ungagged her, and offered the teat of a water skin. Lamiya accepted it in silence, paused, and then spit the entire mouthful into his face. Brian laughed roughly.

Lamiya's gag was slipped back into place, and Kai was offered water in turn. Placing health above satisfaction, he took it.

"Kai . . ." Aidan said. "We have no intention of harming you. Will you swear not to try to escape before we reach the harbor?"

Kai watched the waterway as they slid south. "You will need my advice on navigation. There are places on the river where your boat could founder."

Brian laughed again. "You expect us to trust you?"

"As you wish. I won't offer twice."

Aidan ran his friend's words over in his mind, and made a critical decision. "He wouldn't lie to me."

Brian regarded them both, then grunted assent and freed Kai's hands. "No tricks," he said, as if wishing Kai would try one.

Sophia tried to approach Lamiya. "It is a long trip, ma'am. Some water would soothe the way."

Lamiya glared at her. "I want nothing from either of you."

Sophia backed away. The night was deep and dark. Aidan, Brian, and

Father Leary took turns at the oars, sculling quietly with the current, every stroke taking them closer to Brian's planned destination. To freedom, or death.

Which was, after all, freedom of a sort.

"There is a bend coming up in the river," Kai said. "You should move further toward the deep water."

"A fine suggestion," Aidan said. "You're an excellent helper, Kai. Perhaps I should take you with us. You'd fetch a fine price."

"You find this humorous?"

"It has its moments."

"For instance—when my father was shot?"

"I watched my father die," Aidan said. "Shot by the men you paid to steal me. Your gold bought his blood. Are you sorry for that?"

Wisely, Kai said nothing.

Aidan shrugged. "That was long ago. I am sorry for the Wakil's wounds. I would not have had that happen. Kai—can you tell me that you, or your father, would not have done as much to seek your freedom?"

Kai sat straighter in the boat. "I don't indulge in fantasy while my father lies dying."

"I hope he is fine," Aidan said, the weight of sincerity in every word. "And that you see him soon. I hope that one day you will understand. That there might be some place in this world where you and I could sit, and drink coffee, and watch each other's children play."

Kai wanted to discount the sentiment, but he could not. "Freedom is a dream," he said, and turned away.

CHAPTER FIFTY-SEVEN

IF NOT FOR THE CIRCUMSTANCES, Kai might have found the journey downstream almost peaceful. Frogs sang to them as they floated, and the wings of night insects beat feverishly among the fronds. A salt wind blew from the south, stirring the trees and whispering of freedom.

But that fragile peace was interrupted when, distantly to the north and west, they saw lantern lights burning, heard angry shouts.

"Shhh," Brian whispered. He grinned and set the point of his knife over Lamiya's heart. The rebel seemed almost buoyant, giddy. Kai could feel it from one-eared Olaf and Sophia as well: it was almost as if they were drunken with freedom.

The voices retreated to the west. The rebels whispered among themselves, then Tom Leary pointed east. "Look," he whispered. The eastern horizon blushed rose as the new sun prepared to greet the day. Brian sculled the boat into a sheltered little cove. "Aidan," he said. "You have first watch. Olaf, relieve him in three hours."

Brian covered himself with a blanket, curled up like a cat, and began snoring at once. Kai climbed over him to the back of the boat, carrying a water skin.

Lamiya's hands had been retied in front of her, and her face was unfettered: she had finally promised not to scream if they removed her gag. He thought that she looked tired and strained. At that moment, he would gladly have given his inheritance to comfort her, or free her from this nightmare.

"Here," he said, offering water. "You need this."

She caught the sides of the skin with her bound hands. "You are very friendly with them."

He shrugged. "Any animal caught in a trap will seek freedom."

She sipped again, as if just discovering the depth and intensity of her thirst. "We're going to die, aren't we?" Her tone was coldly matter-of-fact.

"No," Kai answered. *Don't lie to her. Not now.* "Perhaps."

They sat together, sharing the quiet. "I'm cold," she said.

"It will be warmer soon."

"You could run. You could make it, Kai."

"I would never leave you alone."

She looked at him curiously, as if not entirely satisfied by his answer.

"Ali would be very displeased," he offered.

"Ah," she said. "Ali."

"Do you love my brother very much?"

Lamiya sighed. Then: "He is a good man. Our marriage unites two countries."

No answer at all, that. And yet in the pauses between her words, he sensed a meaning he dared not acknowledge. Both of them were weak, and tired. She was afraid, and in that mortal anguish would turn to whatever might comfort her. He was imagining things, that was all.

"'It is low tide,'" he murmured, stirring his hand in the morning's cool water.

"Kai?"

He laughed. "Hafiz," he said.

"Ah." She closed her eyes with pleasure, lashes trembling against her cheek. "One of my favorite poets. Humor me."

Kai reflected for a moment, and then recited:

"Why all this talk of the beloved,
Music and dancing, and
Liquid ruby light we can lift in a cup?
Because it is low tide,
A very low tide in this age
And around most hearts."

Kai felt himself waver. Felt that he was speaking of things better left unsaid. Low tide, indeed. He could not help but continue:

"We are exquisite coral reefs,
Dying when exposed to strange
Elements.
Allah is the wine ocean we crave—we miss
Flowing in and out of our pores."

Kai paused, stopped. That was all he could say to her, even with the shelter of night. But to his surprise, she finished the poem, her voice a honeyed whisper.

"Find that flame, that existence
That wonderful man
Who can burn beneath the water.
No other kind of light
Will cook the food you need."

Kai could not breathe, could not speak. He had no label for the emotions he felt now. Could the slaves' mood be somehow, impossibly, infectious? He should have felt only horror and rage: his father was gravely wounded, perhaps dying! But somehow that fear was less than a sense of . . . freedom. Yes. There it was. Here, upon the river, he was just a man, without obligations, temporarily unable to control his fate and therefore not obliged to a responsibility for others.

He remembered Aidan's words, a dream that one day their children might play together. And his careless answer: *Freedom is a dream.* For Aidan? For himself?

Then what was this moment with Lamiya, so close to her that he could smell the salt of her skin mingling with soap and perfume. A chance for him to feel, even for a moment, that the two of them were together, separate from all obligations and controls, drifting in a tide of the heart.

Only in such a world could either of them possibly ignore the strictures that had guided them from birth.

Kai was suddenly, painfully, jarred by his own thoughts. What was he saying! His mind had strayed into a place of betrayal: of his brother, of his father's wishes, of Nandi's affections. And how presumptuous even to think that Lamiya could ever consider him as anything but a brother. He was deeply embarrassed, confused, prayed that she could not somehow read his heart. "Lamiya . . ." he finally said.

She was very close, both of them hidden in shadow. "Shhh."

He closed his eyes, vanquished by her single word.

Lamiya kissed him. It was not a sister's kiss.

CHAPTER FIFTY-EIGHT

AIDAN KNELT IN THE FRONT OF THE BOAT, preparing to accept a crust of bread from Tom Leary, when he saw Kai come groggily to waking. At first he felt sorry for his old friend, then grinned as he reckoned that the Wakil's son was pretending to be less alert than he was.

Then he relaxed: Olaf would watch the hostages while he took the sacrament. His father had believed in the magic of the river, believed that a thankful heart would draw fish and game, that the woods were filled with spirits, that the moon was a lady and the sun her mate.

But there was magic in Tom Leary's ceremony as well. It was magic that turned crumbs into the body of Jesus Christ, or a sip of water into wine and thence into the blood of the Savior.

Did these things happen? Stranger things abounded in the world. Stranger miracles he had witnessed since leaving the crannog. And perhaps, he thought as he sipped from the water skin, a bit of faith might transform slaves into free men.

Aidan swallowed as Tom Leary said "the body and blood of Jesus Christ," wondering if that salt taste in the back of his throat was God's magic at work. Perhaps, and perhaps there was magic enough for one last, greater miracle.

He rose from his knees and moved toward the back of the skiff as Sophia took his place. Kai was watching him, and Aidan felt a mixture of sadness and dirty triumph. So. Kai knew now that he had lied about conversion, that he had used his friend's faith to gain greater leeway in movement and action around Dar Kush. Could the rebellion have succeeded without such subterfuge? Thinking back over the events of the past weeks, he thought perhaps so. Yes.

But still he could not help but feel a dark satisfaction that the deception had worked.

Aidan felt utterly calm and resigned, almost blissful. One way or another, this night would see the end of it. Moving carefully, cautious not to shake the boat, Aidan came to his friend. "Here," he said. "You should have this back." And so saying he lifted the crescent moon medallion from around his neck and gave it back to Kai.

Kai held it, eyes moving from the moon to Aidan's face. He looked, not angered, but deeply pained. Aidan almost wished that he could feel guilty, or ashamed, but he couldn't.

"You lied to me," Kai said.

"What would you have done?" Aidan asked.

"Found another way."

Midnight in Djibouti harbor.

Oceangoing steamscrews and two sail-ships lay at anchor, in the second largest port in all Bilalistan. During the day it was a bustling, cosmopolitan center of commerce: ships arrived from around the world carrying spices, coffee, silk, exotic fruit, slaves, rare metals and gems, seed stock and livestock. During the day the dockside markets rang with the calls of merchants and traders, auctioneers and agents.

Even if there had not been a sober need for quiet, Aidan O'Dere would not have found words. He was hypnotized by the colossal image of Bilal standing astride a man-made island like some manner of dark angel passing judgment on mankind's sins. Aidan was stunned by the sight. Eight years ago, had it been, since he entered this bay, chained and unable even to read the words emblazoned upon the mighty base?

"The Sun Will Rise in the West," it said. Bilal's promise to his followers. A promise of freedom and plenty.

One of the smaller ships flew Judea's six-pointed star. Hoping for sanctuary, Brian pulled the skiff up next to its hanging rope ladder. Very silently. Father Leary and Olaf scrambled up. There was a brief pause, and then they leaned back over and waved an all clear.

"Go," Brian whispered to Lamiya.

Kai protested. "I should—" Brian pressed a knife to his throat and made a "shhh" sound and grinned.

"No, Kai," Lamiya said. "I will go." And she climbed.

Aidan watched her disappear up the ladder. Somehow, the Empress's niece maintained dignity even in her nightclothes. After she had ascended, Brian made a mocking gesture with the knife. "Now, young sir. We just need ye for a little longer, to gain the cooperation of the captain and the crew. When we reach Azteca, ye'll be free."

"You promised Malik to release us last dawn," he said.

"I lied."

Kai glowered at him, but climbed. He gave a last, accusing look at Aidan, who met his eyes solidly. It did not matter that Kai could not understand, that he could not *allow* himself to understand, Aidan's actions. There were far greater issues at stake than friendship.

Sophia kissed Aidan swiftly, deeply, then gave Mahon to him and clambered up the ladder. After a moment's consideration, Aidan handed his son to Brian and followed Sophia. Brian was stronger and more sure: he trusted Brian to make a one-armed ascent more than he trusted himself.

But when Aidan finally reached the deck, he almost lost his grip and fell. Sophia, Olaf, and Tom Leary stood with their hands clasped behind their heads, trapped at pistol-point by four burly black constables. The biggest of them held a finger to his lips, cautioning silence, and motioned him on board with a wag of his pistol.

For a few seconds Aidan couldn't move. All strength drained away, arms and legs gone numb with shock and despair. Only when the constable pointed his pistol's muzzle at Sophia's head did Aidan find the will to finish the climb. What now? What now?

Lamiya stepped forward and lashed her palm across his face. Aidan grimaced, but did not move. With four guns on him, resistance was suicidal.

One of the constables touched a daub of fire paste to a fuse. It sizzled, sparked, and a signal flare whistled out of its tube and arced into the air.

Aidan turned, looking down on the boat as Brian's gaze followed the arcing rocket. He heard a distant *"Shite!"* as the scarred rebel saw the small boats of the harbor constabulary approaching from all directions.

The trap was sprung.

One black kept Aidan under rifle threat, while others crowded at the rail a few cubits away, rifles at the ready.

As if dazed, Sophia joined Aidan. At first he thought it odd that none of the blacks pulled them away. Then he realized it wasn't necessary. Where were they to go? It was over.

"Damn ye!" Brian cried, seized the oars, and pulled like a crazed animal, trying to escape.

The other boats surrounded him. Brian raised his rifle, but Aidan heard an explosive *crack!* and the rifle spun into the water. Mahon howled with terror.

Aidan screamed "No! My boy!" He gripped at the railing, watching the drama beneath him unfold with a nightmarish clarity.

Brian hauled himself up, tried to strike at them with an oar, and they threw a net over him. He heaved and screamed, and at first Aidan's heart was with him. *Go, boyo! Get free! You and Mahon can still make it—*

Then Aidan realized that Brian's efforts were rocking the skiff. And he had barely comprehended that ugly fact, hadn't even a moment to scream warning, before Brian went over the side, tipping the boat as he did.

With a cry of fear, Mahon, precious Mahon, spilled from Brian's arms, slipped from the net and into the filthy water.

Sophia howled in despair. Already reacting, Aidan never heard her. Distantly, he realized that the constables were training their rifles on his head. He had time only to look Kai squarely in the eyes and say: "My son!" then turned to vault the rail.

As he did, he glimpsed Kai striking down a rifle barrel, heard the Wakil's son yell *"No!"* to the officers. By then he was in the air, diving, struggling to straighten his body so that he wouldn't belly flop and lose precious breath.

The water was warm, warmer than the night itself. He cleft it like a hunting bird, arcing up and stroking toward the last spot he had glimpsed Mahon. When he was within five cubits, he dove.

Blackness, and the stinging waters of Djibouti harbor. It was maddening to be denied sight when his other senses were all but useless. In time, he knew, his eyes would adjust. But there was no time.

Where was his boy? Unless weighted down with clothes or lungs filled with water, human bodies usually floated. There was little tide. Precious Mahon was here, somewhere.

Blackness. Nothing. He stroked for the surface. Just before breaking through he closed his eyes so that the lights and torches of the awakening harbor wouldn't destroy his night vision. Gulped air. Dove again.

Blackness and cold enshrouded him as he went deeper. His eyes were adjusting themselves, and he could look up, see the bottoms of the boats above him, the wavering flames of their torches. And forced himself calm. *There is enough light. Use it. Find him.*

Sophia's hands gripped at Kai's arm like claws, the cords in her throat standing out like taut ropes. Her mouth was half-open, mouthing words too soft to hear. Prayers, perhaps. Kai offered a swift one himself, and then returned his attention to the bay.

Another splashing sound. Kai searched the water, found the place where Aidan had breached for air and then submerged again.

A safely netted Brian had been hauled into one of the other boats. Now, all there was to do was wait.

And wait.

The water bubbled, but nothing appeared. At least forty seconds had passed. Sophia quivered as if in the grip of a seizure. Her hands knotted and she swayed against Kai. "No," she said. "No. You're alive. You have to be. No. Aidan. Please. Oh, God. No—"

Aidan is dead, Kai said to himself. *Merciful Allah, will this madness never end?* Kai put his arm around her and started to draw her away.

Then the bay's black surface burst and Aidan appeared, holding a pale, limp, swaddled body up out of the water.

Aidan did not try to resist the grasping slaver hands as they pulled him back into the boat, water streaming from his mouth and nose. The blackness of the depths still pulled at him, a promise of freedom that he had nearly embraced. Peace. An end to strife and striving . . .

Then his hands had touched Mahon, a pale, limp bundle floating motionless in the water, and all thought of surrender fled his mind and heart.

His son's cheeks were almost blue-white, like some drowned thing that had been days underwater. And yet it had been less than two minutes since Brian's boat had overturned. Fishermen had survived worse.

Gasping for breath himself, Aidan kissed the child's face, then fought to remember things that his father had taught him, half a lifetime ago. He turned his son onto his belly, then pumped at his back with a firm, pulsing stroke.

"It's dead," one of the sailors grunted.

No, not dead. Aidan wouldn't allow his mind to accept that. If Mahon died, then Aidan would die. There was nothing that could keep him in this world, nothing to keep him from simply diving back over the side of the boat and seeking the peace he had glimpsed in the blackness.

He turned Mahon on his back, pumped rhythmically at his stomach, watching the little rosebud mouth tremble with every stroke.

"Ain't that just like a pigbelly? Too damned stupid to know when to quit."

"Looks like your little ghost is a ghost," one wit offered, and the others howled in response.

Suddenly, blessedly, water gushed from Mahon's mouth and nose. The little bundle curled onto his side, spasmed in pain, and vomited up gouts of Djibouti harbor slime. Mahon spewed again and again, and in between gouts of filthy water and curdled milk, the child wailed like the last pure soul on the road to hell. Aidan crushed him to his chest, his own hair plastered over his eyes. *Thank you, God, thank you.*

And suddenly, incongruously: *Praise Allah.*

Whatever might happen to him next, his son was alive.

Alive.

CHAPTER FIFTY-NINE

KAI STOOD AT THE CORNER OF HIS FATHER'S BED, trying to think of a way to say good-bye.

In his stateroom on the third floor of Dar Kush, the Wakil lay beneath the white Persian silk canopy of his bed, weak beyond the capacity for movement. The physician Jimuyu ministered to him with ointment, powder, and lance, his long face sour. Lamiya stood crying near the door, a bandaged Bitta holding her arm.

It is all so perfect, Kai thought. *Like a picture. I have seen many pictures of families gathered at the side of a dying parent. How could I have forgotten how it felt to watch Mother die?*

But then, he thought, men were not intended to remember pain like this. Life could not go on if grief such as that swelling within him did not abate. When he touched his father's rough and ashy skin, it already seemed bereft of life. He could already see how his father would look in the shroud. Kai's heart already stuttered, as if unwilling to beat on when one so dear had crossed the river.

Feebly, Abu Ali gestured to the Imperial Niece. "Child," he rasped. "Come."

Lamiya approached his bedside slowly. The white robe she had thrown over her nightclothes seemed eerily prophetic: mourning would come all too soon. Abu Ali kissed her hand. He reached out his hand for Ali, who gave it. He placed their hands together. "Stand together, as one. Love each other, and this land I have spent my life defending."

"I will, Father," Ali said.

His hand fell away. Abu Ali stared at the ceiling, blinking slowly. "I wish to speak to my sons," he said. "Alone."

Jimuyu, Lamiya, and Bitta bowed and left the room. Elenya's eyes brimmed with tears. "Father?" she asked.

"I will send for you, my flower," he said. "But there are words that no one else must hear."

Elenya bit at her lip but nodded, and left.

Ali knelt at their father's bedside, Kai joining him a moment later. He felt adrift, as weak as a child, but knew that now was the time to show strength and resolution. Their father needed to know that his sons would endure.

For Father, then, he thought, and steeled himself.

Abu Ali labored heroically for each breath, and Kai and his brother waited, giving him whatever time he needed to marshal the strength to speak.

Ali broke the silence. "Father," he said at last. "What is it you would have us do?"

"First, it is time for Elenya to travel to the Imperial Court, to school. I should not have postponed it for so long. Selfishness, I suppose. I knew I would miss her. But there will be troubling days ahead, and you will need the friends she will make. All of the plans are drawn up: you will find them in my office."

"Yes, Father."

"You have done all that would make a father proud," Abu Ali said. "And now there is one last thing you must do."

"Anything," said Kai.

"In time, you punish the slaves for their uprising."

"Tenfold, Father," said Ali. "I swear that I will drench their village in—"

"No!" his father said, wounded voice peaking. He coughed, bringing a bloody sheen to his chafed lips. "No."

"But, Father. Why?"

"Because it is not your mind that speaks those words. Nor even your heart, although I know your love for me is strong."

"What, then?"

"Nassab Asad," he said.

"The knife?" Kai asked in confusion.

"Not the knife. The blood in your veins. All the men of our family have it. The fever, the lust that comes upon us in battle. You will feel it one day." He looked searchingly at Kai, as if already detecting signs of contagion. "I know you fear that when the day of your testing comes, you will not fulfill your destiny."

Had his father's gaze penetrated to Kai's most secret heart? How else could a mortal man, even a father, know such a thing?

"I tell you that not only do you need not doubt your courage, but that the only thing you need fear is the beast within you."

"Father?" Kai began.

"Let me finish. I found it myself, in the Battle of Khartum. Your uncle met it there as well. The lion in his blood. I came home and sought greater union with Allah. Your uncle walked his own path, a path he shared with men like Shaka. Malik was consumed by the sword. He thought that if he was the greatest swordsman, the greatest warrior, that it would keep the beast at bay."

"I don't understand," Ali said.

"I know," the Wakil said. "And I am sorry. You may have to feel it to understand. And so now all I can give you is words. Know this: there is a place in your heart that loves the killing. Feeds upon it. It is a part of the greater void that comes for us all, that yawns for me now. To yield to it gives great power, but that surrender is like yielding to opium, or the green tobacco. It protects a man from cowardice, but has a hunger of its own. And the more you feed it, the greater it grows. It seeks death. The death of enemies."

All the moisture seemed to have been sucked from Kai's mouth. He swallowed twice before speaking. "But is that not a good thing, Father?"

"With each enemy slain, we kill part of our own soul. It grows back, like a lizard's tail. For a time. But Allah has engraved a number on each man's soul, and when we have passed that number, every man we kill kills us just a little bit."

"What is the number?"

"No man knows. Every man is different. Know this: I came very near that number at Khartum. And your uncle Malik passed it."

They were silent in that room, that room where death walked so close to the men of Dar Kush.

"Uncle Malik . . . ?" Kai said finally, wondering if his father would even have the strength to finish. He wanted to emblazon his father's every precious word upon his heart. Soon, he knew, there would be no more.

"Yes. And he did not take refuge in Allah's light. And the hole within him yawned so wide that Fatima's love barely closed it. When she died, I think he felt that he lost what little light remained to him. He looked to me. To us. And borrowed our light. And I was so happy to give it." The Wakil paused, wheezing for air. "But now I go, and Malik will want revenge. Not out of anger, but from fear that he cannot admit, and the blood that boils within him. He will try to take you both with him to hell. Do not let him. Help him. Love him. He is a great man, and as with all great men, has paid a mighty price so to be."

"As you wish, Father," said Ali. "How would you have me punish those who rose against us?"

"You are . . . the Wakil now!" Ali seemed to rock back slightly, almost as if his father had struck him. Kai's own breath seemed to cease its flow. *I am looking at a dead man,* he thought, struggling to keep his eyes dry. *My father is gone already—only his spirit remains.*

"It . . . is your decision," the Wakil said, more softly now, as if that last outburst had drained him. "The way you handle . . . this situation . . . will set the stage for the next fifty years of your life." His chest labored. "Be stern. But be wise. I ask you to trust your heart, not your blood. Can you do this thing?"

Ali nodded. "I can, Father."

"Good. Good," he said, and closed his eyes briefly. When he opened them again, it took him a moment to focus. "Now," said the Wakil sharply, as if sensing the need for haste. "Please send in Elenya."

CHAPTER SIXTY

TWO HOURS PAST MIDNIGHT on the second day following the rebellion, the Wakil's sons and brother left the great house, and in their eyes Aidan saw death. His arms were no longer sore. They were numb now, numb where the ropes had cut into his circulation, numb where they had been drawn behind his back, bound at wrists and elbows, more rope around his knees.

The runaways—Aidan, Brian, Olaf, and Leary—were all bound hand and foot. They lay on their sides, staring up at the possible instruments of their punishment: a row of four wooden crosses erected at Ghost Town's gates.

A row of black guards held the other slaves at bay as they awaited their fate. Ali and Malik had disappeared into the village, returning minutes later with a carved wooden crucifix belonging to Tom Leary.

The guards pushed several of the rebels forward, drove them to their knees, bound their hands. Twelve of them were already bound and tied to stocks awaiting judgment.

"There are two issues here," said Ali coldly, almost as if discussing the price of hay. "One is the rebellion itself, which will be punished." For a moment the passion raging within him burned nearer the surface. He looked directly at Brian, teeth bared. "Have no doubt of that." Brian blinked hard, and broke eye contact. "The other is that some of you pretended conversion to gain freedom of motion. That is a crime against Allah, and for that, you shall be swiftly delivered unto His judgment. Make no mistake: all of the ringleaders will die this day. We know who you are: Brian, Leary, Moira—"

Aidan groaned to see the old woman pushed out into the circle. Her wrinkled face was bruised. She seemed naught but a sack of brittle bones. She fell to her knees, gray hair flagging around her face, but she looked up at them defiantly. "Devil take ye," she spat at them. "I did what I did. I won't beg for what's left of my life. Ye took all the good years. With what's left, I'll speak my mind."

Ali nodded. "You have courage, and even wisdom. You and your people would be better had you used more of the latter and less of the former."

Ali held the crucifix down to Brian. Wiggling to get leverage, Brian sat up and kissed the image of Jesus, glaring at them with his one good eye.

"It is right," Malik said coldly. "Embrace your Messiah. You will have the honor of sharing his fate. I wonder if Allah will rescue you as he did Isu?"

Aidan's hands and feet suddenly itched horribly, the sensation verging on pain, as if he could already feel the spikes driven through his flesh. But Ali had not mentioned him as a ringleader. Did that mean his life was spared? Or merely that he would not be crucified?

One of the guards pushed Molly forward, her hands bound before her, her hair hanging wildly around her face. "You pretended conversion to Islam," said Ali. "Your life is already forfeit. Do you stand before Allah and profess belief in His Prophet?"

Molly sneered at him. "Bring it closer," she said. He did, and she pressed her lips against the cross.

"Good," Malik said. "Soon you stand before your God. This is not a time for lies."

Then Ali stood before Aidan, and he felt as if judgment day itself had arrived. Blood roared in his ears. "Brian swears you were caught up in this, but killed no one, and planned nothing. I can find no one to testify against you. Perhaps you are even innocent. But I cannot bring myself to believe that you have genuinely embraced the Prophet." He leaned closer, his angry breath a bitter perfume. "What say, Irishman? Others have spoken the truth this day, have chosen honor over life. Does the burden of your lie weigh upon you?"

Aidan saw Sophia out of the corner of his eye. She was restrained by Malik's men, and shook her head desperately. *Don't make our child an orphan,* she seemed to say without words. *Live.*

He turned his head away from the crucifix. He wanted it to be over, wished that he had sunk into the depths of the bay with his son.

"What?" Ali said, drawing closer. "I cannot hear you."

Live. For his wife. For his son. For the promise he had made to Nessa, long ago.

Aidan locked eyes with Ali and spoke the hateful words with reverence. *"Lah illah bah illah Llah,"* he said.

"Yes," Ali said. "There is no God but the One God. But by what name do you call Him, I wonder. And what do you really think of the Jew?"

Malik turned toward Kai. "Father Leary admitted that he gave Communion to the Christians, Kai. What did you see?"

Aidan saw Kai's gaze slide away to Sophia, and then to Mahon. He seemed to study the child, who nestled against his mother's breast, asleep.

Then back to Aidan again, and in his eyes, Aidan saw nothing, could read nothing.

Then Kai looked at Babatunde, who had witnessed the entire process without a word, his own face somber and watchful.

Aidan held his breath as Kai reached into his pocket. He withdrew the silver crescent medallion, weighed it in his hand, then bent and placed it around Aidan's neck. "Ash-Shahid as my witness, I saw nothing," he said.

Malik's voice was deadly quiet. "Allah knows if you lie. Would you risk your soul for this pigbelly?"

"You were not there, Malik," said Babatunde. "You cannot say."

"I say you should stay out of this. I am not certain where your loyalties lie, Sufi." Malik glared at Kai, but was unable to force his nephew to break contact, or retract his story.

Now Ali spoke. "Those who led the rebellion must die, as will those who pretended conversion to Islam. All of those will have the honor of dying as did your precious Isu. The others are to be whipped, and returned to the fields." Aidan heard groans of grateful relief.

Ali turned to the slaves. "Be not relieved so quickly." His grin was savage. "There is one thing more I must do."

Hands and feet bound, Aidan stumbled along the dirt path leading to the grove, jabbed from behind by the point of a rifle. Guns everywhere, dark angry hands on the triggers, murder in their eyes.

The entire *tuath* was gathered, every man, woman, and child. He heard the whispers: *Will they kill us? Remember that rice farm out east? Chopped heads off half those poor bastards. Goddess mild, protect us, please . . .*

Ali cantered out in front of them, his face expressionless. "My father, the Wakil, is dead."

Aidan felt leaden. Death, then. So be it, as long as his family was safe. *Sophia will be safe*, he thought miserably. *Safe in Malik's bed.*

The slaves muttered and moaned and tore at their hair.

"Some of you knew of this uprising," Ali said, "and some did not. I should have half of you skinned." He was struggling, fighting some great inner battle. "My father let you keep your names! Your barbaric language. Your deification of the Jew. Your worship of trees. See now what it got him."

Madness burned in Ali's eyes, madness and death, barely restrained by . . . what? Aidan knew not, but felt almost pitifully grateful, whatever it was. Every face was riveted to Ali, all understanding the frailty of the thread that bound them to life.

Ali raised his clenched fists into the sky. "No more!" He smacked his palms together, and his men ran in with torches and buckets of pitch. They doused the trees until their lower branches dripped black, and then set fire.

The flames snaked along the branches, chewed at the trunks, leapt from tree to tree and into the sky.

Aidan had sworn that he would not cry, would not show weakness before these monsters, but as the branches began to burn, as the smoke drifted down in rolling, choking clouds, his eyes began to sting, and he could not stop the tears. All around him, the men and women of the *tuath* watched their beloved grove flaming, branches and trunks consumed, and as a single heart they felt its death. Their past. Their futures. All aflame, soon to be nothing but cinders.

Twin tear tracks glistened on Sophia's face, reflecting the flames ravaging their beloved grove. Over the months she had come to love it, and to understand what this place meant to the captive men and women. Only with its destruction did she fully grasp the enormity of the Wakil's kindness in allowing them this symbol.

Only in loss, she thought, *do we truly understand what we once possessed.*

She was forced to watch as Aidan was locked into the stocks and beaten until the blood ran from his back in rivulets to puddle on the ground. Every whip stroke was like a breath ripped from her lungs, a day torn screaming from her life. Yet her man did not cry out. He took blow after blow, and finally, when his legs could no longer support him, he hung moaning, biting through his lip. He did not scream, even when Malik deliberately raised his voice and ordered, "Bring her."

She was dragged to Malik's waiting cart, where Bitta handed her a bundled Mahon. Her eyes held Sophia's for a moment longer than necessary. There was neither hatred nor pity there. But in that broad, strong face there was something else, a glimmer of the communication that Sophia yearned for, some flash of understanding, perhaps. One woman for another.

Then the moment was gone, and Bitta pushed Sophia brusquely up onto the cart.

Sophia felt utterly numb, beaten, exhausted. She could not even pray for help. Certainly all God's grace had been expended in the restoration of her son, the sparing of Aidan's life. She could ask no more of Him in a lifetime of worship.

But with every breath of her precious burden, she knew it had been worth the price.

Her cart rolled slowly past the village, and the four slaves crucified before its gates: Brian, Father Leary, Molly, and old Auntie Moira. Spikes had been driven through their hands and feet. A small platform beneath the feet allowed them to take some of the strain off their hands, but in time fatigue and despair would weaken them, they would hang by their hands, their chest muscles would grow exhausted, and they would suffocate. It was only a matter of time.

Brian craned his head to watch the smoke curling from the grove, his entire body convulsing with pain and terror. His pants were stained with blood at the crotch. Brian's punishment had been severest of all.

Sophia watched Malik look up into Brian's face. This time, for the first time, Brian could not meet his eyes. Malik laughed grimly, and rolled on.

Sophia watched them all recede: the shantytown, the crucifixes, the stocks, the distant, burning grove. And distantly, just visible, the figure of Kai on his balcony, watching.

PART FOUR

War

"The universe," said the Master, "reflects back the divine in the attributes of the imminent aspects of God."

"The aspects?" asked the student.

"The ninety-nine names of God," said the Master. "Al-Awwal, the First, and Al-Aqhir, the Last. Al-Muhyy, the Giver of Life, and also Al-Mumeet, the Causer of Death. And Al-Rahman, Mercy . . ."

"And Al-Jalal?"

"Yes. And Wrath."

CHAPTER SIXTY-ONE

IT WAS SAID THAT IF ONE HUNDRED of the faithful offered sincere prayers for the soul of the departed, that that pilgrim would be guaranteed entrance to Paradise. If that were true, Kai thought, then his father must be already in the hands of Al-Quayyam, the Eternal Caregiver.

It seemed that not a free citizen in all New Djibouti was about his own affairs that day. The roads outside Dar Kush were crowded with mourners, the grounds filled with coaches and horses, the private cemetery where Kai's sainted mother had rested now for fifteen years ringed with more than a thousand men and veiled women, wearing the white of grieving.

Babatunde spoke to the standing throng, his voice pulling at Kai's heart, which felt as heavy as a stone.

"Ahmad reported," the little Yoruba intoned, "that the Prophet, peace be upon him, said: 'Do not wash those who die as martyrs, for their every drop of blood will exude a fragrance like musk on the Day of Judgment.' The Prophet, peace be upon him, ordered the martyrs of the Battle of Uhud to be buried in their bloodstained clothes. They were not washed, nor any funeral prayer offered for them."

The crowd was hushed. Kai's mind swam, sought firm ground, shamefully fled the reality of the burial.

There was something so . . . final about placing your remaining parent in the ground. Perhaps before that moment, you could deceive yourself that Al-Qahhar, the Destroyer, Death, might pass you by. But when the ground has swallowed both Mother and Father, the lie is put to such childish notions, and what remains is a cold and relentless reality.

He reeled, felt his balance crumbling, almost leaned into Elenya, who stood at his side with Lamiya. His sister seemed to be bearing the burden better than he, shutting away her grief in some part of her child's heart that seemed as old as the seas. Her cheeks, beneath her veil, bore no tear tracks. Her eyes were steady as the Pillars of the Nile. And yet he knew that, if possible, she had loved their father more than any of them. Perhaps in dying the Wakil had lent her some of his strength. He hoped so. He would not wish his own despair and misery on anyone, let alone Elenya.

The washing of Abu Ali's body had been a subject of controversy. He had died protecting his home and family, and at the hands of an infidel. But there were those who said that since there was no *jihad*, no holy war, this made him a lesser martyr, whose body should be washed, who should be prayed over.

Controversy be damned, thought Kai. *Ulema be damned. My father lived in the light of Allah, and there he died. I rest my soul on that conviction.*

"And we ask," said Babatunde in conclusion, "that Allah accept His warrior into His holy arms, and that He hear our prayers. May he dwell always in the fields of Paradise, and may we meet again on a day beyond imagining."

Kai felt coolness as the morning wind dried the tears upon his cheeks, and begged forgiveness of his father's spirit for his weakness. *I have striven to be a good man. I have made mistakes, but you paid for them. Forgive me, I will be a man, Father. I will make you proud. Surely you know my heart now, as no mortal man ever could. Watch me, Father. If there is a drop of your blood in my veins, I will find a way to make you proud.*

Ar-Rahim, the Most Compassionate, help me to be strong. Help me make it so.

In the days and weeks that followed, the house was repaired, and the skeleton of a new barn erected. Servants trudged to their tasks, heads down, shoulders slumped. It was the same with the field hands.

Armed overseers hovered at all times. Watching, waiting. Perhaps even desiring a new cycle of violence to begin, that vengeance, stifled by the last wishes of the dead Wakil, might at last be delivered.

Darkness had descended upon Dar Kush.

Kai concluded his third prayer of the day, rolled his rug, then turned to find Elenya watching from his bedroom door.

Abu Ali's death seemed to have thrust her into the childhood's gloaming. Her face had lost its baby fat. In truth, he thought that she resembled Fatima more than her own mother. Even had she been poor, she would have drawn highborn suitors. "Kai," she said. "You haven't eaten all day."

He did not respond. She came to him and took his shoulders. "Kai! You do nothing but pray."

"I have a great sin to wash away."

"What sin?"

He stared down at her, then softened his gaze and took her small hands in his. "Go, little one," he said. "Forget your brother." From some forgotten well of strength he managed to find a smile. "For now. I will find my way home."

He trailed his finger down her dark, shining cheek. "I will come back."

She backed out of his room, face flushed with alarm.

Quietly, he repeated: *"I will."*

A week later, Lamiya steeled herself and deliberately forced Ali to ride past Ghost Town, where the bodies of the renegades still hung from the crosses. They were rotten now, and when the wind shifted, their stench reached the main house. In the servant village, it must have been unendurable, a constant, nauseating reminder of their sins.

Brian's withered corpse seemed to stare down at her, its face crawling with insects. He had certainly deserved death, but this? Brian had not abused her, had forbid any dishonorable actions toward the women of the Wakil's household. She had feared for her life, but never her chastity. Her upbringing encouraged her to take this haughtily, to assume that Brian had been intimidated by her royal lineage, but she wasn't so certain.

Perhaps he had protected her to use as a trump card, knowing that if he damaged her, Ali's wrath would be impossible to control. Perhaps.

Lamiya had traveled in the wilds of Europe, seen the crazed savages chained in the markets of Alexandria and Tarifa. Most of them were beasts, but a few . . .

Just possibly, the rebel leader had been an honorable man. And if that was the reason she had not been molested, it was unseemly for his body to be displayed so once his soul had departed.

Both eyes were gone now, and flies buzzed about him, crawled upon his tattered lips, his desiccated cheeks. His hair was as limp as bloodstained straw.

Ali laughed. "Not so proud now, is he?"

"Ali," she said, fighting for control. "Hasn't it been long enough? Couldn't you cut them down?"

A pair of servants scurried past them into the village, keeping their eyes to the ground. They had scarves tied around their faces, faint protection against the stench.

"Not yet," Ali said, and smiled. "Not quite."

She rode with him for another hour, but could not keep her mind on the path, or her mount. There was nothing she could do to keep from glancing at her companion. The hard, fine lines of his face, which she'd once found challenging and strong, now verged on cruelty. His eyes, once steady and cool, were now cold.

When they returned their horses to the stable, she made a weak excuse and set off by herself, supposedly to walk some stiffness out of her back, and pick flowers.

But she found herself walking in circles in the woods, faster and faster, her thoughts describing similar arcs behind her furrowed brows.

Why had she never seen this side of Ali before? Or had she, and ignored it? No . . . this was new, something unleashed by the death of his father. Would it accelerate? Fade after a while?

And then, most terribly, she realized that it didn't matter.

I cannot love a man who could smile at such a terrible thing. I cannot. I will not.

A short while later, Lamiya found Babatunde in his room, standing at his reading pedestal, at the window facing the misty blue expanse of Lake A'zam.

"Ah, Lamiya!" he said without turning. "I was just reading a new paper by Quallo, a Dogon astronomer with whom I once shared a wretched balloon ride in Alexandria. He claims optical verification of one of their myths, a story of a 'double star' system so distant its light would require ten or twenty years to reach us. Now, personally I doubt . . ."

He had finally turned, and a glimpse of her stricken face finally seemed to quiet him.

"My child," he said, gliding toward her. "Whatever is the matter?"

She fell to her knees beside him. "I cannot do it, Babatunde." Her words were a rasping whisper. "I know that I say a terrible thing, but I cannot."

"Cannot what?"

"Marry Ali. He has *changed*. His father's death has made him cold, cruel. I cannot." She threw her hands across her face and rocked back and forth on her knees. "Merciful Allah, what will become of me?"

He regarded her sternly, and as much as she wished for compassion, another part of her craved his strength, perhaps realizing that at this moment it was the greatest asset she possessed. "You will do your duty. What you were born to do."

His words scalded. "But, Babatunde . . ."

"You were not born for your own pleasure, but to save your aunt's kingdom."

"But what if . . ." Confusion flooded through her mind. *What if I love someone else?* "What if I do not love him?"

"What do you want?" Babatunde's voice sharpened. "Permission to disgrace yourself? You cannot have it. You think your place is hard. *Life* is hard. For every man whose honor compels him to lay his life on the field of honor, it is hard. For every slave who toils for a family that can be taken from him at a black man's whim, life is hard. How *dare* you?"

Lamiya glared at him, hating the truth in his words, hating even more her own confusion. Then she scrambled to her feet and ran.

The Empress's niece spent a half hour tearing her room apart, emptying her drawers, abortively packing a few belongings, then flinging them onto the floor while loyal Bitta watched in dismay. No matter how she struggled, Lamiya could not stop shaking and crying.

Finally, she stopped, and looked around herself at the room that the Wakil had built for her, designed to remind her of home. Its darkwood paneling, its silken hangings, the canopied bed imported from her homeland, the silvered wall masks of her ancestors . . . assembled at great price and effort by a man who loved her, and believed her to be the future mistress of a great household.

She sank to her knees in the thick warm llama wool rug, sobbing as she had not since childhood. "Allah," she pleaded, "give me strength. If it is Your will that I provide comfort and companionship to Ali, I will try to do so." *To those to whom much is given, much is expected, as well.* "But soften his heart, please, or mine will turn to stone." She paused, another thought, another face flickering briefly through the depths of her mind.

"And please," she concluded, "take from my heart . . . the thoughts that might weaken me."

Such prayers did seem to help Lamiya through her days, and her most secret hope was that they would help her through her nights as well.

And the truth was that in time she knew she might come to view Ali's coldness as strength, and perhaps it was: the kind of strength that had consigned untold slaves to death to build the Pyramids and Pillars. If she could weep with wonder at their glory—and she had—then surely she could find it within her heart to love the kind of man who could bring such marvels into existence.

Surely.

So each day she struggled with her heart, studied with Babatunde, and prepared herself for the day when all such hesitations would become moot.

Three days after she attempted to intercede for the servants, she was taking her morning ride with Ali, a thing that had once been purely pleasure, but was now inevitably combined with business of one sort or another. Today, he supervised as workers repaired the damaged kitchen.

"—and I will have the west wall rebuilt by the end of the day," Ali concluded.

The new supervisor was Yakia Lumumba, imported from New Alexandria to replace the slain Oko. A tall, muscular, shaven-headed civilian of Moorish appearance and military bearing, Yakia snapped to attention. "Yes, sir!"

She stifled a yawn. All of her days were beginning to meld together, as if Abu Ali's death had leached the spice from life. Then she felt her heart leap, and quashed that glad feeling with a little pang of guilt.

Kai was approaching from the direction of Dar Kush's front door. He wore white robes, his hands tucked in his sleeves.

"Kai," Ali said with genuine pleasure. "You leave your room."

"Yes, Brother." Kai seemed not to notice her, but Lamiya was not fooled. "I seek a boon."

"Of course."

"Please. Take the bodies down."

Ali thought for a moment, and then nodded. "I believe the lesson has been learned. It is best to begin healing. We must live with these people." He smiled. "I do it for you, Brother."

Ali called out to Lumumba. "Cut them down."

"Yes, sir."

Ali turned back to Kai. "Are you happy?"

"I am content, my brother."

Without another word, Kai returned to the house.

Ali looked after him, rubbing his chin thoughtfully. "He was always the sensitive one," he said to Lamiya. "Mother's favorite. I hope we never go to war."

"So do I," Lamiya murmured, so quietly that she herself could not hear the words. This family had sustained enough damage. Any more and it might not serve her aunt's purposes, and then Lamiya's life would be rendered meaningless indeed.

Kai prostrated himself before his father's grave. The gravel bit through the thin linen into his skin, and the pain gave him an almost perverse satisfaction. "Father . . ." he said. "I bore false witness before Allah to protect an unbeliever." He searched himself, hoping to find some emotion that burned more brightly than simple self-loathing. He had been startled to discover he could generate sufficient emotion to ask Ali to release the crucified slaves to the dignity of the grave. Even that paltry gesture had drained him. "I feel dead inside," he whispered. "What do I do?"

"You forgive yourself, and move on."

Kai's head whipped around. "Babatunde?"

His teacher approached from the direction of the house. His customary gliding gait seemed today so very smooth Kai would have been surprised to see grass bend beneath his sandaled feet. "We have not spoken in days, Kai. I thought I was your friend."

Kai hung his head. "I am not worthy of friendship."

Babatunde sighed. "Oh, Kai," he said. "The greatest sadness of age is that we cannot give our eyes to the young. Allah sees beyond deeds, beyond words, into the heart."

"Then I am lost."

"Give it time, Kai. Time will heal."

Kai said nothing, merely bent to make a new prayer.

Babatunde sighed, and left.

Kai remained on his knees. He waited, hoping for an answer of some kind, some sign that his prayers might have been heard and acknowledged. After a time, the ache in his knees grew intolerable, and he rose, mounted Djinna, and trotted back down toward the house.

On the way he passed Aidan.

They looked at each other. Each seemed on the edge of words. Neither spoke. They both turned, and each went his own way. Aidan walked as if he had aged twenty years in the past weeks.

Kai felt as if he had never been young at all.

CHAPTER SIXTY-TWO

BY THE FIRST DAY OF THE SECOND MONTH following the uprising, the oppressive air about Dar Kush had, if anything, grown even heavier. There were noticeably more guards about the grounds these days, and they were better armed. There was another difference as well: the general morale of the slaves seemed broken. They usually kept their heads down, and rarely dared to meet squarely the eye of any man or woman whose skin was darker than dawn.

In the mansion itself, dinner was being served under Bitta's watchful eye. Lamiya's bodyguard had temporarily assumed control after Aengus's garroting. The new scar along her shaven scalp only increased her physical authority, and the servants bustled at her approach, hypersensitive to her every gestured nuance.

Lamiya watched as the servants entered with the main dish: an Abyssinian mussel stew served in edible dishes of hot bread—ordinarily a favorite. But the mood was somber as steaming trays conveyed their bounty to the family table.

Ali sat like stone at the head of the table, bearded chin resting on his heavy fist. He did not speak. Lamiya picked at her appetizer, eyes casting about, looking for relief.

Elenya seemed to have become a little old woman in child's clothing since her father's death. She rarely smiled, and never laughed. Ali had decided she should travel to New Alexandria for three months, to be presented to the Caliph; she would be leaving on the morning tide. Tears and bitter recriminations had failed to sway him.

Even Babatunde seemed overwhelmed by the weight of the mood. And poor Kai was no help at all. He seemed to subsist on air and prayer, and had lost almost a sep since the insurrection.

This had to stop. But how?

"Oh, come," Elenya said. The girl seemed to be struggling with her burden, summoning all the brightness she possessed. "We can do better than this! Father would demand it."

She went to the corner of the room, where sat a *bägäna*, a stringed Abyssinian musical instrument of whalebone and wire, played in a similar manner as a harp.

Composing herself, Elenya sat and began to play.

Lamiya was afraid that Ali would request that Elenya desist, so she was delighted when the girl had the presence of mind to choose the Wakil's favorite song, a song from his Abyssinian father's boyhood, "Dännäsa Al-lämä," "I Dream of Dancing." Sweetly, she began to sing and accompany herself on the *bägäna*.

> *I've dreamed beneath a starlit sky*
> *My bed the desert sand.*
> *I've watched as fifty thousand men*
> *Waged war at my command.*

All life's illusions pale beside
The thing I've found most true:
There is no joy short of heaven
Close to dancing, Love, with you—"

"Dännäsa Allämä" was a song of a young prince's love and hope, but concealed within it also was an almost unutterable sense of loss. Not a month had passed since his wife's death that the Wakil had not played that song.

He had danced to it on his wedding night.

In a high, sweet voice, Elenya sang of lovers and lost nights, and despite their individual sorrows and regrets, first Lamiya, then Babatunde, then Kai and finally Ali himself, joined in. Gradually, even grudgingly, the mood shifted to bittersweet, and some of the paleness left the room. Not all, but some.

In the village, a warm but quiet communal cook was in progress in the central square. Aidan looked up from his bowl of fish mush as the first strains of "Dännäsa Allämä" drifted to their ears. The words were in Abyssinian, and he recognized only enough of them to know that it was the late Wakil's favorite.

His spoon fell heavily into his dish, his hand momentarily devoid of strength. He could not afford emotion now. It took every kite of strength he possessed just to survive his days. He could not. He could not . . .

As if those around him were of a single mind, the slaves began singing, as if to drown out their masters' voices.

They did not cry, they sang the prayer that had comforted their people for five generations:

"Sea and stone . . . salt and loam,
Hearth and home, in us resounding . . .
Pressed are we to be slaves unto men,
Yet we be blessed beyond mortal kin,
To be freed and reborn once again
We are bound . . ."

In the dining room, Kai's family ceased singing, and whistled their approval.

"Well done!" Ali cried, striking his palms together smartly.

Babatunde's smile wavered, and then broadened. He cocked his head.

"Listen," he said, and walked to the balcony. One at a time, the others followed.

They looked over to the shantytown. Its lights glowed somberly, the music wafting over the intervening distance.

"They are a simple people, with short memories," Ali said. "I knew that with Brian dead, they would soon forget their troubles."

As Kai walked to his room that night, Babatunde met him, taking his pupil by the arm. "Kai? Would you come with me, please?"

"Of course." Kai felt withdrawn, but was unwilling to offend his teacher, and accompanied him to his room. There, at the little man's directions, Kai rolled the Persian rug back, exposing the delicate geometric complexity of the Naqsh Kabir.

"It has been a long time," said El Sursur.

Kai felt a distant stirring, but kept all emotion from his face or voice. "Perhaps another time."

"Please, Kai. Now."

Displaying no slightest hint of enthusiasm, Kai took his place. Babatunde played the *bägäna*. While Elenya and Abu Ali had been skilled, the Cricket was a master, his nimble fingers plucking the strings like the Sultan's personal weaver working the loom. Regardless, Kai's first motions were halting, robotic.

Slowly, Kai's thrusts and lunges became more fluid, and then almost magically beautiful. He dipped, spun, punched and kicked in slow motion with a dancer's grace, savagely chopped and hacked a dozen imaginary opponents into stew meat. At times his balance seemed almost to defy gravity, as he froze in some impossibly contorted position—then exploded into a lethal whirlwind. When he stopped, he was panting. Kai felt as if a world of ice was breaking up within his chest, and the emotions locked within it were both sweet and unendurably bitter.

Before he revealed his thoughts or feelings Kai turned and fled.

For hours that night Kai lay in his bed, staring at the ceiling, world spinning. He yearned for sleep, but his thoughts returned again and again to Aidan. Wondering how he slept, *if* he slept, in his empty bed, next to his empty crib.

He thought of Abu Ali, cold in the ground now, his immortal soul safe in the arms of the living God. Kai believed that, with all his aching heart. Why, then, the grief and fear? Why the anger?

Aidan had deceived him, and that deception led to the Wakil's death. Yet Kai had protected him. Why? Why couldn't he let the pigbelly bastard hang on a cross with his friends? What within Kai was so weak and corrupt that he couldn't see his way to a simple truth? Ali could see. Ali was strong. It was right that Ali would inherit the majority.

I have not the strength to rule, Kai said to himself. Allah is merciful indeed.

24 Rajab 1290

(August 18, 1873)

Sheltered by the interlaced willow branches above, Kai stood before the weathered black door of Babatunde's mosque, fearing to enter. He had been here before, twice, wanted to enter, to pray, to beg Allah for forgiveness. But as before, his strength faltered. If he could not forgive himself for his blasphemous lie, how could Allah possibly forgive him? Surely, if he entered so holy a place, his very flesh would be blasted from the bone, revealing his secret sins for all to see.

So instead he sank to his knees and lowered his head to the moist earth. He had just begun his usual prayers when he heard a rifle shot at the main gate, a mile and a half distant. He stood and looked southwest. Trees blocked his view, but he heard two more shots.

Only three shots? There seemed no threat, but despite himself, Kai was curious. He mounted Djinna, jumped a fence, and approached the main gate from the north. Another rifle shot, followed by answering shouts from the house.

Now Kai was close enough to see the faces at the gate, recognize horses as well. These would be Kebwe and Makur, longtime students of Malik, the sons of highborn officials in Djibouti harbor. They fairly vibrated with excitement.

"Kai!" Makur called breathlessly. "Great news! Great news! Our regiment has been called up. It's war against the Aztecs! They've taken the Shrine!"

Ali was running from the house, pulling a shirt over his sweat-beaded chest. He must have been interrupted in the midst of his daily exercises.

War? Kai straightened in his saddle. A hard, bright smile widened his face.

War. A thousand opportunities to die honorably, to place oneself before the sword and will of a worthy enemy, that Allah might decide the right and wrong of it all. A chance to reclaim the most sacred relic in their empire. With such an action a life might be redeemed, or honorably lost.

Either conclusion was an occasion for joy, and Kai raised his fist to the heavens, shouting louder than any of them, but for reasons they would never comprehend.

Ali's friends had been joined by a half dozen new arrivals, including Kai's old rival Fodjour. They swaggered and shouted through the halls, Dar Kush's myriad servants seeing to their every need.

"Bring food and drink!" Ali called. "This is a cause for celebration!" Then, corralling his friends Kebwe and Makur: "Tell me where the breakthrough occurred."

They crowded into the main study, and Kebwe flung a map onto the table. He spoke of flaming ranches to the west, Aztecs riding from the south, mounted cavalry, savages as proud and fearless as any army in the world. He told of battlefields strewn with the dead, and most unforgivably, the Shrine of the Fathers with an Aztec banner fluttering high above it.

"The Aztecs broke the line at Swazi River," said Kebwe. "They were beaten back, but then circled around through the mountains."

"That Montezuma is a wily bastard, I'll give him that!"

"I'll give him my sword up his arse!"

"They took the mosque," Kai said quietly. Already, he pictured the site more fully. Could almost smell the gun smoke, the sweat and steel to come.

"Why do they want it?" asked Kebwe. "It could mean nothing to them."

"They see it as a fort on the edge of their territory," said Ali. "From their point of view we could reinforce it with a regiment, and use it to spearhead a march on Azteca."

Kebwe shook his head. "That would be blasphemy. They are insane."

"Mosque Al'Amu," Ali said, humor threading darkly through his voice.

"Father used to switch me if I called it that."

Ali turned to him, all humor fading. "This is our time, Kai. Our children will hear our stories and wonder, as we heard those of Father and Malik. We will drive the *kufurin* into the sea." He drew his sword and lifted it high. "To swift and bloody victory!"

"Victory!" shouted Kebwe and Makur, lifting their swords. Kai lifted his, and opened his mouth, but did not shout. In his mind, he saw a sea of cannibal Aztec butchers, howling for his life. In such a sea he would submerge himself, and blood would either wash away his sins, or drown him forever.

* * *

Aidan paused a moment from his unending, meaningless labor in the bean fields, wiped his forehead with a blistered hand, and stared up at the sun. It was all endless backbreaking drudgery, bending and pulling, chopping and hoeing. The sun broiled the workers, but rest breaks were far apart now, even though it diminished the quality and quantity of their work.

Ali's orders. Obviously, the new Wakil had decided to break every one of them, make them crawl for forgiveness and beg to be treated as slaves and not prisoners.

The Irishman's head felt swollen and heavy. At first Aidan was certain that the ringing he heard was between his ears. Then he realized that the great bell was clanging, calling in slaves from the fields and forests.

Without thought, without sufficient spare energy for anything but the mindless walking pace of the utterly exhausted, he dropped his hoe where it was and joined the flood of living dead staggering along the furrows to the gate.

By the time he arrived, over two hundred of them were already standing in rows. He joined the nearest line. "What's going on?" he whispered.

As if in answer to his question, Ali rode out, Kai trotting Djinna just behind him. The young Wakil wore full battle armor and his gleaming ceremonial sword. His thin beard had been preened to perfection.

"Slaves!" he cried. "I speak to you today not merely as your master, but as one who might also be your friend."

Aidan wondered how Ali could say that word without it choking him. Murmurs rose from the men beside him.

Ali continued, oblivious to their scorn. "The Aztec infidels have broken the peace, and crossed into our territory, as far as the Mosque of the Fathers, where the men who founded and explored our great nation died two hundred years ago. This will not be tolerated. The time has come for war!"

More murmurs. Aidan felt an unaccustomed dizziness, a hollow feeling in the pit of his stomach. What had all this to do with him? Let all the fucking blacks have their hearts torn out by cannibals. Hell, he'd help the Aztecs sharpen their knives.

"You may wish to know what this has to do with you. Well, know this: any able-bodied man who fights with our army, and acquits himself honorably, wins his freedom!" There were the words. *There* was the offer Aidan had dared to hope for.

No one made a sound.

"Who will be a man this day? Who will throw off his shackles and join our cause? That man, should he live, is a slave no longer!"

The servants looked back and forth at one another, eyes wide, shifting weight from foot to foot nervously.

Finally Olaf raised his reedy voice. "We don't know how to fight, sir!"

Judging by his performance during the uprising, Aidan thought, *that* was certainly true.

"You will be taught! All we need from you is your hearts, and your strong bodies. If a drop of true blood runs in your veins, if you commit yourself to our righteous cause, you will be free!"

Olaf and a stout quarryman named Cennedi nodded to each other and stepped forward.

Ali beamed. At this moment Aidan bet he was glad he had spared so many. "Good! To Kebwe, my quartermaster. Who else?"

Two more stepped forward, and Ali motioned them out as well.

In the back row, Aidan was listening, eyes hooded. What were the chances? The blacks would not offer freedom unless they knew few would survive to claim it. But any chance at all was better than the hell his life had become. He stepped forward.

"Ah, good—" Ali began. Then Kai, dressed not in full battle regalia but wearing his sword sashed around a black robe, trotted Djinna forward until he was even with his brother. He whispered in Ali's ear, and the Wakil nodded grimly. "No, Aidan," he said at last. "Not you."

Aidan felt as if the ground had opened beneath him. He forced himself to step back in line, his eyes locked with Kai's, some kind of painful, primal communication passing between them.

This wasn't over.

"Good," Ali was saying. "You, and you, and . . . you."

CHAPTER SIXTY-THREE

KAI STRODE THROUGH THE LUNGING, thrusting, screaming and straining rows of prospective soldiers. All across the lawns and pastures of Dar Kush hundreds of young men, black and white, were pushing their minds and bodies to the breaking point. Black commoners from nearby farms drilled with muzzle-loading rifles, the slaves strove to master their pikes.

Here Kebwe, whose father had been a decorated soldier before retiring to a successful shipping career, pushed them mercilessly. "Points up! Step strong! *You!* That's a pike, not a plough . . . !" Kebwe seemed far more assured and mature than he had during their regiment's monthly drills.

In another part of the grounds, Ali struggled with the black soldiers. "*Squeeze* the trigger—don't pull. And reduce your profile. You're not hunting breakfast. These squirrels shoot back!"

This was good, and right. Kai felt the demons of lethargy burning away in the intensity of preparation for holy war. Alert for the slightest opportunity to teach a willing and capable hand, Kai walked the line of slaves. He saw a pair of Berhar's servants struggling to appear fierce. In trying so hard, they had achieved only low comedy. "No—step as you thrust," he shouted. "And you! Truly Al-Mu'akhkhir placed you behind all thinking creatures! Do you want to be some Aztec's supper?"

The servants were confused and sullen. "No, sir."

"Here," Kai said. "Then—thrust at me. At me!"

"But, sir—"

Kai slapped his face. The slave lowered his pike and charged. Effortlessly, Kai sidestepped him, tossing him to the ground.

"Perhaps you should join the women and cowards!"

"No, sir."

"Then try to learn."

The slave nodded, and Kai strode on, heading to the barn.

There, savoring the rare moment of calm amidst the excitement, Kai fed sugar to his beloved Djinna. "Well, old girl. It looks as if we'll finally see battle after all." She biinked at him, or perhaps at the fly circling her eye. Kai batted it out of the air. "Don't worry," he said. "We'll take good care of each other."

Kai spun as he heard footsteps in the doorway.

It was Aidan. Of course. "Kai," he said hoarsely. "Why did you deny me?"

Kai's expression was cold, but his blood was heating rapidly. *Yes.*

"Why?"

"I don't have to give you reasons."

"Please, Kai. The burden of my days is almost more than I can bear."

Kai was apparently unmoved. "Go back to the village, Aidan. This is not for you."

"Damn you! We were friends once!"

Kai turned away, almost placid amidst the storm. "If anything of that friendship remained, it was discharged when I lied to save your life."

Aidan's head slumped. "Yes. I am so sorry. I wish I could take that moment back."

"You used me."

"As you have used me, all my life. All I ask is a chance to win my freedom."

"So that you can buy Sophia and your child?"

"Yes!"

Kai felt pain that he dared not allow into his voice. "It will never happen, Aidan. You'll die." Despite his best efforts, Kai found himself telling Aidan more truth than he had intended. "All of the mamluks will die. Go away."

"I . . . I challenge you, Kai! Fight me! I'll prove I can do this."

Kai turned his face away from Aidan, not wanting to reveal his emotions. His heart swelled with a strange, pale satisfaction. Truly, he was a child of war, as Malik and Shaka had always said. Aidan was both friend and enemy. In a sick, twisted vining of motivations, he both wanted to save Aidan and to see him die, to proclaim his love and see his old friend crawl.

He had promised no repercussions. He had kept his promise. And now he would have his revenge.

"Very well," Kai said.

He removed his sword, squared himself, and Aidan came at him.

I am a twisted thing, a thing of war. The younger brother, who must make his mark by killing men. This has Allah decreed. And so it is.

I am not my father. I am my uncle, Malik.

As Aidan came at him, Kai did not evade, did not seek to use speed or power or fancy technique.

He stepped in, cutting the line of Aidan's attack, his fist thrusting squarely at Aidan's nose.

The impact sent a jolt along Kai's right arm and into his shoulder, but that right hand was supported by the left, and it was as if Aidan had collided with a swinging beam. His feet went out from beneath him. He went down as if poleaxed.

Aidan rolled over, dazed and shocked by the impact, and rose unsteadily to his feet.

Kai watched him impassively. Aidan circled him, crouched, spiraling closer and closer. In the instant he decided to charge, Kai's right foot lashed out, the toes hardened by years of thrusting into baled straw, then dried beans, and then gravel. They were buttressed by his leather sandals, controlled by a mind that asked no questions and felt no doubts.

The toes speared precisely into Aidan's solar plexus, paralyzing breath and thought, only kites from the pressure necessary to stop the heart itself.

Aidan dropped, face gone pale with shock, vomit surging into his throat and only partially swallowed before gushing sourly out of his mouth onto the straw beneath his hands.

"Stop," Kai said calmly.

In mindless desperation, Aidan fumbled a pitchfork out of the hay and came at Kai with it. Kai sidestepped as if he and Aidan had practiced this dance a thousand times, twisting his right leg behind him as he grasped the shaft, uncorking his hips and twisting the pitchfork so that Aidan's momentum and his grip on the shaft sent him hurtling through the air, smashing through a horse stall shoulders-first.

Aidan lay dazed and beaten, barely conscious. Kai picked up the pitchfork.

"Stay," he said, as if speaking to an animal. "Live."

Aidan was barely able to repress his tears.

"I cannot," he said. "Kill me."

Kai's eyes narrowed. "Our friendship cost me my honor. My father's life." Kai hurled the pitchfork to within a digit of Aidan's head. The Irishman blinked, but did not move, and despite himself, Kai felt a flash of approval. Aidan was a man, and Allah granted every man the right to risk death in a righteous cause. "Go, then. And I hope the Aztecs take your heart."

"They may as well," Aidan said. "It is dead already."

Kai left the barn without reacting. Knowing that it had ended in the only way it could. Because he was Kai.

And Aidan was Aidan.

And the immortal God who had fashioned both had not finished with either of them.

The young nobles, foot soldiers and mamluks lined up, better than four hundred in all, drawn from the surrounding farms and communities. Malik himself had emerged from self-imposed isolation to present Ali and Kai with their captaincies. Despite the solemnity of the ceremony, his uncle struck Kai as somewhat distracted during the entire process. Malik's armor and garb was so polished and pressed that it was almost a caricature of itself. His hair seemed . . . a bit unkempt, his beard ratty, his eyes wild. The mare beneath him was better groomed.

Malik raised his sword. "Nobles! Soldiers! Mamluks! This day you fight for the glory of Allah! I wish I could travel with you, but the eldest in each family must remain to protect the holdings—"

Seated comfortably on Djinna and Qäldänna, Kai and Ali glanced at each other. While what Malik said was technically correct, merely by raising his voice he could have led the Wakil's forces, demanding that either of the Wakil's sons remain behind instead.

One more campaign, he had requested only a few years ago. Physically, he was still the greatest warrior Kai had ever seen, or ever hoped to see. What had happened to him?

"—I believe no Aztec will come this far. I believe that you will end this threat, and run the river with their blood. Send them home with their hearts in their mouths!"

Malik raised his fist to the cheering throng, then walked his horse to Ali and clasped hands with him.

"Are you sure you will not accompany us, Uncle?" Ali asked. "We would happily make a place for you in our tent."

Malik's eyes were just a touch evasive. Just a touch, but enough. "I wish I could, Nephew. But I know you and your brother will do the family proud."

Ali nodded. There were more questions, painful questions, but it did not appear that he would get any answers that day. "Forward!" he called. "March!"

And the troops took to the road. Malik and his men stood to the side, watching.

As Aidan marched by, his eyes met Malik's. Malik smiled a hard, cruel, ironic smile. "Farewell, mamluk. Die with honor."

Kai cringed but remained silent: he had done what he could. Babatunde drew him to the side for a moment. "Kai," he said, "the man you are will change in the weeks and months to come. You have heard many stories about the glories of war."

"Since childhood," Kai agreed.

"There is no law at the western frontier, save that made by strong men. You will be under the hand of Shaka Zulu. I think that in his world, he knows no law but his own."

Kai said nothing, but remembered Cetshwayo's estate, the night hunt and Shaka's killing of the wounded man.

"Would you have me betray my family?" Kai asked brusquely.

"You know me better than that," said the little man. "You go into battle because it is what you were born to do, and it is a righteous cause. But Shaka fights for Shaka's glory, and no other reason. Watch him. Do not let him infect you with his madness."

"He need not," Kai said. "We have madness enough of our own."

Babatunde smiled sadly. "Perhaps I cannot reach you now. But remember my words: Whatever you do, remember that the act is not the impulse. The thing is not the essence. War is the worst thing short of hell itself."

"How do you know?" Kai asked, already sensing the answer.

"There are things in my past I have not spoken of," said El Sursur. "I have not always been a teacher. It is the worst thing," he continued, "but the men who fight it can be good—if they never lose sight of Allah." His voice dropped. "As your uncle has done."

Kai felt a shock run through him at those words, an echo of his father's. Before he could question or probe, Babatunde said, "Know that you are more than a man—you are a spirit. Whatever the man may do, if it is done for Allah, the spirit remains pure. Remember."

"I will," Kai said. What was Babatunde telling him? There was no time left. Teacher and student clasped hands.

Kai turned to see Ali saying good-bye to Lamiya. She kissed his brother on the cheek. He grasped her around the waist, raised her from her feet, and bruised her lips with his. "On my return," he cried, "Lamiya and I will be wed!"

As the men cheered she smiled demurely. Her eyes met Kai's. There was an actual jolt at that instant, an emotional impact that seared him like a firebrand. Then she looked away.

Tightly leashing his mingled sense of pride and shame, Malik watched the troops march out. How proud they looked! He remembered his own first deployment, more years ago than he cared to count. Remembered the doubts and questions, the almost unbearable excitement, the hunger to test his steel in battle.

How long ago that had been. Now he had nothing left to test, nothing left to prove, felt only ashes where once had roared the greatest fire in New Djibouti. He turned to face his men. "Half of you remain here in protection of Dar Kush," he said. "The rest, come with me." He wheeled and headed back to his own estate, an hour's ride north.

When Malik reached his castle, he dismounted and went directly to the greenhouse. In the midst of fronds and flowers he found Sophia, caring for both infants. She seemed shrunken, but calm. He had taken her to bed a half dozen times since her return. Her body had been pliant and warm, but without the feigned passion that had deceived him. And yet . . .

Somewhere within her that passion lived, and the place within him that now held only ashes longed to feel it again. There was a way, yes. He would find it, no matter how long it took.

There were several other slave women in the greenhouse as well, sewing and speaking in low voices.

Malik entered. "Leave us," he said to the other women, who had begun scurrying out even before he spoke.

Shielding her eyes, Sophia bowed before him. He took her shoulders roughly, felt his fingers sinking into her soft, warm skin. "Your Aidan is going to war," he said. "He thinks that he can win honor, perhaps gold. That he will be free, and purchase you from me."

Sophia trembled in his grip.

"He will never return," Malik continued. "And if he does, he will never have you."

He drew his jambaya and placed it against her throat. That lovely throat, whose pulse had fluttered to his kiss. "I would sooner see you dead."

Say something.

She was silent.

I could slit your throat, he thought.

She didn't flinch, and Malik grew uncertain. For the first time it was his eyes that shifted, just a hair. *Damn you!* He screamed silently. She was a witch, to cause so much death, so much chaos and dishonor.

Kill her now, before it is too late.

Before he could do something he would regret, Malik sheathed the knife, and stalked off.

CHAPTER SIXTY-FOUR

THE COMPANY TRAVELED THE ROAD WEST. The noblemen carried breech-loaders and expensive, experimental revolvers, handmade by Beninian craftsmen. At their sides swung swords and jambaya. Common blacks carried muzzle-loading rifles. The mamluk carried pikes, and sometimes sharpened staves and staffs.

As they traveled, they were joined by contingents from other farms, estates, villages, and common households. Now well over a thousand strong, they marched and rode off to the west, to the frontier. To war.

On the evening of the third day's westward march they reached Shaka Zulu's war camp, a vast tent city housing the greatest war machine in the Western empire. It was well patrolled and fully protected, consisting of almost seven thousand men. The slaves were escorted to their rude housing, and the nobles and commoners to theirs. In the freemen housing there were torches and rich savory smells, dancing slave girls and plenty of good food and camaraderie.

Ali, Kai, Fodjour, Kebwe, and Makur were welcomed in.

"Enter!" Shaka roared. "Welcome, warriors. Take food and drink!"

"Meat and water," Ali emphasized. "We are empty and parched."

Shaka grinned. "That is right—you don't take beer. Pity. More for us! Hah-hah!"

Shaka's tent was spread with maps, hung with furs, spears, swords, and knives. Two gigantic redbone Zulu ridgeback hounds gnawed beef joints on his rug.

Kai reckoned that it required a dozen men to break down and erect Shaka's war tent. The colonel himself wore a tailored tunic that combined the black-and-red severity of the Pharaoh's army with the more flamboyant fur trimming and feathered crests of traditional Zulu war garb.

Kai's fatigue dissolved as he concentrated on the maps spread on Shaka's table. He didn't want this war, and yet on some level he needed it. Perhaps in the company of men like Shaka he would find himself.

"What are your plans?" asked Ali.

Shaka swept his hand at the maps. "We'll divide our main force tomorrow, with two-thirds circling to feint at the Aztec settlements *here* and *here*." He indicated spots to the south and southwest of the little model marking the shrine. "We, the core, will proceed directly toward the mosque, capturing and destroying any Aztec forces along the way. Once attacks on their underbelly have drawn away the mass of the shrine's defensive troops, our core force, commanded by me personally, will strike."

Ali seemed unconvinced. "But won't they guess that our strikes at their homes are just distractions?"

Shaka grinned. "Yes—but they'll have to respond just the same. Abu Kwame is dug in at the Drift"—he jabbed his finger at a spot a day's ride northwest of the shrine—"and the Aztecs will be fearful of a pincer movement. The shrine is of tactical value to them, but it is far more precious to us. If they hold the shrine and lose their family lands, they have gained little. Listen and learn: a principle in war is to exploit the difference between a resource's value to your opponent, and its value to you. Understand?"

Ali nodded slowly.

"Good. Now then—once they have withdrawn their forces to protect their bitches and whelps, my core force strikes. A frontal assault by the mamluks, followed by a pincer movement left and right by our elite troops. Your royal forces will remain in reserve. Once the spine is broken, we move in and pluck the heart."

There were general murmurs of approval. Kai continued to study as slaves brought platters of roasted bison and pitchers of water.

"Thank you," he said absently. Ali and the Zulus were laughing, shaking hands, speculating on the morrow. Alongside their solid confidence, his own bravado seemed a thin, frail thing. His gut boiled with acid. *Allah, he pled, do not let the gasses escape, that these brave men know me for a coward!*

Kebwe spoke up. "You are using versions of the same tactic at each location and at each level of engagement? Side feint and forward charge, side feint and forward charge . . . ?"

Shaka nodded. "We will crush them, and the best part is that the mamluks will take the brunt of the casualties. In the entire campaign, we should lose two or three thousand slaves at the most."

There were murmurs of approval, and Ali shrugged. "The Ulema will reimburse us . . ."

Kai heard that number, closed his eyes and saw heaps of savaged bodies. Endless rivers of red. He searched the other faces in the tent. Was there anyone else who was as repulsed by the notion as he?

If there was, no one who was willing to admit it publicly. And heaven help him, neither was he.

Later that evening, Shaka walked the camp with Kai and Ali. He gestured expansively at the troops. His charisma seemed massive enough to bend sky and stars into a mantle.

"I anticipate a swift campaign," he said. "These barbarians have no taste for prolonged warfare." The military organization was roughly organized into a hierarchy influenced by inherited and appointed authority: The officers below Shaka were generally referred to as lieutenants, with their relative status decided by time in grade. The officers were all men of good blood and high social standing. The common soldiers were recruited from all free black men of the empire, the highest noncommissioned rank being the ghazi, then the sergeants, and then the common soldiers.

Shaka's senior ghazi was N'tomi, a man of mixed Zulu and Watusi extraction. Almost seven feet tall, he was abnormally thin, and Kai's first thought was, *A fistful of bones in a sack of skin.* N'tomi towered among them, his long angular face cast in a perpetual scowl. He rubbed his knobby hands together. "We'll send them back across the river, sir."

"A river of blood," Shaka said. "I'll stand on a mountain of their heads."

N'tomi's deep, hollow eyes blazed. "On such a mountain a man might see as far as New Alexandria."

"Heh. Heh, heh." Shaka's teeth gleamed in the night. "He might indeed."

Kai watched them laugh, listened to the hounds worrying their bloody bones, and remembered Babatunde's words, fearing for all their souls.

Kai and Ali slept in one of the officer's tents that night, on narrow cots raised only digits above the ground. When Kai roused himself from bed at dawn, Ali was already gone. He washed with the water in a shallow metal face bowl and then prayed. He could hear the clash and clatter outside his tent, the sounds of steel against wood and steel against steel.

As he exited his tent seeking breakfast, the morning light revealed the rows of mamluks and common soldiers drilling, marching and practicing weaponcraft, being hammered out of their individual identities, formed into the components of a fighting machine. They practiced with spears and pikes, thrusting against horsemen and other footmen.

Ali and Shaka were speaking as Kai approached, and he caught the tail end of his elder brother's discourse. "We are teaching thousands of these slaves to kill."

"And quite efficiently," Shaka replied.

"Not three months ago we repressed an uprising on Dar Kush. Aren't you concerned that these skills might be turned against us one day?"

"Ah?" Shaka said. He nodded, and called to the nearest slave, a broad-shouldered, potbellied lad with a ratty mane of long black hair. "You! Your name!"

"Gunter, sir."

Shaka grunted. "Attack me!"

The slave cringed with fear, but did not move.

"Attack me, Gunter," Shaka roared, "or I will have your life!"

The man quivered, and then attacked wildly. Shaka drew his spear, parried and stabbed just under the left armpit, piercing his heart.

The officers applauded, while Kai lost his appetite for breakfast. Even Ali looked aghast as the unfortunate slave collapsed to the dust, blood gushing from his side.

Shaka merely shrugged. "If he had obeyed my first order, he might have lived."

"I see," Kai said. Disbelief and fear warred within him, and he struggled to keep them out of his face or voice. Ali's eyes were narrowed with disgust. "And you were demonstrating that . . . what?"

"They are training only to cope with straight-line attacks, without lateral motion. They are two-dimensional. Any *gentleman* could kill five of them in his sleep." Shaka stretched and yawned as he said that. Contempt for the slaves? Or for any "gentleman" who would worry about them? "They are fit only for mass attack, with side support."

He flickered his head at one of his fawning lieutenants. "Remove this meat."

Two slaves hauled away the corpse as Shaka swaggered off. Kai watched silently until the Zulus were out of earshot. "The Caliph has entrusted this mission to a monster, Ali," he said, voice low and controlled.

"The Zulus have the greatest strength in New Djibouti. Without their strength, troops would have to be recruited from New Alexandria. Such an action would offend the Zulus, and harmony is vital in these dangerous times."

"You will be the Wakil," Kai said. "Politics is your world, not mine."

Ali rested his broad hand on his younger brother's shoulder. "I cannot do it alone, Kai. If ever I said a word implying I could, discount it."

Kai was warmed by the words, felt closer to his brother than he had in months. Years, perhaps. And the smile they shared was that of two warriors passing through a dark valley, only their sword arms and honor armoring them against the night.

When not sleeping or eating, Aidan and his men drilled without rest. But as Aidan did, he thought of the words he had overheard Shaka speak after slaying the German Gunter. As nauseating as that spectacle had been, he forced the fear and anger from his mind, and struggled to puzzle the words out, to understand what *two-dimensional* meant.

He remembered attacking Kai in the barn, and how easily his former friend had defeated him. Was that it? He thought perhaps he had the answer, but that particular beating might well represent nothing but one man's superiority over another. Then he thought of Gunter attacking Shaka, the Zulu's hideously efficient riposte and counter, and he remembered something he had heard Malik saying about angles . . . depth . . . dimension . . . what had it been? He cursed himself for ever allowing his mind to drift during Kai's lessons.

He looked again at the way the men around him were being trained, and something slipped across his consciousness like a fish in a river. He tried not to grasp for it, and suddenly he had it, saw it. *The masters are deliberately leaving a vulnerability, for fear that their servants will rise against them.*

Of course. Dar Kush's had been but a small uprising. There had been a few larger ones, smashed so viciously that slaves were afraid even to dream of freedom for years to come. But in their hearts, the masters knew that men were men. Aidan looked at the white men about him, and the angles they were being trained to protect, and was aghast.

Kai had spoken the truth in the barn. In his way, his old friend had tried to protect him.

Even now. Even after all that had happened.

"What's on your mind, boy?" asked a red-haired giant training next to him.

Aidan grunted. "Just thinking." The man was almost a head taller than Aidan, with a gentle round face with strong laugh lines. They must have been about the same age. Judging by what Aidan had seen so far, the giant was incredibly strong, but rather clumsy.

"What's your name?" Aidan asked. The giant was studying him carefully.

"Gobe," he said, and laughed. "Means 'tomorrah' in Hausa. That's 'cause my masta always be tellin' me to do things, an' I always be puttin' it off 'til tomorrah."

Aidan laughed. "Good name, then. What was your original name?"

The giant blinked, as if struggling to remember. "Donough," he finally said.

"I once had a friend named Donough," Aidan said, and then looked more carefully into his companion's face, searching. "Have you ever heard of O'Dere?"

Donough's eyes widened in shock and delight. "Aidan? Is that you?"

Stunned beyond words, Aidan grabbed Donough around the waist and began to pummel him about the back and sides, laughing until he felt tears rolling down his face. "Mother Mary! How you've grown, boyo!"

Donough thrust him to arm's length. "And your mother, Aidan?"

"Dead," he said, voice flat. "Years ago."

"Aye, that's the way of it." The great bland face brightened. "But we're alive!"

"And together again." A flood of memories dizzied Aidan. Fishing in the Lady, hunting in the forests. Dancing at festival. Stealing hot bread with poor dead Kyle and Nessa. Crab races at dockside. *All is not lost.* A thousand debens of stone seemed to lift from Aidan's heart. *O'Dere crannog lives!* "Those Aztecs had better watch their arses now!"

Another bout of laughing, this one continuing until they were both weak and coughing.

"Aidan O'Dere," Donough roared again. "I *knew* you looked familiar."

Talk finally gave way to more practice, and then after a while aching muscles were rested while kitchen slaves ladled supper from the stew kettle.

Aidan sat with Donough and a new friend, Devlin, another Irishman, chewing and telling them what he had discerned earlier. "I'm telling you," he said, "the bastards are deliberately teachin' us just enough to get us killed."

Donough grunted belief. "Sounds like the shites."

Devlin hunched in closer. "What do we do, Aidan?"

"Pass the word. Don't let the masters know we know. When they're not watching, practice protecting the flanks."

He watched Shaka, who was on the other side of camp feeding his monster hounds.

Donough spit. "I reckon our time will come."

"It will come," he said. "Every dog has its day."

The next day the troops rolled west. Most of the slaves marched barefoot. Aidan felt slightly self-conscious of his own sandaled feet, but knew that he hadn't the lifelong calluses necessary to march these rutted roads without protection.

Commoners walked as well, or rode on the supply wagons. The nobles were mounted on their strutting warhorses.

Each day, they encountered another string of soldiers and volunteers, and their ranks swelled.

Their numbers fluctuated as the officers conferred, plans were finalized, groups were trained and then split off on flanking, decoy, and harrying missions.

Each night, a vast tent city of interlinking *kraal* circles sprang into existence. Guards patrolled the edges of the camp, lest a nervous slave take the opportunity to slip away into the night and attempt to join the Commanche or Apache.

Scents of roasting meat and boiling coffee filled the air, along with low nervous talk and laughter. As the evening wore on, the fires died down and the men bundled themselves up and tried to sleep.

There were occasional muttered prayers, crying, moaning. Bushes rustled as one man or another urinated or vomited cheap beer from a jittery stomach.

Slaves who could not sleep passed jugs of wine or hemp cigarettes. They huddled in circles, eyeing the guards, eyeing one another. Tomorrow was the day.

Aidan got up and wandered toward the northern edge of the camp, seeking to stretch his legs. Lost in his own thoughts, he wandered until he spotted a familiar profile: Kai, walking between tents with his hands clasped behind his back.

With a mild, ironic smile, Aidan saluted him, right fist to heart. "Hail," he said.

"Aidan." Kai inclined his head.

"How many of us will die tomorrow?" Aidan asked.

"Are you still glad you came?"

"How many of us will die?"

Kai seemed to consider carefully. "Hold yourself as one already dead. Then, if you find yourself alive tomorrow night, thank Allah. Or Isu, if you prefer."

Aidan longed to tell Kai that he knew truth had been spoken in that barn, that he knew Kai had not acted cruelly or capriciously. But he could not. He wouldn't open himself, risk being rebuffed. It was at that moment that he realized fully how much his friendship to Kai meant to him, how much he hated a world that had let them grow close only to rip them apart.

As if he had already said too much, Kai held up his hand for silence, and walked away. Aidan drank the rest of his wine, then poured a little on the ground in honor of the dead. He hung his head, staring out beyond the rope marking the edge of the compound. Whites who passed that line could be shot on sight.

If he half closed his eyes, he imagined that he could see Sophia's face in the ridges and lines of the moon. She held Mahon safe in her arms. Aidan was breathing hard, fast enough to make him dizzy. In his imagination, Malik entered the room behind her, and clasped his hands on her shoulders.

Aidan gripped the rope until his fingers hurt. A hulking half-breed guard approached, grunting, and waved him back into the camp.

Kai entered his tent. Within, Ali knelt in prayer. Ali looked up at his younger brother, face strained.

"I pray, Brother," he said. "It is best you do the same. Tomorrow is the test."

Kai nodded without speaking and unfurled his own prayer rug. When he had finished his formal prayer, he began one of the exercises that Babatunde had given him, the Sufic ritual called the Allah-Hu. With every inhalation, he drew into himself the million complexities of existence. But as he exhaled, he poured forth only the pure essence of Allah, the one true God. On inhalation, he thought, "The infinite forms of Allah." On exhalation, the "Hu," his mind focused on the essence of the divine.

The minutes passed into hours as each, in his own way, prepared for a sleepless night, and a morning in which one or both of them might give up his soul to his immortal God.

CHAPTER SIXTY-FIVE

The clutch
flaming in the smoking wreckage
crushed limbs
and fractured plates
and broken breasts and shattered bones:
bones, and limbs, and plates
and the same, after-all
cartilages and sockets
disjoint at the joint
even before the attack of harmation
Look!
At your blood ablaze in the shred of blades

POL NDU, NIGERIAN POET

27 Rajab 1290
(September 19, 1873)

A SINGLE AZTEC CAMP STOOD BETWEEN Shaka's army and the mosque. It was a makeshift fortress, the kind of structure thrown up in thirty-six hours by a few hundred industrious soldiers without an engineer in the lot. The log walls were twice as tall as a man and in a roughly triangular formation, with small gates in each side. The front gate was open.

It was set in the middle of a plain below the crest of a clear-cut hill. For about sixty cubits from its gates the underbrush had been chopped down to the dirt, but beyond that grass grew thick and shaggy.

A thousand of Shaka's troops had gathered for this attack. Other divisions had split off to attack Aztec encampments to the south and southwest. Before dawn Kai and his brother had crept up to the top of the hill, peering down through powerful spyglasses, evaluating and preparing. Kai knew that the two main divisions of Aztec warriors were known as "Jaguars" and "Eagles." The Jaguars were mobile scouts and fast-attack squadrons, the Eagles shock troops. Judging by their garb he guessed that those now exiting from the front gate were Eagles. They wore plaited armor, feathered headdresses, and moccasins, and carried feathered shields and flat swords with rows of metal teeth on either side. They were stocky and a bit shorter than the average Bilalian, light-skinned but not pale, and tended to move in pairs.

Their armor was unsophisticated in comparison to his own, but as a pair of horses exited the gate for morning patrol, Kai instantly admired the discipline and evident training of what seemed to be Kenyan grays, probably descended from the original horses traded to east coast natives hundreds of years before.

Kai motioned several of the other men forward, and they took up positions.

He could see from his vantage point that the tall grass before the Aztec camp was alive with mamluk warriors, working their way in close. Shaka's plan, again: a buffalo tactic, the head and the horns. The mamluks would draw first blood, engaging the enemy while the "horns" of his cavalry moved in from the sides.

Since awakening this morning, Kai had felt in a bit of a daze, outwardly calm, but inwardly raging with adrenaline. The closer he came to the moment of truth, the deeper the divide within him.

This was the time, the moment for which he had prepared all his life. By the end of the day he might be alive or he might be dead, but he would certainly have killed men.

He had fought, he had crippled robbers on the road. But killing! Ending the life of another human being! Driving his sword into the living body of another child of Allah, no matter how misguided . . . such an action had to change a man, forever. Whoever might live at the end of the day, it would be someone and something other than the Kai who had existed until this point.

No matter if his body lived, Kai was doomed.

He wanted to crawl away and cry for his lost life, but there was nothing in him that could allow such indulgence. There were eyes upon him: his brother's, his friends'. The eyes of his father, in Paradise.

I will not shame you, he thought. *I may die, but our name will live, with pride.*

* * *

Led by Shaka's chief ghazi N'tomi, for the last two hours Aidan and hundreds of other mamluks had crawled through grass and brush until they were almost within rock-throwing distance of the main gates. Aidan peered through the bushes bordering the Aztec camp, mindful of thorns.

The rude wooden wall surrounding the camp was less sturdy than that surrounding his own Ghost Town. Five guards walked the periphery, bearing feathered shields. He guessed that there were platforms on the other side of the wall, from which archers could fire arrows and rifles.

When they were within eighty cubits of the gates, the guards suddenly become hyperalert, staring out into the grass.

As if that was their cue, N'tomi rose and screamed: "At them!" And he charged.

There was a moment's pause, and then a wail from behind Aidan as a ghazi sword pierced the side of a hesitant mamluk. Aidan's companions, as a single man, rose and charged.

The first guards were overwhelmed, faced by a charging wave of half-crazed slaves. Aidan struggled to run fast enough for exertion to drown his fear.

He carried a spear with a short shaft and a long metal head, sharp along both edges, a weapon good for stabbing or throwing. He was just behind N'tomi who had sprinted forward at one warrior, dodging a thin stream of arrows from the top of the stockade. N'tomi jagged left and attacked a group of warriors who seemed momentarily transfixed by the apparition of a skeletally thin black man in black leather armor, feathered and buckled, wielding his sword with no apparent regard for his own life.

Their paralysis served him well, and the first Aztec attempts at defense were simply crushed beneath his onslaught. More brown warriors poured out of the open gate.

That was all Aidan had time to see. His own pounding legs had brought him within spear stroke of an Aztec warrior. The man was half a head shorter than Aidan, but wider. The Aztec crouched, thrust upward with his spear, and would have disemboweled Aidan if he hadn't been able to twist out of the way and counterjab in return. The roar in his ears grew deafening. Thrust and counterthrust, frantic clashing of metal against metal. Then he saw an opening, and clubbed the warrior with the butt of his spear. Without thinking Aidan reversed the spear and drove it into the man's stomach. There was a moment of resistance, and then a sliding sensation as it penetrated. The Aztec's brown eyes went wide. He screamed like a child, and Aidan wrenched the spear free, too busy fighting to feel anything. No regret, no joy, no horror—just the need to move and move and move, and kill, or die.

Warriors streamed out through the main gate, storming their ragtag band like an avalanche. Aidan couldn't breathe, could barely think, completely surrounded by an orgy of unrelenting violence as the whites, driven forward by the blows and oaths of the ghazis, met the Aztecs stroke for stroke.

All around him, men were cursing and struggling, gasping with effort, hewing and being hewn.

But there were too many of them, too many, and as they were surrounded, he began to think: *They're sacrificing us. They're going to let us die. Oh, dear Mary, my life is ended. Sophia, forgive me, I tried* . . .

Atop the hill, Shaka surveyed the action. Kai waited anxiously, his gut boiling. He wanted to flee, wanted to freeze, wanted to join the fray and finally discover who and what he was.

Shaka watched impassively, perhaps waiting for the enemy to commit itself. Finally he signaled to his bugler. "Sound the call," he said. "It is time."

Kai's spine straightened as Wuha pursed his lips to the horn, and it emitted an earsplitting series of bleats. Shaka's mounted cavalry swept in from the sides.

The slaves, hearing the horn, responded as they had been ordered and turned to run, apparently breaking before the Aztecs. Arrows rained down from the parapets, and mamluks fell like teff in harvest season.

The Aztecs had sent a considerable force after the slaves, apparently convinced of the attack's seriousness by the loss of life. Now they were overextended, too intent on chopping down the fleeing whites. By the time they saw the mounted cavalry swooping down from the sides, it was too late for most of them to make it back to the fortified position.

Kai saw this in flashes as Djinna galloped down the hill and into the fight. There was no more thought, no more fear, just a fierce and exultant hunger, so bright that it carried him before it.

His sword arm was raised high, and he leaned forward in the saddle, spurring Djinna to greater and greater effort as he finally reached the battle.

An Aztec looked up. Kai's sword arm swung. A dark-haired head flew.

And in that fashion, Kai of Dar Kush killed his first man. He felt only a fierce, hungry joy, and wheeled Djinna, searching for his next target.

This, then, was war. Aztec, Irish and Frank, black Muslim and Zulu collided on the battlefield, strokes ringing true, man locked with man in single and multiple combat.

He glimpsed Ali to his right, face contorted so that he barely recognized his brother, sword arm deflecting an Aztec battle-ax and replying with a stroke that spattered brains. Only a glimpse: Kai was in a private hell, populated not by demons but by a seemingly endless swarm of brown men seeking to pull him from his horse, or strike at Djinna herself. Djinna seemed to have contracted a battle madness all her own. She bucked and kicked, and Kai watched two Aztecs reel back with shattered ribs. He fought to stay focused, knowing that a moment's loss of attention would mean death. And Kai also knew that if he surrendered to madness there was a place within him—within the fatigue, the horror and the fear—that loved this, that found the sheer brutality an affirmation.

Some void within him embraced it all, and found it good.

And if there had been any reluctance within him, it would have died in the light of Shaka's terrible flame. The Zulu general might have been born on a battlefield. A Bilalian commander would have remained behind to direct the troops, but Shaka had descended with them and was leading from the front. Kai could only glimpse him, but heard his screams and taunts and curses, his hissed exhalations, the sounds of his spear strokes as he rained death on the Aztecs.

Shaka wheeled his Kenyan toward Kai for a moment, and Kai had a brief look at the man's face. It was terribly distorted, as if possessed by some demonic force.

The men around Shaka, black and white, seemed infected by his fever, to vibrate sympathetically to whatever deadly tune played behind those black eyes, so that their entire force was like one giant raging machine, before which the hapless Aztecs had no chance.

A black-haired slave was unlucky enough to stumble into Shaka's path. "Out of my way!" he screamed, and cleft the man to the spine. The white toppled, blood gushing from wounds and mouth.

Kai took a gash on the leg, and answered with a stroke that hacked halfway through the attacker's collarbone. The Aztecs were falling back through the open gate, struggling to close it, even if that meant cutting off some of their own men.

He saw Aidan (alive!) and a clutch of other slaves force open the door, using shoulders and spears to leverage it back, screaming and stabbing through the slats.

Then they were through the gates, and into the camp. Kai had only a moment to glance at a cluster of small huts before the fighting boiled over to ensnare him, and he was lost in the killing again.

An Aztec thrust his spear at Djinna. Struggling to evade disembowelment, the mare rose up and twisted away, throwing Kai. Kai hit the ground with an expert but jarring breakfall. The world wheeled, and it took him a moment to collect his senses, a moment in which an Aztec attempted to spear him. One of the slaves blocked that downward thrust, winning Kai the chance to stand up, take in his surroundings, and begin the battle anew.

Surprised and outnumbered, the Aztecs were being driven into corners and butchered. The entire world was a wheeling, chopping, dizzying nightmare clotted with screams and the smells of blood and fire and spilled bowels.

Kai turned and faced—Aidan. The Irishman was red-smeared and panting, his eyes burning like those of an animal. Kai ripped his jambaya from his belt and threw it underhanded. Shocked, Aidan hurled himself to the side, whipping his head around in time to see the Aztec Kai had stricken through the heart. A brief nod of thanks, and then Aidan disappeared back into the melee.

He came to a strangeness, a place within himself that he had never known, where the clash of steel and screams of the dying could not reach. Rage and fear mingled in his veins, powered him although all physical strength seemed to have fled. Technique, intention, strategy: all forgotten. He watched himself strike blows, deflect blows, heard the steam-whistle sob of his own breathing, from a place where life or death seemed merely two sides of the same coin. And in that still and silent place, two voices whispered.

First, his own:

"We are exquisite coral reefs,
Dying when exposed to strange
Elements.
Allah is the wine ocean we crave—we miss
Flowing in and out of our pores."

And then an answering voice.

"Find that flame, that existence
That wonderful man
Who can burn beneath the water.
No other kind of light
Will cook the food you need."

Now, here, in what might be the final moments of his life, he heard the voice of Lamiya. Not Nandi. Not Sophia. Not his own father, or even Babatunde. A sweet-sour ache swelled within him.

Lamiya, he thought, barely able to raise his sword to deflect a stroke. *I love—*

It was at that moment, at the very end of his endurance, that the Aztecs broke and tried to run.

Kai reeled back against the brush wall of one of the huts, gasping for air, watching the whooping mamluks pursuing the defeated soldiers, hauling many down by hand, spearing others. Those who made it through the gates were felled by Shaka's reserve archers.

Not a single soul escaped to carry the tale.

Drunk and fearsome, Shaka strode the captured enemy camp. The Zulus quaffed beer and reeled as they roared. Despite their intoxicated state, Kai was not fooled: in the morning, they would be ready to run fifty miles and fight to the death, if so ordered by their terrible commander.

Whatever dark tide of madness had carried Kai through the day seemed to have receded, leaving him weak and nauseated, desperately in need of a quiet place to pray, and sleep. Not yet, though. First he found and comforted Djinna, and ensured that she had hay and water. Only then did he find a surgeon to see to his roughly bound leg wound, a gash that smarted but would not hinder.

This was victory, and all of the men were drinking and shouting and congratulating one another on their luck and courage.

Few of them looked at the dead Aztecs, arrayed in feathered heaps around the compound.

Allah preserve me, Kai thought, struggling to keep his innermost thoughts from showing in his face or gait. From the outside, he was just another cocky, grinning black officer. Inside, he was fighting not to recoil from himself and what he had done that day. What all of them had done.

The Muslims were not drinking, but all cheered their commander. "Hail Shaka!"

Ali inquired of Wuha, Shaka's assistant and bugler, a gray-haired veteran campaigner: "What were our casualties?"

"Fifty horsemen," the old man said. "And two hundred of the foot soldiers."

"Does that include the mamluk?"

"Who cares?" shrugged the gray-hair. "Always more where those came from."

Shaka strode up to a great chair that had been erected for him in a central, cleared area of the fortress. The camp was torchlit, the living casting demon shadows across the bloody dead. In the midst of it all sat Shaka, master of all he surveyed, quaffing deeply. He belched and screamed to N'tomi, "Bring them!"

Three bound and battered Aztecs were brought before him. "Beg," he said.

The tallest of them, a scar-face with shoulder-length black hair, spat on the ground. Shaka grunted approval. "Kill them," he said.

One of his men swung his sword. The black-haired head thumped wetly to the ground. Kai flinched. To kill a man in battle was one thing. This was mere butchery, in which no sane man could take pride or pleasure.

Ali stood near at hand, his own sword notched, his shoulder bandaged, his tunic gashed and stained with Aztec blood. He noted Kai's discomfort and shook his head in warning. *Say nothing, Brother.* By some miracle Kebwe, Makur, and Fodjour had all survived, and from their expressions Kai had the sense that their thoughts mirrored his own, although none would speak out.

"Bring them," Shaka said. Several of the slaves who had broken and run too early were brought before him. Kai recognized one of them: Olaf the rebel. To Kai's surprise, two of Shaka's men grabbed Fodjour and led him to the space of judgment as well.

"Fodjour Berhar," Shaka said. "Two of my men saw you retreat from the field without permission. What have you to say?"

Kai's old rival stared at the ground. To his amazement, the young man rasped: "It is as they say. It was my first battle. It will not happen again."

"Indeed," Shaka said coldly. "You are all charged with cowardice."

"Mighty Shaka—" began a slave.

Shaka leapt forward, drew his *umkhonto*, and slashed. Blood spurted, and the body slumped, the head held to the stump of the neck by a frayed thread.

"No slave speaks to Shaka!"

Fodjour blanched. "Allah, be merciful," he whispered.

"Yes!" cried the Zulu. "And I, too, am merciful. I will not kill you for your sin. But my arm is tired: there has been much slaying today. Today your cowardice ends! This night, I make you a man!"

Shaka approached the trembling young noble closely and dropped his voice, but Kai was close enough to hear. "Do you wish to live?"

"Yes."

"Then take my spear, and do exactly what I say."

Fodjour took Shaka's weapon. "What—?"

Shaka pointed, and two guards rushed in, taking the other slave by the arms. He struggled helplessly.

"Thrust it into his belly. Slowly."

Fodjour gaped at Shaka, who drew close. "The thing is simplicity itself. He dies, or you die."

Kai's boyhood friend nodded numbly. He faced the slave, who stared with eyes so wide they fairly bulged from their sockets. "What is your name?" Fodjour whispered.

"Devlin." The man sounded as if his throat were half closed. He stared at Fodjour's spear, trembling.

"Forgive me," Fodjour said, and pressed the spear beneath the notch where his ribs joined his breastplate. Devlin twisted in his captor's arms, strove to pull his flesh away, then screamed piteously as the spear pierced him. Devlin's eyes rolled up, and he went limp. Fodjour turned away and wet yellow curds spilled from his lips. Shaka smeared his fingers in Devlin's blood, then wiped it on Fodjour's cheeks in two parallel rows.

"Thus are men made among the Zulu!"

"What of the other slaves, Colonel?" Kai said. "Surely we have had enough of spears and swords this day."

A great pale wind seemed to pass out of Shaka. Suddenly, he seemed almost peaceful. "So very true," he said.

He paused, and then said: "Impale them."

The slaves were dragged away, shrieking. Olaf wrested his way free and ran to Shaka, prostrating himself. "Please! No more!"

Shaka took a mighty quaff of beer and grinned. "You are quite right." Shaka turned to his lieutenant. "Your whip."

Olaf was bound hand and foot, face pale as whey as Shaka was handed a rhinoceros-hide whip, used for the driving of elephants and the execution of slaves.

Kai looked at Ali, whose jaw was clamped tight. "Brother?" Kai said. Ali glanced at him, and then back to Shaka, still silent.

Shaka's arm flicked up and then out, and the whip uncoiled in the air, blurred and struck Olaf's leg, cutting it to the bone. The hapless slave screeched in agony, tried to pull away, babbled for mercy, but in Shaka's eyes and in the thin cruel line of his mouth there was nothing but unholy wrath.

As the whip came down again, ripping the flesh from Olaf's back, Ali grasped his arm.

"Shaka! Enough!"

Shaka wheeled on him, face twisted in a frenzy of rage. For a moment he seemed not to recognize the man standing before him.

"This man was born on my land," Ali said. "He serves my house. If anyone has the right to kill him, it is I."

Shaka's face twisted in a grim smile, and he handed Ali the whip. "Then do it," he said.

Kai watched his brother weigh the length of braided rhino hide, then, holding Shaka's eyes, he coiled it. "I did not bring our men here to throw them away. There has been enough death today. Olaf has learned his lesson."

Shaka looked from Ali to the slave and back again. For a moment, Kai was absolutely certain that the Zulu was going to strike Ali. All of the Muslim officers were standing now, outnumbered three to one by the Zulus. It was not murder Kai saw in Shaka's face. It was something else, something even uglier.

"If you were not your uncle's nephew," Shaka said, "I would have you flogged." Those were his words, but his voice said *I would kill you.* It was battle madness Kai saw in his face, a thing that was closer to death than life, an abyss that certain warriors found within themselves, leaving them standing forever on its uncertain edge.

Men like Shaka. Like Malik.

Like Kai?

Shaka shook with barely repressed rage, the whites of his eyes wide and gleaming against his black skin. Then he spit on the ground. "Sleep with them, if you wish. *Wakil*," he said mockingly.

The warrior took two steps away, then stopped dead. Without turning, he said: "Do not question me again. Do not touch me. Ever." And then stalked to his tent.

Kai helped a shuddering Olaf to his feet. The wound on his leg gleamed like a pair of wet red lips. "Your fight is over," he said. "We'll send you back to Dar Kush with the wounded."

Olaf nodded gratefully. "I'm sorry, master," he said. "I'm just not the man for this."

Kai nodded, and two of the other whites carried Olaf away. Ali stared off into the darkness surrounding Shaka's tent. Kai rested his hand on his brother's shoulder. "What now?" he said.

Ali sighed. "We prepare ourselves for another day, my brother."

* * *

By the time Kai awoke in the morning, Ali had finished his morning prayers and was inspecting his sword, running its edge along a whetstone with slow, even strokes. As Kai dressed, his brother continued the endless careful strokes, and finally Kai sat on a low folding stool across from him and did the same.

"Brother?" Ali said, not looking up.

"Yes?"

"Do you believe slaves have souls?"

"The Prophet, peace be unto him, said that all men have souls."

He grunted and continued his sharpening for a minute, then stopped. "They volunteered to be here, and must be held to the same standards as any soldier." Although it was phrased as a statement, there was a question lurking there, and Kai wasn't certain what it was.

"I mean," Ali said, "if they are close to animals, we can't expect them to have honor. They should not be punished for what Allah denied them. Does this make sense?"

Ali looked up, and Kai realized for the first time how tired Ali looked. He wondered if he had slept, really slept, since their father's death. And wondered further just what demons had visited Ali in the night.

"What is it, Brother?" Kai asked.

Ali shrugged. "All my life, all I've heard is how glorious this day would be, when we ride into battle for Allah and honor and country."

"You fought valiantly yesterday."

"As I was born and raised to do. As were you. But . . ." he paused, as if there was something he could not say.

"Many of the slaves fought bravely."

Ali nodded.

"You promised them freedom."

"And they are earning it," Ali said. "Some of them. *Some* of them had more courage than some of ours."

"And you protected them," Kai said. He smiled. "Father would have been proud."

"If he had lived to see *you* yesterday," Ali said, "astride Djinna, sword high, surrounded by the infidel and hewing your way clear . . . his heart would have been happy."

Kai dropped his eyes. How could a man be proud of killing? He could still remember the feeling of his sword biting into brown flesh. He should be repulsed. And yet . . . and yet . . .

"And Malik would be proud," Ali went on, and Kai heard a catch in his voice. "And," Ali said, holding Kai's eyes, "I am proud."

Kai looked up. There was something else, something grim and uncertain in Ali's face. Curiously, it made Kai's brother seem younger. So much had happened in the last year, that it felt as though the two of them had lost touch with each other. So many times Kai had longed for the simple days, when he had tagged along after his older brother, who had scolded him, yes, but also played at swords or *satranj*, taken him fishing, shown him how to paddle a boat on Lake A'zam, or taught him how to swim.

How strange that in the midst of death, something gentle and warm had been rediscovered at last, blossoming like a rose in the middle of a battlefield.

By midmorning the troops were pulling out, circling in a pincer movement to attack Aztec outposts to the south and southwest. By afternoon, only fifteen hundred troops remained, and of those, a third were assigned to stay behind to protect the captured outpost.

The remaining men were lined up and ready to proceed to the mosque, Shaka in place at the head of his column. With a lurch, they began their westward progress once again.

As he rode, Kai pulled up alongside Aidan for a moment. "What is the mood of the men?"

Aidan said nothing for a moment, then pointed at one of his companions. "Look at him." The man was ashen, eyes bloodshot. "The men are half dead with terror. Your colonel is a monster."

"He's not mine."

"Who put us in his hands?"

"You volunteered."

"Did I have a choice?"

Kai's lips were pursed too tightly for words to escape. He went back to his place in line, fingering his jambaya. A symbol of power. Sharp as a serpent's tooth, ten digits of lethal steel. He wished it could speak to him.

Or for him.

They rode and marched through an afternoon shower, then on through muddied roads until the sun baked them dry. After eight hours of travel, Kai was relieved to pass along the order to make camp.

Despite a tight stomach he managed a mug of coffee and a few bites of beef at the fireside, and was just beginning to feel human again when Shaka began to address the troops. "Slaves and freemen!" he called, gathering them around. "Tomorrow will tell the tale. Tomorrow we free the mosque. This is why you have come, to fight with Shaka! You who are slaves will win freedom. You who are men will win gold."

Shaka's lieutenants threw handfuls of Centuries, gold coins 1/100 the value of an Alexander, out to the grasping crowd. The soldiers scrabbled for them like starving children fighting for bread.

Gold! "Shaka! Shaka!" they roared, the previous day's nightmare seemingly forgotten.

Momentarily out of the focus of attention, Kai and Ali huddled with their friends, watching as Shaka and his coterie retreated to the tent.

"I notice," said Kebwe, "we were not invited into the august presence."

"Since Ali angered Shaka, no."

Kai drew a line in the dirt with his toe. Wars within wars. No good could come from this. None at all.

The slave encampment was set up in a pasture, against a barbed-wire fence. After eating and washing, Aidan paced its boundaries. Inactivity was a killer, but so was lack of rest. He burned with anxiety and eagerness, fear and doubt. Regardless of the circumstance, many in the camp seemed almost merry. *Freedom tomorrow!* they said, shaking hands and congratulating one another. And for those who would storm the mosque, that was true. Others would be siphoned off to raids of distraction and punishment, and for them freedom might lag a few weeks.

New slaves from northern New Djibouti were pouring in, accompanied by their masters, more black citizens, and even professional soldiers. Each new arrival was sorted, tallied, sent to his proper place, and assigned a position in the chain of command.

Aidan watched as the Zulu officers welcomed the newcomers with open arms and wide smiles. "Find tents for more brave men," they cried. "And meat! And beer!"

A big half-breed sergeant snapped to attention and saluted. Most of the power in the common rank belonged to blacks or half-breed blacks, as if the Muslims wouldn't trust anyone whose mother hadn't been humped by an African.

As Aidan passed one group of newcomers, he overheard a nervous exchange. "Do the Aztecs really eat people?" asked a boy of fifteen or so.

"They'll eat your balls if you don't step quickly," the ghazi said. "Get drunk tonight! Tomorrow we see what you're made of, eh?"

Around a campfire sat a clutch of mamluks, some of them sporting bandaged shoulders or heads. These did not boast or brag. They nursed mugs of beer, smoked cigarettes or pipes of tobacco or strong hemp, and sought to warm their bones. Their eyes were hollow. They had seen death, and knew that very soon they would see more. They shook their heads grimly as the newcomers poured in. "Poor bastards," one of the wounded men said glumly. "Haven't a clue."

"Merry souls," said Donough. "Look how they line up to get dead."

Aidan punched him in the arm. "One of those souls might be guarding your side tomorrow—best keep their spirits up. May be your life on the line. Damn it—let's have some music!"

One of the men found a flute, and another beat a drum, reluctantly at first, and then louder and stronger. Aidan got up and danced a few jig steps, until the acid of fear began to leave him. The fifteen-year-old was watching him, his freckled, tense face filled with unvoiced questions.

He tugged at the boy's arm. "Come on, Mouse—show us some real steps."

The men cheered as the boy stood. Uncomfortably at first he began to shuffle his feet, and then finally to dance a few steps. The other men began clapping along, and some of the new ones took seats by the fire and joined in. They passed beer skins and shouted encouragements and suggestions, some of them creative and highly vulgar. Now there were three, and then four men up and cavorting with the boy Aidan had called "Mouse," and several more musicians joined in.

Aidan saw Kai watching from just beyond the reach of the firelight, and slipped away into the shadows to join him. Kai was walking away, toward the fence, as Aidan caught up. Kai found a rock high and flat enough to sit upon. Although Kai gave him no greeting, Aidan noticed that there was room on the rock for him as well. For a few minutes the two shared a companionable silence, and then Aidan spoke. "Tomorrow is the day."

"Yes. If we . . . if you live tomorrow, you are free."

"And if you live, Kai—what do you win?"

He thought for a time. "A chance to go home," he said finally.

Aidan wanted desperately to reach out to him. "Kai . . ."

But Kai stood, his back to Aidan, as if he needed the wall to hold back some tide of emotion. "Aidan," he said. "I wish you well. Survive the day. Find some way to give your life meaning."

"And you."

"Insh'Allah."

CHAPTER SIXTY-SIX

EVEN AT A DISTANCE, THE MOSQUE of the Fathers was imposing and strange. It seemed to have sprung to life in the middle of nowhere, on a plain desolate enough to call into doubt the sanity of its builders. Its golden dome reflected the morning light. Its mosaic walls, flecked with blue and gold, seemed constructed of coins and gems, as if the architects had struggled to create a structure that was both old and new, that honored a dozen different traditions, that was arresting from any conceivable direction.

Seven hundred years ago, Ethiopian sailors in primitive screwships passed from Africa to the New World, and traded with the brown people there discovered, later establishing a colony.

Bilal's followers soon reached the new land, honoring his instructions. Soon after, two of New Djibouti's eldest and most honored mullahs, Jafari the Moor and Agot the Abyssinian, contracted cancers. Praying together, they shared a sacred vision that drove them to travel further west, accompanied by an army of their followers. When Agot at last was exhausted, and Jafari swore he could travel no further, they proclaimed this to be their burial place, and that this would be the western border of the empire for a dozen generations.

Moor and Abyssinian were buried there, and as the years passed, men volunteered labor to build a shrine above their bodies.

If the architecture was eclectic, and the building materials more often found than imported, still the Shrine of the Fathers was a remarkable achievement. The mosque was rectangular, thirty by about fifty cubits. The flat roof was thirty cubits from the ground, the arched doorways almost eighteen cubits high. The first six cubits of wall were of white rock, the remaining upper ten or so of blue and red rock glazed and polished so carefully that, at a distance, it resembled Benin ceramic.

The ridged golden dome rising in the center of the flat roof looked to be eighteen cubits high by itself, and blazed in the morning sun.

It was, indeed, set in an insane place: overgrown brush and high, dry grass stretched for a mile on three sides, and behind it lay a deep wadi.

Kai watched the flow of men and matériel through the front doors. A makeshift flat-roofed tent city housing perhaps five hundred Aztecs had blossomed before the gates. Kai guessed that another hundred or so might be camped inside.

Ali had been right: despite its ornate facade, the Aztecs didn't understand the symbolic importance of the mosque, or they would have either bypassed it or enlisted more men in its defense.

From their position on a rise almost two miles away, hidden by a stand of cottonwoods, Shaka watched the mosque carefully, then raised his spyglass to peer at the horizon. "Smoke," he said.

"Good," said his half-breed sergeant N'tomi. "Then their villages are burning."

"Their men are here—their women and children are meat by now. My nephews have done well."

As they watched, the gates of the mosque swung open. Armed Aztec riders swarmed out and wheeled their horses south. "Excellent," said Shaka. "Begin the advance."

An hour later, Aidan and four hundred mamluks crept through the brush, led by N'tomi. Shaka and his royal allies remained on horseback, hidden in the woods.

Crawling through prickly brush, Aidan was able to approach within a half mile of the gates before losing cover. There was no way around it: The Aztecs would know they were coming long before they could reach spear or sword range. Every breath burned like fire. The icy nerve that had served him until this point seemed to be thawing. He swallowed, trying to get the sandpaper feeling out of his mouth, but couldn't summon enough spit to coat his throat.

Every half minute now dragged like an hour. He dreaded attacking a fortified position, but if that was the weight he had to carry to win freedom for his wife and son, then he would gladly break his back in the effort.

Sergeant N'tomi rose from concealment. "Charge!"

Like puppets jerked by their heartstrings, Aidan and the others rose, screaming. Shallowly flanking the mamluks were the black riflemen who ran to within three hundred cubits and then fired into the Aztec ranks. After a moment's hesitation, the Aztecs returned fire from the upper levels of the mosque. A mamluk immediately to Aidan's right flopped back, his head a red ruin.

Bullets struck the ground all around Aidan, who was running all out now, nothing on his mind but reaching and killing the enemy.

The survivors made it to the walls. Aidan launched himself at the first row of soldiers, who crouched and waited, their feathered shields clutched before them as if creating some kind of an armored wall.

He remembered some of what happened next. How it was all a dream of chaos, how he seemed to go deaf, but still somehow registered the screams and cries, the sound of shattering bones and the grunts of effort. That he seemed buoyed by a strength not wholly physical, that somehow the vast, gleaming walls of the mosque seemed to look down on all of the bloodshed and battle and silently voice approval.

He fought on, wielding his spear as he had been taught, but adding a bit of the staff craft he had learned watching Malik: butt and point, feint, sidestep, evasion and attack. Grunting with exertion, shaking his head to keep the sweat out of his eyes, gasping with sudden agony as his side was gashed, cursing as his leg was cut, but never stopping, never stopping.

Men to all sides of him were struggling in a red frenzy, rolling on the ground wrestling with club- and knife-armed opponents, howling as they broke ribs or their own bones were broken.

The breath was scalding his lungs like hot metal when he thought: *The retreat! They said they would sound the retreat once the Aztecs were fully engaged. They promised!*

But there was no bugle sound. No retreat. Only the battle, which seemed now to exist in some place outside of ordinary time, in a fairyland of violence. There had never been, nor would there ever be, another reality than this. No wife, no child, no home. Only havoc.

Finally, and distantly, he heard a bugle call, and then a cry of "Retreat!" from the men behind him.

He was engaged with a short, muscular warrior who seemed to be all sinew and lightning. Nothing he did penetrated the man's guard, and he had already taken a blow on his left forearm that threatened to paralyze his fingers.

Gathering his strength, Aidan shoved with desperation, sending his opponent reeling backwards. He used the butt of his spear against the man's knee to drop him. Even in falling, the Aztec kept his guard, but Aidan was not interested in attacking: he had heard the retreat, and intended to obey it.

He turned and sprinted for the tall grass.

Howling, the Aztecs pursued them. Spears and arrows whipped through the air, landing in the dirt, or in the backs of the men around him.

As they reached the grass, and some modicum of shelter, the second bugle sounded. Exhausted, Aidan turned and thrust his left heel into the ground, preparing for the Aztecs. He had not long to wait: they were charging right behind them, outnumbering the surviving mamluks almost two to one.

Aidan's vision wavered with fatigue and terror but he fought, whipping his spear as if it were the tongue of some poison toad, steeling his mind to the carnage and his own growing despair.

A light flared to his right, and he ignored it at first, heard the *fttt fttt* of arrows but assumed they had been fired by Aztecs—

Until the fires began, cutting the Aztec troops off from the mosque.

The flames rose on all sides. Aidan realized that the slave troops had been used more viciously than he could have imagined: Shaka had engaged the Aztecs, then retreated the white soldiers into a death trap, where he intended to burn them all.

Lost! All was lost! And yet, hating everything in the world that had brought him to this terrible place, Aidan O'Dere fought on. It was all there was to do.

As Kai watched, Shaka gave another hand signal, and Wusa called out another series of bleats on the horn. Two hundred cubits away from the fighting, a row of archers with burning arrows launched another flight of fire out into the long grass.

"Go now," Shaka called to his men. "Finish it." Wusa blew the horn again and Shaka's Zulu troops, held in reserve, charged from the flanks, ready to kill any Aztec who escaped the fire. Ready to storm the fortress itself.

Shaka stood on the ridge looking down on the hell he had choreographed, only his bugler, Kai, Ali, Kebwe, and Fodjour beside him.

From here, it all looked like insects scrambling to escape a fire, prodded back in by the sticks of sadistic boys.

"Allah preserve us," Kebwe whispered to Kai. "He's going to kill them all. Soldiers, slaves, Aztecs."

Despite the whisper, they had obviously been overheard. "Is it not brilliant!" Shaka cried. "*This* is why I always win. No one knows the mind of Shaka!"

Kai and Ali watched the fire curl through the underbrush. Watched the slaves and Aztecs fighting in the grass as the fire enveloped them—

Ali's rage and indignation, too long bottled, threatened to explode now. He struggled to control his voice. "Sound the horn," Ali said. His hands knotted into fists. "Colonel, this is madness."

"This is war!" Shaka thundered.

"There are black men out there!"

"There are *soldiers* out there," said Shaka, "and I will brook no interference in my orders!"

Ali wheeled and struck Wusa to the ground, seized his bugle, turned and drew breath to blow the signal.

In a single, eye-baffling thrust, Shaka speared Ali under the rib cage. So swift and savage was the assault that Kai barely saw it happen, and his brother had no slightest hope of defense. Ali buckled to one knee and clasped his hand to the wound. Blood gushed between his fingers, and he collapsed.

Stunned, Kai dropped to his brother's side. The wound was mortal.

"How dare you!" Shaka roared. He glared at the others, face distorted with rage, spear red-tipped and ready. "I knew you Muslim whelps would go jelly-bellied once the killing began. Even your uncle, who was once my brother, no longer has the fire in him. This is *my* war, and it will be fought *my* way, and if any of you would challenge me, make it now!"

Even though there were three of them and one of Shaka, Kai's companions could not move. Shaka's trumpeter raised himself on unsteady legs, eyes wide as he stared at Ali convulsing on the ground.

Ali groped up at Kai with warm, wet fingers. "Kai . . . it hurts," Ali whispered. "Who would think it hurt so much to die?"

"Ali," Kai said numbly. "What am I to do?"

"Be strong," Ali whispered, wheezing through ruptured lungs. "Survive, little brother. Your life is in a madman's hands. He will try to take you to hell with him."

"One coward comforts another," Shaka said behind him. "See how they cry like little girls."

Kai unbuckled his sword belt and let it clatter to the ground. "I am done with this war," he said, turning.

Shaka looked at him incredulously, and then began to laugh, roaring from deep in his stomach, head thrown back, overwhelmed by cruel mirth.

And was still laughing as Kai pulled Nasab Asad from Ali's scabbard. With a single, fluid motion he sliced the tendons in Shaka's right wrist, then spun the blade so that he held it backhanded and plunged it into the Zulu's belly.

Shaka's face widened in shock as Kai drove the knife deep. His spear dropped from his nerveless hand, and his mouth opened. No sound emerged, only a flood of crimson as he dropped to the earth.

Wusa's rheumy old eyes went wide, and he raised the trumpet to his lips to call the alarm. Before he could draw breath, Fodjour had struck him down, so that the two Zulus lay side by side, their blood mingling, only five seconds after Kai struck the first blow.

Kai gazed down at his victim, watching as Shaka quivered and then was still.

He turned to his brother, who looked at him with wonderment. "Who would . . ."

"Ali," Kai said. "Don't speak."

"Who would have thought," Ali said, and his eyes closed.

The nobles gaped. "What have we done?" gasped Fodjour.

"With hope, saved our souls," Kai said. He bent and kissed his brother's unlined forehead. *No more troubles.* Then Kai stood and squared his shoulders. "Up!" he cried. "Would you have glory at the cost of good men's lives? This is *our* fight! *Our* God! Shame upon any of you too proud to spill your blood in His service."

He drew his sword. *"Allah huakbar!" God is Greater!* he cried, leapt upon Djinna, and rode down the hill. Win or die. Win *and* die. It mattered not which.

He glanced back over his shoulder and was heartened to see that the others were following his lead. *Father. Brother. Watch over me.* The nobles charged down and out, into the blaze, through the few gaps in the fire. They joined in combat with the Aztecs amid the blazing grass. The remaining Zulu reinforcements, perhaps convinced that Shaka had ordered the charge, joined the battle.

Suddenly, the conflict was even.

Kai slashed and hacked at his feathered enemy, one of whom ducked down and had time to set the butt of his spear into the ground. Before Kai could react, Djinna impaled herself on it, rearing back and snorting in mortal agony.

Kai went down hard, spinning. He rose to his feet and managed to keep sufficient presence of mind to draw his sword, but was acting on pure reflex, grief and pain and rage melding until he was beyond his ordinary mind, locking in a web of flesh and steel.

That was when something inside Kai splintered into fragments. The Aztecs were no longer human. Shaka was no longer human. The men around him were not men. They were all demons and damned, and he was in hell with the rest of them, acting with reflexes honed for almost twenty years, motivated by instincts older than time.

Aidan hacked his way to Kai's side. It took an instant for Kai to recognize the blurry white face, just identify it as *not brown*, not one of the faces that he was prepared to cleave without hesitation.

Aidan's face was slashed, soiled with dirt and grime, but their eyes locked for a moment, just a moment, long enough to call Kai back from the hell to which he had consigned himself.

He heard a sob break from his throat. His father was dead. His brother was dead. Perhaps even his honor was dead. But Aidan seemed a window to an earlier, more innocent Kai, one who had not come so far down a crimson highway, marching on the backs of the slaughtered.

Aidan still recognized him. And as long as one human being did, then perhaps Kai was not lost forever. Perhaps.

Aidan glimpsed Kai, had looked for him since seeing the disemboweled corpse of poor Djinna. In his heart, he feared that he would stumble over the torn and lifeless corpse of his friend, and was happy that they had shared space on this battlefield, even if just for a moment before the surging tides carried them away from each other.

He broke from the press and charged toward the mosque itself, where black soldiers and mamluks were hammering the Aztecs into splinters. They hurled ropes and grappling irons up to the windows, swarming as swiftly as spiders as soon as one of them lodged into place.

Within the mosque the now outnumbered Aztecs were fighting back, slicing ropes as fast as the whites could fasten grappling hooks in the windows. Black snipers, protected from the Aztec ground troops by fierce swordsmen, fired up at the windows relentlessly, driving the defenders back in a shattering hail of lead and steel.

More Zulus were joining the fight now, and Aidan's heart lifted: Shaka's strategy had drawn much of the mosque's defenses away, divided them again and again, and now he seemed to be subjecting the defenders to an overwhelming assault.

Aidan didn't see how it happened, but the front door of the mosque was suddenly forced open. The mamluks charged in, more and more of them rushing into the interior to kill and die.

Now the Bilalian forces clustered at the walls, protected the gates, and had taken the upper windows. The remaining Aztecs were disorganized now, many of them breaking away and running for the distant forests as arrows and rifle fire poured down on them.

A bugle was sounding—from within the mosque! And the Bilalian troops left the battlefield, surviving horses and horsemen, slaves and soldiers, all pulling in as the remaining Aztecs were slaughtered from the walls.

Then he watched as the gates were closed, and barred, and Aidan stood, stunned and silent to find himself alive and safe in the middle of a crowd of cheering, wildly exultant, blood-smeared warriors who screamed victory to the heavens.

Too numbed and tired to speak or move, Aidan sank to his knees and gave thanks.

CHAPTER SIXTY-SEVEN

KAI STOOD ATOP THE MOSQUE'S FLAT TILE ROOF, in the shadow of the golden dome, marveling at the success of their attack. Everything had worked perfectly: the Aztecs had been distracted and split, and had underestimated Bilalistan's resolve and resources. Shaka had also been brutally shrewd: the Aztecs hadn't anticipated that a commander might deliberately kill his own troops.

But then these troops had only been slaves.

Heaven help us, Kai thought. *If one must think this way to win wars, perhaps it is better to lose them.*

Fodjour reported to Kai with a salute. "As the Wakil's surviving son you are now the ranking officer, Captain. Your orders?"

"Bar the gates!" said Kai. "We now have only to wait for our reinforcements. After the raid on the settlements, the men will circle back to buttress our position."

"Who will arrive first?"

Kai shook his head. "Don't know. It depends on the amount of resistance they've encountered. They have to disengage and circle back. But certainly it can be no more than twelve hours before the first support arrives."

Standing at the edge of the roof, N'tomi called out: "The Zulus come! I must tell Shaka." He grinned, the unaccustomed expression lighting up his skeletal face. Kai dashed away across the courtyard as N'tomi called behind him: "Where is he?"

Allah preserve me. What do I tell the Zulus? It had been no more than two hours since the Zulu prince's death, barely minutes since the fall of the mosque. The soldiers had been so happy to find themselves alive that they hadn't had time to reorient themselves, or ask where their leader was. Kai climbed up a rickety ladder to the parapet, which was lined with lookouts.

The battlefield below him was strewn with black, white, and Aztec corpses. "Keefah and Darbul are here!" Kai called.

Shaka's nephews had led a feint to the south, branching off from the main force the morning of the previous day. In all probability they had avoided contact with the enemy, and would be fresh and ready to fight. The Zulu troops rode toward the mosque, proud and erect, two lines of fifty horsemen supplemented by two hundred foot soldiers, approaching in silence.

"Where is Shaka?" N'tomi insisted, more strident this time.

Kai felt sickened. "Open the gates!"

The great wooden doors swung open. The Zulu horsemen approached . . . and then stopped.

Keefah stared up at Kai, naked loathing in his eyes. Darbul threw Shaka's bloodied tunic to the ground. His face as grim as death, he called out in Zulu, speaking for thirty seconds.

N'tomi stared down at Shaka's nephews, then turned and looked at Kai as if he were a rabid dog, fear and loathing commingled. N'tomi threw his head back and barked commands in Zulu. Then he spit on the roof of the mosque, picked up his spear, and left.

Merciful Allah. They'd found Shaka, Wusa, and Ali. Could they determine that Ali had been killed by an umkhonto, *and Shaka by a* jambaya, *and thereby intuit what had happened?*

What manner of men were these?

As N'tomi passed the other Zulus, to a man they turned and left their posts.

Stunned beyond the power of speech, Kai followed them down a flight of narrow stone stairs and watched as they collected at the gate, a hundred of the remaining two hundred fifty fighting men.

He was honest with himself: the best hundred. N'tomi turned and locked eyes with Kai. There was no doubt in Kai's mind: N'tomi wanted to kill him, and was held back only by lack of indisputable proof. That, perhaps, and a reticence to start a second war while in the midst of the first.

Kai could not hold his gaze. "Let them go," he said.

Heads high, the Zulus filed out and were gone.

Fodjour watched the exit, his hands curled tightly into fists. "Need I ask what Darbul said to them?"

"No," Kai replied. "You don't."

The interior of the Mosque of the Fathers was divided into a large public meeting and prayer room, some private rooms and cubicles to either side, an underground storeroom, and an upper-level sleeping quarters for pilgrims. The actual place of burial was called a *maqam*, a place of great spiritual power surrounded by a low brick wall. Two coffins were arrayed within it, with oversized turbans atop each demarking the status of the dead.

Although the caretakers had doubtless long since been slaughtered by the Aztecs, and the mosque forced to house both troops and Aztec horses, there was no evidence of deliberate vandalism. Within limits, the invaders had been surprisingly respectful.

The Muslims' surviving horses were brought into the mosque and roped into a corner of the room while the Muslims lay down cloaks and blankets beneath them, murmuring *estafghuar Allah* again and again.

Allah Forgive.

A clay-walled communal dining room was packed with young officers, free lowborn blacks, even a few slaves. A hundred or so very tired, discouraged, frightened men.

There was but one question on every tongue: Why did the Zulus leave?

Kai held his hands in the air to catch their attention, and raised his voice. "Shaka is dead. They hold us responsible." The slaves and blacks immediately broke into a nervous clamor. Kebwe and Makur might have been wearing masks, so little did their expressions change.

Kebwe unrolled a map. "There is a contingent of soldiers to the north, here," he pointed, "at the Drift."

Kai nodded. There was indeed a fort a day's ride away, and it would be manned by New Djiboutan regulars. "If they can be reached, they may be able to offer assistance."

"A day there, a day back. Forty-eight hours before help can arrive," said Makur.

Kai nodded. "If we can hold out."

Kebwe pinched the bridge of his nose with his fingers, and looked pained. "Don't say 'if.' Please."

"*When* we can communicate with them," Kai corrected himself, "they will send reinforcements. Their commander is Colonel Wakil Abu Kwame. A good man."

The room was filled with long faces and heavy moods.

"Fodjour," Kai said. "You are the best horseman here."

"Pity it took this to make you admit it."

Kai laughed grimly in reply. It felt good to laugh. It was quite possible that the laughter remaining in his life was finite indeed. "It will have to be you. The rest of us stay to prepare the mosque for assault. What will you need?"

"Two men, six horses, and a devil's luck. We reach Abu Kwame, or we die."

"We will race again one day."

Fodjour turned, then turned back. "Kai—just in case we don't. It was you, that day. The chess game?"

"It wasn't me. It was, however, *my* pepper." The two old rivals laughed and clasped hands.

Fodjour lowered his voice. "Shaka was mad," he said, close to Kai's ear. "You did what any of us would have done, had we the heart."

The words were like a glimpse of sun through a storm cloud. "May the wind be at your back," Kai said.

Kai watched his old friend leave through the front gate. Immediately, the small group broke into a gallop. With luck, reinforcements might arrive by the next evening. Without it, well . . . his father and brother awaited him in Paradise.

For a moment he remembered his brother's mutilated body, then shut that picture out of his mind. There was no time for grief, not if there was to be any chance of survival at all.

With a five-man detail, Kai descended a narrow file of stone steps leading to the cellar. The Aztecs had converted the cool, dry space into an armory. The walls hung with spears and rifles, the floor was crowded with barrels marked in strange Aztec glyphs. "So," he said. "What do we have?"

Makur answered. "The Aztecs kept their powder here—enough for an army."

"If only we had one."

"Hundreds of rifles."

"Of whose manufacture?"

"Ours. All Bilalian or Egyptian design, gained in trade and raids. I see no evidence that they have much manufacturing capacity, although they do seem to make their own gunpowder."

"What the merchants sell, the army has to fight. Food and water?"

"Not enough."

"They must have been expecting a shipment," Kai said. "Well, what there is, work out a system to divide it equally."

"Excellent. And for the slaves?"

Kai glared. "I said: *equally*. They need to keep up their strength as well."

"The nobles will complain."

"They know where to find me," Kai said, turned sharply, and left.

At the very back of the main meeting room was a smaller boxlike structure, like a house set inside a house. This *khalwat* had been the private meditation room of the caretakers, and the soldiers had taken it over as a hospital.

It was Kai's intent to inspect the facilities, and perhaps talk to some of the men, but when he entered he found Kebwe and some of the other men administering to the wounded. Kebwe was halfway through his physician's training, and if he survived the wars would probably travel to Alexandria to complete his education. He had apparently found a supply of bandages, astringent, and opium extract in a cupboard.

Men lay on cots in corners and across the floor, slashed and dying, some with their entrails pressing against makeshift bandages. They groaned for help, and Kebwe was doing his best to stretch the limited resources.

Kai watched, flinching, as Kebwe guided one of the mamluks to apply fire against the stump of an arm. The smell of sizzling flesh filled the air. Kai wanted to gag, but managed to maintain a calm front.

He crouched near as soon as the stump was bandaged. "How are we doing?"

"I need more medicine, and some genuine medical care," Kebwe said, wiping perspiration from his generous brow. He lowered his voice. "We're going to lose maybe ten of them regardless. But we'll lose more if we don't get help."

"God," groaned the stump-armed mamluk. His hair was as red as his blood and hung in limp, wet strands across his fevered forehead. "Why did I come?"

"What is your name?" Kai asked.

"Ndukwana," answered the redhead, mangling a mouthful of glottal clicks in the attempt. Kai almost laughed, and felt a pang of sorrow for the slave who could not pronounce his own name.

"What did your mother name you?"

Red-hair looked at Kai as if no black man had ever asked him that question before. "Caleb," he said, gritting his teeth. His pupils were dilated: the opium was doing its work.

"Let's call you Caleb, then," Kai said. "And I'll tell you why you came, Caleb. To be free."

"And what if I die?" His voice had descended into a slur.

All soldiers deal with fear of death. That was where Malik's offer had not gone far enough. It was not enough to win freedom if you live. To create a warrior, one must see even death itself as a triumph. "Do you have a son?" Kai asked.

"A son," Caleb said. He suddenly jerked his head up. "Two sons."

"If you die, I will free your eldest son. Any man who dies, his freedom is passed to his eldest offspring, or his woman, or eldest sibling."

Caleb looked at Kai, suspicion flaring in his drugged and clouded eyes. "You would do that?"

"On my honor," Kai said.

Caleb closed his eyes and sagged, but a smile shadowed his face.

Kai stood. "Kebwe? Make the same offer to all of these brave men. Find paper. Write the name of the person they would have inherit their bounty."

Kebwe nodded. "It will be done."

Kai had returned to the mosque's flat tile roof, and stood studying the surrounding brushlands, now a smoldering, corpse-littered waste. A detail of men had been assigned to find living soldiers and bury the dead. Occasional screams floated free as Aztec throats met the knife.

As he peered and pondered, Kai made out one familiar blond figure: Aidan, bringing in the wounded. So like his old friend. A warm feeling spread within him at the thought.

Beside him, Makur huffed. "Isn't that pale-haired one your slave?"

"He was, yes," Kai said.

"I've watched him. Arrogant bastard. Why didn't you ever break him? On my estate, he would never dare look me in the eye."

"Would you trust a coward to guard your back?" Kai asked mildly. Makur had no reply. Kai continued to scan, eyes on the horizon now.

"And we will need every atom of courage we can muster. The Aztecs are coming," he said. "They will come. The only question is *when.*"

CHAPTER SIXTY-EIGHT

KAI'S ANSWER WAS NOT LONG in coming.

As the Muslims concluded their evening prayer, a proud line of horses entered the fire-cleared area. They halted just beyond rifle range, forming a line which doubled, then increased into three ranks, and four, until at least two hundred warriors faced the defenders.

Two of them walked their mounts forward. The riders were brown men of noble carriage and warrior aspect, mouths drawn flat in lines as cruel as the slash of a knife, eyes as sharp as the double-edged war axes hanging at their sides. In their feathers, gold ornaments, and leather armor, they were a startling sight.

The lookout sent for Kai, who made swift apologies to Allah for truncating his prayer and ran up the clay steps to the roof. Kebwe joined him a moment later, out of breath. They watched as the two Aztecs waited.

"What do we do?" Kebwe asked. "What do they want?"

"A parlay," Kai said. "I believe that this is a temporary truce."

Unable to completely control their nerves, Kai and Kebwe mounted the best horses they could find and rode out to face their foe.

Much to Kai's surprise, he found himself facing the man his father had aided months before at the Ababa land office. For the first time since the Zulu incident, a tiny spark of hope flared in his heart. The man was taller than his companions, muscular and imposing. He recognized Kai. "You are the son of Wakil Abu Ali."

"Yes." He straightened in his saddle. "I am Wakil Kai Jallaleddin ibn Rashid al Kushi. I remember you."

"I am Cuahutomac, chief of this pride," said the Aztec. "Brother by marriage to Montezuma the tenth himself."

"We met before, in New Djibouti."

"Yes. In better times."

"Your Arabic is excellent."

Cuahutomac ignored the compliment. "I must inform you that you and your men are outnumbered and surrounded."

This I knew already. "We are prepared to fight to the last man," Kai said.

"And that last man will fall, have no false hopes. We outnumber you ten to one. Our engineers will have catapults here by tomorrow night. If we wish to, we will reduce your precious mosque to rubble."

Kai felt sickened. Cuahutomac spoke the truth—such tactics would work well. The Mosque of the Fathers had never been built to withstand siege. And the Aztecs cared nothing for its heritage. He and his men would be dead long before Fodjour could return with reinforcements.

"However," his adversary continued, "a slaughter here, on your sacred ground, would trigger all-out war between the glorious Aztec empire and Bilalistan."

Kai felt a trickle of relief that Cuahutomac understood this. "True," he said.

Cuahutomac met Kai's gaze directly. "Montezuma does not desire total war."

Kai found himself believing the man, and knew that his surge of hope must not show in his face. "What do you want?"

"We merely want the land that belongs to us, and the guarantee of peace for a generation."

Kai shook his head sadly. "I am not empowered to offer these things."

"True," said the Aztec. "But a gesture of goodwill on our part, and your promise to convey my message, would do much to further our cause."

"What gesture of goodwill?"

Cuahutomac leaned forward in his saddle. "I will allow your officers and black foot soldiers to go peacefully."

Kebwe sat noticeably taller, unable to repress a sharp exhalation.

Kai remained far more cautious. "And . . . ?"

"That is all."

There had to be more, but Kai kept his tongue still.

"And, of course," the Aztec said casually, "your slaves must be turned over to us, for sacrifice to great Quetzalcoatl."

Kai started to speak, then restrained his tongue. Now he believed that the Aztec had spoken his mind, and also that the terms were nonnegotiable. Damn!

Cuahutomac seemed to be looking off at the horizon, where a rust-colored dust storm was brewing. "I remember your father," he said. "Is he well?"

"He is dead."

Cuahutomac's mouth tightened in respect. In that moment Kai saw that the Aztec was at least ten years older than he had first thought, small wrinkles at his throat and on the back of his hands betraying the fact that he was at least fifty. "He was a great warrior. You must live to carry his name. You have until dawn to consider my offer."

And the Aztec and his companion turned and left.

"But he offered *life!*" Kebwe shouted, his voice ringing from the walls of their makeshift conference room. "Do you want to die?"

"Of course not. But at what price?"

"A few miserable slaves!" said a second.

Kai tried to keep his voice level, and didn't entirely succeed. "Even if you don't care about the slaves, we were sent to recapture the mosque, to hold it at all costs."

"And we've done the best we could!" Kebwe said, trying to sound reasonable. "We took it once, our forces can take it again!"

"If we give up the mamluks, we desecrate the mosque. We will be blasphemers!"

Kebwe slammed his pistol on the table. "For that I accept the judgment of Allah. Life is precious!"

"*All* life," Kai said. "Not just ours. I won't—can't—win my life at such a price."

"It is not your decision alone!"

Kai straightened. "Following my brother's death, I am the ranking officer."

"Let us not forget Shaka's death, also," Kebwe said quietly.

Kai was unmoved. "This is a holy place. This is now *jihad*. If we die defending the mosque, we die clean in the eyes of Allah. I will not buy my life by violating honor. I am in command. Who would challenge me?"

As the officers grumbled, Kai rested his hand on his jambaya's hilt. Technically, he was correct: the Wakil was appointed by the Caliph, and the title was ancestral, passing to his sons. Although Kai was younger than some of the other officers, he had New Alexandrian authority behind his words.

"Damn it," Kebwe said, but stepped next to his dead friend's younger brother. "Who challenges Kai faces both our swords."

One at a time, the officers ceased their grumbling.

"All right, Wakil," Makur said, tight-lipped. "What now?"

By dint both of his own personality and his relationship with Kai, Aidan had become a leader among the mamluks. Even mamluks with more gray than black in their hair looked to him for advice.

So it had been easy to convince the boy Mouse to spy for them, to send him wiggling between a stack of barrels beside the inner wall, where he could hear the conversations in the conference room.

When he came running back to Aidan and relayed what he had heard, Aidan nodded: war had bloodied Kai, but not changed him.

His mind was buzzing. A few hours ago he had all but given up hope of life. Now he was thinking not only of life, but of freedom, and love, and perhaps more. Yes . . . there might be a way . . .

By the time the officers filed out of the conference room to the main yard, the soldiers, slave and free, had grown restless, had eaten and salved their wounds and begun to recover enough from their exertions to gripe.

"What the hell is going on?" Donough said.

"I don't know," one of the black soldiers spat, "but I'm not dying for you white bastards."

"Bastard?" said Donough, massive fists knotting. "At least my mother could walk on her hind legs—"

Before the argument could escalate to blows, Kai appeared, and all attention focused on him. Aidan thought Kai looked weary, but in command. From the deference shown him by the others, it was as he had suspected: the son of the Wakil had greater authority than any other officer.

This is good, Aidan thought. *Bide your time.*

Kai waited for quiet, and then spoke. "You have questions," he said. "Questions that must be addressed."

"I hear that the Aztecs offered us life!" shouted a black foot soldier.

Kai nodded gravely. "At the cost of our souls."

The soldier was unimpressed. "Will you free us from our bond?"

"The gate is open. You black men—you may leave your weapons and walk out, deserters. If you are right, if we die, then no one will be left to call you coward. You may tell any story you like. But do not expect me to salve your conscience."

He looked out at them fiercely. The men murmured among themselves.

"What of us?" Aidan called, worming his way closer to the front.

"What of you? We are terribly outnumbered. Tomorrow, my brothers, we die. But you, who have fought so bravely, will enter Paradise as free men. Tonight, your chains dissolve. This sacred ground should not be held by slaves."

"And we may leave?" called Donough. *Good lad,* Aidan thought. *Put the pressure on him. Don't any of you see what is happening here? They* need us. *Without us they are lost. Here, for the first time, they are weak and we are strong.*

Kebwe gripped at Kai urgently.

"Yes," said Kai. "Leave your weapons and depart."

Again, there were whispers among the whites.

"You free us, to die here with you," said Aidan. "Or we may leave, without paper to prove our freedom, without land or gold."

"It is life," said Kai.

The moment had come. "It is shite!" Aidan cried.

Kai stared at him, stunned into silence.

"Let me put it another way," Aidan continued swiftly. "What if we win the day? What if we can hold out until reinforcements arrive? What then, Kai?"

Aidan's eyes locked with Kai's. It felt as if there was no one else in the room, as if this moment, this war, was for the two of them alone.

"Any free man who stands with me," said Kai, "if we live, wins land and gold. By my brother's promise, any slave who stands wins freedom. To that I add gold . . ."

Kai took a deep breath, paused as if understanding that he was crossing a critical line. The next comment was directed directly at Aidan. "And his family's freedom."

Yes.

The murmurs were building to a roar.

"Do you pledge?" called Aidan, loath to let the moment pass.

"By my sacred honor," Kai said, "I pledge to buy or obtain the release of every man's family, if that man stands and bleeds with me this day."

The white men around Aidan roared their approval.

"And if we fall, but you survive?" asked Donough.

Even as Aidan watched, Kai seemed to transform, to expand in gravity and force. If he had seemed fatigued at first, he seemed to almost radiate strength now. If before Aidan had assumed that Kai had been granted power by his family connections or rank, now he seemed to swell, to grow in stature and authority. The others stared at Kai with the kind of respect men offer heroes and kings.

"This day," Kai said, "each of you gives the names of your family to my officer. If either of us lives, I pledge that whether you survive or not, your family, up to . . . five members . . . is free for all time."

And there it was. Hope, and a promise for the future. He saw Mahon and Sophia, together in an emerald glade. Free.

Aidan nodded, holding his friend's gaze.

Kai turned to his officers. "Arm them with rifles," he said.

"Mouse," he had been named by his fellows. Abdul was the name given him by his master, who owned a peanut plantation in the north. The boy much preferred Mouse, and in fact had begun to insist that everyone use that name. Mice were clever creatures, survivors, almost impossible to eliminate once they invaded a cupboard.

Now Mouse was one of a press of slaves rushing down stone steps into a cellar armory, where a black man with small, suspicious eyes handed them rifles. Rifles! Mouse had never even *touched* a rifle, and now he was going to have one of his own, and be taught to fire it. And just maybe, when all of this was over, he would take the rifle with him and use it for hunting rabbits and deer.

"One for each man!" cried an officer. "Report to the courtyard in half an hour for drill and practice—"

A big red-hair Mouse didn't know was rolling a barrel away from the wall when he revealed what looked like a rectangular outline etched in the clay. The mamluk looked surprised, disappeared for a moment behind the barrels, and then stood and rolled the barrel back into place swiftly.

One of the others came in close to look as soon as the black officer was looking the other way, and then motioned Mouse to come over. "It's a door," Red-Hair said, offering him a candle. "We need you to find out where it goes."

Now Mouse could see why they asked him: the door was barely big enough for an adult, and beyond it was a passage of some kind, dark enough to give him shivers.

Still, he wondered where it might lead.

Mouse climbed through it on knees and elbows. It was a suffocating journey, all scrapes and head bumps, with a pair of abrupt turns. The candle sputtered, and then winked out. Mouse was suddenly and terrifyingly in total darkness. If he had the nerve to turn and face the mockery of his comrades he might have retreated. At that moment he was convinced that the passage went nowhere, and that he would die here, in the darkness, in the earth, without drawing a single free breath in his entire misbegotten life.

Then he felt the faint tickle of fresh air riffling his hair, and realized that the passage had to end somewhere close. He continued to crawl forward.

The passage tilted down a bit, and he found himself scrambling and sliding the last few feet, and then his face struck a bush.

Yelping, he clawed his way through the obstruction to tumble down into cracked, dried mud.

Mouse wiped his face clean and looked up at the moon. He was out! High earthen walls were on all sides, twisting off into the darkness. This had to be the wadi behind the mosque. He had apparently found a secret escape passage dug by the original builders, who feared that the shrine might be too close to enemy territory.

The boy looked up at the moon almost as if he had never beheld its pale face. "Damn," he said.

The mosque's most sacred and private sanctum was reserved, not for pilgrims, or even for the caretakers, but for holy men making pilgrimage from as far as Abyssinia, come to see what Bilal had wrought. This place, within the great golden dome atop the flat brown tile roof, seemed to Kai like the gateway to Paradise.

The dome arched high above him, buttressed within by cross-beams cunningly designed so that the timbers formed a recognizable Naqsh Kabir. He felt Babatunde's presence, and it was a profound comfort. The hand of the Sufi brotherhood was in play here.

From within, the dome seemed almost to glow, as if the ceramic tile not only conducted starlight, but had a luminescence of its own. Thin matting covered the wooden floor, and just in kneeling there, he felt as if he were part of a lineage of suppliants who had prostrated themselves before the Almighty in this special place.

This insane place.

Mosque Al'Amu. An empty plane. A line on a map between warring empires. How strange that here he felt closer to Allah than at any other place he had known. Here, in the midst of war and death, betrayal and loss, honor and disgrace. Here, where it would be reasonable that a man might cast his eyes upward and see nothing, the glories of Paradise forever withheld . . .

In this place, he felt the hand of God. Knew himself to be in the sight and presence of God. And he trembled.

"Allah, hear my prayer. Here, near the bones of my spiritual ancestors, I feel the nearness of death. And I am so afraid." He knotted his fingers together, trying to stop himself from shaking. "I do not ask for my life. I do not ask that You forgive my actions. Only You know if the things I have done are worthy of forgiveness, and I do not presume to know Your mind. I know that this is where You intend me to die. I ask only that my cowardice not disgrace me. That I may lead my men to some kind of victory, or at least to clean and honorable death."

He paused. "Allah. Let my promise be kept. The men have been true. My friend Aidan has been true. I don't know what is just, or unjust, what Your divine plan is for men in bondage to other men. I only know I gave my word, and if You have to choose between my promise and my life, let my promise be kept, and my life lost."

Another pause, searching for the right words.

"Thy will, not mine, be done."

When Mouse returned through the cellar door, he was covered in rock dust, cut and bruised, and so excited he could barely keep control of his bladder.

The cellar was deserted, and he had to creep up the stairs and out to the main courtyard before he found a clutch of mamluks crouched in a circle, passing a hemp-filled pipe from hand to hand. "It's true!" he told them. "We could escape out the back. We know the Aztecs are watching in the front. That's why he said we could go. He knew no one would. But we can escape!"

The mamluks murmured excitedly, then quieted as Aidan pushed his way into the center of their circle. "True," he said. "You can. Any of you can escape. But I believe Kai. I have known him half my life, and he is an honorable man. This is my only chance to free my wife, my child." He paused. "And perhaps even find my sister, whom I pledged to free. Any of the rest of you who want to flee, do it. I stand here."

The men grumbled, but to his relief only two or three of them stood.

"Good," Aidan said. "Fine. And, Mouse—you're the youngest. Get the hell out of here."

Mouse and three others were heading as nonchalantly as possible toward the back storeroom when they encountered a Moorish foot soldier. "Hey, ghost." The Moor's face was strained, as if offended that he had to share air with them. "Where do you think you're going?"

"Just stretching our legs, sir."

The Moor grunted, mollified, and went his way.

"Should we tell him about the tunnel?" asked an older mamluk.

Mouse considered. All his life, the arrogant blacks had told him what to do. Had worked his father into an early grave, had violated his sister's chastity. He hated them, and hated the fact that he had never been free to tell them. "Fock 'im," he said, and imagined the soldier dead, heart ripped out by Aztecs. Served them right, all of them.

But what of him? He would be free, but where would he go, what would he do? He wanted to be free, but he had no trade except fence mending, could not read or write, and would be hard-pressed even to prove he was a free man.

There was no joy in that future, he was smart enough to know that. But was there another way? Any other way . . . ?

Then another thought occurred to him, and its possibilities were so exciting that again he almost wet himself.

In the holy sanctum beneath the golden dome and the Naqsh Kabir, Kai curled, asleep. Dreaming.

He dreamed of his boyhood, racing on horseback with Ali. Learning to read and write at his father's knee. Playing with Aidan.

Of Sophia, and their first night together.

Lamiya, her eyes glowing in the darkness, whispering: *"Find that flame, that existence, that wonderful man—"*

The sweetness of her soft and parted lips against his mouth.

Uncle Malik, drilling him along the triangle and the square. And Babatunde, tutoring him in the secret lines of the Naqsh Kabir. Babatunde, teaching him in his lab. Babatunde, teaching him the philosophies of men living or long dead.

Then, in the dream, Babatunde seemed to speak to him directly. *"The world is not its symbols, Kai. The form is not the essence . . ."*

"Kai—" he heard a voice call, and the dream receded. Kai sat up suddenly, his eyes bright.

"Kai?" Kebwe called to him again from the mosque's doorway.

"I asked that I not be disturbed," he said, irritated.

"It is your slave, Aidan. He said that, on his life, he must be heard."

A strong oath. Kai prayed the message was worthy of it. "Send him in," he said.

Aidan entered, dressed in battle garb. Two steps behind him was the little one that the slaves called Mouse.

Aidan stopped a respectful distance away as Kai rose.

"Yes? What is it?"

"I believe," said Aidan, "that you should hear what this boy has to say, and hear it *now*."

There was steel in Aidan's voice. Steel and something else: excitement. Kai could not repress a grin. He knew that expression, that tilted, off-center curl of Aidan's lips. There was pure hell in it, and Kai felt his heart's load lighten. Aidan had learned something, discovered something, that could make a difference.

"Then let him speak his piece," Kai said.

CHAPTER SIXTY-NINE

WHEN KAI EXITED THE SHRINE it was only three hours after midnight, but the men had been hustled awake. They grumbled and yawned and stretched, but there was an undeniable thread of curiosity about them.

"Men! Together!" he called. "The new day has begun, and today is our day!"

The men clustered about, and Kai felt his heart swell. "Warriors!" he said. "Those of you still among us this morning have chosen the company of men to the solitary pleasures of the forest."

There was a scattering of grim, tired laughter among them. Kai continued. "This is not a time for sleep, but for arms. It is not the end, but the beginning. The beginning of a legend that will last a thousand years. It will be told, I promise you, that once upon a time there was a band of brothers—white, black, rich, poor—who stood together for the land they loved, for freedom, for Ar-Rahman, the Merciful, and pledged their lives and their souls for something greater than themselves."

He had their attention. The hundred of them were gathered now, and armed. They were a ragtag lot, wearing mismatched armor from Egypt, Abyssinia, and Azteca. Armed with spears and swords, staves and rifles. Born to battle or captured from Frankish homes. These were the men who had placed their lives in his hands. These were *his* men. And they would die, or triumph, together.

"I offer you no pretty promises," he said. "Only that in the coming bloody dawn I will be at your side, my flesh with yours, my sword with yours, and that we will stand or fall together. We. Today, we noble few. I say that every man here has the soul of a free man, of a landed man, that every man here is, today, my brother. And those who did not come with us, or who crept out in the night with their tails between their legs, when they hear the songs and stories of the deeds we shall do this day, they will hold their manhood cheap, and weep that their blood was not shed with ours upon this hallowed ground." He paused. He had them, by Allah. By their shining, uplifted faces, he had them! This was what it was to lead men, to hold their hearts and lives in his hands. They were no longer half asleep. Their trusting eyes believed his words, and something within Kai blossomed. This was the moment for which he had been born, for which his honored father and uncle had prepared him, for which Babatunde had cultivated him. "This is manhood. This is the cost of freedom."

The words were barely out of his mouth before the men began to cheer, and he held up his hand for silence. "No sound," he said. "So many voices together would pass beyond these walls, to the ears of those we would deliver unto hell. Hold your voices closely, let them reverberate within your chests, let them drown doubt, and fear, and confusion." They fell silent, but their faces were alive with the words they did not speak.

"Follow me, my brothers." His whisper carried to every ear. "With the dawn we hold—or we die." He knotted his hand into a fist and raised it high, spread the fingers and clenched them again. "And I say: Hold!"

They did not cheer, but a hundred hands covered a hundred hearts, and pounded against their chests rhythmically. "Kai," they muttered. "Kai. Kai. Kai." Every eye upon him, every mouth speaking his name, as if the only thing giving them hope and life was their belief in him. And the weight and power of that belief made him strong.

He would not prove them wrong.

He would not fail them.

He would not fail.

He would _not_.

CHAPTER SEVENTY

THE MOON HUNG LOW AND PALE on the horizon as the night prepared to surrender to the day.

The brush concealing the secret tunnel quivered and then was pushed aside, and a black, shaven head appeared. The man's name was Kzami, and once upon a time he had been a farmer and trapper on the edge of the Aztec frontier. Kzami was a sharpshooter, a quiet man of lethal skills whose wife and children had been brutally murdered during the Aztec assault on Khartum. When Kai asked for volunteers of skill and courage, Kzami had stood, and no one had challenged his right to lead.

When Kzami picked the men to go with him, to Aidan's surprise, he had asked for hunters, black or white. "I never had a slave," Kzami said. "And any man who fights to avenge my family is a brother."

Aidan O'Dere, Donough, Mouse, two other mamluks, and two more blacks were the final choice, and it was these seven who emerged from the secret tunnel after Kzami. They were scraped, scratched, and dusty, but ready for anything. The whites had Aztec swords and muskets. The blacks, who toted breech-loaders, were two of the best sharpshooters under Kai's command.

Desperately, Aidan wished he was a better shot, that he had had more time, more powder to practice that craft. Easy to understand why the blacks had denied their slaves such skills. But if they wanted mamluks to fight their wars, they would have to change that policy. And if that policy changed, if they were forced to recognize and rely upon the courage and ability of whites, mightn't that one day lead to an end to slavery?

Head feeling like a bottle filled with bees, Aidan crept west along the dried bed of the wadi, choosing stealth over speed.

The Aztecs were camped west of the mosque, just out of rifle range, although it was inconceivable that they had failed to post spies on all sides of the mosque. In intervals, teams of mamluks and blacks exited through the tunnel, positioned themselves, and waited for Kzami's signal.

The trapper was using some kind of internal clock or measurement, and at one point he turned and scrambled silently up the rough, steep side of the wadi, leaving the others behind him. Aidan watched him disappear like a lizard up a tree, astonishingly agile.

After about three minutes the farmer came halfway back down and gestured for the others to follow.

When Aidan reached the top, he saw what Kzami had seen: The Aztec camp was right in front of them. In fact, they had passed it slightly, and would therefore be approaching from the rear. It appeared to be home to between three to five hundred men. Fewer than the thousand Kai had feared, but enough to do the job. They were arrayed in bedrolls and beneath tents, the camp laid out in a rough circle, with a makeshift corral for the horses. Plumed, club-armed guards walked the perimeter in soberly vigilant pairs. He counted up to twenty in the interval between their cycles.

Not long, but perhaps long enough.

Kzami gave silent hand signs to the men behind him, and they began the crawl, following Aidan's lead. The grass between the wadi and the camp was high enough to conceal a man on all fours. Slowly, taking absolutely nothing for granted, they worked their way close.

Brush and grass poked Aidan in the face, and little forest creatures seemed to be crawling up into his armpits. He hoped they were leaf-eaters.

It took the better part of an hour to cover two hundred cubits of grass, waiting until the gap between patrols to traverse any bare patches.

Using hand signals only, Kzami positioned the men. The sharpshooters had their rifles trained on the largest tent.

Willing himself to silence, Aidan crawled into the shadow of a tree, held his breath until the giant Donough appeared beside him. They were committed now. The shadow would hide them from the guard's approach, but as soon as the guards passed them, a single glance back over a shoulder would reveal them and raise the alarm.

Despite the two battles he had already fought, Aidan felt his nerves burning, looked at his childhood friend's placid face and wondered how Donough could be so calm, wondered if they would live long enough for him to ask the question.

Before his next thought had the opportunity to fully form, the guards appeared, walking toward them, speaking quietly to each other. The long night hours had stolen some of their energy and focus. Aidan ducked behind the tree and drew his knife.

The instant the two men passed them, Aidan sprang, trusting that Donough would not hesitate either. There was no need to fear. Aidan's knife was in the man's neck, as Kzami had taught him, at the same moment that Donough landed on his own victim, driving him to the earth with a knee in his back.

His own prey's death cries drowned in blood as Donough's man's spine cracked with a sound like a rotten branch. They dragged the bodies back into shadow.

Step one complete. Two of the men behind him worked their way around to the Aztec horses. A squat, burley mamluk carried a cask of gunpowder as if it were a baby boy.

The men were arrayed very, *very* carefully, and the mamluk set the cask at the edge of the horse corral—the side away from the Aztecs. He applied a daub of fire-paste from each end of the tube, then reached safety just as Kzami signaled that the next set of guards was heading their way.

The fire-paste combined, sparked to flame, and the fuse caught. Then, perversely, the fuse smoked, sputtered, and died.

Behind Aidan, Mouse cursed, then scampered forward. Aidan wanted to scream at him: *There's no time!* But it was too late. Now he could only pray. Mouse hovered over the fuse, probably putting another twist of fire-paste into play. If he could do so quickly enough, he might disappear around the other side of the corral. There was no longer time to cross the clearing into shadow. Just a moment . . .

He was backing away now, making it, when one of the guards saw the flare of light and bounded toward it.

Aidan would never know what went through Mouse's mind at that moment. No one ever would. He could have run, or perhaps remained hidden.

Instead, as the guard headed to look at the flame, Mouse launched himself like a frenzied cat, throwing a rock at the same time. The rock struck one guard in the forehead and sent him reeling back before he could shout an alarm. Mouse hit the second guard on the chest, stabbing with a little knife, the blows deflected by the Aztec's armor.

The guard shucked Mouse off, raised his axe—

The second guard came to his feet, and yelled an alarm—

Mouse raised his arm in a useless defensive motion—

And the powder detonated, and it seemed that Allah Himself had shouted in anger. In an instant, white and brown, Frank and Aztec, friend and foe were obliterated in a thunderclap of light. Chunks of flesh hurtled through the air to litter the grass in smoking heaps, and only the angels could have distinguished man from horse.

Instantly the camp was in an uproar. The surviving horses stampeded in all directions, trampling several of the Aztecs.

Aidan watched as the enemy stumbled out of their tents, seizing weapons as if they had been born with axe in hand.

Two of the mamluks broke and ran toward the west. Howling, Aztecs chased them down and hammered them into red ruin in the grass.

Aidan and Donough stayed flat, knowing that in another moment the soldiers would find them. There was no time to slink back to the wadi. Running west would avail nothing. And the partial safety of the mosque lay on the other side of the awakening army.

This was death, approaching nearer and nearer every moment.

Then the flap of the largest tent opened, and the Aztec chief appeared. Aidan recognized the man from Addis Ababa, and from his conference with Kai the previous day. Even without his ceremonial feathers he was half a head taller than the average Aztec soldier. In the firelight, his skin shone like gold.

Aidan had only a moment to admire the man, who had begun snapping orders in a staccato singsong instantly, as if he had been awake for hours.

Then he staggered back, and then caught his balance again. He looked down at his chest at the same instant that Aidan heard a second shot, and realized that he had heard a first one, but somehow hadn't registered it.

Cuahutomec's head snapped back, his right eye a crimson hole.

A howl of anguish went up from the Aztecs, a cry of mourning and anger arose. For a moment they were disoriented, a thousand-headed beast without a single cogent mind.

"Now! " Aidan screamed, and Donough rose up and ran, probably faster than he had ever run in his life, Aidan close behind him.

On the horizon ahead, dawn's first blush had appeared.

CHAPTER SEVENTY-ONE

ASTRIDE HIS MOUNT, flanked by his five surviving officers, Kai watched the remnants of his sneak attack fleeing toward him, back toward the imagined safety of the mosque.

His riflemen had exited the mosque only half an hour earlier, creeping carefully through the tunnel, circling around into position. Aztec lockouts had been identified and avoided until the explosion, when the mosque's front door flew open and the horsemen emerged. Confused by the chaos in their camp, taking fire from both horsemen and riflemen, the lookouts had wilted and fled.

Now the riflemen were arranged in three standing rows of fifteen, one behind the other, widely spaced and staggered so that each had a clear shot.

It would take a few moments now. There was a gap between arranging his men and giving them their orders and the time, only a few breaths away, that hell itself would be unleashed.

Despite the yelling and frenzied running, the galloping mad horses and the stench of flaming flesh, Kai felt at peace. This, then, was an ending. From the moment of contact with the enemy until this all ended, there would be no more time for thought. His desperate stratagem would succeed, or they would all be dead. And it was all in the hands of Allah, where such things belonged.

As the surviving mamluks passed them, Kai straightened and raised his voice. "On my mark. Fire!"

The first line fired their rifles at the nearest Aztecs, now only ten paces away. Eight axe-wielding foes fell, but those behind them continued on, a few dropping to one knee and preparing hastily seized rifles of their own.

"Second line, fire!" The first line had fallen back behind the second and were reloading: either with premeasured loads of black powder and ball or with manufactured bullets. Less than half his men had seen combat before the current campaign, and considering, their nerves were holding well.

The officers watched, and every time they saw an Aztec take a position to aim carefully, they fired their own weapons. Their fire was lethal, far better aimed than that of either the mamluks, the common black soldiers, or their sleep-deprived, half-dressed Aztec foes.

"Third line, fire!" At his command, fifteen rifles exploded at once, directly into the oncoming Aztecs. The second line had fallen back behind the first and were reloading feverishly.

Still the Aztecs advanced. The officers couldn't spot and hit every enemy sniper. Their rifle line was being smashed, one man after another falling from enemy bullets or war clubs hurled with devilish accuracy. The third line fell back, and now the first was in position again.

"First line, fire!"

One of the rifle barrels exploded in a mamluk's face. He reeled back screaming, flesh peeled away from shattered skull.

The men around him were horrified, fumbled with their weapons, and the Aztecs closed.

"Swords!" Kai roared as the lines collided. Men screamed and killed and died in that first moment. Kai laid about himself with his sword, nothing in his mind except the hacking, brawling melee.

"Hold them!" he screamed. "Hold for your lives—" and he glimpsed the Aztec camp, now fully awakened, charging through the grass toward them. His heart beat so fast he thought it would burst. His war horse bucked and wheeled, obeying its unaccustomed rider but still nervous in the face of such chaos.

He wished that it were Djinna beneath him. And then realized that he might ride his beloved horse again soon, very soon, in the fields of Paradise.

Aidan had found a pocket of calm in the midst of the storm. The Bilalian forces had stolen the advantage, and even though outnumbered, had a better position, their own horses raging through the enemy while the Aztecs struggled to recapture their mounts.

He used that moment to reload. He was one of the few mamluks with a breech-loading cartridge rifle, which enabled him to fire more swiftly. That margin of seconds was all that saved his life. He glanced up just as an Aztec charged him, and blew the bare-chested man out of his half-fastened sandals—

A second sprang at him, and Aidan swung the rifle like a club. Both skull and stock splintered.

He discarded the useless weapon as another Aztec leapt on him, and Aidan went down under the charge. An obsidian knife flashed up and then down. He managed to roll to the side, and the knife slashed his shoulder. He screamed but managed to get his hands around his attacker's wrists. The Aztec chopped at him with the side of his fist. Aidan felt his jaw crack. The world began to swim.

Then mighty Donough was there. He buffeted the Aztec along the side of his head so strongly that the man's eyes rolled up and his grip weakened.

Aidan rolled him over and gripped the man's throat with his good hand. When the Aztec nearly struggled out of his grip Aidan head-butted him once, twice. He clamped his teeth on the man's nose, holding him in place as he fumbled for the dropped knife. He found it in the grass, grasped it.

The Aztec's eyes widened with fear as the knife flashed. Then the fear left his eyes, and they stared up at a cold, uncaring sky.

Aidan rose from his combat, spitting torn flesh. He was trembling, his shoulder gashed and throbbing. He turned to run toward the mosque, and suddenly it was as though a burning stick had been thrust against his leg. *Shot!*

He tumbled, then staggered up with Donough's arm around his waist. Together they hobbled toward safety.

The retreat was desperate now, the Aztecs streamed without end. Kai's mounted cavalry pulled back. Additional snipers provided as much cover as they could, but by now they were breaking and running.

Every step was a nightmare. Even Donough was beginning to weaken, and Aidan noticed for the first time that the side of the giant's face was caked with blood and that half of his scalp had been torn off.

Aidan glimpsed Kai, galloping back toward the mosque. A thin black man, side smeared with blood, clung behind him.

"Retreat!" Kai screamed.

Run, Kai, thought Aidan. *Live.*

The retreating men reached the mosque's walls. Black and white, mamluk, common soldier, and noble, they sought safety behind its gates.

As Kai reached them he felt Kzami finally weaken and slip off the saddle into the arms of waiting mamluks.

"Get him in!" Kai screamed. "And close the gates!"

As dozens of mamluks and soldiers crowded in, the mosque's great gates swung closed. As Muslim riflemen picked at the Aztecs from the second story, others lowered ropes for the men trapped outside the walls. Kai leapt from horseback to one of the ropes hanging from the windows, flaying the skin from his palms as he slid a cubit before finding purchase. Then, feeling more vulnerable than he ever had in his life, knowing himself to be a target for any Aztec with a rifle, he began to climb, muscles cracking from the strain, breath burning in his lungs and heart pounding as the battle raged beneath him.

The riflemen in the window provided as much covering fire as they could as Kai finally reached the window, eager hands helping him through. Then he seized a rifle from one of the mamluks, firing down as the last of his soldiers reached the walls.

Several were dragged down and killed, but most were climbing the ropes now, their horses running wild or captured by the ravening horde.

"Pull them up!" he screamed to the men in the long, low room. His men put their backs to it, straining and pulling as each of the ropes, with several men dangling, began to come up, one man after another scrambling through the window and then helping to pull up his fellows. Kai loaded and fired, loaded and fired, the bullets crashing around his head, fully expecting at any moment to receive a lethal wound.

"Get the hell out of here!" The air filled with stinking smoke, the smell of gunpowder, the screams of men hit by snipers' bullets. The explosions and howls were overpowering, enough to overload his mind and send him into a kind of fugue. There was nothing to be done now but to kill, and kill, and kill, and perhaps to die.

And the dark place within Kai, the place that his father claimed was joined to the majestic beast whose vital fluids had quenched his jambaya's glowing blade, called welcome to him and enfolded him in its dark and living heart.

Outside, Cuahutomec's second in command was enraged. Toaquatyl had stepped from his tent just in time to see his cousin felled by cowardly assassins after they had offered honorable terms of surrender to the blacks.

This was not the behavior of warriors, it was the demeanor of dogs and things lower than dogs. The blacks were not worthy of respect, barely worthy to offer as sacrifice to the Feathered God. And their pale, grublike slaves revolted him. The thought of soiling a sacred obsidian knife with their blood seemed blasphemous. Still, Cuahutomec had been determined to honor them with a great death, and Toaquatyl had bowed to his wisdom.

And now this. Peace be damned, they would kill every one of these sneaking animals, pull their hearts from their chests and lay them in a smoking heap, and all of that would not assuage the pain Toaquatyl felt. Great Cuahutomec, dead and gone.

"Bring ladders!" he cried. They had more than enough men to take this wretched building, with its great ugly walls and dome of gold paint. And if by some miracle they were repulsed, there were a thousand Aztecs not more than a day's ride away. The slaughter would be glorious.

Around Toaquatyl, bullets smashed into the ground, into horses, into men. He laughed at the invisible death. Guns were powerful indeed, but it was the power of the heart that made a warrior great. He might die, but others of his blood would live, and the Aztecs would roll across this land like waves on the golden shore, sweeping all before them.

His own men returned fire, smashing the riflemen back. The fire above them was slowly diminishing. He watched one face after another explode into a crimson mask, watched his own men swarm up the ladders to engage the riflemen with sword and axe.

One of his best screamed down to him: "They've fallen back and barred the door!"

Toaquatyl growled. The enemy would take up another position, hope to use concentrated firepower to keep the superior force from advancing through the halls.

These were old tactics, familiar to Toaquatyl's people since long before the black men had arrived. Then, it had been arrows and blow darts rather than gunpowder-driven lead and steel. The principle was the same. He would not play their game—he would, in fact, use their own dishonorable technology against them.

He had sent several runners back to the camp, and now they returned at a trot, carrying barrels of gunpowder. While Toaquatyl's snipers kept watch on the upper windows, the barrels were pushed against the door and a wool fuse packed with gunpowder thrust into the bunghole.

Toaquatyl's troops scattered, finding shelter where they could. Fifteen seconds later the powder detonated with an explosion that hammered their ears and shook the earth. A vast cloud of dust, metal slivers, and wood splinters erupted from the side of the mosque, and Toaquatyl, who had taken cover behind a dead horse, grinned savagely as the dust cleared and he saw the great doors hanging, shattered, suspended only by their twisted hinges.

There was a moment of silence, and then his men streamed in. The returning fire from inside the mosque was weak and sporadic, as if the blast had completely unnerved the defenders. Toaquatyl's men poured fire into the inner doors and windows, and most especially at the little house at the rear of the main room, from which they could actually see rifle fire.

Black and white defenders fell from the doorways, writhing as bullets riddled them.

A tiny warning at the back of Toaquatyl's mind told him that the fire was insufficient, that they were withholding the mass of their men, that they hoped to trap him, tricking him into thinking that they were so weak.

"Take the second level!" His men raced up the clay stairs, more streaming in behind him. Whatever the accursed blacks had planned, he had more than enough men to handle it.

He led the charge across the courtyard, as rifles from the enclosed area tore into his men. They set shoulders to the door, once, twice, now so enraged that they were ignoring the feeble fire, and the door cracked and swung open—

Within, there were only five or six badly wounded defenders, and perhaps twenty rifles lying about. Preloaded, then, so that a few men in the hutch and a few upstairs could pretend to be many. A ploy, a—

Then Toaquatyl's eyes widened as a stick-thin black man in a fur cap laughed at him. His face was gaunt as death, and he coughed blood. But he was smiling. And holding a torch that he had just touched to a fuse. And the fuse disappeared into a barrel, and the barrel was set atop a dozen other barrels. One of the white men, his right arm a burned, ragged stump, grinned up at Toaquatyl with a mouthful of brown teeth. "Fock ye," he said, and slumped over.

Willing himself out of his shock, Toaquatyl turned to run, but then his entire world turned to light, and there was nothing more except the fragment of a bitter thought:

We were tric—

And then nothing.

CHAPTER SEVENTY-TWO

FROM THE SAFETY OF THE WADI, Aidan watched in awe as the top of the mosque erupted into the sky, smoke and flame arcing a hundred feet into the air as Aztec gunpowder and blasting sticks, piled and linked desperately in the last hours, detonated with a clap like the end of worlds.

For an instant he had time to think of the men who had sworn to escape the pain of their mortal wounds by bringing death to the Aztecs. One moment to ask himself if he could have been so brave, done so much.

Then dust and smoke, driven by the blast wave, belched out of the escape hole like powder from a cannon.

"Get them out!" he bawled, and the men in the wadi dug with their hands and knives and anything they could find, struggling to extract the last few men from the tunnel, praying that it wouldn't collapse.

They pulled out three, and then a fourth, before the tunnel ceiling gave way and the men backed up, despairing. From inside came coughing, and a voice that Aidan recognized. He crawled into the hole at once, pulling rocks out of the way, digging until his fingernails were broken and bloody, until he found a hand, grasped it, and was infinitely relieved to feel the answering pressure.

"Pull me. Pull my feet, dammit!" The men behind him pulled, and he held and pulled, until Kai slid out of the tunnel.

Kai had insisted on being the last out. He was gagging, puking dust, covered with gray powder, gasping for air.

Kai rose on shaky legs, steadied himself, and then said: "Let's see."

"My very thought," Aidan said, and together they climbed up the dirt wall and peered over the lip.

Dust and smoke were everywhere, but a cool, mournful wind blew from the east, and it created gaps through which they could blink and gain a view.

Bodies and chunks of bodies were scattered through the wreckage, shattered men sprawled in postures of death like drowned beetles. The mosque lay in ruins, the entire eastern wall blown out, flames and acrid oily smoke curling up through the remnants of the roof.

A few Aztecs staggered dazedly in circles, trying to help their fellows to their feet—at least, those few whose feet were still attached to legs.

Cuahutomac's army was crushed. A great, primal wail of lamentation and animal rage emerged from a hundred wounded throats. Aidan slipped back down the dirt wall, too shocked at the results of their plan to think or feel or celebrate.

Kai landed beside him a moment later. He gulped a few deep breaths, and then punched Aidan's shoulder weakly. "I guess it worked," he said.

"If you don't mind that the mosque looks just a wee bit . . . damaged."

Kai winced. "There's that, yes."

"We could ask the Aztecs what they think."

"No," Kai said. "Let's not."

Kai directed his men to move their wounded further east along the wadi. The sun was up now, and if one of the dazed and battered Aztecs had glanced into the riverbed, it would have been easy to spot them. Once they rounded an eastern bend, they were safer and better concealed.

"Come on," Kai said to Donough, who held the shoulders of a wounded mamluk as Kai took the legs. The giant's scalp lay open. The crawl through the tunnel had to have pushed dust and dirt into it, and it would be a diseased mass of suppurating tissue within a day or two if they did not get medical aid.

Donough wasn't alone. The survivors were a mess: not a one of them was without cuts, scrapes, bullet wounds, sword cuts, stab wounds, bruises, or breaks. About thirty men had made it out of the mosque alive. Thirty men out of a hundred.

He thought of the men who had agreed to stay behind, to spend what life they had left destroying their enemy. Would he have had such courage? he wondered. He hoped he would never have to know.

"God," Kebwe said, sagging beneath his load as he and one of the mamluks carried a black soldier. "I'm so tired."

"We're all tired. We'll be able to rest soon."

Kai's wounded mamluk clenched a leather strap between his teeth. Kai stumbled and the mamluk thumped against the ground. He bit into the strap and whimpered, but did not scream.

"I'm sorry," Kai whispered. The man did not speak in reply, but the gratitude in his eyes spoke volumes.

Exhaustion made them rest five minutes for every ten minutes of walking, and it was on their third rest break that Aidan, who had acted as scout, scrambled back to them and whispered: "The Aztecs are close. Hunker down!"

The men all retreated to the shadows on the north side of the wadi, backs against the rock wall. All held silent.

And in that silence, Kai heard the soft, deliberate crunch of feet against sand. Two men. Maybe three. The Aztecs were searching for surviving comrades, and retreating Bilalians. Had they additional forces close by? What were their numbers? He didn't know how many had been killed in the mosque explosion, or how many had scattered.

Allah preserve us, he thought. If the Aztec's had received reinforcements, his drastic maneuver would avail little.

"Get ready," he whispered to Kebwe, who closed his eyes, whispered a prayer, then pulled his notched and bloody sword from its scabbard.

Kai reached down inside himself, fighting to find strength. It was there. As long as there was life there was strength, and hope. These were his men, and he would not let them down, would not fail them. They had placed their lives in his hands, and—

Then, distantly, Kai heard the trumpets. Their call drifted on the wind like birds floating on a warm current of air, ethereal and almost unworldly. At first he was certain that he was wrong, that there were no bugle calls, but then he heard shouting from the Aztecs and the sound of running feet, and in the instant after that he heard horses.

Then the air crackled with volleys of rifle fire, and a cry of *"Allah huakbar!"* followed by a hundred answering screams, and another volley.

Kai sagged back against the wadi wall, the breath heavy and hot in his lungs, the late-morning sun beating down on his face.

Happy to be alive.

CHAPTER SEVENTY-THREE

THE COMMANDER OF THE RELIEF battalion was Colonel Wakil Abu Kwame himself, an older Moor with African skin and Arabic nose and cheeks. His face was scarred, his eyes seared clean of illusions. Behind Kwame marched a column of at least three hundred men. His standard-bearer carried aloft the flag of Bilalistan: crescent moon and lion on a field of gold.

Seated next to Kwame was Fodjour, who did little to conceal his confusion and dismay at the destruction encountered on arrival.

Kai faced the mounted colonel with what he hoped was a proper military bearing and saluted fist over heart.

"What in Allah's name happened here?" asked Kwame.

Kai held his salute. After a scowl, the colonel returned it. Kai felt that if he didn't sit soon, he was going to collapse. "Sir. We had no hope to see you before tomorrow."

"Your messenger intercepted our column as it came south, Captain."

"Thank Ar-Rahman, the Merciful. Captain Kai Jallaleddin ibn Rashid al Kushi relinquishing command, sir."

Kwame nodded, eyes boring into Kai like gun barrels. "You report to me in three hours."

* * *

In three hours another company of troops had reinforced the first, guards had been deployed, and a city of tents erected around the fallen mosque.

Hundreds of Aztec bodies were still buried beneath the wreckage. Dozens of dazed and wounded Aztecs had been captured.

Aidan was beyond fatigue, into some twilight zone where his body continued to move as if it were a resuscitated corpse under a sorcerer's spell. It would take days of sleep before he felt human again. If he ever did.

His leg would barely support his weight now, and the fingers of his left hand were as swollen as sausages. His side and back hurt as if someone had thrust flaming pokers into them—but he was alive!

"You've lost blood," said the field surgeon, a black man who reminded him of Babatunde: small, dark, bright-eyed, but round and hard. "And this bone will take weeks to set. But you are strong. You will heal."

"Thank you," said Aidan.

"Some are not so fortunate," said the surgeon. He had treated Aidan as neither better nor worse than his black patients, merely as one more in an endless procession of bodies to be stitched or sawed. "Eyes, hands, limbs—it was very bad?" It was not a genuine question. There was no genuine concern. The little man was on the edge of burnout, as were the survivors of the Mosque Al'Amu.

Donough lay still on the next cot. The pain had driven him out of consciousness. His big body tensed convulsively, as if already in the grip of fever.

The surgeon undid the head bandages and inspected. "Most men would be dead," he said in a flat voice. "If it was an arm, I'd amputate."

"That's what Kai said," Aidan replied. The surgeon looked over at him, and for a moment there was no registration there, as if he had already forgotten of Aidan's existence.

Then he nodded. "Your commander. Well, perhaps he should have been a doctor." He turned to a passing orderly. "Get my pack from my horse. Fetch morphine and tincture of cannabis."

His assistant saluted. "Yes, sir. Immediately."

Kai's wounds had been bound, and he had found time to lie down in a corner for half an hour's sleep. Then he arose, rusty and creaky as an old man, and reported to the colonel's tent.

Kwame and four other officers were seated in a line on a fur rug, cross-legged, backs ramrod straight. So: a board of inquiry had already convened. Kai's mouth tasted of dust. If things went badly in the next few minutes, it might be better to have perished in the tunnel.

Kwame scribbled something on a pad, then looked up. "The strength of the Aztec horde was estimated at four hundred. We intercepted a column of reinforcements with war machines and explosive missiles. Therefore, it is probable that your actions saved lives. Still, you destroyed that which you were specifically ordered to hold. This is a wartime council, and our ruling can be carried out immediately. Do you understand the implications?"

"Yes, sir," said Kai. He could be summarily executed. His father's wealth and political connections would serve him not at all.

"Then what have you to say for yourself?"

Kai took a breath. "It is said, and I quote, that in turning away from the true worship of God, idolaters had 'deprived themselves of the light of heavenly grace and of the showers of divine mercy.'"

"What has that to do with your actions?"

"Our orders were to hold, but with our numbers so reduced, death seemed certain. The Aztecs would merely kill us, and occupy the mosque once again. When men are told to give their lives for an object," Kai said strongly, "that object, made by men, has been placed above the lives of men, who were made by Allah. In such a circumstance, the mosque had become an idol. I was merely following Sunna, the way of the Prophet, to destroy it."

The officers were silent, perhaps stunned by the sheer audacity required to offer such an explanation. Then the moment of paralysis broke, and they buzzed among themselves.

Kwame cleared his throat. "And what happened to Colonel Shaka? His body was not found."

Kai faced him without blinking. "He must have died in the attack, sir. I never saw him after we took the mosque."

The officer to Kwame's left wore Zulu war scars on his cheeks. He seemed alertly neutral to the proceedings, but Kai found it difficult to meet his eyes.

Kwame chewed at his mustache. "There are many strange things here. I heard a rumor that Shaka's body was removed by his regiment—which means that they were here, but did not reinforce the men defending the Shrine of the Fathers."

The Zulu officer seemed nonplussed. "I have no information at this time, sir."

"I see," said Kwame. He conferred again with the others.

"Sir," said a lieutenant to Kwame's right, a big man with a smooth face and a deeply receding hairline. "I believe a formal court-martial should be convened."

Kwame nodded. He stood and walked to the entrance of his tent, gazing out. Kai tensed, as if waiting for the axe to fall, for the blade to plunge into his unprotected back. To what did Kwame's sad, wise eyes bear witness? The shattered mosque, the wounded defenders black and white, the dead and captured Aztecs?

Or the prospective spot of Kai's own execution?

Kwame returned, still without a trace of expression. He took his place on the floor. Although Kai gazed down at them, and they up at him, it seemed that he was at the bottom of an infinitely deep and dark pit.

"I see no evidence of actionable malfeasance," said Kwame. "My decision may not be popular, but this is not a democracy. I will say more."

He looked at Kai shrewdly, tiredly. Clearly, Kwame suspected what had happened here in the last days.

"We may never know exactly what happened here, or why you took the actions you took. But your men are alive, and the Aztecs are broken." He folded his hands together in his lap as he gazed up. "You, Captain, have no future in the military. Nor, judging by your apparent disrespect for religious symbols, have you one among the mullahs."

Kai dropped his eyes, fearing the worst.

"I would not have a man such as you under my command." Kwame paused, and then added gravely, "But I would follow you into battle against Satan himself."

Relief flooded Kai like the waters of an oasis. Kwame rose and saluted him. It took a moment for Kai to collect himself sufficiently to return the salute, pivot, and leave the tent before Kwame saw the tears threatening to stream down his cheeks.

CHAPTER SEVENTY-FOUR

IT WAS A CLEAR, WARM NIGHT, and most of the wounded men were being cared for in the open air, on bedrolls arrayed in the shadow of the mess tent. Kai walked among the injured, supervising the care of his men. "I want food and water for all of them, and clean beds. You will see to that?"

"Yes, sir," said the doctor. "And you haven't slept for two days."

"When the last of my men is cared for, I can sleep."

They lay in rows, bandaged, splinted, bleeding. He passed to help Aidan, who struggled to adjust a bandage on his leg. A medical assistant next to him wound strips of hemp gauze around a black man's fractured shin.

In the moonlight, their skin color was different, but the white bandages glistened the same dark hue. The moonlight, the darkness, the night, seemed to have stolen their color.

Next to Aidan lay a man with an amputated arm and leg. What was his name? Kai searched for it, and could not remember. Allah save him, this man had pledged his life and honor to Kai, trusted him, and he couldn't even remember his name. Is this how it felt to lead men? To see them reduced to butchered animals and never even know who they were?

"Oh, Shareefah. Shareefah," moaned the wounded one. "I'm sorry. God help me . . ."

"Fazul," said Aidan. "Hold on. Life isn't over. You're still a man."

"I lost my leg . . . my arm."

"Half a leg, your left arm. Does your *zakr* still work?"

Despite his injuries, the man laughed. "Better than yours ever dreamt."

"There you have it. Bring that home, your Shareefah will excuse the rest."

The man laughed again, and then coughed blood. He was dying. Aidan had no more comfort to offer.

"Fazul," said Kai. "Where are your people?"

"Upper Djibouti. Master Fakesh."

"I know him. You have family?"

"My wife, Shareefah. Three children."

"Are your mother and father still alive?"

"I don't know. Sold away. Have a sister."

"I promise you that I will find them, and free them. You did your duty. I will do mine."

Fazul sat up as much as he could, grabbed Kai's arm with hard cold fingers. "Do you swear? Do you swear? Ah, Bilal, what's the difference? How would I know . . ."

"Kai never breaks his word," Aidan said, his voice utterly sincere. "And he only lies to help his friends."

The wounded Fazul gripped at his arm as Kai locked eyes with Aidan, seeing nothing in his friend's face but truth. "Tell me my son will be free."

"He will be free," Kai told him, still looking at Aidan.

He searched Kai's face. "You have a good face. I think you are a good man." Despite his weakness, he managed a sly smile. "If you hadn't been born a black bastard, maybe we could have been friends."

"Stranger things have happened," Kai said.

CHAPTER SEVENTY-FIVE

KAI FOUND AN UNUSED CORNER of the supply tent, curled up, and fell asleep at once. When he awoke a day later he found that someone had draped a blanket over him. He never learned who.

He was ravenously hungry, but was only halfway through a meal when he remembered something that his mind had blocked for two days:

Ali.

Without speaking to anyone, Kai took a wagon and a horse and drove out of the camp onto the northern ridge, where a quarter hour's search revealed his brother's body.

At first all he could see was a dark boot, and a still form curled onto its side like a man deep in sleep. A step closer and he could hear the flies buzzing, and after another step a sob broke from his lips as he saw his brother's beloved face, already swollen and puffy. He had hoped to carry Ali back to Dar Kush, but knew that four days in the hot sun would bring Ali's body to a disgraceful state, not fit for proper burial.

So with the short shovel he had thrown into the back of his wagon, Kai dug a trench in the ground, and into it rolled Ali's already bloated corpse. No longer laughing, or prideful. No longer skilled or cynical, no more jests from the fly-strewn lips, no dance steps from the cold and lifeless feet. Just meat now. Like so many others. Just meat.

He covered Ali up and sank to his knees beside the grave, praying.

"Allah," he said. "Your Prophet, peace be unto him, said that a martyr's body should not be washed. My beloved brother was slain at a battlefield, by an unbeliever. Surely that is enough to perfume his wounds, and give him peace."

He stopped, listening to the wind whispering through the tall grass. If he was very still, was that not the sound of laughter? A strong, clear voice that had once teased and chided and led him? For a moment it was, and then it was gone. Kai grew quieter still, barely breathed.

Nothing.

He stood, looking down at the narrow mound. So silent. Such a strange and lonely place for Ali's restless heart.

"Farewell," he said quietly. And then after a time, he returned to camp.

Later, his heart opened, Kai allowed himself another thought that he had pushed far away: *Djinna.*

The horses had already been dragged from the field, pulled into a pit where they would be burned and buried. He spent two hours searching but could not find her corpse. His beloved Djinna, dumped in a grave, buried in a strange place, her huge, brave heart forever silenced.

He stood at the edge of the excavation, gazing down at the dozens of dead horses piled in its depths, and something that he hadn't allowed to break open when burying his brother finally tore free, and tears ran hot and free down his cheeks, spilled salt onto his lips.

He prayed Djinna would not think less of him.

Kai stood out at the wood and brush fence surrounding the new encampment, gazing at the shattered husk of the mosque. More soldiers were arriving now, being informed that the mosque had been taken and Shaka Zulu killed in the process, the current whereabouts of his corpse unknown. Rumor said that the Aztecs might have taken it, to tear his dead heart out to offer to their dark god.

Kai felt empty, but strangely light, as if he were on the verge of floating up above all of the turmoil. He heard a scratching sound, and turned as Aidan, unsteady on his crutch, limped up to him.

"More men arriving," Aidan said. "They'll hold. This wasn't all for nothing."

Aidan said nothing more. Kai studied him. "You have a question, but you won't ask it."

Aidan remained silent.

"Because you don't want to offend me by asking if I intend to keep my word. To Fazul and Shareefah. To the men. To you."

"I'm sorry," said Aidan.

"No. You have every right to question. I have no right to demand faith." He took a deep, cleansing breath. "Yes, I will keep my word. But do not trust my words. Believe only my actions."

"Sometimes words are all men have," said Aidan.

Kai turned and looked back at the makeshift infirmary, the rows of wounded, black and white. The men shared coffee, and bread, and for those few moments, they were just men. "Words legitimized stripping the honor from honorable men," he said gravely. "Justified turning their women into whores. Words that I spoke myself justified using thoths to pursue men seeking the same freedom I would have sought, were I in your place."

Aidan started to speak, but Kai motioned him to silence.

"I am sorry that words are all I have. For now. But there will be actions. I swear to you."

He turned to walk away, but Aidan called to him. "Kai!"

Kai turned slowly. He felt as if his face was frozen, as if the silver thread connecting soul and body had been severed. "Yes?"

"I'll take the words," Aidan said.

Kai dropped his eyes, then with great effort brought them level with Aidan's. "I'm sorry, Aidan. More than I can say. Hopefully not more than I can show."

"*Insh'Allah.*"

There was a pause, and then Kai stepped forward and the two men embraced as they had once upon a time, long ago, before reality had awakened two lonely boys from a dream of brotherhood.

Next to the ruin of the mosque, a new fort was under construction, logs hauled from thirty miles away to form high, straight walls. Rubble was being carted and carried away. The encampment was now an orderly structure, almost eight hundred armed men, cannon and spiked wire fences surrounding an area nearly a mile square.

The survivors of what was already called "Kai's Maneuver" were being loaded on wagons and horses. They were a raggedy bunch, but as the wagons began to roll, the relief soldiers saluted them.

Kai hauled his weary bones up onto the lead wagon, grateful that he wouldn't have to ride a strange horse all the way back to Dar Kush. He just wanted to rest, and think.

Colonel Kwame and two of his lieutenants approached. Kai saluted him, and Kwame returned it, then pulled a scroll from his belt and handed it up to Kai. "The entire district is under military control now," he said. "This document is all the authority you need." He looked at the mamluks, crowded on the wagons with their black compatriots. "A promise is a promise."

"Thank you, sir," Kai said.

Kwame turned smartly and walked back to his tent. Kai felt an almost overpowering wish to thank Kwame for his kindness, but ultimately words, or perhaps nerve, failed him. If fate was kind, there would be another time and place. For now, he had to get his men home.

"Roll out!" he called, and the wagons began to move.

Two days later, they arrived at the gates of the first plantation, a wide iron gate barring a dirt road that wound back between a stand of walnut trees. The blacks and mamluks hobbled down from the wagon.

Before they could ring the gate's bell to announce themselves, there was a shout from down the private road, and little white boys in threadbare pants came running, followed a moment later by three black men on horseback.

After introductions, Kai showed the document to the master, a graying, broad-browed man named Jaffari Fakesh. A thick-waisted man in his sixties, Fakesh nodded soberly, calling for several slaves to come forward.

Dozens of whites had gathered now, men and women, boys and girls.

Heart heavy, Kai pulled the sheet back from one corner of the third wagon, exposing the still, pale face of Fazul.

A stout, handsome woman screamed and rushed forward, sobbing and gripping at her dead husband. *Shareefah*, Kai thought. Three children clutched at her legs, moaning.

The eldest child was a son, and the spitting image of his father. "You are the son Fazul spoke of," Kai said.

The boy's face, ruddy with emotion, tilted up, jaw clenched.

"Your father fought bravely," Kai said. "He was a hero, and he wanted you and your family to be free. Free you are, all of you. By my order, and order of the Caliph, you will receive a homestead and a year's stipend."

The boy's eyes were filled with tears, but they did not spill. He reached up to take the scroll that Kai offered. "If you have any other questions, or needs, come see me at my home, and I will ensure that they are answered or fulfilled." The boy nodded, clutching the papers of emancipation. Freedom. At the cost of death.

And doubtless wishing he could remain a slave, if only his father would come marching home again.

On the third day they made camp by the banks of the Tankwa canal. Only twenty survivors now remained: black and white soldiers had dispersed as the caravan traveled east, each to his own home and people. There were strained good-byes: for a short time they had simply been men who had survived an extreme experience. As they reentered the normal world the whites grew quieter, the blacks more distant, until finally they no longer shared songs and jokes and memories, just waved quietly as men who had saved their lives, or fought at their sides, returned to the roles they had inhabited before the Aztecs took the mosque.

Kai and Aidan sat side by side at the edge of a campfire. They talked, laughed, and sometimes shared a companionable silence, as they had in the old days. "Remember the hemp beer?" Aidan laughed.

"Remember?" Kai said. "My head rang for a week the first time. An evil brew." He paused, then added, "I could use a mug of it now!"

They laughed together until they were nearly sick. The camp had quieted down.

"How is your leg?"

Aidan slapped it, and winced. "Happy to still be part of my body."

"I think Sophia would kill me if I brought you back without all parts in working order." Kai stirred at the fire with a long branch. "You are officially ordered to immediately begin work on a collection of fine, strapping boys."

"And girls," Aidan sighed. "Sophia would like girls."

Kai crinkled his nose. "Do you really want girls, knowing that there are boys like us lurking about?"

"I'm a veteran now," Aidan said. "I can kill without mercy."

They laughed again, and talked more as the night wore on, and at length the campfire burned low. Kai and Aidan stretched their bags out beneath the stars, their heads close together.

"Remember those stars?" Aidan asked.

The night sky seemed infinitely clear, stretching up above Kai like some vast, eternal fire viewed only through pinpricks in black velvet. He thought the sky had never seemed so clear and deep. "I haven't seen them in a long time."

"They've been there," Aidan said, "waiting for us to notice them."

Kai let his gaze wander among those stars, feeling his fatigue reaching to swallow him, and with that fatigue a rare and treasured sense of contentment. So many stars. Could each of them really be a sun like that bringing life to Earth, as claimed the learned Dogon? And had almighty Allah gifted them with planets? And life? And if there was a plan that kept them all burning, all spinning, mightn't every living thing on all those worlds feel confusion, fear, anger, love, the need to find truth?

If there was, then no matter how things seemed to him now, how impossibly confused, he had to believe that there were answers as well as questions. Solutions as well as problems. He had to.

"I see them," Kai said. "I'll try not to forget them again."

CHAPTER SEVENTY-SIX

"If you would not fear the lion, you must be a lion yourself."

SWAHILI PROVERB

AFTER TWO MORE DAYS, only a weary dozen of Kai's men remained to cross over onto his ancestral land. Another half-day's travel brought them, by late afternoon, to the moat surrounding Malik's castle.

The fields, roads, and even the castle itself seemed almost deserted. The teff fields surrounding the castle looked ill worked, although a few slaves were hoeing among the rows.

The slaves saw them, but there was no joy in their faces, and no waves of greeting. They registered the newcomers, then turned back to their tasks.

Kai drove the lead wagon personally now, Aidan hunkered beside him on the thinly padded seat. "It's quiet," Kai said.

"Aye," Aidan replied. "For the moment."

After they crossed the moat Kai dismounted, and approached the main house. Just when Kai was beginning to wonder if Malik had taken his entire household on some manner of outing, horsemen appeared from around the side of the castle into the courtyard.

Malik's guard Quami was dressed almost formally, as if their arrival had been anticipated.

"*Asslaamu alaykum,* Kai," the Afari said, and saluted. "Welcome home. Word of your victory precedes you."

"*Waalaykum salaam.* Where is my uncle?"

Instead of answering him, they held their positions. He knew Malik's men were merely arrayed as an honor guard. Why, then, did his eyes keep roaming to their swords?

Finally, the lead guard said: "He comes."

Malik appeared from his castle's front gate, wearing light ceremonial armor under a white hemp robe. A red and white moon crest graced his chest. Its steel mesh and interlinked ringlets gleamed in the waning light. He saluted Kai, fist to heart. "Nephew!" he cried, approaching. "You make me proud. How your father would have wished to see you now."

They embraced, but in the instant before they did Kai saw that the armor was only partially polished. There were specks of cleaning compound caught in the mesh. Some ringlets gleamed, others were clearly tarnished.

"I am sorry to hear of Ali," Malik said. His face was a bit puffy. If Malik had been an unbeliever, Kai might well have thought him a drunkard. But Malik would not touch spirits, so whatever had affected him so had to be something deeper and more damaging. "We will mourn together."

Kai nodded, cautious and alert. In Malik's speech and carriage there was something too expansive, too deliberate. Behind his black beard, his eyes were too bright.

"Come, now," said Malik. "I have prepared a feast for you. Your men may take their horses to the barn—I will have food and drink brought to them."

Kai respectfully rested a hand on his uncle's shoulder, and set his feet more firmly. First things first. He pulled the scroll from his tunic. "Uncle Malik. I have an order here—"

Malik waved his hand dismissively. "Oh, that? Yes, I heard. Well, we can discuss that later. First, let me feast and celebrate you. Come!"

Kai held his ground. "Uncle? No. This must be settled now."

Malik became very quiet. His men were silent, as were Kai's. Even the wind refused to blow. Kai swallowed hard, his sense of alarm growing. Malik held his hand out, taking the scroll from Kai's hand. He read the scroll hurriedly. "This is not binding—my land was ceded to me for government service. It needs to be countersigned by the governor. When you do that, come back. But for now, let us feast!" He whirled, the hems of his robe swirling as if in a whirlwind.

Perhaps Kai would have followed his uncle in, shared meat and drink with him and delayed more serious discussions until later, but a pale, slender figure in the castle's main doorway caught his eye, a flicker of motion that made his heart glad.

"Aidan!" Sophia called. She was dressed in a kind of gold wraparound dress, something combining both Abyssinian and Moorish influence. Her eyes went to him with an uneasy mixture of greeting, joy, and fear. She ran from the house toward the wagon, and Aidan began to clamber down.

"Restrain her!" Malik said to his men. Qwami grabbed her arms.

"Sophia!" Aidan started forward, and Malik's men bristled, moving swiftly to form a curtain between the mamluk and his bride.

Kai's men, black and white, straightened on their horses or sat erect in the wagon. Several of them half pulled knives and swords before Kai raised his arm in brisk command. "Hold!"

Suddenly, whatever lethargy Kai had sensed in his uncle was gone, as if he had awakened from a twilight dream. Malik was as still as stone, his eyes flecks of arctic ice. "What is this? Your men draw arms in my house?"

"Uncle, I beg you," Kai said. "This is a simple case. This man has done service to the state—"

"As have I!" his uncle thundered.

"No one disputes that."

"No?" Malik asked, voice twisted with scorn. "*No?* Then why do you come to *my* home, telling me which of *my* possessions I may own and which I may not?"

"Please, Uncle. Obey the law . . ."

"The law? Obey the law?" Malik grabbed Sophia and pulled her forward. There was a blur of motion, and his jambaya was at her throat. Aidan froze. On horseback and in the wagons, Kai's men ceased all motion. Kai raised both hands, showing his palms, desperate to stop the situation's dreadful momentum.

"No one," said Malik, "will take what is mine, and she is *mine*. You want a slave? What—five slaves? Take five. Or twenty-five. But you cannot have this one." He paused, and Kai sensed that Malik was not merely telling him. He was, in his way, pleading with his nephew. "She is mine. You *cannot*."

"I can have the signature within a day," said Kai.

Malik's eyes gleamed. "Yes. And much can happen in a day. Due to the excitement, she might run away. We might never see her again."

Sophia's face was white with terror. The edge of the blade was tight against her throat: she could end her life merely by nodding her head.

"For love of Allah . . ." Kai whispered.

"Yes," said Malik. "For the love of Allah."

No one dared to move. Then, haltingly, Aidan limped down from the wagon. All eyes turned to him. Wounded, he could barely hobble, and each step seemed wrenching.

Silence, and then Aidan spoke. "As a free man," he said, "I have the right to trial by combat for the mother of my child." He seemed to search for words, and finally said, "May God decide which of us is righteous."

"Aidan," Kai begged. "Don't do this."

Aidan ignored him. "Malik Jallaleddin ibn Rashid al Kush, I challenge you to a duel."

Malik stared at Aidan in stark disbelief. Then his knife left Sophia's throat. Malik threw back his head and roared. Tears sparkled at the corners of his eyes when he finally desisted. "You must have lost your head as well as your heart. I accept."

The instant the words left Aidan's mouth, Kai felt as if someone had removed all of his internal organs and replaced them with ice. It was as if he had fallen down some kind of chute, sliding into a black, cold, pitiless place, a place without hope.

Aidan was a dead man, and everyone there, especially Aidan, knew it.

Malik called two servants, spoke to them briefly, and then stood, watching without speaking as several more brought a wide selection of weapons from his training hall.

Swords, pikes, battle-axes, knives, whips, staffs, shields—weapons Kai could name but had never trained in, and some he could not name.

Ali had allowed Aidan and Sophia to spend their waiting time together, and was behaving in an expansive, almost solicitous manner.

As Aidan limped along the line of weapons, Malik stripped to the waist. His chest hairs were grayer than Kai remembered, but his body itself was still like chocolate poured over rock.

"Aidan," Sophia whispered, the urgency in her voice carrying her words to Kai's ears. "You can't do this!"

"Yes," he said grimly. "I can."

"You're so badly wounded."

"Not as badly as you think," Aidan said, voice low. "Or *he* thinks. Don't worry, little one."

Kai backed away from Aidan and Sophia, stared with disbelief at his uncle, still stunned that this was actually going to happen. He felt as if he were watching the entire disaster through a telescope.

Malik whipped the air with his sword, then turned to Aidan. "Would you like more time to make your selection?" he asked. "Allow me to recommend the Gupta blade—it is a man-killer, and beautifully balanced. Or perhaps . . . the Turkish. Unusual design, but excellent for a man of strength and courage."

Aidan looked at Malik, and chose a blade similar to Malik's Moorish rapier, three and a half feet of Benin steel honed to a razor edge, with a full hand guard and contoured grip. He balanced it in his hand, chopped with it like an axe.

Kai winced. He knew that Aidan had more skill than that. Did he think that Malik would be lulled by such a charade?

Malik's smile broadened, almost as if he could read Kai's mind. "Shall we call for my surgeon?" he asked. "We could have your wounds rebound."

"No," Aidan said.

"And you are resolute in this?" Malik raised his voice. "All present hear clearly that this man, of his own free will, has challenged me for this woman's hand?"

There were murmurs of assent from the gathered.

"I can understand, of course. She is most exceedingly tender. But I fear it has been many, many nights since last she lay with you. Her body has, in all likelihood, forgotten yours—"

Howling, forgetting whatever stratagem he might have devised, Aidan attacked fiercely, wildly. Barely moving yet somehow completely avoiding the attack, Malik flicked his sword contemptuously, and pinked Aidan's left shoulder. Then, before Aidan could wheel, he transferred his blade from his right to his left hand. "It is good to give the weak side occasional practice," he said to Kai, as if the entire affair were of no more import than a training exercise.

Aidan attacked again. Malik was so far above the wounded mamluk that there was no competition at all. Aidan turned, swinging his sword like a club. Malik slid back a lightning step to gain a moment's time to adjust tactics, then sliced the tendons in Aidan's right arm. Sophia screamed but Aidan backed away, grimacing as he ripped off his shirt and wrapped it around his wound. Blood dripped to the ground, puddled on the tiles. Then, limping, Aidan picked the sword up with his left hand and stood before Malik again, who was warming to his work.

The next time Aidan lunged, Malik slipped the tip of his blade along Aidan's forehead. Blood streamed into his eyes.

Kai had had no hope for any positive outcome from this disaster, but with Aidan blinded, this had descended from butchery into some darkly, sadistically comic theater.

He watched his uncle touch Aidan again and again, each time with absolute fluidity and control. At any instant Malik could have set the blade in Aidan's throat or heart. He wanted to vomit: no slaughterhouse cow would be tormented like this.

Kai was stiff, unmoving, disbelieving. He met Sophia's eyes. She sagged with grief, her moment's crazed flare of hope extinguished. Her dark hair half masked her face. Her eyes streamed tears and she had turned her head away from the sight. Her man was so weak he could barely stand, meeting his death pointlessly.

Even Malik seemed to understand this. "It is time this nonsense ended," he said, and shifted his balance. Set his heel firmly against the ground. The next motion would be a half-speed feint to draw a sluggish block, followed by a disengagement and a killing lunge. Everyone knew it, even if they had not seen Malik perform a thousand times in the past. It was in his posture, in Aidan's grim resignation as he wiped blood from his eyes and prepared himself for one final effort. Sophia stifled a scream—

"Hold!" Kai heard someone scream, and then realized the single word had emerged from his own throat.

Even Malik was taken aback as he stepped back out of range. "What? Do you plead for this man's life?"

"No," Kai said, holding his voice steady. "No. As his commander, as an officer in the federal forces, as inheritor of the Wakil's manor and mantle, I proclaim that this man, honorably wounded in holy war, is unfit to continue this trial."

"My honor was challenged. You cannot merely end this."

"I do not. But you will."

Malik's right eyebrow raised in astonishment. "Or . . . ?"

"By right of arms, by all that is holy, I say that this man and his family are under my protection." Some small part of Kai struggled frantically to seize those words, reel them back before they passed the gate of his lips. This was insanity, and would avail nothing, lead to nothing but death.

"This is my house," Malik said. "I will not release her."

Moving in part to conceal the trembling of his limbs, Kai removed his cloak. "Then I must proclaim myself Aidan's champion," he heard himself say.

Malik stared at him. "This is madness."

Yes.

"Kai," Aidan gasped, on hands and knees. "No—"

Aidan staggered to his feet, blinded, crippled, exhausted, and pushed Kai away. Without taking his eyes from Malik, Kai caught Aidan's left arm, spun him, wrenched the sword from his hand and swept his feet from beneath him as if he were but a child. Aidan struggled to rise, and Kai kneed him under the jaw. Aidan flopped to his back and lay dazed.

"Well done." Malik, ever the teacher, seemed to be trying to smile. "But as always, your back was not straight."

"I apologize," Kai said. "After all your patient tutoring, I should know better."

Kai faced his uncle, fighting the growing sense of being separate from himself, floating above and beyond himself. *You're going into shock,* he thought. Breathe. Breathe. His uncle beckoned Kai forward until their faces were only digits apart. "You are superb, Nephew. But you of all people know that you are not my equal. I beg you to reconsider."

Kai inhaled, held it in the pit of his stomach, exhaled slowly. *Inhale the complexity of the world. Exhale Allah's essence. Allah hoo.* "Uncle," Kai said, judging every word carefully. "This man saved my life. He is the best friend I have ever had. He was wounded fighting for *our* mosque, when he could have gone free." He paused. "When you yourself were forced to remain behind." Malik flinched at that, and Kai knew he had struck a nerve. "There is no other course open to me. But you can end this honorably. Free Sophia."

Malik wavered. He looked back at Sophia, and she at him. The four of them seemed to exist in a place without sound, without time. Kai's troops, Malik's guards receded until they were all but vanished.

Malik seemed engaged in a titanic struggle. With what part of himself? What had he really lost in the Battle of Khartum? What was the gap between the outer man, the hero of a hundred battles, slayer of a thousand men, the great and invulnerable Malik, and the inner man, the man who had held his dead wives, who had so lovingly nurtured his nephew?

Sophia faced Malik: proud, beautiful, at the very height of her power as a woman. Kai remembered her gifts, even now was moved by the brand she had placed on his heart. And when Malik turned away from her, dropped his face, Kai knew that her strength had conquered his uncle when he was most vulnerable, knew before he spoke what his answer would have to be.

"Allah preserve me," Malik whispered. "I cannot." Almost a minute passed, and still the witnesses were frozen, suspended in time by the shocking turn of events. "You know that you cannot survive this."

Kai said nothing, but felt his jaw incline a fraction in assent. "Then let us pray together a final time."

Malik nodded. Without taking his gaze from Kai, he commanded: "Quami—bring my *kilim.*"

As Malik's chief guard hurried to the house, Kai went to his wagon, brought down his pack, obtained his own prayer rug, and unrolled it in the courtyard. Malik's rug came, and he laid it beside Kai's. They began to pray as the others watched.

"*Lá illah ha ill Allah.*"

Kai made two *rakats*, and then made *du'a*, supplication. *Holy Father*, he prayed. *I know not what You wish. I cannot follow my heart. My heart says to run, to turn away from this terrible thing in my path. But honor is a thing of the spirit, and it tells me that there is no other way through this. Help me. Help us both. Show us another way, or if not, let he who walks most fully in Your eternal light win the day.*

And if not that, let us die together.

Thy will be done.

When done they rolled the rugs up. Malik looked at Kai, trapped by his own madness. He took his nephew's shoulders and kissed his forehead.

"Good-bye," he said.

They buckled their sword belts around their waists, drew their swords, and faced each other, the breadth of an imaginary square between them.

Kai's insides had turned to water, but were now frozen. The fear had swollen to such a size that it was no longer a fire burning in his body. He now lived *within* the fear, was smaller than the thing that had eaten him. But in one sense that total envelopment helped. It was no longer a thing to be fought. It could not be fought.

He felt as if he were sitting cross-legged on the bottom of a lake, and the lake's surface burned with fire. Breathe. Focus. Stay at the bottom. To drift back into the real world meant floating back toward the surface. Meant rising into the flames.

Breathe.

Dimly he saw Aidan and Sophia at the corner of his vision. She had lifted him up, pulled her husband to the side, and held him tightly, his head in her lap, arms wrapped tight around his shoulders.

Malik fixed his baleful glare upon them. "Comfort your man well," he said. "After my nephew is dead, the *kufurin* will die a death few have known."

"Luck, Kai," Aidan managed to say.

There is no luck here. No victory. No hope.

Only honor, and dishonor.

Kai never took his eyes from Malik. "Allah preserve us both," he said.

Then he walked the circle, sword held perfectly at the center line of his body, pointing precisely at his uncle's center line. Malik walked in absolute syncopation, maintaining his fencing measure and position effortlessly.

Slowly, the circle evolved to a converging spiral. One digit at a time the distance between them closed as Kai brought himself into proper distance. Then, for the first time, Kai lunged. Malik parried with a barest flick of his wrist.

One final lesson.

Kai's opening gambit was purely exploratory. Weeks back, Malik had said that old war wounds were plaguing him. Kai now reckoned that it was emotional, not physical, ills that had prevented his uncle from accompanying them, but he needed to be certain. At Kai's level of skill, imperfections in balance could be detected in the smallest hesitations. Balance was never static. It was the product of a thousand tiny shifts, invisible to the untrained eye, looming large as the moon to an expert.

Malik's body still responded as sound and echo, light and shadow, in perfect proportion to stimulus. He was not aggressive—yet. Kai knew that Malik must be as reticent as he to commit, to make a move that would lead to a fatal wound for either of them. He knew his uncle. Despite his obsession, there was no question in Kai's mind that Malik hoped that this thing could be ended short of death.

Then in the next instant Malik had changed not lines but levels, dropped low as Kai corkscrewed his blade around, seeking reengagement. Kai dropped his stance and Malik disengaged with blinding speed and fluidity, changed levels again and cut Kai's forearm, returning to guard before Kai had time to feel the pain.

He cursed to himself, shifted his balance back, and in the instant that his weight was balanced equally between his feet Malik lunged. In the blink that it took Kai to shift his balance Malik's blade had touched his right shoulder, and then his lower pectoral. Pain flared as each cut ripped skin but spared muscle.

Kai whirled away, turned—and found Malik's sword at his throat.

"Submit, Nephew. I would not kill you."

Kai was terrified, the nearness of death wrenching him from his desperately woven cocoon of concentration. Without turning his head he could see the petrified Sophia and Aidan. He spun and parried and then exploded forward with every bit of speed he could muster. Malik chose to deflect rather than retreat, and the two men found themselves face-to-face, blades locked. Malik smashed Kai across the cheekbone with his sword's guard.

Firebursts blinded Kai as he reeled back, losing his grip on his weapon. Malik took a step back rather than pursuing. His eyes were narrowed and calculating, almost as if he were merely giving a lesson.

Kai scrabbled for his sword and then stood unsteadily, vision wavering. This wasn't working. What had he hoped for? That he could force his uncle to relent, to change his mind? To do that he had to gain his respect, to gain sufficient stature in Malik's eye that he would listen to his nephew. If not that, then to . . .

To . . .

Kai's mind refused to look further than that. There was no alternative, except death. But how to gain Malik's respect? Mere courage? Malik would expect no less. No, it was skill that might force Malik to see him differently. But Malik knew every move he could make, every tactic he might devise . . .

Or did he?

Kai quieted the ugly voices in his mind. He concentrated on Malik, who stood on the other side of the square, sword balanced lightly in his hand, its tip pointing down.

Calm. Waiting. Darkly amused.

Kai couldn't hold his gaze, and his face dropped to the square. His vision clouded again, and to his surprise he saw Babatunde's Naqsh Kabir superimposed over the square, its lines intersecting the square at oblique angles.

The Naqsh Kabir. Yes.

He attacked, lunging beautifully along a line of the square, then changed line to one of the Sign of the Presence of God's lesser angles. His leverage seemed stronger, and for the first time Malik exerted himself in the deflection, moving back and to the side, and the tip of Kai's sword came within a half-digit of Malik's chest.

Malik's eyes narrowed again, and he nodded, the barest hint of a smile creasing his lips. Malik lunged in again, and this time—Kai was certain— using his maximum practice intensity. There was a phrase of motion so fast and dangerous that Kai's conscious mind ceased functioning, and he was lost in a world of reflex, Malik's virtuosity forcing him to respond in similar pattern, until he was unable to remember his chosen tactic.

He felt himself leaving the bottom of the lake, drifting up where the water boiled, his survival instinct flaring and flashing and burning away his forced calmness, panic hammering at the doors of his resolve.

Kai jerked back as Malik slit his cheek, then fell as a deliberately broad stroke swept with decapitating speed toward his neck. He sat on the ground panting, looking up at the dark, massive figure looming over him, the sword in its hand already freshened with his blood.

If he had not yielded ground, had not in fact fallen before his uncle, that last stroke would have slain him. Malik's eyes were dark, huge. Cold. He knew his uncle's physical endurance, knew that he could not have tested it to any degree, and yet Malik's breaths were sharp and deep. He was sweating, and the iron bands of his chest rose and fell like the gears of some massive machine.

"Your last chance, Kai," Malik panted. "The fever is almost upon me. The men of our family burn with it. Your father knew its heat, and it has been my curse. Turn back now, before it is too late."

As Kai stood again the world was wavering, concussed. He charged, came straight at his uncle, then stopped, veered, engaged swords with delicacy then slid to the side and, before Malik could adjust lines, charged again. The change of lines, tempos, intensities and tactics, all in the blink of an eye, confused the sword master just enough to get Kai close before Malik could disengage blades and skewer him.

For an instant Kai was at close range, and before his uncle slid away he slammed a knee toward Malik's groin, a blow Malik twisted to avoid. In that instant Kai dropped his sword and gripped Malik's right wrist with both of his hands, wrenching and torquing desperately, disarming his uncle with a move that left him open for a countering elbow.

But Kai knew that response, had seen it and felt it a dozen times, and was already moving away from it as it arced in over his shoulder and splintered his jaw. Agony exploded, but instead of moving away Kai came in, head-butting, hammering with fists and knees in a blind whirl, until a short blow to the pit of his stomach dropped him. Kai hit the ground, rolled out, and came up—between Malik and the swords.

The side of his face ached and he spit what felt like a splinter of cracked tooth. Kai blinked blood out of his eyes and managed to focus.

His uncle's nose bled, and there was a gash in his scalp across his left eye. He stood in a crouch now, all trace of avuncularity vanished. In his right hand he held his jambaya, fourteen digits of gleaming death.

Kai drew Nasab Asad. Again, after a moment of clarity, he had descended into dream. He held his father's blade. His brother's. And faced the deadliest warrior in New Djibouti.

His uncle.

The two men circled, each slashing at the other's exposed limbs. Kai let Malik rip the back of his left arm to get a nick in on his uncle's right wrist.

It was a beautiful move. A warrior's move. The two men fell into a rhythm of steel, a dance so deadly that few men could even follow the pace, let alone survive or triumph.

Blend. Break. Evaluation. Blend. Malik's blade, lightning quick, scarred

Kai's face just above the eye, but Kai kicked Malik's knee. Malik smashed Kai's foot, but then his uncle hobbled back. Kai was half blind now. Malik tested his knee, and found it good. He circled Kai to his blind side, and Kai turned to face him.

He knew what would happen now, now that he had, through terrible and near total exertions, damaged Malik. Now his uncle would kill him. Now would come an ending.

But if that was his fate, he would face it as a man. And if necessary, perhaps the very nature and manner of his death would awaken that compassion that his words and efforts had not.

Insh'Aallah.

Malik's face, crimsoned and cold, flickered for a moment, and Kai was not certain if that was merely his vision, or whether something had, for a moment, broken through the wall around Malik's heart. Like a fish in a frozen pond, something had come near the surface for just a moment, and then vanished.

Then Malik began the ending, creeping closer, his blade held low and extended in his right hand, the left back a length, his entire body a weapon.

Kai abandoned his life, and joined the dance.

What Kai had seen within Malik's eyes was indeed a phantom: the phantom of his own image, lost in the mist of years.

Never had Malik intended to kill or even to cripple his nephew. A swift disarm followed by a beating that would warn him from future misadventure, then to reckoning with the rebellious slave and the woman Sophia.

But nothing was working right, not since the night his brother died. No, that was wrong. Not since the night of Fatima's death, when he had taken the witch Sophia in her room, and in some way she had taken him in return. Abu Ali's death had widened the wound, so that it seemed he could not heal, could not mend, could only stanch the dark outflow of his life force with Sophia's body. Malik hated himself for his weakness. And that very hatred increased the flow.

When he sat alone in his study, he could hear the voices of the men he had slain. If he closed his eyes he could see their faces, and their cold, bloody fingers seemed to grip at him from the pit of hell. He had been at the edge of death, had peered into the depths. Had seen no light. Felt no sheltering touch of a loving God.

The faith that sustained Abu Ali was not his. Malik had knelt in prayer fifty thousand times, and never felt Allah's grace. Not for a moment. He had felt the fire of hell, and knew that it burned for him. There was no God, no force of light in the universe. There were only men and their endless struggles to make meaning.

And there was Satan, who had taken his wife, had taken his brother and his nephew, had brought the witch into his heart so deeply that he had come to this.

Only her flesh held back the dead. Only her lips offered salvation. Only in her arms could he find dreamless sleep.

So he would humble this boy, and then kill the slave. And Malik would continue down the road to hell, taking nightly solace in unwilling arms.

He had made his devil's pact, but then . . .

In his vision, for a disturbing instant, he faced not a man of twenty, but a boy of eleven, with the full promise of life before him. Such a clever boy was Kai! So quick to learn, so nimble-minded. A lover of books, but deep within those mischievous brown eyes burned the same fire that had raged in his father, before Abu Ali turned so fully toward Allah. The same fire that had consumed Malik's soul when Allah had denied him His light.

All creatures seek the light, and if denied the glory of heaven, they will warm themselves at the fires of hell.

It was not a boy he faced, but a man! A man who had defied him, whose men had drawn arms in his house. A man who had wounded Malik in the presence of his retainers, and had to be punished, severely.

But . . .

He saw that boy, and in that vision time seemed to yield. No longer were they in a courtyard, fighting for life and honor. They were in his exercise chamber, practicing. Malik's beautiful wife Fatima watched them, beaming.

See how young Kai holds his sword! A small sword, a child's sword, smaller and lighter than a man would carry, but still a thing of good steel and sharp edge. And Kai used it so earnestly, thrusting and blocking and dancing through his paces at Malik's command.

How exciting to be so young, just taking the first halting steps along the road of life. As the younger brother, Kai shared a bond with Malik that most could not understand. And there was within him a spark of genius, a spark that Malik would nurture into a full flame. Ali would become Wakil, but it was Kai, studious Kai, who would carry on the true family tradition, winning honor and glory, expanding the ancestral lands with grants from Alexandria. And when the moment came to strike for independence, General Kai would join voices with Wakil Ali, and lead their country into the future.

And how proud Malik would be. Abu Ali had provided the fleshly spark, but he, Malik, had actually fathered the boy.

How proud.

Then his vision wavered, and he saw the adult Kai again. The precise same expression: fear, determination, the fierce pride that marked the men of his family.

The boy was wounded, had fought bravely, but had slowed down now. That was inevitable, although he had displayed sheer genius in the middle game. The way he had changed lines of engagement! And that disarm, sacrificing the jaw that now swelled like a melon, on the off chance that fortune would favor him better with knife than sword!

Kai's life fluid puddled on the tile beneath his feet. His legs trembled, and he raised a hand to wipe blood from his brow.

He is almost finished, Malik thought. To test his theory Malik probed the outer edge of Kai's circle. Kai attempted a clumsy riposte and evaded.

No, no, young Kai. When a man attacks, he leaves an opening. Find it!

Kai seemed to be swaying. From exhaustion, or . . . ? Almost as if he could hear music, notes dancing magically on the wind. He moved almost like a belly dancer. A trap? Intrigued, Malik slashed, and Kai evaded with a bit more grace, actually invited Malik to overextend, and then swept his foot from under him.

Malik rolled away and Kai lunged after him, slashing and stabbing. An exquisite, hopeless move. Malik spun, nearly sweeping Kai's legs from beneath him as his nephew scrambled back. Malik rose. His courageous, doomed, beloved Kai had spent himself, could barely hold the three debens of steel aloft.

A single tear rolled down Malik's cheek. "Yield," he whispered.

Kai lunged at him. Behind them, the witch Sophia screamed. It was Kai who lost his concentration for a moment, and Malik cut his wrist, disarming him.

This was the moment. He could close, could cripple the boy without killing him . . .

He closed for the death stroke, but was suddenly overwhelmed by the image of young Kai again, looking up at him, face smeared with blood. Then young Kai's face was clean, and beautiful, staring up with respect and adoration at a younger, better man, the man that Malik once had been.

"Kai," Malik whispered.

*   *   *

Malik hesitated on the death stroke. Kai's head crashed forward, a final, desperate move, striking Malik on his already broken nose. Malik stumbled back, dazed, pulling Kai with him. As Kai went down he scooped up the fallen knife, and they collapsed together. There was a single sharp, despairing cry.

And then silence.

Sophia and Aidan were shocked and motionless, his fingers locked with and nearly crushing hers. His blood mingled with her tears. He had barely breathed since Kai had stepped in to take his place, had never dared hope that any such miracle might delay his death. Certainly he did not believe in salvation. Not at this late date.

To lose his woman, his life, and his best friend on the same day . . . that was an unholy joke, that was the cruelest twist since that cold morning, half an eternity before, when dragons had glided out of the mist and destroyed his world.

He felt Sophia's breath, hot against his cheek, her fingers clutching his hard enough to crack a nut.

Kai and Malik lay tangled on the ground, limbs splayed like the dead. Neither moved. Then Kai pushed himself up, rose tottering on unsteady legs, his shirt covered with blood. He took a single step, then staggered and fell. Malik rolled him away.

The sword master stood, gazing down at his nephew, eyes filled with grief. "Look—" he said, then blood gushed from his open mouth, and he collapsed to his knees, and then fell onto his side, Kai's knife in his back.

Kai rolled over onto his side and looked at his uncle. Gingerly, as if each was afraid of breaking the other, the two men held each other. Malik's face held no more anger, no more pain. It was soft, and proud. He reached out with a single bloody finger and traced a crimson line along Kai's swollen jaw. "Care for Azinza. Present her to the Empress."

Kai swallowed, and it felt like shards of broken glass scraping down his throat. As the adrenaline of combat began to retreat, pain rumbled through his body like an avalanche. "As if she were my own."

"I remember your first step," Malik said. "How proud . . . how proud your father . . ." His face softened as the muscles went slack. Suddenly, strangely, Malik's head felt . . . *lighter.*

There was silence in the courtyard as Kai laid his uncle's head gently on the tile. Very slowly, he tugged at Nasab Asad's handle until the blade slid free of Malik's body. Fighting for every digit of motion, Kai stood.

He looked like a scarecrow dipped in blood. He wavered, almost fell, and then caught himself again. "By right of combat and inheritance, by law and will, I proclaim myself lord of this manor. The woman Sophia and her child are free." He raised his chin, faced Malik's guard defiantly. "Is there challenge? Is there?" The tip of his jambaya trembled. "If there is challenge, I . . . by Allah, I . . ."

Kai spiraled and fell to the ground.

PART FIVE

The Wakil

"Why are we here?" asked the student, who was in crisis.

The Master saw his pupil's genuine pain, and considered his answer carefully. "God said: 'I was a hidden treasure, and I loved to be known, so I created the universe that I might be known.'"

"If God made the world, with all its pain, how can God be good?"

"He gave us not only pain, but joy. And more, that which births and reconciles both."

"Which is . . . ?"

CHAPTER SEVENTY-SEVEN

After a war life catches
Desperately at passing
Hints of normalcy like
Vines entwining a hollow
Twig

CHINUA ACHEBE, NIGERIAN WRITER

1 Shawwal 1290
(November 22, 1873)

WITH THE PASSAGE OF TIME, life on Dar Kush returned to normal. The servants worked the beans and teff and hemp, and the Kikuyu grazed their cattle in the fallow quarter. Hammers rang sparks in the quarries, and horses and colts ran through the glade.

The workers prepared for the feast of Idd-el-Fitr. Cattle were roasting on spits over deep beds of coals. Tables and chairs were set in neat rows, linen picnic squares spread for visiting commoner families, bowls of fruit and piping fresh bread were heaped in abundance. And the neighbors arrived, royalty and commoners alike. The festivities began.

Near the balcony, the dirt farmers and poor laborers of the district gathered. On this night, it was customary for the lord of the manor to make speeches and distribute alms.

One of the guests, a round-shouldered man with a dark, creased face and a frayed hemp shirt, was impatient. "When do we begin?"

"The master speaks first," said Olaf. His wounds had healed, and since returning from the war he had been emancipated. He had been given the option of a payment in gold or a job as a foreman on Dar Kush. Ironically perhaps, he had chosen foreman. "It's tradition."

"I hear that he hasn't been seen since his return from the wars!" said Khadija, one of Djidade Berhar's three slender, small-hipped wives.

"Mommy," her youngest child said. "I'm hungry!"

"Soon, Mada. I hope." But then, feeling her own stomach rumbling, "Where *is* the Wakil?"

The hundreds of guests on the lawn began a chant:

"*Kai! Kai!*"

"*Kai! Kai!*"

The chant echoed in the great house, through the busy halls bustling with servants, up the stairwells and even in the Wakil's athenaeum, as Aidan entered with Sophia and their child, Mahon, now seven months old.

He blinked rapidly, willing his eyes to adjust to the darkness in Wakil Abu Ali's study. No. He corrected himself. *Wakil Kai*, he thought.

Kai stood before the great desk, speaking with an Ibo nurse who held Kai's niece, Azinza. His eyes were sunken and he had lost five pounds from his spare frame. It seemed to Aidan that the things Kai had seen and done and lost in the last months had stolen what remained of his boyhood. If he heard the shouting outside his window, he didn't or couldn't respond.

"Her mother's eyes," Kai said, his voice as flat as hammered copper. "Nurse, please take Azinza to the nursery. Care for her well."

Sophia and Aidan stood waiting, uncertain. Unspeaking. Aidan had not spoken to Kai for weeks, and felt awkward and oddly nervous.

"Aidan," Kai said. "Your wounds are healed."

"Most, yes. The others, given time. But some . . ."

"Some wounds never heal completely," Kai finished. His fingers scraped lightly at his desktop, as if digging his uncle a second grave.

"There will always be scars," Aidan said.

"Yes." A pause, and then: "What have you decided?"

Sophia pointed to the map on the study's main wall. "We've decided to seek the northwestern frontier," she said. "Wichita province. There is good land there."

Kai grew quiet, and somehow smaller. "There is good land here as well, should you want it. Should you wish to stay."

Pause. How many hours had Aidan and Sophia spent talking about this? In his heart, Aidan knew how much Kai had done, what he had sacrificed, in order to keep his word to the mamluks. To keep his word to Aidan. Had Kai slept a full night since that awful day?

Part of Aidan wanted to stay, to help his friend heal, to help him make a life.

But . . . he just couldn't. Too much death and degradation, too much wealth built on the sweat of men and women who didn't own their own bodies. Too many graves. Too many memories.

"We want to make a new life together, Kai," he said. "Eire and Andalus are both alien to us now. This is our country. We would make our own world."

Kai's eyes closed. "You could stay for the feast," he said. "It is nearly sundown. Perhaps you could make a start in the morning?"

Sophia shook her head. "We are meeting with another family tonight, five miles up the road. They're expecting us, Kai."

Aidan's heart ached, and he wondered what visions played against those tightly shut lids. They opened. "Well, then, this is good-bye. There are papers for you to sign." Kai's words were so devoid of emotion, so tightly controlled, they might have emerged from a puppet.

Aidan examined the first paper, and his breath caught:

DECLARATION OF EMANCIPATION it said, continuing on in cursive script to detail how one Aidan O'Dere and his family were free for all time, with all of the rights of citizenship, earned through distinguished service to the throne.

Hand shaking, he signed, and then Sophia signed.

Kai managed the ghost of a smile. "And there is a matter of finance," he said.

Aidan held up a protesting hand. "We don't need anything."

"Please," said Kai. "Consider it a gift. From a grateful nation, and one who wishes you well."

He opened a desk drawer, extracting another parchment, and a leather sack. Again, his every motion was measured and precise. Sophia opened the sack, and as she did her eyes widened. Aidan took the parchment.

"What is this?" he asked.

"A piece of land on the frontier. Sophia spoke to me of Wichita province some weeks back, and I made an investment in property. I would like you to evaluate it for me. If you would be my eyes and ears, a piece of it is yours. A trading post half a day away holds a year's supplies for you on credit."

Aidan wanted to protest, but his senses swam. His own land! And if he knew Kai, it was fertile, and defensible. Dear God, even in the midst of his anguish and loss, Kai had provided for his friend. "Kai . . ."

"Please," Kai said. "There is farming, and fishing there. A trusted broker says that there is a mountain so green it glows in the morning. That the lake's waters are fed by a stream so thick with fish a man can catch them by hand." His eyes were far away, crinkling at the edges, his voice slightly warmed by whatever they saw. "I hope it will remind you of home."

"I'm sure it will," Aidan said. He reached across the desk and shook Kai's hand. It felt hard, and cool. "Perhaps we'll meet again."

"If it is the will of God."

Sophia rounded the desk. As she approached, Kai's eyes dropped to the desktop. She took his face in her hands, turned it, and gently kissed his lips. "You are a good man, Kai, and I love you for what you have done."

His face softened a bit, just for a moment. Aidan swore he glimpsed something raw and screaming behind the mask. Then the moment was over. Sophia stepped back. "Good-bye," she said.

Aidan gripped her hand as he turned, needing her to take him out of that place, needing her to carry him away from darkness and the past, toward a new life together.

He heard, but did not see, Kai release all strength with a deep and despairing sigh, then collapse heavily into the chair behind the desk.

Aidan and Sophia descended the stairs, Sophia balancing Mahon easily against her hip. As they passed the first landing, Lamiya and Babatunde emerged from a side hallway. The imperial niece was radiant in her white mourning gown, a single gold braid circling her slender neck. She and Sophia faced each other, and then Sophia bowed, hand over her heart. Lamiya inclined her head graciously.

"You are leaving now?" asked Lamiya.

"Yes, mistress," Sophia said automatically. She caught herself almost in midsentence and bit her lip, perhaps wondering at the proper mode of address.

"You should call me Lamiya." A smile curled the dark, lovely lips behind the veil. "You are free now. Enjoy your lives together. I wish you well."

"Thank you," Aidan said. How strange. He had known this woman since she was a girl, and had never thought to call her by her name. Even now it seemed stuck on the tip of his tongue. "Lamiya. I do not wish to presume, but . . . what of you? Will you stay?"

"I am called home," she said.

"And Kai will marry Nandi?" asked Sophia.

"The Zulus have broken communication," Babatunde said quietly. Lamiya glared at him. Babatunde folded his fingers together, saying nothing more.

"Lamiya," Aidan said, and shook his head ruefully. "I can't believe I have known you all these years, and never called you by name." He laughed uneasily. "In many ways Dar Kush is my home, and it hurts to leave, but I must."

"I understand."

"But, Lamiya . . . isn't this your home as well?"

"I am called home," she repeated, but now looked a bit uneasy. Aidan noted her reaction with interest. He had often seen the way Kai looked at Lamiya, but had never seriously asked himself what, if anything, she might feel for him in return.

"We should be on our way," Sophia said.

"Travel safely," said Babatunde, with a slight bow of his head.

"Long life," said Lamiya.

Aidan took Sophia's arm and led her gently away. In many ways the boy he had grown up with was dead and gone. Any obligations between them had been thoroughly discharged. What remained were the affairs of the nobility, and those he could not pretend to understand.

But as he descended the stairs he thought, *Luck, Kai. And life. And love, my friend.*

Babatunde watched Aidan and his family depart. He felt an unexpectedly deep contentment, as well as a sense of gratitude to be witness to a tiny part of Allah's great design. Beside him, Lamiya sighed.

"It is good to be free," Babatunde said. "To go where one will, to marry whom one wants."

Lamiya's small, perfect teeth gnawed at her lip. "Babatunde," she whispered. "I have been raised all my life to do as the Empress bids."

"Yes."

"I am a *feqer näfs*. A soul mate. With Ali dead, I must never marry, must live a celibate, or the Empress will have me declared a nonperson. I would never see my family again."

Babatunde closed his eyes. "Freedom is not a gift. It is a responsibility. The Empress has given her command, but you must decide your own course of action. Tell me, child, if the Empress was motivated as much by politics as spirit, what did she wish from your union with Ali?"

"The wealth and influence of Dar Kush," she answered.

"History has shown," he said, "that kings and queens find ways to justify that which increases their power and security. And I know the woman who sits on the throne of Abyssinia well enough to know something that you do not."

Lamiya turned to Babatunde as he opened his eyes. "What is that?" she said, voice full of hope.

"That the Empress will be furious if you follow your heart."

"Yes." Lamiya lowered her head.

"But, my child," Babatunde said, "your aunt will understand, and love you always."

CHAPTER SEVENTY-EIGHT

In the end, a man is alone with his own fate.

SWAHILI PROVERB

KAI SAT IN HIS FATHER'S CHAIR, fingering the edge of his father's knife and counting his heartbeats. How many of them a day? How many more in a dishonored life?

He had hoped that Aidan might stay, might see that Dar Kush could be his home as well, but that hope had been dashed. He couldn't blame his old friend. If he himself could leave, he would.

But this place, which had been his home for so many years, now promised to be his prison. As his word of honor had been his prison. As had his heart. He listened to its beats, counting them. So many dead now, so many gone.

His father. Dead at the hands of a man now dead.

His brother. Dead at the hands of a man now dead.

His uncle. Dead at the hands of a man who wished he was dead.

The study door opened. Kai glanced up, only faintly curious. Lamiya stood in the doorway. Once upon a time, the sight of her had made his heart happy. Now he tasted only ashes.

Kai did not rise, or offer her greeting. She would probably leave within the week. He wished her well. He wished he could remember the boy who had loved her so deeply. *That was a good lad,* he thought. *Rest easy. You were my heart, and you are dead. The rest of me will follow as swiftly as possible.*

Distantly, he realized that Lamiya had begun to speak. "—can only say this once," she was saying. "I have not the strength or the will to repeat it. My marriage to your noble brother was born of necessity. My aunt needs Bilalistan's minerals and resources, and your father needed our political support."

Yes, yes. All of these things were true. Why was she telling him things that he already knew?

"I was born and raised to be the link between our nations," she said. "There is only one way I can fulfill that destiny, Kai, and that is as your wife."

What right had she, a guest in his house, to mock his pain? To twist the knife that should have pierced his heart, not Malik's? He must send her away. *Do it, now,* a voice within him said.

Before you believe what she just said.

Kai's hands tightened upon the hilt. So sharp, the blade. So eager to drink deep. A swift journey to the darkness that haunted his family, had taken everything he loved.

He listened to his heartbeat. It had doubled. His head felt flushed, and his hand, so steady it barely seemed a living thing, shook like an opium addict denied his poison.

"Everyone wants to know what the new Wakil will do," he whispered. Why had he said that? Said *anything* to this woman who tormented him with what he dared not even hope he could have?

"What do you want?" she asked.

His sigh was as vast and deep as the ocean. "To leave this world," he said, voice completely reasonable and calm. "It has shown me nothing worth the price of living."

His throat closed. His head fell upon his crossed arms, and he felt the tears burning down his cheeks. Disgraceful. He had kept them away, fearing that once they began they would not stop, and now this woman, in her infinite cruelty, had broken the dam.

"Damn you," he whispered.

He felt something, like a butterfly grazing his shoulder and then fluttering away. He knew that she had come close, had almost touched him, then had pulled back. Of course. Who would not be repelled by such a spectacle?

"How *dare* you," she said, voice filled with scorn. "You who have spoken so often of honor and duty. Who spoke of a slave's obligation to those who feed and support him. Well, what of the obligations of the master? What of the obligations of you who slept on silk at the right hand of your father? You have lost much. Your father and brother and uncle watch you, now, at this moment, wondering what manner of man it is who has inherited their world. *This*," she stormed, "is the moment you were born and bred for. This, none other. Who is the man to whom I have offered my sacred honor?"

Now he looked up. Her words were full of wrath but behind them was something even hotter. Not pity, for which he might have struck her dead with the knife in his hand. Not love, which he could not have believed or accepted. No, something else.

Fear. But of what? Of him? Or herself?

"Who are you, Kai?"

Who are you, Kai? Indeed. And who was she? Who was Lamiya Mesgana, behind her veils and gold and the shadow of the Empress? Hidden in her words, behind her words, was another ocean, seething with unspoken emotion.

Then suddenly he heard himself say the words he had no right to ask, a question to which he wished no honest answer. "Do you love me?" he said, the words fumbling from his lips. "Could you?"

"I belong," she said, "to the man who is master of this house."

He could not answer, could not move. Her words. Her eyes, the richness of her lips hypnotized him. What was she saying? The entire world seemed suspended.

Suddenly her hand blurred, cracking him across the cheek. "Damn you!" The pain was distant, but roared and swooped. Ringing through his head to disperse the ensnaring fog.

Lamiya slapped him again, and this time he blinked. *Allah preserve me. What is this? What is she saying? Does she realize . . . ?* His emotions rose, swelled, vanquished reason.

When she raised her hand a third time he grabbed her wrist and lurched to his feet. Their faces were very close, and no mortal force could have stopped him from pulling her to him, tasting her lips, finding there the meaning he had found nowhere else. He broke away, gazing deeply into her eyes, looking for lies, evasion, manipulation . . . or love.

Seeing nothing but fear. And then, when he kissed her again, something else.

Hope.

"Pick up the knife," she whispered.

Moving stiffly at first, and then with greater purpose, Kai thrust his father's blade into his belt and strode to his balcony to face the waiting crowd.

It was just sunset, but the torches cast their wavering brightness into the long shadows.

As he stepped out, the crowd went silent. He looked out upon his father's estate, on the people now relying upon him, on all he had inherited, for good or ill.

If he squinted, he imagined he could see Aidan and Sophia, traveling the northern road toward whatever fate awaited them. Yes. There they were, translucent in the dimming light, traveling just beyond the gate. Aidan seemed to stop, and turn. To search the house until he saw Kai. He waved.

Slowly, Kai waved back.

Perhaps thinking that the gesture had been intended for them, the crowd roared in response.

Kai looked back into the study, and saw Babatunde standing in the doorway, face placid. Things were what they were, nothing more or less. Had the little Yoruba always known that life could play such horrific tricks? Something in the trace of a smile on the round dark face told him the answer was *yes*.

He beckoned Lamiya forward onto the balcony. Her hand slipped into his. It was small and strong and warm. She would marry him, and he would do all in his power to ensure that Bilalistan's wealth continued to flow to the throne of Abyssinia. That if war came, Bilalistan's armies would not fight against the Empress.

Lamiya would bear him children, and in time the wounds of the past might heal. Might.

Allah, why have you brought me to this place? What man could be worthy of such damnation and such grace?

Then, left hand joined with the hand of his future wife, jambaya raised in his right, Kai spoke aloud: "Welcome to all who wish us well. There has been strife, and war, and care, but now is a time of feasting. Let all men be brothers this day," he said, his voice rolling resonantly unto the multitudes, "breaking bread and lifting our glasses in celebration. Let the feast of Idd-el-Fitr begin!"

And he looked out over the estate, and the vast holdings bought with the sweat and blood of good men, and the crowd, and the road which now held only ghosts and promise . . .

The purpled fields and shadowed mountains as the last glimmering of the sun disappeared in the west . . .

And his eyes closed, the warm pressure of Lamiya's hand the single thread connecting Kai of Dar Kush to the things of this world.

EPILOGUE

FOUR TIMES IN AS MANY HOURS Aidan and his family were stopped by road patrols and forced to show their documents to men with small eyes and angry mouths. It seemed almost physically painful for these patrolmen, most of low birth, to admit that their documents were genuine, the Wakil's seal and signature unimpeachable, and grant them the open road.

Sophia said almost nothing the entire trip, but held their child and leaned against his shoulder, holding his arm as if the sweet contact itself were almost more pleasure than flesh could bear.

They carried more than the documents of freedom: they carried a map detailing their entire passage west, showing places where free whites might find shelter and food along the way.

It was almost dark before they reached the first spot on the map, designated as a small town.

It was all clapboard and cheap, straw-heavy brick, only four buildings off a tiny path branching from the main road. CONOR'S, read the sign.

There were a cluster of wagons and horses outside the longest and lowest of the buildings, and a white man with heavy jowls and substantial girth sat next to one of the horses, foot in a puddle of horse piss, swilling from a brown bottle. He seemed on the thin edge between sleeping and consciousness. Aidan reckoned he'd have no trouble from the drunk, but still lashed up their horses to a tree some cubits away. He helped Sophia down from the wagon and entered the main building.

As they approached the door he heard fiddle music, and almost couldn't believe his ears—it was a song he hadn't heard since it was played by the red-haired witch, a lifetime ago in O'Dere crannog. Could it be . . . ?

But when they came through the doors the music stopped, and every head in the room turned to face them. Now that the sun had set, the only light came from a pair of oil lamps. There were a dozen whites in the room, two children, a pair of oldsters, and eight or nine souls of prime working age.

His eyes sought the source of the music, and was vaguely disappointed to see that it had been played by a toothless old man. Though gray and balding, his hands were nimble enough with the bow.

At the back of the room was a table shaped like half a wheel, with a well-upholstered woman behind it. She regarded them suspiciously.

"Are ye free?" she asked. "We 'ave no need a' mischief 'ere."

Aidan showed her his papers, and she squinted at them, and then nodded. The mood in the room seemed to change completely, smiles and nods now that they knew he was no runaway who might bring the law down upon them.

"Aidan!" thundered a voice behind them, and he turned into Donough's crushing embrace. The two men buffeted each other mightily. Then the giant just hugged him, and Aidan squeezed him back, fighting not to let the tears fall from his eyes.

"You made it, little man," Donough said, grin splitting his bandaged face.

"I made it."

Donough shuffled his feet shyly. "And this must be Sophia?" He held out a bearlike hand, and she took it.

There was a giggling sound behind Donough, and he stepped aside as a tiny woman with a sharp, sunburnt face came forward, carrying a bundle of baby. Donough seemed even more nervous. "This is Mary," he said.

Something shifted in his demeanor, became challenging. "And this is my son, Donough," he said. Several of the drinkers roused themselves sufficiently to make appropriate cooing sounds.

Mary let them peel the blanket away. Donough was large for a child so obviously young, with dark eyes, dark hair . . . and dark skin.

There was silence in the room. Donough's arm tightened around Mary. One of the drinkers spit on the floor, muttered something under his breath, and waddled away.

Sophia was the first to speak. She reached out with a long, slender finger and traced the sleepy child's cheek.

"He has his mother's eyes," she said. "And will have your strength, Donough."

Aidan slammed an Alexander on the bar. "Drinks!" he cried. "All around! Tomorrow we head for the frontier, but tonight, we celebrate life and friendship!"

The woman behind the bar's eyes went round and wide. "We canna make change for that, and 'ave nothing worthy of it," she said. "Not if ye paid for every mug in the house."

"You're a pretty liar," he said. "It will be the first taste I have had as a free man. You could piss in a cup and it would taste like nectar."

She grinned at him. "We can do better than that," she said, and dragged up a brown jug. "Me 'usband makes it 'imself. Ain't much, but it's the best we got."

"It'll do," Aidan said. She poured four cups, and then four more, and then for the entire house.

"To tomorrow," Aidan said. And toasted his wife, and his old, newfound friend, and Donough's elfin wife. The core of the new crannog he would build. Yes. He would make safety for his family, and then he would make money in this wild land, and he would use every penny he could squeeze to find Nessa.

Keeping my promise, Ma. Here's to you, and to everyone who ever loved me. The best is yet to come.

He took a swig, and almost spit it out. Choked it down. The liquor was pure liquid fire as it burned its way down his throat, dizzying poison fit only for cleaning armor or filling lamps.

It was also, he decided, the very finest draught of his entire life.

AFTERWORD

THE SYMBOL OF THE NASQ KABIR, "The Sign of the Presence of God," which figures prominently in this work of fiction, is indeed real, and might be considered a "paper computer" diagramming nonlinear process. In the Western world it is often called the Enneagram, and is little known other than through several books on personality, which present less than 1 percent of the actual teachings. Traditionally, one must find a master to receive oral instruction. One of the very few genuinely informative works on this subject is A.G.E. Blakes's *The Intelligent Enneagram*.

Among the other books which provided blessed assistance in the writing of *Lion's Blood* are the following:

On Islam and Sufism: *Essential Sufism*, edited by James Fadiman and Robert Frager, *The Sun Will Rise in the West*, by Shaykh Taner Ansari, *The Prescribed Prayer Made Simple*, by Tajuddin B. Shu'aib, *Principles of Islamic Teachings*, by the Islamic Education Center.

On African culture: *The Rise and Fall of the Zulu Nation*, by John Laband, *The Golden Age of the Moor*, by Ivan Van Sertima, *Encyclopedia Africana*, edited by Henry Louis Gates and Kwame Anthony Appiah, *African Kings*, by Daniel Laine, *African Ark*, by Carol Beckwith and Angela Fisher, *Bless Ethiopia*, by Kazuyoshi Nomachi, *The Washing of the Spears*, by Donald R. Morris, *The Anatomy of the Zulu Army*, by Ian Knight.

On Irish Culture: *A Literary History of Ireland*, by Douglas Hyde, *The Celtic World*, edited by Miranda Green, *Life in Celtic Times*, by A. G. Smith and William Kaufman, *The Glories of Ireland*, edited by Joseph Dunn and P. J. Lennox. Of particular interest (considering this author's limitations) was *The Complete Idiot's Guide to Irish History and Culture*, by Sonja Massie.

And on the nature and nurture of cultures and civilizations themselves, Jared Diamond's wonderful *Guns, Germs and Steel*, without which, to try to understand why history played out as it did, one must resort to the loathsome, politically motivated reductionism of *The Bell Curve*.

The poem shared by Kai and Lamiya on their way to Djibouti harbor was indeed written by the fourteenth-century poet Hafiz.

Major events in this alternate chronology given Gregorian dates might well map in the following fashion:

400 B.C. Socrates leaves Athens for Egypt.

380 B.C. A wounded Alexander has visions of completing his life as a pharaoh.

200 B.C. Egypt and Carthage defeat Rome.

A.D. 623 Treaty of Khibar: Muhammad approves a nonaggression mutual assistance pact with the Jews. Establishment of Judea follows.

632 Death of Muhammad.

650 Bilal rescues Muhammad's family at Karbala.

701 "Black Barges on the Nile"—germ warfare against the royal house of Egypt. Establishment of Fatimite Caliphate.

1000 Discovery of the New World.

1100 Fatimite Caliphate trading with Aztec/Toltec Empires.

1700 Colonization of Bilalistan.

1863 *Lion's Blood* begins.

Steven Barnes
Longview, Washington
16 Safar 1422
(May 10, 2001)
www.lifewrite.com
www.lionsblood.com